W9-BMD-099

WILD
ANIMALS

PETER STRAUB

WILD ANIMALS

ANIMALS

THREE NOVELS

JULIA

IF YOU COULD SEE ME NOW

UNDER VENUS

G. P. PUTNAM'S SONS
NEW YORK

Copyright © 1984 by Peter Straub
All rights reserved. This book, or parts thereof, may not be
reproduced in any form without permission in writing from the
publisher. Published on the same day in Canada by
General Publishing Co. Limited, Toronto.

Designed by Richard Oriolo

Library of Congress Cataloging in Publication Data

Straub, Peter.
  Wild animals.

  Contents: Julia—If you could see me now—Under
Venus.
  I. Title.
PS3569.T6914A6   1984   813'.54   84-13237
ISBN 0-399-13013-6

Printed in the United States of America

CONTENTS

INTRODUCTION

For me, this collection is principally an opportunity to make *Under Venus*, my secret book, available to the public.

In many ways, it was the novel which cost me most—I don't think this is uncommon with second novels—and it taught me lessons I was able to use only much later in my career. *Under Venus* lurks behind virtually everything I have written since, an unquiet ghost, by turns rancorous and helpful, instructive and condemning, reproachful and outmoded and inspiring: an old love, more comic than I knew, who won't let go.

If it were not for *Under Venus* I would be a very different man, and if it were not for what happened to it, I think I would have been a far different writer—I think that if this second novel had been accepted by the publishers who had indulged me with *Marriages*, it would have taken me even longer than it did to find my true direction. When my editor at Coward, McCann & Geoghegan, an entirely admirable woman named Pat Soliman, asked me to think about it again, she shocked me into compressing perhaps a decade's anxiety, growth, and introspection into a fifth of that time. It may be that this was the only time in the history of the often adversarial relationship between writer and publisher that the publisher rejected a book with sufficient merit to be publishable, did so quite properly, and with wholly beneficial results.

Of course it did not seem that way to me at the time. I had been working on the novel for more than two years, and my wife and I were living in a tiny bed-sitter in Belsize Square, London NW3—I'd begun the novel in the bedroom of a "garden flat" in Dublin, for which read "basement," and had finished it, more than six hundred handwritten pages later, on the drop-leaf dining-room table that came with the bed-sitter. We'd come to London from Dublin on the strength of the acceptance of *Marriages*, and the price of London rentals meant that we lived, ate, slept in one room. I was entirely committed to writing. I think the only break I'd had during the past two years had been the trip back to America which was to provide the first chapter and much of the detail of *Under Venus*, then called *The Scarred Girl*.

This trip had been subsidized by our parents. Unhappy with academic work and feeling as though my first novel had bought me just enough time to finish writing the second, I had quit the PhD program at University College, Dublin. By the time the book had brought me to its conclusion, I needed it. It had to work. It was much better, more ambitious and more accomplished, more novelistically solid, than *Marriages*. Editing and revision, I thought, could straighten out whatever might be wrong with the book: I felt too close, too surrounded by it, to be objective about its flaws. What I mainly knew about the book was that it felt strong and alive to me. After I had cut sixty or seventy pages from the manuscript and typed the rest, revising as I went, on that same wobbly table, I brought it to my English agent. He promised to read it over the weekend. Several days later I walked the few short blocks from our building to the pay telephone in the Belsize Washeteria. Wonderfully, the dam broke. The agent told me that the only reason the novel would not win England's biggest literary prize was that I was an American, hence excluded from consideration. Did Hilary tell me that he was proud to agent such a wondrous book, or have I invented that sentence? The book was sensitive, beautiful, exciting, etc. I floated home on the melting of an immense knot of anxiety I'd lived with for so long that only its disappearance brought it to my attention.

Yet the novel came back postpaid, and so did the anxiety. I cut and pasted the typescript, taking out another big wad of pages. It remained *Under Venus*, tighter but the same book that had told itself to me from 1970 to 1972. I cut and pasted again. It was just more itself, not something different. Finally I thought of rewriting it in the first person—*Marriages* had been in the first person, I enjoyed the rhetorical possibilities it opened up for me; perhaps I should try speaking in the lyric, go-for-broke voice (for so it seemed to me) of my protagonist, Elliot Denmark.

Rewriting *Under Venus* in an arbitrary first person was a mistake born of desperation—the book had become a tar baby. It was not dead for me, though sometimes it had pretended to be dead, but I could not continue to work on it and be alive myself. The book resisted all the changes I made to it, and the more I wrote, the more it loosened and sagged. In the end I stopped—put the whole thing in a folder and tried to submerge in a new project my exhaustion with the book and my deepening doubts about myself. The new project became *Julia*, which I think almost nakedly reflects the psychological condition of the thirty-year-old man who wrote it. It is a dark book, driven and gloomy and cynical in the raw, startled manner of adolescence. It is a kind of retreat from the world, after the expansiveness of *Under Venus*, and its assurance is more than half bravado. But the man who wrote it was having a wonderful time. He was inventing again, saving his life.

And *Julia* did save my life; and having saved it, improved it too. In one afternoon my agent sold English and American rights for more money than my wife and I had jointly earned in our last year in America; not long after, the film rights were sold, enabling us to buy our first house.

Of course *Julia* was a novel in the genre that had produced *The Exorcist*, *The Other*, and *Rosemary's Baby*—horror, supernatural fiction, or whatever it was called (gothic fantasy?) was in 1975 more popular than ever in its history. More commercial, that is, which is why a clearheaded English publisher and author named John Knowler told me months before *Julia*'s hardback publication that I'd have to do that sort of thing again, you know. He was smiling, and my agent smiled too, across the table in the French restaurant on Theobald's Road, but this calm declaration rather distressed me: I had no idea of what I wanted to work on next, but I'd assumed that I had a choice. And friends who had read *Marriages* and knew of the struggles involving *Under Venus* wondered when I'd get back to writing "real" novels. It seemed not to matter that *Julia*, for all its sometime messiness, was in almost every way more mature than *Marriages*. These friends took a position precisely opposite John Knowler's, that for the sake of my soul I had to (*had* to, you know) stop writing horror (or whatever it was called). Some of them were kind enough to say that I had to stop because I wrote it too well, presumably meaning well enough to write something else, and have been kind enough, by their lights, to go on saying it ever since.

Satisfy your publishers (and by extension their accountants); or satisfy yourself. "Another, ah, book like . . . you know . . . another *scary* book?" Yes, I say, another scary book: but I was trying to do more than that. "Are *all* your books going to be like, um, *Ghost Story* and *Shadowland*? That kind of book?" No, I say, only until I think I've done everything I can do with that kind of book.

My now no-longer-secret book, *Under Venus*, and the change of tone from the first to the second ghost story here, should show you why. It doesn't matter which side of the argument you're on—what I hope is clear when the three books in this collection are read is that, if I was wounded by the lack of enthusiasm for my second, very odd novel, the wound stung me forward onto the path I should sooner or later have found for myself. The story of Elliot Denmark and his heartsick, frustrated, skeptical love for Anita Kellerman is really very similar to the story of *If You Could See Me Now*'s neurotic Miles Teagarden, widowed and obsessed with the memory of his cousin Alison. Miles is a kind of failed Elliot—if Miles could have written fiction himself instead of having to write a book about other books, he would have been as happy as it would have been possible for him to be. Both men return to the critical landscapes of their youth, one in a triumph more than half ironic and the other sidelong, hidden, and both must contend with their old obsessive attachments. The deepest connection between the two books, however, is not the situation of their protagonists but the so-called attachment herself. Anita Kellerman is Alison Greening grown up, or a version of her. *If You Could See Me Now* is *Under Venus* from another angle; but this time the disturbingly intense feeling in the book has a focus.

There is no concealing the fact that *Under Venus* was written by a very literary young male in his mid-twenties, and many readers will think also that he is remarkably primitive in his attitudes toward sex. Unless they are wives or mothers-in-law, women are magically powerful. Sex objects all, they yearn for his surrogate's body but become remote and threatening once they have it. They are treacherous, fickle, dangerous, even when they are middle-aged professors of psychology. A strongly irrational impulse, as powerful and irrational as worship, and probably as fearful too, lurks within Elliot Denmark—the impulse to mythologize his loved one, to give her a kind of totemic psychic power. In the light of his behavior it seems impossible that Elliot Denmark should consider himself an essentially rational being, but since he does, he must reject that side which responds to Anita Kellerman—he must decide that she is flawed.

I wish I could read Anita Kellerman's *Under Venus*.

That at least would be free of its real author's literary influences. The thumb-prints of nearly everyone I was reading, and had just read, crowd these pages. Certain sentences and opinions are obvious imitations of Saul Bellow (especially *Mr. Sammler's Planet*), certain paragraphs are pastiche Updike. Toward the end of the book there is a joke involving piano-playing which I stole entire from Alison Lurie's novel *Love and Friendship*—I'd discovered her not long after we'd moved to London, and read her straight through. Part of what I was after was the social sweep, the inclusiveness, of the later John O'Hara novels. I wanted to get a lot of Plechette City, Wisconsin, into the novel; so perhaps it is due to O'Hara's influence that I included the political battle over the fate of Nun's Wood. Wattman and Donadio, the objectionable musicologists, were almost certainly born while I read Richard Stern's brilliant novella *1968*.

But the deepest influence, I am convinced, was Iris Murdoch. (Some obvious traces of Murdoch's influence also crop up in *Julia*). I still look forward every year to reading the new Iris Murdoch novel, and in those days I read them in great fascinated gulps. Especially impressive and important to me was the way dreamlike events, sometimes actual dreams, jostled the more naturalistic and comic events in her fiction—changed them by their proximity, jarred them *loose*. (*Under Venus* contains a very Murdochian dream.) I wanted that too, in my book, that quality of the dreamlike which would contribute to the intensity of Elliot's baffled love. The owl, the wounded fox, and the wolf, if it is a wolf, were meant to push the novel a bit outside naturalism, to add some of the qualities of Romance.

Under Venus drifts toward the gothic without quite knowing what to do about it. If I were to write it now, I *would* do it in the first person, I would remove the Nun's Wood subplot and Ronnie Upp and Anita's son, and I would have Anita Kellerman be dead—perhaps in an accident that might have been a contrived suicide. When Elliot returns to Plechette City, he finds that he keeps driving past her old house, cannot suppress his memories of her; finally he succumbs and knocks at her door. A young woman with a scarred face opens the door—in the scene that follows we learn that she had been in the car when Anita drove off the bridge. Elliot is shocked that anyone else was in the car, because he's sure it was suicide. Anyhow, Elliot is even more shocked the next day when . . .

You'd better finish it yourself, because I'm not interested in that story any-more. It has a different face and body, but the same bones, as *If You Could See Me Now*.

I must now give my grateful thanks to two men whose help and advice were invaluable during the writing of the two novels which followed *Under Venus*, and who in more general and probably more important ways helped me to find my direction.

Thomas Tessier, a fellow writer and close friend from the Dublin days of poetry readings, shabby flats, and pub-crawls along Lower Baggot Street, gave me expert counsel about supernatural fiction during this long period—by 1973 he had become a publisher in London, and talking with Thom also gave me a crash course in what happens to novels after the novelist drops them into the mail slot. It was from Thom that I first heard of H. P. Lovecraft, Fritz Leiber, Robert Bloch, and Richard Matheson; and through Thom that I began to understand how publishing actually works.

David Machin, who was with the English firm of Jonathan Cape during these years, helped not by giving an *ad hoc* seminar about the realities of book publishing but simply by being a wonderful editor, tactful, supportive, and wise. It was always a pleasure to work with David, even when he had it at the back of his mind that I ought to cut several cherished chapters from a typescript—part of the measure of his tact is that he always let me think that it was *my* idea to amputate those chapters. I think of David Machin as the model editor, I suppose, and the qualities that made him so valuable in that way were I think identical to those that made him admirable as a man. But if I go on like this I will embarrass him. I will only say that David Machin contributed significantly to both *If You Could See Me Now* and the novel that followed it, *Ghost Story*. He helped the books find their shape. And me to find mine, as it were, by treating me all along as though it were just possible that I might amount to something one day—for a young writer, still uncertain of that himself, such treatment is better than gold.

I am happy to see these three early books together in one volume, and hope that they will give much pleasure to those who come to them, whether for the first or the second time.

P.S.

JULIA

I

THE HAUNTING

1

The little blond girl, about nine or ten—Kate's age—and enough like Kate to make Julia feel dizzy, ran floating up from nowhere along Ilchester Place and, windmilling her arms at the street corner, flew into the path to Holland Park. Standing on the steps of the house with the man from Markham and Reeves, Julia's first sensation was the sharp, familiar ache of loss, now so strong as to make her feel that she might shock the man from Markham and Reeves by being sick into the wilting tulips; but the real-estate agent, who had clearly decided that his customer was precipitate and eccentric to the point of lunacy, might have done no more than mutter something about the heat and pretend that nothing out of the ordinary had occurred. That Julia had already twice lost the keys to Number 25, that she had written a deposit check for twenty thousand pounds on the first day she had seen the house (the first house he had shown her), that she was buying, as well, all the furniture from the previous owners, a retired carpet manufacturer and his wife already in Barbados, that she intended to live alone in an eight-bedroom house—but he had his own ideas on that point—had prepared him for almost any conceivable vagary on her part. Conscious of her haste and her oddness, and a little fearful of the man's subtle contempt for her, Julia yet felt it possible that the estate agent attributed some of this behavior to her being merely another comically "rich American"; and so she felt, with a little flare of independence, only the smallest qualm about obeying her second response to the sight of the running blond girl, a feeling that she must follow her. The impulse was overwhelmingly strong. The man from Markham and Reeves was holding her by the elbow, very delicately, and beginning to produce the third key from his waistcoat pocket—he had tied a bright yellow ribbon through the hole at the top of the key.

"Yellow for remembrance, Mrs. Lofting," he was saying, the edge of condescension clear in his voice. "Confess I pinched the idea from a pop song. May you—"

"Excuse me," Julia said, and went quickly down the steps to the pavement. She did not want to run until she was out of the man's sight, and restrained herself until she too had rounded the corner to the park and was shielded by the wall. The girl looked remarkably like Kate. Of course she could not be Kate. Kate was dead. But people sometimes caught sight of friends in a crowd or riding past in a bus when those friends were in reality thousands of miles away—but didn't that mean that the friends were in danger or about to die? Julia ran a few awkward steps into the children's play area and, already panting, began to walk. Children were everywhere, in the sandboxes, racing around on the patchy grass, climbing the trees she could see from her bedroom window. The blond girl could be far into the park by now, Julia realized, either on the long sward of green to the right or on one of the paths up ahead, or over toward the Orangery. The child might not even have taken the path into the play area but run straight up the long lane to Holland House. Surely Holland House *was* that way? Up there past the peacocks? Julia did not feel sure enough of the park's geography to pursue her phantom—who in any case was just an ordinary little girl on her way to meet friends in Holland Park. Julia, who was still unthinkingly walking up the path past the sandboxes, stopped. Chasing after the child had been unreasonable, perhaps hysterical: typical of her. I really am losing my grip, she thought, and said "Damn" so loudly that a stout man with a brushy gingery mustache stared at her.

She turned about, embarrassed, and looked up across the back walls of gardens to the upper row of windows in her new house. The house was monstrously expensive: she could not allow Magnus to know that she had purchased it, that she had signed every paper put in front of her. For a moment the thought of Magnus—the idea of Magnus, enormous with rage—drove everything else from her head, and she felt a second of terror. She might have been unreasonable, even unbalanced—he would be quick to say it—but about Magnus, reason was not possible. The long, restrained lines of the house, which she had thought beautiful the moment she had seen it, helped her to quiet her feelings.

Holding one hand to her chest, Julia walked back down the path to the corner of Ilchester Place. She remembered the man from Markham and Reeves only when she saw him leaning against the front door, his expression one between confusion and boredom. *He* had written her off when, telephoning her bank from his office, he had learned how much money she kept in a checking account.

She expected the man to say something, but he appeared to be past courteous formulas. He merely straightened his shoulders and offered the key, holding it by the flagrant yellow ribbon. Now he did not look so much bored as weary. And in any case, what could Julia say? She could not explain her sudden action by telling him that she had wanted to look again at a girl who reminded her of her dead daughter: he did not know anything about Kate or about Julia. She did the best she could.

"I'm so sorry," she said, looking up into his gray, rather compressed-looking face. "I wanted to check on something around the back before you left."

He looked at her oddly: to examine the back, of course, she would have gone through the house rather than around the corner.

"Not a lot of children on this street, Mrs. Lofting," the man said. "They play in the park of course but you'll find that Ilchester Place is a quiet sort of neighborhood, as I've told you." Was this, too, more tired sarcasm? But the man had noticed the girl, and was making an effort to be courteous. He had looked straight through her weak excuse.

"Thank you," she said, taking the key and putting it in one of the short pockets of her dress. "You've been very patient with me."

"Not at all." The man looked at his wristwatch, then for a moment at his car, and than at the Rover, where suitcases were piled up on the backseat, crowded in with some potted plants, two short stacks of books tied with string, and a box of floppy dolls she had had since childhood. These were the only things she had taken besides her clothing, and they were all from the room she had been using since leaving the hospital. The books were an indulgence, but they were hers, not Magnus'.

"No, you needn't, please," Julia quickly said. "I couldn't dream of asking you, after . . . everything."

"In that case," he said, palpably relieved, and began to go down the steps, "I have some things to attend to at the office, so if you'll excuse me, I'll be leaving you to your new house." He glanced up at the long, warm brick exterior. "It *is* a beautiful house. You should be quite happy here. And of course you have our number, should anything arise. Am I correct in thinking that you do not know Kensington thoroughly?"

She nodded.

"Then you have before you all the pleasures of investigation. Where was it you were living before? Before today? Hampstead, wasn't it?"

"Yes."

"You should find this part of Kensington very sympathetic."

He turned away to walk toward his car. When he had opened the door he faced her again and called across the pavement and lawn. "Do ring us if you have any problems, Mrs. Lofting. By the by, I think you might have some spare keys made for you at one of the shops in the High Street. Well, good day then, Mrs. Lofting."

"Bye." She waved from the steps of the house as the man drove away. When his car was out of sight, Julia went down to the Rover and looked back up at her house—now truly her house. Like all the other houses on the short, elegant length of Ilchester Place, it was neo-Georgian, brick, secure. There she would be safe from Magnus. The house had spoken to her need for quiet and for restful seclusion the moment she had seen it: almost as if it had in fact spoken to her. Buying it had been as much a compulsion as following the little Kate-like girl had been. She *could* live in it, apart from Magnus: in time she could telephone him or write a note, after he had got used to the idea of her bolting. She had spent the previous night in a Knightsbridge hotel, afraid that every step meant the approach of Magnus, his face red with false sympathy, with the effort of trying to contain his violence. Magnus could be terrifying: it was the other side of his impressiveness, that huge male authority. No, she would let Magnus be for a while. Her note had explained all that could be explained.

Now the suitcases and the rest of her things had to be got into the house somehow. She pushed the button beside the door handle and, when it resisted her, pushed it again harder. The car was locked. Julia pulled a key from her pocket, but it was the house key on its taunting yellow ribbon. She bent over to look through the window and saw the rest of her keys dangling from the car's ignition. *Helpless.* She felt the oncoming of tears. For a moment she experienced an intense gratitude that Magnus was not beside her. "Julia, you are completely incapable." "I wonder if you ever do anything right." Or a short, brutal condemnation: "Typical." A barrister, Magnus had an arsenal of techniques for suggesting that other people, especially his wife, were weak in the head.

"Oh, thank God," she said aloud; she had noticed that the window on the passenger side of the Rover was rolled down, although that door too was locked. "Typical" as that might be, Julia took it as a good omen for the first day she was to live in her new house. Perhaps Magnus really might be kept from finding her—for a week or two, at least.

As if the two were related, the thought of Magnus recalled the girl again, and Julia, opening the other door by reaching in through the window and pressing down on the inner handle, thought of trying to find her inside Holland Park. She fought down the image of herself and the girl, sitting together on a bench, talking. Beneath this lay another image, an image of horror and despair, and Julia, sensing it coming to her consciousness as it had during the weeks in hospital, deliberately made her mind empty. She would think about the luggage and the plants; one of the pots had broken, shearing away a section of clay nearly seven inches long and exposing granular black soil webbed with thin white roots. Julia had, she realized, bought the house on Ilchester Place the same way she had taken Magnus for her husband, in a rush.

But she had spent *her* money on *her* house: it was the first utterly free thing she had done since she had married Magnus eleven years before. Then, in 1963, she had been twenty-five, a rather more than pretty young woman with striking reddish hair and a soft, unlined, contented face: "the face of a girl at an Impressionists' picnic," her father had said. She had gone through her private school and Smith College, it seemed to her now, in a sort of trance, at a great distance from herself. Little but her courses and a few professors had moved or touched her. She had lost her virginity to a boy from Columbia, a tall, intense Jewish student of English. Most of his courtship had consisted of anecdotes about Lionel Trilling and the sex lives of famous poets; they had seen a great many French movies together.

Afterward there were other boys, but none of them came any closer to the inner Julia than the Columbia student; she slept with none of them. When she graduated from Smith, she took a job with Time-Life, in the clipping library at *Sports Illustrated*, but quit a year later when she overheard another young woman, one she had thought of as a friend, describe her as a "fucking heiress." Quitting was a relief: she knew that she was incompetent at the job, and had lasted a year because the head of her department, a married man named Robert Tillinghast, was fond of her. She liked him, but not enough to remove her clothes in his company, which was clearly what he had in mind. For six months, then, she lived in her parents' home, reading novels and watching television, feeling more and more afraid of any world beyond the front door or the Smith campus; then she ran into a Smith friend in a restaurant and heard that the publishing company she worked for was looking for a young woman to do editorial work; in a week she had another job. Here, she enjoyed an almost mechanical, rootless pleasure in the work, editing academic books in the firm's college department; she was fond of saying that she learned things from each new book. She took an apartment in the West Seventies. She seemed to be settling into a dazed, busy, thoughtless life: taking the bus to work (on principle, she rarely rode in taxis), doing her correspondence, working with manuscripts, eating with one man or another, she often thought that she was merely watching herself perform, as though life had not yet truly begun. Then one morning she woke up in her bed beside Robert Tillinghast, and decided, panicked, to leave New York and go to England. "I'm moving horizontally since I'm not able to move vertically," she told her friends. Robert Tillinghast drove her to the airport and said, Good God, he wondered what would become of her. "I guess I do too."

In London, she first took a room on Drury Lane, and six months later, after she had found a job with a publisher of art books, moved to a two-room flat in Camden Town. "You're living in a kennel," her father had blustered when he flew across to inspect her new life. "Where the hell are the want ads?" He found her a self-contained, large-windowed flat with two bedrooms ("You need a room to work in!") in Hampstead, three times the cost of her place in Camden Town. One night several months after she had moved in, she met Magnus Lofting at a party given by a married couple who both worked for the art-book publishers.

They were Hugh and Sonia Mitchell-Mitchie, both Julia's age; Hugh, who wore denims and T-shirts and the golden curl of an earring in one ear, was the head of the art department. Sonia, like Julia, did editorial work. In manner, both were bright and inconsequential; Julia, who liked them while she was a little unsettled by them—both seemed to spend an abnormal amount of time discussing their love affairs—had not known that their idea of a party was to spend two hours drinking as rapidly as possible and the rest of the night playing parlor games.

When the others began to play, Julia faded backward in the room, hoping to go unnoticed: she was made insecure by all games. Sonia began to taunt her; in a moment, twenty people were staring at her. Julia felt cruelly exposed.

"Don't be a bully, Sonia," a man said. "I'll talk to your friend."

Julia turned to the source of this authoritative voice, and saw a big rocky-faced man in a pinstriped suit; he was years older than anyone else at the party. The hair above his ears was already going gray. "Sit down next to me," the man ordered.

"You saved my life," she said.

"Just sit down," Magnus ordered.

She gladly sat.

Ten years later, she could not remember the conversation they had had, but she knew that, immediately, there had been something impressive about him: he was purely male, with a suggestion in every gesture that he could take her as easily as he could light a cigarette. With the instincts of someone who had grown up surrounded by prosperous people, she recognized that he was successful at whatever it was he did; he seemed to understand her utterly, or to be utterly indifferent to anything he did not understand. In a chilling way, he was fascinating. They spent the rest of the evening talking to one another, and while Hugh and Sonia and the rest of the party were beginning another game, one in which a "murderer" assassinated his "victims" by winking at them, Magnus said quietly to her, "I think I'll be going. Shall I give you a lift? How did you get here?"

"I took a bus," she confessed.

"Too late for a bus now." He stood up. He was a head taller than she and too big to be merely burly. When he raised a hand, she flinched; but he carried it to the back of his head and smoothed down his hair. "I'll take you home unless you live somewhere unreasonable. Blackheath or Guildford are out of my range."

"I live in Hampstead," she said.

"Grace abounds. So do I."

They walked to his car, a black Mercedes, parked on the Fulham Road; she learned that he was a barrister, and that he had once lived next door to Sonia Mitchell-Mitchie, who had become a kind of adopted niece. He asked few questions of her, but Julia found herself talking compulsively. For some reason— a reason she was not to understand for years—she even mentioned Robert Tillinghast when describing why she had left New York.

It was only when she knew that she was going to leave Magnus that she recognized that she had married him—had fallen in love with him—in large measure because he reminded her of her father. And they were both prodigal, casual adulterers. Julia saw very early that Magnus had other women: he was brutally offhand about them. On the ride back to Hampstead, he had said that he wanted a drink, and drove to a club behind Shepherd's Market, where he signed her name in a guestbook and led her into a dark, half-filled room in which elegance was still a few paces in advance of shabbiness. The waitresses wore long pastel gowns revealing outsize, separated breasts. A third of the men were drunk; only two women, besides Julia and the hostesses, were in the club. One of the drunks put his arm about Julia as soon as she entered the room. Magnus pushed the man away without looking at him. He ordered drinks and began to look aggressively about the room as if he were looking for another man to knock down. Both of the other women, Julia saw, were looking at him. She felt pleasantly excited, stimulated, sipping at her drink.

"Do you gamble?" Magnus asked her.

She shook her head.

"You won't mind if I do?"

"No," she said. "I suddenly feel very awake."

Julia followed him through a door at the end of the lounge and continued, following his broad back, to a grilled-in counter where Magnus took money from his wallet and bought chips. She watched as he placed two hundred-pound notes on the counter, and, after hesitating a second, a third. He seemed to get a surprisingly small amount of chips for all this money.

Together, they skirted various gaming tables and went up to a roulette wheel. Magnus placed four of his chips on red. Breathless, Julia watched the ball spinning across the ratchets. It landed, clattering, on red. Magnus left his chips where they were, and the ball landed again on red. Then he moved everything he had won to black; again he won. How much money did those chips represent? Five hundred pounds? More? As she watched Magnus glowering down at the stack of chips, she felt exhilarated, slightly disoriented: he must have loathed the party, she realized. The next time the wheel spun, he lost some of his chips, but his face remained immobile.

"Your turn, Charmaine," he ordered. He shoved a stack of chips toward her. With desperation, Julia realized that they were worth at least two hundred pounds.

"I can't," she said. "I'd lose your money."

"Don't be cowardly," he said. "Bet any way you please."

She pushed the chips onto the red, since that was what Magnus had first won with. This time the ball clattered down onto the black. She looked up at him, stricken.

"Doesn't matter," he said. "Put more on it." He slid chips toward her.

She did as he said, and lost again. She stepped away from the table.

Magnus continued to gamble, seemingly indifferent to her. She stood beside him, watching chips pile up before him. Winning seemed not to affect him in any way; he simply stolidly stood there, scowling at the table, moving piles of red and white chips back and forth. Several times men approached and spoke to him, but Magnus replied with short, curt sentences and turned away from them.

After half an hour, a thin black-haired woman Julia remembered seeing in the lounge came up and kissed Magnus. "Darling," she said, "you haven't been here in ages. You might lose all your old friends." Saying the last two words, she looked tauntingly at Julia. Julia felt at once undressed.

Magnus whispered a few words to the black-haired woman, and then turned back to the table. When he cashed in his chips, Julia saw that he had won nearly a thousand pounds.

In the car she said, "Was that woman your mistress?"

It was the first time she had heard him laugh.

When he left her at her door he asked for her telephone number and, after she had given it, brought two twenty-pound notes from his jacket pocket and put them in her hand. "I'll ring you Wednesday," he said, and moved out the door before she could protest. Julia put the money in a drawer, intending to give it back when she next saw him; two months later, when she found the two notes again, it was too late to return it. Eventually, she gave one note to Oxfam and the other to Amnesty International.

At work the next Monday, she learned two things about Magnus: he had been Sonia Mitchell-Mitchie's first lover, and Julia had been expected to sleep with him. "Magnus always does that, picking up some girl at a party and then taking her home and ravishing her," Sonia said to Julia. "Weren't you ravished?"

"He barely touched me," Julia protested.

"He must have been off his feed," Sonia said.

In the following weeks, Magnus came to occupy more and more of her time; but he made love to her only when she had begun to wonder if he ever would. He was certainly the biggest man she had ever gone to bed with. By that time, two months after the Mitchell-Mitchie party, he had become a reference point in her life. She tended to judge other men by Magnus' standard, or by trying to guess if Magnus would like them. Certainly no other man was as exciting as Magnus Lofting: he had an absolute assurance a younger man could not possess, still trying to consolidate both his manhood and his career.

Yet it was only after he had described his childhood to her that Julia, already in love, knew that she must marry him. He and his sister—"poor Lily," a year older than he—had been raised by monumentally distant parents. Entirely absorbed into themselves, entirely indifferent to the opinions or sensibilities of others, the Loftings had traveled much, leaving the children at home with a succession of tutors: before she drew Magnus out on the subject of his child-hood—he was seemingly callous about it now—Julia had not known how far off, therefore cruel, it was possible for parents to be. Except for the tutors and "poor Lily" Magnus had grown up in near silence, abandoned in the glassy marble tomb of a house in Hampshire. His childhood was heartbreaking for Julia, whose own father, unlike Sir Greville Lofting, had been intrusive, verbal, and commanding. Magnus' childhood, that early isolation, she thought, went a long way toward explaining Magnus' compulsions; as a young man, he had apparently been ruthless about his professional life, and even now he invested it with enough psychic energy to power a steam engine. Magnus' childhood not only helped to explain Magnus to Julia, and thereby make him more ac-cessible, but it also helped to humanize him. At first, that Magnus had once *had* parents seemed impossible, slightly shocking; that he had "poor Lily" and a much younger adopted brother, Mark, seemed a revelation.

She was further surprised by the depth of his attachment to "poor Lily." But again, their childhood made it accessible. Magnus and Lily had grown up a society of two, intensely devoted to one another, each other's only company. They had invented a language ("Durm") in which at playful moments they could still converse. They were "Magnim" and "Lilim." They had constructed elaborate games using every portion of the house and grounds, games in which Magnus apparently from the age of five or six had taken the commanding role—king, general, prime minister, Coriolanus, Odysseus, Priam. This had endured up to the time Magnus entered Cambridge. Lily had never married, and Julia learned that Magnus spent at least one afternoon or evening a week with his sister. In fact, she thought that the inevitable usage of "poor Lily" had been adopted less from an intrinsic absurdity of Lily's than from a wish to counter any jealousy Julia might be expected to feel. Despite her oddities, her spiritualism, her general appearance of genteel dissipation, Lily did not deserve the epithet. She proved, when Julia finally met her, gray-haired, undoubtedly lovely, and so finely made that separate facial muscles were visible beneath her skin. Lily made Julia feel awkward and hot, probably smudged in some conspicuous place. And it was only two years later, after the birth of Kate, that Lily became friendly.

Mark, the son of a young friend of Sir Greville's, a consular official in Africa who had killed himself, was another matter. The Loftings had adopted the child, then two years old, out of an uncharacteristic generosity, having promised his mother, dying in a tropical hospital, that they would care for him. Their notion of care was to send the child and nurse to England, with only a telegram and a breezy following letter to warn fifteen-year-old Magnus and sixteen-year-old Lily that a new brother was to be dumped in among them. They hated him. Their world had been a sacred alliance of two for too long to admit a third. Magnus invariably referred to Mark as a "waster" and a "troublemaker"; Lily too remained suspicious of Mark. Sometimes he was "bad, very bad," which Julia supposed was a reference to his having impregnated a girl in the Hampshire village when he was fifteen. It might also have referred to the first action of his adult life, having his name altered by deed poll from Lofting back to Berkeley—a mute comment on the Lofting methods of childrearing. Mark was a disappointment: he had never learned their secret language, never having been given much chance to learn it; he had obtained a third-class degree at Cambridge; he was now lecturing at a polytechnic in sociology, a field Magnus claimed did not exist. Mark had flirted with fringe political groups all his life, he had marched and passed out leaflets, and he was now supposed to be a Maoist—Magnus had once scornfully seen him carrying a copy of *Red Star Over China*.

—Well, I don't see what's wrong with reading any book. And neither do you.

—I didn't say he was reading it. He was carrying it. For effect. In his circle, it's the equivalent of a Rolling Stones record.

—Now, honestly, I'm not defending Mark, but you are being malicious and unfair. You condemn him whether he's reading the book or not.

—Does it matter what I say about some Notting Hill Maoist?

Mark generally dressed in blue jeans and a chambray workshirt; he lived in the same rooms in Notting Hill Gate he had taken after leaving Cambridge, sleeping there, in a fabulous mess, on a mattress on the floor. Julia had heard most of this from Lily, with Magnus grunting disapproving asides, over a period of three or four months. She herself did not meet Mark until the day he appeared at Magnus' house on Gayton Road, three weeks before Julia's wedding, saying that he wanted to meet the victim. She heard his light, wry voice—a very un-

Lofting voice—from the front steps, and then heard Magnus say, "The what? I take it you mean my fiancée."

"Your victim, Magnus."

She heard Magnus sigh. "Well, you might as well come in then, since you're here."

"You are typically generous, Magnus."

Julia had thought of Mark as a potential ally since she had heard Lily and Magnus first disparage him; he was at least flawed and might be expected to be sympathetic to her. Her heart beating a little quickly, she thrust the *Guardian* behind her chair and stood to meet him.

Magnus came scowling into the room, leading a tall young man with long, shining black hair. Julia saw Magnus' grimace at the sight of the wrinkled newspaper, wadded up behind the chair; then she saw that Mark Berkeley was the kind of man women might turn around to stare at in the street. He was beautiful—sexually beautiful. The long dark hair framed a face a few shades lighter than olive, with high Mongol cheekbones and a full, curving mouth. Beneath black eyebrows, in the dark amused face, his eyes were unbelievably blue. When he held out his hand, she noticed that his fingernails were filthy.

"You're almost as pretty as Lily said you were," he said. "I wish I'd seen you first. Be nice to have another beautiful woman in the family, won't it, Magnus? Now that Lily is getting a bit past it."

Holding his rather grubby hand, Julia felt, as an undercurrent to Mark's remarks, that he was looking straight through her; he might be an ally, but not of the sort she had anticipated. Mark too was formidable. Yet he seemed far from unsympathetic. As Julia felt herself warming to her fiancé's younger brother, a number of impressions went rapidly through her mind. Mark seemed more like Magnus' son than his brother: he had an air of irresponsibility which seemed nearly cultivated. It was impossible to imagine Mark holding a job— any job but lecturing. And she considered, still holding his hand, that perhaps she was being conned by an expert. It was certainly all too easy to find oneself instantly liking someone so attractive. She disengaged her hand. She was not sure that she approved of men as beautiful as this.

"Really, Magnus," Mark said, "doesn't she look like a vision Lily might see in one of her crystal balls? What an extraordinary person she must be to want to marry you."

"Oh," she said, trying to save the situation, "sometimes I think half the women in London want to marry Magnus."

But Magnus had turned impatiently away from her. The rest of the afternoon had staggered painfully along, Mark taunting Magnus, Magnus becoming increasingly blustery. Julia had not known at all how to read Mark.

A year later, when Julia realized, sickened, that Magnus had not ceased to see his other women for as much as a month, she had angrily, furiously proposed to him that she could begin taking up with his brother. "Why should you have all the fun?" she had demanded, raging.

Magnus had gripped her hard enough to raise bruises on her arm: she saw, trembling with both fear and anger, that he was barely restraining himself from clubbing her. Then the pressure lessened, his jaw unclamped, and he moved a step backward. "I'd happily kill you if you ever slept with Mark," he said. His tone was so cold that she believed him at once: despite all that talk about "unbalanced" Mark, she had never before seen that he hated his brother. At least, that was what she thought she had seen.

It was not long after this explosion that they began to discuss having a child.

Kate was born the following summer. For the next nine years, the Loftings lived conventionally in Hampstead, traveling abroad—Magnus bought a farmhouse a mile from the Dordogne River, and they spent three summers doing it up—seeing Lily at intervals, seeing Mark two or three times a year when he dropped in unannounced. Clearly, he was kept informed of events in the Lofting house by Lily: he sent a beautiful dollhouse on Kate's first birthday, he frequently telephoned when Magnus was out of town, and conducted cool, flirtatious conversations with Julia. Magnus undoubtedly carried on his affairs, but they had lost much of their power to wound Julia. They seemed entirely peripheral, taking little away from Julia and Kate. Still unpredictable, still sometimes frightening, Magnus loved Kate absolutely. Julia spent the nine years of Kate's life in a homebound trance, superficially content. Once, at a party, she had heard herself say, "Can't live for another person? Of course you can live for another person, I live for my . . ." She was on the verge of saying "daughter," but saw Magnus staring at her, and substituted "family."

Now she thought: I'm going to start being myself, freely myself, and discover what that means. And if I go crazy that's okay too.

Julia stood at her bedroom window, the shades parted, looking out at the play area, filled with desultory children, and the green of the park beyond. She pushed up the window and leaned out, thinking *a woman on the verge of a new life leaned from her window.* . . . The room was unbearably stuffy. The air drifting across Holland Park seemed cooler, more invigorating despite the warmth of the day. Unpacking her clothing, untying the books, Julia had felt damp, sticky, and oddly ruthless—the clothing could go anywhere, since the bedroom, like the entire house, was solely hers. When she put the box of dolls for the moment in one of the bedroom closets, she sat on the edge of the bed for a moment, feeling heat rise from her in layers like steam. Julia felt the presence of the house about her, for a moment almost oppressive in its size. Yet she had wanted it, and she had it. The McClintocks' furniture was old-fashioned and a bit worn, but comfortable, tending toward plush and cushions. In time, she would get rid of it and buy new furniture, but for the moment she was as pleased with the old furniture as with the house, since it had the same settled, familial look of prosperous comfort.

It was odd, the way this house had claimed her. At first, she had thought of moving to a service flat, probably somewhere in Knightsbridge; the temporariness of such a home depressed her, however, even in imagination, and she had gone to a real-estate agent's office, thinking vaguely of buying a lease on a flat. But having seen the house on Ilchester Place—"Quite unsuitable, of course," the man had said—she had known that she had to have it. It was nearly the first time in her life that Julia had used her money in a high-handed, reckless fashion. With Kate dead, did it matter how much she spent? The image of Kate's last minutes threatened to rise up again, and to put it off Julia moved quickly away from the window. She had been half-consciously looking for the girl she had seen that morning, the blond girl. How lovely it would be if buying the house brought her into contact, friendship, with another child, a girl like Kate, with whom she could have an easy, relaxed companionship.

But that was impossible: she could not make a stranger's daughter her own. She really was getting less realistic, less responsible to the world of ordinary truths. Was it possible that instead of beginning a new life, she had merely further confused and muddled the old one?

She could not afford to think that way. If she had been garrulous, disorganized, sloppy, everything that Magnus had accused her of being, perhaps these qualities were wrong only to Magnus: she had a right to her own foibles. And even now, free from him for only two days, Julia could simply feel how oppressive Magnus—Magnus' values—had been. She said to herself, I think it means my marriage is over, and surprised herself with the thought. Leaving Magnus had everything to do with Kate's death, of course, that horrific scene on the kitchen floor, Kate's blood everywhere, boiling out of her panicked body—but leaving him, Julia now thought, might also come from a deep knowledge that marriage to Magnus was no longer possible. Really, Kate had kept them together. Kate had been their focus.

Interesting, she thought, and then realized that she had spoken the word aloud. "I'm going to be the kind of woman who talks to herself," she said. "Well, why shouldn't I?" She turned to the McClintocks' mirror and began to arrange her long hair, which now glowed a little in the light pouring in the bedroom window.

When she had put everything away, scrubbed the already spotless kitchen and vacuumed the living-room carpet, Julia took a shower and afterward left the house. She had been making up her mind that she would see Lily after all—Lily now lived in Plane Tree House, just across Holland Park. Surely she could persuade Lily not to betray her to Magnus. "Poor Lily" had become, during the past nine years, a good friend: one of the attractions of Ilchester Place was that it was so close to Plane Tree House. In fact, Julia had moved near to both of the other members of the Lofting family. Mark's flat in Notting Hill was so close that she could walk to it.

Julia made sure she had her key in her pocket, and then turned up into the park. Almost immediately, she saw the blond girl again. The child was sitting on the ground at some distance from a group of other children, boys and girls, who were carefully watching her. Julia stopped walking, almost fearing that she would interrupt whatever performance was going on if the child should notice her. The blond girl was working intently at something with her hands, wholly concentrated on it. Her face was sweetly serious. Julia could not see what it was that required such concentration, but the other children were as grave as the little girl, indeed scarcely breathing. This was what gave the scene the aspect of a performance. Thinking of Kate, who could keep a dozen other children still while she loosed some fantastic story from her imagination, Julia, smiling, stepped off the path on the side opposite to the play area, so that she was perhaps twenty yards from the girl and her audience, and sat on the grass. The girl was seated, her legs straight out before her, in the sandy overspill from one of the sandboxes: a sort of pit like a golfer's sand trap. She was speaking softly now to her audience, ranged on the scrubby grass before her in groups of three and four. The other children playing in the sand took no notice of them. They were certainly unnaturally quiet, completely taken up by the girl's theatrics.

Julia forgot that she was going to see Lily: she forgot all about Lily. It was five-thirty and still very hot; Julia felt the sun's great weight on her forehead and arms. Like most London women, she was as white as if she lived under permanent clouds, and for a second considered that for the first time in years, she might get some color. Watching the child continue her intricate movements and brief, admonitory-looking bursts of speech, Julia felt peaceful, slowed by the sun, her tension for the moment gone. She *had* been right to buy the house; she had turned a corner, and could begin to live differently. For a second she thought the blond girl had darted a quick glance at her, but it was far more likely that she had merely looked sideways, aimlessly. There could be no doubt that she was the same blond girl Julia had seen before, floating along up the street: she did not really look like Kate, except for the accident of that silky, innocent, nearly white shade of hair, but she somehow suggested Kate. Oddly, watching her was not painful for Julia: Instead, there was a rootless exhilaration in it. Julia felt disconnected from everything, watching the girl, a pure, happy, sun-struck disengagement. The girl's face, at Julia's distance, looked aristocratically fine featured: her profile was heartbreakingly clear. She seemed to be not so much storytelling as lecturing—holding the others by force of personality.

Her hands were moving; something was held in her right hand. That was where the other children were looking. The girl laughed excitedly, and Julia saw some object flash in her left hand. She applied it to the thing in her right hand, apparently a square of green. The green square flipped in the air; it was like a rag. A little girl in the audience bent her head, and Julia saw her shoulders shake, as if she were overcome with giggles. The blond girl spoke a few sharp words, and the other girl raised her head. Now the group of children had a huddled look; they were creeping forward, fascinated . . . but fascination, Julia saw, was not quite the correct word. It was as though, almost, they felt trepidation about getting nearer the girl: she was undoubtedly their leader.

Now the girl spoke quickly to the others, pointing an index finger. It was extraordinarily like a classroom. She gestured with the limp green thing. One of the other girls flinched. Then the blond girl continued working with her hands, the other children slowly gathering about her. Julia strained her neck to see what they were doing, but could see only the crown of the girl's head. One of the smaller children began to cry.

In another second the performance had ended. The other children drifted away, some of them running, excited, shouting. Others moved slowly, going toward the first sandbox, where they aimlessly milled about, scattering sand. These continued to glance at the blond girl, who remained sitting where she had been, her back to them. She was smoothing the sand with the palm of her hand, seemingly filling in a hollow she had made. It was clear from her posture that she knew she was being looked at, and that she expected it; she was at once self-conscious and unconcerned. When she had patted and smoothed the sand, she stood up in one motion and briskly wiped her hands. She seemed regal, lifting her head, and Julia's heart contracted for her. The girl walked out of the little sand trap toward the path, moving directly toward Julia. Her face still bore an expression of watchful self-awareness. What complicated roles and rituals children have, Julia thought. She knew the girl would not look at her, and she did not. Once on the path, the girl turned deeper into the park, and after walking a few determined steps, broke into a run. In a moment she was traveling at top speed, racing up the path; in another moment, she had vanished before a knot of teenage girls whose long straight hair flipped like the tails of horses.

Julia stood—less gracefully than the blond girl had done—and went across the path into the play area. She still felt a little disoriented, as if she had just awakened after deep sleep. The sun felt unusually strong on her face. She wanted to see where the blond girl had been playing.

A small black girl, two or three, with a curly ruff of hair and huge mournful eyes appeared directly in front of Julia. She clasped her hands before the bib of her overalls and tilted back her head, staring up at Julia with her mouth open.

"What's your name?" she asked.

"Julia."

The girl's mouth opened a fraction wider.

"Doolya?"

Julia raised her hand for a moment to the child's springy ruff of hair. "What's your name?"

"Mona."

"Do you know the girl who was just playing in here? The girl with blond hair who was sitting and talking?"

Mona nodded.

"Do you know her name?"

Mona nodded again. "Doolya."

"Julia?"

"Mona. Take me with you."

"Mona, what was that girl doing? Was she telling a story?"

"She does. Things." The girl blinked. "Take me with you. Pick me up."

Julia bent down. "She does what? What does she do?"

Mona expressionlessly backed away a few steps, continuing to stare at Julia. "Poo," she said. She giggled, revealing small perfect teeth. "Poo." She turned away too quickly, fell on her bottom, and then struggled up on her feet and staggered off.

Julia looked after Mona for a moment, wobbling in the direction of the next sandbox, and went to where she thought the blond girl had been sitting. Julia knelt down above the spot. For a second she hesitated, wondering if she were trespassing on a secret or a code, and then she drew her hand along the sand as the girl had done. Her hand met no resistance. She repeated the action. Then she delicately scooped a little of the sand out of the hollow she had made. Very slowly, she continued to drag her fingertips through the little hollow. When the depression was three or four inches deep, her fingers touched something hard and metallic, and she dug cautiously around it, still using only one hand. Gradually she uncovered a small knife. Gummy sand was sticking to its blade. Julia looked at the knife in puzzlement and then scraped more sand from the hollow. Her fingers caught an edge of something hard, and almost without any pressure, she levered up from the sand the corpse of a small turtle of the size that had been sold to children for a quarter in Julia's own childhood. It took her a moment to see that it had been mutilated.

Vomit rushed up from the floor of Julia's stomach, and dropping the mutilated turtle and the small knife back into the hollow, she swallowed the bitter stuff back down again. With her foot she scattered sand over the turtle and the knife. Julia left the sand trap quickly, fearing she might faint, and moved toward a shaded bench on the main path through the center of the park. I'll just sit here and catch my breath, she thought, before I see Lily. She unthinkingly rubbed her hands on her dress, and after a few minutes noticed that she had left a small smear of blood along one seam. Sweat had broken out over her face; Julia blotted it on her sleeve, which instantly showed a series of dark crescents and ragged blotches. She made her mind empty: she concentrated on the sun, on the prickling she felt along her forearms and on her forehead. She was unable to look at the children.

After some minutes had passed, Julia raised her head and closed her eyes against the strong sunlight. She needed sunglasses. Somewhere, she had sunglasses. They were back at Gayton Road. She could visualize them, their bows crossed, lying on a formica counter in the kitchen. She'd buy another pair. Yes, she thought, I jumped into reacting, I did not think. There was no proof the girl had killed the turtle or cut it up that way. Julia may even have been probing the wrong spot in the sand. Little girls so pretty did not do things like that: it was an unfair psychological rule that handsome children were healthier and more stable than ugly ones. In fact—Julia allowed the idea to seep cautiously into articulation—she had been upset because the sight of the turtle reminded her of what had happened to Kate.

She could speak of none of this to Lily. Making that resolution, Julia stood up from the bench and cut across the long stretch of grass, going toward Plane Tree House. She really did feel peculiar.

2

The two women sat on Lily's terrace in the sun, now milder than it had been an hour before. "Poor Lily's" hair, prematurely gray like Magnus', had been cropped since Julia had last seen her sister-in-law, and it lay flat and short as a boy's, emphasizing the fragile lines of her face and making her look more than ever at an oblique relationship to the rest of the world. Yet Lily had remained unruffled by Julia's news and Julia's highpitched, taut mood. For half an hour, Julia had considered that Lily might be pleased that she would have Magnus to herself again, but she knew that this was grossly uncharitable: Lily simply did not respond as other people did. In the end, her news given, Julia had allowed herself to relax, cosseted by Lily's hospitality—she was now drinking her third gin and bitter lemon, served in a tall glass chiming with ice—and Lily's unpredictability.

"You *are* extraordinary, though," Lily was saying. "Extraordinary and precipitate. You're a regular heroine. I can't imagine myself ever doing anything so reckless and brave."

"God knows I'm not brave," Julia said, laughing.

"Oh, but you are. You have a brave soul."

"Then I'm a coward with a brave soul."

"You mustn't think it is cowardly to fear Magnus. Magnus is not like anyone else. He has always been a terribly apart sort of person. He has *command*. Sometimes I think that Magnus is not from this world at all, or that he is thousands of years old, preserved by some black magic. I've had a reservoir of fear of Magnus since he was three years old. Even then, Magnus had an ancient, powerful soul. Of course, I think you were wrong to leave him, and I hope with all my strength that you will return to him." Lily was drinking tea, and she followed these words by taking a birdlike sip at it, making it clear that she had at least one more thing to say. Julia, listening to this description of her husband, wondered how many times Lily had pondered in just this way on Magnus' "ancient, powerful soul." It was typical of her romanticizing of her brother. "But as my advice is universally ignored, I don't suppose that you will immediately follow it."

"You heard from him, Lily? What was he like?"

"Desperate, simply desperate. Of course, I couldn't give him a crumb of solace. And his solace, you know, would be mine—I'd be desolate for him if I thought you were never going back to him."

"I can't."

"He loves you. Since the only other person, apart from Kate, that Magnus has ever loved is myself, I am able to be quite certain."

"Lily," Julia insisted, "please don't. I can't take that now."

After a moment while both women looked away from one another toward the park, Julia asked, "Was he angry?"

"I wouldn't call it anger," Lily said. "He was distressed."

"Lily," Julia said, "you have to promise me that you won't tell him where I am. Never mind what you think is in my best interest or Magnus', please don't tell him. Promise me. Please."

"I'll promise you anything you like. But I'd be happier about it if you made me a promise too. I'd like you to tell me that you will consider going back to your husband."

"Lily, I've bought a house," said Julia, almost laughing. "I've bought *furniture*. It's just . . . just impossible for me to face Magnus. I can't make a promise like that to you. I can't even think about Magnus."

"On the contrary, it is my impression that you think of him all the time." She looked interrogatively at Julia.

When Julia said nothing Lily went on. "It was no one's fault about Kate, darling. You both very bravely did what you had to do. Magnus and you were both commended at the inquest, you know."

"I can't help that."

"But it's a pity that you were unable to hear it." Conscious that she was too crudely leading Julia into an area she would be unable to enter for perhaps months, Lily resisted the impulse to be Magnus' advocate in the matter of Kate's death. The facts of her niece's death were at least as clear in Lily's mind as in Julia's, and Lily knew, and could fully understand, that Julia had broken down afterward. In fact, Lily realized, she must have begun looking at houses only a day or two after she had come out of the hospital where she had been kept under sedation. Julia had left the hospital only to attend Kate's funeral; even that had been a mistake. That pale, confused, drugged creature stalked through the rain by photographers—it was unlikely Julia had any memory of that morning. Apparently she had begun to make arrangements for bolting on her first day back at Gayton Road: Lily supposed that she had been unable even to look at Magnus straight. Of course, Kate's death had been horrible. She had choked on a piece of meat, and Magnus and Julia, after dialing 999 and waiting minutes for an ambulance while their daughter fought uselessly for breath, had frantically decided to attempt an emergency tracheotomy. Kate had bled to death by the time the ambulance arrived. By Magnus' report, Julia had been very calm, very controlled throughout: only the next day did she get funny. Even now she looked flushed and breathless; and was drinking far too much gin.

"Well, tell me about this house of yours," Lily said. "What number in Ilchester Place is it?"

"Twenty-five."

"How odd that you should move to that street. Perhaps it is not odd at all, given that London is the sort of place in which all sorts of recurrences and coincidences occur."

"Lily, what are you trying to say?"

"My brother used to visit a house in Ilchester Place, a long time ago. It was while he was at Cambridge. I believe he had a friend there."

This comment fed a familiar stream of bitterness in Julia, who said, "Magnus and his friends. How boring all of that is. Maybe it comes from his having such an old, powerful soul."

"Yes, it does," said Lily, who seemed to be a little hurt.

"Lily, I'm sorry," Julia quickly said. "Can't we two be friends, without any relationship to Magnus? I want to begin a new life, I have to live on my own, I can't stand to think of Magnus and I'm afraid to see him, so that's done, but I want your friendship very much."

"Why, my dear," said Lily, "of course you have it. I want what is best for you. We *are* friends."

Julia felt close to tears. "I'm going to have a new life," she said, almost defiantly. "I want your help."

"Of course," Lily said, reaching out and taking Julia's hand. It was cold from her icy glass, and some grains of sand still clung to it. She allowed Julia to weep for a few moments in silence.

"You need something to do, you know," she said after Julia's noiseless crying had ended. "Only bores suggest their interests to other people, but how would you like to attend our next gathering? Mrs. Fludd is our new interpreter. She was a real find, the most *sensitive* sensitive I've met since poor dear Mr. Carmen died. Not personally, of course. She is a real old cockney, tough as a boot. But she has the gift to an astounding degree. I am very enthusiastic about her—but if you scoff at these old-fashioned performances, my feelings won't be bruised. It would be something for you to do, however."

Ordinarily Julia would have made some excuse, but she was touched by Lily's kindness, and this made her feel guilty for her earlier deliberate rudeness. "Just tell me where and when," she said. "It might be fun." Then a troubling thought occurred to her. "They won't . . . she won't . . . do anything about getting in touch with . . . I mean . . ."

"There's no question of it," Lily said firmly. "Really, people have the most obsolete idea about what we do. I suppose you expect ectoplasm leaking from shadowy cabinets."

"Okay," Julia said, smiling. "Just call me whenever your gang has its next meeting."

"Fine," Lily said, clearly pleased. "Now I think I want to give you a present. In return, I hope you will allow me to snoop enviously through your house as soon as possible. Now excuse me."

Lily left the terrace, and Julia closed her eyes for a moment. We make a wonderful pair, Lily and I, Julia thought, we're both out of our tiny minds. She thought of going round to see Mark, and then she ceased to think of anything at all.

Lily awakened her by stroking her shoulder. She was carrying a large yellow book under her arm, and had a pair of scissors in her other hand. "My dear, you've been asleep for half an hour," she said.

"I've just been thinking about Mark," Julia said. "I'd like to see Mark." She felt once more full of energy.

"That might not be very clever, dear," Lily immediately said. "You'd be far wiser to leave Mark alone."

Lily, having lost one brother to Julia, did not wish to lose the other; she had come closer to her adoptive brother over the past ten years, as Magnus had not; "poor Lily's" defensive psychology seemed quite clear to her sister-in-law.

"Mark is so interesting," Julia said, "and I hardly feel that I know him. Magnus scarcely let him in the house. He used to telephone me sometimes and we'd have these long, sweet conversations. He's probably the only man I've flirted with since I married Magnus."

"He would be," said Lily. "Let me give you these presents. I'm sorry I haven't more to welcome you into your new house, but it's on such short notice. First, here's a lovely big book full of pictures, and it's all about your new neighborhood." She held the big volume before Julia's eyes: *The Royal Borough of Kensington*, by Eda Rolph. "Full of astonishing tales. Haven't read the book in years. The other present is some of these flowers." She waved her hand at the small, vibrant garden growing in boxes at the end of her terrace.

"Oh, I can't let you cut these beautiful flowers," said Julia, who disliked all cut flowers. "That would be a terrible crime. You can't cut them for me."

"But I can," said Lily, bending down and beginning to snip off nearly a dozen flowers. "Some tulips, some of these beautiful begonias, some of my favorites here, these monstrous pinks, and a few more of everything else. Now. Take these home and put them in water," she said, giving Julia the double handful of bright flowers, "and they'll stay fresh for as long as you like."

Julia looked apprehensively at the flower boxes, but was relieved to see that the loss of her dozen scarcely affected their appearance at all: the flowers grew there in such abundance that only a few small gaps were now visible. The massed scent of the flowers in her hands made her light-headed. They were overwhelmingly sensual. One of the fleshy tulips brushed her face.

"I don't mean to look as though I'm sending you away," Lily said. "These flowers can always be put in water here until you leave. Why don't you have dinner with me tonight? I've got . . . let's see, some nice little chops. Or was this one of my vegetarian nights? There is enough food, anyhow. Afterwards we could watch a delicious new series on the television. One of those wonderful costume dramas. I've never read much Trollope, you know, but it means so much more all acted out. And the language is so beautiful, none of the vulgarity the younger playwrights go in for now. Will you watch it with me? It's fascinating, and I could tell you what's happened in the earlier five hundred episodes."

"I'm out of the television habit," Julia said, smiling. "Your brother wouldn't allow one in the house. I do think I'll go home. Thank you for everything, Lily."

"Have you a telephone?"

"I'm not supposed to, but I do," said Julia. "It's still in the name of William McClintock. But I could practically shout across the park to you."

Lily nodded, apparently satisfied.

Julia slipped the book under her arm and, still holding the flowers with both hands, turned to leave the terrace.

"Now remember your promise!" she called over her shoulder to Lily.

Later, Julia regretted that she had not accepted Lily's offer of nut cutlets and the *The Pallisers*. She had fallen asleep on the McClintocks' enormous gray velvet couch just after lying down on it to rest her feet; she had been trying to read a novel she had bought and begun in the Knightsbridge hotel the night previous, a Penguin edition of *Herzog*, but had fallen asleep after two pages. When she awakened, the smell of Lily's flowers pervading the large room, her mouth felt unpleasantly thick. She was very hungry, despite a dull pain just behind the frontal bone of her forehead. She marked her place in the book with a wrinkled tissue from the pocket of her dress and went through the long room to the kitchen.

The light bounced, harshly white, from the gleaming surfaces of the oven and refrigerator. Julia looked in the cupboard for a glass, but realized despairingly that the McClintocks had taken all of the kitchen and dining things with them, as well as all the linen. The kitchen held no food, no drink. And now it was hours past closing time for shops. Julia turned on the cold water from the taps over the sink and applied some of it to her face; then she cupped her hands and tried to drink from them, but she could not hold enough water in her palms. Eventually she reduced the flow of water from the tap and bent her head so that she could drink directly from it. The water tasted metallic and brackish: she let it run for a minute, and tried it again. Now it was slightly better, but it still tasted as though it were full of metal particles. She supposed she would have to buy bottled water; but maybe she would get used to the taste.

Julia dried her hands and mouth on the long reddish drapes over the outsize hall window. While doing this, she remembered the bloodstain from the morning and looked down at the side seam of her dress. The light-blue seersucker showed a stiff brownish crescent an inch long. The stain seemed larger than it had that afternoon. What an odd scene that was, reflected Julia; surely she had found those things in the sand by some bizarre accident, she had probably been nowhere near the place where the girl had been playing. No child would do a thing like that—well, a boy might. She could imagine Magnus cutting up live turtles as a boy.

Did hot or cold water remove bloodstains? She had been told a hundred times, but could never remember. It was the one you didn't think it was, so she decided to try cold water. Julia went back through the hall to the big ground-floor bathroom, the one the McClintocks had lined with rose-tinted mirrors. (The McClintocks, in most ways utterly conventional and even a shade stuffy in their tastes, had revealed a secret decadence in their bathrooms. The tubs and sinks were marble, the upstairs tub shaped like a huge sunken shell; the taps were swans' necks, gold. Most surprising were the walls, lined with tinted mirrors. Julia's bathroom upstairs had black mirrors, against which the gold faucets dully gleamed.) Julia took off her dress and draped it over the edge of the sink, so the stained portion would soak, and then filled the sink with water. Cold was right, she thought.

She turned away from the sink and caught sight of herself in the wall mirrors. Funny to see yourself front and back, half nude. Julia wore only underpants and tights. *My shell*, she thought. She was beginning to get a little fat: she would have to be careful about pants. But, she told herself, you don't look so bad, considering: if no Playmate, no matron either. The rose tint made her skin look darker and healthier than it was; Julia decided to get more sun this summer. It was a vision of Magnus-free peace—to be able to sprawl in the sun in the park outside her home.

Leaving the bathroom, she sprinted up the stairs to the bedroom she had chosen that morning. Though it was still not dark, she turned on the lights in the hall and bedroom. This gave the house a cavernous, echoing aspect which made Julia realize how little she knew her new dwelling. She crossed to the windows of the bedroom, pulled the drapes together, and began to dress. In a few minutes, buttoning on a floppy blue blouse she had always liked, Julia realized that it had become very warm in her bedroom; she was perspiring as she had outside. The rest of the house had not seemed so warm. She drew apart the drapes and opened the window by pulling it up from the bottom. The air which streamed in seemed magically cooler than the air within the room. It could have been because the house had been empty for a month; or could it have been something else?

Julia went to the storage heater set against the wall and touched it with the flat of her hand. She snatched it back in pain. The heater had been turned up to the full. The real-estate agent must have turned it on, Julia thought, so that he would not be showing customers a chilly house. Perhaps some of the down-stairs heaters were on as well. She switched off the bedroom heater at the wall and went into the black-mirrored bathroom to comb her hair. The small heater in this room, she discovered, was also on. She flicked it off at the wall, and straightened up to look at herself. In these bathrooms it was impossible *not* to look at oneself. Julia wondered what sybaritic tricks the McClintocks had got up to before these sinister black mirrors. Yet her hair shone in them: and she supposed that she looked good enough for a restaurant. There was a decent-looking French restaurant, she remembered, just off Kensington High Street on Abingdon Road. And hadn't she seen a Chinese restaurant too? Now, she was embarrassed that she had cried, however briefly, before Lily; Lily had, though, demonstrated an almost otherworldly kindness. It seemed to Julia that she had very little to weep about—the sensation of debating between restaurants was one she had not had since her wedding, and it was charged with a nostalgic, delicious liberty. Still drowsy, hungry as she had not been in years, Julia felt for the moment young and capable of anything.

She decided, once on Kensington High Street, to try the French restaurant, remembering that it had been awarded a Michelin rosette some months before. On this first night, she could afford to be lavish with herself. She had, in the past, argued bitterly with Magnus about restaurants; spending twenty pounds on a meal for two at Keats was obscene; but surely tonight she had something to celebrate. Julia drifted down the busy street, looking in the shop windows, conscious of the multitude of cars surging past on her right, noting where she might buy things she needed for the house. She saw a bank: she would transfer her own account here and leave Magnus what she had put into their joint account. Up ahead was a W. H. Smith for buying books. She noticed a surprising number of package stores. At length she reached Abingdon Road and crossed the High Street to walk up toward the restaurant. The night air moved languorously about her, slipping past her skin. As she opened the door of the restaurant, a beautiful black-haired girl wearing large tinted glasses coming down Abingdon Road smiled at her, and Julia smiled back, feeling as though the girl had given her the liberty of the neighborhood. She too was a capable young woman, living alone in Kensington.

After dining luxuriously and slowly, relishing every mouthful of her snails, then half a seafood pancake, and finally a *suprême de volaille*, Julia paid for her meal with a check and walked back along the crowded street. Traffic seemed perpetual here, gnashing and snarling past as if it too were on its way to a meal. Only when she reached the quiet corner of Ilchester Place did she remember she had left the house key in the pocket of the dress now soaking in the sink.

"Christ," she moaned. She went up the steps and tried the front door. It was locked. Julia looked up at the windows and saw that she had left lights burning in the bathroom and bedroom. At the rear of the house, she had left the bedroom window open, but it was far out of reach. Perhaps a window in the kitchen or dining room might be unlatched. Julia walked around the side of the house, pushing randomly at the windows she could reach. After she had walked down the entire length of the right side of her house, she looked down in frustration and saw that she had trampled many of the little flowers the McClintocks had grown in a border around the house—small, brilliant flowers with thoughtless, optimistic faces. They lay crushed and broken in a weaving line down the side of the house, just visible in the darkness. Julia felt as though the massive dark bulk of the house were rebuking her—it was a strong but momentary impression: she did not deserve this house and the house knew it now. "Oh, please," she breathed, and pushed at another window. It resisted her.

Julia rounded the corner at the back of the house and found herself in her moonlit back garden. The grass looked spectral, some color between green and black. Indeed, the entire garden looked unearthly in the dark light, the flower banks at the far end massive and colorless, like stationary clouds. Behind them reared the brick wall at the end of her property. Julia had a momentary tremor of fear that someone besides herself was concealed in the garden, but pushed this from her mind by the decisive action of vigorously trying each of the windows in turn. At the far end she discovered that the small window in the bathroom was opened out at the bottom, unlocked and with its ratchet set so that the window protruded two or three inches beyond the frame.

She reached in and released the ratchet, freeing the window so that it swung freely, opening a space about a foot high and fifteen or sixteen inches long, set in the wall at the height of her head. When she threw up the window and poked her head beneath it, she could see, in the rose mirror opposite, the light space of the window filled with the black orb of her head. Ordinarily, she would not think it possible that she could lift and squeeze her body through this small space, but now she had no other choice. The air in the bathroom felt silkily warm to her face; she had to crawl in this way. The only alternative was to break a window, and she shrank before doing violence to the house.

On the verge of pulling her trunk up to force her shoulders through the window, Julia again sensed that another person was somewhere in the back garden: her stomach frozen with fear, she whirled about. No one was visible. The grass, tinted that expressionless color, lay unbroken to the mass of the flowers. Nothing moved. Julia narrowed her eyes and tried to see into the McClintocks' flowers. She braced her legs and felt some of the zinnias of the border crush beneath her feet. "I know you're there," she said. "Come on out. Now." She felt both foolish and courageous, uttering these words in as commanding a voice as she could summon. Still there was no movement from the featureless dark bank of the flowers. After another long scrutiny, she felt safe enough to turn her back to the garden.

Again she felt the heavy warmth emanating from her house. She braced her elbows, bowed her head, and scrabbled up the wall with her feet while pushing her shoulders through the window frame. The window, let loose, dug her painfully in the back of the neck. Hitching up on one arm, she banged the aluminum border of the window with her other hand; this gave her enough leverage to push herself through the window nearly to her waist.

She wriggled, dropping her upper body so that her weight might drag her bottom through. Instead, she stuck in the window like a swollen fruit. She jerked forward twice, abrading the skin at her hips: from sudden though tolerable pain, she knew she had begun to bleed. Julia pushed with all her strength at the wall, bending with as much torque as she could muster, and felt her hips slide through another half inch. With one further push and bend, she came through, banging her heels on the protruding window, and fell to the bathroom carpet on her right shoulder. She had lost both shoes.

She lay for several minutes on the bathroom floor, breathing heavily. Her fingers found the cool marble of the tub. Her hips ached; her stomach fluttered.

For some minutes Julia was unable to move, fearing she might be sick. The skin of her face and hands felt very hot. Eventually she sat upright and rested her back against the bathtub. Through the material of the blue blouse, the marble felt very cool. Modern urban people, peaceful and sedentary, are crippled by shock when they receive otherwise ordinary physical distress; Julia had read this theory in a magazine recently, and she now ruefully reflected that it seemed true in her case. She could nearly feel the blood beating in her face.

Supporting herself with one hand on the rim of the tub, she unsteadily stood up. The wall mirrors reflected a tangle-headed, stooping female figure in pale, ripped trousers. Everything glowed darkly, pinkly, as if through a haze. What she could see of her face looked black. Julia moved slowly to the sink. She tugged at the seersucker dress and let it drop wetly to the carpet; then she pulled the plug, not moving until the standing water had been sucked away, and ran fresh water, which she splashed on her face. The water smelled like greasy coins. When she peeled off her trousers, she saw that she had scraped skin from both hips; the trousers, bloodied, were ruined. By morning, she would have the beginnings of spectacular bruises on both hips. Julia bent down to the sodden dress, extracted her key from the pocket, and turned on trembling legs to the door. Then she had a second thought, and patted the heater by the door. It nearly burned her fingers, and she flipped up the wall switch to turn it off. Before leaving the bathroom, she remembered to place the blue dress back in a sinkful of fresh water.

The entire house seemed sluggishly hot; Julia thought it might take her an entire morning to find all of the heaters. Yet the warmth spread seductively throughout the living room, and she sat on the gray couch to relax for a second before attempting the stairs. Her hips ached. One of the downstairs heaters was set into the wall beside the big windows; yet another smaller heater was in the kitchen. Julia leaned back in the couch, stretching her legs out before her. She closed her eyes. Her hips smarted, but at least had stopped bleeding from the abrasions. Then she blinked, imagining that she had heard a series of sharp clicking noises from the dining room. Perhaps they had come from the kitchen: refrigerators made all sorts of noises. She heard one sudden, definite clicking noise, and her eyes opened involuntarily. It had come from the dining room—the noise had sounded like someone tapping at the window. Julia looked across the width of the living room into the dining room, directly off it. Its large French windows were set in line with the living-room windows, so that a passerby could look through the house into the garden. The dining-room drapes hung a foot apart. Through the gap, Julia could see nothing but black. She felt an extreme disquiet; she wore only the blue blouse and underpants, and sat in view of the window. Perhaps someone had been hiding in the garden after all.

Her heart accelerated. Julia bounded up from the couch and ran through the hall to the bathroom and latched the window through which she had crawled. Then she crept back through the warm house to the dining room and peered out, concealing her body behind the drapes. A second later, she thought she had distinguished a standing figure—it was a darker shape posed before the mass of the flowerbeds. It moved slightly. She had no impression of height or sex; she needed none. Julia knew that it must be Magnus. She fell to the floor as if by instinct. Julia lay there for some minutes in a panic before she recognized that she must have been wrong. Magnus did not know where she lived.

If it were Magnus, and he wanted to hurt her, he would have assaulted her in the garden. He could scarcely have missed her scramble through the bathroom window. And it was possible that no one was in the garden. The motion might have been a bush, moved by some breeze.

Julia opened her eyes and peered out to the garden, her face at ground level. The garden held nothing untoward. Her heart had begun to beat normally once again, and Julia sat up, blotting her face with the heavy drape. The grass still had that spectral, shining blackness, and she could see the brick wall quite clearly. Nothing between the house and the wall was moving. Julia stood up and, holding one hand to her chest, went back into the living room, moving slowly in the darkness. *Heaters*, she thought, and glided across the room to the big storage heater set into the wall. It too had been turned on, and she flipped up the switch set into the wall.

Julia woke with a start several hours later: she had been dreaming, and the dream eluded her from the second of her waking. She could hear noises from below; at the same moment she was aware of the noises, she became conscious of the heat in her bedroom. The window remained open, but the bedroom had not cooled since Julia had left for the restaurant. Her entire body was perspiring; this connected in some way to her dream, which had been frightful. She went taut with attention, listening, but heard nothing more. But there had been noises. She had not imagined them—rustling, soft, hushed noises, as of some person moving about in the dark. Her first thought was *Kate's up*, but this was only a half-conscious formulation on the surface of her mind when she thrust it away, aware that Kate had been in her dream, somehow threatened. Spurred by the image of Kate in peril, Julia sat up in bed, listening. She could hear no further noises. She rose from her bed and moved to the doorway. Standing halfway out into the hall, she loudly said, "I'm going to telephone the police. Did you hear me, Magnus? I'm telephoning the police."

Not knowing if she were to be attacked in the next instant, she hung in her doorway, listening with her entire soul. Sweat ran in a distinct line down her back to her buttocks. The hall seemed a shade cooler than her bedroom, less concentrated and dense. Julia remained poised in the doorway a long moment, hearing nothing, her mind empty of all but physical sensations. She began to count silently to one hundred, forcing herself to pause between numbers; when she reached one hundred, she went on to two hundred. Still she heard nothing. She must have been mistaken; yet she was too frightened to go downstairs to check. In the end, she went back inside the bedroom and locked the door. Then she thrust up the window and let the cooler night air pour over her. In her garden, in the visible areas of the park, all was still. Eventually she returned to her bed and lay down on the damp mattress.

The next morning, while Julia was writing a provisional shopping list on the back of her checkbook, the only paper she could find in her bag apart from a few wrinkled tissues, the telephone shrilled in the living room. Her first thought was that Markham and Reeves were ringing with some question about the house; but realizing that Markham and Reeves were likely to ignore her until she annoyed them with yet another request, Julia thought that Lily must be telephoning her. She put down her checkbook and went from the kitchen into the living room. Light streamed slantwise through the big south windows and the front of the house. The terrors of the previous night had seemed unreal and slightly hysterical to her, waking uncovered in the sunny house and moving through it during the morning, deciding what she needed to buy—food, dishes, glasses, pots and pans, sheets, towels, blankets, eating utensils. For the time being, bottled water. Books and whiskey.

"Hello?" she said, looking at the windows across the street. A man down the block washed his car, sluicing water across its top. Who were these people, who were her neighbors?

In the next instant all the optimism was battered out of her by the sound of Magnus' voice. "Julia, I expect you know who this is. I want you to leave that building and come back to Gayton Road. That's where we *live*. I've been on to the estate agents, and I made it clear to them that no contract you could sign would be considered binding, so we might just emerge from this ludicrous deal of yours with only a small loss. At the moment, Julia, I consider you incompetent to handle your own affairs, and certainly incompetent to make decisions about our future. In the meantime I want you here where you belong. You must leave that house. It is unthinkable—"

She hung up.

When the telephone rang again, she plucked the receiver from the hook and held it away from her ear. Magnus' voice went harshly on, but she could distinguish only isolated words. *Irresponsible . . . featherbrained . . . Kate . . . marriage . . .*

"I don't consider myself married to you any longer," she said into the receiver. "You frighten me. You're a bully. I can't think of you without seeing Kate. So I can't look at you, live with you, be married to you. Please leave me alone, please. Stay away, Magnus."

"Like hell I will," she heard him say. "You're disturbed—when you face up to certain things—"

She shouted, "If I catch you hanging around my house, in the garden or anywhere else, I call the police." Then she snapped the receiver down.

She stood over the telephone, waiting for him to ring again, threatening, bullying, lying to her. When a minute passed without his making a third call, she thought: he ripped the phone out of the wall.

Yet, a few seconds later, he did ring again.

"Julia, Magnus. Don't ring off. I was so angry I couldn't telephone back immediately. Julia, I want you here. I want you with me. I fear for you. You're in danger down there, alone."

Julia felt herself stiffen. "Why am I in danger, Magnus?"

"Because you're alone. Because you need help."

"On the contrary, Magnus," she said. "I feel safe for the first time in two months. Lily promised me she wouldn't call you, and now that she has, the only danger I can imagine is from you. Maybe I'll move again. I know you were here last night. You were watching me. When we have something to talk about, I'll invite you to my house. Until then, stay away. Or you will be in embarrassing trouble."

She could visualize his response to this: his hands tightening into fists, his face reddening, his mouth compressing.

"Damn you," he said. To Julia, it was as though the weight of their ten years together was behind his curse. She made no reply; a second later, Magnus hung up. Now she felt as though in battle with Magnus—perhaps the chiefest effect of eleven years of marriage was that threats and curses were no longer suppressed by politeness. They knew each other too well for politeness.

Twenty minutes later when for the first time she heard the sound of her doorbell, Julia started violently, spilling the contents of her bag. It was just long enough since her telephone call for Magnus to have driven down from Hampstead, intent on forcing her back to the house—or back to the hospital. There was no question that Magnus was capable of clapping her back in a hospital bed, muddled by drugs: in the meantime he could find some legal maneuver that would make her his prisoner. This was a new thought, and Julia, stuffing things back into her bag, resolved that she would fight him physically, violently, rather than submit to being dragged away.

She crept behind a large brown chair and peered around the drapes to the front steps. She could see only a squat, foreshortened shadow. Then the person took a backward step and came into view. It was Mark Berkeley. Julia jumped up from behind the chair and hurried to the door. She threw it open just as Mark, still walking backward and looking up at the house, had reached the steps to the pavement.

"Mark, you darling," she said. "What a wonderful surprise. I thought you were Magnus. Please come in."

Mark stood in the sunlight grinning at her. He really was incredibly handsome. His denim shirt and trousers were so faded they might have been the same ones he had been wearing when she first met him.

"Do you mind my knowing your secret?" he said. "Lily rang me yesterday evening. She's full of admiration for you, and I must say I am too. What a beautiful house. It's perfect."

"Lily has a terribly big mouth, but in your case, I don't mind." Julia held the door as Mark came into the hall beside her. For a moment she had a strong impression that he was about to embrace her, and she moved fractionally away from him. Mark put one warm hand on her back.

"She called Magnus too? So he knows where you are?" Julia nodded.

"He rang me up two nights ago, in an utter rage. He accused me of hiding you from him."

"Damn him." Julia was shocked, and then considered that such a suspicion was characteristic of Magnus. "Oh, I'm so sorry, Mark. I don't want you to be bothered by him. Well, come on in and sit down. Can I get you anything? Actually, I can't. I don't have a thing in the house and I was just about to go shopping. Oh, I'm so happy to see you, you're just like fresh air."

"Why do you keep this house at nursery temperature? It's warmer in here than outside." Mark flopped onto the couch. "Julia, you know you needn't be apologetic about Magnus with me—I've known him even longer than you have. In fact, I was never quite sure why you stayed with him all those years. I suppose I can say that now."

"You can say anything you like," said Julia, though she did not actually wish it, and disliked his remark. Almost against her will, she added, "We did have Kate," and then thought that her marriage really was over if she could make such a statement. Seeing handsome, banished Mark at rest in her home, his scuffed boots crossed on her carpet, Julia felt alarmingly free of Magnus. She said, "I can't bear to think of him right now, Mark. I'm still frightened of him. But I'm getting stronger. You do think I did the right thing?"

"Julia released from bondage," Mark said, laughing. "Of course you did the right thing. I'm just worried that he won't let you be. Do you think he won't bother you?"

"I don't know," Julia admitted. "I think he might have been sneaking around the house last night. It was just an impression, something I saw out in the garden, a figure. In fact, he as much as admitted it this morning on the telephone. He scared me out of my wits." Mark was regarding her very seriously, which gave Julia's narrative some impetus: she would have hated Mark's easy dismissal of her fears.

"But that's terrible," he said. "That's just what I was afraid of. You have to keep him away. To be frank, I wouldn't trust anything he says. It would be just like Magnus to try to frighten you into returning to him."

"Oh, let's not talk about Magnus," Julia pleaded. "I want to show you my house. Do you really like it? I bought it in such a rush that I'm not sure myself. I've never done anything like this by myself before."

"It's perfect for you," he said. "But where did you get all this astounding furniture?"

"It belonged to the people who used to live here," she said. "I like it. I don't want to have to think about furniture."

"Then you're all right," he said, smiling.

Julia led him through the house, taking him into each room in turn until they came finally to her bedroom.

"But it's roasting in here," Mark said. "Even with the windows open. You must have the heaters on. Where are they?"

"No, I switched them off yesterday," Julia said, going across the green carpet to the big gray block of the heater. She looked at the wall outlet and saw that the switch was in the down position. "That's funny, I thought . . ." She paused. "Maybe I switched it on. No, I couldn't have, because it was so hot when I moved in. I must have been mistaken in some way." She bent down and flipped up the switch. "Up is off, isn't it? On these switches."

"Usually," Mark said. He went across the room and lightly touched the top of the heater. "Well, that's on, anyhow. It's turned up all the way. Maybe you have a poltergeist."

"Oh, I hope so," Julia said. "That's nice. You just smile when I say something drippy and girlish like that. Magnus would look disgusted."

"Magnus has Standards."

"And a powerful soul."

"Hah! Do you forgive her for letting me know your secret?"

"For telling you, but not for telling Magnus. He gave me a wretched night."

"Let me go shopping with you, and I'll help you put Magnus right out of your mind."

"You're a dear. I'll need lots of help carrying heavy things."

"Consider my back yours." These words, coming from Mark, had an almost explicit sexual overtone; Julia took his arm as answer. No one as irresponsible as Mark could ever be threatening.

"If you help me, maybe I'll return the favor by helping you clear up that legendary mess of yours in Notting Hill."

"Agreed," Mark said.

3

Even later, Julia could look back on that afternoon of shopping with nostalgic, regretful pleasure. It had been as though she really were free of all ties, unattached, spendthrift and carefree—the girl she might have become ten years ago if she had not been mesmerized by Magnus Lofting. She and Mark had taken the Rover first to Oxford Street, where Julia bought towels and sheets and some kitchen things she needed, and then to Harrods. Mark had insisted on buying her an odd little green bracelet, not expensive by Harrods standards. Finally they had gone to Fortnum and Mason, where Julia spent a ridiculously happy, ridiculously costly hour buying exotic groceries. Julia several times caught other shoppers looking at her queerly and realized she was making a lot of noise but for once did not feel embarrassed or rebuked; Mark, for his part, seemed delighted by her effusiveness. His enjoyment of her high spirits fed them: Julia felt nearly intoxicated with pleasure, uncomplicated and cloudless. She and Mark had tea at Fortnum's; then they abandoned the laden Rover in a parking garage and went to a pub; in the evening he took her to a small restaurant in Notting Hill. Magnus had never entered a pub in all his adult life—Magnus would have fled The Ark (provided that he could have been coaxed into any restaurant in Notting Hill) at first sight of the menu which was chalked on boards hung on the walls. After dinner, now in a second pub, Mark rather shyly invited Julia to his flat: "Room, actually. You've never been there."

"Some other time, dear Mark. I have all those things to put away. And I've had too much liquor to trust myself in your room."

That night her dreams were lurid. She was walking slowly, ploddingly, through Holland Park—a Holland Park full of statues and bronze monuments. She was alone; Magnus had vanished somewhere, and Julia knew that he was seeing another woman. Kate gamboled up ahead, her head bobbing, her white dress winking in the gray-green light. Julia tried to walk faster, in order to protect Kate, but each step took enormous effort, as though she was walking through a bog. Then, looking ahead, she saw that Kate had a companion, the blond girl she had seen on her first day in the park. The two girls danced ahead of her, unheeding. Their identical heads, each white gold, flew through the dense air. Far ahead of Julia, on a long hill, they sat down. Julia tried to run, but her legs were as if paralyzed. The second girl was speaking rapidly to Kate, uttering some vile business—Kate sat enthralled. When Julia came nearer, the girls turned their faces toward her, their identical eyes glowing. "Go away, Mother," Kate said.

Then she was carrying Kate's body through a city. The blond girl, as before, danced ahead of her, leading. Julia followed after, crossing busy streets in bright sunshine, until they had left the crowded downtown part of the city and were in a sinister, dilapidated area: grimy, sunless courts and filthy brick buildings with boarded windows. A hunch-backed man scuttled past, grinning at her. The blond girl entered one of the buildings through an open arch. Julia, frightened, forced herself to follow. She found herself somehow on a rooftop, stared at by shabbily dressed, lounging men. Her arms were in great pain and Kate had got very heavy. The blond girl had vanished through another arch. Julia understood that she would have to stand on the rooftop, holding her daughter's corpse and gazed at by the shabby men—she would have to stand there for hours. The entire scene had a despairing, criminal atmosphere of moral failure; Julia wanted to leave, but she could not.

She awakened in the hot room. The despairing flavor of the dream still clung to her. Julia missed Kate terribly: at the moment, as she stared up into blackness, her life seemed empty of anything but loss and uncertainty. With a tiny shock of disapproval, she realized that she wanted Mark's company, not sexually, but for the fact of his sleeping near, his chest rising and falling. She turned over on her other side and buried her head deep into her pillow, which still smelled of the shop; the single blanket she had put on the bed had been kicked off during her sleep. She closed her eyes, trying to overcome the mood of the dream. Then she heard the noise which had awakened her the night before. It was a soft, rustling, rushing noise, coming from the hall or the stairway. Julia tightened, then relaxed. It must have been a breeze on the drapes in the hall.

A crash from downstairs made her sit bolt upright in bed—she immediately thought that Magnus had broken in and was now storming about, breaking things. At first she felt her familiar fear of him, but as she listened, her fear hardened into anger: she would not have Magnus in this house. She lifted her wrist near to her face and squinted at her watch. It was past two in the morning. If Magnus were out at this hour, he was probably drunk. In the past years, he had begun to drink more heavily and often came home to Gayton Road smolderingly intoxicated, incensed by something that had happened in the night. She slid from bed, pulled a nightdress over her head, and then wrapped herself in her bathrobe. When she opened the door to the hall she listened intently, cautiously, but heard nothing.

Julia left her bedroom and crept into the hall, moving as quietly as possible. When she reached the head of the stairs, she heard the rustling noise again, and her heart nearly stopped. She flailed out with her right hand and banged the switch for the stairway light. No one was there. She could see the edge of the drapes over the downstairs hall window; they hung straight and still. The rustling noise had suggested rapid movement, a two-legged presence; yet it was a feminine noise, and it was impossible to imagine Magnus producing it. Julia went quietly and slowly down the stairs and paused in the hall. She heard nothing from any of the rooms. Still using the light emanating from the staircase, she pushed open the door to the living room. Moonlight lay over the couch and carpet, silvery and weightless. The yellow cover of Lily's book shone from the floor. "Magnus," she enunciated, taking a step into the room. "*Magnus.*" There was no answer. Julia became aware that her eyes hurt; her flanks, too, throbbed where she had abraded them the previous night. "Say something, Magnus," she said. It would be very unlike Magnus to crouch silently in a dark room. Much more in his style would be to seize her, shouting.

Julia glanced rapidly around the room, but saw nothing amiss; the living room looked drugged, impersonal, not hers; the McClintocks' furniture lay like heavy beasts sleeping around a water hole. She walked through the moonlight to the dining room. These drapes too were open, and she could see out into the garden, eerie in the silvery light. There too nothing moved. Julia turned around to look into the corners of the room.

And then she saw what had made the noise. Lily's flowers lay in a puddle on the carpet, the vase she had put them in shattered into four or five large irregular pieces. Julia stifled a scream rising in her throat, and put one hand to her mouth: someone had smashed the vase against the mahogany table and then thrown the flowers to the carpet. She ran to the windows and tugged at the handle; it moved smoothly down, and the window swung out into the garden, admitting a wave of cool night air. It was unlocked. Last night, outside, she had pushed at the handle, and it had not budged. Now she turned the key, locking the window again. Magnus must have entered somehow—had found his way in here—and after smashing the vase, had fled through the garden. The scene, in her imagination, had the same stench of moral failure, the same hopelessness, as the moment on the rooftop in her dream—it was overwhelmingly despairing.

Julia bent to the soaking carpet and picked up the sections of the McClintocks' vase. These she took into the kitchen and set on the counter. Later she would try to glue them together. When she returned to the dining room she gathered the foolish broken flowers, took them into the kitchen and pitched them into the small bin beneath the sink. She thought of Magnus reeling home, furious, talking to himself, staggering bearlike up Kensington High Street. She supposed that he would visit one of his women.

After she had blotted up some of the water with a dish towel, Julia went back upstairs to her bedroom. She felt flushed and restless and lay down in her bed to await morning. It would be impossible to sleep, she thought, but her eyes, heavy, began to close almost immediately. Just before she dozed, she imagined she heard far-off laughter—an unfriendly, mocking noise. Heat settled on her in layers; in one of the broken dreams she had between intervals of wakefulness, she dreamed that she and Kate were birds, gliding birds, riding currents of warm air. Up there, they were free: no one would notice them. She desired anonymity, apartness, isolation. Perhaps, she thought, she really did want to go mad.

"Well, I told you I wanted to see your house," said Lily. They were speaking on the telephone, shortly before noon. "And it would be a heaven-sent answer to our problem. Normally we meet at Mr. Piggot's rooms in Shepherd's Bush, but he's been doing some painting and the flat simply reeks of it— extremely unsuitable, as you can imagine. Mrs. Fludd won't come to Plane Tree House because she insists on working in a ground-floor room, and I don't imagine we should occupy the lobby, do you? Miss Pinner and Miss Tooth live together in a bed-sitter in West Hampstead, but that too is on the second floor. Mr. Arkwright says his wife won't hear of having our session at his house. So, my dear, you see our position. Might we meet at your house? I know it's an intrusion, especially as it's your first experience, but I'm at my wit's end trying to invent a ground-floor room which simply does not exist."

"No, it's my pleasure, really," said Julia, who was in fact dubious about having Mrs. Fludd and the rest of Lily's circle in her house. Then she thought that if Magnus were hanging about outside, watching the house, it would serve him right to see a crowd of people drive up. She saw the house from his point of view, all its lights blazing, cars parked outside on both sides of the street: it would be an emblem of her independence from him. She said, "I'd be happy to help out. What time do you usually meet?"

"You *angel*," breathed Lily. "Nine o'clock. The others will be so gratified."

"Should I have any refreshments? Anything to eat?"

"Coffee or tea. Some biscuits. We're not a very particular set."

For the rest of the morning Julia sat out in the sun in her garden, alternately reading *Herzog* and dozing; after lunch she went again into the garden, taking with her an iced glass of gin and bitter lemon. The drink, the hot sun, reminded her of summer afternoons in America, at home or at Smith, afternoons of Nat Cole on the radio, boys appearing to sprawl on the grass. In this mood of nostalgic, sun-drugged leisure, Julia passed the afternoon, reading steadily through *Herzog*.

At four, struck by an idea, she went into the house through the dining room and telephoned Mark.

"It's probably totally crazy," she said, feeling a little dishonest. "Lily practically insisted that I join her gang of devil-worshipers or whatever they are, and now that they're meeting here I feel sort of swamped by them. Could you come over to hold my hand?"

"Lily won't like that," said Mark.

"Bugger Lily. I haven't even mentioned to her that she broke her promise to me by telephoning Magnus. I know she couldn't help it. Besides, I don't know that she wouldn't like it if you were here. Aren't you two friends these days? I thought you and Lily were getting on?"

"She's got some peculiar ideas about me," Mark laughed. "I think Lily fancies herself my warden."

"As mine too," she said. "Please come. We're all meeting at nine, but you could come over earlier."

"Done. Do you want me to bring anything?"

"Bring yourself," Julia said.

Lily and a squat, red-faced woman in a flowered dress covered by a shapeless, ancient gray tweed overcoat straining at one large button arrived at eight-fifty. As a pair they were unavoidably comic: Lily like some aging, silky moth accompanied by this little bulldog of a woman who needed only a carthorse's straw hat to complete her ensemble. And Julia could not keep from smiling at the two of them when she had opened the door. Of all the women who looked like Lily, she thought, only Lily would appear in public with this person. They looked like a vaudeville team—Lily would be the "aristocrat" who is doused with water and slapped with cream pies.

"Mrs. Fludd and I had a lovely walk through the last of the sun," Lily said. "Julia Lofting, Mrs. Fludd."

"How do you do?" Julia said. "Please come in. Did you walk through the park?"

"Holland Park is locked at sunset," said Lily. "It's tight as a drum. Mrs. Fludd wanted to see the neighborhood."

"It ain't half hot," said Mrs. Fludd. "It's tropical, I call it. Still, it's nearer than Shepherd's Bush. Not exactly cool in here either, is it?"

Julia apologized, explaining about the heaters.

"You want to go to a nice air-conditioned bingo," said Mrs. Fludd.

She bumped to a halt following Lily into the living room. Mark rose from the couch, grinning. "Nice to see you again, Lily," he said. "And you must be the wonderful Mrs. Fludd I've heard so much about."

Lily glanced at him, and then at Julia; her disapproval clear, she turned to attend to Mrs. Fludd, who appeared to have become even redder and more squat in shock.

"There's two new ones," she complained. "You said one. You never said two new ones. I come all this way for nothing. Too much interference with two new ones."

"This is my brother, Mark Berkeley," Lily quickly said. "He's a friend of Mrs. Lofting's. Mrs. Fludd, please don't say it's impossible. All the others will be arriving soon. And I wanted Mrs. Lofting to witness our transcendences."

"No transcendences with two new ones," Mrs. Fludd said firmly. "No transformations, no interpenetrations, and no consummations neither. This one"— she pointed at Julia with a stubby finger—"is skeptic. All the vibrations will be muddled. Aren't you skeptic, dear?"

Julia looked at Lily, not sure what to say. Lily was no help. She was still upset by Mark's presence. "I suppose I am," she finally said.

"Of course you are. Your aura's dark—dark as pitch. Confusion and despair in the seventh plane. That's the plane of domesticity. Right, dear?"

"Well . . ."

"Right, then. And there's another cloudy aura," nodding to Mark. "Dirty as an old pond. But that one's open to things. He's receptive. Maybe too open. Pretty men are like that. He needs special care, he does."

"Does that mean you won't do it?" said Julia. She was charmed by Mrs. Fludd.

"Did I say I wouldn't? I said, no transcendences, no transformations, no interpenetrations and no consummations. You couldn't follow them proper anyhow, being skeptic. But *he* could—he's open. He wants to be filled, like a bottle."

Mark laughed delightedly and said, "Mrs. Fludd, you're a genius. You're worth twice your fee."

"Don't take money," said Mrs. Fludd, unbuttoning the single button and permitting the front of the tweed overcoat to spring apart. "Money soils the gift. I take tea, though. PG Tips is my drink." She moved unhesitatingly toward the couch. "Mr. Piggot makes a wonderful cup of tea." She sat, exposing thick white calves and a pair of tight, black policeman's boots, and looked expectantly at Julia.

"Oh, I'm sorry," Julia said, "but I don't have any tea. I bought coffee, thinking . . ." She looked again at Lily, who merely shrugged, still distressed by Mark's presence. She had moved far across the room from him, and after her gesture to Julia, pretended to examine the garden through the long dining-room windows.

"Can't drink that muck," said Mrs. Fludd. "Sometimes I take a little Ribena. Smashing for the upper regions, Ribena is."

"I don't have any Ribena either," Julia said, nearly wailing.

"Humph."

"Sherry?"

Mrs. Fludd cocked her head and considered. "Well, as there's to be no special tricks tonight, I could accept a tiny amount of sherry, yes. Next time, you want PG Tips, love. We all drink tea here. Miss Pinner and Miss Tooth dote on Mr. Piggot's tea. Here's my coat, love."

When Julia was going toward the kitchen for the sherry the doorbell rang, and she asked Lily to open it for her. When she returned to the living room, a tall spindly man in his sixties with a severe long face and a little Hitler mustache was regarding Mark with an expression of grave disquiet. "Two will never do, Miss Lofting," he was saying. The man had thrust his hands into the pockets of his long tan canvas coat—a coat like a park attendant's or a movie IRA man's—and showed no inclination to remove it or his large-brimmed hat of the same color. Mark, perfectly at ease, merely smiled back at the man.

"Now, Mr. Piggot," Lily coaxed, "Mrs. Fludd is willing to go ahead, and so . . . And here is Mrs. Lofting, our hostess. Mr. Piggot, Julia."

Mr. Piggot glanced sharply at Julia, softened a bit, and removed his hat. His hair grew in a graying mousy fringe above his ears, leaving a high, mottled bald scalp which looked as fragile as an eggshell. "Well," he said. "Looks like she makes a good cup of tea."

"Have a nice glass of sherry, Mr. Piggot," Julia said, trying desperately to win over the old scarecrow.

"Sherry, is it? We generally imbibe tea at these gatherings. PG Tips, I use. Mrs. Fludd fancies it, don't you, Mrs. Fludd? But I won't say no to a nice sherry, not from your hands. British, is it?"

"Uh, Spanish," Julia said. "Manzanilla."

Mr. Piggot's face contracted. "Well, it'll wet the whistle. I feel a bit dry after cycling over here from Shepherd's Bush. We generally have these sessions at my place, you know. Expect your—aunt?—has told you that. But Mrs. Fludd won't go into a place that's been painted too recently. Distorts the reverberations."

"Something horrible," Mrs. Fludd cheerfully agreed, accepting her sherry. "Throws me whole system off."

"There's Mr. Arkwright," said Mr. Piggot when the bell rang again. "Punctual as the Irish Guards is Mr. Arkwright."

Julia said, "Will you let him in, Lily?" She took a third glass of sherry to Mark, who said something sardonic about filling up his bottle and moved over to sit beside Mrs. Fludd. Mr. Piggot still gazed at him with affronted blue eyes, spaced rather too closely together.

"Hullo, all." A compact little gentleman in a frayed gray gabardine suit bounced into the room a few paces ahead of Lily. He too had a mustache and a bald head, but his mustache was larger than Mr. Piggot's, and his cranium seemed almost aggressively solid. Julia noticed a medal pinned to his jacket before she saw that one of his sleeves was pinned up. "Am I the last?" He looked around briskly, paused at Mark, and then made for Julia. "See the West Hampstead ladies aren't here yet. You must be Julia Lofting. Pleased to meet you. The name's Arkwright. Nigel Arkwright. And you have sherry, how thoughtful. Lovely house you have here, eh? My cousin Penny Grimes-Bragg took a house in this neighborhood many years ago, over in Allen Street. Not far from here, is it?"

"No, not at all," Julia said, wondering if Mr. Arkwright got out of the house much. But she had decided that he was an "ally" against the unpredictable Mrs. Fludd and the as yet unknown West Hampstead ladies.

"No more than a brisk walk," he was saying. "Driving my old bus down here, I was just thinking of the old days when Penny and I—"

"Do join me, Mr. Arkwright," Lily broke in. Her innate sociability had apparently overcome her resentment of her brother's presence, for she smiled at Julia once Mr. Arkwright turned his back.

"With pleasure, Miss L.," he chirped. "Ah, Mrs. Fludd, two new ones tonight. That'll limit the old bag of tricks, won't it?"

"Drink your sherry, Nigel," said Mrs. Fludd amicably. She had moved some inches away from Mark, who was now slumped far down on the couch so that his bottom seemed in danger of slipping to the floor. He looked profoundly bored, but Julia sensed some area of tension—unreleased, concealed—in him. Mrs. Fludd too appeared to have been accumulating psychic power, for she glanced toward the door a second before the bell rang again.

Julia went into the hall and opened the door. Two women, both thin and elderly and dressed in long, threadbare black coats, stood on the doorstep. Behind them Julia glimpsed an ancient black bicycle propped against the curb, and an even older-looking, rusty Morris Minor behind it which must have been Mr. Arkwright's "bus." The West Hampstead ladies had presumably taken a combination of buses. If Magnus were lurking outside, watching the various arrivals, the effect would not be what she had intended. In fact, she saw, the effect would be the reverse of her intention: Magnus would suppose her to have slipped over the edge into total incompetence. Still, she found a smile for the two women.

"I'm Julia Lofting. You must be Miss Pinner and Miss Tooth."

"Such a long way."

"But not as far as Shepherd's Bush."

Miss Pinner and Miss Tooth entered Julia's house, remarking upon its niceness. When they reached the living room, they darted in tandem across to Mrs. Fludd, spoke a few words to her, and then turned around to smile at the others of their group. When Miss Pinner finally saw Mark, her smile disappeared. Miss Tooth, however, cast him a glance full of vague benevolence.

"Who is this young man?" asked Miss Pinner.

"Now, Norah," said Miss Tooth.

"Who is he?"

"Mrs. Lofting's brother, Mark. Very dark in the aura, he is. *Your* aura's very strong tonight, Miss Pinner. Bright orange, the color of powerful movements in the fourth house. Perhaps we shall have luck tonight." Saying this, Mrs. Fludd looked about the room, her attention visibly distracted from Miss Pinner; she had grown, since Julia had last looked at her, slightly apprehensive.

"There will be no question of the higher states with two new ones," said Miss Pinner.

Lily said from Mr. Arkwright's side, "Mrs. Fludd has very graciously agreed to limit herself to the elementals."

As Julia looked at the two old women their faces, which had seemed so similar at the doorway, separated. Miss Pinner bore a certain resemblance to Mr. Piggot, at that moment engaged in describing to Lily and Mr. Arkwright how he caught fish in Hyde Park by fixing bread to his fishhooks: both of them had long narrow faces and small bright-blue eyes like chips of sky. Miss Tooth looked rather dusty and faded, with her small, deeply lined face the image of a retired governess. Miss Pinner could have been an exheadmistress noted for her disciplinary acumen. Julia took all the coats to the hall closet and returned with sherry for the two women. Miss Tooth glanced at Miss Pinner before accepting hers and, receiving a nod, took the glass in her small, trembling hand.

Mark gave Julia a despairing look and rose from the couch to join Lily, listening to Mr. Piggot describe his illicit fishing experiences. For these old people the spiritualist gatherings were social occasions; Mr. Arkwright kept punctuating Mr. Piggot's adventures with loud bursts of soldierly laughter. His rush of talk hadn't denoted any special sympathy for Julia, but demonstrated instead pleasure at his release from loneliness. Julia's house was filled with people whose company she could not enjoy; even Mark was sullen. Miss Pinner and Miss Tooth were now examining Julia's furniture. They were in an ecstasy of approval, everything being "so nice." Julia wished she could leave and lock the door behind her; but she took a sip of her sherry and sat beside Mrs. Fludd on the couch.

"I shouldn't stay here," said Mrs. Fludd.

"No? Mrs. Fludd, I'd be so grateful if you could. Lily has been looking forward so much . . ."

"You needn't be false to me, Mrs. Lofting, you'd be happy if the lot of us went home. But you don't take my meaning. I shouldn't stay here if I were you. Shouldn't stay in this house."

Julia looked at the woman's red puggish face in surprise; she was further surprised to notice that Mrs. Fludd's eyes were shrewd and perceptive, not at all vague. It was as though she had seen that Mrs. Fludd was actually a man, wearing that absurd clothing; the shock was as great as that. She had been seeing Mrs. Fludd as a "character," someone not to be taken seriously, and this quick glance of recognition made her blush for her assumptions. If the others of Lily's gang were lonely eccentrics, Mrs. Fludd's cool, startling gaze revealed a person composed of flintier materials than the gibberish about transcendences and interpenetrations had suggested.

"Something's funny in this house," she said.

"You think I should leave?" said Julia, transfixed.

"Do you see anything? Hear any noises? Has anything unexplained occurred?" Even her diction had altered.

"I don't know," Julia confessed. "Sometimes I think I hear things—"

"Yes." Mrs. Fludd nodded sharply.

Remembering something Mark had said, Julia asked, "What are poltergeists, exactly? I feel sort of foolish, asking you, but is it possible that there might be one here?"

"Never any harm in a poltergeist," replied Mrs. Fludd. "They move things, sometimes break a mirror or a vase—mischievous creatures. You'd be in danger only if you were very receptive, like your pretty friend across the room. Or if you were dominated by some strong destructive emotion. Hate. Envy. Then, if the spirit wished revenge, it might influence you. That's rare, but it does happen, if the spirit is particularly malefic. Or if some coincidence links you to it. In Wapping, a thief dead for fifty years set fire to a house containing a burglar's family. Killed them all."

"But how do you know?" asked Julia.

"I felt it. I knew."

Such monolithic assurance always influenced Julia. In any case, it permitted no argument. "You feel something here?" she asked.

Mrs. Fludd nodded. "Something. Can't pin it down yet. But I don't like this house, Mrs. Lofting. Who lived here before you?"

"A couple named McClintock. He made carpets. I bought this furniture from them."

"Any deaths in their family? Any tragedies?"

"I don't know. They were childless people."

"But you've seen something. Things in this house."

"Well, I'm afraid it might be my husband," Julia said, and laughed.

Mrs. Fludd immediately closed up, separating herself from Julia; then, relenting, she took Julia's hand. "Ring me if you ever want advice," she said. From her bag she extracted a white card which read *Rosa Fludd, Interpreter and Parapsychologist*. Printed at the bottom was a telephone number.

Mr. Piggot approached the couch, followed by the perky Mr. Arkwright. "It *is* time?" said Mr. Piggot. "I'm eager to investigate some theories I had at the shop since our last meeting."

"Of course, love," said Mrs. Fludd, firmly back in her former role. She clapped her hands together twice and conversation in the room ceased. Miss Pinner and Miss Tooth turned their white faces raptly to the couch.

"*Time*," breathed Miss Tooth.

At opposite ends of the room, Lily and Mark also turned to face Mrs. Fludd; Lily with an expression combining eagerness with satisfaction, Mark wearily. Julia had time to wonder what was wrong with Mark before Lily asked her to turn off the lights.

She jumped up and went quickly to the light switch. Glowing gray light entered the room from the big windows; in this soft diffused semidarkness, Julia could see the fixed, rapt expressions on the faces of the "group." She and Mark were outsiders here, and she moved to his side.

"Have you a candle or small lamp, Mrs. Lofting?"

Julia went into the dining room and turned on a little ceramic lamp in the shape of a toby jug.

"Move it further away, please," commanded Mrs. Fludd. "I must ask you all to join hands at the beginning. Look at the light behind me. Cleanse your minds."

The little lamp cast only a feeble light into the living room. Julia, joining the group, found herself being gripped by Mark on her right; he was holding her hand tight enough to hurt her. On her left Mr. Piggot's hand was surprisingly soft and damp. His wafery skull shone palely in the twilight.

The group members, once they had joined hands, moved to sit on the floor, awkwardly, pulling Julia and Mark down with them. Only little Miss Tooth accomplished the move from standing to sitting with grace, seemingly floating to a cross-legged position; Miss Pinner moved with a machinelike efficiency. Julia, covertly watching her, thought she could smell oil and gears.

Once on the floor, the group members looked past Mrs. Fludd's head to the soft light emanating from the toby jug lamp. Mark, brooding, had set his face into a mask of weary tolerance. Both apprehensive and skeptical, Julia too looked at the lamp. After a bit her eyes began to burn. When she glanced at the others, she saw that the group members had closed their eyes; their faces hung in the air like death masks. Mrs. Fludd sat in a perfectly ordinary position on the couch before them, her hands folded in her lap. In the pane of the tall back window, her head and the lamp glowed against the darker glass. Whitish clouds scudded above the flamelike, dissolving orb of the lamp.

"Close your eyes," said Mrs. Fludd, her voice very slow and quiet. Mr. Piggot, to Julia's left, sighed and slumped backward, tugging her hand. "You may open them later if you wish."

She closed her eyes. About her she heard breathing. Mark gripped her right hand harder, and she shook her hand in his, signaling him to loosen; he pinned her hand yet more tightly.

"One of us is having trouble," said Mrs. Fludd. "Who is it?"

Mark said, "I'm getting out of this." He broke contact with Julia and stood up.

"Close the group," said Mrs. Fludd. "Mr. Berkeley, you will sit quietly outside the group and observe."

Julia hitched sideways and grasped Lily's cool hand. It lay passively in hers. Lily had not opened her eyes when Mark had spoken, though all the others had. Mark now sat behind them, still facing Mrs. Fludd.

"I need your help, Mrs. Lofting," said Mrs. Fludd softly. "Make your mind empty, completely empty and white. Let nothing enter it." Her voice was slowing and becoming deeper in timbre. Julia opened one eye and saw, looking up toward the couch, Mrs. Fludd's heavy jowls outlined by the soft light behind her. Her hair was a white gauze. She seemed to have become heavier and older. Julia closed her eyes again and thought of a white saucer.

Miss Tooth, at the left end of the seated line, began to breathe stertorously. Lily's hand still lay utterly passively in Julia's. After a bit, Julia felt an ache in her thighs. Her eyes closed, she began to see flashes of scenes, people's faces or landscapes appearing momentarily before her and then melting into other scenes. Moses Herzog, his face that of an elderly English professor at Smith, metamorphosed into Blake's flea. The hideous features of the flea in turn were transformed into Magnus' face. By an effort of will, Julia dismissed this last vision—she thought of clouds covering that big, powerful face, obscuring it. When the clouds blew off, they revealed one of the lounging, shabby men who had been in her dream. Now the man was her father, and he examined her with an expression of exhausted pity. She could see herself standing on the black tarpaper of the rooftop, Kate dead in her arms. Both of her thighs ached; the right was on the verge of cramp. Julia lurched to one side and twisted her legs out before her. Mr. Piggot twitched at her hand in rebuke.

Opening her eyes, Julia again saw Mrs. Fludd, who now sat slumped in the chair as if she had fallen asleep. Her mouth was open, black and toothless in the fleshy mass of her face surrounded by the penumbra of her hair. The woman's squat body was as if compressed—"slumped" was the wrong word, for she appeared to be under gathering tension.

"Close eyes," she said in a gravelly voice. Julia, startled, immediately pressed her eyes shut. She heard Mrs. Fludd's heavy boots scuffing on the carpet. She was again on the rooftop, now alone with the men. Her father, who had died one summer while she and Magnus were in Perigord, turned his face from her. Internally, she began to speak to him, as she frequently did when moved by guilt. *You were a decent man, but too forceful. I can see that now. I married Magnus because he had your power, he could dominate like you, and then I saw what a weapon your power was. But, Daddy, I loved you. I would have gone to your funeral if I had known, I want you to forgive me for being away, I loved you always, please forgive me, grant me that.* . . . As the words became rote, the vision dissolved. She was alone on the roof, oppressed by the comprehensive atmosphere of moral loss. All was grimy, all was inferior and flawed. She bent her head. The scene turned to opaque blackness through which she fell: Julia was dizzied, and seemed actually to be slowly falling. The room seemed to have turned about; surely she was now facing the front window instead of Mrs. Fludd? She resisted the temptation to open her eyes. Again, she imagined the white saucer—cool, without blemish, entirely surface—and filled her mind with it.

For a time the only noises in the room were Miss Tooth's strained breathing and the hushing noise of Mrs. Fludd's boot scuffing the carpet. Julia grew calmer and wondered what Mark, behind them, was doing and thinking in the darkness. He had begun to be uneasy after he had crossed the room to sit beside Mrs. Fludd. She must have said something to him—as she had to Julia. And now how did they look to him, seated on the carpet like fools before the massive image of Mrs. Fludd? She could scarcely restrain the impulse to turn her head to look for him. Mr. Piggot's boneless hand, stirring momentarily in hers, returned her to her context.

"*Agh. Agh.*" The soft choking noise came, Julia thought, from Miss Tooth. Then she heard a wail which was unmistakably Miss Tooth's and realized that the insistent choking noise was made in Mr. Arkwright's throat. Lily too was making a noise; the most mothlike, ladylike of noises, an exhalation of breath carrying the slightest coloration of voice. This was astonishingly sexual. Julia's hands were tugged forward and back, and soon she too began to rock. Her legs had once more begun to ache, but she could not think of interrupting the resistless rocking motion to swivel them back under her. Daringly, she slitted her eyes and saw, as in a haze, the dark heads on either side bobbing forward and back. Each was making some low noise, rhythmical and insistent. Miss Pinner was growling like a cat. Before them sat Mrs. Fludd, her feet now still, her face distorted. Mr. Piggot's hand had grown very sweaty. Julia closed her eyes and resumed rocking back and forth. Not wishing to remember the image of Mrs. Fludd's face, she made her mind utterly void of thought. She thought of the thought of nothing. Soon she was a rocking particle of nothing.

Then she saw Kate—Kate with her back turned to her.

A deep croaking voice stopped them all. "*Aah, stop.*" Jolted back to herself, shaken by the vision of Kate, Julia withdrew her hand from Mr. Piggot's while still clinging to Lily's. She opened her eyes. Mrs. Fludd was pressed back against the cushions of the couch, her face nearly purple. She had none of the repose Julia associated with the notion of mediumistic trance: her eyes bulged, her mouth worked. "*Stop. Stop.*"

"Something's wrong," whispered Mr. Piggot.

Together they watched Mrs. Fludd struggling, not knowing what should be done. Lily tugged at Julia's hand, indicating that she was not to rise. Gradually Mrs. Fludd's face cleared of purple and her eyes closed; she lay back drained and apparently powerless, her face heavy and dead. As Julia watched, the old woman's face became chalky. "It's over," she uttered, her voice low as it had been earlier in the evening. Yet it seemed to shake. Her hands, too, trembled as she placed them on her chest, forcing herself to breathe regularly.

"Over?" inquired Miss Pinner. "Why, we were just—"

"This must stop," said Mrs. Fludd in her trembling voice. "I'm sorry. I can't do more. I can't finish." The woman, Julia saw, was terrified. "Get my coat," she ordered. She was trying to struggle up from the sofa. "No more tonight. My coat. Please." She fell back exhausted, and Julia saw with horror that the old woman had begun to blink back tears.

The group members stood about in the darkness, uncertain and disturbed. Only Miss Pinner seemed indignant. While she hissed something to Miss Tooth, Lily approached Mrs. Fludd. "Get my coat," said Mrs. Fludd. Now she was openly weeping.

"Somebody get some water, please," Lily said, and Miss Pinner looked up from her intense talk with her companion. Julia stood by, frozen, incapable of movement.

"What happened?" she asked. "Mrs. Fludd, what happened to you?"

"Get out of this house," Mrs. Fludd whispered. She lolled back on the cushions, her mouth dryly opening and closing. Tears continued to roll down her meaty cheeks. "Some water." She began to whimper.

Miss Pinner exasperatedly went from the room. Julia noticed that she was going not to the kitchen, but in the direction of the hall bathroom.

"She's frightened," Lily whispered to Julia. "What was that she said to you?"

Julia shook her head. Mrs. Fludd was again trying to speak. She bent near. Foul breath assaulted her. "Danger. I'm in danger. You too." The woman was trembling violently. A sharp, acetic odor floated up to Julia, and she recognized it only when Mrs. Fludd gasped and made a violent, thrashing attempt to get up from the couch. Now she was both humiliated and terrified, and Julia, the sour odor swirling about her like ammonia, could not hold her to the couch. She looked into the dark recesses of the living room, over the heads of Miss Tooth, Mr. Piggot and Mr. Arkwright, but Mark was nowhere in the room. He had left the house unseen.

Miss Pinner's shriek stopped her speculation and froze her as she stood, her arms on Mrs. Fludd's shoulders. Miss Tooth rushed from the room. Mrs. Fludd too had heard the scream, and sank back into the couch, closing her eyes. Julia ran after Miss Tooth. When she reached the bathroom, she saw Miss Pinner supine just inside the door; Miss Tooth was cradling her friend's head. Julia stepped over Miss Pinner's body and entered the bathroom. The mirrors reflected her startled, wide-eyed round face, making her look unnaturally healthy and beautiful. Then, momentarily, flickeringly, she saw someone behind her move out of her field of vision: she whirled around, but no one else was in the room. And if anyone had been there, Miss Tooth would have seen him. Julia turned back to the mirror; and there the figure was again just slipping from sight. Yet Julia, like everyone, had seen this happen before: it was a common experience brought on by nerves. It was no more unusual than hearing one's name called in the street. Surely, this or something similar had startled Miss Pinner. Julia approached the sink for a glass of water and saw that her blue seersucker dress, forgotten, still soaked; the water in the basin had turned the color of rust, but the dress still bore its stain.

4

When Julia finally returned home that night, shortly after eleven, she went early to her bed. She felt as though she would be apprehensive all the rest of her life—and half of the disquiet lay in the inability to be definite about what was its source. She and Lily had taken the quaking Mrs. Fludd to her flat in a taxi; driven through the grim, hopeless streets which were so much like the streets of her dream, they had come to Mrs. Fludd's block of flats, in a cul-de-sac off the Mile End Road. The streetlamps had all been broken, and whitish shards of glass shone up from the dirty pavements; the road too was littered with broken glass, the pebbled green spray of shattered windshields. A lighted plaque on Mrs. Fludd's building announced that the gray, prisonlike structure, one of a series of similar buildings forming a compound, bore the name Baston; before Baston, roving gangs of boys in rolled-up Levi's passed back and forth, shouting in raucous voices. Several of them stopped to gape at the taxi. When they saw Mrs. Fludd they began to hoot. "Bloody ol' witch! Bloody ol' witch!" Mrs. Fludd had not spoken a word during the long ride from Kensington, though Julia had twice asked her what had happened to her, what had she seen. The old woman's mouth had tightened with such pressure her upper lip went white. The gang of boys terrorized her even further, and she initially refused to leave the cab. Lily, on the street side, got out and at first disconcerted the boys. When they began again to hoot, it was at Lily. She ignored them and, together, she and Julia coaxed Mrs. Fludd from the taxi. "Wait for us," Lily said to the driver, and the two women helped Mrs. Fludd into the open court. Several of the boys trailed along behind, calling out obscenities. "Here," said Mrs. Fludd, flipping up a hand at an entrance: she lived on the building's ground floor, as Julia had expected.

Julia supported her through the small, antiseptic flat to the tiny bedroom where a dusty budgerigar slept in its cage. The bedroom, no larger than a big closet, contained a single bed and a dwarfish chest of drawers. On the white walls hung crosses, star charts, a dozen odd paintings which Julia scarcely noticed. Lily had gone into the kitchen to see if anything could be found for

Mrs. Fludd, and Julia helped the old woman down onto the cramped bed and bent to unlace her boots.

Bending and struggling with the tight knots, Julia felt a pudgy hand settle on the nape of her neck. "Get out of here," Mrs. Fludd croaked.

"I just thought I could help," Julia said, looking up into the old woman's flaring face—she wondered if Mrs. Fludd's heart was all right.

"No. I mean, get out of this country," muttered Mrs. Fludd. Her breath was like a buzzard's. "Go back to America. Where. You belong. There's danger here. Don't stay."

"Danger here in England?"

Mrs. Fludd nodded as if to a backward child, and rolled onto her bed.

"Does it have to do with what we were talking about? What did you see?"

"A child and a man," Mrs. Fludd said. "Be careful. Things could happen to you." She closed her eyes and began to breathe heavily through her mouth. Julia, looking up at the wall, found herself looking at a Keane print.

"Is the man my husband?" she asked.

"The house is yours," Mrs. Fludd said. "You must leave."

Then she turned her heavy face again directly to Julia and gripped both of her hands. "Listen. I do. Fake things. Frauds. For the others. Mr. Piggot and Miss Pinner. Expect it. Not all. All that about transcendence—it's fraud. But I do see. Things. Auras. I *do*. But I hypnotize them, like. Now I'm scared. They were a man and a girl. They put you in danger. Me. In danger. They're evil. Just evil."

"Is the man my husband?"

"Get out," Mrs. Fludd groaned. "Please."

"Please, Mrs. Fludd, who is the girl? You must tell me."

The old woman rolled on her side, groaning. A wave of corrupt air rose from her body. "Go."

On the ride home Lily demanded to know what had happened. "She was frightened out of her wits. What did she say to you?"

"I'm not sure I understand it," Julia defensively said. Soon after this the cabdriver confessed that he was lost, and they switched back and forth on dark, oppressive streets before finding their way again. Julia got out of the taxi at Plane Tree House and paid the fare over Lily's protests: it took most of the money in her purse. Then she walked home, skirting the park, where voices and laughter came to her from the dark regions beyond the locked gates.

Once in her house, she went into every room, looking for she knew not what and finding nothing: most of the lights had been left burning, and the house had a blank, emptied, waiting air, as if no one lived in it. Half-filled sherry glasses adhered to the tables. One had tipped over, and poured an irregular dark stain onto the carpet. Probably because of what Mrs. Fludd had said to her, the house seemed malevolent: "malefic"—that extraordinary word the old woman had used.

In the unused bedrooms, where the furniture had been covered with dust sheets and vacancy lived like a guest, Julia felt insubstantial, drifting without purpose, looking for what she knew she would not find. Dusty and untouched, these rooms seemed chilled by their emptiness. When she checked, she saw that the heaters here had been left in the "off" position. Yet the house was a giant structure, a huge form, which hedged her out and kept her at bay: it would resist her impositions, it would not yield to her. Her sense of the house's obduracy was immense. She felt, more than ever, that she was living inside a comprehensive error, the mistake that her life had become: bigger forces lay without, waiting. A child and a man.

This hopelessness drove her finally to her hot, claustrophobic bedroom. She undressed quickly and threw her clothing over a chair; before she got into bed, she looked at the heater's wall switch. The switch was down. Julia remembered having flicked it up yesterday morning when Mark was in the room; certainly she had not turned it on since. She touched the metal surface of the heater, and found that it was as hot as if it had never been turned off. That meant that it had been on last night, since these heaters did not function during the day; yet hadn't she looked, last night? She cursed her memory. But last night Magnus had been *in the house*. Could he be so childish as to go about turning on the heaters?—but if he could stoop to smashing things up, terrorizing her as bluntly as the boys had Mrs. Fludd, it was impossible to say what he might not do. Angry, Magnus was capable of anything. She turned the heater off once again; then, on an afterthought, took a roll of tape from her closet and taped the switch to the fixture.

Though she shrank from the very idea, Magnus had to be faced: as did her feelings about him. What *were* those feelings? Julia felt at once as though she were on the crumbling lip of a precipice; her control, her hold on things sound and normal, was fragile; she knew that much of her seeming calm and placidity was a performance. Horror lay beneath the surface—horror was what inhabited the abyss below the precipice. The image of Magnus murdering Kate, that sight of him plunging the knife into Kate's throat while she thrashed on the floor, could rise in her at any time, as it had before she had been taken to the hospital and drugged into insensibility. Even then she had been tortured by waking dreams. Over and over, her wrists strapped to the side of the bed, she had imagined grasping Magnus' arm and turning the knife to her own throat. That image too had haunted her. Dying for Kate—she would gladly die for Kate. Instead, she had passively watched the clumsiest of murders. Magnus was inextricably tied to this horror, the horror of inanition, of drift which meant loss, of lying, of emptiness without end or meaning: that was death indeed, and it seemed to crawl forth from the walls of this house.

A child and a man. Kate and Magnus. Mrs. Fludd had seen them. And what had she said, before the trance? It had been something about hate or envy— they were what made a spirit "malefic." Kate was present; Kate lay behind Magnus' mad forays into Ilchester Place. She was unforgiving. Logic took her relentlessly to this illogical conclusion. Julia began to rock from side to side on her bed, moaning. She was breaking down. It was an image, again, of the precipice where she had so carefully walked, of clods and pebbles shredding away, breaking up on the long fall down. It was Kate. Mrs. Fludd had seen Kate. In some vivid, dreamlike way, Magnus was dominated by Kate; he was an unthinkable danger to her mind.

Unable to sleep, unable to control her thoughts, Julia snapped on the reading lamp at the head of the bed. She forced herself to extend her arms alongside her body. Flatten the fingers so the palms touch the sheet, extend the thumbs. Relax. She breathed deeply, twice. She would talk to Mrs. Fludd. If she had to leave the house to escape the danger Magnus posed, she was capable of leaving. For now, sleep was impossible: but she would not leave this bedroom. This room was hers. If she were to be driven from the room, she would leave the house.

Julia turned her head to see the books on the little stand beside the bed. She had finished the Bellow novel, and now had *The Millstone, The White House Transcripts, The Golden Notebook* and *The Unicorn* on the table; she needed something less stimulating than any of these. Kate and Magnus: Mrs. Fludd's hints and warnings outlined a dread possibility. Kate's spirit still living, hating her and using Magnus' anger, feeding that anger, Kate's spirit seething through this house. . . . All of this was real, happening to her.

Julia had to call Miss Pinner as well as Mrs. Fludd; before the departure of the West Hampstead ladies, Miss Pinner had been too shaky and distraught to describe what she had seen in the bathroom.

Then she saw another book which she had recently placed on the bedside table, hidden behind the little stack of paperbacks. It was *The Royal Borough of Kensington*, Lily's present to her. A sober, judicious list of facts, a few anecdotes, color plates—it was just what she needed, a book about as tangy as a suet pudding, a sleeping pill of a book. She lifted the heavy volume into her lap and began to flip the pages, reading paragraphs at random.

Prominent inhabitants of Kensington in the eighteenth century . . .Kensington as a village . . . political history of the royal borough . . . the planning of Kensington Gardens . . . merchant princes included . . . a notorious Mr. Price, hanged for the theft of a whippet. . . . Flipping a page after reading about the fate of Mr. Price, Julia saw a heading which read "Crime, Ghosts and Hauntings." At first she turned over several pages, not trusting herself to read such a chapter, but her curiosity was too great, and she went back to the heading and began to read.

At first she found nothing more exciting than had been the lists of prominent Kensington aldermen and merchants; the author had tracked down a number of conventional haunted-house anecdotes and set them down in colorless straightforward style. The ghost of a headless nun in a "manorial" building on Lexham Gardens; two sisters who had killed themselves in adjoining houses on Pembroke Place and had been seen crossing the gardens, hand in hand, by moonlight; the Edwardes Square "paterfamilias" of 1912 who had been possessed by the spirit of his mad great-grandfather and taken to dressing in the extravagant style of a century before and had finally murdered his children; Julia read all of these stories with a dulled interest.

Then a sentence and a street name burst from the text.

One of the most vexed and troubling of all Kensington murders [Julia read] was that of the case of Heather and Olivia Rudge, of 25 Ilchester Place. One of the last women to be sentenced to death in England, Heather Rudge, an American, had purchased the house on Ilchester Place from the architect, who had built it for himself in 1927 but in two years wished to move, due to family troubles; at the time, Mrs. Rudge, who was separated from her husband, had a reputation as a brilliant, rather reckless hostess, and was considered by many inhabitants of her social world as "fast." [Eda Rolph implied a fondness for handsome younger men and wealthy businessmen from the City.] One contemporary, the author of several mild books of verse and a once-popular series of theological novels, described her as possessing "a small, vivid, distinctly alarming face in which beauty and avidity fatally conjoined. *Vanitas* indeed: yet we found in her a helter-skelter charm." The birth of a daughter, Olivia, twelve years after the purchase of the Ilchester Place house, occurred in wartime, and so did little to affect her already damaged career as a hostess—the morals of a rich, aging playgirl whose greatest notoriety had passed six or seven years before interested only a few.

The parties continued, at intervals and with considerably less splendor than previously, and then ceased altogether; little was heard of the Rudges until 1950. In that year, the nine-year-old Olivia Rudge was mentioned in connection with the death by suffocation in Holland Park of a four-year-old child, Geoffrey Braden of Abbotsbury Close. Olivia Rudge and what the popular press briefly referred to as the "Holland Park Child Terror Mob"—a group of ten or twelve children apparently led by Olivia—had been seen tormenting young Braden on the day before his death. The following morning, Olivia and several others, according to a park attendant, had again pursued young Braden and abused him. The attendant had chased away the gang of older children and advised young Braden to go home; when he had returned to that area of the park, he had found the boy's body lying in a shadowed place beside a wall. Public and police interest shifted from the gang of children when it was learned that young Braden had been sexually injured before his death; and subsequently a vagrant was hanged for his murder.

Two months following the execution of the vagrant, Heather Rudge telephoned the Kensington police station to confess to the murder of her daughter. Police arriving at the house found Olivia stabbed to death in her bed; the coroner later reported more than fifty stab wounds to the body. Mrs. Rudge was immediately taken into custody and hence was protected from the crowd of journalists who wished to harry her—the murder of Olivia Rudge had quickly become a front-page speciality of the scandal press which had soon unearthed the past of Olivia's mother. ("Society Sex Queen Murders Daughter.") In time, Heather was convicted of murder and sentenced to death. Later her sentence was commuted to life in prison.

Certain questions remain. Why did Heather Rudge kill her daughter? Why was her sentence commuted? Was there a connection with the murder, a year previous, of Geoffrey Braden? Certainly the press had implied such a connection. Newspapers had seized on the case, claiming that Heather Rudge had been driven mad by her daughter; the more sensational papers asserted that Olivia had taunted her mother with her knowledge of the Braden murder, and that Heather had decided that her daughter could not be permitted to live. In time, Heather, now represented as a victim herself, was found to be insane by a special examining board. She is at present an old woman living in the permanent seclusion of a private mental hospital in Surrey. The questions remain unanswered. Heather Rudge will take the secrets of her daughter's involvement in the Braden case to her grave. Forgotten by the public, her mind shadowed and confused, Heather Rudge is a living ghost.

Julia's first thought, after reading this, was an irrelevance: so that's where those mirrors came from—Heather Rudge, with her wild parties staffed with young men, not the proper McClintocks. Then in the next half second, she knew that she would find out, that she was compelled to find out, everything there was to know about Heather and Olivia Rudge. She read the two pages over again quickly, then flipped back and read them once more, slowly and carefully. Eda Rolph nowhere stated directly that Olivia Rudge had murdered or had helped to murder the Braden boy: what grounds were there for the implication? Julia immediately began to think of how she could discover information about the Rudge case. Newspapers: surely the British Museum, if not a branch library, had newspaper files on microfilm. Could Heather Rudge be living still? She turned to the first pages of the book to look at the publishing information. *The Royal Borough of Kensington* had been published by the Lompoc Press in 1969, five years ago. She might easily be still alive. ". . . a private mental hospital in Surrey." How could she find the name of the hospital? Heather Rudge had lived in this house, she had slept in this bedroom; in sleep, her body had occupied the very space Julia's body now did. Julia seemed to be spinning through time; time seemed plastic, distorted, unsafe: the past seemed to rise up all about her, like a foul gas.

Then she sat upright, her heart speeding. Perhaps Heather Rudge had stabbed Olivia in this very bedroom. Olivia dying as Kate had died, bleeding as though blood willed to depart the living body, her blood foaming out over this spot around a hidden corner in time. . . . Julia nearly bolted from her bed.

But it could not be true. This must have been Heather's bedroom, she thought; her daughter would have had one of the smaller bedrooms down the hall. And that was where the murder would have been done.

Why am I so interested in this, in these people? Julia thought. Because it will be an explanation.

Julia felt wide-awake, as stimulated as if she'd just had three cups of strong coffee. She wanted to telephone Mark, to see Lily—she wanted to telephone

Eda Rolph, to ask her the name of the hospital where Heather Rudge had been kept for the past twenty-four years. But she is here too, Julia thought, she is part of the character of this house, and she lives here still, moving up and down the stairs, her skirt rustling, turning down a bed, running to the door to greet a lover or a friend, locked in the bubble of her time. Every moment lives parallel with every other moment. What *had* Miss Pinner seen, to make her faint?

As if in answer, a clicking noise came to her from downstairs. It was the same noise she had heard before when, crouching beside the drapes, she had seen Magnus standing motionless in her garden. It was the noise of something outside wishing to come in. Julia realized that, paradoxically, she was now less afraid of Magnus than she had been before reading about Heather and Olivia Rudge—Magnus was flesh, Magnus was blood. All about her moved intimations of the past of the house, those echoes of her own past. She lay in bed listening to the soft rapping at the downstairs windows. Some minutes later she picked up *The White House Transcripts;* she read doggedly for two hours, getting through very nearly half of the book, before she finally fell asleep, her light still burning. The rapping, patient and insistent, continued to sound through the house.

Sweating, she dreamed of Kate.

Julia came drowsily awake two hours later feeling that she had just been touched: no, caressed. Her light still burned. She reached up to switch it off. The bedroom was even hotter than it had been when she had first come in; her entire body seemed filmed with sweat. The bedroom curtains hung straight and unmoving; in this room, air refused to circulate, but piled atop itself, densely. The sky shone through the window, lighter than the dark of the bedroom. Julia could still feel, along her bruised left side, the afterimage of a hand, stroking lightly. The caress was gentle, seductively soothing. Of course there was no one else in the room; she had conjured up the caress herself, summoned it up out of her needs.

Julia settled down into the sheets again, deliberately relaxing. The rapping from below had ceased: Magnus had gone home, unable to bring her wandering and calling through the house, having failed at least this once. She closed her eyes and crossed her hands on her midriff. Perhaps Heather Rudge had nursed Olivia in this room, talking to her daughter in baby talk . . . perhaps Mrs. Fludd had seen Heather doing violence to her daughter. Surely such an event still lingers in its physical setting, still reverberating there. . . . Julia's mind began to drift. She heard a snatch of music playing: it was big-band music, tinny, as if on a radio, and then it dissolved, along with everything else. She fell immediately into dreams which were indistinguishable from semiwakefulness. Once again she was being caressed. She was being touched by lingering, stroking hands beside her own hands. Small hands moved lightly down her body. They paused, and began again, stroking. Julia saw Kate beside her: they clasped one another. Kate was with her. The caresses were like music—soft, moving, layered. Julia felt infinitely quietened, infinitely soothed; the small, moving hands were like tongues, lapping at her. She gave herself to this comfort.

Broken dreams, fed by these long caresses, filtered through her mind. She and Mark sat side by side on the gray couch, speaking words she could not hear. Mark's hand surrounded hers. She was swimming in warm water, a pool of water as warm as a bath. She wore no bathing suit, and the water slipped about her like oil. Her skin was opening. She was beneath strong sun. The flickering touches ran insinuatingly over her opening body. Mark and Kate: then, shockingly, only Kate. "*No*," she said, groaning, and her voice brought her up through sleep. "No." She could still feel the last touch of the hand, stroking between her thighs: she felt sickened and frightened, roused. Now she was absolutely awake.

She had been dreaming of Kate. What horrible thing had she dreamed? She listened for the sound of Heather Rudge slipping down the stairs. Now, the thought of Kate was fearful: Kate, she realized, must hate her. She was caught in a terrific dislocation, her body moving toward its resolution, her consciousness stunned by what was logically inexplicable. Slowly, feeling as though soiled for life, Julia slipped her hand to the part of her body which needed its touch, and with hard circular movements of two fingers brought herself over the edge. She felt like the unappeased ghost of the living Heather Rudge. Her body smelled of loss and failure, of airless exertions.

The next morning, with trembling hands, she dialed the number Rosa Fludd had left with her. For the first time in her life, she had taken a drink in the morning—a smoky, unwatered slug of malt whiskey, choked down while she was still in her robe. She had immediately wanted another. The quick explosion of warmth, intimating relaxation and pointing to an eventual extinguishing of consciousness, was uncannily like being back in the hospital, seconds after her morning injection. Now, she thought, I know why people drink in the morning. It's better than breakfast. She had quickly screwed the top back on the bottle and gone to the telephone. Beside it was the white card Mrs. Fludd had given her.

She heard the telephone going *brrr brrr* in Mrs. Fludd's white antiseptic flat. It trilled six, then seven times without answer. Was she still there, watched over by her budgerigar and the huge sentimental eyes of the girl in the Keane print? It was imperative that Julia speak to her: what would the old woman have said to her—admitted to her—if Julia had known about Heather and Olivia Rudge last night? On the tenth ring the telephone was answered.

"Yes," said a young woman.

"I'd like to speak to Mrs. Fludd, Rosa Fludd. My name is Julia Lofting."

"Wait a minute." Julia heard muffled voices; the young woman had covered the receiver while turning to speak to someone else in the room.

"My aunt says she can't talk to you."

"Is anything wrong?" Julia asked.

"Anything wrong? You should know. You were one of them brought her home." The girl's accent was so strong that Julia had difficulty distinguishing the words. "You're one of them put her in a state."

"A stite? Oh."

"A *state*. You and them others. You bunch of airyfairies near drove her out of her mind, didn't you? That's not proper, is it? Poor woman don't even take money to jolly you lot along, and . . ."

Another voice was raised in the background and the hand again clamped over the receiver.

"Tell her I have more information," Julia said. "This is terribly important."

". . . she says she has more information. You sure? You want to?"

In a moment Mrs. Fludd had taken the telephone. "I'm here," she said. Her voice sounded tightly contained.

"Mrs. Fludd, this is Julia Lofting. Are you all right? I've been worried about you."

"You can't waste your worry," said Mrs. Fludd. "What did you want to tell me?"

"Well, I read, just by accident, a story about my house in a book on Kensington, and I had to tell you what it said. Mrs. Fludd? This house used to be owned by a woman named Heather Rudge, an American, who had a daughter named Olivia. Mrs. Fludd, she stabbed her daughter to death. My own daughter was stabbed to death—my husband wanted to save her life, she was choking to death, and he killed her. The other little girl was killed right in this house more than twenty years ago. Is that what you saw? Is that what Miss Pinner saw in the bathroom?"

"Don't know about Miss Pinner," said Mrs. Fludd.

"Mrs. Fludd, could—could my own daughter be haunting me? Could she try to harm me? Is that what you meant the other night? Did she try to harm *you?* Is my daughter behind this?" Hysteria and tears mounted in her, and she stopped talking to force calm into her voice. "Can't you help me, Mrs. Fludd?"

"Go back to your own country."

"Can't you tell me what you saw?"

"I didn't see anything."

"But you said—a child and a man. Kate and Magnus."

"I saw *nothing*. Miss Pinner is a old fool, and she saw nothing either. Get out of that house, get out of this country. That's all I can tell you."

"Mrs. Fludd, please don't hang up. I've been doing so much thinking—I have so many things to ask you. How . . . how do people in the past work through people in the present? How do dead people control living people? Is that possible?"

"I told you that," said Mrs. Fludd. "You're wasting my time. Good-bye."

"You said hate or envy," Julia quickly said.

"You remember, then. Sometimes they might want to take something of yours, and to give you something. It helps the malefic spirit. But strong spirits don't need help, Mrs. Lofting. They does what they want to do. I can't talk, Mrs. Lofting. Please leave me alone."

She hung up and Julia kept the telephone pressed to her ear until she heard the dial tone.

She pressed the button, wanting to dial again, but in that instant her instrument shrilly rang. Julia released the button.

"Yes," she said softly.

"I'm going to get you back," came Magnus' deep voice. "You can't get away from me. Do you hear me? Do you hear me, Julia?"

Julia clapped the receiver down. Some figure behind and beside her seemed to move quickly away, just out of the line of her vision, and she whirled around, her breath caught in her throat. No one else was in the room. "Kate," she whispered, "Kate, don't."

When Julia went into the kitchen for a glass of water, she recoiled as soon as she turned on the tap. What gushed from the faucet was a foul brown stream, stinking like ordure. Julia clapped one hand to her mouth, then twisted the knob and shut off the flow. Now it smelled like metal, like coins. After a moment, testingly, she turned it on again: the greasy stuff foamed from the taps. Frantic, Julia again twisted the knob to make the flow cease. Malvern water from the Safeway, a dozen bottles, ranked beneath the sink, and she took one, pried off the cap, and poured a glassful. It tasted incredibly sweet: drinking it, Julia realized how close she had come to being sick. Even now from the sink rose the stench of that rushing brown fluid, making her stomach contract.

Then she remembered something, brought back by her physical discomfort. The night she had climbed through the bathroom window, she had lost her shoes; they had fallen outside when she had finally pushed herself through the little frame. And out there they had lain, to be found by Magnus: something taken, something given, Mrs. Fludd had said. Nearly everything she owned had been given her by Magnus. She wore his ring; he had bought earrings, pendants, beads, clothing for her. Julia would nearly have to walk naked to divest herself of everything given her by Magnus.

But how long had those shoes lain outside? Three nights and two days. They might still be below the bathroom window. Julia ran out of the kitchen into the hall and down the hall to the bathroom. Reflected in the rose mirrors, she threw the rod off its ratchet and lifted the window out. On tiptoe, she leaned forward, holding the window with her left hand, and put her head out. She looked down at broken white and yellow flowers, some snapped off at their stalks, others trodden into the soft dirt. She could not see her shoes. Julia leaned farther out of the window—she leaned forward as far as she could go. Still she could not see the shoes. They were gone: someone had taken them. It seemed like a proof. A girl and a man. They wished to do her harm.

For some moments Julia thrashed back and forth in the bathroom, out of control. She knew she was making some low, dreadful noise; the noise could not be stopped, and it echoed within the mirrored room, bouncing back and forth like her body. *I have to stop this,* she told herself, and forced herself to sit on the floor. The noise came out in hiccoughs and then concentrated itself in her throat, where she could stop it. When she became aware that she had been drooling, she wiped her mouth.

She looked dumbly around the bathroom. She was sitting, glassy-eyed, her mouth open, near the tub: her face in the rose mirrors looked slack, exotic. Magnus had taken the shoes.

Julia unsteadily rose, gripping the sink with both hands. Within it, the seersucker dress still lay in an orangey-brown pool. She could still see the bloodstain; it seemed to have got larger. Now it appeared to be several inches long. Julia tore the dress out of the sink, pulled the plug, and squeezed the soaked material while the discolored, odorous water was sucked away.

She was not really thinking. She knew that she had to destroy the blue dress, and the knowledge instantly became action, bypassing thought. She had to burn the dress.

Julia carried the dress through to the kitchen where she picked up matches and then continued on to the fireplace in the living room. She dropped the dress onto the grate and applied a lighted match to a dry corner of fabric. The dress did not light. Julia lit a second match and held it to the same point; this time, the thin material flared up, crumpling and darkening beneath the spreading corner of flame. An acrid odor spread into the living room, followed by smoke. About half the dress burned before the flames guttered out on sodden material. The room stank of charred fabric—it was the smell of burning fur. Julia scarcely noticed this stench. She tried holding matches beneath the wet remaining half of the dress, but the fabric merely blackened, still wet.

Then she saw the morning's *Guardian* on a table near the couch and moved across the room to get it. She shook four pages loose, and stuffed them beneath the dress in the grate. When she picked up the sodden lump of dress, ashes and soot clinging to it, she saw the large, rust-colored bloodstain leading out from the seam. She thrust papers over the dress and tossed matches into them. Greasy yellowish smoke boiled out from beneath the papers. Julia threw match after match onto the smoldering newspaper, but the damp fabric would not burn. Her hands were black with ash.

Abandoning the effort to burn the dress, Julia went into the kitchen for one of the big black plastic garbage bags, which she flipped open and carried back to the fireplace. Using the small ornamental shovel, she scooped the mess of ashes and charred spongy fabric into the mouth of the bag. She then twisted it shut and carried it outside into the path beside the house.

Sunlight and warmth surprised her. The past half hour—hour?—seemed to have been visited upon her. She had been dominated by an urgent, thoughtless revulsion she had been unable to resist. Julia felt her pulse slow; she became aware of sensation again, the light defining a million blades of grass, the sun's warmth penetrating her hair. Julia began to breathe more regularly, suddenly conscious that she had been panting. That *thing* in the black bag: she had had to destroy it as though it were alive. Now, grasping the neck of the bag, she felt all of her revulsion once more and thrust it into the bin and clapped the lid over it. Big smudges of ash dirtied her quilted robe. Other smears of ash covered her legs. Julia felt as though she had just run a race.

Magnus: she had lost all reasoning consciousness when he had appeared, as if by evil magic, on the telephone. Now she could not even remember his words, but she remembered their import. They had been threatening. He had her shoes. She flew back into the warm confines of her house.

Twenty minutes later, another visitation: this young woman standing before her, a neighbor, living in Number 23, the house next door. Smaller than Julia, her hair nearly as short as Lily's, a creamy, shy, smiling face only just beginning to show wrinkles. Her name, Hazel Mullineaux. From the woman's first words ("I don't know if I should bother you now"), Julia suffered from an acute awareness of her smudged robe and blackened hands. Her face too—from Mrs. Mullineaux's glances at her cheeks and forehead, Julia knew she was a patchwork of filth. She hid her hands behind her back.

"You seem so busy that I don't know if I should take up your time like this." A smile.

Julia, bent on appearing normal, did not think to invite this hesitant young woman inside. "Oh, I have all the time in the world," she said, and then cursed herself for overstatement.

"It's just that we thought we should ask. We thought you should know," she amended, and then gave a further amendment. "And of course we wanted to meet our new neighbor."

"Thank you."

"I didn't really catch your name, I'm sorry."

She had not given it. "I'm Julia Lofting."

Hazel Mullineaux peered past Julia to see the interior. "You are a Canadian? I'm trying to catch the accent. . . ."

"I'm American," Julia said. "But I've lived here a long time."

"That explains why it isn't so broad."

"Oh," Julia said, "I never think about it at all, it's changing all the time, I guess. My husband used to say that I sounded like an Iowa farmhand, and I've never been in Iowa in my life, but then neither was he." She babbled, smelling the reek the burning dress had made: for ten minutes, she had fanned a news-paper in the living room, but the smell hung on, as though she had burned a cat.

Mrs. Mullineaux seemed disconcerted by this chatter about Iowa. "Well, as I said, we thought you should know about it. Last night my husband saw a man standing outside your house."

Julia froze. "What time was that?"

"At ten, when he came home from his office. Like all publishers, he works too late. Then at ten-thirty he happened to look out the window, and he saw you going into your house and the man was still there. Perry said he didn't look like a criminal, but he had moved further down the block and was beside the tree in front of number seventeen, the Armbrusters' house. Perry was curious, so he kept watching the man, and after you'd gone in, he began to come up the block toward your house again. Then he just stood across the street and watched the house. Perry said he stood there for at least an hour.

Of course, there's no law against looking at a person's house, but it did seem odd. He asked me if I thought he should have telephoned the police. I said I would speak to you about it. In case he returns. I hope you don't think we have been prying into your—circumstances."

"No, oh, no," Julia said. Now she could smell the burned-cat odor all too definitely, and she saw that Hazel Mullineaux also had caught it: the creamy little woman looked at her oddly, and moved a step backward. "I've been doing some cleaning," Julia said. "I know I'm a mess."

"Yes. I mean, no, of course not. But *as* this man seemed to hang about so long, I did want to tell you. I hope you don't think we did wrong not to ring the police."

"It was my husband," said Julia. "I think he's watching me. I know he is."

"Watching . . . ?" Hazel Mullineaux's face expressed a perfect incomprehension.

"He doesn't live here," Julia supplied, feeling herself slip into a bog of explanations and not knowing how to avoid it. "You see, I bought this house for myself. I can't see him—he's been bothering me, making telephone calls. I think he broke in here one night. . . ."

Mrs. Mullineaux now radiated shock and disapproval.

"Oh, please, I want us to be friends," Julia said. "Neighbors should be friends, don't you think? I haven't even invited you in. Would you like a cup of coffee? You were so kind to tell me what you saw. I don't know if the police should be called or not. I don't know if there's any danger. . . . Everything's gotten so confused in the past couple of days, it's because of Kate, our daughter, I mean late daughter. . . . Really, I'm terrified of him, but I don't think I should call the police, it's not a story they'd understand. But thank your husband for me, for worrying about me, that was a friendly act. . . ." She looked at Hazel Mullineaux's rather dazed expression. "Won't you come in for a cup of coffee? I'll have to air out the living room to get rid of that terrible smell, but we could sit in the kitchen, or even in the back garden."

"I can't right now, thanks," said the other woman. She was already moving down the steps. "Some other time."

"Oh, I have to ask you," Julia said before the other woman could get away. "Did you know the people who used to live here?"

"Of course we knew the McClintocks," said Mrs. Mullineaux. "They were older, and a bit remote, but quite nice, really."

"No, not the McClintocks," Julia broke in. "I mean the ones before them. Mrs. Rudge. Heather Rudge. She had a daughter."

"Before the McClintocks? We moved here in 1967, and the McClintocks had been here for twenty years, we thought."

"Yes, of course. Of course. You couldn't possibly have known her."

Mrs. Mullineaux turned away, went down the steps, and before walking down the pavement to her house, looked back at Julia. Her face twitched into a grimace approximating a smile.

That woman thinks I'm crazy, Julia thought. And then she thought of Magnus, patrolling the street. He had rapped at the dining-room window for hours last night—Magnus was trying to push her over the precipice. She wanted Mark's easy presence, Mark's careless masculinity: he was a talisman against Magnus. Even Lily could not be trusted to save her from Magnus. She heard Hazel Mullineaux slam her front door. Against that, too, Mark would stand as protection.

"I think you need help, darling. You're under so much pressure, and I can't blame you for being apprehensive, even suspicious."

"Apprehensive, Lily? Of course I'm apprehensive. That performance the other night put me right at ease. . . ."

"That's *just* what I mean. I rang poor dear Mrs. Fludd this noon, and the telephone just kept ringing. She never goes out, never, except for her sessions. Something terrible has happened, I'm sure. I can't help it, I'm worried for the old dear."

"Well, I'm worried for myself. Magnus was seen loitering outside the house last night. I'm sure he broke in here two nights ago. He's trying to drive me back to him. He's out of his mind, and I think I might be too. Do you want to know what I think? I think Kate is punishing me. It's what Mrs. Fludd said—a man and a girl. Kate is in Magnus' mind. Sometimes she's in this house too, and she hates me. She believes Magnus' lies."

"Oh, darling . . ."

"You want him for yourself, don't you? You want Mark for yourself too. You'd like Magnus to think I'm going crazy. I suppose you'll call him right now and tell him what I said, but you won't get him because he's probably hanging around here, watching the house."

"Julia, you can't think that of me. . . ."

"You called him. You broke your word."

"Because I wanted you to be back with him."

"But you do want him for yourself, don't you? And Mark."

"Julia, this does us no good. That is terribly unfair. Please listen, Julia. Kate has no reason to hate you, nothing you did was meant to injure her. You were brave."

"Magnus killed Kate. Magnus hates me for leaving him, and now Kate hates me. Mrs. Fludd saw them."

"Julia, why don't you come over here so we can talk about that day? Please come over. That's at the bottom of everything. . . ."

"What do you mean by that? What are you trying to get me to say?"

"Nothing, Julia, nothing. I just thought that talking about it would do you good—if not to Magnus then at least to me—but if you're not ready yet, that's fine. I still think you should come over and stay with me for a few days so . . ."

Julia had a sudden, clear vision of a man in a white jacket jabbing a hypodermic into her arm.

"Good-bye, Lily. Sorry."

She hung up, trembling so severely the receiver rattled out of the cradle and fell to the floor. She had to get out of the house.

Julia ran upstairs to her bedroom and threw off the filthy robe; in her bathroom, she hurriedly showered, avoiding looking at herself as much as she could avoid it, afraid that a glance into the mirrors would show a slight figure just flickering from her sight. The telephone began to ring as she was toweling herself, and Julia let the bell shrill, counting the number of rings. After twenty, it stopped. She continued dressing, deliberately not thinking of what Lily had said to her. She thought, instead, with longing of more books—of buying books—of slipping into a narrative of other people's lives. *That* was release.

It led her, as she went rapidly along Kensington High Street twenty minutes later, her damp hair adhering to her neck, to sudden, vivid memories of her girlhood: of summers at their home in New Hampshire, where it had been as warm as this every day. Her great-grandfather had bought the estate after he had retired from the board of his railroad company, having made several hundred million dollars in the boom; the soil itself, the texture of the air had seemed different there, wholly, innocently absorbed into her family's life. For an instant, Julia ached to be back in America. She stood on Kensington High Street, between a package store and W. H. Smith's, the sound of car horns dividing the air, and was transfixed by the particular memory of a New Hampshire valley. And beyond the valley, the endless innocent unrolling of the continent: but it was not like that anymore, she knew. It was her own past for which she had ached. Yet there lay in her an undigested yearning for the visionary and fruitful continent; her childhood, it seemed to her, had been spent there. She turned into W. H. Smith's and bought a fat paperback of *Gravity's Rainbow*.

Toting the book, Julia passed through the crowds on the High Street. It really was as hot as New Hampshire in August. She debated walking up Kensington Church Street to Notting Hill Gate, to see if Mark were home. She remembered his address, and thought she knew where the flat was; it was on one of the long curved streets, Pembridge something, intercepting Notting Hill Gate, one of the streets lined with large houses now broken up into bed-sitting-rooms and two-room flats. Mark's was a "garden flat": it was in the basement. She imagined a flight of steep steps down from the pavement into a dank lightless room—the vision was enough to turn her back to Holland Park, where she could lie in the sun. She did not feel ready, yet, to visit Mark's flat. To go there unbidden would entail a chain of consequences of which she was a little apprehensive.

As she walked along past the row of shops, Julia scanned the crowds for a glimpse of Magnus. He could easily be facing a window, unseen, tailing after her; certainly she had to assume that Magnus had taken to such tactics. Or, even more unsettling, perhaps he was now forcing his way into her house. But she could not rush back to inspect the house, she would never catch him there, she was sure of that. Still, Julia could not rid herself of the image of Magnus hovering behind her. In front of the long piazza of the Commonwealth Institute, she whirled around quickly, and caught a priest in the stomach with her elbow. While they each apologized, they recognized one another as Americans; the priest, a neat dark man with a witty face, looked at her oddly as they swapped pleasantries. She could only surmise that he was responding to something in her own manner or regard. What was wrong with her, that even a pleasant stranger found her peculiar? Julia brought one hand up to wipe her forehead and saw the hand tremble. Her forehead dripped sweat. "It's nothing," she said to the priest. "Just anxiety. I'm a normal person. I don't usually punch men in the stomach."

She turned up into Holland Park. The paths were crowded, and every five feet of ground supported a new body. A pack of children ran squealing on the long sward, breaking apart into pinwheeling clusters and then, clamoring, re-forming. Boys in jeans, girls in long filmy dresses, girls in jeans, Germans strapped into cameras and expensive clothes. She skirted a party of twenty Japanese, singing to one another. A young couple directly before her exchanged a long kiss while the boy rubbed and kneaded the girl's buttocks, uncaring of the crowds. Julia felt a hot, direct physical pang until she saw the American priest, walking quickly up ahead without looking back. She deliberately thrust down the memory of her last night's dream and its aftermath. Without purpose, she began to drift after the American priest. The book felt very heavy in her hand.

The priest turned off the main path to enter the smaller walk which, Julia recalled, passed the area where peacocks and other birds strutted beneath dark trees. Julia followed, watching the black suit as if it held a meaning. The priest paused to look at the peacocks for a second and then continued walking toward the woods which circled the top half of the park. He strode along briskly, and soon was disappearing around a corner into the sparse woods. Three women pushing baby carriages, accompanied by a single man carrying an open wine bottle, crossed before Julia, and the priest was gone from sight. Then she saw Magnus.

He was sitting on a bench, not looking at her. He looked very tired. Julia froze; she took two cautious steps backward, and then turned around, the vision of Magnus in a light-gray suit, bending forward, his face rumpled, burning into her: if he turned his head, he would see her. At first she took light quick steps, gliding up the path; when she passed around the bend, she moved more slowly until she dared to look over her shoulder. He had not followed her. Julia looked across the park—an exit lay ahead to her right, just before Plane Tree House. She would circle the park to get home. Julia trotted down the path, ignoring the stares of men she met, setting her face.

There was no longer any question of staying in the park to read her book: she had to get home and lock the door. But just before she reached the final stage of the path to the side gate, she saw the tiny black girl who had been in the park that first day. The girl was staring up at her just as she had that day.

"Hello, Mona," Julia said. "Do you remember me?"

"Poo," said Mona, smiling openmouthed at Julia. Her eyes shone.

"That's not a nice word."

"Poo. Shit." Mona giggled and turned away. "Fuck you."

Julia stared at the tiny girl.

"Fuck you. Shit. Fuck."

"What . . ." Julia turned and found herself looking into the face of the little blond girl. She was touching a bicycle which was leaning against the fence bordering the park, and she was looking straight into Julia's face. No other children were near; the closest people were a man and a woman twenty yards away, asleep on the grass with their faces to the sun. About Julia and the blond girl a charged timeless vacuum seemed to exist. The child wore curiously old-fashioned denim trousers, with a high elastic waist and floppy legs. The resemblance to Kate made Julia's heart pulse with fear. They stood looking at each other, not speaking; Julia had nearly the sense that the girl had been waiting for her in this secluded place.

Then the girl smiled, and her resemblance to Kate vanished. One of her front teeth had been broken in half, chipped away in a rising arc which left her smile uncentered and asymmetrical.

"Who are you?" Julia said.

The girl's smile tightened in a curiously adult, challenging way. Her joined hands moved, or something in them moved. When Julia looked at her hands, she saw that the girl was not actually touching the bicycle, but holding her hands near the rear wheel. It took her a moment to see what the girl held captured between her cupped palms. Only when the small brown creature quivered did Julia see that it was a bird.

"Is that bird injured?" Julia asked.

The child made no response, but continued to stare at Julia, smiling her adult, unbalanced smile. The whole being of the child seemed hurtled together, compacted.

In one quick sure movement the girl thrust the bird into the wheel of the bicycle, jamming it securely between the spokes and the metal rods which held the mudguards to the wheel. The scene printed itself with utter clarity on Julia's mind: as in the second before some foreknown disaster, time seemed as fixed as the girl's smile. Julia stared at the bird, the instant before the girl jerked the bicycle forward—it was held between the two metal rods, not in the wheel as she had first supposed. Its body projected through the spokes.

"Don't . . . no . . ." she stammered.

The girl jerked the bicycle and the bird instantly became a pulp of bloody feathers. Its head fell softly to the ground.

Julia snapped her head up to look at the girl, who was now mounting her bicycle. She did not immediately ride away but straddled the bike, intently staring at Julia.

Julia opened her mouth to speak, but caught sight of the bird's head lying with open eyes beside the rear wheel, and felt her stomach irresistibly begin to draw itself upward. She turned away and vomited into the dust.

When she had finished, the girl was no longer beside her. The bicycle was rolling away through the gate, the girl pedaling slowly and unconcernedly; soon she had slipped into crowds and traffic.

Julia took a step and found that her knees shook: she forced herself to run. Heedless of Magnus, she raced directly toward her home, her mouth open, her body jouncing, her breath straining at her ribs. She flew across the green, narrowly missing the curious who parted to let her pass, and into the path which curved around past the children's play area. By then her mouth had turned to cotton and her side felt pierced by swords.

She came racing around the corner of Ilchester Place and stumbled to a walk. Her breath dragging in her, face pumping with blood, she went up the three steps to her walk. The house seemed impassive, unwelcoming; she wanted no more than to fall into her bed and close out the whole world in sleep. The book in her hand seemed to have tripled in weight.

When Julia reached her front door she felt in her pocket and touched a used paper tissue, an earring with the pin broken, a loose mint, two small coins. The key, she remembered, lay at the bottom of her bag, on a counter in the kitchen. Her knees seemed to disappear altogether. Her body pitched into the springy grass. Before her eyes went shut, she saw the creamy startled face of Hazel Mullineaux staring at her through a side window of Number 23.

The old woman sat up in her narrow bed; a long, white page of moonlight lay folded at the juncture of wall and floor. Pulling her gently from sleep, a low voice had uttered her name repeatedly, lightly, as if teasing her. It came again, this time from a greater distance, somewhere else in the house. The woman did not want to follow the voice; she clung to the sheets, resisting. But she knew that she could not resist long. The voice was cool water, long blue slices of water she needed. The weak muscles in her arms began to tremble. And she knew who it was. Her tongue dryly scraped her teeth. Her name issued teasingly from the hallway. At last her body ceased to strain. Without her guidance, the woman's arms parted the upper sheet from her body and folded it back. Her legs swung over the edge of the bed.

She rose on unsteady legs which knew where to take her. The voice seemed the only thing in her mind. Her feet found her low shoes and slipped within them. She moved out of the hallway and saw the open door. Just outside, luminous in yellow light, stood her visitor, calling.

The woman moved down the hall. Knowledge lay ahead, knowledge and peace. Her hand moved to grasp the heavy tweed coat as she passed the coat hooks. Silly hand; silly coat; not needed. It was only to cover her nightdress. She pulled it across the bulge of her belly and fastened the single button.

Teasing, gentle, the visitor waited. Seductive—extraordinarily seductive. The woman padded toward the door, then passed through it into a wide familiar space.

The visitor moved quickly, walking backward, beckoning. White light on hair, on the beckoning backs of hands. All about the visitor was indistinct and hazy. Other voices filtered to her, but she did not turn her head.

The teasing voice was the last thing she heard.

II

THE SEARCH FOR HEATHER

5

"I almost understood everything," Julia said. "I was lying in bed, reading that book you gave me, and when I came to the bit about Heather and Olivia Rudge, I knew that I was getting close to understanding what's been happening to me—because I *haven't* just been making it up, Lily. It was all mixed up with Kate and a little girl I saw before I fainted—I was so close, I had this amazing rush of energy and I almost called you, I had so many ideas. There's something about the house that Mrs. Fludd saw, and it's important because of what Magnus did to Kate. Somehow, the energy in this house is focused on me because of that. Mrs. Fludd *knew* she was in danger, and she said I was too. Doesn't that convince you I'm not just making it all up?"

There was a long pause on the line while Lily balanced the effects of several statements. Finally she said, "Darling, Mrs. Fludd was killed in an accident. It was a hit and run, very near her house. Apparently she just wandered out into the traffic on the Mile End Road, and the car was gone before anybody knew what had happened. It's always best to look for a reasonable, rational explanation before . . . before deciding on the other."

"I know. But some things don't have rational explanations."

"Darling, there is nothing supernatural about a hit and run. As tragic as it is."

"Evil isn't rational. Lily, I know that something hates me—something in this house. Mrs. Fludd felt it too—it's what she kept saying to me. I was so close to understanding everything that night I read about the Rudges. I almost broke through—I had all of these thoughts and ideas—I could feel the past all around me. The past is *in this house*. Don't you see that I'm connected to that story? Because of Kate? It's the key to everything."

"Well, as to the key to everything," Lily began, and then stopped. She had promised Magnus (they had worked it out together, with some strong advice from Julia's doctor) that she would not lead Julia into that territory; if Julia were ever to admit the truth about Kate's death, she would have to come to it herself. So she finished her sentence by saying, "I think it is in your state of mind." Immediately she regretted her choice of words.

"My state of mind? That's nice of you, Lily. Thanks."

"I didn't mean that the way it sounded. That's the truth, my dear."

"I can't believe that you of all people won't even discuss the possibility that something out of the ordinary is happening. Lily, if Mrs. Fludd saw something or felt something, as she did, isn't that just in your line? Isn't that just the sort of thing you *do* accept?"

"Only under the proper circumstances, Julia. You know I have a firm belief in the supernatural, but . . ."

"And how about Heather and Olivia Rudge? Lily, there are no accidents. *There are no accidents.* These things have been happening to me for a reason. Maybe it takes a coincidence to set it off, maybe there's some kind of plan, I don't know, but I've been doing a lot of looking into the Rudge case for the past few days, and I'm sure that's the direction I have to go. I found out the name of the clinic where Heather Rudge has been kept, the Breadlands Clinic, and I wrote to her, asking if I could see her."

"How did you find it?"

"It was in an old copy of the *Times*. My neighbor, Perry Mullineaux, got me a reader's ticket for the British Museum's periodical collection, and I've spent the past three days going through old newspapers. Remember telling me that I needed some interest? Well, I've sure got it. I tell you, sometimes I almost see the two of them, I can feel them all around me in this house—I hear the music they listened to, sometimes I think they've just left a room the moment before I entered it—did you know about the heaters? I kept turning them off without ever turning them on, someone else was doing that, I thought Magnus, but eventually the only room where it happened was my bedroom and I taped the switch to the wall and the heater still wouldn't go off. So I cut the wires, and the thing still stays hot. That's just a small thing I know, but then there was that bloodstain on my blue seersucker that wouldn't go away and kept getting bigger, there are the flashes of someone I keep seeing in the mirrors and the way the water has been getting so foul, it simply reeks, it's like shit, like diarrhea but full of *money*, sometimes it smells like greasy old American pennies, I haven't taken a real bath in a week. Then there are the noises and the whole general feel of the house—it wants me here, but it doesn't like me. Lily, why did I buy this house? *This* house? Don't you think I have a right to find out? That's why Mrs. Fludd was killed, it's horrible, it's awful, that intelligent old woman was killed to keep me from knowing too soon. I'm going to see Heather Rudge, and I'm going to find everyone I can who knew Olivia—I keep seeing signs of evil in children, not just malevolence but real evil, Lily. Kate's behind all this, she's evil now she's dead and I have to work at it, I have to see what I can do, it's so unfair. . . ."

"Julia," Lily said when Julia's voice had broken down into a series of excited hiccoughs, "I want you to move over here with me. I don't think you should be on your own."

"I can't leave. Everything I'm interested in is here."

"Julia, have you been drinking?"

"Not much. Why? It doesn't matter. Magnus drinks."

"I want you to come to stay with me, Julia."

"That's funny, everybody wants me to live with them. I'm very popular with the entire Lofting family. I can't tell you how wanted that makes me feel."

"Are you sleeping?"

"I don't need sleep anymore. I'm too excited to sleep. Well, I suppose I get a couple of hours a night. I've been having the most amazing dreams—I keep dreaming about that girl I saw in Holland Park. She's a sort of metaphor for Kate, I guess. She seems totally without any redeeming virtues."

"Julia, guilt shouldn't . . ."

"I have no guilt. I leave that to your brother."

Julia hung up.

Worried, Lily took her watering can into her efficient little kitchen and filled it at the tap. She carried the can out onto the terrace and began to sprinkle water over the flowers, which had lately showed the effects of the past month of hot dry days—particularly intense weather for a London summer. Eventually the weather would break, she supposed. Lily's clearest memory of such a long spell of hot weather was a summer more than twenty years before; she remembered it because that had been the year Magnus bought the house on Gayton Road. He had not been so fat then, and he had told her that he liked to go on Hampstead Heath and take off his shirt. One day she had met him in Gayton Road and walked over the Heath with him; in a green sloping vale Magnus had removed his shirt and fallen asleep in the sun. He had looked enormous, hieratic to her, his big pink trunk and massive, handsome head against the brilliant green of the grass. Lily had watched him for an hour, admiring how even in sleep Magnus seemed more powerful, more authoritative than other men. Of course, he was cruel, though not to her. "Magnim," she had said, stroking one of his bristling eyebrows—it was his name in their private language. She had been happy that he had women, but equally happy that he seemed incapable of marriage. Lily, in those days, had thought that most women would know better than to desire marriage with Magnus.

Julia had been a shock: at that time, an innocent, radiant girl with beautiful hair and a modest manner absurdly at variance with her general air of healthiness, she had been eminently the type of girl Magnus seduced (physically, she was rather an American Sonia Mitchell-Mitchie, then Hoxton), but far from the kind of woman he might reasonably have married. Lily had for some reason always thought that were Magnus to marry he would take a woman older than himself. "It's her Burne-Jones eyes," Mark had suggested—poor envious Mark would have wanted any woman Magnus claimed as his own, even if she had looked like Mrs. Pankhurst. Later she had discovered the extent of Julia's wealth, and Magnus' marriage had become far more comprehensible.

But not for years did it become less painful. Really, Kate had helped with that reconciliation, had perhaps effected it, since Magnus, while altering little in other ways, had revealed a surprising capacity for fatherhood. He had loved Kate so deeply that Lily could not herself do otherwise; and eventually she and Julia had become friends. That Julia from the beginning had wished for that friendship encouraged it; but perhaps the change had begun when Lily arrived one morning to find a nursing Julia reading not a baby manual but *Middlemarch*. Julia might have been absurdly young, almost too wealthy, but at least she had good taste in fiction. Eventually, Lily had given her some volumes on the occult—books recommended by Mr. Carmen and Miss Pinner—and had been pleased that Julia had read them carefully. (Though she had thought more of Mr. Carmen's Roheim and Mircea Eliade than Miss Pinner's books on astral projection.) Later, she had more reason to be grateful for Julia, though Julia was unaware of it, for she had purchased the flat in Plane Tree House largely with money allotted to her by Magnus from his joint account. And she knew without asking that it was Julia's money which paid for most of Magnus' expensive presents to her.

The main thing, Lily thought, was to get Julia back with Magnus—never mind how much money was lost on the house and its contents. Both of them needed healing. Lily knew perfectly well that she was at times jealous of Magnus simply because he was a man, and jealous of Julia because she had come between herself and her brother as even Mark had never done, but it was in everyone's interest that they begin to knit themselves together again. Magnus, this past week, had been worse than Lily had ever seen him. Sometimes he did seem almost to hate Julia—though, proud as he was, he needed no supernatural assistance in that—while he desperately wanted her cured, wanted her back.

And Julia needed Magnus far more than he needed her. She had begun to look shockingly weak and ill. Her marvelous hair had gone dull and limp, and her face soft and pouchy. Sometimes she seemed hardly to be listening to what you said to her. Julia was running on sheer nervous energy. It was no surprise that she saw evil children everywhere or that she had built up a sick fantasy about Kate.

And now this obsession with the Rudge case, which was perfectly explicable in the light of what Julia was determinedly repressing. Lily imagined Julia in a reading room, flipping crazily through old newspapers, making mad notes— she must look like Ophelia floating downstream on a sea of newsprint.

I have a duty to Julia and to myself, Lily thought. When she had finished watering the plants she put the can down on her terrace and went inside to telephone Magnus.

Most importantly, she had to keep Julia from Mark. There was something missing in Mark, a moral space filled by his resentment of Magnus. Lily knew that Mark would miss no opportunity to humiliate Magnus. Julia, now weakened and perhaps hysterical, would be more open to Mark's entreaties than she had ever been. That must be blocked.

She first dialed Gayton Road. When there was no answer, she tried his chambers, where a secretary had not seen him all day and had been told not to expect him. She knew what that meant. Lily went down a list of his drinking clubs, and finally reached him at the Marie Lloyd, a certain sign of trouble. Once at the Marie Lloyd, the least prepossessing of all the little clubs he patronized all over the city, he began looking for a fight—he had once knocked down a truck driver outside the club who had sneered at him. She had to carefully judge the state of his intoxication, and calibrate her statements to it. Magnus' spy, she also saw herself as Magnus' protector. From his first words, she knew that it would be dangerous to irritate him, and so Lily omitted from her account of her conversation with Julia most of the material about the Rudges.

"Yes, she's much better," she said. "I think she fainted from exhaustion, and she's been getting some rest. She has a project she wants to begin working on, and that will help her fill her time. It seems harmless enough. Magnus, you must not go to that house anymore. That is absolutely the wrong tactic."

"Were you there when she fainted? Did you see her?" This meant, Lily knew, that Magnus wished to ignore her advice.

"A neighbor saw her faint," Lily said. Now was not the time to inform Magnus that Mark had come along moments later. "Someone got word to me, and we helped her get inside. She'd locked herself out, but the French windows at the back were unlatched and we helped her in that way."

"Those damned windows are always open," Magnus grumbled. "I'm going to go down and see her. Take her home."

"I wouldn't," Lily hastily said. "In her frame of mind that would only hurt things."

"Bugger that."

"I think you should go home. I think you should let things go their own way for a few days, my love, until she has settled down a bit more. She's a terribly confused girl."

"She looks like hell," Magnus said. "I saw her. But who isn't confused?"

"Magnus, before long she will have to face what really happened to Kate. I know it is dreadfully unfair to you that she blames you for what happened, and my dear, I feel your pain, but I do think now that the best thing for you would be to go straight home and perhaps telephone her later and try to speak calmly to her. I'm certain that is the best tactic, in the long run."

"I have the feeling you're hiding something from me, Lily."

"No. I am not."

"What's this project?" Magnus belched loudly. "Christ, I have to pee. What's this project she's working on?"

"I gather it has something to do with that house she's taken."

"Christ," Magnus said and brutally rang off.

Julia, hanging up the telephone, still kept her mood of excited elation. This had little to do with liquor, despite Lily's implication, for she had only sipped at a watered whiskey during the afternoon after her return from the periodical collection in Colindale. Yet the feeling was akin to that of one stage of drunkenness—an optimistic, impulsive sense that wheels had begun to move, that a resolution was near. She had no doubt that this would have a connection with the Rudges: the Rudges were to help her exorcise Kate, help her finally lay Kate to rest. How this was to happen she did not know, but she felt a certainty that it would happen. In any case, she no longer had any choice—she was driven to discover the truth about Olivia Rudge.

The old copies of the *Times* and the *Evening Standard* she had read had convinced her of at least one thing. Olivia Rudge had been psychotic. One member of her group, the gang of children in Holland Park, had been anonymously quoted as saying that Olivia was "bent"; even a detached reporter had called her "disturbing." If Julia could determine the truth about the murder of young Geoffrey Braden, perhaps that would appease Kate. Wasn't proof of that the extraordinary change in her mood since she had read those pages in *The Royal Borough of Kensington?* She still had trouble focusing her mind on remembering what she was supposed to do from one moment to the next, but she felt as though she were riding a great wave, borne along on it resistlessly. She burned her dinners, left half-filled cups of coffee all over the house, but since she had thought to ask Perry Mullineaux to help her get a reader's card, she had one great sustaining purpose—even Magnus had receded in importance. Let him skulk about the neighborhood; he was merely in the present; he had no connection with what mattered.

Turning, still pleased with herself for her parting shot at Lily, vaguely toward the dining room and the doors to the garden, Julia reminded herself of an idea she'd had at the end of her day's stint at the library. Before she talked to Heather Rudge—she had no doubt that she would hear from her—she would look through old copies of *The Tatler.* Surely, in the hostessy period of her life, she had been photographed for that magazine; there might even be pictures of her parties.

Then she remembered something Mark had said when he had appeared, as if by sympathetic magic, at her side when she had fainted. She had come conscious to find herself cradled by Hazel Mullineaux, Mark holding her hand. Even then, groggy and confused, she had been aware that Mrs. Mullineaux was not blind to Mark's appearance, and she had tried to fight her way upright into parity. Mark had taken her hand more firmly and said to Hazel Mullineaux, "I don't know who you are, but as you're being so kind, do you think you could go across the park to fetch Julia's sister-in-law, Lily Lofting?" He gave her Lily's address and said he'd "stay on" to watch over Julia—a little bemused, but glad to be of use, Hazel had left them.

"That was neat, don't you think?" asked Mark.

"Do women always do what you tell them?"

"Nearly always. They're usually thoughtful enough not to terrify me, too. I thought you were about to live up to your mortuary eyes. Like that Burne-Jones girl at the Tate you've always reminded me of."

"Mortuary eyes? Burne-Jones? What are you going on about? I feel better already." Julia straightened up, her grogginess nearly gone.

"The girl in *King Cophetua and the Beggar Maid.* Same eyes. I noticed it years ago, when I first met you. What brought on this fit?"

Then she had told him about the blond girl in the park, rushing to finish the story before Lily's arrival. The incident was so private that, at least then, it could be shared only with Mark.

Julia threw some things in her bag and rushed out of the house just as a taxi appeared at the far corner of Ilchester Place. When it came near she hailed it and told the driver, "The Tate Gallery, please." Better than driving: she felt too excited to trust herself to the Rover.

When the taxi pulled up before the Tate she gave the driver a pound note and went quickly up the gray stone steps, passing the usual crowds of tourists, and went through the entrance and turnstiles. She said to a guard, "Could you tell me where to find the Pre-Raphaelites? I'm looking for a specific painting. A Burne-Jones."

The man gave her detailed directions, and she went down the stairs and eventually turned into the room the man had indicated. She saw the painting immediately. The girl sat, backed by a cushion, on a long shelf, shyly holding some flowers; the King, seated on gold beneath her, gazed up. She did look like the girl Burne-Jones had painted. Mortuary eyes. Were hers so round? But the King: the King, but for his short sharp beard, was Mark. She gasped with pleasure. Julia stood before the painting for ten minutes, and then, still looking at it, moved to a bench where she could sit and keep looking at it. The little room endured several waves of spectators, swelling in, circling, and then draining out again. Julia shifted her place on the bench whenever her view of the painting was blocked. Eventually, alone in the room once again, she silently began to cry.

She had Mark—at least she had Mark. Both of them were Magnus' victims. Mark's phrase encapsulated the futile history of her marriage; she did not know if she were crying for her nine wasted years or for relief that Mark, however slightly, had shown her a way out of them.

Mark, Mark.

When the next dribbling of strangers entered the room, Julia dabbed at her eyes and went up the stairs back through galleries to the entrance. She walked outside into warmth and light and the noises of automobiles, went down the stone steps, crossed the street to the embankment and began to walk along the river. After a time she ceased to walk and leaned on the railing to stare at the gray and sluggish water. Low tide had left some scraps of weed, a bicycle tire, a battered doll and a child's cloth cap stranded on the mud and gravel of the riverbed. Julia was certain that she would soon hear from Heather Rudge; she felt oddly disembodied, as though she were floating above the river muck. She found herself adopting the expression of the girl in the Burne-Jones painting.

That girl is going to pieces, Lily thought, and if she does, she'll ruin everything for all of us. Drying her hands, Lily tried to think if any explanation had been given for Mark's appearance by Julia's side. Had he been invited? Was he in the habit of calling on Julia? The first possibility was less dreadful than the second, but only marginally. In any case, she had to talk sense to Julia, she had to try to break her out of her wild and irrational mood. Julia had almost certainly come out of the hospital too soon. Magnus would be able to correct that. The girl had become fixated on the sordid Rudge case, of which Lily had a dim memory. It had been in the newspapers for several weeks a long time ago—now that she thought of it, all of that had happened the same summer

Magnus had purchased his house. But it was merely one of those newspaper sensations, having no connection with herself. Surely it was a reflection of Julia's loss of control that she had focused on that ancient story.

No connection. Unless . . . no, that could not be. Despite Julia's frantic assertions, accidents and coincidences occurred all the time. You had only to think of Rosa Fludd to see that. Poor dear Rosa Fludd. Poor Rosa. The horrid niece had been very rude to Lily on the telephone.

Lily went through the living room to her bedroom, stopping on the way to regard the Stubbs drawing which had been Magnus' last birthday present to her. Perhaps she could still persuade Julia to sleep in the spare bedroom. She had to make some sort of assault on Julia—all of them had been too easy, too lenient with her brother's wife. The image in Lily's mind was of a butterfly battering itself against a window: to keep its colors safe, the butterfly had to be pressed between glass. Once Julia was safely in the extra bedroom at Plane Tree House, Magnus could be brought in to make her see good sense. Thinking of this, Lily thought of asking Magnus about the coincidence she'd had in mind a moment before, just to see if it could possibly be true—and if it were, might Julia discover it? Lily cursed herself mildly for her lack of knowledge of the details of Magnus' life. Where exactly had he gone when he had visited Ilchester Place? But surely it was stretching things to suppose . . . ? Lily shrugged the idea away and turned to her wardrobe closet. She had already decided to change her clothes.

The more soberly she were dressed, the more convincing she would be. Flipping through her clothes, Lily pulled a dark blue linen suit from the closet. She'd owned it eight years, and it still looked elegantly crisp. Then she opened her scarf drawer, sighed, and began to change.

Wearing the blue linen suit and an off-white blouse Julia had given her the year before, Lily returned to her scarf drawer. She tried on three before settling on a long rectangular Hermès scarf in a red and white pattern; then she regarded the effect in her long mirror. She looked slightly more practical than usual—like a retired lady lawyer, or the wife of a prosperous professional man. Now she had to rehearse what she would say to Julia. She glanced at her watch and saw that it had been half an hour since she had spoken to Julia on the telephone. Surely she would still be at home.

Use the Rosa Fludd story, Lily advised herself. Remind her that Mrs. Fludd told her to leave the house; now was the time to take hold of herself, very firmly, before things got utterly out of hand. She must not mention Kate unless Julia did so first. It was monstrously unfair to Magnus, but, as Lily reminded herself, Magnus had taken up the doctor's suggestion more quickly than she had herself—Lily would have to put an end to Julia's fantasy.

Now Lily supposed that she'd have to use the plural. One fantasy had burgeoned into half a dozen. "Wants a little cold water thrown over her," Lily muttered, and checked the angle of her skirt in the mirror. She was ready.

Outside in the warm sun, she strode into the park. It was Friday afternoon, and Holland Park seemed always to be more crowded then than at any other time save the weekends. Lily's neat figure moved, her bag swinging in time with her heels, through crowds of young people. Layabouts, most of them. Students. Though what they found time to study she couldn't say. Of course there's one famous subject, she thought, seeing a couple kissing on the grass. Magnus should really have married someone his own age: a man like Magnus needed a respectable woman for a wife. And certainly not an American. Americans failed to understand so much, for all their automobiles and electric toothbrushes. Magnus should have been Queen's Counsel by now, but any chance of that had disappeared when Julia became Mrs. Lofting. She *was* a dear girl, of course, and no one could say that all that money hadn't been helpful. But even that had its shady side. The old rogue who'd made it was a sort of pirate, from what Lily could gather. Julia's great-grandfather had been one of those ruthless railroad barons of the end of the last century—he had blood on his hands up to the elbows, Magnus had said. The grandfather was cut from the same cloth, apparently: whole forests had been felled for him, rivers spoiled, wars fought and companies stripped and men killed to increase his holdings. There was a taint, an historical stain, to Julia's money. Lily lifted her head and turned, her heels making a neat staccato sound on the asphalt, deeper into the park.

Descending a short flight of steps beside the little gardens, Lily noticed a small blond girl leap up from one of the benches where old people sunned themselves and run in the direction she was now walking. After a few yards, the girl began to walk. What a sweet old-fashioned-looking child, Lily thought: she even looked a little like Kate, at least from the back. After a moment she recognized that it was the girl's trousers which gave her the old-fashioned aspect: they were high-waisted and elasticized around the top, like children's trousers of twenty-five years before. The girl seemed almost to be leading Lily to Julia's house. She began to skip ahead of her, slowing to a walk whenever she got more than fifteen or twenty yards away, and then, Lily approaching, skipped and ran once more—just as if, Lily thought, she were on a leash.

When they reached the children's play area, within sight of Julia's house, the girl vanished. Lily checked her stride for a moment, puzzled. She looked over the children playing in the sandboxes and sporting beside the trees, but saw no flash of that astonishing hair—that hair like Kate's. To her left, on the long stretch of grass, she saw only three small wailing children, none of them the girl.

Lily glanced from side to side once more, then shrugged and was about to resume walking when she felt a quick chill over her entire body. She had seen, she was now looking at, a stout elderly woman seated on a green bench, her profile to Lily. It was Rosa Fludd. She was far off to Lily's right, staring straight ahead of her, unmoving. She wore the hideous tweed coat she had worn the night of the last gathering. Lily slowly turned in the woman's direction; her stomach felt frozen, and the ends of her fingers were tingling. She realized that she was unable to speak.

By a violent effort of will, Lily turned her head away from Mrs. Fludd and looked back at the children. They played on, scrabbling in the sand. Their voices came clear and sweet to her. She snapped her head back to look at the park bench. It was now empty. Like the girl, Rosa Fludd had disappeared.

Lily's breath gradually returned to her body, as if it had been suspended for some minutes in the air before her. She self-consciously straightened her back and patted the back of her head. She looked once again at the bench. No one sat there. No sad gray fat lady. Of course. No one had ever been there. What an extraordinary thing, Lily thought. And to have an hallucination just at the time when she was preparing herself to drum sense into Julia! A less stable person than herself might immediately join Julia's fantasies and condemn himself forever to unreality. Lily permitted herself a smile at the thought of the response of Miss Pinner or Miss Tooth to the resurrection of Mrs. Fludd. Then she wondered just what Miss Pinner had seen in the bathroom on that awkward night; and then reminded herself on no account to bring up the subject with Julia. She found herself, she reflected, in the position of a priest taking a hard line on miracles with an overenthusiastic new convert.

By now Lily felt recovered; well, nearly recovered. The experience had been decidedly *dégoûtant*. She glanced once more at the bench—empty—and firmly marched on her way down the path.

On the corner of Ilchester Place Lily paused, trying to marshal her arguments. She had nothing in mind as to her exact words, but she knew she must have a lever—Julia in effect had to be pried from that house. Perhaps she could use Magnus. Some subtle threat was needed. If she could drop the word "hospital" in the proper way . . . Lily stood for a moment, enjoying the unaccustomed flavors of power and connivance.

She glanced up at Julia's bedroom windows. Or were those for the unused rooms? The house did have an empty look: more romancing, Lily thought. That damnable hallucination had upset her. Yet she could look obliquely through the side windows and see that at least half the living room was empty. From directly across the street she'd be able to look straight through the house: and if the drapes were drawn, wouldn't that mean that Julia was probably at home? Lily felt an inexplicable reluctance to begin her crusade immediately.

She took the ten paces across the street and looked through the double set of windows to the garden which glowed greenly, as if reduced in scale, through its frame. She'd have to ring the bell. Why this odd reluctance? Some memory pulsed below the level of consciousness and then opened to her: Mrs. Weatherwax at a postwar cocktail party (in the Albany, she remembered). A giant hulk of a woman, the wife of a Minister, the queen of her set, Mrs. Weatherwax had been in particularly foul mood, and had occupied a settee, her face frozen into disapproval—she had nearly dared anyone to approach her. Absurdly, the house had reminded her of Mrs. Weatherwax, exuding hostility from a flowered settee in the Albany. Those crushed flowers along the side of the house: had it been some sort of visual pun? Yet pun or not, the impression had been clear and strong.

What nonsense, Lily thought, and took a step off the pavement. Then she saw Magnus' face appear in the light square of green at the back of the house, and she froze in the attitude of taking her second step. She quickly retreated backward. After a second, she moved as far to one side as she would go while still watching the windows at the rear of the house. Magnus was jerking on the handle, his mouth working. As Lily watched aghast, he took some sort of card from his wallet and slipped it into the frame where the two halves of the window joined. His arm pumped rapidly; the windows parted, and Magnus climbed into the house. Lily could watch no more.

6

Magnus stood in the sunny dining room, listening carefully. Somewhere in the empty house a switch moved, inspiring a hum from machinery hidden behind the walls. Magnus fumblingly replaced his Access card in his wallet. He lurched forward a step, then paused again and listened like an animal. Perhaps the buzzing noise came from inside his head. He'd had no more than seven or eight hours' sleep all week, fueling himself with whiskey, keeping his adrenaline flowing by imagining scenes with Julia—sleep was caught in his office between clients, on park benches; once he'd fallen asleep in the flowerbed in the garden, keeping watch on Julia's window. He could imagine beating Julia, making love to her, waking her up an hour before dawn and talking to her urgently, cogently. Like many gregarious men, Magnus hated to be alone, and at times this week, locked into his house, patrolling from room to room with a bottle in his hand, he had talked to Julia so earnestly that he seemed to see her before him, her own ghost. Twice he had heard her calling his name in distress or pain and sped drunkenly across town to park before the dark house on Ilchester Place. He didn't know what he expected to see—unless it was Julia pinned by Mark, fighting him off a final desperate second before yielding. That scene came into his dreams and sent him rocketing awake, his heart thudding. He had begun to masturbate again, as he had not done since adolescence. There was a woman five minutes from this house, a former client who lived in Hammersmith, another woman nearly as close, the wife of a man in prison, but Magnus knew that he went to them largely because he frightened them; and they made sense only as temporary alternatives to Julia. Without her, they were useless to him. So he had come to lurk outside this house at night, his anger and frustration undimmed by whiskey, with no plan other than to speak to Julia the words he could always find when alone. On the telephone he could not control himself: she sounded snippy and pert, dismissive. It infuriated him.

Now the memory of that anger, and the tone of Julia's feigned coolness which inspired it, momentarily helped Magnus to quiet his apprehensions. That, of all the houses in London, Julia had chosen this one was nearly enough to encourage belief in all of Lily's mystical claptrap. Twenty-five Ilchester Place contained too many frustrating memories for him to feel comfortable with Julia's living there. Even after all these years, it was the past stirring again, wretchedly.

Now, Magnus thought, I should burn this place to its miserable roots. This idea gave him a shade more courage, and he moved around in the dining room, picking up things and putting them down. He would not be spooked by the place. And now it was bright day, unlike the other times when he had crouched outside, tapping at the windows before trying to force his way in. Then he had felt the house beating at him, almost—it was the only way he could describe it.

Magnus pulled the little bottle of brandy from his pocket and took a long swallow before entering the living room. Noticing that he had begun to perspire, he loosened his tie and swabbed at his forehead with his handkerchief. In the old days, the house had never been so hot—if anything, it had been rather cold. Someone had installed these damnably ugly storage heaters. This warmth was unpleasant, oppressive. Magnus tore the tie from his neck and balled it up in his trouser pocket.

He called Julia's name. When no answer came, he staggered toward the couch and leaned on its cushiony back. He bellowed her name again, then swore when he heard only the soft, buzzing noises of the house. Looking toward the staircase, he saw double for a moment and forced himself to stand straight upright. He focused his eyes. Of course all the furniture was different. Years ago the room had been brighter, with satin wallpaper—could that be right? It had looked like satin. Her sheets had been satin too, and silk. Down here had been small couches, bright paintings: the room had looked much larger. Everything gets smaller as we age, Magnus thought. This isn't a bit like the room where I came years ago—that room had been cheerful, frivolous, a bit silly. And we silly young men had thronged here. As an alternative to Cambridge, the house had attracted him by its carelessness, its perpetual atmosphere of carnival, the license he had thought of at the time as American. That was not to neglect the attractions of his hostess. He could visualize Heather Rudge slipping through the arch of the doorway with a cocktail shaker in her hand, a Sobranie cigarette wobbling in her charming mouth.

But all of that was what he wished to keep Julia from discovering. And what he must not think of. Magnus pushed himself away from the couch and went toward the kitchen.

There too everything had changed. Now all was white—white as a hospital. Magnus threw open several cupboards. Bottles of Malvern water, plates, glasses. A drawer of new silverware. To one side beneath the sink he found a clutch of whiskey bottles. The malt he'd taught her to like. He touched one of the bottles. They were somehow reassuring.

She must be dead by now, he thought. Then his mind blurred, and he thought he had meant Julia. The fear he had felt on the night he had broken the vase began to leak back into him. No, it was the other one who was dead, not Julia. She must have died in that place where she'd been put. That weak, foolish woman. He'd sent her money for years. Presumably other men sent her money too. She kept the same claim on all of them. Magnus slammed the door to the liquor shelf, hoping to chip away some of the white paint or damage the catch.

From the kitchen he stalked into the downstairs bathroom. He hovered just within the door, sensing that someone was near. Cunningly, he glanced into the rose mirrors. Something was just flickering out of sight. He was drunk. There was nothing to be afraid of. His head seemed to hum in sympathy with some deeper vibration. Watching himself in the mirrors, he took another pull at the brandy. And there it was again, just vanishing from sight. "Damn you," Magnus uttered. His thick gray hair lay across his forehead; his suit was spattered and wrinkled. He combed his hair with his fingers. "You're not there," he said aloud. "Bugger yourself."

What was it that had frightened him that first night he had come in from the garden? He had been slightly more sober that night: he'd half wanted to pound sense into Julia's fuzzy mind, half simply to sit in her house and relish her atmosphere. He had lifted the vase of flowers to smell them. The house was a particularly *taut* web of noises, none of which he could identify. But he'd thought he could hear Julia moving about upstairs, talking to herself. Then, at first quietly, almost modestly, a feeling had grown in him that he was being watched, as if by some little animal. A feeling of eyes on him. Irrationally, this had grown: the mouse had become a tiger, something baleful and immense and savage. He had never felt such sudden terror. And it was as much despair as fear—an utter and complete hopelessness. Gripping the vase, he'd been afraid to turn around, knowing that something loathsome crouched behind him. Kate's death. That very second seemed to hang behind him, about to engulf him. His head had hurt intolerably. Something rushed toward him, and he threw down the vase, making an awful clatter, and raced outside into the little garden without looking around.

Now he repeated "Bugger yourself," and left the bathroom to stand at the foot of the stairs.

If Mark were up there he'd . . . he'd strangle him.

Magnus put a foot on the lowest stair.

Something was up there. His skin seemed hot.

He stepped back down to the carpet and felt an immediate release of pressure. Even the buzzing in his head diminished. The upstairs of the house was full of noises. A running, rushing noise: for reasons Magnus could not begin to define, this meant an appalling danger to him. He put his foot back on the stair and felt the atmosphere thicken about him. An iron band clamped about his forehead and tightened; his chest pulled for air.

He backed away further into the hall. Now the house almost palpably lay about him—to stay there would kill him. He felt it with utter certainty. He tried to pull his handkerchief from his pocket and found that his fingers were unable to close properly. His hand shook. The fingers could not coordinate. He was afraid to turn his back to the staircase. Eventually he made his way to the door.

When he stood outside on the front doorstep in the sun, Magnus wobbled a
little and touched the bottle in his pocket, stroking it as a man pets a dog. Out
of the side of his eye he saw a face peering through a window at him and he
wheeled to face it. The woman's face, as pretty and mild as a saucer of cream,
hung there by the drapes for a second and then jerked back. Magnus contracted
his face at the spot where she had been. If he saw Julia, he'd beat the life out
of her. Someone had to pay for this—humiliation. He'd batter anyone who got
in his way.

The day after these events Julia drove her car south along the motorway,
following the directions given her by the director of the clinic. She felt bright
and illuminated with sleeplessness, her consciousness high and clear. She was
driving very fast, and became aware of her speed only when she accidentally
glanced at the dashboard. It seemed to her that she had never driven so well,
with such confidence. Below the bright center of her consciousness, her body
piloted the little car like an extension of her nerves.

In Guildford, the sight of a restaurant made Julia suddenly aware that she
was hungry. She had not eaten since receiving the letter; two letters, actually,
the short scrawled note from Mrs. Rudge folded within a typed sheet from the
director. The first of these had read:

> Julia Lofting,
> Is that your real name and do you live in my old house? You remember
> my case. Visit me if you wish.
>
> HR

In her excitement she had been able only to skim the covering letter, which
claimed for its writer a great pleasure that Mrs. Rudge was to be visited after
so many years and that no official impediment would block such a visit. There
had once been a problem with the press, who had treated "the patient" badly.
It would be a further pleasure to the director if he could meet Mrs. Lofting
after her talk with "the patient." This had the whiff of a laden desk and busy
secretary, behind them the stronger odor of hospitals and ammonia, and Julia
had thrust it away after memorizing the directions to the Breadlands Clinic.
She had reread Heather Rudge's scrawl a dozen times, looking for whatever
she might find in her cramped, spidery letters. It was, most noticeably, an
American handwriting, without the copperplate flourishes and separations of
that generation's hand in England.

Julia had spent that morning and afternoon foreseeing her meeting with Mrs.
Rudge—she was like a greyhound pulling at its leash, blind to everything but
what had just scrambled out of the bush. She had let the telephone ring unanswered, had finally left her home and walked until dark, through dingy
sections of Hammersmith and Chiswick; past eleven, she realized that she was
wandering near Gunnersbury Park, and took the underground back to Kensington. Not even the increasing noises and furies in the house had frightened

her: they were a sign that she was indeed getting closer to whatever was directing her life. She was at last able to act.

And the poltergeist, the spirit, was pleased. It was almost showing itself. Of course if it were Kate's spirit, it could not reveal itself until the very end—she was certain of that. But the heat in her bedroom had doubled in intensity and the noises at night—the rushing and rustling—were almost frantic. At times Julia heard voices, a woman's and a girl's, muttering from the hall. Snatches of music. Magnus had dwindled in her imagination. He was merely an outside force—baleful but not central to her. Magnus was a tool. Julia felt as though she were approaching the center of a blinding light too burning and intense to permit fear; she had to stand in the full clarity of that light, she had to understand all. Otherwise, Mrs. Fludd had died in vain. Perhaps even Kate's death would be for nothing. She felt the full weight of the past impelling her toward this hot center of light.

Just out of the center of Guildford Julia saw a Jolyon restaurant and her stomach again cramped savagely. She pulled up to the curb and went inside. Going down past the ranks of cafeteria food, she grabbed at whatever fell beneath her hand, at the cash desk finally paying for yogurt, chips, two sausages, an egg, toast and coffee. She carried her tray to one of the room's few clean tables and, scarcely bothering to look around her, began to bolt the food. After a few bites her hunger ceased as abruptly as it had begun, but she continued to eat until the sausages and egg had been consumed. The rest lay untouched on the table as she hurried out.

Half an hour later Julia saw the brass plate identifying the Breadlands Clinic and turned into the long narrow drive, which circled through a small wood before ending at a gray manor house. Julia's mouth was very dry: her heart seemed to be skipping beats, skittering. To calm herself she called up the photographs she had seen of Heather Rudge. Finally she was able to open the door of the Rover and walk across the crunching gravel to the steps of the manor.

An elderly woman in white greeted her. "You are Mrs. Lofting? Mrs. Rudge is *so* pleased that you wrote. And you know that Dr. Phillips-Smith wishes to see you afterward? Good. It's rather a long way away, so please follow me— of course, the poor old dear's not so difficult, not anymore, but we have to obey all the regulations, don't we? Of course. And she does have her rough spots. Keeps going on about her daughter, as I expect you'll know. You look as though you could use a rest, dear. Do you want to take a minute before you see her?" Small, bright squirrel's eyes.

"No, please, no," Julia got out.

She received a professional smile which seemed to conceal a good deal of metal. "Then please come this way, Mrs. Lofting."

They went briskly down a featureless corridor, past numbered doors. All was eggshell-white. "We *were* able to move her into E wing," the elderly woman said.

"Oh? How—how does she look?"

"Much better."

"Better. . . ."

As the nurse inserted a key into a locked metal door, Julia turned her head and looked into a small white room where a motionless form lay beneath a sheet. Beside the bed stood a steel table crowded with ampules and hypodermics. Julia nearly stumbled. The food bounced in her stomach like an angry cat.

"Just through here." At the end of the corridor, another heavy metal door. A large bald man in dirty white hoisted himself from a stool. His stomach wobbled as he came forward.

"Will you fetch Mrs. Rudge, Robert? I'll take Mrs. Lofting to the visitor's room."

Robert nodded and moved slowly off. The nurse led Julia through a small room bright with watercolors—a few old men working about a scarred table gaped at them. The men looked frightened, their faces oddly smooth and unmarked. One wore dark glasses which froze his face into granite.

Why am I here? Julia thought. I can't stand this place.

The feeling grew as the nurse brought her through two more chambers, each with the unsettling contradiction of bright, haphazard walls and pale, stunned-looking inhabitants. Faces which fled from experience. . . . Julia felt trapped by their hunger.

"Here we are, dear." The nurse had turned another corner and was holding open a door to an anonymous little room where two chairs stood on either side of a green metal table. Gesturing at a tattered pile of magazines, the nurse said, "She will be right with you."

Julia took the far chair as the nurse pivoted from the room.

A second later footsteps came. The door opened on Robert, who then stood aside to allow a woman to pass by him. Julia at first thought he'd brought the wrong woman. The flabby creature in the faded housedress bore no resemblance to the photographs of Heather Rudge, who had been trim and oval-faced in her forties, clearly sensual. Julia glanced at Robert, but he had moved to the stool in the corner of the room and now sat with his hands locked across his belly. He stared at the floor.

The woman still stood just inside the door. She was the sister of the faded, hopeless women Julia had seen in the other rooms.

"What is your name?" the woman asked. Her words scattered Julia's first impressions.

"I'm sorry . . ." said Julia, rising from her chair. "I've wanted so badly to meet you. You are Heather Rudge?"

"Mrs. Lofting?"

They've tricked me, they've given me someone else, thought Julia.

"Mrs. Lofting?"

"Yes," Julia said. "I'm sorry, it's just such a moment, meeting you—I bought your house, you know. I think about you. I think about you a lot."

The old woman shuffled across the floor and sat facing Julia. Her jowly face sprouted a few white whiskers.

"Why were you interested in my name?"

The woman looked slyly at Julia. "Nothing."

Julia leaned forward. "I don't know quite where to start. . . . Do you like having visitors? Do they treat you well here?"

"It's bad here. But better than prison. I was in prison, you know." Julia could hear in her voice the flat vowels of the Midwest. "You don't have to tell me about outside. They let us read—things."

"Oh, I should have brought you something, a book, something, or magazines, a stack of Penguins—I didn't think."

The blunt-faced woman stared impassively at her.

"I came to talk about you."

"I'm nothing. I'm safe here. Nothing happens to you here."

Julia could not speak. Finally she blurted, "My daughter is dead too. We have things we share, things in common, important things."

"You think mine is dead?" The old woman shot a quick sly glance across the table. "That's what they all think. But they didn't know her. Olivia isn't dead. And why should I care about your daughter, Mrs. Lofting?"

"Not dead? What . . . ?"

"It isn't 'what.' It's what I said. Why are you interested in Olivia? Didn't you come here to talk to me, Mrs. Lofting?" Unexpectedly, the old woman chuckled. "You poor cunt. You don't know where you are."

The heavy food churned in Julia's stomach. "I have to begin at the beginning. . . ."

"First you have to know where it is."

"Something's been happening to me and I have to tell you about it. I've been reading about your case in the old newspapers, I've been reading them for days, I believe there is some connection between us. . . ."

"Look at me, Mrs. Lofting," said the other woman. "I'm the one who is dead, not Olivia. Mrs. Lofting. Nice Mrs. Lofting visiting the crazy woman. Eat your own shit, Mrs. Lofting. Rub yourself with your shit. Then you'll know what I am."

Julia threw herself into it again. "I think I can help you too—part of you is caught in my house, I can hear you there sometimes. Does that make me crazy? Why did you talk about being safe?"

Now Mrs. Rudge's attention was wholly fixed on Julia. "I can't do anything for you, Mrs. High-and-Mighty Lofting. I scorn you." Her face grew distorted; she nearly spat her words. "Live in your house. I'll tell you about Olivia, Mrs. High-and-Mighty, Mrs. Nice. Do you want to know? Olivia was evil. She was an evil person. Evil isn't like ordinary people. It can't be got rid of. It gets revenge. Revenge is what it wants, and it gets it."

"What—what was her revenge?"

The silence was better than scorn.

"Do you mean that she made you do what you did?"

"She's laughing at me. She's laughing at you too. You hear her, don't you? You don't know anything." The flabby white face, contracted about a writing mouth and narrowed eyes, loomed before Julia. "*I* did what I did, Mrs. Shit, because I saw what she was like. Do you have to ask me what her revenge was?"

"Mrs. Rudge," Julia pressed, "did she do what people thought she did?"

"What she was was worse than what she did. Ordinary people can't touch it. I'm happy to be in here, Mrs. Lofting. Do you want to know a secret?" Malevolence gleamed from her distorted face.

"I want to know," said Julia. She was leaning across the table, straining to hear the thick words.

"You'd be lucky to be me."

Robert snorted from the corner.

"You're stupid, Mrs. Shit. As stupid as us in here."

Julia bowed her head. Spittle shone on the table's battered surface. The room seemed horribly small. A rank odor floated about her and for a moment she felt dizzy, assailed.

"Who else can I talk to?" she brought out. "Who else knew you?"

"The Braden bitch," snarled Mrs. Rudge. "Talk to that sauerkraut eater. Talk to my daughter's friends. They'll have found out."

"What are their names?" Julia softly asked.

"Names. Minnie Leibrook. Francesca Temple. Paul Winter. Johnny Aycroft. Do you want more? David Swift. Freddy Reilly. Hah! Go ask them about your problems, Mrs. Shit."

"Thank you," Julia said.

"You're just what I thought," said Mrs. Rudge. "You belong in here. Stupid cunt. Now get out."

"You have eight minutes," said Robert from the corner.

"No, I'd better . . ." Julia began. She stood up.

"Stupid cunt bitch. Stupid murdering cunt bitch."

Julia bolted around the body of the old woman and threw open the door. Robert looked up startled and held out a pudgy hand. Julia ran down the corridor and turned blindly at a corner. When she saw a large door with a light over it, she rushed through; impelled by a vision of Mrs. Rudge's sullen, working face and Robert chasing heavily after her, Julia fled the hallways and spun into a long hall filled with men and women.

Their faces were sagging and gray, or drawn and gray. They had all swiveled to stare at her entrance. Julia at first stopped, and then moved quietly among them toward the far end of the hall. The men were bent; their faces mooning and unconscious, they shuffled aside to let her pass, some of then fumbling toward her with unsteady hands. One cadaverous man grinned slackly from beneath wild hair. Julia only half saw the Ping-Pong table, the metal chairs pushed together to form rows. The odors of clean linen and sour flesh and disinfectant swam about her, as if Heather Rudge had leaped on her back. These faces—they looked as though they would leak sawdust. A hand with enormous knuckles brushed at her wrist, snatching at her. Julia flinched, and the elephantine man at her left hissed at her. A squashed-looking woman with terrible bright hair joined his hissing. A man whose face was all drawn to one side, as if snagged by a hook, scuttled before Julia and grabbed for her elbows as she twisted to pass him. She felt as if drowning in grotesque, stinking flesh. . . . She pushed at the man in blind revulsion and ran to the end of the hall just as Robert appeared at the far corner.

She was in a long dim corridor. Behind her she could hear lurching bodies, heavy footfalls. She ran. At the corridor's end there was a flight of steps down to a narrower, darker hallway with a rough stone floor. Here she ran in darkness for half its length; then, holding her side and gasping for breath, Julia walked quickly to a large barred wooden door. She pushed aside the bolts and swung the door open, grunting with the effort. Three broad stone steps led upward to a grassy lawn. At the far end of the lawn, the wood began. The names Heather Rudge had spat at her came thrillingly into her mind. *Braden. Minnie Leibrook. Francesca Temple. Paul Winter. Johnny Aycroft. David Swift. Freddy Reilly.* She looked into the dark tangled wood and moved up over the steps toward the wood's darkness, repeating the names.

Magnus stood in shock beside the sandboxes, children all about him. He was staring up at the window of Julia's bedroom. It was impossible, what he had seen there for a moment. He touched the bottle in his jacket pocket. A little boy brushed against his legs and Magnus stepped backward, feeling sand grind beneath his heel. His pulse seemed to have stopped. Gradually, into the silent vacuum which had dropped over him like a bell jar, sounds began to come. He heard children's piping voices and the far-off booming wash of a jet. One of the children pressed against his left leg. He had walked through the park from Plane Tree House, irritated. Lily had been more than usually coy with him, as if she were keeping a secret. She'd assumed her you're-such-a-naughty-boy manner, as she sometimes did when she had learned something upsetting about him, but she had refused to speak directly about his supposed transgression. Instead, she had babbled about Julia's "privacy," about her need for "an honest meeting" with Magnus, about "the needs of all concerned," all the while her eyes shining with bright, needling admonition. He had supposed that all this had to do with his drinking.

Then she had got onto his not being a Queen's Counsel again.

"For God's sake, Lily," he had said. "I've explained this to you a hundred times. If I wanted to be a QC I could be one. But all I would do would be to double my prices and drop my cases down to a fourth of what they are now. You don't understand what a Queen's Counsel is. For a man in my position it would be a ludicrous mistake."

"I want my distinguished brother to be a QC."

"You mean you want to be the sister of a QC without first understanding what it means. Absurd. And it has nothing to do with Julia. Can you get that into your head?"

"Magnim. . . ."

"And don't start to stroke me with Durm."

She had brightly pulled back. "You should have your clothes looked after. That suit looks as though you've slept in it."

"I probably did, damn it."

By the time he had left Lily's flat, he had a headache and the sour beginnings of indigestion. He had walked gloomily through the park, irritated with the sunshine and the loafers sprawling on the grass. The newspapers predicted a change in the weather in the next few days, which suited him. He wanted rain. He longed for clouds and cold blustery weather. Eventually he reached the play area and stepped off the path onto the springy grass. Then he looked angrily up at Julia's window and saw Kate—the back of her head shining through the glass. In the next second she had disappeared. But it was Kate. He knew the color of that hair better than he knew the color of his own. For a long moment Magnus forgot to breathe.

He extracted a grinning black girl of two or three from his leg and, gulping air, stepped forward on the grass. His stomach burned. His tongue was a wooden oar lodged in his mouth. He could not have seen Kate. Yet he *had* seen her—that hair shining like the hair of a princess in a fairy story. For a moment Magnus felt one of the strongest and most unselfish emotions of his lifetime, an overriding fear for Julia's safety.

His legs took him over the lawn, racing, to the road out of the park. He ran a few laborious steps into Ilchester Place and then, puffing, began to walk quickly. He scanned the expressionless facade of the house. Impossible to tell what was going on inside. The great moment of the fear had receded, but it lay close enough to bring Magnus up the walk, leaping the three steps, to the door. He pushed the bell. From far within the house Magnus heard the bell's chime, falling away: the house was empty.

He jumped off the doorstep and half circled the house, peering in the windows. The interiors he saw looked motionless, tomblike, immaculately dead. He pounded on the window of the kitchen until its whiteness and sterility repelled him; then he continued around to the back of the house where he tried the handle of the French windows. They were locked. He leaned forward and looked past the parting of the drapes, cupping his hands about his eyes. The stolid furniture bulked on the floor as if it had come from a taxidermist's show window. Before taking out his Access card he glanced at the house next door and saw Julia's kittenish little neighbor staring down at him in horror from an upstairs window.

He shook his fist at her before noticing the tall, weedy man cutting around the corner of Julia's house to come toward him. The expression on his face, that of a policeman about to dress down a tramp, infuriated Magnus, as did everything about the man, his modishly long blond hair and his velvet jacket and glinting ascot. When the man glanced suspiciously at Magnus' rumpled and stained, tieless exterior, Magnus whirled to face him, balling his fists.

"Just a minute," the blond man began. "Just a minute there, you."

Glowering into his face, Magnus saw, with the sureness of years of sounding witnesses and juries, an essential weakness beneath the bluster. "Piss off," he growled.

The man stopped, as if hesitating, and then approached to within two feet of Magnus. "I don't know what your game is, mister, but you shall be in trouble with the law if you don't leave this house alone. I've seen you here before and I don't like the look of you."

"You utter twit," Magnus said. "Piss off and leave me alone. My name is Lofting. My wife lives here. I don't know who the bloody hell you are and I don't care. Now get going."

Amazement came into the well-cared-for face. "My name is Mullineaux," he blurted. The admission caused him anger and Magnus, seeing it, braced himself. "I live next door to this house you were about to break into. Now I must ask you to leave."

Magnus leaned his forehead against the windowpane, grinning ferociously. "You have a lot of guts for a Golden Wonder," he said. "I'm going inside. I think my wife is in danger." He straightened up and smiled at the man, knowing despairingly that he would have to fight him.

"Your wife isn't here," said Mullineaux. "And I doubt if you could do anything for her, in your condition." He lifted an admonitory finger. "If you go away this instant, I promise you that against my better judgment I will not speak of this to the police. Now please go."

" 'Now please go,' " Magnus mimicked. "Now *you* will please go, twit, because I'm going inside. You can stand here and watch or you can help me."

"I must say . . ." the man said, advancing and placing a hand on Magnus' arm.

An absolute conviction of his size flashed through Magnus, and he punched the man on the side of his head, knocking him aside. Because Magnus had used his left hand, the blow was weak, but Mullineaux crumpled to the ground. At that instant Mark's face floated into Magnus' mind. He ground his teeth, enraged, and took a step toward the pale figure now groveling on the grass. He lifted his right boot back, intending to kick Mullineaux on the point of his jaw, but looked upward at the neighboring house and saw the pretty little woman inside shrieking through the glass. "Come and get this idiot inside," he muttered, his fury dissipating, and stalked off back around to the front of the house. He had left his car at Plane Tree House.

Kate? Kate? As he stormed through the park, the slightly hazy, glowing summer air seemed to darken about him.

7

Mark came awake in darkness, the dirty sheet twisted about his hips. He had been dreaming about Julia, a variation on a dream he had been having regularly for the past three or four years. Usually the dream began with his entering a classroom, perching on the desk, and suddenly realizing that he was totally unprepared. Not only had he no lecture or plan for this particular class, he could not even recall which course he was supposed to be teaching. Students from various years and classes regarded him quizzically, already bored: if he could not think of something to say, soon the whole hour, an hour he hadn't the barest idea of how to fill, would be lost. Was this *Working Class Movements in England*, Monday, Wednesday and Friday, 9:30–10:20? *New Trends in Socialist Thought*, Tuesday, Thursday and Friday, 1:30–2:20? *Crowd Theory*, Monday and Wednesday, 4:00–5:25? He would realize with growing desperation that he did not know what day it was. Last night, the dream had progressed to this point, and then Julia had risen from one of the chairs and, pulling a sheaf of notes from her bag, began to lecture brilliantly on the London Corresponding Society and its Secretary, Thomas Hardy. He had resented her usurping his class at the same time as he had listened dazzled to her initial summary of information and the cascade of her ideas, which defined exactly what he had been struggling to express to this class over the past year. He had been certain he would remember everything she said so that he could use it in the first chapter of the book he wanted to write, but all of it had vanished in the first second of wakefulness. Instead of her ideas, he would remember how she had looked—dressed in a white blouse and yellow skirt, her hair hanging softly about her shoulders, she was the Julia he had seen that first morning at Magnus' house. She looked enchanted, like a woman who conversed with fairies: a woman to whom clung the last bewitching traces of childhood. Mark stared up at the low ceiling of his room, realizing that the dream had caused in him a terrific sexual arousal. He wanted Julia very badly. She could not consider herself married to Magnus after his brutal appearance at her home yesterday afternoon; the thought gave him energy to roll over and punch the light switch beside the mattress. Magnus seemed to have at last exploded. Both Julia and Lily had described the incident to him, each of them advising him to stay away from Magnus for the time being. Well, when *hadn't* he avoided Magnus? One of the first utterly clear impressions of Mark's life was that his adoptive brother detested him.

Maybe loathing was more the word for it, he considered, and giggled.

Still grinning, Mark untangled his legs from the sheet and stood up beside the mattress, carefully avoiding the stacks of plates and half-empty tins strewn over the floor. He had begun eating in bed the previous winter, when his bed was the warmest place in the flat, and had not yet got out of the habit. A pile of clothing lay atop a chair near the mattress, and Mark extracted from it a shirt and trousers, which he pulled on over his body, taking great care with the zip of the trousers. From the pocket of the shirt he took a pack of Gauloises and a lighter and applied the flame to the tip of the cigarette, relishing the smoke's occupation of his mouth and lungs. Then he felt beside the mattress and found his watch. It was eleven o'clock. He glanced for a moment at his desk, set below the window at the opposite end of the room, and immediately felt the loss of all sexual desire. There lay his typewriter, some pencils in a small bottle, a stack of paper, a few sheets of notes and a dozen books in two piles—all the material for beginning work on his book. They had lain there since the previous summer, when he had deliberately not taken any teaching work so that he could write. But that summer had passed in a series of casual meetings with women, daydreams, grandiose plans which had never come to anything. He had spent an alarming amount of time asleep, as if exhausted by inactivity. After another three terms of teaching, Mark had thought that he could at last get down to the book, but now he could not look at his desk without feeling a panicky fluttering of guilt. He was less sure of his ideas now than when he'd first thought of writing his interpretation of working class social movements. When he could bring himself now to think about the book, he chiefly visualized the reviews it would earn. "The breakthrough in socialist thought achieved by this brilliant young lecturer . . ." "This classic of Marxist praxis . . ." He snubbed out the Gauloise on a plate and went down the hallway to the bathroom.

When he returned Mark separated the curtains above his desk and let a drained, weak version of the sunlight enter the room. Well below street level, the little flat required electric lighting at all times of day. Forever gloomy, on overcast days it held large areas of brownish obscurity. The windows, like the smaller window in the kitchen—the flat's second room—looked out onto a wall of concrete which had once been white. Soon his headache would return. It had first come nearly a month ago, just after he had awakened. Ever since, he had been haunted by it, an insistent throbbing behind his temples and a feeling of constriction over the entire top of his head. On mornings when he had dreamed of Julia, it seemed worse. These sensations, never actually painful, had affected his concentration. Even if he were able to sit at his desk and begin work, he thought, he would be unable to construct a decent paragraph: he found himself losing the thread of conversations, of suddenly being aware, as in his classroom dream, that he was uncertain of what he had planned to do next. Several times on the street, he had been unable to remember where he had been going. He often found himself brooding about Julia and Magnus. A displaced, lost child himself, Mark had lately begun to see Julia—whom he had for years thought of as no more than a sweet, moderately pretty housewife—as his counterpart. Magnus' possession of her seemed a cruel and blatant injustice. No man as bastardly and arrogant as Magnus deserved any sort of wife, certainly not one as sensitive as Julia. And Julia's money, which he could use to further a thousand worthwhile purposes—the writing of his book only the most immediate of these—had been squandered on drinks and bourgeois dinners, and almost certainly funneled off to Lily. At times, Mark nearly hated Julia for tolerating so long her brutish parody of a marriage. And the money had come from that old crook, Charles Windsor Freeman, Julia's great-grandfather, one of the classic American plunderers and exploiters: Mark could turn it against that very class and cleanse the money of its stain.

It was time for his exercises. Mark extended himself on the carpet, which showed strands of thread beneath its scuffy greenish tufts, and deliberately emptying his mind, first lifted one arm and then the other straight upward. He tightened his muscles and pushed upward with all his strength. He repeated this with his legs. Loosened, he sat in the lotus position and attempted to touch his forehead to the ground. He extended his tongue until its roots ached. Then he sat blankly, expectantly. He closed his eyes to a furry darkness.

He stared deeply into the opaque darkness, letting it take shape around him. No movement, no thought. He was a vessel to be filled.

Within ten minutes the chaos of the flat had spun away, leaving him in a vibrant, circling universe. He was a dancing point of light in darkness, a slit of entry for spirit. Stars and worlds moved about him like spheres. The single burning lamp was a glorious golden wheel of consciousness toward which he flew, circling. It breathed and pulsed, trembling with life and knowledge.

His body, no longer tiny, became immense. His whirling encompassed worlds, galaxies. Mark-body became Mark-self, breathing in gusts of spirit. Time cocooned him, light as dust. Everything was holy. He could blow time away and fracture the world, leaving only Mark, only holy light. His hands lay across continents, weightless as the buzzing of a fly. His arms lifted themselves, and extended through vast distances. Wordless chanting filled the glowing space about him. Disembodied peace indistinguishable from tension illuminated and lifted him. Muscles, birds, flight. He was up. Now he was traveling toward a swarm of bright particles which coalesced as he traversed the great distance separating himself from them. He ached for union. He saw first a golden city, then a face he knew to be Julia's even before it came fully into focus. He was creating her from spirit. Space began to hum with energy, to sing. He was dissolving into flames and candles, into sheer brightness. The face he saw was not Julia's, but that of a beautiful child. The brightness unbearably, gloriously intensified.

Outside, far away and to his left, a taxi blared. Mark began to spin downward, heaviness invading his body's vast molecular spaces. He collapsed forward onto the carpet, his thighs cramping. His tongue caught a dusty web of hair. Mrs. Fludd, sitting beside him on a couch in Julia's living room, said to him, "You are being blocked." With the repetition of the taxi's bright, horrid noise came his headache, settling like night over his scalp.

"I'm so grateful that you agreed to see me," said Julia to the pleasant, smiling middle-aged woman who had opened the door of the large white house at 4 Abbotsbury Close. "It's very important that we talk, important to me—I was so surprised to see your name in the directory, I thought you would have moved after your tragedy. Do you remember speaking to me on the telephone, Mrs. Braden? I'm Julia Lofting. You said I should come over this morning before lunch. . . ."

The woman opened the door further and admitted Julia to deep gloom. All of the house she could see appeared to be dark brown; a far wall held a cluster of old photographs layered with dust. "I am not the one you spoke to," the woman whispered to Julia. "Mrs. Braden is upstairs in her room. She is waiting for you. It is about Geoffrey, yes?" Her German accent sounded like that of the voice Julia had heard over the telephone yesterday: but this woman's voice was higher in pitch, silvery. Julia immediately, irrelevantly thought of it as the voice of a hypnotist.

"You're not . . ." Julia glanced up toward the staircase, which ended at a darkened arch.

"I'm Mrs. Braden's companion," said the woman, her voice insinuating, lulling. "I am called Mrs. Huff. I have known Mrs. Braden only since the tragedy. At first there were so many, those men from newspapers, the police, many wicked people coming to pry—the curious. I kept them away from her. Now no one comes for a long time. She wants to see you."

Mrs. Huff, moving with a stiff efficiency that recalled Miss Pinner, and which Julia only now recognized as arthritis, pulled open a door at Julia's left and revealed a musty parlor. Brown overstuffed chairs faced each other across a mottled carpet. Beside each rose a hairy plant. "Please to wait here until I return. It will not be long."

"Is there a Mr. Braden?" Julia stood uneasily beside one of the fuzzy chairs.

"He died in the war," Mrs. Huff said, and was gone. The door clicked behind her.

Julia did not want to sit in the chairs; they reminded her of some sticky plant that trapped insects and then digested them. She turned in the dark little room and began to pace, too excited to take in the room's furnishings, which seemed to hang in the dusty gloom. Her steps took her to a wooden bookcase; Julia looked at the titles, odd in some way, uniformly stamped in gilt on the thick spines. Then she saw that they were all in German. She ran her hand along the books, and her fingers came away black. Wiping her fingers on a tissue from her bag, Julia walked in small circles on the dark carpet. Surely it was

Turkish? Her grandfather had owned a carpet much like it. She became aware of a pressure in her bladder. Where was the bathroom? It was only the excitement, she knew, and it would soon pass away if she could take her mind off it. She began to pace more rapidly; if the pressure increased, she would have to sit cross-legged in one of the awful chairs. Then her steps took her immediately before a small canvas, and she stopped pacing, puzzled by its familiarity. It was not a painting she had seen before, but surely she knew that arrangement of uptilted table, pipe and gash of newsprint. Braque—it was a Braque. She peered at the little painting more closely. It had to be a reproduction; but when she read the signature she saw the buttery raised strokes of paint. Surprise dissipated the urgency in her bladder.

She turned about just as the door opened. Mrs. Huff beckoned stiffly with one hand, smiling. "Mrs. Braden will see you now. Please follow me."

"This painting—I can't believe it!" said Julia.

"Please to come. I know nothing about painting."

Julia hurried from the room, propelled by the silvery, lulling voice. Mrs. Huff gestured toward the staircase, smiling, and then began to ascend. Julia followed. When she had passed through the darkened archway, she saw Mrs. Huff opening a door halfway down a lightless hall. Julia had time to notice rows of paintings lining the walls, but the obscurity within the corridor effaced them. She went hurriedly through the door Mrs. Huff was holding open for her.

"Please sit down, Mrs. Lofting," said the large gray-haired woman dressed entirely in shining black who had risen at Julia's entrance. "I am Greta Braden and it was I to whom you spoke on the telephone. Please take the chair to your left. I think you will find it comfortable. Thank you, Huff." The door closed softly behind Julia.

She found herself staring at a painting encased in a gold frame from which depended a sliding red velvet drape, now pulled to one side to reveal a fleshy naked woman whose skin seemed to absorb all the room's light. It was, unbelievably, a Rubens. The rest of the bedroom shared with its occupant the atmosphere of elegance gone down in neglect. The flocked wallpaper, once red-gold, had been darkened by grime to a mute shade of brown. Books and newspapers lay over the floor, many of the papers yellowing with age. On the worn black velvety expanse of material covering the massive bed lay a tray holding the ruins of breakfast. Mrs. Braden's large angular face seemed to have caught dust in every fold. The gray hair was stiff with grease. Looking at her, Julia was not sure that Greta Braden was quite sane.

"You wish to talk with me about my son. Why is that, Mrs. Lofting?"

Julia sat on the chair Mrs. Braden had indicated, and felt the cushions slither beneath her weight. Now she was looking at a photograph, hung on the wall above the huge bed, of a small frail-looking boy in spectacles. Beside it hung a second photograph, of a tall, gaunt man wearing pince-nez and a Norfolk jacket.

"That was Geoffrey," said Mrs. Braden. "My husband stands beside him. What is your interest in me, Mrs. Lofting?"

"I saw Heather Rudge two days ago," said Julia, and saw the woman's body stiffen inside the shiny black shell of her clothing. "She was abusive and disturbed, but she did mention that I might speak to you." Overriding a curt, dismissive gesture from Mrs. Braden, Julia hastily added, "I am not working for Heather Rudge, not in any way. You see, I recently bought the Rudges' former house. I was—I was recovering from a long illness. Something about the house demanded that I buy it. Since then I've been looking into the past of the Rudge family—the past of the house. It's been something like a compulsion—I want to know everything I can find out about them. I don't think the truth ever came out about your son's death, Mrs. Braden. There's a lot more, but you might think I was crazy if I said it all. The chief thing is, I have to find out about the Rudges."

Mrs. Braden was looking at her very shrewdly. "And then you will perhaps write about what you find?"

"Well," said Julia, afraid to risk expulsion by uttering the wrong answer, "I'm not sure about that. . . ."

"Twenty-four years ago I would not have talked to you," said Mrs. Braden. "Especially if you mentioned the name Rudge. Now much time has passed, and I have waited for someone to speak the truth about my son's death. Many have gone unpunished. When my tragedy happened, the police would not listen to me. I was a foreigner, a woman, and they thought me suspicious, foolish. They ignored me, Mrs. Lofting. My son's death has gone unavenged. Now do you understand why I am speaking to you?"

"I . . . I think so," said Julia.

"My world is in this room. I have not left my house since twenty years. I have become old in this room. Huff is my eyes and ears. I care for nothing but my husband's collection of paintings, his memory, and my son's memory. Even Huff does not know everything about my son's murder—doesn't that word sound awesome and terrible to you, Mrs. Lofting? Do you know what murder is? That it is the greatest crime against the soul, even the souls of the living? It is an eternal crime."

"Yes . . . I feel that," Julia breathed. "But what I need is proof. Or knowledge more than proof."

"*Proof.*" The older woman expelled the word from her mouth as if it were rotten meat. "I need no proof. That man the police executed was a harmless vagrant. He was a simple man, a child himself. He liked to talk to the children. What proof did the police have when they killed him?"

"So you *are* convinced he was innocent," Julia said.

"Of course, of course! Listen to what I am saying to you. There were no secrets between Geoffrey and myself, Mrs. Lofting. I know what they did to him in that park. Those others tortured him daily. They made his life a hell because he was sensitive and because he had asthma. And because he was partially German. They called my son the Kraut, the Jerry, the Hun. They were all bad children, those others."

"And you knew Mrs. Rudge?"

"That one. She laughed at me. She scorned me. I begged her to help me for

Geoffrey's sake, but she was blind and foolish. She could not see what was happening within her own house. She could not see she was defending a monster. I have no doubt about what happened to my son, Mrs. Lofting. The Rudge girl mutilated him and then killed him. And the others helped. Now. Do you think that I am wrong?"

Julia gently touched the sheeny material of Mrs. Braden's sleeve. "What did Olivia look like, Mrs. Braden? Can you describe her?"

The reply destroyed her expectations. "She was just a girl. Her exterior was unimportant. She looked like one of a hundred girls. She has been dead as long as Geoffrey. You must be aware of that."

"I am aware of it, yes, but there are reasons—I have to know what she looked like. Did she have blond hair? How tall was she?"

"Those are foolish details. Blond, yes, she may have been blond. But you couldn't tell she was evil by looking at her, Mrs. Lofting."

"That's the same word her mother said."

Mrs. Braden smiled. "That stupid woman," she said. "That rude common little fool. No, Mrs. Lofting, you must not dwell on the wasted lives of the Rudges. You must find the others. You must make them confess."

"I have to find them," Julia agreed. "I know some of their names. Minnie Leibrook and Francesca Temple and Paul Winter. . . ."

"And John Aycroft and David Swift, yes. And the Reilly boy. You surprise me, Mrs. Lofting. Those were the children who helped Olivia Rudge kill my son. If you want your proof, talk to them. And I can help you."

Julia waited tensely, unable to guess what would come.

"Some of them have died. None of them have prospered. As you can imagine, Mrs. Lofting, I have been interested in the lives of this group. I have 'kept up,' as you would say. I can tell you that the Reilly boy disappeared in America, your country, ten years ago—he is lost. John Aycroft killed himself when his business went bankrupt. Minnie Leibrook died in an automobile accident while drunk. Francesca Temple was very wise and became a nun. She now lives in the Slaves of Mary convent in Edinburgh, under a vow of silence. Paul Winter became a professional soldier, as was his father, but was cashiered by his regiment. He lives in a flat in Chelsea. David Swift ruined his family wine business and lost his wife in a freak accident—she was electrocuted. He lives above a pub in Upper Street, Islington. Talk to those two men, Mrs. Lofting. If you can make them talk, you will have your proof."

Julia was stunned. "How did you find out all this?"

Mrs. Braden flexed her shoulders, making the cloth creak. "My eyes and my ears. Huff. I pay Huff very well. She has many talents. I will ask you to leave now, Mrs. Lofting. But first I will give you some advice. Be very thorough. And be careful."

"Well, careful is what you'd better be," Mark said that evening. "I never heard such a tacky idea. You mean you really intend to march up to those two people and grill them about a twenty-four-year-old death? For which a man has already been executed? Look here, have another drink instead and forget all about it. God knows what you'd be getting into."

"I'll have another if you let me pay for it. Please, Mark."

"If you insist, I reluctantly accept." Mark had counted his money a few minutes before in the men's room, and knew that the last round had left him with sixty-three pence. He owed twenty pounds to a colleague, and when he'd paid that, his next check from school would leave him just enough to pay his rent and buy a month's food and drink. Still, he supposed, he could always put off Samuels for another month—maybe he could put him off until the second term. He watched hungrily while Julia withdrew a small purse from her bag and took from it a ten-pound note. With a start of anticipatory pleasure, Mark realized that he already thought of Julia's money as his own. "That's sweet of you, darling," he added. He took the note from her fingers.

When he came back from the bar with the two drinks he put the pile of bills and change on the table between them. He said, "Are you bothered about the change?"

She looked up at him, startled. "Why, do you need money?"

"Just something to tide me over. I've had a tight month."

She pushed the bills at him, her face beautifully focused on his. "Mark, please take it—please. Do you want any more? It's silly of me to have so much when you don't have enough. Really, do you need more?"

"We can talk about that later," he said. In the soft light which filtered through to the back corners of the pub, Julia looked much better, he thought. Her face still seemed milky from lack of sleep, but she was more confident, vibrant, like the Julia of old, before Magnus had sunk his claws into her.

"Are you feeling well, Mark?" she asked.

"Just a headache. It comes and goes." He adjusted his face to put on his most endearing expression, what an old girl friend had called his "sheep-in-wolf's-clothing face." "I have to say," he went on, "that I think you should just drop the whole business right now. I don't think you should have upset yourself by visiting those two old grotesques. I don't understand your worry about Kate. You still have Kate, my love. Kate is part of you. She can't hurt you. I blame Magnus for planting all that fear in you. I could kill him for what he's doing to you. You should have let Perry what's-his-name go to the coppers." His headache had tightened up a notch, but he kept his face steady, putting, if anything, more warmth into his eyes.

"You hate Magnus, don't you?" Julia sounded faintly startled.

"Magnus is a bastard."

"I do think of you as my protection against him. It was magic, how you appeared that time I fainted. And you and Lily are the only people I can talk to about what's been happening to me. If it weren't for poor Mrs. Fludd, I probably wouldn't be able to talk about it at all. Did you hear about her?"

Mark nodded, and his headache made the pub swirl. "Lily told me. Too bad. Funny old girl."

"*She* saw something, and she knew she was in danger. I think she was killed so she couldn't tell me what it was. Mark, I'd think I was going crazy if it weren't for her—I have to make her death mean something." Julia took a big swallow of her drink. "She was murdered. I'm sure of it."

"She walked in front of a car, didn't she? That's what, manslaughter, not murder."

"Why did it happen, though? And if it was a straightforward accident, how did she know she was in mortal danger? Mrs. Fludd said there was a man and a child—I've been thinking all along that they were Magnus and Kate, I thought Kate was haunting my house, but there's another possibility. Of course the man is Magnus, I know that much—he's completely irrational—but the girl might be someone else. That girl I saw. And that's why I have to see those people."

Mark rubbed his temples. "I think you're making a mistake. I think you should forget about the whole business." Julia had got an exalted, excited look which rasped on his nerves.

"What did Mrs. Fludd say to you that night? I have to know, Mark. It might help."

"Nothing. It was nothing. I can't even remember."

"Oh." She seemed chastened. "Really? Please try."

"I can't tell you how much my head hurts. Well, I think she said something like, 'You're being blocked,' and then she said that I should leave your house."

"It's what she told me! Oh, Mark, she wanted to save you too." She reached toward him and stroked his woolly hair. The pain seemed to ebb. He looked at her flushed face and her brimming eyes and saw that some of her exaltation was from the whiskey. "Dear Mark," she said. "Your poor head."

"Maybe she was trying to keep me away from you." That was in fact what he had felt.

"I went to the Tate this week," he heard her say. Her fingers continued to caress his hair. "I looked at that painting. The Burne-Jones. You're in it too. I am so grateful for you."

When he looked up from his cupped hands he saw that Julia was crying. "Finish your drink and let's go," he said. The headache had resumed its normal proportions.

Then they were standing in the squalor of his flat, holding one another. Carefully adjusting his stance to support Julia's weight while avoiding a crusty dish on the floor, Mark stroked her long, rather unkempt hair. He saw a profusion of split ends and wiry single hairs thrust up in a fuzzy corona. "Mark, I don't know what is happening to me," she was saying. Each word floated out into his collar and burst in a haze of whiskey. "Sometimes I'm so frightened. Sometimes it's like I'm not in control of myself. Ever since I read about the Rudge case I've been kind of *dominated* by it—it's all I think about. Because it would mean that Kate . . ." Her back shook with her sobbing.

"Don't talk about it," he said. He slipped his right hand between them and began to stroke her breast. Julia gasped, and then tightened her hold on him.

"Stay with me," he said. "I need you."

"I want to," she uttered into the side of his neck. His back was beginning to ache from supporting her. Julia was heavier than he had thought. "You're the only man I've ever wanted, except for Magnus. But . . ."

"I need you," he repeated. "You're beautiful, beautiful, Julia." He swung her body around, kicking a plate and knocking over an empty, clouded milk bottle, and, grunting a little, lowered her to the mattress. "Please, Julia. Stay with me." He bent and began to unbutton her blouse, brushed his lips on the mound of her belly. In the light from the single lamp beside the mattress, her face looked blotchy and flushed.

"I can't," she moaned.

"You can do anything you want." He peeled her blouse away from her breasts and put his mouth to one of her nipples. Then he leaned sideways, rolled one hip onto the mattress beside her, and kissed her mouth. It was warm and fleshy, with the feeling of crushed fruit.

"Mark . . ."

"Shh."

"Mark, I can't." But still she did not move. "Just stay beside me," she said.

Mark pulled the blouse over her shoulders and slipped it down her arms, then tossed it aside. He rapidly stripped off his own shirt, and gave her another long kiss. Julia lay inert, her eyes glazed and bloodshot, out of focus, in the light of the lamp. After undoing his belt and pulling off his boots, Mark shed his trousers. "I will," he said. "I'll just stay beside you."

"Promise. Please."

"Yes."

He discarded his underwear as she distractedly, uneasily, removed the rest of her clothing. "Your house is a mess," she said, laying her skirt atop the blouse.

"Touch me." He guided her hand.

"You're soft." She smiled into his face. "Sweet. Big soft Mark."

"I still have my headache," he confessed. "This doesn't usually happen to me." Julia's hand warmly cradled his penis, holding it hesitantly. "No. Keep your hand there." Now he was beginning to feel a fractional urgency, and he stiffened a little. Her hand jerked him awake. He tongued her nipples, sliding his hand between her legs. Julia's body seemed an immense, fruitful meadow of warmth.

"My God," he said. "What happened to your thighs?" They bore enormous purple bruises.

"I hurt myself crawling in a window one night when I lost my key."

"Damn it," Mark said. He had lost the small erection he had just gained. His headache throbbed. He lowered his head to the place beside hers on the pillow and reached down to pull the sheet up over them. He touched a warm knee, the curve of a calf, then looked down to see that the sheet lay tangled at their feet. He closed his eyes again and felt her hands pulsing warmth into his back. He slid one hand between her thighs and caressed a bush of long coarse hair.

"Don't," she said, suddenly gripping him tight. "Don't. Just stay with me."

But Mark was incapable of anything else. His head seemed to have grown to twice its size. There was a whirling vacuum between his legs. He punched the button on the lamp and held to Julia's warm body because it anchored him in the room. His head found the cushion of her breast. Everything spun about him. He tried to create an erection by willpower, but his brain could not retain the necessary images. His body felt as though it were traveling—traveling great distances toward a cluster of lights. Julia's voice brought him closer to his real size, but he could not focus upon that either.

". . . keep seeing grotesques. Did you see that man in the pub? He had a red stump instead of a hand—just scar tissue—and his mouth . . ." He forced himself to think: he had not seen a man with one hand in the pub ". . . a roomful of blank, flabby people reaching for me . . . that old woman at Breadlands . . . swearing . . ." Her voice slipped away altogether.

In the morning she was gone, and his body stretched uselessly, achingly, into air. Beside his head on the pillow he found a note which read *You're a darling. I'm off to do my detecting. Love.* Beneath it was a check for a hundred pounds.

8

The spirit did not like her leaving the house for an entire night. When Julia entered her home, wanting to wash and change clothes before looking for Paul Winter and David Swift, she saw with little surprise that some of the furniture had been tumbled about, chairs overturned and cushions flung to the corners of the living room. From upstairs came an angry knocking and banging that she knew would disappear when she set foot on the staircase. In the midst of the din, she could hear a radio playing some vapid forties dance tune, and that noise too would vanish. The odd, fumbling night with Mark—he had lain against her unmoving all night, as unconscious as if drugged—slipped away. As much as tenderness for Mark, she had felt all during the long hours after the alcohol had worn off an acute awareness that she was not in the *real* place, the place where the important things happened. Mark's inability to make love had been a relief; apart from her house, deflected from her quest, she wished only for comfort from the desolation. Back in her house and close again to the source of the mystery, she felt that desolation as her familiar element—it was the gray commanding sea in which she swam. What was happening to her was necessary; she was at home.

Julia went into the kitchen and experimentally turned the tap. A pipe clamored in the wall like a trapped owl. A viscous brown jelly plopped at the mouth of the faucet, and she hurriedly twisted the knob of the tap. Into the air she softly said, "You're angry with me." The hullabaloo upstairs quieted for a moment. When she had poured three bottles of Malvern water into a pot for heating, she quickly went through the living room, uprighting chairs and replacing the cushions.

"You're not Kate," she said, tilting her head back. "You're Olivia. I'm going to prove it. I'm going to find out, I'm going to *find out*—it's what I'm here for, isn't it?"

The toby jug lamp crashed to the floor and shattered.

"I'm going to help you," Julia whispered. The house seemed to get warmer with each word. "You are very powerful, but you need my help. And when I find out, I'll find out everything. I'll know why you are torturing Magnus. And then I'll be free too."

She waited for another bang from upstairs, but the house seemed to hover about her, expectant.

"I'm going to free us," Julia repeated softly. "You want Magnus to hurt me, but I'm going to set you free. That's why I came, isn't it? You needed me. You had to have me live here."

A heavy painting thudded to the floor, cracking the glass with a sharp noise like a pistol shot.

"I'm not afraid," Julia said, and then added, "I don't have to be afraid until I know." She was lying—at any moment she expected something to fly at her head—but it was a lie which contained a glowing corner of the truth. Fear could not keep her from the hot center of the truth: fear was only personal.

After she had washed at the sink, scrubbing herself in armpits and private parts with a sponge, Julia ascended to the throbbing heat of the upstairs. Her bedroom door gaped open. An elbow of noise seemed to pulse from the walls. The heat from her room gusted out in a breeze which lifted her hair and dried her skin as she entered the bedroom. The paint on the storage heater had blistered, leaving brown ulcerlike disks on its surface, curling upward in serrations. Julia heard rustling footsteps in the hall where she had just been. The closet door hung open. She went toward it, pulled it fully open and looked inside, her throat clenched. Some of her clothes had been pulled from their hangers and lay tumbled and twisted on the closet floor, mixed up with her shoes. Then she saw the box of dolls. It had been burst open, and the dolls scattered all over the back of the closet. Their floppy, uncomplicated bodies were torn and slashed. Ancient gray wool foamed from their chests. The terror poured back into her, and she fell gasping to her knees. Her certainty blurred with her vision. Kate had treasured the dolls; a malevolent Kate would destroy them. For a moment she was sick with yearning to be back in the hospital.

When she dashed into the bathroom, she first noticed that the figure in the black mirror—*her?*—looked haggard and old, her hair a mess and her eyes big with shock. Then she saw that the large untinted mirror over the marble sink had been heavily scored with soap. She stared at the lines and slashes until they coalesced into a list of obscenities. All the details of lying next to Mark flamed in her mind, dirtied by the words glaring at her from the mirror. The spirit knew, and hated her for what she had done. The last word jumped out at her: MURDERESS. "*Liar,*" she snarled, bone-jolted, and seized the nearest heavy object—a large ovoid rose-veined stone, polished to glassy smoothness—and with it shattered the mirror. Her heart froze, contracted. Magnus seemed all about her, wrapping her in a chill, despairing blanket of deception. That accusing word still burned in her sight. After a few minutes she breathed deeply and began pushing together the long silvery shards of the mirror. Her mind skittered away from her as her hands mechanically brushed at the smaller pieces of glass. Had she written those words herself? Had she mutilated the dolls? For a moment she was certain that she had.

* * *

Winter, Capt. Paul S. 2B Stadium St. SW 10. Both of the men had been in the directory. Stadium Street occupied the seedy lower end of Chelsea, near the four wharves and World's End: Julia drove the Rover down the crowded carnival of King's Road from Sloane Square, and after inching through the packs of young people parading in costume from one boutique to another, crossed Beaufort Street and found herself in a different world. The brilliant, nervous crowds had vanished, the restaurants and boutiques replaced by factory walls and the peeling facades of bed-sitters. Here, the few clothing stores hung their wares from their awnings; bent old women with shopping carts trudged along the pavements, mumbling to themselves. When she turned the corner of Cremorne Road she fleetingly saw through the side window a grossly fat man in a ripped topcoat bunched at the waist by string struggling to force a terrified spaniel into a paper bag. He was gripping the dog by the throat, working the bag around the dog's frantically kicking legs . . . *murderess* in letters of crusty soap appeared in Julia's mind.

The bright red side panel of a bread van blocked her windscreen, and she wrenched the wheel to avoid a collision. The letters MOTHER'S PRIDE wheeled off; the Rover fishtailed to the right, ticking a parked car, and then swung back in its lane. Car horns and shouts erupted about her. She sped away.

On desolate Stadium Street she left her car and immediately caught the smell of the Thames. Its sunless, oily odor seemed to settle on her fingers and hair. She felt as though she were inhaling damp cobwebs impregnated with the smell of fish. Julia peered at the door nearest her, and made out through encrustations of paint Number 15. She moved slowly down the block, hearing blinds rattle as she passed the row of mean, dwarfed houses. The rusted frame of a bicycle lay beside the curb like the corpse of a monstrous insect. 10, 8, 6. Number 5 had been painted in swarmy patches of red and blue and yellow across which had been written in large black letters REVOLUTION IS THE RIGHT OF ALL and HENDRIX; the front door was fixed by a big gray padlock. Julia crossed the street and pushed open the small stiff gate to Number 2. At the end of the line of cracked paving stones, the front door was festooned with a rank of bells beside nameplates. She went up the walk and read the names scrawled on the plates— Voynow, a blank, Mertz & Polo, Gandee, Moore, Gilette, Johnson. No Winter was listed, and she felt unable to ring any of the unidentified bells. Her confidence sinking, Julia stepped back and saw on the pitted concrete facing a glossy black letter *B* above an arrow. In relief, she looked upward and truly noticed for the first time that the weather had changed. The sky held a shifting mass of clouds, obscuring the sun and piling toward a top layer of hard, thin gray.

B was a narrow door set into the rear of the house. Through it seeped a trace of some tinny music. When Julia knocked the door almost immediately opened upon a thin figure dressed in black turtleneck and black trousers. The music, swelling past him, resolved into Ravi Shankar. Julia first took in the man's prominent, bitter cheekbones and then that he wore an obvious wig several shades lighter than his hair.

"Captain Winter?" she asked, unsure.

"It's been ages since anyone called me that, dear," the man said. "I suppose you're Roger's outraged sister. Well, you'd better come in."

Julia stepped across the threshold into a heavy musk of incense. "I'd better explain," she said. "I'm not who you think I am. My name is Julia Lofting, Captain Winter—"

The man groaned. "*Please* don't. Call me anything, but don't call me Captain."

"Mr. Winter."

"Paul."

"Paul. Thank you." Looking at Winter's alert, essentially dishonest face, Julia was surprised to see that the man was roughly her own age. She realized that he must have been about thirty when he had been forced to leave his regiment; though, looking at his crowded, exotic little room crammed with paisley cushions and African wall hangings interspersed with reproductions of paintings and bright Druze rugs, she could not see Paul Winter as a member of any sort of army. But she permitted herself the disloyal thought that Winter had solved the problem of how to live in a single room better than had Mark. Except, she saw, that this was the kind of room which implied that it was forever night beyond its door: it was a room which denied daylight.

"You can't be Roger's sister," he said behind her. "She'd never take such a time appreciating my little collection of things. You like my chambers, don't you?"

"Yes, I do," she answered simply.

"When I close my door," he said, "I close out the world and exist here in a world I've created. It's my oasis, my haven. In fact, I rarely leave it. It contains all my needs—beauty, peace, art, refined sensation. And it does have a Chelsea address, which is important, don't you think? I wouldn't live anywhere else, and I've lived all around the world. The army, you know." He was preening himself before her, and Julia caught an odd mixture of failure and arrogance in the man; he saw himself as an Oscar Wilde, but the absurd vanity of the toupee made him pathetic. In a minute, she sensed, he'd begin inventing weak epigrams. "But of course you know," he said. "My distinguished military history," and his cheekbones seemed to sharpen into points. "All in the past. Would you care for a cigarette? They're Turkish."

"No thank you," Julia said. "I'm sorry to bother you like this, Capt—Paul, but for personal reasons I am interested in something in your past."

"Oh, God," he groaned theatrically. "The past doesn't exist." He considered that a moment, and revised it. "No intelligent man believes in the past." Finally he satisfied himself. "Those who believe in the past are condemned to live in it."

Julia seemed to catch a justified suspicion in the man's glance. "Well, the past has everything to do with my present," she said. "It's very difficult to explain." For a second, she saw before her the box of ripped dolls and the accusing words soaped across the mirror, and her blood swung heavily downward.

"Say, you look about to faint," Winter said, alarmed, and pushed a chair toward her. When she sat, he moved to one of the cushions and perched on it. "What's the matter?" he asked.

"I'm being haunted," she blurted out.

"My *dear*," he cooed. "Turn yourself into a tourist attraction and charge admission."

She smiled at him.

"Am I to understand that this delicious condition has something to do with me?"

Julia nodded. "Yes. . . ."

"How fascinating. Ask away. I have no secrets anymore, my dear. I simply *am*, and people must accept me or reject me, for it's not worth the trouble to conceal one's inner nature. One's truth always wins out in the end. I only joined the army because my father wouldn't hear of anything else, you know, and I found it simply rife with hypocrisy. That was why they got rid of me, I must tell you, because I could no longer tolerate their petty restrictions and poses. I had to be myself. It made it pretty awkward for them, I can tell you, my being a general's son. Like Rimbaud, was it? The French poet. I say, you're not taking some sort of survey, are you? I couldn't bear that. Or doing research for a book?"

"No, this is personal," repeated Julia. "I've become involved with something you can help me with, if you would be so kind."

"I've always been so interested in the spiritual side of things—I'm Virgo with Aries rising."

"I want to ask you about some people you might remember."

"Fascinating." He scrunched down further into the cushions. "Ask away. I'm *so* glad you're not Roger's sister."

"I don't know how to begin. Do you remember, um, Francesca Temple? Or Freddy Reilly?"

He blinked. "Good heavens, you are going back. I used to play with them."

"You do remember."

It was too intense for him, and he backed away from a definite statement. "Barely. Just faintly . . . one catches the outlines, as it were. One isn't oneself in childhood. Childhood is a lie adults tell themselves. The man fathers his own childhood, if you see what I mean. Now let me see. Francesca Temple. A very modest little girl, with the loveliest brown curls. Yes, I can"—he pivoted a hand in the air—"catch her now. She was a follower. *She* was a soldier, if you will. Do anything you told her to. Freddy Reilly was a bit butch, if you understand me. A great one for games. Don't tell me you're being haunted by Freddy Reilly!" He silently clapped his hands together and revealed an even row of small, slightly discolored teeth.

She took up all her courage. "Can you tell me anything about any of the others? For instance, do you remember Olivia Rudge?"

He gaped at her, then toyed with the fringe of the cushion. "Can't remember her very well, I'm afraid. Rather a strange little girl, I seem to recall." He suddenly stood up and straightened the crease of his trousers. "Would you like a cup of anything? Tea? I make an excellent cuppa—half China, half India. Exquisite."

"No, please," said Julia. "What can you tell me about her? Olivia?"

"I think," he said, "I think you're beginning to be just the tiniest bit boring." He radiated an emotion it took Julia a second to recognize as fear. "Childhood is our least interesting period, I've always thought. I don't think I wish to answer any more questions about mine."

"I have to plead with you," said Julia. "You won't be in any trouble—there are just some things I have to know."

He ostentatiously examined his watch. "I don't think I have time for any more of this fascinating reminiscence. That woman was supposed to be here at two, and I can't tell you what a bother she'll be—now *there's* trouble for you."

"Mr. Winter—Paul—how did Geoffrey Braden die?"

He went nearly white with shock. Or was it shame? "I'll have to retract my invitation to tea, darling. I must ask you to kindly push off before my visitor arrives. Can't say I really heard your last question. Did you have a jacket?" He was prodding her shoulder with the tips of his fingers. "Really, dear. It's a waste of time asking me about ancient history. That was always my worst subject." Julia reluctantly stood.

"Could you just describe Olivia . . ." she began.

"I know I'm an old fool for being in such a flap," he said, urging her toward the door, "but that is one subject on which I do not propose to expound. The book is closed, my dear."

She was standing outside the narrow door, looking at his painfully contracting face beneath the cheap blond wig. The Indian music built to a frantic climax behind him.

"She wants me," she said. "Olivia."

"I believe it," he said. "Don't come back, please. Leave me alone, whoever you are."

"Julia Lofting," she said, but the door was closed.

The two of them sat on the terrace at the beginning of the evening, watching the rain pelt down onto the park, bending the leaves and tormenting the small bushes outside the walls. When a gust scattered drops onto the floor of the terrace, she delicately hitched her chair back out of the rain's territory; he ignored the spattering of drops and allowed it to dampen his shoes. They were, Lily noticed, already caked with mud and webbed with cracks. Magnus' whole being seemed in disrepair, and she experienced a moment of sheer distaste for Julia, who had done this to him, and for her brother, who had allowed it to be done.

"So it was *that* house," she said. "This is a fine time to discover it."

"I didn't think it was any of your business."

"Magnus," she said in exasperation, "how do you expect me to help if you conceal things from me? Concealment amounts to a lie. Is there anything else you've been hiding from me which might affect Julia?"

"An impossible question," he grunted. He stared dully at the rain. "I like this weather. It's more English than all that sunshine."

"Oh, you're simply maddening. Don't you realize that she has been looking into that wretched old case? I don't think she even bothers to eat anymore. She's convinced it's got something to do with Kate. In fact, she told me she was being haunted. Haunted! In her condition, every detail becomes exaggerated and blown up and inflated—Magnus, you must tell me if there is anything else she is likely to discover."

"I don't know. What *has* she discovered?"

"I'm not sure she would tell me."

"She'd tell that bloody psychotic Mark."

Lily tactfully ignored this remark while silently agreeing with it. "If you want your wife back, and I can only assume that is the motive behind your extraordinary performance this past week, you must tell me whatever you know so that I can use it for your benefit."

"You mean that you want to use Julia for *your* benefit."

"I will ignore that remark." She glanced at him before saying, "If you don't move out of the wet you'll catch pneumonia."

Sighing, Magnus shoved himself backward in his chair.

"Is there any way you can be connected to that house? That would push her right over the edge, you know. Well. At least then we could put her in hospital, where she belongs."

"Is that what you want?" Magnus stared at his sister in genuine surprise. "She's coming home with me, not back into hospital. But no, I don't think there's anything. All of that was so long ago."

"What about the daughter? Did you know her well?"

"Never met the little lady."

"You're sure."

Magnus winced. "Of course I'm sure. Now stop grilling me. Have you anything left to drink?"

"It was drink almost put you in jail, remember. That and your temper. But help yourself, if you want something."

He said, "I don't want it, I need it," and went across the terrace and into the kitchen. A few moments later he returned with a tumbler half filled with amber liquid.

Lily waited until he was settled again in his chair before saying, "Well, what did you do this last time? Leave notes about?"

"I threw some of the chairs around. That's all. She'll know it was me." He drank with visible satisfaction.

"And I suppose you think that will help. Magnus, there are two things that I regret. One is allowing her to keep her fantasy about Kate's death. She needs to be shocked out of it. I'd tell her now if she were here. The other thing is introducing her to poor Mrs. Fludd. Those two together got her started on this ghost business."

"Mrs. Fludd? Oh. Your guru."

"Before her death she stirred Julia up with all sorts of dark hints. Rosa had the gift, but she could never resist playing to her audience. And she died at the most unfortunate time."

Magnus was clearly not interested in the fate of Mrs. Fludd. "I think Julia needs a psychotherapist," he said. "Maybe I do too. I don't know what's been happening to me lately. I have funny blackouts. I see things. One day I saw Kate."

"Poor baby," said Lily. "So you agree with me that we must get her back into hospital?"

"Maybe I do," Magnus mused. He looked at Lily for a moment with perfect complicity.

"Tell me something," Lily said, now that was settled. "What did you feel when you went back inside that house again? Did you feel no shame?"

"No," he said. "It was simpler. I felt fear. I was scared out of my wits. It made me want to murder someone."

"You should have married someone your own age," said Lily.

"Someone like you, you mean."

"We do have a marriage of a kind," said Lily. "We understand each other."

Mark Berkeley stood beneath the awning of the package store, watching the rain spill down the gutters and gradually form a black slick pool which would cover all that part of the street. He still had in his pocket about seventy pounds, after cashing Julia's check and buying some tins of food, a pair of boots and a snakeskin belt—and just now, the two bottles of whiskey. He could remember deciding to put Samuels off until next term, for the sake of the boots; he could remember shopping and dialing Julia's number several times that afternoon; but he could not remember leaving his room in the rain to walk to the package store. He stared down at the blocked drain by the side of the curb—the street-lamp revealed on the surface of the water the shifting, mesmeric pattern of an oil slick—and tried to reconstruct the walk from his building. His shoulders and hair were soaked with rain. Maybe, he thought, these lapses were somehow derived from his exercises, lately far more successful than ever before. He was more than slightly fearful of where these long, otherworldly sessions might take him; but weren't they proof of what the old woman had said about his "recep-tivity"? This, he was certain, lay behind his headaches—proof of a power he hadn't known he possessed. He was Mark, he was special, he was the child of luck.

A tall girl whose name he could not remember stepped out of the rain and stood beside him. She shook her hair and smiled, and he knew the shape and taste of her mouth.

"Going to a party?" she asked. "Good night for it."

"What?"

"A party. The bottles, Mark. Are you going to a party?"

He looked at the bottles in the white bag. "I couldn't tell you what I was going to," he said. "I sort of don't remember."

She looked at him bristlingly. "I suppose you're on something."

"No. No. I've been meditating. I'm doing it a couple of hours a day."

"Well, it's too late to meditate now," she said firmly. What was her name? "Do you want to come back to my place? We could have our own party."

Then he remembered: Annis. Annis was one of last summer's girls. Looking at her wide, greedy black eyes and hair in which drops of rain sparkled, he felt a spasm of sexual interest, but then Julia's face superimposed on hers. His mind seemed to waver. "Annis, I can't tonight," he said. "There's someone I have to see."

"Well, do me a favor and fuck yourself," Annis cheerfully said, and ran off through the rain.

Swift, David N 337 Upper Street N1. Julia stirred restlessly on the passenger side of the Rover's front seat, trying to find a comfortable position while still looking directly at the inconspicuous door immediately beside The Beautiful and Damned. She had already tried to fill in the time by trying to remember how many other pubs in London were named after novels, but could only recall The Cruel Sea in Hampstead, which Lily had entered once and decreed "puerile, like its namesake." Julia had come to Swift's address at eight, driven aimlessly around Islington before returning at nine, had again found him not at home and driven on impulse over to Gayton Road, where all the lights burned and open drapes revealed empty rooms, and then returned to wait for Swift's return. Now it was just past eleven, and her back was beginning to hurt. From time to time she thumped her feet on the floor of the car to keep her legs from falling asleep. When a man in a shabby overcoat and tweed cap loitered before the door beside the pub, Julia switched on the windshield wipers and leaned forward, tense. The man turned his back to the street. Not daring to breathe, Julia waited for him to open the door. But the man merely hunched his back against the rain and stood spread-legged beside the door. Finally Julia understood what he was doing, and she looked away in exasperation.

More people slouched past the pub, and Julia idly watched them until they had gone into the Wimpy bar down the block. At eleven-fifteen the pub disgorged a group of young men who hung, half in and half out of the rain, beneath the small canopy, wrangling and stuffing their hands into the pockets of their jackets. They obscured Swift's door, and Julia groaned, silently praying for them to break up and go home. More young men left the pub. They formed a desultory, nearly unmoving mass all along the side of the building. If Swift were to come home now, she could easily miss him. "Please," Julia whispered. David Swift was her last chance.

As she watched, one of the men began to shout. A friend gripped his arm, but the man violently pushed him away, sending him sprawling off the street. In a second, half of the crowd had vanished; a third man circled the first, who still shouted, and then they were brawling. Julia watched them slipping on the wet pavement, clutching at each other's wrists and shoulders before separating to begin punching again. The street had become wholly quiet around them, except for the rain's spatter. One of the men—Julia was not sure which—gave a solid, thunking blow to the face of the other, who went down in the heap of his clothes. His attacker kicked him savagely once, then again. Julia, terrified, put her hand to her mouth. The attacker picked the man up from the pavement and began to strike him again and again in the face. *He's a Magnus*, Julia thought, and in desperation stabbed at the switch for her headlights. The attacker turned his head into the glare of the lights—Julia saw a bearded chin and a prominent nose—and then pushed the bleeding face away. He turned and ran slap-slapping along Upper Street. His victim lay alone on the pavement, his clothing soaking in the rain. All the others had scattered. As Julia watched, the man's body trembled, and then inched across the pavement like the hulk of a wounded boar. The man rolled against the side of the pub and sat up. His face was a gash of red.

Julia pushed down the lever in the door and leaned out. She had to call for an ambulance—she looked frantically about for a phone booth, but rain, flying directly into her face, blurred her vision. She wiped her eyes and saw, far up the block, a red booth outside a darkened cinema. She crossed the empty road and began to run toward the booth. A burly coatless man cradling a dark clanking bag passed her, but she scarcely noticed the man until she was within the kiosk. Then, looking through the streaked glass, she saw the man set down his bag before Swift's entrance and dig out a key from his pocket. She hung in the booth for a moment, deliberating, and then slammed down the receiver just as the man disappeared from the street.

She pounded down Upper Street to the pub. The beaten man now crouched over the pavement, his elbows planted in his own blood. He was moaning incoherently, perhaps drunkenly. She pressed Swift's bell rapidly several times, then held it down. The man against the pub rolled over on his side and clamped his hands to his face.

Heavy footsteps thumped down a staircase. When the door jerked open, Julia saw a man's bulky frame in the shadow of the tiny hallway. Far above, a single light burned, illuminating the top of the dingy staircase. "Mr. Swift?" she asked.

"That's me," the man said. Julia caught a pungent whiff of whiskey. "What is it?"

His upper-middle-class accent both surprised and comforted her. It was the accent of Magnus and his friends—the accent Mark had consciously discarded.

"I have to talk to you. And there's been a fight. This man's been hurt. We must telephone for an ambulance."

"I don't clean up after drunks," Swift said. He thrust his head out the door, revealing in the reddish light from the pub a broad, pinkish face and close, rather curly black hair. His jacket looked oily and frayed. "Let him rot. You said you wanted to talk to me?" He looked at her appraisingly, and Julia nodded. "I'm willing. Come on into the fleapit."

As Julia stepped into the hallway, again catching the clear, biting odor of whiskey, she promised herself to telephone for an ambulance no matter what Swift said. He was already moving a bit unsteadily up the stairs. "Come on and talk, if that's what you want," he called down.

At the top of the stairs he was holding open the door to a shabby sitting room. Blotchy yellow wallpaper, a stained green carpet as threadbare as Mark's, battered furniture she recognized as coming from a discount warehouse—it was like the furniture in her Camden Town flat, years before. Swift was standing at a low table, pulling bottles out of the paper bag. Grunting, he broke the seal of one of them. "Drink?"

"May I?"

"I asked you."

"Then yes, please."

Swift removed two glasses from a wall shelf and poured several inches of whiskey into each. He gave Julia her glass, and she saw above the line of the whiskey fingerprints, water spots, smears. She set it down on the table.

"Can I telephone first? That man downstairs . . ."

"No," Swift said. In the electric light, his pink face was scrubbed with hot reddish spots, as if scoured. "Fuck him. What did you want? Who are you, anyhow? A solicitor?"

Julia moved to one of the unsafe-looking chairs and sat. She wiped some of the rain off her face. "My name is Julia Lofting, Mr. Swift."

"You must be a solicitor."

"No, I'm not, I promise you. I'm interested in—involved in something you can help me with, if you would."

"Don't tell me it's a business deal." Swift snorted. He was still standing, holding his glass in one hand and the bottle in the other. "I'm afraid Swift and Company is no longer. Three generations of sharp practice end in the wreck you see before you. Do you want some sort of towel?" He gulped down whiskey as she shook her head. "Well, don't just sit there looking all confused and sexy and helpless."

"It's about your childhood," Julia quickly said. "I have to know about something that happened then. I promise you that I won't divulge anything you say to me to anyone else—that I'm interested for purely personal reasons." I won't tell this man I think I'm haunted, she vowed, he'd throw me out. She had to avoid the mistakes she had made with Winter. "I'm not a writer or anything like that," she said. "Or the police."

He rolled his eyes up toward the ceiling. "I'd better sit down." He moved heavily to the couch and fell into it facing her, still holding the glass and bottle. "My childhood. I suppose I had one. Now what the devil do you want to know about my childhood?"

Julia knitted her hands together, stared at the filthy carpet, and then looked directly at Swift. He had a froggish, unlined, well-brought-up face. She could easily see him in an expensive suit, ordering secretaries about. That she disliked him on sight somehow made it easier to talk to him.

"I live at Twenty-five Ilchester Place," she said. "Olivia Rudge's old house. I want to find out all about her."

Swift was momentarily shaken. His head bobbed toward his drink; but he made no move to throw her out. "God," he said. "That wicked little bitch.

She's been dead over twenty years." He gazed at the liquid in his glass, clearly not intending to offer more information.

"This afternoon I spoke to Paul Winter."

Swift brightened. "That poof. I bet *he* wouldn't say anything."

"You're the only one left," Julia said. "The Aycroft boy killed himself and Minnie Leibrook died in an accident. One of you disappeared in America. Another girl is in a convent. And Paul Winter made me leave his house."

The man facing her snorted. "I don't suppose he liked the idea of having a woman in his room. I relish it, I can tell you. He was probably expecting one of his chums. That's why they pitched him out of his regiment, you know. He fell in love with his driver, but the driver wouldn't reciprocate. Paulie got a little too passionate, the driver kicked up a fuss, and they rubbed Paulie out as if he were a little foul spot on the rug. Bang. Finish." He took another swallow and repeated, "Finish. General's son in disgrace. As for Aycroft, he put paid to himself when he was found embezzling money from his firm. Excuse me, bank. His bank. Good-bye, Aycroft. And Minnie Leibrook . . ." He caught himself short. "What do you want to know about all this for, anyway? So you live in the old Rudge house. Congratulations. What's that got to do with me?"

"It's personal," said Julia. "I just want to know about Olivia."

"You're fascinated." He poured more whiskey into his glass. "You've been looking into her short and nasty life and now you're keen on her. How do I know that you won't use whatever I say against me?"

"I promise," said Julia, and inspiration came to her. She dug in her bag and withdrew two ten-pound notes and put them on the table. Swift's eyes gleamed at her. She put down another note. Her heart fluttered. "I want to buy information from you."

He snaffled up the notes. "I guess you do. A woman like you doesn't come up here every day and offer me money." He leered at her. "I'll talk to you if you come over here and sit beside me."

Julia hesitated, and then went around the little table to the couch. Cautiously she sat beside him. "Now you have a drink," he said. "You're behind." Julia sipped from the bleary glass. "More." She did as he commanded.

"Tell me about Olivia," she said. "Please." She allowed his hand to rest negligently on her knee.

"You'd never forget her if you ever met her. She was really wicked. It was the most impressive thing about her. It was the reason all of us, the kids you know about, followed after her. We had a club. Do you want to know the rules?" He squeezed her knee, and Julia nodded. "Have another drink." He poured more whiskey into her glass, and she sipped at it. "The first rule was you had to kill an animal. Aycroft killed his dog. He brought it to her and she ripped it open with her knife and made him drink some of its blood. Proper little ceremony. We all did it. I brought a neighbor's cat. Same folderol. I was clever—just touched my tongue in the blood. Then we had to light fires. We had to burn a house or a shed, something in that line. We did that together. She watched us and told us what to do."

"You did it?" Julia asked.

"We tried. She stole a can of petrol from somewhere and we soaked the porch of a wooden house behind the High Street. The bugger wouldn't burn. Olivia was madder than a hen—she looked just like a witch. Maybe she was a witch. We all thought she was. Anyhow we burned most of the porch, but the firemen came before the rest of the building went. Then we had to do lots of thieving and give it all over to her. You see, we had to see her every day—we had to spend all day with her in the holidays. We all had a crush on her, I suppose, even the girls, and she had us scared out of our wits. We knew there wasn't anything she was afraid to do. We learned all about sex from her, in her bent little games. If you didn't do what she wanted, she'd tell your parents about everything else. She had ways. If you told anyone in authority, she'd kill you."

"Yes," said Julia.

"She would, too. She would have. She was evil. She made the Temple girl—who did everything Olivia wanted—lick her. You know what I mean, lick her?" He stroked Julia's knee. "She could beat up any of us."

"And she killed Geoffrey Braden," Julia softly said.

The hand tightened and released on her knee. "A man was found guilty of that and executed."

"A harmless vagrant," said Julia. "He liked the children. He used to talk to them. You know he didn't do it."

Swift turned his pink face toward Julia and drained his glass. "You were a fool to give me that money," he said. "You were a fool. Nobody's thought about Geoffrey Braden in twenty-five years. Nobody's going to do anything about it now."

"That's not why I have to know."

"I don't care," he said, and her heart sank. Then he added, "I was going to tell you anyhow. You were stupid to give me that money. I was innocent. I didn't do anything."

"You just watched," Julia guessed. She could feel her pulse thrumming in her neck.

He grinned at her. "I watched."

"So she *did* do it," Julia whispered.

"Of course." He looked at her with an expression like triumph. "She covered his head with a pillow. She tried it twice before, but an attendant heard his yelping and ran over. She hid the pillow just in time. Then one afternoon she did do it. Three of the bigger kids held him down and stuffed things in his mouth. Then she put the pillow on his head and sat on it. It was what she always wanted to do. To kill someone. You could see that. It was what she was all about. I'll bet the little bitch had an orgasm."

"What did she look like? Was she blond?"

"Sure. Blond. A color anyone else would have to get out of a bottle. It was the most beautiful hair I ever saw. And a sweet little face. Oh, she was charming. Sometimes I think about the way she'd look if she were still alive—Christ, that bitch would have changed the world." His hand slid over her leg. "I like talking about this, you know. If I weren't drunk, I'd probably chuck you out, but I like telling you about it. It was funny. She made us feel that we were all in a war. Soldiers."

"Her tooth," Julia said. "Didn't she . . . ?"

"How did you know about that? The first day she tried to do little Braden, he hit her mouth with the top of his head—broke one of her front teeth. He didn't have a chance after that. She had to have him. But he never really did have a chance, the little bugger. Do you know what happened afterward? With Paulie? Your poof friend?"

He was gripping the underside of her thigh, and she put a hand on his wrist. It was feverishly hot. She shook her head.

"Paulie was bent even then. She liked that. She made him bite him after he was dead."

"Bite him?"

"Bite him. Bite his cock. She made him bite his cock."

He leaned over and snared her wrist. His mouth slurred on her cheek. "She said if he didn't do it, she'd do it to him."

Julia twisted away and stood up. She broke her hand away from his grip and tottered backward toward the door.

"You're not leaving," Swift growled. "You're going to stay with me." He struggled to stand.

"I have to talk to Olivia," she said, facing him.

It stopped him long enough for her to seize the doorknob and pull it open.

"You're crazy," he shouted, half-crouching before the table. His trousers bulged at the fly.

When she fled down the stairs she heard him yelling above her. "Cock-teaser! Remember—nobody cares anymore, you bitch. You can't do anything."

She slammed the street door. The beaten man no longer lay beside the pub, but still some blood remained, tinting the puddles of rain. Julia ran toward her car. She knew, she knew. It had been Olivia Rudge all along: Kate was safe. Once in the car she began to sob, whether from horror or relief she could not tell.

YOU KNOW. The words had been smeared in soap on the black mirror above the bathtub. From the atmosphere of tense quiet within the house—for the first time in two weeks, Julia had not heard the rustling noises from upstairs—she had expected some atrocity, and had been fearful of leaving the ground floor of her house. She had no idea of what Olivia intended to do with her now that she had discovered the truth. Julia mounted the stairs, looking for signs of triumph or outrage. In her throbbingly hot bedroom, all lay undisturbed from the morning: the burst dolls sprawled at the back of the closet, sprouting gray curls of wool, their power to frighten her gone. Every time she looked over her shoulder, she expected to see Olivia Rudge. That adult, challenging smile. Or she feared to see Magnus, controlled by her. But all she found were the two words of confirmation. YOU KNOW. She scraped them off with a table knife, and wiped the remaining flecks and smears with a towel until the black mirror held only a foot-long blur which translated her reflection into cloud. There would be more, much more. This lull, this truce, and the two words were more frightening than Olivia's displays of power.

Julia gazed out of her bedroom window into night and rain. Out there, everything had disappeared into darkness. Reality lay within.

She snapped off the light, undressed in the dark and felt her way to the bed. Then she lay beneath the burning sheet and watched the darkness move. A black plane composed of millions of particles sifted down toward her, withdrew, and sifted down again. Perspiration trickled into the hair above her ears.

She stabbed the reading light on in sudden fear and the plane of darkness disappeared. There was nothing. There was no giant pillow of dark. She switched off the light, and saw it return.

When the first touch of small hands came, she went rigid, aware that she had somehow fallen asleep. A cool hand slid up her inner thigh, and she rolled over, twisting in the sheet. The hand returned on her buttocks, caressing, probing. Julia gasped at the violation and spun around, rolling to the other side of the bed. Arms braced her shoulders to the bed. They held her immobilized; her legs, trapped in the twisted sheet, were as if pinned to the mattress. The cool small hand found her pubic hair, then her cleft. It began, delicately, to rub. Her body felt naked to the dark air, though the sheet bound her. Julia groaned as the hand pressed toward her clitoris and stroked. Feathery: feathers, tongues. She was a fly caught in a sticky cocoon, ministered to by the spider. Against her will, with horror, she felt her body build up a rhythmic tension. The relentless hand stroked, rubbed, as if dipped in oil; it circled, insinuated into her. Her back arched. She felt her nipples harden. Sweat broke out on her chest. Julia inhaled a gulp of burning air. She seemed to be falling into a deep well. Her knees twitched. The tight sheet, wrapping her like a shroud, was itself the lightest of caresses, palms on her taut nipples. The pressure, arching her back, subtly increased and began to beat outward in circles. Suddenly she saw Mark before her, his body taut with longing. The oiled rubbing hands were the huge tip of his penis. The embracing arms were his. Her legs moved wide apart and his shaft slid deep within her. She bared her teeth. Arms, legs, hands, deep velvet held her. She saw, felt him stiffen and plunge and a sound died in her throat as everything burst.

And the next morning when Julia tottered sick with nausea into the bathroom, Olivia showed herself within the house for the first time. She did not jump out of sight at the last second; she did not flicker away. She stood, a small blond smiling child, behind Julia as Julia looked into the black mirror opposite her. Julia placed a protective hand over her abraded, sore cleft and whirled around. Again, the child appeared behind her in the facing mirror.

As Julia watched, Olivia gave her asymmetric, challenging smile and slowly drew an index finger across her pale throat. Her other hand gripped the pulped, still trembling body of a headless bird.

*   *   *

A Thames gull slapped into the window late at night, making a noise like a train wreck, and startling into wakefulness the man who reclined on a fluffy Indian cushion. Uneasy—he had been close to fear for the past twenty-four hours—and not as yet quite certain where he was, the man extended one hand and knocked over the bottle of Calvados. His room, crowded with details of his life, reassuringly came together about him; the needle of the record player crackled and hissed in the final grooves. He righted the bottle, shaking his head. None had spilled, for he had consumed most of what was left during the night, after his guest had left. His mind seemed thickened, syrupy; the aftertaste of his heavy cigarettes coated his mouth.

From beyond the door, his name quietly sounded. He sat up straight, pulling his legs under him, and listened to the sound of the voice. It uttered his name over and over, beseechingly, in a voice neither male nor female. "Foolish little scut," the man muttered, and for several seconds considered his promise not to open the door again. But that too was foolish. Both had had far too much to drink. The man bent forward and stood in one motion, feeling the muscles in his thighs protesting. Upright, he patted his hairpiece and straightened his pullover. He moved to the door as slowly as he could, relishing the sound of his name, half whispered, urgent, full of need.

He opened the door to a stranger—a stranger? The voice was a voice he knew. The visitor smiled, and he knew the contours of that smile.

Too late, he saw the knife slide from beneath the coat. His mind fluttered with bright, hopeless panic and he stepped backward as the visitor moved through the doorway, still voicing his name.

III

THE CLOSING: OLIVIA

9

Julia moved hesitantly up Kensington High Street at the end of day, buffeted by the crowds returning home late from work, unsure of where she was going. Confused, she had taken the wrong way, and was dimly aware of this. Her left wrist was still oozing blood, and she dabbed at the deep cut with a wrinkled yellow tissue, hoping it would stop; but the cuff of the blouse was stained and smeared with blood, as her sheet had been. Because of the pills, her mind had difficulty in retaining images, and she looked at the sky twice before being certain that it had stopped raining. All of the sky was a vast dark undifferentiated gray. *No holes*, she thought, *no air spaces*, and saw herself beating at the under-surface of gray cloud as if it were a thick layer of ice trapping her in arctic water; the pavements and street were still filmed with black rain. Ascent, escape, ascent, escape, revolved in her brain. But she could think of no escape. Olivia held her fast.

She thought of the beggar maid's king, Cophetua, his face immobilized by love. Mark. Was he safe? He had rung immediately after the grinning specter of the girl had vanished from the mirror.

Take some pills and go to sleep, he'd said. Do you have anything?

—Yes. Pills? Yes.

—You need rest. Take a couple of pills and get a really good rest.

—I have to see you. I'm in danger. Like Mrs. Fludd said. I am, Mark.

—Listen to me. Ghosts don't kill. Your danger is entirely from Magnus, and you're staying away from him. Julia, love, you're overtired. Lock your door and knock yourself out for the rest of the day.

—I need you, Mark. She wants me.

—Not half as much as I do, he had laughed. I'll see you this evening, sometime tonight.

—Save me.

Had she said that, *save me?* Perhaps she had imagined the entire conversation. All that was clear, besides gulping down two pills—memories of the hospital making her shudder—was running back upstairs and heaving the polished, rose-veined stone at the walls of the bathroom. Heaving it, again and again, until the black mirrors had showered down, leaping off the walls and shivering past her face. Then she had slipped on a large panel of glass and gone down into the mess, gashing her wrist. She had barely felt the pain. *Now she can't come in here*, Julia had thought, uncaring of the blood which welled out of the gash and down across the palm of her hand. The walls were unreflecting gray-white plaster marked like a graph with small black studs, to a few of which adhered an inch of mirror. Broken glass, some of it catching muted light from the ceiling, was strewn over the bathroom carpet, tumbled in long snaky shapes in the sink and tub. She felt warm blood falling onto her bare feet and snatched a towel from the rack and wound it about her wrist. Pebbles of glass snagged at her cut. Then she had swallowed the two pills. And staggered across twelve feet of broken glass to her bedroom.

(Thus she did not hear the bell seven hours later when Lily and Magnus came together to her front door.)

As in the hospital, she was visited by long fluent dreams. Those had been of turning the knife on herself, of sacrificing herself for Kate, that Kate's vibrant little life could be restored: her blood for her daughter's, a barter. She had felt Kate's forgiving approach at such times. But now her dreams all had the same flavor; they were as ashy as failure and loss. Even as she began to slip steeply into them, she resisted, sensing the approach of that hopeless territory. She was again walking through the gritty streets, carrying her daughter's corpse. The child she knew to be Olivia lurked ahead, unseen, and it was her duty to find her. The sky above the blackened roofs of tenements was lurid, red and orange shot with black streaks. Again, her long, burdened wandering took her to a mean courtyard. She moved across the filthy cobblestones and past abandoned, bricked-up warehouses and passed through the arch of the yard. A hunched leering man in a tattered coat winked at her, summoning from a doorway a small black girl with a curly ruff of hair. Julia ascended broken stairs and came out, as she knew she would, on a flat rooftop. A little woman in a large brown coat sat alone on the rooftop, her weight supported by a rickety chair. The woman was Mrs. Fludd. Seeing her, Julia felt tears welling in her eyes.

—I'm sorry, she said. I put you here. And I still need your help.

—I cannot help you.

Kate's body was taken from her; it had been needed to bring her here, and now it could vanish.

—You called her up.

—Yes, said Julia.

—You invoked her. She needed someone to call her back, you see, and you were chosen. This happened because of your daughter.

—What do I have to know?

—She won't like you knowing her secrets.

Mrs. Fludd turned sideways in her chair, refusing to speak further.

—Talk to me.

The old woman's face, heavy and washed of color, turned again toward Julia.
—She will have your friends.

Then she had been running into a long tunnel, noticing even as she ran that the tunnel led nowhere, that it narrowed the further and deeper she went. At the end was Mark, the New Hampshire valley, peace . . . but she knew that at the end of all her running would be only a black narrow hole. About her rang Heather Rudge's coarse, wheezing laughter.

She had awoken with this laughter still reverberating above her, joining the other noises of the house. The towel had been dragged off her arm, and the left side of the bed was stained by irregular red blots. For a moment she sensed that, as in her dream, Olivia Rudge hung nearby, just out of sight, waiting to appear. It would not be long. Mrs. Fludd's final words had then come back to her. Struggling to impose firmness and direction on her dream-tattered mind, Julia had wrapped her wrist in the top sheet and groggily sat up. She looked out the window across the room and saw rain drizzling down from a ghost-gray sky. A scarf of cool wind reached her from the open window and instantly vaporized in the heat. For the first time, Julia was consciously aware of the hot, feral smell pervading the bedroom, the reek of a lion's cage.

Throwing aside the ruined sheet, Julia had risen and looked at her watch: now it was eight, and she had slept through the entire day. *Your friends.* Mark, her truest friend, was in danger. Her mouth filled with dust. When she had glanced into the closet and seen again the ripped, scattered dolls, she staggered away from the bed and felt blood begin to move sluggishly down her wrist. She tore several sheets of Kleenex from the box near her bed and clamped them over the slash, which had begun to pulse and complain. When she struggled into her robe, she buttoned the left sleeve to fasten the Kleenex to the wound and went down the echoing stairs to telephone Mark.

Olivia was abroad; Olivia would have anyone she wanted. *It can't be got rid of. It wants revenge*, Heather Rudge had said. *It wants revenge.*

Mark's telephone had shrilled a dozen times. She would have to go to his room.

So now she walked blearily along Kensington High Street, the wad of sodden Kleenex dropped somewhere behind her and blood seeping into the cuff of her shirt. Between the flat gray sky and the rain-blackened streets, the streetlamps had already switched on, and cast an acid yellow light over the crowds through which she pushed. From time to time, a wave of oblivious men carried her back a few paces, making her stagger as she was thrown, almost unseen, from one comfortless shoulder to the next. She looked in all their faces for Mark, and found instead—it seemed to her—only sneers and laughter. Julia realized that the men thought she was drunk. Sleeping pills had never affected her so strongly before. Maybe it was due to lack of food. But the image of food—a greasy pile of pinkish-gray meat—made her stomach lurch and tighten.

A heavy curtain of dark appeared before her vision, blotting out the bunched, jostling crowds and the snarling jungle of traffic beyond them. Julia tottered, blind, and fell sideways against the rough facing of a building. For a moment, as the people sweeping past brushed her elbows and knees and trod on her feet, she lost all awareness of her identity and surroundings. The wave of nausea and dizziness was nearly a relief, sucking responsibility from her, and she gave herself over to it, forgetting why she was out on the street and where she was going. Her mind fled back to the image of the drained Mrs. Fludd, seated on a rickety chair alone on a rooftop. *Your friends.* Then the long, long flight down a narrowing tunnel. Kate had been her nearest friend. Her thought bucked like a rearing horse.

She opened her eyes to a dark burned with acid yellow. I'm in her world now, she thought. Soon I will meet her again. I nearly know it all. The two imprisoned women, the two ruined men had nearly brought her to the full knowledge she sought, and she had to make her way through Olivia Rudge's world to find the rest. Men like beasts rutted past her, each eyeing the stricken woman leaning against the brick wall of a bank. A high thin red line—a scream—traced the sky.

Men followed her with their eyes. Before her, as she watched them quicken with lust or amusement (*What in the world can I look like?* she wondered), they drew their faces into the masks of beasts, boars, bulls, wild dogs. Bristles jutted from their snouts, their feet were hooves tearing the ground. Their skin burned in the yellow light, unhealthy and sallow. In the babble of voices, she thought she discerned Magnus' low growl, and started, her mind a fluttering rag.

Her hands brushed her thighs: cotton. She was wearing cotton trousers. She could not remember dressing. Looking down, she saw that she wore a pale shirt, a short tan jacket. She touched her hair and felt oil. The voice was not Magnus', merely that of a man shouting to another man in the street.

Four young men passed before her, their hair languorously curled; as they turned to stare, she saw their faces inflamed with pustules, death in the pouches of their cheeks, their eyes like razors cutting pieces from her body. In the high, curved, bald forehead of a man thrusting past she saw death, the skin tightening on his skull; and she saw in a woman's colorless lips death, as they parted over her teeth. And she saw they were all dead, sweeping past her in the noise of raised voices and automobiles. The dark gained on them all.

Bone-shining foreheads, skeletal umbrellas against the dark, now nearly invisible sky and the wash of yellow from the lamps and headlights. It was the world of her dream life.

Julia fought to right herself steadily on her feet. Simple movement would cure this dreadful trick of vision. The boys, now further down the block, were only boys; the men and women merely weary from work and the journey home. She felt a familiar pang—an echo from her old personality—as she realized that the little tan jacket would probably cost two weeks' wages for any of the men crowding past. Magnus had persuaded her to buy it: or had he bought it, using her money? After so many years, it made little difference, but she wanted him to have bought it. Possessions were shameful. Then why had she bought the house?

She had been chosen. In that was the last mystery.

One step, another; she tugged at the hem of the jacket and straightened her back. No one was looking at her, in all the sweeping flood passing by. Julia began to walk more steadily, and recognized she had come over half the way to Kensington Church Street. It was one way of getting to Notting Hill, though roundabout. She hung unmoving on the crowded pavement for a second, debating whether to go back and take the walk along the side of the park which went directly north and ended at Holland Park Avenue, but then decided, in the cool gauzy air, to continue on the long way. The unaccustomed coolness would clear her head. She moved on again, passing W. H. Smith's, a package store, a clothing shop where mannequins flung out their arms as if wailing.

Then she caught sight of herself in a shop window and hurried past, unable to look away. Her face was a formless white puddle, with discolored blots beneath her eyes—it was the face of one of the women in the Breadlands Clinic, the face of a dazed animal fleeing experience. For a moment she saw how she would look when old, and she turned wildly away and rushed down the street, her bag bumping at her side.

A known face at a queue at a bus stop across the street from Biba's made her shorten her stride. The old woman in the long black dress hadn't yet seen her; Julia turned her back to the line of people at the edge of the pavement, feeling an instinctive desire to escape. . . . Still, she might have been mistaken. She edged sideways and back, and dared to turn around. The long narrow face now in profile, the dogmatic chin, tendrils of white hair escaping from beneath a black hat: it was Miss Pinner.

Her first response had been panic: perhaps she did not want to know what the old woman had seen in the mirror that disastrous night. Perhaps she already did know.

But her curiosity about that evening was too great to be dismissed; she could not flee from Miss Pinner too. Julia's decision seemed to help her dispel Olivia's world, for the tired people at the bus stop all appeared reassuringly ordinary, and she waited until two or three men had walked between them and then crossed the blackly shining pavement to tap the old woman on the shoulder. She pronounced her name, and heard her voice emerging levelly, distinctly.

"Yes? Yes?" The old woman started out of her reverie and turned her headmistress' blue eyes on Julia.

She doesn't recognize me, Julia thought. "Excuse me," she began, and saw the old woman purse her mouth expectantly, as if she were about to be asked for directions. "I'm surprised to see you here, Miss Pinner," she said.

Fear jumped for a second in the woman's eyes, and she stepped out of the queue. "Mrs. Lofting?" she said. "I'm sorry, I didn't recognize you at first, you see . . . you look ill, my dear. Yes, you are quite right, I am not here often . . . and I am afraid that I shall have to be getting off home." She lifted a small brown parcel. "We used to enjoy shopping here, and since Miss Tooth's birthday is approaching soon, I wanted to see if I could find anything for her at Derry and Tom's—but I found that they had been replaced by that very curious store across the street, and the little restaurant on the roof was shut, so I bought her something elsewhere." As she chattered, she glanced down the street obviously looking for her bus. "I'm late already. I must be home in time to prepare our dinner. Heavens, it's past eight."

"Do you have time to talk to me before your bus comes, Miss Pinner?"

"I can't say, I'm sure." Then the little flicker of fear was replaced by something like cunning. "I'm sorry that I was taken ill at your charming house, Mrs. Lofting. It was a very distressing evening for all of us, I'm sure . . . and then poor Mrs. Fludd's sudden demise . . . her niece forbade any of us to attend the funeral . . . but I was remiss in not writing to thank you for your hospitality. Miss Tooth and I were entertained in many grand houses years ago, when Miss Tooth could still follow her career, as you know, and we never sinned against hospitality in that way. I do hope you can forgive me."

"You were taken ill?" said Julia, focusing on the one sentence she had been able to follow.

"A spell of faintness," said Miss Pinner, showing the faint but detectable embarrassment honest people bring to their untruths. "I've been kept very busy these past months, going through all our old scrapbooks." She hitched up her shoulders painfully, in the movement of one adjusting to the twinges of a long-standing arthritis. "I can't do it in the mornings anymore, so my afternoons are very tiring. But Miss Tooth"—here the dogmatic face forgot all embarrassment—"Miss Tooth can still do her exercises."

"Can she?" said Julia, wondering if the drug were still clouding her perceptions.

"She can still work at the barre," said Miss Pinner with great satisfaction. "Miss Tooth is very supple yet."

"At the bar?" said Julia, trying to visualize little Miss Tooth serving up pints of bitter in a public house.

"Oh, yes. Of course she hasn't the stamina she had when she was younger, but she has all of her grace. We are preparing a book from the scrapbooks. Many people still remember her, as I see you do yourself. Of course, you would only have heard of her. You're too young to have seen her dance."

"Unfortunately, I was too young, yes," said Julia, seeing it at last. She remembered how, during the séance, Miss Tooth had seemingly floated to the floor in one effortless motion. "But she was very famous, wasn't she?" Julia guessed.

"How kind of you to remember," said Miss Pinner, and now her manner was entirely friendly. "Rosamund was a great artist. I was her dresser for twenty-five years and we retired together. After working for Rosamund Tooth it was impossible to work for anyone else. And I wouldn't touch any of the young lot. All technique and no poetry."

"Did Miss Tooth see anything in the mirror after you'd fainted that night?" Julia said brutally.

Miss Pinner's face trembled into an utter blankness of expression.

"I thought I saw something when I followed her in," Julia added. "And I know what it was."

Miss Pinner looked aghast, and Julia felt a twisting of guilt for making the old woman confront her lie. "Perhaps you saw it too."

"No—no—Mrs. Lofting, you should not be asking me about that night. I was tired from the long ride down from our home and from putting the scrapbooks in order. I don't know what I saw." She stepped nervously back into her place in the queue, and Julia followed her.

"Was it a little girl? A blond child? She is, she was, a wicked person, Miss Pinner. Please tell me, Miss Pinner." But she was already confused by the expression of mixed astonishment and relief on Miss Pinner's angular face. "Wasn't it the blond girl?"

"I am afraid to tell you, Mrs. Lofting," said Miss Pinner. "Oh. There's my bus down the road. Please don't detain me. It'll soon be here."

Julia, afraid that she would never know, gently touched the thick black stuff of Miss Pinner's coat with her right hand. "Wasn't it the little girl? She does horrible things. She once made me faint too."

Miss Pinner shook her head. "I don't think . . ." she began. Down the block, the bus swerved into traffic and came toward them, its headlamps beaming yellow through gathering dark.

Julia suddenly felt a sick certainty that her assumptions had been wrong; she was again at the edge of the abyss, afraid to look down. The bus swung heavily toward the curb, a wing of yellow light flashing below the upper deck. In his cage behind rain-streaked glass the driver looked totemic.

"I must get on now or wait another twenty minutes," said Miss Pinner. The queue moved forward slowly, a crippled insect laden with parcels and umbrellas. "I would not have said so much except that you knew about Rosamund." She was nearly at the steps of the bus, kept from them by only a fat woman struggling with two small dogs and a little girl with the face of a pampered pig.

"I have to know," said Julia as the woman swung the pig-child up onto the steps and gruntingly lifted herself and the dogs into the bus. "I have to know." She raised her hands, as if praying.

Miss Pinner looked in shock at Julia's left hand and shirt cuff, and then gazed straight into her face with a tense compassion. "I saw you," she blurted, and the conductor raised her up onto the platform and the bus was gone.

Earlier that day, brother and sister were sitting across from each other at Lily's table, two empty wine bottles and soup bowls and plates littered with bones between them. Magnus sat slumped in his chair, staring at the unappetizing remains of his lunch. He looked flushed and puffy, but he had changed into a clean suit and shirt, and wore immaculately polished shoes. He was impressive. Locked into his face, at a complicated level beneath the features but informing them, was a combination of authority and power and malice which she had seen in him all her life.

She said, "Magnus, you are a beautiful man."

"What!" His head jerked up and she saw his bloodshot eyes. "For God's sake,

Lily. I am fifty-three years old, I'm nearly three stone overweight, and I have not been sleeping well. I am tired."

She wanted to reply, but he cut her off. "And I'm not sure about this. I think you're rushing it."

Enjoying this moment as she did each of those rare occasions when she was stronger than he, Lily said, "Yesterday you agreed with me. We both know that she must be put back into professional care as quickly as possible. Magnus, your wife is in danger—she may do permanent harm to herself. Not to mention the damage she is doing to you."

"Humph." Magnus shook his head.

"I trust you wish to keep her from Mark," she said slyly.

"Mark is a wretch. He is a failure. There has always been something wrong with him. You know that."

"You are what is wrong with him, and of course I know it. Does Julia? Magnus, she scarcely knows him at all."

"Yes, I do want to keep her from him."

"Have you ever told her about his breakdowns?"

He shook his head. "They were a long time ago."

"Well, you see my point," she said, "she really only knows Mark's surface. And that is very seductive."

Magnus was not ignoring her now.

"You do take my point, and you needn't pretend that it hasn't been preying on you as it has on me. If we can get her back into the hospital, we shall have taken care of *that* problem. Now. As I see it, we must first persuade her to leave that house, by whatever means, and to move into my spare bedroom. It's possible to—I mean to say that the door locks from the outside."

"Yes," he said. "Are you certain—are you absolutely certain there couldn't be anything in that story of hers? I saw Kate in the window of her bedroom one afternoon. That afternoon I struck that ninny. I'm certain it was Kate. I couldn't be wrong about her. I know it was Kate. It knocked the breath out of me. And I have felt—things—in that miserable house. I don't know how to describe it. All I know is that I want her out of there. That place upsets me."

"You upset yourself," Lily said calmly. "You see your daughter, whom you miss terribly; Julia is obsessed with a case a quarter of a century old in which a mother stabs her daughter to death. You haven't been eating or sleeping regularly, and Julia is burning herself up. Of course the two of you see things. But as far as Julia actually being in touch with spiritual manifestations, any such thought is absurd."

"How can you be so certain? I was certain too, until I saw Kate."

"Experience," she said dismissively. "Ghosts are seen all over this country by people who are upset, or have had too much to eat or drink. Magnus, this is my field as the law is yours. I assure you, if a spirit were to appear to anyone in this family, it would appear to me. An untrained, inexperienced person like Julia would simply not have the faintest idea of how to interpret an authentic sighting. Magnus, with respect, do let me tell you that when an untrained person gets it into her head that she is in contact with a spirit, a sort of hypnosis begins to take effect—the untrained person has all sorts of fancies—wild thoughts—and she can easily persuade others to share them. I'll confess that I had a small trace of this myself."

"Lately?" Magnus said with interest.

"Yes."

"So you saw Kate too." His big face was suffusing with blood.

"No, but if I listened long enough to you and Julia I very well might. I saw—I supposed myself to see—something far more mundane."

"*What?*" Magnus seemed to be increasing in size, and Lily felt a thrilled, appreciative trace of her fear of him.

"Actually, I imagined that I saw Mrs. Fludd," she said, and Magnus slumped back into his chair. "Which simply proves how careful we must be not to be swayed by Julia's delusions."

"But what if she *is* right? What if I was right, and not merely overtired?" But even in his tone of voice, Lily heard that he did not want to believe it.

"Then I expect that we should *all* be endangered. Any truly vengeful, destructive spirit, once set free, draws strength from its own evil. It might even control any mind weak enough to be open to it. But such cases occur very infrequently. There isn't one in a century. Genuine evil is as rare as that. Most of what we call evil is merely lack of imagination."

"Most murderers are an unhappy lot," Magnus agreed. "I've defended several who didn't so much commit murder as fall over it."

"Precisely," Lily said. "So I think we can dismiss the possibility of this being a case of genuine manifestation."

"What did I see in the window, then? And what did I feel in that house?"

"You saw and felt your own fear. If that can happen to my commanding brother, then I think this has gone far enough. I should never have introduced Julia to Mrs. Fludd. Neither of us should have permitted Julia to indulge her ill fantasies about Kate's death."

"That's enough of that," Magnus said warningly, and pushed himself away from the table.

"Except for this," said Lily. "We—you and I—must accept the truth. We are going to institutionalize Julia. For her own good and for ours. Do you think that she might be suicidal?"

"I don't know," Magnus said.

"There you have it. We don't know. You can't afford to have her divorce you, and you don't want her to die. She must be put back into the hospital, and kept there until she is docile. And I suggest that you take whatever steps are appropriate to ensure that her money is accessible. You must be able to control her money. You must be able to control *her.*"

Magnus was leaning forward, his elbows on his knees, staring directly at her. "You are being very frank, Lily."

"It is too late to be anything else," she said straight to him. "In truth, Magnus, we all desire to own her. That is what we wish. You, I—and Mark. We wish to possess her."

"I wish to save her," he flatly said.

"Did I say differently?"

"Fine, then," Magnus said.

"I adore you when you're reasonable," Lily half sang, "and there'll never be a time when I don't. I think we should go over there now. We can walk across the park."

"I'll begin to look into things tomorrow," Magnus said, and shrugged; he stood up and dropped his napkin beside his plate.

When Julia had numbly watched the bus disappear around the corner and up Kensington Church Street, exhaustion seemed to invade her with every breath, weighting the marrow of her bones. Her body seemed very heavy; she no longer felt able to trudge up to Notting Hill; she wanted to lean on Mark's arm. She thought with longing of her bed, of long sleep, of reading a book propped against the blanket while a light kept her safe from the dark. She saw me dead, she thought. Or had Miss Pinner seen—an idea fragile as a moth's wing, but freighted with all of Olivia's darkness, flickered for a half second at the borders of her consciousness and was then tamped down, forgotten, and her mind veered away, not recognizing what it had done.

And with it she veered, turning to her side, blinking, knowing only that she wished to be at home.

She got halfway back up the street before her burning feet could carry her no farther. A few steps away was a bench, and she limped toward it and collapsed onto it, sighing. A man in a black raincoat with the collar turned up sat beside her and brushed her legs with his. Very lightly, he brushed her leg again. Julia peeked at him, hoping he would leave, and saw—thought she saw— that the man had no lips. His face seemed to be chopped off below the nose, and to begin again at the chin. Between was a white scream of teeth, a permanent snarl of rigid teeth and blackened gums. She was afraid to look again and was too tired to move on, so sat hunched within herself, staring directly ahead of her, seeing nothing. He too hunched in his black raincoat, the collar turned up, and stared ahead. His leg hung against hers, with almost no pressure save that of the thin black cloth of his trousers. After what seemed an hour the man shifted, and she glanced quickly at him and saw that his face was, after all, utterly normal, rather pudgy and full-lipped. She realized that she had been holding her breath, and noisily inhaled. The man pressed his leg to Julia's but now he was just an ordinary man, and she moved down the bench, pretending to look for something on the wet sidewalk, so that she would not offend him. After a time he moved away, leaving behind a copy of the *Evening Standard*. Julia unthinkingly picked up the newspaper and numbly walked home. Noises and screams drifted across from Holland Park.

The house pulsed with heat and expectant, waiting quiet, its lights flaming. Julia walked through rooms which seemed alien and dead, utterly apart from her. She heard none of the by now familiar noises of the trapped echoes and spirits of the Rudges. Julia thought, as she sat wearily on the McClintocks' ugly couch, that Olivia might have withdrawn, leaving Julia in her world forever:

that was the strength of evil, she saw, its absence of hope, its stink of moral failure. For a moment she saw the tramp on Cremorne Road savagely stuffing a dog into a bag; from an accumulation of these sordid, hopeless moments evil was condensed.

She bent her neck backward and closed her eyes and suppressed a half-formed image which threatened to flood into her mind.

To distract herself, Julia took up the newspaper she had taken from the bench. In time she would have the energy to face the stairs and her bedroom. Then she remembered the carnage she had made of the upstairs bathroom— bare white-gray walls like dead skin and skeletal shards of black mirror over everything. That mess: Olivia seemed alive and present in its midst. She could not bear to look at it now.

Julia skimmed the news on the front page—it seemed remote and irrelevant. She read the names of politicians, looked at their photographs, and scarcely remembered who they were. They had nothing to do with her, nothing to do with Olivia Rudge. Why was she reading this? It was the first current newspaper she had looked at in weeks. She felt the atmosphere of the house intensify around her, and turned the page.

At the bottom of page four she saw the little headline. Paul Winter had not been judged worthy of much space. The headline read GENERAL'S SON FOUND DEAD IN CHELSEA FLAT.

> Captain Paul Winter, 36, son of General Martin Somill Winter, second in command to Montgomery at Alamein, was found dead this morning by a friend in his small flat in Stadium St. SW 10. Captain Winter, who had left the army several years ago, suffered multiple stab wounds. General Winter was informed of his son's death soon after discovery of the body. The General and his son are said to have not been on speaking terms for many years. Captain Winter was unmarried.

Julia's first thought was of David Swift: he had to be warned. As she began to move dazedly across the room to the telephone, she heard the sound of chattering, high-pitched laughter—gleeful hiccuping childish laughter. "Damn you, damn you, damn you," Julia screamed, at the same time recognizing with a part of her mind that Olivia Rudge could never produce a sound so innocent. It was the delighted laughter of a young child.

Where was it? For a moment it seemed to ring all about her and pervade the house. She forced herself to be still and quiet, and then heard that it came from beyond the kitchen. She knew where. If she had not shattered the black mirrors, it would come from upstairs. Julia ran through the rooms, her warning to David Swift forgotten, and rushed down the hall to the bathroom.

Some figure lurked in the mirror, pouring out that delighted laughter. When she banged open the door she saw its shape crouched on the side of the tub, darkly reflected in the rose mirrors. She stabbed on the light.

The little black girl, Mona, perched on the side of the mirrored tub, rocking with glee. From her upturned throat poured gasping high trills which bounced off the shining walls, redoubling. Mona saw her and raised a short pointing finger and continued to screech.

"What . . ." Julia uttered, and spun around. Olivia Rudge passed the bathroom door and was proceeding calmly, her back to Julia, into the kitchen.

"*Stop*," Julia shouted. She sprinted out of the bathroom, Mona's screams of glee locked in her inner ear, and saw Olivia, in jeans and a red shirt, going out the side door of the kitchen into the dining room. As Julia reached the door Olivia twisted the handle of the French windows and disappeared out into the garden. Rage flashed through Julia's entire nervous system, and she followed.

She went around the side of the house and saw the blond child moving easily and swiftly, well ahead of her, down the street. You won't get away from me, Julia thought, not with that highly visible hair, and began to walk quickly down the street after her in the direction of Kensington High Street. Olivia's hair shimmered in the dark air like a beacon, drifting twenty or thirty yards ahead of Julia. The child turned left on the High Street and was lost from sight.

Alone in the darkness, Julia ran to the corner, hearing her shoes clapping on the pavement. At the corner she looked to the left and saw Olivia moving resolutely up the street, two blocks ahead. A cocoon of silence seemed to have descended over the two of them. Julia was unconscious of the babble of voices and traffic sounds which had so penetrated her earlier; the other people on the street, now merely evening strollers, were insubstantial specters between herself and the girl's flickering hair. She crossed an intervening street and came up onto a long block, following Olivia. Anger and determination were joined presences, thin, high and sweet, thrumming in her blood.

The girl drifted ahead of her, slowing whenever Julia was detained by a knot of people or by traffic at an intersection. When Julia tried to gain on the girl and ran for the length of a block, Olivia effortlessly and without seeming to increase her pace quickened her movement and maintained the distance between them. Around Julia, the cool gauzy air, still smelling of recent rainfall, seemed to congeal into a glowing envelope which contained only herself and Olivia Rudge. Energy—Julia's energy—burned within this envelope, beating at the pulse of her blood.

After a time Julia ceased to be aware of the stream of traffic, to see the other people on the pavement. When her view of her quarry was blocked, she crossed to the other side of the walk and saw her moving easily and determinedly up the street, jeans and red shirt beneath the pale flame of her hair. There was no one else in the world; there was no other movement in the world.

At the long terrace of the Commonwealth Institute Olivia paused and turned. A block away, Julia saw her unsmiling, intent face and for the first time did not find in it a challenge. It was nervous and blank, waiting for her to come closer, almost fearful. Julia pushed off a curb to give leverage to her running and nearly went headlong into an oncoming car. "Look here," came a man's outraged voice, but Julia barely recorded the protest. Olivia was leading her somewhere; Olivia seemed almost to be pleading to her.

From her right she heard the clang of gates and knew that the attendants were locking the park. It was nine o'clock. As if it were a signal for her, Olivia turned her face from Julia and scampered up the steps to the terrace, passed through a line of columns and began to move quickly up the lane running north alongside the park. A few stragglers emerged just as Julia reached the path and blocked her view of Olivia; and then they were alone again, walking rapidly up the long dark path. The girl's hair shone.

"Olivia!" she shouted as the girl slipped into the darkness between the rows of trees. Again she followed, trying to lessen the distance between them, and began to jog, feeling her muscles catch like gears. Olivia was now far ahead, lost in the dark.

Then she appeared in the flaring circle of a lamp, still moving effortlessly between the twin rows of trees. Julia passed the lower portion of the silent green length of park and reached the gate to the youth hostel just within the grounds. Olivia had vanished again. She shouted her name; silence. Making a frantic guess, Julia pushed through the wooden gate and ran up another smaller, twisting path: far ahead, confirmingly, she thought she heard the sound of Olivia's footsteps.

At the bar of the metal gate pulled across the path she hesitated for only a moment, and then swung her trunk over, awkwardly lifting her legs, and half tumbled into the locked park. Her body was a weapon, an arrow for Olivia. Before her, the path wound darkly past the side of Holland House and the wooded hostel. It went far up into the area of the park Julia did not know, a woods traced with many small unpaved paths. Olivia was moving resolutely, unhesitatingly up the narrow way toward the woods.

"Olivia! Olivia!" Julia screamed, but the child did not turn. Julia went after her.

After a few minutes she had left the path and was running across soft grass. Olivia's shining hair appeared flickering between the trees, moving steadily forward. Julia's cuff snagged on a low branch, and then ripped away. Her shoes sank in loamy earth, and admitted chill moisture. In the sparse wood she lost her quarry, then saw a gleaming flash of white up to her right, cutting through bushes and across a barren dark space. They went deeper into the wood, Olivia floating over the low wooden fences and Julia tripping over them, staying on her feet by sheer momentum. In this way, Olivia seemed to lead her for nearly a mile, tricking her into loops to one side or the other, disappearing behind trees and surfacing in wide clearings, tracking back to the right.

Where the wood ended Julia saw the girl racing through low bushes to a wire fence, and ran after. When she reached the fence Olivia was already beyond it, going slowly down a pitted asphalt walk. In the darkness Julia saw only a shimmer of white, pale as breath, to mark her going.

She would have to get over the fence, which was chin-high. Pulling at the top bar with her hands, she lifted herself up to place a toe between the links of chain, then her other foot, and pushed on straining leg muscles so that her torso was above the top bar, where sharp twisted strands of wire prevented her from rolling over. She tremblingly balanced herself, leaned out across the bar, and raised her right leg over the top. Down the sloping path she would find Olivia: this conviction allowed her to swing her other leg over the top, catching the ripped cuff on one of the strands of wire. She tore it impatiently away, and pushed herself off the fence onto the lightless path.

From ahead of her came the sound of running. With all of the breath left in her, Julia forced her body into a trot; the downward slope of the path carried her into a run she was unable to control. It was as if she were running down a mountain, her legs flying out to keep her body upright. Gravity brought her forward, falling like a boulder, toward the sound of Olivia's movement.

Light, noise, astonished faces met her as she tumbled out onto the street below the path. Still ahead of her, she heard Olivia's noise, and she bounced off and around a metal containing fence and raced out into the middle of Holland Park Avenue. Headlights fixed her like a pinned butterfly; her upper body, head, arms and shoulders were still traveling faster than her legs. When she fell, a car squealed to a stop, horn blaring, only inches from her body.

10

Olivia had murdered Geoffrey Braden; she had murdered Paul Winter; she had murdered Mrs. Fludd; and she had tried now to kill Julia. She had been called upon from whatever rank, resentful obscurity she had inhabited: Julia's appearance on Ilchester Place had clothed her in flesh, and now she was a bodily presence in the house. Or so Julia had felt: she could not enter a room without imagining that her tormentor had just quit it. When alone in her bedroom, she locked the door, knowing that Olivia could reach her at any time she wished. The long run through the park had been something like playfulness. Olivia had been toying with her, trying to reproduce Rosa Fludd's "accident."

They were in a new configuration: the screw had tightened, and Olivia wanted her blood. Julia stood on weak, aching legs in the kitchen, waiting for her coffee to boil. It was as dark beyond the windows as if it were still night; the sky, a patch of which Julia could see above the wet brown boards of a fence, hung motionless and woolly, looking as if it might snag in the trees. A few small drops dashed against the window.

Paul Winter. Someone had visited his room and butchered him. Someone under Olivia's control, some man driven by hate so that Olivia could enter him; a man whom absurd, touching little Paul Winter had trusted. Someone who was his Magnus. Whoever it was would not know that he had killed a man for talking to a woman named Julia Lofting. Maybe he wouldn't even remember committing the murder—maybe Olivia could sweep into a mind and then flow out again, leaving no real memory of her occupation. This thought weakened Julia's legs, and she leaned against the counter on shaking knees, perspiring.

The disturbed, reclusive woman in Abbotsbury Close would read the newspaper item or hear of it from Huff, and be savagely glad. She too was Olivia's victim.

And David Swift would be the next, if she understood what Olivia was doing. Julia immediately left the kitchen and went into the living room. She had to check in the directory to find Swift's number. Would her story convince him of his danger? He had seen Olivia at work, but Swift was a stupid and arrogant man. She had no choice, she had to persuade him. She dialed the number and listened intently as the telephone shrilled at the other end. She prayed for him to answer it, but the telephone continued to ring. He might be outside, she thought, or in his bed, sleeping off a hangover.

Julia did not want to look at the third possibility, but neither did she evade it. In the A-D directory she found the listings for police departments, and rang the Islington police. "A man may be dead," she intoned. "Look at Three Thirty-seven Upper Street, the flat just above a pub called The Beautiful and Damned. His name is Swift. This is in connection with the murder of Captain Paul Winter. Hurry."

"What is your relationship to Mr. Swift, madam?" inquired the policeman's drawling voice.

"I'm afraid for him," Julia said, and hurriedly hung up. Relieved that she had at least done something, she went back into the kitchen, where the kettle full of Malvern water was emitting its high shriek. She promised herself to telephone Swift later.

She drank her coffee standing at the white counter, trying to decide how to act, what to do to meet Olivia's challenge. Olivia would try again to kill her. All the previous night, after she had been aided by the puzzled, half-solicitous, half-furious man who had nearly hit her, she had lain atop her sheet in the steaming bedroom, afraid to close her eyes. Then, she had vowed to leave Ilchester Place; Olivia's secret was known, there was nothing left to find; she had to defend herself. Yet in the morning she had realized that Olivia could reach her anywhere. No house was any safer than her own. She had cleaned up the bathroom, filling pails and bags with sections of black glass, with that certainty lodged in her mind.

She thought of it just as she finished her coffee: if freedom from Olivia were anywhere, it would be in America. It was time to return. Her marriage was finished. She did not want Magnus or need him. She was closer to Heather and Olivia Rudge than to anyone else in England—save Mark. But she and Mark had almost never had even so much as a serious conversation. Would he like to live in New Hampshire? She realized with dismay how little she knew about him.

But the thought of him gave her courage to answer her telephone when it began to ring in the living room. She braced herself, thinking that she might hear for the first time the voice of Olivia Rudge. But it was Lily's voice she heard.

"Julia, I hope you won't mind my asking you how you are?"

Julia found that she could speak to Lily only in the coolest, most detached manner. Lily seemed to have emerged from another era.

"Good morning, Lily. How am I? I don't know. I feel sort of suspended. I feel very odd. A lot's happened. I know how Mrs. Fludd was killed. Olivia almost did the same to me. I think it was her idea of a joke."

"My darling, if you are saying . . ."

"That Olivia tried to kill me. That's right. Next time, she won't be so playful. What would you do if your life were in danger?"

"I'd go to Magnus," Lily said simply.

"Well, so you would. But I can't. The next time, it might be Magnus trying to run me over. So I can't do that, Lily, can I? No."

She could almost hear Lily's patience snapping.

"I understand that you're overtired, darling," said Lily. "But you should realize that you're being almost absurdly unrealistic. Magnus loves you, Julia. Magnus wants you for his wife. He wants to begin rebuilding your marriage. We—Magnus and I—went to see you yesterday, just past lunchtime. I wish you had been at home, so you could have seen how pathetically distressed he is."

"I was at home, I was asleep. I'd taken two sleeping pills. Olivia had just given me a message. Do you believe me, Lily? And last night she tried to put it into effect—she lured me outside and ran me into traffic. I was almost killed. It was like being hypnotized. It's what she did to Mrs. Fludd. Would you have called it an accident, Lily?"

"Have you ever wondered why it is to you that all these things are happening? Why is it you?"

"You're clever, Lily. That's all I have left to find out."

"You have been very active and you have been through a great deal, my dear. How long has it been since you've been out of the hospital?"

"I don't know," said Julia, feeling her artificial detachment begin to recede. "What difference does it make? A month, maybe."

"Not as long as that, I shouldn't think. My dear, darling Julia. You've had such a rotten time of it. Don't you think you really deserve another rest? Don't say anything now, but I do want you to think about it. And I want you to consider moving in with me for the time being. All alone over there, you might be hurt, or injure yourself in some way, and no one would know anything about it. That's what Magnus and I wanted to talk about with you yesterday afternoon. We wanted to beg you to move in with me for the time being."

"You and Magnus," Julia said. "You and Magnus wanted, you and Magnus thought, you and Magnus this and that. So you're afraid I'll hurt myself. What do you mean by that, Lily?"

"Nothing, darling, we were simply . . ."

"I want you to know something, Lily. I was just thinking, this morning, right before you called, that I would like to go back to America. There's nothing here for me anymore, unless it's Mark Berkeley. I want to divorce Magnus. He seems impossibly remote to me. If I live through this siege, I'm going to divorce him. There. What do you think of that, Lily?"

"I think it's calamitous," said Lily. "It's psychic disaster. You still blame Magnus for what happened, and you should not be permitted to do that."

"I see," said Julia coldly. "I think you'd like to have me back in the hospital, Lily."

"I just want you, darling, to *think*," wailed Lily. "How much sleep do you get? How well do you eat? Can you take care of yourself? Why, why, why do you think this Olivia person wants to kill you? You—out of all the people she might have chosen."

Julia listened, her mouth open, almost thinking that Lily would tell her.

"We're not making any progress," Lily said finally. "Please think about staying in my guestroom, darling. You don't truly want to return to your troubled country and leave dear old England and Magnus. You need Magnus. You need help. Julia, none of us shall be happy, none of us shall be what we were until you accept some basic truths. The truth about Kate—"

Julia shouted into the telephone, "You don't know the truth about Kate, you don't know the truth about Magnus!" Then she hung up.

Lily rang back several seconds later. "Julia, you are still heroic, I respect you in every way, darling, but you are also a bit erratic. Did you ring off on me?"

"Give up, Lily," said Julia. "Give up on me. I'm not in your world anymore. I'm in hers. Ask Miss Pinner."

"You'd better begin thinking very quickly and very well," Lily said five minutes later to Magnus, having roused him from sleep with her telephone call. "She wants to divorce you. And she mentioned that she is thinking of returning to America."

"Good God," Magnus managed to utter. "Is she mad? She can't divorce me."

"I should imagine, brother dear, that she has grounds sufficient to divorce you fifty times, should that be necessary. But, yes, I think she is mad. This Rudge affair has utterly unhinged her. She has snapped, Magnus. There is surely some way that you can have her put away in the hospital. Put away for good, if necessary. Or at least until she is capable of listening to reason."

"Lily," Magnus wheezed, his voice foggy and menacing, "what the devil did you say to her? Did you wave Kate in front of her again?"

"No," Lily said, "at least not directly. She is much too full of this Rudge matter to consider Kate. Will you go to your chambers and look up in your musty old books whatever law you can invoke to get her safely put away? Because if you do not, you will not have a wife at this time next year. She could go to Reno, or wherever it is Americans go to be especially vulgar."

"I'll see what I can find," Magnus growled. "I'll look up what's needed for an involuntary commitment."

"You might have done that when she left you," Lily offered in her sweetest tone.

"I needed you to suggest it, Lily."

One question of Lily's stayed with Julia. *Why is it you?* She could have answered, because it was I who bought the house, but that merely pushed the question back a step. She was not satisfied with what she already knew; it seemed to her that the force which had taken her out to Breadlands and had led her to Olivia's group had not yet released her.

What she most wished to do was to take two more pills and sleep out the rest of the day. But there had been something, some idea she had not followed up. . . . Her mind traced the flicker of memory back, almost catching it. A magazine. Then she had it: *The Tatler*. She had been going to look for pictures of Heather Rudge's parties in *The Tatler* on the day she saw the Burne-Jones painting.

Well, she thought, why not? Since making the discovery of Olivia's role in the Braden boy's death, she had felt occupationless. Now it seemed that she was only to wait—wait for Olivia to decide in what way she would move. Leafing through magazines in Colindale was far more attractive. Let Olivia appear in the reading room, let her wave her knife over bound stacks of *John O'London's* and *Punch*. The image was so bizarre that Julia, for the second time, caught at the fluttering tails of her sanity. Was it possible that she *had* ripped the dolls and written on the mirrors? Turned on the heaters? Perhaps she had imagined seeing Olivia. Her doubting mind bent back on itself.

Yet someone had killed Paul Winter. She had not invented that. Olivia was no delusion. Aware that she was on the verge of feeling grateful for Winter's horrible death, Julia dressed in her hot silent room, went out to her car, and drove through drizzle and glittering streets to Colindale and the periodical collection.

Her reader's card was inspected with almost insulting thoroughness by a uniformed guard; as she walked down the symmetrical rows of desks she obliquely saw two young men seated behind a large heap of Victorian magazines smirk at each other as she passed. Julia supposed that she looked more than ever like an actual beggar maid. Her shoes were mud-stained from the chase through Holland Park, her tights were ripped, and she hadn't washed her hair in a week.

The desk she was accustomed to using was occupied by a large black man wearing gold spectacles which seemed to emit fierce light. His long flat cheeks bore triple raised scars, purplish black. He glanced aggressively at Julia, a bear defending his territory, and she wandered to the other side of the room, looking for a vacant desk. Two or three men tracked her with their eyes, looking benignly amused.

At last she found a desk near the wall and dropped her spattered raincoat over the top of the chair. After filling in a request slip for all the copies of *The Tatler* from 1930 to 1941, she took it to the desk and gave it to a new librarian, a dark-haired young woman with large tinted glasses. Julia watched the young librarian take her card to one of the runners, and realized that, two weeks ago, she had seen her outside the French restaurant on Abingdon Road. It was the girl with whom she had felt a sympathy, the girl who had smiled at her. They had been members of the same species. Now she felt nothing of the kind. She had nothing in common with this pretty young librarian.

With her hair a reddish mass of tangles, in her ripped black tights and muddy shoes, dark circles beneath her eyes, Julia sat behind her blond desk, her mood lifting. She would not feel sorry for herself. A boy set half a dozen fat black volumes on the desk before her. "They'll send up the others when you have finished with these," he said, nearly apologizing, as if he expected this strange woman to shout at him.

She knew that she would find something. She felt morally renewed. Julia pulled the top volume off the stack and began to leaf through it, staring hungrily at the pictures of men and women in evening dress, remembering her childhood. Almost, she could hear them speak.

The first hour she found nothing, nor the second; it was slightly before noon when she had even a faint success. She had flipped halfway through the volume for 1933–34 when a picture, a face, on an earlier page burned back to her, and she tore backward in the book to November, 1933. There on the right-hand side of the book, grinning up at her, was Heather Rudge, holding a cigarette and a champagne glass, her shoulders gleaming; the sexuality of the woman scalded Julia's bowels. On both sides of her dangled young men. Julia rushed to the caption. "The well-known American hostess Mrs. Heather Rudge at Lord Kilross' party, here seen with Mr. Maxwell Davies, Mr. Jeremy Reynolds, Lord Panton, the Hon. Frederick Mason, and Viscount Gregory." That was all. None of the young men, who glittered with an identical infatuation, were familiar to Julia, and she saw no other photographs of Heather at the party.

She went slowly through the remainder of the volume, but Heather did not reappear. Nor did she for another forty-five minutes, when Julia saw her oval, challenging, vain, sensual face again rising up from her dazzling shoulders on a fluted neck. More young men surrounded her—Mr. Maxwell Davies, Viscount Gregory and the Hon. Frederick Mason among them. They looked unchanged. The occasion, Julia read, was a party given by Lord Panton, who appeared beside a frilly little blonde, the Hon. Someone-Someone, all teeth and curls. These were her young men, undoubtedly: Julia wondered which of them had owned the honor of siring Olivia.

Thrice more, in the volumes leading up to 1936, Julia found photographs of Heather. She seemed to travel usually in the company of the same young men, with a slight mixture of mustached older gentlemen with straining bellies and popping eyes. Oliver Blankenship, Nigel Ramsay, David Addison. But every time one of these older men appeared, he was shadowed closely by several of Heather's younger set. Heather was always "the well-known (or popular, or famous) American hostess" in these photographs, but there were no pictures taken of her parties.

Julia signaled to the runner to take the six heavy volumes and return with the later set. Her face was warm and hectic, flushed, and she began to drum her fingers on her desk and look wildly around the quiet room, where men bent their heads over books as though drinking from them. Her watch said three-thirty. She'd had nothing to eat or drink since morning coffee.

One wing of the library contained a small cafeteria. Julia wondered if she should get a sandwich before going on. The impulse grew out of her rising mood, the optimism she had begun to feel, and she decided to follow it, even though she felt no hunger. She scrawled a note for the boy and went quickly down the aisles and out of the reading room, giving a bright, unfocused smile to the guard at the door.

Julia flew down the long lightless hall to the cafeteria, selected a tray from beneath the gaze of a bored Indian woman wearing a hairnet, and looked over the available food. "Too late for hot lunch," the Indian woman announced from her stool. Julia nodded, examining the sandwiches. "No hot lunch now, only sameges," the woman insisted.

"Fine," Julia said. She took from the rack a cheese-and-tomato sandwich wrapped in thin cellophane; touching the whispery layer of cellophane, Julia instantly imagined it plastered across her face, adhering there, stuck to her nostrils and mouth. She dropped the sandwich on the tray.

"Coffee?" Julia said, standing before the shining coffee machine.

The woman shook her head. "No coffee. Too late, coffee again at half four."

"Fine," Julia said, and plucked a container of orange drink from a carton.

When she reached the cash desk, the Indian woman left her stool and moved slowly past the racks of food, audibly sighing. At last she reached the register and rang up Julia's purchases.

"Two pounds."

"That can't be right—one sandwich?"

The woman stared deeply into Julia's face, then looked with great boredom back at the tray. She punched more buttons on the register. "Thirty-two pence."

Julia took the tray to a clean table, and looked back at the waitress, half expecting to be ordered to one of the uncleaned side tables. The woman was shuffling back to her stool, conspicuously not taking notice of Julia.

The orange drink felt cool and sweet on her tongue, and it opened a channel all the way down into her stomach. She chewed experimentally at the dry sandwich; its bread seemed poreless, synthetic, and the cheese did not separate between her teeth. For a few moments she continued to chew distractedly at the stale sandwich, lubricating it with orange drink.

When her insides contracted, she quickly left the table and rushed across the room to the door marked LADIES. Inside one of the metal cubicles she vomited neatly into the bowl, and tasted the heavy sweetness of orange drink; when her stomach contracted again, only a thin yellowish drool came up.

She went to a sink and wiped water across her mouth. The mirror showed a drugged-looking, raddled harridan of indeterminate age; gray showed clearly in the frizzy hair at the sides of her head. Her lips were cracked, and beside her right eye was a small bruise she'd got when she had fallen down in Holland Park Avenue. Julia tried to comb her hair with her hands, and managed to coax it back into mere disorder before she left the washroom and returned to the reading room.

The five fat volumes sat atop her desk. Within minutes, Julia was lost in the first, examining all the photographs on a page and then flipping it over. By four o'clock she had seen two more pictures of "the famous American hostess," once in company with Mr. Jeremy Reynolds and the other on the arm of Viscount Gregory. Heather was unchanged, but the young men, five years older, were visibly coarser and meatier, beginning to show double chins and jowls.

In the volume for 1937–38, Julia found a photograph of Heather standing beside a wheelchair. Strapped in the chair, incredibly shrunken and frail, was David Addison, one of the portly, pop-eyed older men who had customarily accompanied her; on the other side of the wheelchair stood Mr. Maxwell Davies, his earlier slender and dark handsomeness now softened and blurred by fat. Davies' face was opened in a thoughtless, greedy maw of a smile—it made Julia shudder. It seemed to her that she could smell his breath, taste the thin flavor of the man's mouth. Heather Rudge glinted, smiling a cool winner's smile, between the two ruined men.

There were no further pictures of Heather in that volume, and none in the next. Some of the young men, Lord Panton and Viscount Gregory and others, appeared at balls and dances, grown fatter, gross of face, with the ruddy look of once-athletic alcoholics. She closed this volume at five o'clock. The library closed at five-thirty, and Julia debated whether or not it was worthwhile to leaf through the remaining two big volumes.

She decided to skim through them in the half hour left to her, and then to telephone David Swift again. Julia hefted the volume for 1939–40 and turned to the first number and began to flip through the issues more quickly than she had before. When she reached the issue for May 19 she glanced down at a page of Cambridge photographs and gasped aloud. A young Magnus Lofting, standing erect in a dinner jacket, beamed out at the world from the page; beside him stood Mr. Maxwell Davies. "Two Cambridge men discuss the Blues," read the caption and gave their names.

From that moment Julia burrowed into the last two volumes, looking for the picture she knew she would eventually find. Even isolated shots of Heather, or of Heather with her familiar retinue, did not long delay her; Julia flipped through, scanning the pages for one inevitable photograph.

The photograph appeared at the end of the 1939–40 volume, in an issue for February, 1940: the year before Olivia's birth, Julia remembered. "Wartime Spirits Kept High in Kensington," the article was headed. One of the pictures showed, unmistakably, a corner of the living room at 25 Ilchester Place. The wallpaper looked gaudy, and instead of the McClintocks' heavy furniture, graceful small chairs and lounges stood against the walls. Men of various ages seemed to fill the room, many of them in uniform. Heather, looking as young and sensual as she had in 1930, appeared in over half of the photographs. She danced with Lieutenant Frederick Mason and Captain Maxwell Davies, and was seen in ardent conversation with Colonel Nigel Ramsay; but the photograph at which Julia stared until the bell clamored throughout the reading room was on the second page of the set, and showed an elderly couple, wildly out of place at the party, smiling somewhat tremulously into the camera. They were identified as Lord and Lady Selhurst. Behind them, in one of the corners of the room, twenty-one-year-old Magnus Lofting had his right arm about Heather Rudge's bare shoulder.

She looked up as the African at her old seat was rising from his chair and gave his ferocious countenance a glance of such peculiarity that he dropped a sheaf of paper. She thrust the volumes to the back of the desk and stood up—only she and the African were in the reading room, apart from the pretty librarian and the last two or three stragglers already passing the guard. Her heart seemed to blaze. Now she knew how to answer Lily's question, *Why is it you?*

"Because," she thought, "Magnus is Olivia's father. Because both of his children were stabbed to death. Because Olivia wants revenge. Because the patterns are clear."

Light-headed, she left the library and entered a steady gray falling of rain. Chains of black clouds printed the dark sky. Julia absently searched her bag for her keys, unlocked the car door, and bent in behind the wheel. Her face felt chilly and slick with rain, and her hands were cold, wet. These sensations, like the bitterness at the base of her tongue, skidded off the reflective surface of her mind; at that moment, if asked, she would have hesitated before answering in what country she was. All of the puzzle had finally been connected, it had clicked into place, and the answer to Lily's question had been found, as it must have been, in the past. Julia did not need Magnus to confirm or deny her knowledge: she knew that she was right. Magnus was Olivia's father; he'd had a youthful affair with Heather Rudge and then deserted her. It explained everything. And it clarified Heather Rudge's conduct when Julia had met her at the clinic. Now she knew why the old woman had thrice asked her, *Is that your real name?* Julia leaned back in the car seat and looked up at the black chain mail of the sky, seeing each of the pieces fall into place. What could make more sense than that Olivia Rudge would seek to kill her deserting father's second wife, Olivia being what she was? That she would make a deadly rhyme of her own murder?

There was a place she had to go. One area of her mind knew this with utter clarity, even while all the rest still floated, stunned by Olivia's symmetries. Ordinarily she would not have trusted herself to drive—she felt as though she'd had half a bottle of whiskey—but there was no other way of getting where she had to go. She pulled the key over in its slot and heard the Rover's engine kick into life. She slammed the car into gear and shot forward across the parking lot. Rain blurred across the windshield, and Julia flicked on the wipers at the same moment as she turned out into the street. The map in her head would lead her where she had to go, though she did not know how to get there.

Olivia, Magnus.

Olivia, Magnus. She had known from the night of her meeting with Mrs. Fludd, but only now did she see how the connection worked, how she was a part of Olivia's web as she was of Magnus'. Olivia could have been Kate, she thought, and the Rover rocketed forward, just scraping past a yellow Volkswagen. She meant, Olivia could have been her daughter. She and Heather Rudge were interchangeable.

"*No,*" she said aloud, and swerved her car out into the passing lane, stepping on the accelerator.

Sisterhood. They were sisters. Women of the same man. Mothers of murdered daughters.

Julia brought the car to a squealing stop when she finally saw the red light, and ignored the curious glances from beneath umbrellas on the sidewalk. She sat, her mouth slightly open and moistureless, behind the wheel, looking upward, waiting for the light to change. Magnus seemed more incalculable than ever, a sea of possibilities and surprises: she could never encompass him nor dismiss him. The poison which was Olivia came from a level deep within him, from some power stunted and sent awry in his childhood. (Like Mark, said a disloyal cell in her mind.)

Horns erupted behind her, and she threw the car into gear and shot across the intersection. She knew where she was going. The sky's darkness leaked down, staining her hands on the wheel.

Had she hit a dog? She could not remember: indeed, she could not remember most of the drive. There had been a dog, in the vicinity of Golders Green and the Finchley Road, a rust-colored dog bounding out into the road; Julia had cramped the wheel immediately, instinctively to the side, and had sent the Rover into the side of a parked car, crumpling one of its doors; but she thought that when the Rover had ground its way out of the parked car, a second thudding sensation had come from the left front tire. Speeding away, she had been afraid to look in the mirror.

Now she stood beside her car in Upper Street, a steady rain dripping into her hair, thinking about how terrible it was to kill a dog. She could not look at the Rover. Magnus' present to her (bought with her money), it had been importantly clean and sleek, feline: an exemplar. It was like Magnus to buy something for her with her own money and then use it against her. From the side of her eye she caught an impression of a wrinkled rear end and a back bumper curled in like a ram's horn. She hunched her shoulders against the rain. Where was her coat? Not in the car. She had left it slung over her chair in the periodical library. She hoped that she had not hit the dog. It would leave no marks, but still be dead.

Across the street the lights of the pub burned softly red through the windows; glasses hung upside down, bat-fashion, gleamed like Christmas, points and blurs of red. Rain jumped in the street and ran in rivulets toward the drain. The streetlamps produced a shining streak along the pavement, a harsh acid yellow, a color which eats the skin. Water caught in Julia's eyebrows and lashes. She looked above the pub and saw no lights in the windows.

She had to go up to the flat; she had to see.

There were no police, what did that mean, no police?

Julia moved across the street, forgetting to turn off the lights of her car or to remove the key, pausing to let half-seen cars splash by before her. She came up on the pavement before David Swift's door, and knocked twice. Then, her head and neck streaming with water, she found the bell and pushed it down.

When no one came, her insides seemed to freeze. What had happened to the police? Hadn't they understood her message? Julia pushed at the door. It held against her. Numbly, in baffled frustration, she turned her head and saw the Rover's headlights shining at her from across the street; she was pinned within them. They were all of the car she could see.

Frantic, she turned again to the door. Something Magnus had once described to her came back to her in miraculous detail: he'd been defending a housebreaker, and he had told her how the man had used a plastic card to slip the catches on locks. He had used her check card to demonstrate. She dug in her bag for her wallet and pulled the card out, spilling loose papers and bills into the bottom of her bag, and inserted the top edge of the card between the door and the jamb. She pushed it up and in. A hard sloping edge floated back: she heard a loud click. When she pushed at the doorknob, the peeling door swung in. She slipped inside, escaping the beams of her lights.

It was the dingy staircase where he had called to her, shouting. From the top she heard a muffled noise. Julia's heart clenched, and then released her, though fear poured through her like cold water, and she went up the filthy stairs. She had dreamed of doing this, though she could not remember when. Her fingers shook on the wood of the door at the top; muttering came from the other side, a meaningless series of syllables. She pressed her trembling fingers to the wood, and pushed the door gently in. Her fingers left small dark stains on the wood.

She was conscious of Olivia: that tense, webbed atmosphere of waiting tension. Olivia's air seemed to fill the room. Her lion's smell. She was here, or had just left. Julia saw the knife first. Wonderingly, she picked it up from the floor, feeling her palm adhere to the handle. She remembered—as though it too were dreamed—the penknife she had uncovered in the sand on her first day in the house. Holding the knife, she could feel sand in her palms, grinding at her skin. Olivia.

She whirled about, certain she had heard Olivia calling. But it had been a noise from the couch, the repetition of that whiffling noise she had heard on the staircase. As if truly in a dream, Julia walked smoothly across the bare carpet to the couch and saw David Swift lying on his back, his eyes open and his mouth working. Broken syllables came from him. He was sleeping, Julia thought, talking in his sleep.

As she looked, his head snapped to one side and his chest seemed to bloom. A red slot opened up from his breastbone to his belt, and redness spurted out, foaming over his shirt. It was as though a flower had opened, revealing a sudden configuration of great complexity and intricacy. More blood flowed from beneath his chin and sheeted across his neck. He stared up into Julia's eyes and tried to speak. Blood filled his throat, and it welled from his mouth, garbling his words.

"She . . ."

"She's just left," Julia finished for him. He had already lost an appalling amount of blood; Julia took up a cloth from the little table and pressed it over the long wound on the man's midriff. She must have seen it wrong, she thought, her mind surprisingly calm; he had been dying when she had come in. As Julia held the useless cloth over the long wound, David Swift thrashed on the couch and sent a wave of blood over her hand and then fell back. Julia dropped the knife into the sticky fluid beside the couch. She stood up, blinking. Olivia had got here first and had killed him while he slept. Her stink was in the room.

She washed her hands at the sink, her back to the dead Swift. When she was free of blood, she fled down the stairs and left the street door ajar, so that a policeman would look within. Through increasing rain she ran in the beam of the Rover's headlights toward her car. Laughter and music from the pub followed her.

The horror of what she had seen broke over her when she sat again in the car, rain sliding down her collar from her hair, and she shook back and forth, slamming from the seat to the steering column, yanking and pushing back with her arms, her hands locked on the circle of wood. She had been too late; even the police had been powerless against Olivia. Julia slammed the Rover's door and cowered within, shaking and freezing. Her mind cleared long before she was able to control her body. Images of America, of valleys and green distances, invaded her.

11

She drove through dark, rain-slicked streets, her window wipers thumping, on what she knew was the wrong side of the road. She should have been on the right, because she was driving through the back reaches of a city like Boston, which was familiar to her in a surrealist, dreamlike fashion; yet all the other traffic was on the left, and that too was dreamily familiar. Julia went with it, driftingly, faintly pleased by her knowledge of this strange city, and faintly annoyed that she could not get her bearings properly. She saw a spot of blood on her thumbnail, and in reflex wiped it on the seam of her trousers.

Her turnoff, the access road to the expressway, lay somewhere nearby; from there it was only a couple of hours' drive to New Hampshire. She knew that because she had never in her life been more than a couple of hours' drive from her family's valley: Julia could visualize all the roads, the highways and expressways and turnpikes and seal-coated county roads and gravelly tracks used by farmers, which formed a lacy web of connections between where she was and the valley. And she could visualize with a perfect wholeness the last turning before the valley, the sweep of the exit ramp from the freeway down through dark hills, a few mysterious lights shining in deep vales, far off the glow of a town. She could see every inch of that dark access to the valley, and she knew where the river was, though you couldn't see it. She wanted to see it now, before her.

She was driving through an American city, a city like Boston, bearing generally south. Nineteenth-century houses, built of red brick, now a grimy brown, stood on either side of narrow streets. Cold rain rattled on the top of the car.

Driving through an American city, driving through America. London was a furry patch in her memory; London did not exist. She was in Boston, and there was no London. Soon she would find the Berkshires, and that lovely long highway through banks of trees. Tanglewood. Julia pressed hard on the accelerator and her car slewed on wet Pentonville Road, fishtailing in its lane. Except for all these cars, it looked like the outer edges of Boston. She knew that people drove on the wrong side of the road here. It was habit with her by now. Why should that be? She pushed the question down.

She was of no age, she was going home, nothing had happened to her. Her father waited, dressed in an elegant dark gray suit; her grandfather had just died, and that was why she was going home from Smith. Boston was a mistake, she should not be in Boston; but she knew the way to go.

Now she was near the Fens, she thought. It would look much different, for everything had changed, and she had not been at Smith for years. She wheeled the car around a corner, blindly, her mind fluttering. A vision of a man's chest gouting fluid. . . . It meant nothing, though her feet had slipped on red blood. Nothing. Julia forced herself to smile at a young man striding across the road, walking on broad white stripes, and he returned the smile. He had an American face, round beneath floppy hair. Wet with rain. A slippery face, a face which left no traces.

The Rover jolted forward past the boy. Soon she would find the way, and then she would be sailing, with no mental effort at all, down the turnpike, leaving the city behind, moving toward the sloping bank of the exit, turning down between hills, passing small ghostly lights deep in a vale where the winding of the road shone under the trees.

At the same time, she knew where she was going, though her mind seemed to detach itself at times and go floating through Boston. As she drove down Marylebone Road, she noticed on the back of her left wrist another smear of blood, and hurriedly, disgustedly, wiped her wrist on the car seat.

But she could not rid herself of the feeling of being in Massachusetts until she had left her car parked outside a house in Notting Hill, rushed up the path in the rain, gone down six steps at the side of the house. Her mind seemed to be flying apart, a wispy cloth tugged by birds. She pounded at the bell. A basement, a valley. Breath caught and tore, chugging, in her throat. Her mouth open and cottony. Finally the door opened, and she rushed against the man who stood within, touching his wet face with her hands. He held her tightly while he struggled to remove his coat. Raindrops coursed down her face, and she butted against his chest, shaken by what she recognized as crying only after what seemed a long time of it.

Mark stood just within his door, letting her sob. His damp coat hung uncomfortably on his shoulders, and while he cradled Julia he shrugged first one arm out of its sleeve and then the other. He allowed the coat to fall squashily to the floor and hugged Julia tighter. She trembled against him like a trapped bird, her elbows and forearms whipping at his chest.

"Oh, thank God you're home," she finally uttered. "I was so afraid I wouldn't find you and then I'd have to . . ." Her voice became too damaged and soft to continue.

"I just got home, just this minute," he said down into the wet hair on the crown of her head, plastered down on either side of a natural part. "Good Lord," he said, "I never thanked you for that money. I really shouldn't have taken it, but it came just when I was short, and—"

Julia's distorted face tilted back to look at him confusedly. She had obviously forgotten all about the check.

"Never mind," he quickly said, and hugged her to him again. "What's happened to you?"

She rested her cheek on his shoulder, and breathed heavily for a moment. "Everything's happened," she finally said. "She's going to kill me. I saw—I saw—" Julia stared at him with blurred eyes, her face looking directly into his without recording it.

"You saw?" Mark stroked her cheek, but she made no response.

"I thought I was in America all the way here. I thought I was driving through Boston. I was looking for the turnpike, so I could get to New Hampshire. I was going to my grandfather's place, in the valley. Isn't that funny?"

"You're under strain," Mark said.

"I'm going to be killed," she said again. "Nobody can stop her. I don't want to die. Can I stay with you tonight? You're all wet." She touched his face. "Why are you wet?"

"I was out," Mark said. "I was having a chat with Lily. About you." He smiled at Julia. "I got in just before you came crashing in. Come in."

He led her into his room and helped her to sit on a cushion and removed her shoes. Then he dried her feet with a towel and wiped her hands. He finished by dabbing at her face.

"You have another bruise."

"I fell down. In the street. She was playing with me then."

"And what's this on your wrist?" He stared at the thick dirty bandage under the cuff of her blouse.

"I cut myself. Not on purpose. It was after I saw her. I called you." Julia was looking straight before her, as if now that she had come to him, he could offer no further help. "She wanted me to be hit by a car. Like Mrs. Fludd. She doesn't care about murder. She likes it. She makes other people like it too."

"Hold on," he said, taking her hands and chafing them. Mark was squatting down before her, looking at her unfocused eyes. "Who's this 'she'? That girl you were talking about earlier? Olivia Rudge?"

Her eyes snapped into clarity. "I didn't tell you her name," she said, staring at him and beginning to snatch back her hands.

"Lily did," he said. "Just now."

"Lily doesn't believe me. She can't. It's because of Magnus."

"Don't worry about Lily. What about this girl?"

Julia watched in fascination as an ant crawled out of Mark's shirt and traversed one of the wings of his collar. The ant, small, red and very quick, sped down the collar and across his chest and fled again into the interior of Mark's shirt.

"She wants to murder you."

"Yes."

"She knows that you found out about that child, whoever it was, twenty years ago."

"Geoffrey Braden." Julia thought of the ant struggling through the hair on Mark's chest. She felt astonishingly light-headed.

"And now she wants to kill you."

"She's killed two other men. Paul Winter and David Swift. I just came from

Swift's flat." Julia spoke in a level voice, looking straight at his shirt front. "May I lie down on your mattress?"

"You'd better," he said, and lifted her up and helped her across the room to the mattress. Sheets and blankets lay rumpled at its foot, and Mark pulled them up over her legs. Then he sat on the floor bside her, shoving clothing and plates to one side.

"I'm going to find you some sleeping pills," he said. "They'll help you relax, Julia."

"I don't need sleep," she said.

"You need to rest," Mark said. He lifted her head and pulled the grimy pillow across the mattress to place beneath it. Then he left her staring up at the ceiling and went to his kitchen for a vial of pills and a glass of water. "It's just Valium," he said.

"Take too many pills," Julia mumbled, but swallowed one anyhow. Then she focused her gaze on his eyes—he could see her pupils contract—and said, "I found out that Magnus is her father. That's why it's me. That's why she wanted me from the start."

"Just close your eyes, Julia," he said, "and we'll talk about it all in the morning. We have a lot to talk about. You'll see."

She obediently closed her eyes. "I washed my hands because I had blood on them." She turned her head toward Mark and opened her eyes to look at him. "I want you to protect me. Just tonight. Please."

Against his will, Mark was looking at the outline of Julia's thighs beneath her trousers. He noticed a smear of some dark, brownish substance along the seam of the wool, and felt everything within him leap as though touched by a live electrical wire.

"I think I might be sick," he heard Julia say. "I feel so funny. I don't want to die. I don't want to die, Mark."

After Mark had switched off the light, he threw off his clothes in the darkness, unsure of where to sleep. Julia lay unconscious and fully dressed across his mattress. He did not dare to move her—Julia's condition seemed dangerous to him, fully bearing out everything Lily had said. It was as though she could spin off into outright lunacy if she were as much as touched. And her suggestion about Magnus had upset him, reminding him again that she was his adoptive brother's wife, despite the events of the past week or two. Mark knew all too well that Magnus was stronger than he, and would not hesitate to beat him senseless if he suspected him of sleeping with Julia. Magnus had beaten him twice during his youth, and Mark shied away from the memory of these experiences. He pulled a patterned Indian rug, given him long ago by a girl whose name he could no longer remember, from the closet and arranged the stiff scratchy thing over his body as he lay back in a chair.

Magnus seemed to be everywhere, behind every rock and round every corner: Magnus' virility, according to Julia, had spawned Olivia Rudge, Julia's fantastic wraith. Though they were approximately the same height, Mark invariably thought of Magnus as much taller than he, twice as massive, twice as serious a presence. Was it really possible that Lily could control him? Her offer had been a neat instance of payment for services rendered, but it would be a valid offer only if Magnus agreed that his efforts to persuade Julia were worthy of recompense. Mark knew that Magnus considered him an incapable, nearly insignificant man, but he did not think that Magnus would cheat him. Certainly none of them could permit Julia to leave England.

Mark lay back in the chair, his head lolling and the blanket scratching his skin as if it were sandpaper. Julia still lay motionless beneath the sheet. Magnus and Lily were right about her needing a long rest, under supervision. All he had been doing was humoring her along any direction that seemed to lead away from Magnus, but perhaps it was now time to be more thoughtful. His academic career, in truth, was at its nadir; Mark could not imagine enduring much longer the boredom of teaching. His book was a phantasm, a dead thing which had lived only in illusion. Teaching was his only income, apart from the beggarly amount Greville Lofting had bequeathed him. There had been no nonsense about equal division of wealth in that old bastard's head. Not that, in comparison to Julia, he'd had much anyhow.

She groaned from the mattress, and muttered something.

He had expected his headache, which had descended on him when he was leaving Plane Tree House and had not left for four hours, to return with Julia's arrival, but he was surprisingly free of it. It was, he thought, because of her condition: a Julia so weak, so dependent, could not pull whatever trigger it was that launched his headache. (For in these past few days, it felt like that, as though a bullet, a red-hot foreign substance, had tumbled into his brain.)

He heard Julia's voice: "Mark?"

"Here," he grunted. "In the chair."

"Why aren't you with me?"

"I was thinking."

"Uh-huh," Julia offered, already half asleep again.

Had she used to talk in the night, half muttering, to Magnus? Wanting him to come to her bed? This thought stirred Mark, and he sat up in the chair and examined Julia's sprawl beneath his sheet. Her face was dug deep into the pillow, her hair bursting out around it. With her hair disarranged and uncombed, she looked far more like most of the other women whose heads had rested on that pillow.

She pronounced his name, very clearly, in her sleep.

Involuntarily, Mark suddenly imagined Magnus' heavy, serious body straddling hers, Magnus' belly pressing on Julia, Magnus opening her legs, Magnus' confidence taking her. She was his. Mark could see Magnus' arms circling her, her legs bent at his hips. His penis surged forward against the roughness of the cloth, and he threw the blanket off and crossed the room to climb onto the mattress beside Julia. A little later that night, after a quick struggle with buttons and elastic, he felt his mind traveling over enormous distances as he plunged atop his brother's wife. It was like making love on LSD, but even that had been a pedestrian experience beside this, for during all of the night remaining, hallucinations and visions lifted and inspired him: he was a gorgeously sexual bird, fertilizing the air. Innocence irradiated the air, canceling odors of sweat and old cooking.

In the morning Mark left the flat to shop for eggs, bacon and bread, and Julia, alone in the squalor of his room, began to weep. She felt abandoned and helpless, beached on a gray shore. Even Mark could not restore her to the ordinary human world or save her from the bleakness. She cried for a few minutes, and then arranged the sheets atop the mattress. They bore ridges of dirt and crusty stains, which Julia rather consciously overlooked. She was wondering if the police had discovered the body of David Swift; and if they had, if the papers would carry a story about the death. Swift was not a general's son. Someone had to be told what had happened. Mark had only pretended to believe her; and she had been too weary and shocked to fully explain the events of the night. She realized that she knew only one person she could telephone.

Lily picked up the receiver on the first ring, thinking that Magnus had discovered what had to be done to have his wife safely hospitalized.

"Yes," she said, and looked dartingly around the room at her Stubbs horse, her vases, the Persian screen. Julia's voice came to her, tired and faint, making each of her possessions seem locked in its place.

"Lily? Lily, I have to tell you some things. Listen to me."

"Where in the world are you?" Lily swiftly said. "Magnus and I tried to talk to you last night. You weren't at home."

"Well, now I am," Julia lied. "I was out last night."

"Do you think that's wise, darling? All of us feel that you should get as much rest as possible. I'd be happy to help you move some of your things over here, so you wouldn't be alone. . . ."

"It's too late for that, Lily," came Julia's faint voice.

"Darling, speak more directly into the mouthpiece."

"You must believe me, Lily. No one else will. I can't talk to anyone else." She sounded far-off and desperate, and Lily for a moment visualized her sailing off westward, a figure in an airplane getting smaller and smaller in the sky.

"You've been fretting again," she said. "Why don't you come over and tell me about it?"

"Lily, Magnus is Olivia's father. I know it. He used to meet Heather Rudge— in my house. There's a picture of them together here. Taken less than a year before Olivia's birth. He's Olivia's father, Lily. That's why she picked me. I saw her kill someone last night. David Swift. He knew her, and he talked too much, like Paul Winter. She made someone kill them. I came in just after, and he was dying. I'm next, Lily, there's no one left but me. I'm next."

Lily scarcely heard the latter half of this announcement. When Julia had said Magnus was the girl's father, Lily had immediately felt that she was speaking the truth. Rage at Magnus' deception and lies flashed through her like an electrical explosion. She felt completely betrayed. "You're certain about Magnus," she managed to say.

"I'm sure," came Julia's bruised voice. "That's why it was me she wanted. It's the pattern."

"My God," said Lily, immediately seeing another pattern. "Do you see what you are saying? Julia, if what you are saying is true, there *is* a reason why you were chosen by Olivia. Magnus . . ."

"Magnus and Kate," Julia whispered. "Magnus and Olivia. The difference is that Olivia was evil. And she can work in people's minds."

"Julia, this is important," said Lily, her mind spinning among possibilities.

"Look for that man's name in the newspapers," Julia said, not listening to her. "Swift. He was one of her gang. He told me about Geoffrey Braden's murder. She had him killed. I saw his body—I saw his blood, all over him."

"Ju—"

But Julia had hung up. Lily dialed her number and, her mind still whirling, listened to the phone ringing in Julia's house. "Pick it up," she urged, "pick it up, pick it up." Eventually she depressed the button with a finger and after hearing the dial tone again, tried Magnus' number at Gayton Road.

"Lily," he said. "I can't just flick a switch, you know. There are a couple of options. It'll all happen. I'll let you know tonight."

"That's not what I rang you about," she said angrily. "I want to ask you something, and I want you to tell me the truth, Magnus."

"What now?" The boredom in his voice made her furious.

"Were you the father of that wretched child? The Rudge girl? I've just spoken to Julia, and she says she has proof you were her father."

"Syntax, Lily," Magnus said. "Did you say proof?" His voice came through with an amused incredulity that was as good as a confession.

"She knows that you were—I think those were her words. I want you to tell me the truth, Magnus."

He said, "I don't know the truth."

"Meaning?"

"I don't know if I was her father. I could have been. So could two or three others. She bled us all for money. Perhaps the child was a committee effort. Some weekends, one nearly had to punch a clock."

"You are a fool, Magnus. You could have told me that a week ago, and perhaps done a deal of good. Now I expect that you shall be lucky ever to see Julia again."

"Can't you do *anything* while I find out about the paperwork? I can't do it all myself."

"You petulant fool," she snarled at him. "At the moment, I am going to see if I can find anything in the morning papers about a fellow named Swift. Your wife says she saw him killed."

"For God's sake, now you're going mad too."

"Good-bye." Lily delicately put the phone back in its cradle and went to the couch, where the morning's *Times* and *Daily Telegraph* had been folded over one of the arms. She ripped the two papers off the couch and spread them on the carpet. She flipped through the *Times*, scanning the headlines on each page. When she had reached the sports news, she went through it backwards, making sure. No mention of a David Swift, no unexplained deaths at all.

With great relief, she turned to the *Daily Telegraph*. It was a hallucination of Julia's, another reason for locking her away. Nothing, of course, on the first page, and nothing on the second. Lily scanned the third page with a growing certainty that she had been rushed into a foolish panic; she would have to find a face-saving formula for apologizing to Magnus. A headline on the fifth page, two inches from the bottom, put an end to these thoughts. KNIFE DEATH, it read.

> The body of David Swift, 37, was discovered by police in his Islington flat during the early hours of Thursday morning. Police were investigating the open doorway to the flat when they found the body of Mr. Swift, who appeared to have died from multiple stab wounds. Witnesses located by Islington police say that an unidentified woman was seen leaving Mr. Swift's flat approximately one hour before discovery of the body.

Lily hastily read the short paragraph again, and then stood and dropped the paper to the floor. It was true: Julia had been seen running from that man's flat. Magnus was Olivia's father. The pattern she had seen while talking to Julia became clearer and clearer to her. Julia was unable to see it, and so had invented another pattern to suit the facts she could acknowledge. All along, Lily had dismissed Julia's stories because there had been no compelling reason for her to have been the object of a genuine manifestation. Now the reason seemed so obvious—so glaring—she could not think how she had failed to guess it. (But she shamefully knew how much her dismissal of Julia's story had to do with pride.) Blood rushed to her face. Lily walked to her window and looked down at the empty park. Rain leaked from a dark sky.

Now more than ever it was important to get Julia out of that house. Suppose Olivia Rudge were to appear there . . . Lily shuddered, and returned to the telephone. She was afraid, she recognized, for all of them. If Julia were right, none of them were safe. Suppose Rosa really *had* seen something, and had died for it? Lily groaned, and picked up the telephone to ring Mark.

Julia knew that Lily would call her back at the wrong number. Then what would she do? Look in the paper, she hoped. Surely a man could not meet a violent death in London and not have a paragraph written about him. Someone has to believe me, Julia thought, and now there's only Lily. Mark's attitude, whenever he wasn't in bed, was distant, doctorly, calming; she had seen that he hadn't believed her, and had been surprised that, even in shock as she had been, she was not more wounded by his disbelief. It was confirmation of her isolation: what was Olivia's atmosphere if not that? The atmosphere of the rooftop dream.

She sat on the edge of the mattress, her mind vague, uncertain of what to do. Eggs and bacon had been Mark's idea. For Julia, the thought of food was almost anthropological in its remoteness. What she wanted, though her vagina throbbed, was to cling to Mark again, to put her arms about him and nest beside him without thought, in a deep blankness.

She allowed her eyes to rove over his incredible flat. The floor was crowded with articles of clothing and plates and cloudy milk bottles. Books were heaped in odd places. Underlying the general odor of Gauloise cigarettes was an odd grainy smell like that of an uncleaned birdcage.

She unsteadily stood up, having decided to do something about the floor. When she bent to pick up several plates stacked together, blood pounded into her head and she saw moving blots of red and black, and sat heavily on the mattress again until her vision cleared. The room seemed to wobble about her. She touched the plates. Brown stuff had hardened on the top surface, and glued all the plates into a single unit. Julia held them in her lap until the room ceased to vibrate and then carried them into the kitchen. The sink was already jammed with china and glasses submerged in cold greasy water, so Julia set the plates on top of the little fridge and returned to the other room to pick up more things. When she came back to the kitchen with two glasses and two milk bottles, she found two dozen webby milk bottles ranked on a ledge behind the sink. Complex green spidery growths and furry tendrils linked the bottles. Julia rattled them backward and squeezed in her two bottles.

The telephone shrilled from the other room and Julia hesitated before she left the kitchen to stand over it. Perhaps Lily had guessed where she was: did she care to hide it any longer? Indifferent, she lifted the telephone. A rich breathy female voice floated into her ear. "Mark, what *have* you been up to lately? Annis said you were positively rude to her, and garbled something about meditation; well, *we* think you've got some Great Love taking up all your time, it's just not like you, why don't we all meet sometime at the Rising Sun to—"

"He's not home," Julia said and hung up on a whoop of startled laughter which caused her to drop the telephone. When it hit the floor, the plastic base cracked apart like the shell of a snail.

Julia wandered across the room to Mark's desk. She sat in his chair and pulled the drapes to one side. Rain fell into the gray well before the window, flattening the few spears of grass which had struggled up through the concrete. A wedge of gray sky hung in the upper corner of the window, seeming out of perspective, crazily tilted. Julia touched Mark's typewriter and then licked the dust off her finger. She could not make sense of the telephone call. Now, behind her, the broken phone began to buzz periodically like an angry bee. Great Love? Annis? Was that a girl's name? Julia could not make her mind understand the words of the girl on the telephone. She felt as though she had been jeered at, made fun of, by the whoop of laughter. Even that had been in a Knightsbridge accent. She put her head down on the cool keys of the typewriter.

His desk, his books, his papers. He was working on something. She felt intense gratitude for his working, for his being part of that comfortable line of men who did things, who made bridges and books and decisions. She caressed the stack of paper beside the typewriter. Mark. His name seemed to heat in her chest. He could not be blamed for his inability to accept her mad story. Later in the day she could show him a newspaper and prove that she had not invented the death of David Swift.

The afternoon seemed an impossible distance away; even thinking seemed to require an unreasonable amount of effort. She was sure that the breathy woman on the telephone had laughed at her. Again, she thought of leaving for America.

She rolled down onto the mattress, hoping that Mark would soon return. The door of a wardrobe gaped open beside the mattress, and Julia idly looked at Mark's few clothes hanging on wire hangers. He seemed to possess only one necktie, nearly six inches wide, silvery in color, with a sunburst painted on it in orange. Julia thought of Magnus' neat rows of striped ties, hundreds of them, and managed to smile. Mark owned a green tweed suit which clearly derived from the late fifties and looked as though it had not been worn since then. Magnus had seemed not to care for clothes, but he had owned a lot of them. He had, for instance, owned seven pairs of shoes, all exactly alike and made by the same bootmaker on Cork Street who had made his father's shoes. Mark appeared to own only boots, no shoes at all. Black and brown boots, one pair of each, with zips up the side. One pair of sandals. Something brown and partially hidden by a bag at the back of the wardrobe caught her eye, and she looked closely at it. The particular woody shade of brown was familiar, and even as she registered its familiarity, she felt the beginnings of alarm, as if a bell had begun to ring.

She reached from the edge of the mattress into the closet and twitched the bag aside with her fingers. She was looking at the backs of a pair of shoes with chunky low heels and a benchmark stamped discreetly into the leather just at the bottom of the back seam. It was a small letter *D*, and stood for David Day, who had made the shoes. She had purchased them four years ago, and even now she could remember how much they cost. They were the shoes she had lost climbing in her window on her first night in Ilchester Place.

Julia stared at the backs of the shoes for a moment, panting slightly, her mind unable to reckon with what she was seeing. She reached into the wardrobe as though it contained a rattlesnake and extracted the shoes. Their uppers were water-stained and scruffy from their two days outdoors. It was Mark, not Magnus, who had taken them.

"Wait," she told herself, touching the brown shoes. Her heart had begun to thrum. She looked at her right wrist where she wore the little green bracelet Mark had given her. Something taken, something given, Mrs. Fludd had said. Julia tugged off the bracelet and dropped it onto the dirty sheet. Mark had appeared in Olivia's wake several times; sympathetic magic, she had once thought it was. But he had appeared every time, every time.

Could he have just found her shoes? Then why would he hide them in the wardrobe?

Receptive, Mrs. Fludd had said. *He wants to be filled, like a bottle.*

Julia became aware she was making a noise in her throat, but found she could not control or stop it. Her heart seemed to thunder, banging her rib cage like a noisy drum. She plucked at her bandage and tore it off her wrist. She could feel herself breaking, as though she were a thin bone. The long wound on her wrist pouted, a ragged weal along the skin, and she tore it apart with the fingers of her right hand, separating the lips of the wound. A bright surprising ribbon of blood appeared in the gash.

He'll know, her mind said. She tore at the wound and the ribbon of blood bannered out across her hand and onto Mark's bed. She rubbed the shoes in her blood and left them on the bed. Her arm began to throb. She realized that the noise in her throat had subsided to a choked gurgling noise, half a snarl. She printed the mark of her wound on Mark's sheets.

When she stood from the mess she had made, she wound the bandage around her wrist again, ignoring the fresh stains on her trousers, and then ran toward the door. She had to get out before Mark's return. Her vagina throbbed in the same rhythm as her wrist. Wounds. She gasped, realizing that five minutes before, she'd been thinking about safety. There was no safety, only its illusion.

Julia opened the door and looked fearfully up the steps, as if she expected to see Mark Berkeley smiling down at her. Rain filtered gauzily down onto her face. Julia went up the six steps to the street. Within seconds, the thin material of her blouse had adhered coldly to her skin. She ran down the block, pursued by Olivia's taunting smile and the thought of Mark. Only one escape, only one safety, existed. Kate was there before her. In her haste and fright, she forgot the Rover until she had reached the end of the block.

Her house seemed as hot as Ecuador. Julia slammed the front door and bolted it, knowing that Hazel Mullineaux had seen her come limping up from the sidewalk, her hair streaming and her clothing soaked. Her neighbor had been standing at the side door of her home, her face white and gleaming beneath the cover of a wide black umbrella. She had looked like an advertisement for skin cream. Breathing hard, Julia waited behind the door for what she knew would happen. Before thirty seconds were out, the bell rang down the hall. "Go away," Julia whispered.

Hazel Mullineaux knocked on the door, then rang the bell again.

"I'm all right," Julia said, a little louder.

After knocking again, Hazel Mullineaux bent to lift the flap of the mail slot and called, "Mrs. Lofting? Do you need any help?"

"Go away," Julia said. "I don't need your help."

"Oh!" Julia could tell that Hazel was kneeling outside the door. She probably looks adorable doing that, Julia thought.

"I thought you looked . . . well, upset," came the low voice through the slot.

"Leave me alone," Julia said. "Get away from my house."

"I don't mean to intrude."

"I'm glad to hear it. Please go." Julia remained leaning against the door until she heard her neighbor's footsteps go reluctantly down to the pavement. Then she went into the dark living room and yanked the cord of the telephone out of the wall. Holding the severed telephone in her hands, Julia noticed that the weeks of abnormal heat had effected some chemical change in the walls of the house, for the wallpaper had buckled in places; one strip curled down from the ceiling like a dog's tongue. The whole room seemed to have aged during the weeks of heat, to have become wrinkled and shabby. The McClintocks' furniture had lost its solid fat Victorian look, and now appeared to be peeling, like sunburned skin. The glue had cracked in one of the dining-room chairs. The carpet lapped up at one end of the room.

Julia dropped the useless telephone to the floor. Her wounded wrist, the muscles in her calves, and her vagina all ached. The flesh on her face felt as though it were blubber, puffing out from the bones. She could trust no one.

Upstairs, she sat on the edge of her bed, waiting. The house hung emptily about her. No one could telephone now, and she would not answer the door. The others knew what they needed to know. It was Mark or Magnus, one of them. One of them had been used by Olivia Rudge, and Mrs. Fludd had seen it weeks before. She had been tricked by Mark. It was Mark. It could be Mark.

Julia got up and moved to her desk and pulled a sheet of paper and a pencil from a drawer. Someone would have to know, or Olivia would never be stopped, she would keep on filling people's minds, using them, going from one to another like a disease.

If I am found dead, she wrote rapidly, *it will be no accident. If I am found dead in this room or anywhere else, whatever the cause of death may appear to be, I shall have been murdered. The murderer will be either my husband or his brother, Mark Berkeley. One of these two is planning to kill me. This same person will have been the cause of the death of Rosa Fludd, and will probably have killed Captain Paul Winter and David Swift. (But maybe not.) This is because— This has to do with a dead child named Olivia Rudge, who died in the same way as my own child. My husband Magnus was also the father of Olivia Rudge. Look her up in the newspapers for the year 1950. But leaving the supernatural aside—since it may prejudice the opinion of whoever reads this, I beg you to know that I am not suicidal, and that my death will in no way be an accident. PLEASE KNOW THIS.*

Without rereading what she had written, Julia folded the paper and inserted it into the pages of her address book, and then slid the book between two sweaters in a drawer. Then she lay down on her bed and stared up into the heat and watched patterns move across the surface of the ceiling. She waited. Gleeful noises seemed to well up from other parts of the house. Hot air and a feral stink blew about her. Eventually she swallowed three of her sleeping pills.

12

Once, everything had been different. There had been a pretty, rather placid young woman named Julia Lofting, who had lived in North London with her successful husband and their beautiful daughter, and all three of them had unthinkingly led happy, contented lives, each devoted to the unity they made, each devoted to the other . . . once there had been a girl with a great deal of money named Julia Freeman, and she had married an older man, an Englishman named Magnus Lofting, and lived with him in London, tolerating his infidelities and his angers for the sake of their daughter (her daughter) . . . once a confused, uncertain American woman named Julia lived in a house with her daughter, seeing her husband late in the evenings when he came home from one of his drinking clubs . . . there had once been a beautiful and imaginative child named Kate Lofting . . . but she was dead . . . once there had been a couple, Magnus and Julia, with a nice house but not as nice a house as they could afford because they (she) hated extravagance, and with two cars and one daughter, and they'd had few friends outside the family because many people did not like Magnus and because Julia was a bit shy and their daughter was all they needed, really . . . once an American girl had thrown herself at a man named Magnus and made a daughter with him, she used her money to make him sleep with her (marry her) . . . once there had been a girl everybody liked. Julia looked up at the cracked ceiling of her bedroom, thinking of the girl she had been, her father's darling (her hair was her best feature). She waited. Her best and truest self was in the past which had sent her Olivia Rudge. Whose father she had married. She was too tired to move from her bed, and her mind spun from version to version.

From downstairs came the noise of a rampage—she could hear glass breaking, a series of popping, hollow explosions, and ripping noises, fabric being torn. The noises had started in the kitchen and then moved into the dining room. It sounded now like chairs being thrown up against the wall. I wanted to set you free, Julia thought, meaning that I wanted to send you away in peace. But you don't want peace. You want control. You hate all of us, and you hate this house.

I did set you free, but in the wrong way. Wood splintered somewhere in the house, and this sharp sound was immediately followed by another series of popping explosions. The cups in the dining room. Then the broader, flatter sound of the china plates being broken. A bottle of some kind smashed against a wall? Wine? Whiskey? Julia, half in a daze, sniffed at the air but caught only a faint odor of excrement.

"It's settled."

"In what way?"

"We need a certificate signed by her physician and one other. Two doctors at the hospital, Dr. Whatever and another one, will agree to sign it. Then she goes in for a period of examination. It's a temporary order, but it gives me time to look into ways of keeping her there out of trouble. Does that satisfy you?"

"I don't know what would satisfy me now."

"Lily, don't go soft on me. This was really your idea, you know."

"My idea for your good, brother."

"For ours. And hers."

"Chiefly yours."

Magnus looked across the room to where Lily sat on her delicate little couch beside the Persian screen. She was staring at him oddly. Her eyes seemed slightly larger than usual, and the hazel irises appeared to swim in the surrounding white. Lily's whole face was pale. "For God's sake, Lily," he said, "are you still angry with me about that wretched child? You're making it all up, you know, I did not lie to you. I never did see the child. Anyone could have been her father."

"Anyone wasn't."

"It's a trifle late for a blood test, Lily."

"I wish you weren't so obtuse at times."

He looked at her in complete puzzlement. "Lily, let me explain our position. Julia can be put into the hospital as soon as I have the doctors' signatures. That should be no later than Tuesday. I have control over all monies, whether held jointly or separately, in case of Julia's hospitalization or death. I mention the latter only as the extreme case. The legal point in question is mental incapacity— which shall be proven by the doctors' authorization of our request that she be involuntarily hospitalized. It is very simple."

"Try to ring her," Lily ordered. "Right now."

"What? Do you want to bring her here? There's really no need for that now, since the doctors—"

"*Try to ring her.*"

"Lily, what in the world is going on?"

"I'm terrified, you idiot," she said. "She has been telling us the truth all along, and I was too stupid and vain to recognize it. She is in mortal danger."

"What in the world . . ." Magnus stared at her in disbelief. "Are you telling me that you believe in that cod's wallop now? Didn't you just assure me, two days ago, that it was all fantasy? Didn't you say that?"

"Yes," she admitted. "But I was wrong. We have to try to save her life. Please ring her, Magnus. I want to know that she is still safe."

Magnus reluctantly lifted himself heavily from his chair and padded across the room to the telephone. He dialed Julia's number and listened silently for some time. "No answer," he said. "What's this all about, Lily?"

"Revenge," she answered. "Olivia Rudge's revenge."

That was it, Julia thought, listening to the savage noises from downstairs. It was revenge. She hated being thwarted, and Heather had cut off her career: so Heather was part of her revenge, Mrs. Braden immured in her bedroom was part of her revenge, and all of her gang had shared in it too, seeing their lives disintegrate or grind to powder, nothing accomplished except by the severest penance.

She had been meant to buy the house. Olivia had reached out and found her, the only woman who could release her into the world again.

If only Kate had not tried to swallow that piece of meat . . . if only she and Magnus had waited longer for the ambulance. Julia seemed not to be lying on her bed, but to be suspended above a thrashing seacoast, sharp upthrust rocks and seething water. Her skin was boiling, as with fever. She imagined holding Kate in her arms. But Kate was in that small deep hole, in that small box in the deep, deep hole. In wretched Hampstead cemetery. She wanted to carry Kate away from here. To float with her, far above the sea and the rocks.

Then she saw Kate with her back turned to her. It was what she had seen before Mrs. Fludd stopped the séance. *I am responsible,* she thought, without knowing what she meant.

A black bird zipped past Mark's head and muttered some message to him, as it would to another bird. It was a single word. *Brief,* perhaps, or *free.* Or *be.* He watched the bird whirl off into the glowing area above the tops of the trees, where the sky was unnaturally pink. The cottony undersides of the thick clouds, which had just ceased to release their drizzle of rain, seemed to reveal some incandescent color laid across their upper surfaces. They looked as though they had been painted by Turner, and Mark, thinking this, was moved to the edge of tears. His scalp tingled. Birds spoke to him, he walked beneath Turner clouds. Since completing his last meditation, he had felt almost unbearably, uncomfortably happy—he had reached ecstasy. Colors of the grass and trees boomed out at him, as if they were shouted through loudspeakers; so many different greens! He felt that he had never truly seen any of these shades before, how they rippled next to each other, jumped forward or receded in space. Color was a stupendous bounty.

Julia had bled on his sheets. That too seemed a sign of grace. Blood after making love. He felt as though Julia were his other half, as though they shared the same limbs, or the same heart. She had dug the shoes out of his closet, knowing in what love he had spirited them away from her garden after finding them one morning. He'd had to look at her house, he'd walked all round it, passing his hands over the rough brick, almost swooning. Even his headache had not diminished his joy. Julia had left Magnus, and she would be his.

She was his. He moved dazedly through Holland Park, nearly alone on the paths, chiming with this knowledge. He had flown deep into her; he knew her bones and joints. Julia was light and vision. And a creature of blood, a furnace of it. *Be,* the bird had said to him. Traveling toward Julia, he was traveling toward blessedness. A pure greedy joy smashed drunkenly at him. Queenly, she was waiting. *Be.* He staggered under the impact of it.

A girl walking slowly in front of him lowered her umbrella with a motion of such grace that he nearly sobbed aloud. He recognized the back of her head and neck, where black hair fell down over a brown leather jacket. Mark quickly crossed the ground between himself and the girl and linked his arm into hers, laughing. When she twisted toward him, startled and a little frightened, he kissed her familiar mouth and felt his soul expanding with a scream of happiness.

"I can't believe this," Magnus said, still holding the telephone. "I tried to persuade you that there might be something to Julia's story, recall that? And you were certain that it was all a delusion. You convinced me. I cannot be convinced back again, Lily." He set the receiver back in its cradle, very gently, a sign Lily knew quite well: he was rapidly reaching the demarcation between annoyance and outright irritation.

"Perhaps not," she said. "It makes little difference whether or not you are persuaded. But do think back, Magnus—what did you see on that day you thought you saw Kate?"

"How can I answer that? I don't know what I saw. The reflection of a cloud, a flash of sun on the window. . . ."

"No. I mean, what did you think you saw?"

He looked at her in disgust. "I am not going to be made a fool of, Lily."

"Tell me. Just tell me what you saw."

"Kate. Standing in the window of Julia's bedroom."

"How do you know it was Kate? Was she facing you?"

"She needn't to. In fact, the girl I thought I saw was facing the other way, and I saw only the back of her head."

"It might not have been Kate! It might have been the other one!" Lily half-started from her chair. "Magnus, that's it. You saw Olivia Rudge. She wanted you to see her, and to think that she was Kate. She wanted to hurt and confuse you."

"Lily," Magnus said slowly, "I have never interfered with your enthusiasms, and I have never jeered at them. But if you are telling me that I saw an apparition in that window—"

"What did you feel when you went into her house that day? Didn't you tell me that you were terrified?"

"I was spooked. You told me that yourself. I was also drunk."

"No, Magnus. You felt her. You felt her evil. She hates you too."

"My God," Magnus said. "This is a nest of ninnies. What reasoning is behind all of this? Why should this little demon out of the past suddenly appear again?"

"Because of Julia," she said. "She needed Julia to free her. Both of your daughters were stabbed to death by their mothers. Julia was what she needed."

First I gave birth to Kate, Julia thought, and then I gave birth to Olivia. But part of Olivia is still in me. I complete her. The sleeping pills and lack of food made her mind swim about a general focus, which was her awareness of the noises from the ground floor. Things were still being smashed. The suffocating heat that dried her throat and burned her eyes seemed to carry her some inches above her bed and leave her floating above a vast, undefined space into which she could be spilled at any moment. Julia knew that this was due to a warp, a wrinkle in her mind that was a part of Olivia. She wished to read, to bring herself back into gravity, but she was too weak to pick up any of the books on the bedside table. A wind seemed to blow through the house, hot and African. The glass across one of the McClintocks' paintings shattered, accompanied by screams of laughter. Then she heard the thunking noise of the painting's being kicked in.

Maybe all this is just in my head, she thought. *Would that make it less true?* Indeed, everything in the world seemed crowded into her head. The smell of beasts and burned skin settled about her.

"A rape, Mark? Not in your style, I should have thought." Annis stood before him, breathing a little heavily, her face flushed. He could see the place on her full lower lip where he'd bitten it. "I thought I was being sent away, anyhow," she said.

"Lovely, sweet Annis," Mark said, holding her again, "darling, lovely, gorgeous, sexy Annis, how could I send you away?" He laughed at both her absurdity and his own, bubbling up within him.

"Is meditation responsible for these moods? I think I'd advise a little rest. Are you up on something?"

"On you, Annis, on you," he chanted, and swung her around.

She pushed at his arms. "Mark, put me down. Mark, I don't like this."

He whooped with laughter, seeing himself from both within and without, and nearly fell down. "Are you going somewhere? Let's go to a pub. Let's go to a pub and hold hands. I was just noticing how the sky looks like a Turner. Don't you think?"

She looked at the sky half with genuine interest, half with bemusement. "It looks like a slate roof, if you want my opinion. You know, you don't have to act like this with me. I'm perfectly willing to start seeing you again. But I thought you had some new interest in your life."

"On the contrary, dear Annis, I am shedding some of the old interests. I decided to quit teaching. I'm just going to travel for a while. Travel with me, Annis. You'd look lovely on a boat." He began to laugh uncontrollably, and fell onto a bench. Annis and Julia shared one substance, and Mark giddily witnessed Julia's features shining through the other's face. When she turned away from him in irritation, he caught her wrist and pulled her down beside him. "I'm serious, let's have a drink and talk about it." He looked into her wide, beautiful, hungry face and felt himself turn on all the voltage he possessed. Annis' face broke over him like a wave.

"Well," she said. "I'm going somewhere now. How about lunch at one?"

"Lunch at one, what fun," he sang. "Only an hour away." Joy seemed to smash at his ribs again, and he gripped her hand. "Name two places you want to go to, Annis."

"Well, I've never seen California," she said. "I can't think of any other place I'd like to go."

"Europe?"

"Europe is boring. I'd settle for California."

"You'll have it."

"Doesn't it take a lot of money to get there?"

"Doesn't everything come through meditation? Lord Buddha provides, Annis, Lord Buddha provides."

"We're going to have everything," Magnus said, having by now passed firmly into outright anger, "we're going to have the lot, and you decide to get mysterious and orphic. Aren't we going to have everything you wanted? I have a mad wife who's going to be locked away for God knows how long, but you'll have the bleeding lot, Lily. What do you think you're trying to do to me?"

"Self-pity isn't your most attractive trait," she said. "What I think I am trying to do, as you put it, is to tell the truth at last. Look, Magnus. Suppose that Julia came to you with some idea about a point of law that you'd been thinking about for months? Suppose she said something about it at breakfast?"

"Bugger the analogies," he said, even angrier, and causing her more fear than she knew she could afford to reveal.

"I'll tell you what you'd do. You'd ignore her, and resent her incursion on your special territory. That's the way I felt."

"The law is not a ridiculous bundle of lies and fantasies!" he shouted.

She merely looked at him, not daring to speak further.

When he turned away and slammed his fist into the countertop, she waited for him to settle down again—she could see his shoulders sinking back to their normal level, and his neck lose its swelling, as if it were shedding layers of tissue—she said, "Try to ring her again. I am afraid for her, Magnus."

"Damn you," he said, but said it quietly.

She said to his back, "Someone killed those two men. Julia knew about it before they were in the papers."

"Are you sure? She's no fortune-teller."

Lily thought back to her last conversation with Julia. "I *think* so. She told me about the second one, certainly. The Swift man. She was in his flat."

"Then I'm glad he's dead."

"She was there to warn him about Olivia Rudge—I think that's what she said. Or I may have gathered it."

"That's two things you're vague on. You're not terribly persuasive."

"And Mrs. Fludd was killed because she saw Olivia."

"Nonsense. Wait. Did you imply that Julia was in the Swift man's flat when he was killed?"

"That's what she told me."

"She told you that she saw him—what? Die? Be killed? What did she say?"

"I can't remember. She said that she was there."

"*Damn*," Magnus said loudly. "Didn't she inform the police?"

"I shouldn't imagine that she thought they had much chance against a ghost."

"Ghosts don't murder people," Magnus said and went quickly back to the telephone. After dialing and listening intently, his lips working in and out, he said, "Still no answer."

"Then she has either drugged herself to sleep or she's gone out," Lily said. "We must do something quickly, Magnus. Olivia is after her. I know it. She's already tried to kill her once."

"I wonder if Julia is actually madder than you. You should both be put away." He considered a second, containing his anger, and said, "Think about this, Lily. If Julia was right, then aren't we all endangered? You and I as well as Julia? After all, we know about Olivia too."

"We're all touched by it, we're all soiled," she answered him. "Mark too, I should imagine. We may be in as much danger as she is."

"Rubbish."

"Remember how you felt inside that house," she said. "She hates you too, Magnus. She's enjoyed torturing you."

Julia was carrying Kate, a bundle no heavier than an armful of leaves and twigs, to the hospital. Kate was injured, and it was urgent that Julia find the hospital immediately: she could feel some warm fluid soaking into the sleeves of her blouse. Down grimy, vacant streets she was wandering, looking up at barred doorways for the name of the hospital. It was her fault that she could not find the hospital, that instead she was trudging through these gritty hopeless streets, looking exhaustedly into one filthy sunless court after another, dirty cobblestones . . . she had failed, and she knew that Kate had already died, that the merest breeze would lift away the feather of her body. Soon she would be on the bare rooftop, surrounded by failure and loss, carrying them within her. She saw herself turning the knife from Kate's body and turning it toward herself.

Footsteps ran through the house, raising the smells of heat and lions.

She wandered through these hopeless streets, looking for the hospital that could undo what already had been done.

"Where are you going?" She watched tensely as he rushed around her flat, gathering up his raincoat and umbrella.

"I have to get out of this room," he said as calmly as he could. "Before I deliberately break something, I am going to take a short walk. *You* ring her."

"Will you be back? Magnus, please . . ."

"I'll be back," he said harshly, almost barking the final word. As she watched, half-cowering by the door to the kitchen, he turned away from her and thundered across the floor like a bison. When he left he banged the door with such force that he split a section of the jamb.

Julia moved fractionally toward consciousness, her heart thudding, aware that the hand she had turned toward herself had not been Magnus'. It was a woman's hand, like hers. It was hers. Her mouth flooded with pain and a residue like tar, and she realized moments later that she had bitten halfway through her tongue. She had recognized her hand from the dream. She swallowed a trickle of blood, not really feeling the pain for longer than the time that lay between the vision of the woman's hand with the steak knife in its fingers and the recognition that it was hers. Instead of pain, there was a drumming sensation through her tongue. Her entire body seemed as dry as a cracked riverbed. Kate's twig-light, leaf-light body lifted out of her arms. Her lips went numb.

In the next instant she had fled back into the condition of the drugs, and was walking up filthy stairs to the bleak rooftop. She knew every discoloration and stain on the walls, every warp of the stairs.

Mark lay sprawled on wet grass, feeling the ground damply claim his shoulders and buttocks. He was dimly aware of the burnished tips of his new boots, gleaming a dark rich brownish gold all the way down the length of his body. His head was filled with birds. That he had just met and spoken to someone appeared miraculous to him, an unbelievable effort of coherence and will.

But I've seen her too, thought Lily, still facing the door and listening to Magnus go noisily down the stairs. It was the day I saw Rosa Fludd sitting on the park bench. She led me across the park. Was Rosa really there, or did she conjure her? She wanted me to see Magnus breaking into Julia's house. She wanted me to feel that sick disappointment. Perhaps Rosa came to me as a warning. She had warned Julia, and that day she was warning me. Lily sagged against the counter, felt the metal strip along the top of the wood dig into her hip.

Mark was moving at the center of a golden, glowing haze, a bowl which had settled down over him as he lay on the wet grass. He knew that this humming golden aura was the outward form of his headache, given him by his most successful meditations, and that it was transformingly beautiful proved the rarity, the absolute value of his mind. It proved also the absolute value of his exercises, even of the headaches, since they had transported him bodily into euphoria. Into paradise.

The trees past which he moved burned at him, the bark blistering in his vision and the leaves rattling like gold. He had felt like this before, but he could not remember when. His boots made the path shiver. If he hit hard enough with his heels, he could open a crack all the way to the planet's red, seething core.

Asleep now, Julia reached the opening to the roof and walked out onto baking tar paper that adhered tackily to the soles of her shoes. The sky into which she moved was a flat field of gray striped with vibrating, humming pink. The strange union of colors gripped the pit of her stomach and made her bowels full and watery. Her mouth drummed, lined with a bitter substance like tobacco juice. A pine needle pierced her tongue. She wanted Kate, but Kate was dead. Olivia raged beneath her in the empty house screeching with laughter. Even up on the flat roof, hopelessness pouring into her like salt, she could hear the noise from downstairs: hoarse screams, shouts, loud breakage. It no longer made any difference. She was watching herself as in a mirror. Her skin burned in anticipatory shame.

Lily pushed herself away from the counter and went unsteadily into the living room. She knelt before the telephone and with a shaking hand dialed Julia's number. Now instead of the ringing she expected, she heard only the bottomless space, filled with the echoes of static, which precedes the dial tone. She punched the button and the gray depthless space hung in the receiver. When she struck the button again, the depthless sound mercifully gave way to the dial tone. She tried Julia's number again, and heard the digits slot into connection; then a sound like that of a man falling through deep space, spinning away from life.

Lily banged the receiver down, waited until she felt safe enough to lift it again, made sure of the reassuring, chunky dial tone, and then dialed 100. She gave the operator Julia's number and waited.

"I'm sorry," the operator's twanging voice came back a minute later. "That number appears to be temporarily out of service."

"Why?" asked Lily. "What do you mean, out of service?"

"We are not permitted to offer that information," the operator disdainfully said. "You may speak to the supervisor."

"Yes."

"Hold, please."

Lily licked her lips and waited again. The silence in the telephone was furry and dense, more solid than the other. She listened to it for what seemed entire minutes before she could bear the waiting no more and hung up. Then she paced nervously in her living room, waiting for Magnus to return. She would not go to Ilchester Place alone.

Something flew along the upstairs hall, something infinitely despairing.

Slowly, with merciful intent, the knife in her hand slid into Kate's blocked throat. Her hand, the hand she had dreamed of turning toward herself, gripped the sleek little knife between thumb and finger, blade up. Kate uttered a half-conscious, choking noise and opened her eyes at the instant Julia began to carve into her throat. Kate's eyes were clouds. As in a mirror, the scene glinted at her from where it was happening at the flat edge of the roof, two figures bent together in a clumsy parody of love. She heard the door to her room bang open, and the hot wind gusted about her, making the scene before her and the pink-striped sky mist over, like a mirror. The one who wanted her was with her, and she whirled about on the roof and saw only desolation, dirty tar paper and a ruined sky. A white column of air blew toward her. She could see dust and scraps of paper whirl about inside it, spinning crazily. From somewhere below in the streets or from another side of the bedroom came a chortling sound she knew was the suppressed laughter of a small dark-skinned child whose name she could not remember. Strong arms braced her, and Olivia's smoldering odor invaded her nostrils and the white column of air whirled her into it, caught up with dust and scraps of old newspapers, dust and paper.

November

"You said you'd heard from Mark at last."

"Yes."

"Still in California?"

"Still in California, yes. Los Angeles."

"With that girl?"

"What was her name?"

"Annis."

"Odd sort of name for a girl. Or is it her patronym?"

"I don't know. He said that he was working at last. He'd found a job as maintenance man at something called a free school. Annis apparently has a little money each month."

"Do you think he will marry her?"

"I don't know whether she would marry him."

"I suppose that means you are becoming liberated, Lily."

She sniffed, and returned to her novel. When she was certain that he was not looking at her, she peeked across the room to the Sisley. Magnus had bought it for her in October. It hung in the place of the Stubbs drawing of the horse, although she had actually preferred the Stubbs horse. That had been relegated to the dining room.

"Mark has found his level at last," Magnus was saying. "Maintenance man. That means cleaner. I'm surprised that in the city of the angels the position is not referred to as maintenance engineer."

"He said he is also taking classes at a yoga institute."

"And belongs to the Che-Mao-Lumumba Revolutionary Tactics Chess League, no doubt. Didn't he tell you sometime before the inquest that it was yoga—those damnable exercises—which had finally pushed him over the edge? I should think he'd stay away from that sort of thing."

"You know very well it wasn't that. I don't imagine I need particularize."

"Please don't," said Magnus, sounding rather wounded. "But even he said that it played a part in his crackup."

"Julia played a larger part," Lily said maliciously.

"I think I just said that I did not require reminding. A very nasty shock, finding that my wife spent her last night before committing suicide in another man's bed. Especially that lunatic's bed. And the bloody fool didn't even possess the wit to see what Julia was going through." Magnus stared at his hands, which he had clasped tightly in his lap.

"We can be very grateful she left that—letter," Lily said, substituting the last word for "note." "It really did make things much clearer. I did think the coroner was right, don't you? To think that it proved instability of mind and was a clear indication of suicidal intent?"

"It offends me to see any man lead a jury to that extent," Magnus growled. "Coroners have far too much power in this country. Little gods. But yes, Lily, for the thousandth time, yes. I do think the coroner was right. Of course he was bloody right. There's no doubt about it. Any fool looking at the condition of that house and her car would know that her mind was gone. Now do you suppose we might have some tea? Actually, I'd rather have a drink. Would you get me one? No, I'll get it myself." He rose and moved toward the drinks trolley.

"Do have some cheese and biscuits, Magnus. There's a bit of Stilton on the sideboard."

"One cannot get a real Stilton anymore," he said. "Only supermarket rubbish. And have you seen or, heaven forbid, tasted what they have the gall to refer to as Sage Derby? It should be fed to birds. A decent pig wouldn't touch it."

"I just thought you might like a bite of some nice cheese and bikkies," she said, watching him splash whiskey into a tumbler. He took even more than she had expected. "I didn't mean to upset you."

"I . . . am . . . not . . . upset."

"Magnus, you know that I am deeply, truly grateful to you for not being affected by my silliness on that last day. Your steadfastness was simply remarkable. I lost my head, I was an utter fool, and you were so strong, you wouldn't be shaken, not in the least, and I am enormously grateful to you for that. I am grateful for your clear head and for your strength."

He glanced at her, and took a long swallow of his drink. "You shouldn't be grateful that I avoided being an ass. That's a negative sort of compliment." But she saw that he was calmer.

"And I shall never cease to be grateful that she wrote that note," she said. "If she hadn't given the game away by naming two of you, well . . ."

"Well," he said. "Tellingly put, Lily." He went back across the room and sat carefully in his chair. Magnus seemed to Lily to be gaining weight with every day. "I should have been in the soup, at least until they tried to 'pin it on' Mark."

"Do you know, I think that I appreciate how she felt. Not about you or even Mark, of course, but how she must have felt about *life*, when I was being so foolish on that day, I experienced the most remarkable sensation of utter hopelessness and despair. It was quite total. I felt utterly gray and washed-out, as though everything bright was long behind me. Julia must have felt something of that kind."

"Julia was not in a rational frame of mind. None of us can know what she thought about anything, much less something so vaporous as *life*." He looked at her sourly. "You didn't see the condition of that house."

"I couldn't go in there," she said. "I just couldn't do it." She switched to a safer topic. "Have you had any luck with the house?"

"Nobody is buying houses now, especially not houses as criminally expensive as that one. That officious twerp at Markham and Reeves told me the market is worse than it's been for fifteen years."

"Have you been to the cemetery yet, Magnus?" She had been earlier in the week, to see to the flowers.

"No, not really. Not since the funeral. I can't abide Hampstead cemetery. It looks like a suburb of Melbourne."

"Julia never liked it either."

"Rot. Utter rot. How can you claim to know such a thing?"

"Because she told me on the day of Kate's funeral. She said that she wished Kate could have been buried in an older cemetery. In Highgate."

"I don't believe that Julia held a firm opinion on a boneyard she saw only once, and then so exhausted she could scarcely stand upright."

Lily shrugged, irritated with him.

"Anyhow, nobody seems to want the damned house," he said. This was an oblique apology to her, and she peeked again at the Sisley painting. He was still talking, of course. "People look at it and they don't like it, for some reason. Did I tell you that that McClintock person wrote wondering if Julia would sell him his furniture back? Said he couldn't find any furniture like it in Barbados. He'd have had a shock if he could have seen his precious furniture."

"That frightens me," she said. "Please don't dwell on it."

"I wasn't about to dwell on anything," he said and gulped at his drink again. "Anything good on the goggle box tonight?"

"Nothing," she said. "I thought I might try reading one of those books Julia had. I'll be finished with this novel by tonight, and I thought I'd try one of hers. That's an odd coincidence, isn't it? I didn't have time to look at them for ages, and then I didn't want to. But it seems a pity to let them go unread. There's a nice long one about a rainbow. I think I'll begin with that, it looks a lovely read. She did have a lot of books, didn't she?"

"It was because she was friendless," Magnus said flatly.

"How can you, Magnus?" she said, genuinely surprised. "Julia had friends. You and I were certainly her friends. And I suppose Mark was a friend of a sort."

"Bloody Mark. I hope he falls under a bus."

"Mark has suffered a great deal."

Magnus turned away in impatience. "Are you sure there's nothing on the box? I'd like to watch something tonight."

Lily knew that this meant that he wished to spend the evening with her, and that he would fill it by insulting the television and all who watched it. She wished that he would leave—Magnus was in one of his carping moods, which lately annoyed Lily more than they once had. "Nothing you would care for, Magnus. You despise the television, as we both know. But," she added more from habit than desire, "you might stay for dinner. This is one of my vegetarian nights. I'll make a big salad."

Magnus shuddered. "I could get something from a restaurant and bring it back. I don't like these meatless Tuesdays of yours."

As neutrally as possible, she said, "If you wish."

"Right, then."

In exasperation, she thrust down her book and went over to the window on the terrace. Her flowers still bloomed vigorously, and were dazzlingly, violently colored in the damp gray air. To Lily, they looked like little flags of content-ment—they said *we, at least, have no problems.*

Behind her, Magnus cleared his throat. "Just out of curiosity, my darling, do you still go to those groups of yours?"

Lily looked into the deep green of the treetops.

"Not as often as before," she said.

"Why is that? Don't you fancy the new swami?"

She let her gaze travel down the rough, pitted bark of the trees. On this cold, cheerless November day few people lingered in the park, and the men and women on the long path rushed by, their hands deep in the pockets of their coats. They looked gray and insubstantial before the great trees, like smoke blown past.

"Oh, Mrs. Venable is acceptable," she said, not paying much attention to what she was saying. "I don't feel the same about the meetings." Now she was watching a child in a blue hooded coat recklessly ride a bicycle down the path, which was forbidden. None of the people on the path seemed to care, as if their opinions were smoke too. "But I don't like to disappoint the others," she said. The child swung off the bicycle and propped it against one of the trees. A girl's bicycle, Lily noticed. "Rosamund Tooth is such an old dear, and Nigel Arkwright can be quite charming when he doesn't babble on so," she said. The child on the path had turned around and was now apparently scrutinizing the ground, her cowl making her look like a dwarf-ish monk. "But I'm not as interested as I once was," Lily said. "Mrs. Venable's speciality is communing with the departed, through a control named Marcel, and I've always thought that was a shade—you know." Irritatingly, Magnus snorted, lumping her with the class of people who sought information from controls named Marcel. She could now see the pale glimmer of the girl's face. The child was staring straight ahead, as if counting to herself. Then she tilted up her face and looked right at Lily. Her eyes were blue and expressionless. With both hands, still holding Lily's eyes with her own, she swept back the hood and revealed hair the color of white gold.

Lily jumped back from the window, whirled around, and uttered the first sentence to appear in her mind. She said, "We should never have buried Julia in Hampstead cemetery."

Magnus said, "What?"

IF YOU COULD SEE ME NOW

I

JULY 21, 1955

"Winter has already started," said Alison.

"Huh?"

"Winter started a month ago."

"I don't get you."

"What day is it?"

"The twenty-first of July. Thursday."

"*God*, look at those stars," she said. "I'd like to take a big step off the planet and just go sailing through them." He and Alison, cousins from opposite ends of the continent, lay side by side on their grandmother's lawn in that part of rural Wisconsin nearest the Mississippi River, and looked up past the dark massive heads of the walnut trees to the sky. Oral Roberts' country voice came drifting to them from the porch of their grandmother's house. "My spirit is passing into you," Oral Roberts was shouting, and Alison's mother, Loretta Greening, softly laughed. The boy turned his head sideways on the coarse, springy grass and looked at his cousin's profile. It was fox-sharp, ardent, and if will could lift her off the earth she would already be sailing away from him. He caught her smell of cold, bracing water. "God," she repeated, "I'd just buzz around up there, wouldn't I? I feel that way sometimes when I listen to Gerry Mulligan. Do you know about him?"

He did not.

"Boy, you should really live in California. In San Francisco. Not just because we could see each other more, but Florida is so damn far away from everything. Gerry Mulligan would just slay you. He's really cool. Progressive jazz."

"I do wish we lived near you. That would be neat."

"I hate all my relatives except for you and my father." She turned her head toward his face and gave him a smile of brilliant, heart-stopping whiteness. "And I suppose I see him even less than I see you."

"Lucky me."

"You could look at it that way." She turned away from him again. They could hear their mothers' voices mingling with the noise from the radio. Their grandmother, Jessie, the shrewd center of the family, was doing something in the kitchen, and from time to time through the crossweave of the sisters' conversation on the porch slid her softer voice. She had been closeted all day with cousin Duane (pronounced *Dew*-ane), who was about to be married. Their grandmother opposed the marriage, the children knew, for reasons tenuous but forceful.

"You got into trouble again last year," Alison said.

He grunted assent, embarrassed, not wanting to talk about it. She was not supposed to know about the side of him that got into trouble. Last time it had very nearly been serious, and the entire messy context of the trouble raged in his dreams several nights a week.

"You get into a lot of trouble, don't you?"

"I guess so."

"I get into a little trouble, too. Not like you, but enough to make them notice me. I had to change schools. How many times have you changed schools?"

"Four times. But the second time was—the second time was just because one of the teachers hated me."

"I had an affair with my art teacher."

He looked at her sharply, but could not tell if she were lying. He thought that she probably was not.

"Is that why they made you leave?"

"No. They kicked me out because they caught me smoking."

Now he knew that it was true—lies were never as anticlimactic as that. He felt intensely jealous and intensely interested. Both of these feelings were mixed with a large measure of admiration. At fourteen, a year older than he, Alison was part of the passionate adult world of affairs and cigarettes and cocktails. She had previously revealed to him her enthusiasm for martinis "with a twist," whatever a twist was.

"Old Duane would like to have an affair with you," he said.

She snickered. "Well, I'm afraid old Duane doesn't have much of a chance." Then, rushing at him with all of her unexpected, ardent force, she rolled rapidly over onto her side and faced him. "Do you know what he did yesterday? He asked me if I wanted to go out for a ride in his pickup, this was while you and your mother were visiting Auntie Rinn, and I said sure, why not, and he took me for a drive and he put his hand on my knee as soon as we left the driveway. He only took it off when we passed the church." She laughed again, as if this last detail were the conclusive proof of Duane's unsuitability as a lover.

"You let him?"

"His hand was *sweating*," Alison said through her laughter—indeed said it so loudly that the boy wondered if Duane could hear it—"and it felt like he was rubbing tractor grease or something all over my knee. I said, 'I bet you don't have much luck with girls, do you, Duane?' and he pulled over and made me get out."

"Are there any boys you like up here?" He wanted her to give a flat negative, and her reply at first made him flush with satisfaction.

"Here? Are you kidding? First of all, I don't like the boys very much, they're so inexperienced, and I don't like the aroma of the barnyard that surrounds most farmboys. But I think Polar Bears Hovre is sort of good-looking."

Polar Bears, so called because of the whiteness of his hair, was the son of the Arden Township policeman, and he was a tall, rather chunky boy of nearly Duane's age who had several times driven over to the Updahl farm to ogle Alison. He was a famous tearaway, though as far as the boy knew, he had not yet been made to leave any schools.

"He thinks you're good-looking too, but I suppose even a lout like Polar Bears would notice that."

"Well, you know that I only love you." But she said it so lightly that the phrase seemed smooth with overuse.

"I'll accept that," he said, thinking it sounded sophisticated—the kind of thing her art teacher might say.

Duane had begun to shout in the kitchen, but they, like their mothers on the porch, ignored it.

"Why did you say that about winter? That winter was starting?"

She touched his nose with a finger, and the gesture made his face blaze. "Because on this day last month we had the longest day of the year. Summer's lease is fading, dear one. Do you like Auntie Rinn? I think there's something spooky about her. She's really off the wall."

"Yeah," he said vehemently. "She's eerie. She said something to me about you. When Mom was out looking at her herbs."

Alison seemed to stiffen, as if she knew that the old woman's comment would not have been complimentary. "What did she say about me? She listens to my mother too much."

"It was . . . she said I should watch out for you. She said you were my snare. She said you'd be my snare even if we weren't cousins, even if we didn't know each other, but since we are cousins, that it was much more dangerous. I didn't want to tell you."

"*Snare*," Alison said. "Well, maybe I am your snare. It sounds like a nice thing to be."

"Nice for me, you mean."

She smiled, not agreeing or disagreeing, and rolled back to look again at the shining starry sky. When she spoke, she said, "I'm bored. Let's do something to celebrate the beginning of winter."

"There's nothing to do."

"Polar Bears could think of something," she said sweetly. "I know. Let's go swimming. Let's go up to the quarry. I'd like to go swimming. Hey? Let's do it."

It seemed like a dubious proposition to him. "They won't let us do it."

"You wait and see. I'll show you how we swim in California."

He wondered aloud how they would travel the eight miles to the quarry. It was in the hills just outside Arden.

"Wait and see." She jumped up from the grass and began to march toward the farmhouse. Oral Roberts had ceased faith healing for another week, and now the sounds of a dance band mingled with the voices of their mothers. He ran to catch up with her and followed her through the screen door of the porch.

Loretta Greening, a softer, taller version of Alison, was sitting on the porch sofa with his mother. The two women looked very much alike. His mother was smiling; Alison's wore her perpetual look of nervous excitement mixed with discontent. After a moment the boy noticed Duane seated on a wicker chair at the far end of the porch. Slapping a fist noiselessly against his thigh, he appeared to be considerably more discontented than Mrs. Greening. He was staring at Alison as though he hated her, but she blithely ignored him.

"Give me the keys to the car," Alison said. "We want to go for a drive."

Mrs. Greening shrugged to her sister.

"Oh, no," said the boy's mother. "Alison is too young to drive, isn't she?"

"It's for practice," Alison said. "Just on the back roads. I have to practice or I'll never pass the test."

Duane was still staring at her.

"I have this theory," Mrs. Greening said to the boy's mother. "You always let them do what they want to do."

"Because I'll learn from my mistakes."

"Well, don't you think—" his mother began.

"Here," said Mrs. Greening and tossed her the keys. "For God's sake watch out for that old fool Hovre. He'd rather give you a ticket than chew that disgusting tobacco."

"Oh, we're not going anywhere near Arden," Alison said.

Duane had put his hands on the arms of his chair. The boy realized with sickening certainty that Duane was going to invite himself along, and he feared that his mother would insist on their allowing him to drive the Greening Pontiac.

But Alison acted too quickly for either Duane or his mother to speak. "Okay, thanks," she said and wheeled back through the door of the porch. By the time the boy could react, she was already sliding into the car.

"We pulled that one off all right, didn't we?" she said minutes later, as they were swinging out of the valley road onto the state highway to Arden. He was looking out the back window, where he thought he had seen the lights of Duane's pickup truck. But it could have been any truck from one of the farms in the valley.

He was about to agree with her when she spoke again, strangely counterpointing his thoughts. It was a common experience between them, this access to each other's thoughts and fantasies, and the boy thought that it was what Auntie Rinn had noticed.

"Old Duane was just about to invite himself along, wasn't he? I wouldn't mind him if he wasn't so *path-et-ic*. He sort of can't do anything right. Did you see that house he was building for his girlfriend?" She began to giggle. The house had become a subterranean family joke, unmentionable before Duane's parents.

"I just heard about it," he said. "It sure sounds funny. He didn't want me to see it. Duane and I don't really get along. We had a big fight last year."

"And you didn't even sneak out there just to take a peek? Jesus H. Christ, it's amazing. It's . . ." She broke down into giggles, unable to characterize the house any better. "And," she said gasping, "you're not supposed to mention it to Duane, you can't make just the teeniest tiniest little comment . . ." She was laughing uncontrollably.

Because the car was weaving in and out of its lane, he said, "How did you learn to drive? My parents won't even let me touch the car."

"Oh, from these greasers I sometimes hang around with."

He merely grunted, having no idea what greasers were, and thinking that they sounded even worse than the art teacher.

"Do you know what we should do?" Alison said. "We should make a pact. A really serious pact. A vow. To make sure that whatever happens, you know, no matter who we marry, since we can't really marry each other, that we stay in touch—no, stay together." She looked at him oddly for a moment, and then swung the car to the side of the road. "Let's make a vow. This is important. If we don't, we can't be sure."

He looked at her dumbly, amazed by this sudden emotion. "You mean, promise to see one another when we're married?"

"Married, not married, if we're living in Paris or Africa—anything. Let's say—let's say we'll meet here on some date. On this date in ten years. No, that's not far away enough. In twenty years. I'll be thirty-four and you'll be thirty-three. That's lots younger than our mothers. July twenty-first, um, 1975. If there's still a world in 1975. Promise. Make me a vow." She was looking at him with such intensity that he did not even attempt to turn the absurd promise into a joke.

"I vow."

"And I vow. At the farm, twenty years from now. And if you forget, I'll come after you. If you forget, God help you."

"Okay."

"Now we have to kiss."

His body seemed to become lighter in weight. Alison's face seemed larger than its true size, more challenging and masklike. Behind the mask her eyes shone at him. With difficulty, he made his body move on the car seat. He bent toward her. His heart began to gong. When her suddenly enormous face drew near his, their lips brushed. His first sensation was of the unexpected cushiony softness of Alison's lips, then this was supplanted by an awareness of her breathing warmth. Alison pressed her mouth harder against his, and he felt her hands at the back of his head. Her tongue darted through his lips.

"This is what Auntie Rinn is afraid of," she whispered, her mouth publishing warmth over his. She kissed him again, and he became a pinpoint of sensation.

"You sort of make me feel like a boy," she said. "I like it."

When she withdrew, she glanced down at his lap. He looked dazedly into her face. He would have given her anything, he would have died for her on the spot.

"Did you ever go swimming at night?" she asked.

He shook his head.

"We'll have so much fun," she said, and started the car again. With a flourish, she pulled out into the road.

He turned his head to look again out of the rear window, and saw the high headlights of another vehicle swing out thirty yards behind them. "I think Duane is following us."

She hastily looked into the rearview mirror. "I don't see him."

He looked back. The headlights had disappeared. "But he was there before."

"He wouldn't dare. Don't worry about old Du-ane. Imagine having a name like that anyhow."

As he laughed, relieved, he was stopped short by an appalling realization. "We didn't bring our suits! We'll have to go back."

Alison glanced at him oddly. "Don't you wear underwear?"

Again, relief made him laugh.

When they reached the rutted dirt road leading up the hill to the quarry, the boy quickly checked for the following headlights, but saw nothing except the lights of a farmhouse far down the road. Alison flicked on the radio, and "Yakety Yak" blared out at them. She sang the words as they sped up the hill. *"Don't talk back."*

A thick screen of bushes separated the irregular steps to the quarry from the grassy, rock-strewn flat space where she stopped the car. "Oh, this is going to be good," she said; on an afterthought, she snapped the radio back on. "—and for Johnny and Jeep and all the A.H.S. gang at Reuter's Drive In, Les Brown and His Band of Renown playing 'Lover Come Back to Me,' " came the announcer's low oily voice. "And for Reba and LaVonne in the Arden Epworth League. Les Brown and 'Lover Come Back to Me.' "

From the flat space where workmen's sheds had once stood, a beaten trail of dust and grass led through an opening in the screen of bushes to the rocky steps down to the lip of the quarry. When he had followed Alison down the steps, they stood on the slablike platform, two feet above the black water. As with all quarries, it was said that this one was bottomless, and the boy could believe that—the black skin of water seemed inviolate. If you broke through it, you would never cease to fall, you would go down forever.

No such reflections troubled Alison. She was already out of her blouse and shoes, and was now removing her skirt. He realized that he was staring at her body, and that she knew he was staring, but did not mind.

"Get out of those clothes," she said. "You're awfully slow, cousin. If you don't hurry up I'll have to help you."

He quickly pulled his shirt over his head. In bra and pants Alison stood and watched him. Shoes, socks, and then his trousers. The night air drifted coolly down onto his shoulders and chest. She was looking at him with approval, grinning.

"Do you want to do what we do in California?"

"Uh, sure."

"So let's skinny-dip."

"What's skinny-dip?" Though he thought he knew.

"Watch me." Smiling, she pushed her pants down over her hips and stepped out of them. Then she reached up and unhooked her bra. The car radio sent them Ray Anthony playing a languid torchy song. "You too," she said, smiling. "You won't believe how good it feels."

A sound from above them, from near the rocks, made him jump. "Was that someone coughing?"

"Do birds cough? Come on."

"Yeah." He removed his underpants, and when he looked up at her, she was just diving into the water. Her body gleamed whitely beneath the dark surface of the water, gliding for a long time out toward the center of the quarry. Then her head broke the water and she flipped back her hair, a movement full of competent womanly life.

He had to be near her. He went to the lip of rock and made a flat dive into the water: the shock of the cold seemed to flash through his nervous system and burn his skin, but the simple womanly efficiency of her gesture had been a greater shock. More than her talk of greasers and art teachers, it made her a foreign creature.

By the time he got to the surface, his body had adjusted to the temperature of the water. Alison was already knifing away from him, moving smoothly through the water. He realized with chagrin that she was a better swimmer than he, who was proud of his swimming. And she was a stronger swimmer too, for when he set out after her, she effortlessly increased the pulse of her strokes and widened the distance between them. At the far end of the quarry she flipped under the water in a racing turn and came up gracefully and powerfully, her shoulders and arms gleaming in the darkness. The rest of her body gleamed too, mysterious and warped by the water. He began to tread water, waiting for her.

Then he heard, muffled by the drifting snatches of dance music from the car, another sound from above them, and he looked up sharply. Something white ran flitting behind the sparsest of the bushes. For a moment he thought it was a white shirt, and then it stopped and was too motionless for it to have moved at all—moonlight on a rock. From the other side of the quarry's top, up above and behind him, came a short calling whistling sound. He looked up over his shoulder but saw nothing.

Alison was now near him, making her beautiful strong strokes which barely disturbed the surface of the water. She bent at the waist, her bottom flashed for a moment, and she was gone. He felt her hands braceleting his calves and he managed to hold his breath before he went under.

In dark water, Alison was clasping him now at the waist, grinning. He touched her cold smooth hands. Then, bravely, dared to touch her spreading hair and round skull. She gripped his middle more firmly and, using her shoulder muscles, levered him down and slid her body along his until her arms were clasping his chest. Her mouth nipped at his neck. Their legs lay parallel, twin forks, touching. Trouble started in his mind.

When what she had caused to come to life brushed her stomach, she released him and went smoothly up to the surface. Holding the final seconds of his air, he saw her body dangling headlessly down, an unbelievable bounty of almost mystical perfection. Her small breasts bobbed in the water, her legs bent to a heartbreaking curve of calf. Her hands and feet were white stars, flashing. The trouble spread thickly through his mind, canceling all else. He glided up beside her, bruising all that foreign heartland and wilderness of skin.

For a second he was unable to see, and Alison's arm clamped about his neck: when his eyes cleared, he was looking into a sleek wet fall of hair. Her hard cheekbones pressed his jaw. Using all his strength, he broke the hold of her arms and turned her into him. His head went under water, forced to the hollow of her neck, and he heard her yell of laughter. His legs kicked around hers. They were back under, thrashing, and the trouble in his mind forced them to roll deeper into the cold water. His ears boomed as she struck them.

Booming was everywhere. The water blanketed him, her slippery perfection fought him. They reached the surface again and gulped air a second before the water exploded with trouble. Her laughter ceased and she gripped his head, crushing his ears forward painfully and then there seemed to be more than two of them, fighting the trouble, fighting the water and fighting for air and fighting *for* trouble. The water boomed and whenever all their bodies, their one body, broke the surface, geysers of spray were booming too.

II

TO GET TO ARDEN

1

No story exists without its past, and the past of a story is what enables us to understand it (perhaps that I believe this is the reason I teach novels and not poems, where the internal history may be only a half dozen slewfoot lines), but because—precisely because—I am so aware of the past pressing in on my story, I wish to allow it to leak in when it must, and not butter it over the beginning. I know, and here speaks the lecturer in literature, the sort-of professor of contemporary fiction, that each story, however freighted with history, is a speaking present unit, a speaking knot, a gem. We may appreciate a diamond more if we know its history of association with bloody feuds and failed dynastic marriages, but we do not understand it better. The same point could be made of love, or of lovers—the history of indifferent wives or loafing husbands, even the paraphernalia of personality, is strewn about there on the floor, waiting to be put on with their clothing. So I begin this story, so far along in this maladroit paragraph, with myself driving my car, a decade-old Volkswagen, from New York to Wisconsin in the last breathless weeks of June. I was in that limbo between youth and middle age when change is most necessary, when new possibilities must replace the old dying visions, and I had been divorced a year. Divorced spiritually, not legally: because my wife had died six months after she had left me, I would never need the formal decree. (Impossible to conceal the bitterness, even after Joan's death.)

I had been driving for a day and a half, going as fast as my Volkswagen and the highway patrol would permit, and I had spent the intervening night in an Ohio motel of shabby aspect—a motel so characterless that I forgot its name and the town on the heel of which it squatted the moment I rejoined the freeway. Having had a particularly disturbing nightmare, I was gasping for freedom, for new air. Every cell and nerve of my body was choked with malignancy, the residue of gasoline fumes and repressed outrage; I needed dull green peace, fresh days in which to finish (actually, to write most of) the dissertation which would enable me to keep my job.

For as I have said, I am not a professor: not even, to be truthful, a "sort-of" professor. I am an instructor. An instructor of the last gasp.

Automobiles, especially my own, make me irritable and prone to accidents of temperament. Each man sits alone in his six-foot metal coffin, and traffic jams are like noisy graveyards. (I may be mechanically incompetent, but I can reduce death to a metaphor—the day after dreaming of it!) I am likely to *"see"* things, whereas normally all my hallucinations enter through another organ— I mean my nose. (Some people see things, I smell 'em.) In Massachusetts once, during a time when I was teaching *Tom Jones*, I was driving late at night on a country road well out of Boston. The familiar road sign picked out by my headlights indicated a sharp curve. Entering it, I saw the road begin to ascend steeply, and pushed the accelerator down hard to the floor. I like to go up hills as fast as possible. When I had swung fully into the curve and had begun to ascend—little Schnauzer engine barking furiously—I heard a terrific clatter from the brow of the hill. A second later, my blood thinned: just beginning to career down the hill was a stagecoach, obviously out of control. I could see the four horses racing in the straps, the carriage lamps flickering, the driver hauling uselessly on his reins. His face was taut with panic. The high wooden box of the coach jounced down at me, veering crazily across the road. It seemed like my last moment on earth. I fumbled in fear at the controls of my car, not knowing whether to change gears, shut off the engine, or risk my luck on speeding past the plunging carriage. At the last moment my mind began to work and I turned sharply to the right. The coach sped past me, missing the car by four or five inches. I could smell the sweat of the horses and hear the creaking of leather.

When I had calmed down, I continued up the hill. It must have been a fraternity or club prank, I thought, college madmen from Harvard or B.U. But after I had gone on no more than a quarter mile, I realized that it was very late for that sort of prank—past three in the morning—and that you don't race stagecoaches downhill. They crash. And I could not be sure that I had seen it at all. So I turned around and went back. I followed the road five miles the way I had come—long enough to catch up, more than enough to find the wreck. The road was empty. I went home and forgot about it. A year later, idly listening in my bath to a phone-in program about the supernatural, I heard a woman say that while she had been driving on a country road well out of Boston, she had turned up a hill late at night and seen a careering stagecoach racing toward her. My asthmatic heart nearly folded in half with shock. Driving, I still remember this. When the other world comes up and slaps me in the face, it will happen when I am in a car.

Teagarden's the name, pomposity's the game.

I was sweating and in bad temper. I was perhaps thirty miles from Arden, and my engine was rattling, and on the backseat noisily shook a carton of books and papers. I had to do that book or the Advancement and Promotions Committee—seven well-padded scholars on Long Island—would fire me. I was hoping that my cousin Duane, who lives in the newer farmhouse on what used to be my grandparents' farm, would have got my telegram and had the older wooden house cleaned up for my arrival. Duane being himself, this seemed unlikely. When I reached a town I knew called Plainview, I stopped at a lunchroom for chili, though I was not hungry. Eating is affirmation, greed is life, food is antidote. When Joan died, I stood up beside the refrigerator and gobbled an entire Sara Lee creamcake.

Plainview is where my family always stopped for lunch when we drove to the farm, and I had to make a longish detour to get there. In those days, it was a hamlet of one street lined with feed stores, a five and ten, a hotel, a Rexall pharmacy, a tavern, our diner. Now I saw that the town had grown, and the second feed store had been replaced by the Roxy cinema, which itself had bankrupted so that the marquee read C ARLTO HESTO IN HUR. Good work, Carlto! The diner was externally unchanged, but when I stepped inside I saw that the churchy wooden booths along the wall had yielded to new banquettes padded with that plastic luncheonette leather which is forever gummy. I sat at the far end of the counter. The waitress idled over, leaned on the counter staring at me and missed a few beats with her gum while I gave my order. I could smell baby oil and tooth decay, mostly the latter.

Though she smelled of nothing of the kind. As I've said, I have olfactory hallucinations. I smell people even when I'm talking to them on the telephone. In a German novel I once read about this phenomenon, and there it seemed almost charming, pleasant, a sort of gift. But it is not charming or pleasant, it is disquieting and unsettling. Most of the odors I catch hook the nerves.

She wandered away, scribbling on a pad, and rejoined a group of men attending to a radio at the other end of the counter. The men were huddled together, ignoring their plates of hash and steaming cups of coffee. I could see it was a matter of serious local interest, both by the men's attitudes—anger in those hunched shoulders, anger and bafflement—and by the broken phrases which came to me from the radio. "No progress in the shocking . . . discovery of the twelve . . . a bare eight hours since . . ." Some of the men glanced sullenly at me, as if I hadn't the right to hear even so much.

When the waitress brought my bowl of chili I asked, "What the devil's going on?"

One of the men, a skinny clerk in rimless glasses and a shiny double-breasted suit, clapped his hat on his elongated pink head and left the diner, slamming the screen door.

The waitress blankly watched him go and then looked down at her stained blue uniform. When she brought her gaze up to my face I saw that she was older than the high-school girl I had taken her for; her sprayed white bubble of hair and bright lipstick rode uneasily on her aging face. "You're not from around here," she said.

"That's right," I said. "What happened?"

"Where're you from?"

"New York," I said. "Why does it matter?"

"It matters, friend," came a male voice from down the counter, and I swiveled to look at a burly young moonface with thinning blond hair and a high corrugated forehead. The others grouped behind him, pretending not to hear, but I could see their bicep muscles tensing in their short-sleeve shirts. My friend with the football forehead leaned forward on his stool, palms on knees so that his forearms bulged.

I deliberately took a spoonful of chili. It was warm and bland. Greed is life. "Okay," I said, "it matters. I'm from New York. If you don't want to tell me what's happening you don't have to. I can hear it on the radio for myself."

"Now apologize to Grace-Ellen."

I was dumbfounded. "For what?"

"For swearing."

I looked at the waitress. She was leaning against the wall behind the counter. I thought she was trying to look offended.

"If I swore at you, I apologize," I said.

The men sat staring at me. I could feel violence thickening about them, not sure which way to flow or whether to flow at all.

"Get the shit out of here, wiseass," the young man said. "Wait. Frank, get the number of bigshot's car." He held up a massive palm in my direction while a small man in suspenders, a natural flunky, jumped up from his stool and ran out and stood in front of my car. Through the window I saw him pull a piece of paper from his shirt pocket and write on it.

My friend lowered his meaty palm. "I'm taking that number to the police," he said. "Now are you gonna sit and bullshit me some more or are you gonna leave?"

I stood up. There were three of them, not counting no 'count Frank. Sweat ran coldly down my sides. In Manhattan such an exchange might last fifteen minutes with all parties knowing that they will do nothing more violent at the end than walk away. But the muscular balding blond young man had no trace of New York relish in insult and feigned toughness, and I risked only one further remark.

"I only asked a question." I hated him, his distrust of strangers and his manner of the village bully. I knew I would hate myself for fleeing.

He looked at me with flat eyes.

I walked slowly past him. All of the men were looking at me now with expressionless faces. One of them edged a contemptuous half inch out of my way so that I could open the door.

"He's got to pay for that chili," said Grace-Ellen, coming to life.

"Shut the fuck up," said her defender. "We don't need his goddamn money."

I hesitated for a second, wondering whether I dared to drop a dollar on the floor. "Whatever it was," I said, "I hope it happens again. You deserve it." Then I wheeled through the door and flipped the little pinwheel catch on its outside and sprinted toward the Volkswagen. Grace-Ellen's voice was screaming *don't bust that door* when I got the car started and drove off.

Five miles out of Plainview, my mind was a stew of fantasies. I imagined retorts witty and threatening, attacks sudden and brutal. I saw a hundred things I might have done, from reasonable discussion to mashing my bowl of chili into Wrinklehead's face. Eventually, I was trembling so severely that I had to stop the car and get out. I needed release. I slammed the door so hard that the whole car vibrated; then I raced to the back and kicked one of the rear tires until my foot ached. For a while I hammered on the beetle's engine cover, pounding with my fists, seeing Wrinklehead's face in my mind. When I was exhausted I half-fell into the dust and grass at the side of the road. Hot sun scored my face. My hands throbbed, and I noticed finally that I had torn a triangular flap of skin from my left hand. The palm was filling with blood. I clumsily wound my handkerchief around it. When I held the handkerchief tightly, the wound throbbed more but hurt less, both satisfactory sensations. A memory hit me and came pulsing out with my slow blood.

This was a memory of marital disharmony. A memory of disorder. Most of my marriage was disordered, in fact, the blame for which was neither Joan's nor mine but lay in the mismating of two wildly divergent temperaments. It was tomaytos–tomahtos, eether–eyether in every possible sphere. My favorite movies had people shooting guns, hers had people speaking French; I liked to read and listen to records in the evening, she liked parties where she could pick fights with stuffy gents in white shirts and striped ties; I was monogamous by nature, she polyandrous. She was one of those people for whom sexual faithfulness is simply not possible, for whom it would be something like death of imagination. Seven months before Joan died, she had gone through, to my knowledge, five lovers during our marriage, each of them wounding to me: the last of these was one (let's call him) Dribble. She was swimming with him, drunk, when she drowned. On the occasion I remembered, we had gone for dinner at Dribble's house. Amidst the usual posters of the time (Che's iconic face, War Is Unhealthy for Children and Other Living Things) and the paperbacks by Edgar Rice Burroughs and Carlos Castaneda, we ate chili and drank Almaden Mountain Red. Only during the musical part of the evening, while Joan and Dribble were dancing to a Stones record, did I realize that they had become lovers. Once home I became a Mars of the coffee table and the dining-room curtains—I had thought we were in a good patch, I felt betrayed. I accused. She denied hotly and then hotly refused to deny. I slapped her. Oh, these errors of an optimistic heart. She gasped, then called me a "pig." She said that I had never loved her, that I had stopped loving anything but Alison Greening. It was all that could be said, it was a deliberate foray onto my sacred territory. She stormed off to Dribble, I drove to the all-night university library and played clown to students in the corridors. My six years' marriage was over.

It was the memory of that last messy scene that assaulted me while I sat in the dust beside my car. I almost smiled. It may have been from shame—it makes me blaze with shame, that I struck her—and it may have been in response to an odd and powerful sensation which visited me then. This sensation was, centrally, of freedom: of having a purer vision of myself settling down upon me, of being cast out forever from my old life. It felt like cold air, like blue cold water.

The connection between these two scenes, as you will have noticed, is anger—as it was anger, I only now observe, which rebounded back on me to grant the sensation of a central freedom. Anger is an emotion not typical of me. Generally,

I mess through life, seeing everybody's point of view. But the month to come, certainly the strangest of my life, brought as much anger as it did fear. In my normal life, back on Long Island, I was shy and something of a clown, a clown from shyness. Since my adolescence, there seem to have been secrets of competence and knowingness from which I was locked away. Innocently, I had always imagined that anger created its own moral authority.

I rose from the dust and got back into the car, breathing hard. Blood had seeped through to the outer layers of the handkerchief, and I was vaguely aware of blood on my shoes, which I scuffed against the backs of my trouser legs. An echo of a dream caught in my mind, dislocating and severe. This I shook off by attempting to start the car. My assault on the engine must have offended the touchy little motor, because it sputtered and tut-tutted a long time and then eventually flooded. I sat, still breathing noisily, for a while and then tried it again: it chuffed, and went back to work.

When I had gone about half of the distance to Arden I turned on the radio and twisted the knob until I found the Arden station. Then I discovered what the peculiar scene in the diner had been all about. My up-to-date reporter, Michael Moose (so it sounded), was coming to me with the news and all the news on the hour and the half-hour with a full five minutes of local roundup and world events. In his deep hollow announcer's voice, he said, "Police report no progress yet toward discovery of the perpetrator of the most shocking crime in Arden's history, the sex-murder of Gwen Olson. The discovery of the body of the twelve-year-old sixth-grader was made early this morning by fishermen crossing a deserted area of waste ground near the Blundell River. Chief Hovre reports that he and his team will be working on this case full time until it is solved. A bare eight hours since . . ." I turned it off.

Though any urban American gets this story with most of his breakfasts, it was not callousness that made me switch off the radio, but the flicker of a penetrating certainty—the certainty that I would be seeing Alison Greening again, that she would honor a pact we had made twenty years before. My cousin, Alison Greening—I had not seen her since that night, when the consequence of a nude swim had been our total separation.

I cannot explain this sudden half-conviction that Alison would keep her vow, but I believe it had its birth in that earlier flood of wonderful high feeling, that grip of freedom as I bled into my handkerchief. When I knew and loved her, she embodied freedom to me, freedom and strength of will—she obeyed only her own rules. Anyhow, I savored this sensation for a moment, my hand still on the knob of the radio, and then I packed it away in my mind, thinking that what would happen, would. I knew that the keeping of my half of our vow was an equal part of my return to Arden.

Eventually the four-lane highway ascended a hill I knew, and then, going sharply down, traversed a high metal bridge which was the first true landmark. Going down the hill, my father would say, "We'll fly over it this time," and pull back on the wheel while accelerating. I would scream with expectation, and even as we raced past the bolts and girders of the bridge it was as though we had for a moment taken flight. From here I could have jogged to the farm-house, bad heart, thick waistline, suitcases and cartons and all, and I glanced at the long flat cornfields on both sides with spirits momentarily high.

But between the bridge and my grandmother's farmhouse were many more landmarks—I knew the roads, the few buildings, even the trees by rote from my childhood, when they had been all washed in the glow of being on vacation— all of them important, but at least three of them vital. At the first crossroads past the bridge I left the highway, which continued, going over another, low metal bridge, on to Arden, and joined the narrower road into the valley. At the very edge of the entrance to the valley, when one first becomes aware of the wooded hills sloping up from the far side of the fields, was the yet narrower and rougher road to Auntie Rinn's house. I wondered what had happened to that sturdy little wooden structure now that the old woman was surely dead. Of course children have no proper idea of the ages of adults, forty to a ten-year-old is only a blink away from seventy, but Auntie Rinn, my grandmother's sister, had always been old to me—she was not one of the fat vital shouting farm women conspicuous at church picnics in the valley, but of the other common physical type, drawn and thin, almost stringy from youth on. In old age, these women seem weightless, transparencies held together by wrinkles, though many of them work small farms with only the most necessary assistance. But Rinn's day had long passed, I was sure: my grandmother had died six years before, aged seventy-nine, and Rinn had been older than her sister.

Rinn had owned a considerable reputation for eccentricity in the valley, and visiting her always partook a bit of the adventurous—even now, knowing that the old wraith's home was probably inhabited by a red-faced young farmer who would prove to be my cousin at several removes, even now the little road up the hill to her house looked eerie, winding up past the fields to the trees. Her house had been so thickly surrounded by trees that little sunlight had ever fought through to her windows.

I think Rinn's oddness had been rooted in her spinsterhood, always something of an anomaly in farm country where fertility is a sign of grace. Where my grandmother had married a neighboring young farmer, Einar Updahl, and prospered, Rinn had been tenuously engaged to a young Norwegian she never met. The match was arranged by aunts and uncles in Norway. It is the only sort of engagement I can imagine Rinn accepting—to a man thousands of miles away, a man in no danger of impinging upon her life. The story, as I remember it, was that the young man ceased to threaten Rinn's independence at the very time he drew nearest to it: he died on board the boat bringing him to America. Everyone in the family, save Rinn, thought this was a tragedy. She'd had a house built for her by her brother-in-law, my grandfather, and she insisted on moving into it. Years later, when my mother was a child, my grandmother had visited Rinn and come upon her talking volubly in the kitchen. *Are you talking to yourself now*, asked my grandmother. *Of course not*, said Rinn. *I'm talking to my young man.* I never saw any sign that she was on excessively familiar terms with the departed, but she did look as though she were capable of tricks not available to most of us. I knew two versions of the story of Rinn and the heifer: in the first, Rinn was walking past a neighbor's farm when she looked at his livestock, wheeled around and marched up the track to his house. She took him down to the road and pointed to a heifer in the pen and said that animal will die tomorrow, and it did. This is the predictive version. In the causal version, the neighboring farmer had offended Rinn somehow, and she took him into the road and said, that heifer will die tomorrow unless you stop—what? Crossing my land? Diverting my water? Whatever it was, the farmer laughed at her, and the heifer died. The causal version was certainly mine. As a child I was scared to death of her—I had half-suspected that one glance of those washed-out Norwegian blue eyes could turn me into a toad if it was a toad she thought I deserved to be.

She must be imagined as a small hunched thin old woman, her abundant white hair loosely bound by a scarf, wearing nondescript farm dresses—working dresses, often covered by various amazing coats, for she had kept poultry in an immense barnlike structure just down the hill from her house, and she sold eggs to the Co-op. Her land never was much good for farming, being too hilly and forested. If her young man had come, he would have had a hard time of it, and maybe when she talked to him she told him that he was better off wherever he was than trying to plant corn or alfalfa on a heavily wooded hillside.

To me she had chiefly spoken of Alison, whom she had not liked. (But few adults had liked Alison.)

Six minutes from the narrow road to Rinn's old house, set off the main valley road on a little dog-leg behind the valley's only store, was the second of my landmarks. I spun the VW into the dirt parking area before Andy's and walked around in back to have another look at it. As comic and sad as ever, but with all of the windows broken now and its original slight listing become a decided sprawl of the whole structure, it sat in a wilderness of ropy weeds and high grass at the edge of a vacant field. I see now that these first two landmarks have both to do with marriages frustrated, with lives bent and altered by sexual disappointment. And both of them are touched with strangeness, with a definitive peculiarity. I was sure that in the past fifteen years, Duane's monstrous little house had acquired among the valley children a reputation for being haunted.

This was the house that Duane built—my father's apposite joke—the house he had single-handedly built for his first love, a Polish girl from Arden detested by my grandmother. In those days, the Norwegian farmers and the Polish townsmen mingled very little. "Duane's Dream House," my parents had said, though only to one another: his parents pretended that nothing was wrong with the house, and any jocularity about the subject met with insulted incomprehension. Duane had worked to plans in his head, and they had evidently been stunted there, for the house he had lovingly built for his fiancée was about the size of a small granary—or, say, a big dollhouse, a dollhouse you could stand up in if you were under five-foot-seven. It had two stories, four equal tiny rooms, as if he had forgotten that people had to cook and eat and shit, and all of this weird construction now leaned decidedly to the right, as if the boards were stretching—I suppose it was about as substantial as a house of straw.

As was his engagement. The Polish girl had fulfilled my grandmother's worst expectations of those whose parents did not work with their hands, and had run off one winter day with a mechanic at an Arden garage—"another shiftless Pole without the brains God gave him," my grandmother said to my mother. "When Einar was trading horses—Miles, your grandfather was a great horse-trader here in the valley, and there never was a lazy or a stupid man yet who could see what a horse was made of—when he was going off for a few days with a string, he always used to say that the only thing an Arden Pole knew about a horse was he was supposed to look at its teeth. *And* that he didn't know which end to find them at. *And* that if he found them he didn't know what he was supposed to see. That girl of Duane's was just like the rest of them, running off into damnation because a boy had a fancy car."

She had not even seen the house he had just finished building for her. As the story gradually came to me, Duane had wanted the girl's first sight of her house to be as he was carrying her into it after the ceremony. Had she come out with her mechanic one night for a look and run off on the spot? Duane had gone into Arden to see her, the week before Christmas in 1955, and her parents had been weepy and hostile. It was a long time before he learned from them that she had never come home the night before—they blamed him, a Lutheran and a Norskie and a farmer, for the loss of their daughter. He ran up to her room and found everything gone: all her clothes, everything she had cared for. From there he raced down to the five and dime where she clerked and heard that she had told the supervisor that she wasn't going to come in anymore. And from the store he went to the filling station to meet the boy whose existence had never exactly been confirmed. He too had disappeared: "Run off last night in that new Stude," the owner said. "Musta been with your girl, I spoze."

Like a character in a parody of a gothic novel, he had never spoken of the girl again, nor had he ever visited this terrible little house. It was never mentioned before him: he was pretending that his engagement had never happened. Four years later he met another girl, the daughter of a farmer in the next valley. He married her and had a child, but that too turned out badly for him.

The absurd frame structure was leaning as though a giant had brushed against it, in a hurry to get somewhere else; even the window frames had become trapezoidal. I walked across the dust and into the thick high weeds and grass. Burrs and bits of fluff adhered to my trousers. I looked in through the two windows facing the rear of Andy's store and the valley road. The room was, to be straightforward, a mess, a mess of desolation. The floorboards had warped and rotted so that weeds thrust up at various places into the room, and bird and animals droppings littered the floor—it looked like a filthy vacant coffin. One corner held a tangle of blankets from which radiated a semicircle of dead cigarette butts. On the walls I could distinguish the scrawls left by felt-tip pens.

My spirits began to dwindle as I looked in at my cousin's folly, and I turned away, snaring my left foot in a thick fist of weeds. It was as though that malignant dwarf of a house had snatched at me, and I kicked out with all my force. A thorn stabbed my ankle as decisively as a wasp. Swearing, suddenly cold, I walked away from Duane's little house and went through the dust around to the front of Andy's.

This, the third of my landmarks, was much more comfortable, much more touched with the grace of normality. My family had always made a ritual stop at Andy's before continuing on to the farm, and there we invariably loaded up with bottles of Dr. Pepper for me and a case of beer for my father and Uncle Gilbert, Duane's father. Andy's was what people used to mean when they said general store, a place where you could buy almost anything, work-shirts and trousers, caps, ax handles and heads, meal, clocks, soap, boots, candy, blankets, magazines, toys, suitcases, drills and punches, dogfood, paper, hoes and rakes, chicken feed, gasoline cans, silage formula, flashlights, bread . . . all of this ranked and packed and piled into a long white wooden building raised up on thick stilts of brick. Before it, three white gas pumps faced the road. I reached the steps and went up through the screen door to the dark cool interior.

It smelled as it always had, a wonderful composite odor of various newnesses. When the screen door banged behind me Andy's wife (I could not remember her name) looked up at me from where she was sitting behind the counter, reading a newspaper. She frowned, glanced back at her paper, and when I began to thread my way through the aisles of things, turned her head and muttered something toward the rear of the store. She was a small dark-haired aggressive-looking woman, and her appearance had become drier and tougher with age. As she glanced suspiciously back, I remembered that we had never been friendly, and that I had given her reason for her dislike of me. Yet I did not think that she recognized me: I have changed greatly in appearance since my early youth. The chemistry of the moment was wrong, I knew this; my earlier elation had ebbed away, leaving me flat and depressed, and I should have left the store at that moment.

"Anything I can do for you, mister?" she asked, in her voice the valley's lilt. For the first time it sounded unfriendly and alien to me.

"Andy in?" I asked, coming closer to the counter through the massed smells of newness.

She wordlessly left her chair and disappeared into the cavernous rear of the store. A door closed, then opened again.

In a moment I saw Andy walking toward me. He had grown fatter and balder, and his pudgy face seemed sexually indeterminate and permanently worried. When he reached the counter he stopped and leaned against it, creasing his belly. "What can I do you for?" he said, the jokiness of the phrase out of key with his rubbery defeated face and his air of country suspicion. I saw that gray had eaten nearly all of the brown in his fringe of hair. "You're not one of the drummers. Reps, they call themselves now."

"I wanted to come and say hello," I said. "I used to come in here with my parents. I'm Eve Updahl's boy," using the shorthand that would identify me in the valley.

He looked at me hard for a moment, then nodded and said, "Miles. You'd be Miles, then. Come back for a visit or just a look-see?" Andy, like his wife, would remember my little errors of judgment of twenty years before.

"Mostly to work," I said. "I thought the farm would be a peaceful place to work." An explanation when I had planned to give none—he was making me defensive.

"Don't think I recall what kind of work you wound up doing."

"I'm a college teacher," I said, and the demon of irritation made me take pleasure in his flicker of surprise. "English."

"Well, you were always supposed to be brainy," he said. "Our girl takes shorthand and typing over to the business college in Winona. She's getting on real good up there. Don't suppose you teach around here anywhere?"

I told him the name of my university.

"That's back East?"

"It's on Long Island."

"Eve always said she was afraid you'd wind up back East. So what's this work you got to do?"

"I have to write a book—that is, I'm writing a book. On D. H. Lawrence."

"Uh-huh. What's that when it's at home?"

I said, "He wrote *Lady Chatterley's Lover.*"

Andy swung his eyes up to mine with a surprisingly roguish gesture which was somehow girlish at the same time. He looked as though he were about to lick his lips. "I guess it's true what they say about those colleges out East, huh?" But the remark was not the invitation to masculine revelation that it could have been: there was a sly malice in it.

"It's only one of a lot of books he wrote," I said.

Again I got the wink of roguishness. "I guess one Book's good enough for me." He turned to the side, and I saw his wife lurking in the back of the shop, staring at me. "It's Miles, Eve's boy," he said. "Coulda fooled me. Says he's here writing a dirty book."

She came forward, glowering. "We heard you and your wife got divorced. Duane said."

"We were separated," I said a bit harshly. "Now she's dead."

Surprise showed in both their faces for a second.

"Guess we didn't hear that," said Andy's wife. "Was there something you wanted?"

"Maybe I'll pick up a case of beer for Duane. What kind does he drink?"

"If it's beer he'll drink it," said Andy. "Blatz, Schlitz, or Old Milwaukee? I guess we got some Bud around here too."

"Any one," I said, and Andy lumbered away to the back room where he kept his stacked cases of beer.

His wife and I looked uncomfortably at one another. She broke the contact first, darting her eyes away toward the floor and then out to where my car was parked. "You been staying out of trouble?"

"Of course. Yes."

"But you're writing filth, he says."

"He didn't understand. I came here to write my dissertation."

She bristled. "And you think Andy's too dumb to understand you. You were always too good for us up here, weren't you? You were too good for ordinary folk—too good to follow the law too."

"Wait, hold on," I said. "Jesus, that was a long time ago."

"And so good you don't think about taking the Lord's name in vain. You haven't changed, Miles. Does Duane know you're coming?"

"Well sure," I said. "Don't be so bitchy. Look, I'm sorry. I've been driving two days and I've had a couple of funny experiences." I saw her glance at my handkerchief-wrapped left hand. "All I want here is peace and quiet."

"You always made trouble," she said. "You and your cousin Alison were just alike that way. I'm glad neither of you was raised in the valley. Your grandparents were our people, Miles, and we all took to your father like he was one of us, but now I think maybe we got enough trouble without having you here too."

"Good Lord," I said. "What happened to your hospitality?"

She glared at me. "You wore out your welcome here the first time you stole from us. I'll tell Andy to take your beer down to your motor. You can leave the money on the counter."

Portion of Statement by Margaret Kastad:

July 16

I knew he was Miles Teagarden when he first set foot in our store even though Andy says he didn't know until he said he was Eve's boy. He had that same look he always had, like some bad secret was on his mind. I used to feel so sorry for Eve, she was straight as a die all her life, and I guess you don't know what will happen to your children if you bring them up in funny places. But Eve never was to blame for that boy Miles. Now we know all about him, I'm glad Eve passed away before she could see just how bad he turned out. On that first day I just turned him out of the store. I said Miles, you ain't fooling none of us here. We know you. Now you just get on out of our store. Andy'll take that beer of yours down to your motor. I could tell he was in a fight or something—he looked weak or scared, the way they do, and his hand was still bleeding. I told him, and I'd tell him the same again. He never was any good, was he, for all those brains they said he had? He was just funny— just funny. If he was a dog or a horse you'd have penned him up or just shot him. Right off. Him and that sneaky look and that handkerchief around his hand.

I silently watched Andy load the beer into the backseat of the Volkswagen, shoving in the case beside the paper boxes full of notes and books. "Hurt your wing, huh?" he said. "Wife says you paid up there. Well, give my regards to

Duane, and I hope your mitt gets better." He backed away from the car, wiping his hands on his trousers as if he'd dirtied them, and I wordlessly got in behind the wheel. "Bye now," he said, and I looked at him and then took off out of the dusty little lot. In the rearview mirror I saw him shrugging. When the curve in the road by the red sandstone cliff took him out of sight I snapped the radio on, hoping for music, but Michael Moose was droning on again about Gwen Olson's death and I impatiently turned it off.

When I had got as far down the valley as the shell of the school where my grandmother had taught all eight grades I pulled over and tried to relax. There is a special feeling in the mind that represents the creation of alpha waves, and I deliberately sought that mild state. This time I failed, and I merely sat in the car, staring alternately at the road, the long green field of corn to my right, and the shell of the schoolhouse. I began to hear the buzz of a motorcycle, and soon I saw it flying down the road toward me, growing in size from the dimensions of a horsefly to the point where I could see the black-jacketed, helmeted rider and the blond passenger behind him, her hair whipping out in the wake and her thick thighs gripping him. At the curve by the sandstone cliff the sound altered, and then it died away altogether.

Why should your old sins be permanently pinned to your jacket? For all to read aloud? It was stupidly unfair. I would do my shopping in Arden, despite the inconvenience of making a ten-mile drive whenever I wanted anything. The making of this decision helped to dispel my temper and after a minute or two of further brooding I began to feel as though I might be producing an at least feeble tranquillity.

Where, you might ask, was the clown, the reluctant wag I have proclaimed myself to be? My own abrasiveness surprised me. A woman like Andy's wife would think the word "bitch" scandalous applied to any sphere but the canine. It was an emotional morning. My former thefts! Yet I supposed that it was too much to expect anyone to have forgotten them.

A hundred yards past the deserted school was the church: Gethsemane Lutheran church is a red brick building with quite a sturdy, pompous, peaceful air to it, probably conferred by the Palladian columns at the top of the stairs. For the sake of my grandmother, who was already very weak, Joan and I had been married in this church. (My mother's idea.)

After the church the land seems to open up, and the corn takes over. I passed the Sunderson farmhouse—two pickup trucks parked on the high sloping lawn, a rooster strutting in the red dust of the driveway—and saw a burly man in overalls and a cap just coming out of the house. He stared at me and then decided to wave, but I had not generated sufficient alpha waves to return his greeting.

Half a mile past the Sunderson farm I could see my grandmother's old house and the Updahl land. The row of walnut trees at the edge of the lawn had put on weight, and now they looked like a row of heavy old farmers standing in the sun. I drove by the front of the property and swung into the driveway, passing the trees and feeling the car jounce on the ruts. I expected to feel some strong upwelling of feeling, looking at the long white house again, but my emotions seemed flat and dull. It was just a two-story house with a screen porch, an ordinary farmhouse. Yet when I got out of the car I smelled all the old odors of the farm, a rich compound of cows and horses and fertilizer and milk and sunshine. This pervades everything: when people from the farm had visited my family in Fort Lauderdale, it hung on their clothes and hands and shoes. Smelling all this again made me momentarily feel thirteen years old, and I lifted my head, straightening out the kinks in my neck and back, and saw a heavy form moving down the screen porch. By his shovel-handed, lumbering walk I knew it was Duane, who had been sitting invisible in the corner of the porch just as he had been on that terrible night twenty years before. When Duane came out of the porch into the sun I tried to smile at him. What the first sight of my cousin had brought back to me was how much hostility there had always been between us, how little we had liked one another. It would be different now, I hoped.

2

"Have a case of beer, Duane," I said, mistakenly trying for a bluff friendliness.

He appeared to be confused—really, confusion was stamped all over his big plain face—but his mechanism was set for holding out his hand and saying hello, and that was what he did. His hand was huge, a true farmer's hand, and so rough it felt made of a substance less vulnerable than skin. Duane was a short barrel-like man, but his extremities might have come from someone a foot taller. As we clasped hands and he blinked at me, half smiling, trying to figure out what I meant about the beer, I noticed that he had obviously come in from a morning's work: he wore heavy stained denim coveralls and workboots crusted with mud and excrement. He radiated all of the usual farm odors, compounded with sweat and underlain by his true odor, his inner smell, which is of gunpowder.

Finally he released my hand. "Did you have a good drive?"

"Sure," I said. "This country isn't as big as we think it is. People zip back and forth on it all the time." The persistence of habit: although he was nearly a decade older, I had always taken this tone with Duane.

"I'm glad you had a good drive. You sure surprised me when you said you wanted to come out here again."

"You thought I was lost among the fleshpots of the East."

He distrusted the word "fleshpots," being not quite sure what it meant. That was twice I had taken him off balance. "I was just kind of surprised," he said. "Say, Miles, I was sorry about your wife. Maybe you wanted to get away?"

"That's it," I said. "I did want to get away. Did you take time off from your work to greet me?"

"Well, I didn't want you to come in and find nobody to home. The kid's gone out somewhere, and you know kids, you can't count on them for anything. So I thought I'd wait around after lunch and say hi. Make you feel welcome. And I thought I might listen to the radio in the porch there, see if anything new happened on that terrible business. My kid knew that Olson girl."

"Will you help me get these bags and things inside?" I said.

"Huh? Oh, sure," and he reached in, bending over the seat, and lifted out two heavy boxes of books and notes. Upright again, he asked, "Is that beer in there for me?"

"I hope it's your brand."

"It's wet, ain't it?" He grinned. "I'll put it in the tank when we got you squared away." Before we went toward the porch, Duane twisted his head and looked at me with a surprisingly embarrassed expression on his face. "Say, Miles, maybe I shouldn't have said that about your wife. Because I only met her that once."

"It's all right."

"No. I should never open my mouth about anyone else's woman troubles."

He was referring, I knew, to his own history of marital disaster and to something else as well. Duane was suspicious of women—he was one of those men, sexually normal in every other respect, who are at ease only in male company. I think that he had a radical dislike of women. For him they primarily had been sources of pain, with the exception of his mother and grandmother (about his daughter I could not then speak). After his first disappointment, he had married a girl from one of the farms in French Valley, and this girl had died giving birth to their child. He'd had one numbing humiliation at the hands of a girl (the humiliation not salved by his grandmother's evident satisfaction in it) followed by four years of being between women, his romantic life joked about in Arden bars, then eleven months of marriage and the rest of his life without adult feminine companionship. I suspected that his suspicion of women contained a fair portion of hate. For Duane they had approached and then abruptly withdrawn, still holding whatever mysterious sexual secret they possessed. In the old days, when the Polish girl had been giving him trouble, I had often sensed that his attitude toward Alison Greening was edged with something darker than mere desire. I think he hated her, hated her for evoking desire in him and for finding his desire laughable, a thing of no consequence or value. Alison *had* found him absurd.

Of course Duane was physically vigorous, and his celibacy must at times have been a torment: yet I suspected him of being the kind of man who is shocked and upset by his own fantasies, and is comfortable with women only when they are safely married to his acquaintances. He had submerged his sexuality in work for so long that he expected other men to do the same, habit had become transformed into principle, and he had his success to justify him. Duane had purchased two hundred neighboring acres, and was now at the limit of what a man could farm by himself if he worked ten hours a day; as if to demonstrate the physical law that actions have equal reactions, sexual starvation had fattened his bank account.

The immediate evidence of his prosperity struck me when we carried the boxes and suitcases into my grandmother's old house. "My God, Duane," I said, "you bought new furniture for the place!" Instead of my grandmother's spare old wooden furniture, her threadbare old sofa, the room held what I suppose could be called nineteen-fifties lounge furniture: heavy patterned chairs and matching couch, a blond coffee table, starkly functional table lamps instead of kerosene lamps, even framed reproductions of mediocre paintings. In the setting of the old house, the nondescript new furniture had a tactless chic. The effect of all this on the austere farmhouse living room was to make it resemble a freeway motel bedroom. But there was another resemblance I did not immediately identify.

"I suppose you think it's funny to get new stuff for an empty house, don't you?" he asked me. "The thing is, I get people stopping up here more often than you'd think. In April, George and Ethel were here, and in May Nella from St. Paul, and—" He went on to enumerate a lengthy list of cousins and their children who had stayed in the house for a week or more at a time. "Sometimes this place is like a regular hotel. I guess all these city folks want to show their kids what a farm looks like."

While he talked I noticed that the old photographs of the grandchildren still hung on the walls, as they always had. I knew them all: I identified a picture of myself at nine, my hair in a cowlick like a ruff, and one of Duane at fifteen, scowling suspiciously at the camera as if it were about to tell him something he wouldn't like. Below this was a photograph of Alison which I sensed glowing at me but lacked the courage to look at directly. The sight of that beautiful wild face would have knocked the wind out of me. And then I noticed that the house was immaculately clean.

"Anyhow," Duane was saying, "up over to Arden, a warehouse full of office furniture had a clearance sale just when I got my rebate. So I thought I'd do the old place up since all the furniture was going pretty cheap. Took the truck down and just humped all this stuff back with me."

This was the resemblance I had been unable to name: the room looked like an office in a down-at-heels concern.

"I like the modern way it looks," said Duane, perhaps a shade defensively. "And it cost less than a secondhand disc." He glanced at me, then added, "Everybody seems to like it."

"It's great," I said, "I like it too," distracted by the throbbing and glowing of Alison's photograph on the wall. I knew this photograph well. It had been taken in Los Angeles near the end of her childhood, before the Greenings were divorced and Alison and her mother moved to San Francisco. It showed only her face. Even when she was a child, Alison's face was beautiful and complicated, magic, and her father's photograph showed it all, the beauty and the magical complications. She looked as though she knew and embraced everything. The thought of that overwhelming expression on her childhood face made my stomach tingle, and to avoid looking at the photograph I said, "I wish you had picked up a desk while you were at it. I need a desk to work at."

"That's no problem," said Duane. "I got an old panel door and a couple of sawbucks we could lay it across."

"Well," I said, and turned toward him. "You're a good host, Duane. The place looks clean, too."

"Mrs. Sunderson down the road, you remember her? Tuta Sunderson? Her husband died a couple of years back, and she lives up there now with her boy Red and his wife. Red farms pretty near as good as Jerome did. Anyhow, I talked to Tuta and she said she'd come over here every day to cook your breakfast and dinner and clean for you. She was in here yesterday." He paused, having something further to say. "Said it would be five dollars a week and you'd have to buy your own groceries. She can't drive since she had her cataract operation. That okay?"

I said it was fine with me. "Actually, let's make it seven dollars," I said. "Otherwise I'd feel like I was stealing from her."

"Whatever you say. She said five, though, and you probably remember her. Let's get that beer into the tank." He clapped his hands together.

The two of us went back outside into the hot sun and the farm smells. Duane's gunpowder odor was stronger in the open air, and to escape it I reached into the car first and pulled out the case of beer. He trudged beside me up the long path past the baking metal of the pole barn, the granary, and well past that, his white clapboarded house, to the tank beside the cattle barn.

"You said in your letter you were working on a book."

"My dissertation."

"What's that on?"

"An English writer."

"Did he write a lot?"

"A lot," I said, and laughed. "A hell of a lot."

Duane laughed too. "How'd you pick that?"

"It's a long story," I said. "I expect to be pretty busy, but is there still anyone around here that I used to know?"

He considered that as we passed the brown scar where the summerhouse used to be. "Didn't you know Polar Bears Hovre? He's the police chief over to Arden now."

I almost dropped the case of beer. "Polar Bears? That wildman?" When I was ten and he seventeen, Polar Bears and I had spitballed the congregation from the choir loft at Gethsemane church.

"He settled down some," Duane said. "He does a good job."

"I ought to call him up. We used to have fun together. Even though he always liked Alison a little too much for my taste."

Duane gave me a peculiar, startled look, and contented himself with saying, "Well, he keeps pretty busy now."

I remembered another figure from my past—really, the sweetest and most intelligent of all the Arden boys I had met years ago. "What about Paul Kant? Is he still around? I suppose he went off to a university somewhere and never came back."

"No, you can see Paul. He works in Arden. He works in that Zumgo department store they got over there. Or so I hear."

"I don't believe it. He works in a department store? Is he manager or something?"

"Just works there, I guess. He never did much." Duane looked at me again, a little shyly this time, and said, "He's a little funny. Or so they say."

"Funny?" I was incredulous.

"Well, you know how some people talk. Nobody would mind if you called him up, I guess."

"Yes, I do know how they talk," I said, remembering Andy's wife. "They've said enough about me. Some of them are still saying it." Now we were at the tank, and I leaned over the mossy rim and began putting the bottles down into the green water.

Portion of Statement by Duane Updahl:

July 16

Sure, I'll tell you whatever you want to know about Miles. I could tell you lots about that guy. He never fit in up here, you know, when he was nothing but a shrimpy kid, and I could tell right off that he wasn't going to fit in any better this time. He looked weird, I guess you could term it. He talked like he had a crab hanging on his asshole, city fashion. Like he was making jokes at me. When he said he wanted to see Chief Hovre you coulda knocked me down with a feather. (Laughs.) I guess he got his wish, didn't he? We were carrying beer to put down into my little tank I got there beside my barn, you know, and he said that about Polar Bears, I mean Galen, and then he said he wanted to see Kant (laughs), and I said, sure, you go ahead, you know (laughs), and then he said something, I don't know, about people talking about him. Then he damn near popped those beer bottles slamming them against the bottom of the tank. But when he really acted strange was when my daughter came in.

The cap on one of the last beer bottles caught my handkerchief when I was pulling my hand out of the tank, and the wet cloth separated from my hand and sank down on top of the bottles. Chilly water tingled and ached in the exposed wound, and I gasped. Blood began to come twisting out like smoke or a flag—I thought of sharks.

"You meet up with something that didn't like you?" Duane had insinuated himself beside me and was staring heavily down at my hand bleeding into his tank.

"It's a little difficult to explain." I snatched my paw out of the cold water and leaned over the tank and pressed my palm against its far edge, where moss grew nearly an inch thick. The throbbing and stinging immediately lessened, inhibited by application of magic substance. If I could have stayed there all day, pressing my hand against that cool slimy moss, my hand would have healed, millions of new cells would have formed every second.

"You dizzy?" Duane asked.

I was looking out across the road to his fields. Alfalfa and tall corn grew in alternate bands on either side of the creek and the line of willows and cottonwoods; a round shoulder of hillside further up was perfectly bisected by the two crops. It was for silage—Duane had years before given up everything but beef cattle. Up from the bifurcated hillside grew the woods climbing to the top of the valley. They seemed impossibly perfect, like a forest by Rousseau. I wanted to take a handful of moss and go up there to camp, forgetting all about teaching and my book and New York.

"You dizzy?"

Blood was oozing down through the thick moss into the water. I was still looking at the edge of the field, where the rise of trees began. I thought that I had seen a slim figure duck momentarily out of the trees, glance toward us and then slip back into cover like a fox. It might have been a boy. By the time I was fully aware of it, it had vanished.

"You okay?" Duane sounded a little impatient.

"Sure, I'm fine. Do you get many kids wandering around up in those woods?"

"They're pretty thick. Nobody goes in them much. Why?"

"Oh, nothing. Nothing, really."

"We still got a few animals up there too. But they're no good for hunting. Unless you got a rifle can shoot around trees."

"Andy's probably got a few of those." I lifted my hand from the moss. It immediately began to sting and pulse. Due to removal of magic substance.

Portion of Statement by Duane Updahl:

July 16

He was planning something all along, something that had control of him, you could say. You should have seen him grab onto the tank with that cut mitt of his. I should have known there'd be trouble up in those woods, just by the way he was staring at 'em and asking funny questions.

Magic substances are those with a sacred, soothing and healing content. When Duane said, "Let's go up to the house and I'll bandage that mitt of yours," I surprised him by ripping out a handful of the thick moss, exposing a gray, rusting section of the tank, and by gripping the green slippery stuff in my wounded hand. I squeezed it tightly, and the stinging pain lessened a bit.

"Used to be an old Indian woman around here who'd do that for you," Duane said, looking at the pulpy mess in my hand. "Make medicine out of herbs and like that. Like Rinn did, too. But what you got there is liable to get pretty dirty. We'll wash her out before we put on the gauze. How'd you get a thing like that, anyhow?"

"Oh, it was just a stupid fit of temper."

The moss had become dark with blood, an uncomfortably soggy thing to hold, and I dropped the messy handful onto the grass and turned to walk up the drive to Duane's house. A dog lying panting by the granary looked attentively at the bloody pad.

"You get into a fight?"

"Not really. I just had a little accident."

"Remember that time you totaled that car just outside Arden?"

"I don't think I could forget it," I said. "I just about bought it."

"Wasn't that after that time out at the—"

"It was, yes," I broke in, not wanting him to utter the word "quarry."

"That was a hell of a time," he said. "I was in my truck going down the road right after you, but when you turned right on 93, I went the other way toward Liberty. I just drove around. After about an hour—"

"Okay, that's enough."

"Well, you know, I was going to—"

"That's enough. It's all in the past." I wanted to shut him up and was desperately sorry we had ever got on this topic. Several steps behind me, the dog began growling and whining. Duane bent down and picked up a stone and threw it at the animal; I kept walking straight ahead. I was holding my hand out from my side, letting my blood drip steadily down my fingers, and I imagined that skulking creeping black-and-white beast crawling toward me. The stone connected; the dog yelped, and I could hear it pelting off to a safe distance. I looked around and saw a trail of bright drops on the grass.

"You gonna call Auntie Rinn today?" Duane had reached the cement steps to his house, and was standing down there, his head tilted up at me. "I told her you were coming, Miles, and I guess she understood. I think she wants to see you."

"Rinn?" I asked, incredulous. "Is she still alive? I was just thinking that she must have died years ago."

He smiled—the infuriating disbelief of an insider. "Dead? That old bird? Nothing can kill her."

He came up the stairs and I followed him into his house. The door opened onto a hallway off the kitchen, which was much as it had been when Uncle Gilbert had been alive: patterned linoleum on the floor, a long Formica-topped dining table, the same porcelain stove. But the walls looked yellowish, and the entire room had an air of dirt and neglect only partially explained by the greasy handprints on the refrigerator and the stack of dishes by the sink. There was dust even on the mirror. It looked like the sort of room where an army of ants and mice are poised behind the walls, waiting for the lights to go off.

He saw me gazing around. "The damn kid's supposed to keep the kitchen clean, but she's about as responsible as a . . . ." He shrugged. "A cowflop."

"Imagine what your mother would say if she could see it."

"Oh, I'm used to it this way," he said, blinking. "Besides, it don't do to hold to the past like that."

I thought he was wrong. I have always held to the past, I thought that it could, would, should be repeated indefinitely, that it was the breathing life in the heart of the present. But I couldn't speak of this to Duane. I said, "Tell me about Auntie Rinn. Were you hinting that she's deaf?" I went to the sink and held my dripping hand over it.

"Hang on while I get the gauze and tape," he said, and lumbered away toward the bathroom. When he returned he took my hand and held it under a stream of cold water from the tap. "You couldn't say she was deaf. You couldn't say she was blind. The way I make it out, she sees what she wants to see and hears what she wants to hear. But don't mess around with her. If she wants to hear it, she'll hear. She's sharp. She knows everything that's going on."

"Can she get around?"

"She doesn't leave her place much. Neighbors buy her groceries, the little she needs, but she still has her egg business. And she rents out her little field to Oscar Johnstad. I reckon she gets by. But now she's in her eighties, we don't even see her at church."

Surprisingly, Duane was a good nurse. As he talked, he quickly dried my hand with a dishtowel, pressed a big pad of absorbent cotton onto the wound and wrapped a broad strip of tape around the base of my hand, winding it around both sides of my thumb. "Now," he said when he was finishing. "We're gonna make you look like a farmer."

Farms are notorious for accidents: slings, bandages and amputated limbs are commonplaces in rural communities, as are suicides, mental instability and sullen temperaments. In the latter particulars, but not the former, they resemble academic communities. Both are usually thought of as havens of serenity. I entertained myself with these reflections while Duane made his final pass with the roll of tape, tore it with his blunt fingers, and anchored the loose end firmly at the base of my hand. I looked like a farmer: a good omen for the completion of my dreadful work.

Oh, for it was dreadful, an insult to spirit. As the fingers of my left hand began to tingle, suggesting the possibility that Duane might have wound the tape overtightly, I realized how much I disliked writing academic criticism. I decided that once I had finished my book and had made my job secure, I'd never write another word of it.

"Anyhow," Duane said, "you could call her up or just go over."

I would. I thought I would drive over to her farm in the next day or two, after I had settled in at the old farmhouse. Auntie Rinn, I thought, was inhabited by spirit, she *was* spirit in one of its forms, like the girl whose photograph could make my tongue a stone. I heard the door open and close behind me.

"Alison," Duane said matter-of-factly but with an undertone of anger. "Cousin Miles has been wondering where you were."

I turned around, aware that I did not look normal. Gazing sardonically, even contemptuously at me, though with a trace of interest—the contempt seemed defensive and automatic—was a rather thickset, thoroughly Nordic blond girl of seventeen or eighteen. His daughter. Of course. "Big deal," she said. She was the girl I had seen that morning, clinging to the rider of the motorcycle. "He looks sick. You threaten him or something?"

I shook my head, still trembling but beginning to recover. It had been stupid of me not to remember her name. Heavy-breasted in her T-shirt, large in hip and thigh, she was still an attractive girl, and I was aware of what an odd figure I appeared to her.

Duane looked over at me, then looked again, observing that I was shaken. "This is my girl Alison, Miles. You wanta sit down?"

"No," I said. "I'm fine, thanks."

"Where were you?" asked Duane.

"Why is it your business?" said this stocky warrior with lank blond hair. "I went out."

"Alone?"

"Well, if it's any of your business, I was with Zack." Again, that flat glass-breaking glare. "We passed *him* on the road. He'd probably tell you anyhow, so I might as well."

"I didn't hear the bike."

"Jesus," she groaned, her face an ugly mask of disdain. "Okay. He stopped down by the other house so you wouldn't hear. I walked up the road. You satisfied? Okay?"

Her face twitched, and I saw that what I had taken for disdain was only embarrassment. It was that torturing embarrassment of the teens, and aggression was her weapon against it.

"I don't like you seeing him."

"Suppose you try and stop me." She strode past the two of us into another part of the house. A television set went on a moment later; then she called from another room, "You ought to be out working anyhow."

"She's right," Duane said. "What do you want to do? You look a little funny."

"I just felt a little faint. What's wrong with Zack? Your daughter—" I was not yet ready to call that surly warrior Alison; she seemed, in my imagination, to be stalking and slashing through a forest, lopping trees off at their knees. "She seems to know her own mind."

"Yeah." He managed to smile. "That's one thing she really does know. She's a good girl though. As good as you can expect anything built female to be, anyhow."

"Sure," I agreed, though the qualification made me uneasy. "What's wrong with Zack?"

"He's no good. He's a weirdo. Listen, Alison's right, I ought to be out doing some work, but we still should set up your desk. Or I could just tell you where everything is and you could set it up yourself. It's no work."

Over the noise of the television set, Duane told me where to find the door and the trestles in his basement and then said, "Make yourself at home," and went outside. I watched him through the side windows of the kitchen as he lumbered toward the pole barn and emerged from it atop a giant tractor. He looked comfortable and at ease, as some men look natural on a horse. Somewhere he had acquired a peaked cap which I could see when the tractor had taken him behind the tall rows of corn up in the far field.

The sound of the television drew me into the unexpected room where Alison Updahl had gone. When I was a child this room had been cramped, linoleum-tiled like the kitchen, and occupied chiefly by a sprung davenport and an inefficient television. Duane had evidently rebuilt it; his skills had grown since the days of the Dream House. Now it was three times its former size, thickly and luxuriously carpeted, and furnished in a manner which suggested a great deal of expense. My cousin's daughter, sprawled on a brown couch and watching a color television, looked, in her T-shirt and jeans and bare feet, like a teenager in an affluent suburb of Chicago or Detroit. She did not look up when I entered. She was rigid with self-consciousness.

I said, "What a nice-looking room. I haven't seen it before."

"It stinks." She was still looking at the television, where Fred Astaire was sitting in a racing car. After a second I saw that the car was up on blocks in a closed garage.

"Maybe it just smells new," I said, and earned a glance. But no more than that. She snorted through her nose and returned to the movie.

"What's the film?"

Not bothering to look up again, she said, "*On the Beach*. It's great." She waved off a fly which had settled on her leg. "Suppose you let me try and watch it?"

"Whatever you say." I went to a big comfortable chair at the side of the room and sat. I watched her for a minute or so without either of us speaking. She began to jerk her foot up and down rhythmically, then to toy with her face. After a while she spoke.

"It's about the end of the world. I think that's a pretty neat idea. Zack said I should watch it. He saw it before. Do you live in New York?"

"On Long Island."

"That's New York. I'd like to go there. That's where everything is."

"Oh?"

"You should know. Zack says everything is going to end pretty soon, maybe with people throwing bombs, maybe with earthquakes, it doesn't matter what, and that everybody thinks it'll happen in New York first. But it won't. It'll happen here first. There'll be bodies all over the Midwest, Zack says."

I said that it sounded like Zack was looking forward to it.

She sat up straight, like a wrestler on the mat, and took her attention off the screen for a moment. Her eyes were very pale. "Do you know what they found at the Arden dump a couple of years ago? Just when I was starting high school? Two heads in paper bags. Women's heads. They never found out who they were. Zack says it was a sign."

"A sign of what?"

"That it's beginning. Pretty soon there won't be any schools, any government, any armies. There won't be any of that shit. There'll just be killing. For a long time. Like with Hitler."

I saw that she wished to shock. "I think I can see why your father doesn't like Zack."

She glared at me and returned her gaze sullenly to the screen.

I said, "You must have known that girl who was killed."

She blinked. "Sure I knew her. That was terrible."

"I suppose she helps prove your theories."

"Don't be creepy." Another pale-eyed, sullen stare from the little warrior.

"I like your name." In truth, and despite her foul manners, I was beginning to like her. Lacking her confidence, she had none of her namesake's awesome charm, but she had her energy.

"Ugh."

"Were you named after anybody?"

"Look, I don't know and I don't care, okay?"

Our conversation seemed to be concluded. With an air which suggested that she would stay in that position for life, Alison had returned to the television set. Gregory Peck and Ava Gardner were strolling across a field arm in arm, looking as if they too thought the end of the world was a neat idea. She spoke again before I could rise and leave the room.

"You're not married, are you?"

"No."

"Didn't you get married? Didn't you used to be married?"

I reminded her that she had been at my wedding.

Now she was staring at me again, ignoring Gregory Peck's twitching jaw and Ava Gardner's trembling breast. "You got divorced? Why?"

"My wife died."

"Holy cow, she died? Were you upset? Was it suicide?"

"She died by accident," I said. "Yes, I was upset, but not for the reasons you're imagining. We hadn't lived together for some time. I was upset that another human being, one to whom I had been close, had died senselessly."

She was reacting to me strongly, in an almost sexual way—I could almost see her temperature rising and I thought I could smell blood. "Did you leave her or did she leave you?" She had curled one leg beneath herself and straightened her back on the couch so that she was sitting up and staring at me with those flat sea-water eyes. I was better than the movie.

"I'm not sure that's important. I'm not sure it's any of your business, either."

"She left you." Accent on both pronouns.

"Maybe we left each other."

"Did you think she got what she deserved?"

"Of course not," I said.

"My father would. He'd think that." I saw the point of these odd questions finally, and felt an unexpected twinge of pity for her. She had lived all her life within her father's suspicion of womankind. "So would Zack."

"Well, people can surprise you sometimes."

"Hah," she grunted. It was a proper rejection of my cliché; then she twisted herself back around, almost flouncing on the couch, to watch the movie again. Now my audience was truly over, and this complicated little warrior queen was bidding me leave.

"You needn't bother to show me the way out," I said, and left the room. On the other side of the kitchen, in the little vestibule before the door, was the entrance to the basement. I opened this second door and fumbled for the light. When I found the switch and flicked it up, the bulb illuminated only the wooden staircase and a pool of packed earth at its foot. I began carefully to descend.

It still bothers me that I did not go to Duane to discuss his daughter's loony theories. But I have heard proposals more bizarre from my students—many of them my female students. And as I navigated Duane's basement, stooping over, hands extended, going to what I hoped was the west wall, I considered that he had surely heard it all by now, his daughter's ventriloquial act: he had said this Zack was a weirdo, and I was inclined to agree. We had presumably judged on the same evidence. And their family problems were secondary to me, or tertiary, or quaternary, if I counted Alison Greening, my work and my well-being as my interlocking priorities. *Mea culpa.* Also, I would not have given Alison Updahl more problems than daughterhood had.

The pad of my bandage bumped a clean flat surface and sent it rocking. With my right hand I reached to steady it, and grasped by accident a smooth long wooden handle. It too was swinging. The object, I realized after a moment's further groping, was an ax. I saw that I could have jostled it off its peg and severed my foot. I swore aloud, and felt gently around for more axes in the air. My hand brushed another long depending handle, then another, and after it a fourth. By this time my eyes had begun to adjust to the cellar's darkness, and I could discern the four shadowy handles hanging down in a row from one of the ceiling supports; rakes and garden hoes hung beside them. I worked my way around them, threading through bags of cement and Qwik-Ferm. I stepped over a stack of equipment catalogs. Beyond them a row of things like skinny dwarf mummies leaned against the wall. After a second I knew they were rifles and shotguns in soft cases. Shell boxes were stacked up at one end of the row. Like most farmers, Duane did not find it necessary to put his guns on display. Then I saw what I was looking for. Leaning against the wall, just as Duane had described it, was an old white paneled door, a perfect flat surface for a desk. It had odd doorknobs, but they could easily be taken off. Perhaps Duane would want them—as I got closer to the door, I saw that the knobs were glass, thousand-sided. Beside the door were stacked two trestles, Duane's sawbucks, like insects in the act of copulation. And beside these was a case of empty Coke bottles, the old eight-ounce variety. The top had been ripped off to expose the open, sucking mouths of the bottles.

I thought of calling for Alison Updahl's help, but decided not to. It had been a morning of mistakes, and I did not wish to commit another and upset the delicate peace between us. So I took the trestles up first and put them on the grass outside Duane's back door, and then went back down for what would be my desktop.

The long heavy wooden rectangle was far more awkward to handle, but I managed to get it up the stairs without knocking down a shotgun or dislodging an ax or shattering the old cello-hipped Coke bottles. After I had muscled it up the steep wooden steps, I was sorry I had not called for Alison's help, for my chest leapt and pounded as though a trout were dying in it. My torn hand ached. I slid the door across the linoleum, crumpling several small hooked rugs, and then banged the screen door open with my elbow and wrestled the door outside and down the concrete steps. I was sweating and breathing hard. Mopping my forehead with my sleeve, I propped the door against the trestles and looked at it in dismay. Spider webs, dust and insects made scurrying lacy patterns over the white paint.

The solution, a garden hose, lay at my feet. I twisted the knob set into the base of the house and played the hose over the door until all the filth had been sluiced away. I was tempted to run it over myself. My hands were black and my shirt was ruined, and sweat poured out of my scalp. But I merely held my hands one after the other in the jet of cold water, wetting the bandage as little as possible. Application of magical substance.

Cold water!

I dropped the still-spurting hose and went across Duane's patchy lawn in the direction of the barn. When I looked to the right I could see my cousin's head and upper body grinding along atop the invisible tractor, as if he were floated by a perverse, bumpy wind. I went over the gravel and dust of the drive. The dog began to curse me with big windy arrogant curses. I reached the tank and plunged my good hand into the greenish water and closed it over a beer bottle to which clung my bloody handkerchief. This I threw into the weeds. I extracted the dripping bottle. I had just twisted off the cap and begun to pour into me the tingling liquid when I saw the blond-fringed face of the Tin Woodsman staring at me from the kitchen window. She winked. Suddenly we were grinning at each other, and I felt the snarl of emotion which the day had caused in me begin to loosen. It was as though I had found an ally. Really, it could not have been easy for a high-spirited girl to have my cousin Duane for a father.

3

After I had stripped it of the knobs and set it up in the empty upstairs bedroom of my grandmother's house, the desk looked sturdy and serviceable, a present-day echo of all the desks I have known and used. The room itself, small, white and pine-floored, was a perfect place for literary work, since the bare walls offered vistas for contemplation and the single window which faced the barn and the path to Duane's house, opportunity for distraction. Soon I had all my paraphernalia arranged on the desk—typewriter, paper, notes, the beginning of my draft and my outline. Typex, pens, pencils, paperclips. The novels I placed in several neat piles beside the chair. For a moment I felt that spirit lay in labor, in hard work, the more recondite and irrelevant the better. My dogged dissertation would be my linkage with Alison Greening; my work would summon her.

But that day I did no work. I sat at my desk and looked out of the window, watching my cousin's daughter cross and recross the grass and the path as she went to the equipment shed or down to the barn, glancing curiously at my window, and then watching Duane ride up from the road on his giant tractor. He put it in the pole barn and then lumbered back across to his house, scratching himself on the bottom. I felt—I suppose I felt—lonely and elated, primed for an event and still flat and hollow at the same time, as though I were not what I was pretending to be, but were merely an actor waiting for the role to begin. It is a feeling I often have.

I sat there watching the sky darken over the barn as the path lost its definition and the tops of Duane's house and the barn first stood out with greater clarity against a background of darkening blue and then were absorbed into the sky, as if bites were taken out of them. Lights appeared in Duane's house in series, each window lighting up as though it were timed to go on a moment after its neighbor. I thought Alison might appear on the path, her T-shirt shining in moonlight as she sulkily walked toward me, the lank ends of her hair swinging in rhythm with her heavy thighs. After a time I fell asleep. I could have been out no more than an hour, but when I opened my eyes only one light was on in Duane's house and the territory between our two dwellings seemed as dark and pathless as a jungle. Hungry, I groped my way downstairs and into the kitchen. The house was clammy and musty, and everything was cold to my touch. When I opened the refrigerator I found that either Duane or Mrs. Sunderson had stocked it with enough food for that night and the following morning—butter, bread, eggs, potatoes, two lamb chops, cheese. I fried the chops and wolfed them down with slices of bread and butter. A meal without wine is not a meal for a grown man. I gnawed at the block of cheddar for dessert. Then I dumped the dishes in the sink for the cleaning woman and went burping back upstairs to the bedroom. When I looked in at my workroom I saw a single light still on in Duane's house, but at its far end. Alison's bedroom, presumably. As I stood looking at it I heard the buzz of a motorcycle going up the road. It increased in volume until it came about level with my position and then it abruptly shut off. My desk looked malevolent, like the fat black center of a spider web.

My bedroom, of course, had been my grandmother's. Yet I see that it is not of course, for she had moved to the chillier, smaller bedroom upstairs only after the death of my grandfather; for this reason it had a newer bed, and for that reason I chose it. It was as far as you could get from the old bedroom and still be in the house—on the opposite side and up the narrow stairs. My grandfather had died when I was a small child, so all my memories of my grandmother are of her as a widow, a wrinkled old woman who climbed the narrow stairs to go to bed. As some old women do, she swung in size between extremes of heaviness and thinness, alternating every three or four years, and finally settled on being thin, and died like that. Given that the narrow little room had this history, it is unsurprising that I had a dream about my grandmother; but I found the emotional violence of the dream shocking.

I was in the sitting room, which was furnished not with Duane's office contraptions but in the old way. My grandmother was seated on her wooden-backed sofa, nervously looking at her hands.—Why did you have to come back?

—What?

—You're a fool.

—I don't understand.

—Haven't enough people died already?

Then she abruptly stood up and walked out of the room onto the porch, where she sat in the rusty old swing.—Miles, you're an innocent. She raised her fists to me and her face contorted in a way I had never seen.—Fool, fool, fool! Fool innocent!

I sat beside her. She began to beat me around my head and shoulders, and I bent my neck to receive her blows. I wished for death.

She said—You put it in motion and it will destroy you.

All the life went out of me, and the setting receded until I was suspended in a blue fluid, far away. The distance was important. I was in a far blue drifting place, still weeping. Then I understood that it was death. Distant conversation, distant laughter filtered to me, as though through walls. When I became aware of other bodies floating as mine was, hundreds of them, thousands of bodies spinning as if from trees in that blue horror, I heard the sound of loud handclaps. Three of them. Three widely spaced loud claps, unutterably cynical. That was the sound of death, and it held no dignity. It was the end of a poor performance.

Sweating, I rolled over on the bed, gasping. The dream seemed to have lasted for hours—I seemed to have been caught in it from the first moments of sleep. I lay panting under the great weight of guilt and panic. I was held responsible for many deaths; I had caused these deaths, and everybody knew.

Only gradually, as I saw light begin to crawl through the window, did rationality appear. I had never killed anyone. My grandmother was dead; I was in the valley to get work done. *Easy*, I said out loud. Only a dream. I tried to produce alpha waves, and began to breathe deeply and evenly. It took a long time for the enormous sense of guilt to dissipate.

I have always been a person with an enormous excess of guilt. My true vocation is that of guilt expert.

For three-fourths of an hour I tried to fall asleep again, but my system would not permit it, my nerves felt as though doused in caffeine, and I got out of bed just past five. Through the bedroom window I could see dawn slowly beginning. Dew lay silvery over the old huge black iron pig trough in the field near the house where my grandfather had kept hogs. The field was now used for grazing a horse and a neighbor's cows. Beside humped cows, the tall chestnut mare was still asleep, standing with its long neck drooping down. Further up began a sandstone hill, pocked with shallow caves and overgrown with small trees and intensely curling vines and weeds. It looked much as it had during my childhood. A very light gray fog, more like a stationary mist than fog, hung in the lowest parts of the field. As I stood by the window, absorbing peace from that long green landscape edged with fog, two things happened which made me momentarily and at first without realizing it hold my breath. I had let my eye travel up across the road and the fields—the colors of Duane's corn were beautifully muted by the gray light, and the woods seemed blacker than in the sunlight. Light fog like smoke came curling out of the mass of trees. Then I unmistakably saw a figure emerge, embraced by the fog, and hover for a moment at the boundary between wood and field. I remembered my mother telling me of seeing a wolf come from those woods forty years before—of seeing a wolf pause perhaps at that exact spot and stand tense with hunger, leveling its muzzle at the house and barn. It was, I was almost certain, the same person I had seen the previous afternoon. Like the wolf, it too stood and paused and looked toward the house. My heart froze. I thought: a hunter. No. Not a hunter. I didn't know why not, but not. In the same second I heard the bee-noise of a motorcycle.

I glanced at the empty road and then back up to the tree line. The figure had disappeared. After a moment, the motorcycle entered my frame of vision.

She was hanging on behind him, wearing a blanketlike poncho against the morning chill. He wore uniform black, jacket to boots. He cut the engine just after they passed out of my sight, and I wrestled myself into my bathrobe and hurried down the narrow stairs. I quietly stepped onto the screen porch. They were not kissing or embracing, as I had expected, but were merely standing in the road, looking in different directions. She put her hand on his shoulder; I could see his skinny intense enthusiast's face, a wild face. He had long upswept old-fashioned rock-'n'-roll hair, raven black. When she removed her hand, he nodded curtly. The gesture seemed to express both dependence and leadership. She brushed his face with her fingers and began to walk up the road. Like me, he watched her go, walking along with her stiff Tin Woodsman's walk, and then he jumped back on his bike, gunned it, wheeled around in a flashy Evel Knievel circle and roared away.

I stepped back inside and realized that the inside of the house was as cold and moist as the porch. On my chilled feet I went into the kitchen and put a kettle of water on the stove. In a cupboard I found a jar of instant coffee. Then I stepped back outside onto the damp boards of the porch. The sun was just beginning to appear, huge and violently red. After a minute or two Alison reappeared, coming quietly around the side of her house, taking long slow strides. She crossed the back of her house until she reached the last window, where the light still burned. When she stood before it she levered the window up until she stood on tiptoe and then she hoisted herself into the bedroom.

After two cups of the bitter coffee, gulped while standing in bathrobe and bare feet on the cold kitchen floor; after two eggs fried in butter and a slice of toast, eaten at the old round wooden table with the sun beginning to dispel the traces of fog; after appreciation of the way cooking had warmed the kitchen; after adding more greasy dishes to those in the sink; after undressing in the bathroom and with distaste scrutinizing my expanding belly; after similar scrutiny of my face; after showering in the tub; after shaving; after pulling clean clothes out of my suitcase and dressing in a plaid shirt, jeans and boots; after all this I still could not begin to work. I sat at my desk and examined the points of my pencils, unable to rid my mind of that awful dream. Although the day was rapidly warming, my little room and the entire house seemed pervaded with cold breath, a chill spirit I associated with the effect of the nightmare.

I went downstairs and took the photograph of Alison off its hook in the living room. Back upstairs I placed it on the back of the desk, tilting it against the wall. Then I remembered that there was another photograph which had hung downstairs—indeed there had been many others, and Duane had presumably packed most of them away with the furniture after our grandmother's death. But only one of all those photographs of various grandchildren and nephews and children of nephews concerned me. This was a photograph of Alison and myself, taken by Duane's father in 1955, at the beginning of the summer. We were standing before a walnut tree, holding hands, looking into the incomprehensible future. Just thinking of the picture now made me shiver.

I looked at my watch. It was still only six-thirty. I realized that it would be impossible to get any work done in my mood and at such an hour. At any rate, I was unused to doing any sort of writing before lunch. I felt restless, and had to get out of my workroom where the typewriter, the pencils, the desk itself rebuked me.

Downstairs, I perched on Duane's uncomfortable sofa while I sipped a third cup of coffee. I thought about D. H. Lawrence. I thought about Alison Updahl's nightime excursion. I rather approved of that, though I thought her company could have been better chosen. At least the daughter would be more experienced than her father; there would be no Dream Houses for her. Then D. H. Lawrence began to rant at me again. I had written much of the middle portion of the book, but I had saved the beginning and ending for last—the ending was fully outlined, but I still had no idea of how to begin. I needed a first sentence, preferably one with several scholarly clauses. From which forty introductory pages could eloquently, commandingly flow.

I went into the kitchen, once again cold and damp. I lowered my cup into the sink with the other dishes. Then I walked around the table and took the telephone book from its shelf beneath the old wall phone. It was a thin volume, about the size of a first collection of poems, and on the cover was a pastoral photograph of two small boys fishing from a pier. The boys were surrounded by blue cold-looking river water nicked by a million ripples. Though barefoot, the boys on the pier wore sweaters. Across the river massed a thick unbroken line of trees—like an eyebrow across a thug's face. When I had looked at it for longer than a second, the photograph seemed less pastoral than ominous. It was menacing. My own feet had been bare on cold boards; I too had been suspended above indifferent blue water. In the photograph the sun was dying. I folded the cover back and flipped to the page I wanted and dialed the number.

While the phone trilled at the other end I gazed dumbly through the window facing the lawn and the road, and through the trunks of the walnut trees saw Duane already mounted on his tractor, plying majestically across the field near where the trees began. He reached one end of his course and made the heavy tractor twirl around as easily as a bicycle. On the third ring the receiver was lifted. She did not say hello, and after a moment I spoke myself.

"Rinn? Is that you, Auntie Rinn?"

"Of course."

"This is Miles, Auntie Rinn. Miles Teagarden."

"I know who it is, Miles. Remember to speak loudly. I never use this terrible invention."

"Duane said he told you I was coming."

"What?"

"Duane said—Auntie Rinn, could I come up to see you this morning? I can't work, and I couldn't sleep."

"No," she said, as if she already knew.

"May I come? Is it too early for a visit?"

"You know farm people, Miles. Even the oldsters get up and doing early in the day."

I put on a jacket and walked across the dew-sodden lawn to the Volkswagen. Condensation streamed off the windshield. As I swung into the road where I had seen the Tin Woodsman make her curious and emotionless departure from the boy who could only be Zack, I heard my grandmother's voice, speaking quite clearly some words she had uttered in my dream. *Why did you have to come back?* It was as though she were seated beside me. I could even smell her familiar odor of woodsmoke. I pulled off to the side of the road and wiped my face with my hands. I wouldn't have known how to answer her.

The trees which began toward the end of the rutted road to Rinn's house, just where the valley begins to climb up into the hills, had grown taller and thicker. The pale early sunlight came slanting down, spangling the corrugated trunks and the spongy, overgrown earth. A little further along the narrow road, some of the rags of light struck the side of Rinn's chicken coop, the top of which was fully illuminated by sunlight. It was a big barnlike structure, long and high as a two-story house, painted red; little comic-strip windows like missing pieces of a jigsaw puzzle arbitrarily dotted the side facing me. Further up the rise stood her house, which had once been of white boards but now badly needed paint. The three-room structure looked as though a cobweb had settled over it. The trees had marched right into her tiny area of lawn, and big thick branches wove together over her roof. As I got out of the car, Rinn appeared on her little porch; a moment later she opened the screen door and came outside. She was wearing an ancient blue print dress, calf-high rubber boots and an old khaki army jacket with what seemed to be hundreds of pockets.

"Welcome, Miles," she said, with that Norwegian lilt in her voice. Her face was more wrinkled than ever, but it was luminous. One of her eyes was covered with a film like milk. "Well. You haven't been here since you were a boy, and now you're a man. A nice tall man. You look like a Norwegian."

"I should," I said, "with you in my family." I bent to kiss her, but she held out her hand, and I took it. She wore knitted fingerless gloves, and her hand felt like loose bones wrapped in cloth. "You look wonderful," I said.

"Oh, goodness. I have coffee on the stove, if you're a coffee drinker."

Inside her tiny, overheated kitchen she thrust sticks of wood down into the heart of her stove until the iron pot bubbled. Coffee came out in a thin black stream. "You're not always up so early," she said. "Are you troubled?"

"I don't really know. I'm having trouble getting started on my work."

"It isn't your work though, is it, Miles?"

"I don't know."

"Men should be workers. My young man was a worker." Her good eye, almost as pale as Alison's and a thousand times more informed, examined me over her cup. "Duane is a good worker."

"What do you know about his daughter?" I was interested in her opinion.

"She was misnamed. Duane should have named her Jessie, after my sister. That would have been right, to name her after his mother. The girl needs to be guided. She's high-strung." Rinn peeled a cloth off a plate loaded with round flat discs of a breadlike substance I knew well. "But she is much nicer than she wants you to think."

"You mean you still make lefsa?" I said, laughing, delighted. It was one of the great treats of the valley.

"Lefsa and sonnbockles. Of course I make them. I can still use a rolling pin. I make them whenever I can see well enough."

I spread thick butter on a piece and rolled it up into a long cigar shape. It was still like eating bread prepared by angels.

"Are you going to be alone this summer?"

"I'm alone now."

"It's better to be alone. Better for you." She meant me specifically, not mankind in general.

"Well, I haven't had much luck in my relationships."

"*Luck*," she snorted, and hunched further over the table. "Miles, do not court misery."

"Misery?" I was genuinely startled. "It's not that bad."

"Miles, there is great trouble here now. In the valley. You have heard the news. Do not associate yourself with it. You must be alone and apart, doing your work. You are an outsider, Miles, a natural outsider, and people will resent your being near. People know about you. You have been touched with trouble in the past, and you must avoid it now. Jessie is afraid that you will be touched by it."

"Huh?" It was with talk like this that she had terrified the wits out of me when I was a child.

"You are innocent," she said—the same words my grandmother had used, in my dream. "But you know what I am talking about."

"Don't worry. No matter how provocative they get, little girls don't tempt me. But I don't get what you mean by innocent."

"I mean that you expect too much," she said. "I think I am confusing you. Do you wish more to eat or do you care to help me gather my eggs?"

I remembered her comments about work, and stood. I followed her outside and through the trees down the slope to the henhouse. "Go in quietly," she said. "These birds can be excited easily, and they might suffocate each other in panic."

Very gently, she opened the door of the tall red structure. A terrible stench came to me first, like ashes and dung and blood, and then my eyes adjusted to the dark and I saw hens sitting on their nests, in tiers and rows like books on a bookshelf. The scene was a parody of my Long Island lecture halls. We stepped inside. A few birds squawked. I was standing in a mess of dirt, sawdust, feathers, a pervasive white substance and eggshells. The smell hung acrid and powerful in the air.

"Watch how I do," Rinn said. "I can't see in this light, but I know where they all are." She approached the nearest nest and inserted her hand between the bird and the straw without at all stirring the hen. It blinked, and continued to stare wildly out from either side of its head. Her hand reappeared with two eggs, and a second later, with another. A few feathers were glued to them with a gray-white fluid. "You start at that end, Miles," she said, pointing. "There's a basket on the floor."

She covered her half before I had coaxed a dozen eggs out of half as many unhappy hens. Duane's thick bandage made for clumsy work. Then I went up a ladder where the air was even denser and stole more eggs from increasingly agitated birds; one of the last ones pecked me in the hand while I held her three warm products. It was like being stabbed with a spoon.

Finally we were done, and stood outside in the rapidly warming air beneath the looming trees. I inhaled several deep, cleansing breaths. At my side, Rinn said, "Thank you for helping me. You might make a worker someday, Miles."

I looked down at the thin hunched figure in the outlandish clothes. "Did you mean to tell me that you talk to my grandmother? To Jessie?"

She smiled, making her face look Chinese. "I meant that she talks to me. Isn't that what I said?" But before I could respond, she said, "She is watching you, Miles. Jessie always loved you. She wants to protect you."

"I guess I'm flattered. Maybe—" I was going to say, maybe that's why I dreamed about her, but I was hesitant to describe that dream to Rinn. She would have made too much of it.

"Yes?" The old woman was looking alerted to a current inaudible to me. "Yes? Did you say more? Often I don't hear properly."

"Why did you think I would get involved with Alison Updahl? That was a little farfetched even for me, don't you think?"

Her face shut like a clamp, losing all its luminosity. "I meant Alison Greening. Your cousin, Miles. Your cousin Alison."

"But—" I was going to say *But I love her*, but shock choked off the startled admission.

"Excuse me. I can no longer hear." She began to move away from me, and then stopped to look back. I thought the milky eye was turned toward me. She appeared to be angry and impatient, but inside all those wrinkles she may just have been tired. "You are always welcome here, Miles." Then she carried her basket and mine back up to the little house darkened by trees. I was already past the church on the way home when I remembered that I had intended to buy a dozen eggs from her.

I parked the car in the gritty driveway and went along the porch and through the front room to the narrow staircase. The house still felt damp and cold, though the temperature was now in the upper seventies. Upstairs I sat at my desk and tried to think. D. H. Lawrence seemed even more foreign than he had the previous day. Auntie Rinn's final words about my cousin both thrilled and upset me. To hear another person allude to Alison Greening was like hearing someone else recount your dreams as his own. I riffled the pages of *The White Peacock*, far too nervous to write. Mention of her name had set me on edge. I had used her name as a weapon against Duane, and Rinn had used the same trick on me.

From downstairs I heard a sudden noise: a door slamming, a book dropped? It was followed by a noise of shod feet hushing across the floor. Alison Updahl, I was sure, come around to flirt while expounding her boyfriend's crazy philosophy. I agreed with Rinn, Alison was a far more agreeable person than she wished anyone to know, but at that moment I could not bear to think of anyone casually usurping my territory.

I thrust my chair away from the desk and went thundering down the narrow steps. I burst into the living room. No one was there. Then I heard a rattling noise from the kitchen, and imagined her nosily exploring the cupboards. "Come on, get out of there," I called. "You tell me when you want to come over, and maybe I'll invite you. I'm trying to get some work done."

The clattering ceased. "Get out of that kitchen right now," I ordered, striding across the room toward the door.

A large pale flustered-looking woman appeared before me, wiping her hands on a towel. The gesture made her large loose upper arms wobble. Horror showed on her face, and in her eyes, magnified behind thick glasses.

"Oh my God," I blurted. "Who are you?"

Her mouth worked.

"Oh my God. I'm sorry. I thought you were someone else."

"I'm—"

"I'm sorry, I'm sorry. Please sit down."

"I'm Mrs. Sunderson. I thought it would be all right. I came in to do work, the door was open . . . You're—you're Eve's boy?" She backed away from me, and almost fell as she stepped backwards over the step down into the kitchen.

"Won't you please sit down? I'm honestly sorry, I didn't mean to—" She was still retreating from me, holding the dishtowel like a shield. Her eyes goggled, the effect made even worse by her glasses.

"You want cleaning? You want me to clean? Duane said last week I should come today. I didn't know if I should, what with, I mean since we, since this terrible . . . but Red said I should, take my mind off, he said."

"Yes, yes. I do want you to come. Please forgive me. I thought it was someone else. Please sit for a moment."

She sat heavily in one of the chairs at the table. Her face was going red in blotches.

"You're very welcome here," I weakly said. "I trust you understand what I want you to do?"

She nodded, her eyes oily and glazed behind the big lenses.

"I want you to come early enough to make breakfast for me, wash all the dishes, and keep the house clean. At one I'll want lunch. Is that what you agreed to do? Also, please don't bother about the room I'm working in. I want that room undisturbed."

"The room . . . ?"

"Up there." I pointed. "I'll be up and working most mornings when you arrive, so just call me when you have breakfast ready. Have you ever done any work like this before?"

Resentment showed in the puffy face for a moment. "I kept house for my husband and son for forty years."

"Of course, I should have thought. I'm sorry."

"Duane explained about the car? That I can't drive? You will have to do the shopping."

"Yes, okay. I'll go out this afternoon. I want to see Arden again anyhow."

She continued to stare dumbly at me. I realized that I was treating her like a servant, but could not stop. Embarrassment and a fictitious dignity made me stiff. If she had been the Woodsman, I could have apologized.

"I said five dollars a week?"

"Don't be silly. You deserve seven. I might as well give you the first week's wages in advance." I counted seven dollar bills out onto the table before her. She stared resentfully at the little pile of bills.

"I said five."

"Call the extra two dollars hardship allowance. Now you don't have to worry about making breakfast this morning since I got up early and made my own, but I'd like lunch somewhere around one. After washing the lunch dishes, you'll be free to leave, if the downstairs rooms look clean enough to you. All right? I really am sorry about that shouting. It was a case of mistaken identity."

"Uh," she said. "I said five."

"I don't want to exploit you, Mrs. Sunderson. For the sake of my conscience, please take the extra two."

"A picture is missing. From the front parlor."

"I took it upstairs. Well, if you will get on with your work, I'll get on with mine."

Portion of Statement by Tuta Sunderson:

July 18

People who act like that aren't right in the head. He was like a crazy man, and then he tried to buy me back with an extra two dollars. Well, we don't work that way up here, do we? Red said I shouldn't go back to that crazy man, but I went right on going back, and that was how I learned so much about his ways.

I wish Jerome was alive yet so he could give him what-for. Jerome wouldn't have stood for that man's way of talking nor his ways of being neither.

Just ask yourself this—who was he expecting, anyhow? And who came?

I sat dumbly at my desk, unable to summon even a single coherent thought about D. H. Lawrence. I realized that I had never liked more than two of his novels. If I actually published a book about Lawrence, I was chained to talking about him for the rest of my life. In any case, I could not work while imagining that guilt-inducing woman shifting herself about through Duane's furniture. I bent my head and rested it on the desk for a moment. I felt Alison's photograph shedding light on the top of my head. My hands had begun to tremble, and a vein in my neck pulsed wildly. I bathed in that melting, embracing warmth. Application of you know what. When I got up and went back downstairs, I found that my knees were shaking.

Tuta Sunderson peeked at me from the corners of her eyes where she knelt before a pail of water as I went wordlessly by. Understandably, she looked as though she expected me to aim a kick at her backside. "Oh, a letter came for you," she uttered. "I forgot to tell you before." She gestured weakly toward a glass-fronted chest and I snatched up the envelope as I went out.

My name was written in a flowing hand on the creamy outside of the envelope. After I got into the baking interior of the VW I ripped open the letter. I pulled out a sheet of stationery. I turned it over. Confused, I turned it over again. It was blank. I groaned. When I grabbed the envelope up from the floor of the car I saw that it bore no return address, and had been posted the night before in Arden.

I shot backwards out of the driveway, not really caring if another vehicle were coming. At the sound of my tires squealing, Duane far off in the field turned his head. I sped away as if from a murder, the blank page and envelope lying on the seat beside me. The car's engine began to sputter, lights flashed as if the hand of Spirit had momentarily thrust in and touched them; by instinct I looked up across the fields to the woods. No one stood there. No figure not a hunter but a wolf. If it was a trick, a worthless joke, who? An old enemy in Arden? I wasn't sure I still had any; but I hadn't expected Andy's wife still to carry hostility toward me like a raised knife. If a sign, of what? Of some future message? I grabbed the envelope again and held it clamped to the wheel with both hands. "Damn," I muttered and dropped it back on the other seat as I floored the accelerator.

It was from this moment that all began to go wrong, askew. My mistake with Tuta Sunderson, the maddening letter—perhaps I would have acted more rationally if the threatening scene in the Plainview diner had never occurred. Yet I think I knew what I was going to do in Arden long before it was a conscious thought. My old response to stress. And I thought I might know the handwriting on that envelope.

Speeding, I recklessly zoomed up the twisting hilly road to Arden. I nearly forced a tractor off the road. Bunny Is Good Bread; Surge Milking Machines; This Is Holsum Country; Nutrea Feeds; Highway 93; DeKalb Corn (orange words on green wings); Broiler Days: the billboards and roadsigns flashed by. At the crest of the long hill where the road opens into a view like that in Italian paintings, endless green and varied distance dotted with white buildings and thick random groups of trees, a tall sign with a painted thermometer and pointer announced that the goal of the Arden Community Chest was $4,500. I switched on the radio and heard the hollow, spurious voice of Michael Moose. ". . . report no progress in the shocking—" I turned the dial and let loud rock music assail me because I hated it.

An area of frame Andy Hardy houses, the R-D-N Motel, and I was going down Main Street, past the high school, where Arden lay at the bottom of the last hill. Pigeons were circling over the brick fortress of the courthouse and town hall, and in the odd quiet of the moment I could hear their wings beating after I had swung into a parking space before the Coast to Coast Store and shut off the motor. Wingbeats filled and agitated the air like drumming; when I got out of the car I saw that the birds had wheeled away from the courthouse/ town-hall and bannered out over Main Street. Apart from an old man sitting on the steps to Freebo's Bar, they were the only visible living things. A tin sign clacked and banged somewhere behind me. It was as though some evil visitation had drawn everyone in Arden inside behind locked doors.

I went into the store and picked up enough groceries for a week; the two women in the aisle looked at me oddly, and would not meet my eye. The atmosphere in the grocery seemed almost ostentatiously hostile, almost theat-rical—those women glanced at me, then quickly lowered their eyes, then pierced me with covert glances from the sides of their eyes. *Who are you and what are you doing here?* It was as though they had spoken. I counted my money down onto the counter and went hurriedly back outside and locked the grocery bags in the VW. I had to get a bottle of whiskey.

Down the street, just passing the corner of the Annex Hotel and the Angler's Bar, walking toward me with his hunched bustling walk, accompanied by his sour-looking wife, was Pastor Bertilsson. He was my least favorite clergyman. He had not yet seen me. I looked around in panic. Across the street was a two-story building labeled Zumgo, a name I recalled having heard before. It was here Duane had said Paul Kant was working. I turned my back on the Bertilssons and hurried across the street.

Unlike the Plainview diner, Zumgo's had resisted any efforts to bring it up to date, and my first response was to relish the old-fashioned fittings of the store—change was sent enclosed in metal cylinders, racketing down on wires from an office suspended below the ceiling, the counters were wooden, the floors of boards worn smooth and sent rippling by time. A moment afterwards I noticed the threadbare, depressed look of the place; most of the tables were only scantily covered by goods, and the salesladies—even now staring at me with displeasure—were aged shabby horrors with rouge enameling their cheeks. A few overweight women desultorily picked at underwear strewn across a table. I could not imagine Paul Kant at work in such a place.

The woman I approached seemed to share my attitude. She drew her lips back over false teeth and smiled. "Paul? You a friend of Paul's?"

"I just said, where is he working? I want to see him."

"Well, he isn't working. Are you a friend of his?"

"You mean he doesn't work here?"

"When he's in he does, I guess. He's home sick. Least that's what he told Miss Nord. Said he couldn't come in today. Looks funny, I think. You a friend of his?"

"Yes. I used to be, at least."

For some reason, this caused her canine, hungry interest in me to become merriment. She gave me a glimpse of her plastic-coated gums and called to another woman behind the counter, "He's a friend of Paul's. Says he doesn't know where he is." The other woman joined her laughter. "A friend of Paul's?"

"Christ," I muttered, turning away. I went back to ask, "Do you know if he will be in tomorrow?" and got only malicious staring eyes for my answer. I noticed that two or three of the customers were staring at me. Auntie Rinn's advice came back to me. Certainly some of the women seemed to resent the presence of a stranger.

Baffled, still angry, I paced around the store until even the first old woman had ceased to giggle and gossip about me with her partner. I had a purpose I did not then wish to admit to myself. I examined unspeakable clothing; I regarded sad toys and dusty envelopes and yards of material best suited to the backs of horses. The old response to stress became conscious: I took a five-dollar bill and folded it into my palm.

I was helpless before my own advice to *get out*.

On the second floor I spun a rack of paperback books. One of the jackets and titles snagged my attention. My Ph.D. supervisor, a famous scholar, had written it. It was Maccabee's most popular book, *The Enchanted Dream*. Actually a mechanical treatise on nineteenth-century poets, it had been tricked out with a jazzy cover showing a long-haired young man apparently inhaling an illegal substance while a slightly less beautiful nude maiden coiled lambent legs and tendrils of hair about him. Unable to control the impulse which was my purpose—I hadn't thought of such amazing luck—I took the book off the rack and slid it into my jacket pocket. It had been Maccabee who had suggested I write on Lawrence. Then I turned cautiously around (when it was too late for caution) and saw that no one had witnessed my theft. My chest thumped with relief; the book hung unobtrusively in my pocket. I twitched the pocket flap up over the top of the book. When I passed the cash register I dropped the bill on the counter and continued out onto the street.

And nearly into the arms of Bertilsson. That hypocritical pink moonface and wet smile were directed, I swear, toward the pocket with Maccabee's book before Bertilsson decided he wished to favor my face with them. Balder and fatter, he was even more repulsive than I remembered him. His wife, several inches taller than he, stood stock-still beside him, her posture suggesting that I might be expected at any moment to commit an act of disgusting perversity.

As I suppose I had, in her eyes. When Joan and I were married, Bertilsson had taken pains to incorporate into his homiletic address some allusions to my past misdeeds; later, on a drunken night during our honeymoon, I wrote him an abusive letter and posted it on the spot. I think I said that he did not deserve to wear his collar.

Perhaps the recollection of that statement was what put the malicious icy chips in his eyes, far behind the sanctimony, when he greeted me. "Young Miles. What have we here? Young Miles."

"We heard you were back," said his wife.

"I'll expect you at tomorrow's services."

"That's interesting. Well, I must—"

"I was grieved to hear of your divorce. Most of my marriages are of the enduring kind. But then few of the couples it is my privilege to unite are as sophisticated as you and your—Judy, was it? Few of them write notes of thanks as distinctive as yours."

"Her name was Joan. We never did get divorced in the sense you mean. She was killed."

His wife swallowed, but Bertilsson, for all his oiliness, was no coward. He continued to look straight at me, the malice behind the sanctimony undimmed. "I *am* sorry. Truly sorry for you, Miles. Perhaps it's a blessing that your grandmother did not live to see how you . . ." He shrugged.

"How I what?"

"Seem to have a tragic propensity for being nearby when young women are lost to life."

"I wasn't even in town when that Olson girl was killed," I said. "And Joan was anything but nearby when she died."

I might as well have been speaking to a bronze Buddha. He smiled. "I see I must apologize. I did not intend my remark in that way. No, not in the least. But in fact, since you bring up the matter, Mrs. Bertilsson and I are in Arden on a related mission, a mission of mercy I think I may describe it, of the Lord's mercy, related to an event of which you seem to be in ignorance."

He had long ago begun to speak in the cadences of his tedious sermons, but usually it was possible to figure out what he was talking about. "Look. I'm sorry, but I have to get going."

"We were just with the parents." He was still smiling, but now the smile expressed great sad meretricious gravity.

My God, how could he think that I had not heard of that?

"Oh, yes."

"So you do know about it? You have heard?"

"I don't know what I've heard. I'll be going now."

For the first time, his wife spoke. "You'd be wise to keep going until you get back where you came from, Miles. We don't think much of you around here. You left too many bad memories." Her husband kept that grave, falsely humble smile on his face.

"So write me another blank letter," I said, and left them. I recrossed the street and stepped over the nodding drunk into Freebo's Bar. After a few drinks consumed while listening to a half-audible Michael Moose compete with the mumbled conversation of men who conspicuously avoided catching my eye, I had a few more drinks and attracted a little attention by dismembering Maccabee's book on the bar, at first ripping out one page at a time and then seizing handfuls of paper and tearing them out. When the barman came up to object I told him, "I wrote this book and I just decided it's terrible." I shredded the cover so that he could not read Maccabee's name. "Can't a man even tear up his own book in this bar?"

"Maybe you'd better go, Mr. Teagarden," the bartender said. "You can come back tomorrow." I hadn't realized that he knew my name.

"Can tear up my own book if I want to, can't I?"

"Look, Mr. Teagarden," he said. "Another girl was murdered last night. Her name was Jenny Strand. We all knew that girl. We're all a little upset around here."

It happened like this:

A girl of thirteen, Jenny Strand, had been to the Arden cinema with four of her friends to see a Woody Allen movie, Love and Death. *Her parents had forbidden her to see it: they did not want their daughter to receive her sex education from Hollywood, and the title made them uneasy. She was an only daughter among three boys, and while her father thought the boys could pick things up for themselves, he wanted Jenny to be taught in some way that would preserve her innocence. He thought his wife should be responsible: she was waiting for Pastor Bertilsson to suggest something.*

Because of the death of Gwen Olson, they had been unusually protective when Jenny said that she wanted to see a friend, Jo Slavitt, after dinner. —Be back by ten, her father said. —Sure, she agreed. The picture would be over an hour before that. Their objections were silly, and she had no intention of being restricted by anyone's silliness.

It did not bother her that she and Gwen Olson had looked enough alike to be taken, in a larger town—one where everyone's family was not known—for sisters. Jenny had never been able to see the resemblance, though several teachers had mentioned it. She was not flattered. Gwen Olson had been a year younger, a farm girl, in another set. A tramp had killed her—everybody said that. You still saw tramps, bums, gypsies, whatever they were, hanging around town a day or two and then going wherever they went. Gwen Olson had been dumb enough to go wandering alone by the river at night, out of the sight of the town.

She met Jo at her house and they walked five blocks in sunshine to the theater. The other girls were waiting. The five of them sat in the last row, ritually eating candy. —My parents think this is a dirty movie, she whispered to Jo Slavitt. Jo put her hand to her mouth, pretending to be shocked. In fact they all thought the movie was boring.

When it was over, they stood on the sidewalk, empty of comment. As always, there was nowhere to go. They began to drift up Main Street toward the river.

—I get scared just thinking about Gwen, said Marilyn Hicks, a girl with thin fair hair and braces on her teeth.

—So don't think about her, snapped Jenny. It was a typical Marilyn Hicks comment.

—*What do you think happened to her?*

—*You know what happened to her,* said Jenny, *who was less innocent than her parents supposed.*

—*It could have been anyone,* said another girl in a shuddery voice.

—*Like Billy Hummel and his friends over there?* said Jenny, *ridiculing the other girl.* She was looking across the street, where some of the older boys from AHS, football players, were wasting time hanging around the telephone-company building. It was getting darker, and she could see the white flock of the letters on their team jackets reflected in the big phone-company window. In ten minutes the boys would be sick of watching themselves in the window and would drift off down the street.

—*My dad says the police better watch someone real close.*

—*I know who he means,* said Jo. They all knew whom Marilyn's father meant.

—*I'm hungry again. Let's go to the drive-in.*

They began to trudge up the road. The boys took no notice of them.

—*The food at the drive-in is junk,* said Jenny. *They put garbage in it.*

—*Sourpuss. Look at ole sourpuss.*

—*And that movie was dumb.*

—*Sourpuss. Just because Billy Hummel didn't look at you.*

—*Well, at least I don't think he murdered anyone.*

Suddenly she had had enough of them. They were standing in a circle around her, waiting for her to move, their shoulders slumping, their faces empty. Billy Hummel and the other boys in team jackets were walking the other way, back into town. She was tired and disappointed—with the boys, with the movie, with her friends. For a moment she wished passionately that she were grown up. —*I'm fed up with the drive-in,* she said, *I'm going home. I'm supposed to be home in half an hour anyway.* —*Awcomeonnn,* moaned Marilyn. The whine in her voice was enough to make Jenny turn decisively away from them and begin to walk quickly down the street.

Because she could feel them staring at her she turned into the first side street. Let them gawk at an empty street, she thought, let them "my goodness!" one another.

She walked straight down the middle of the unlighted street. Windows shone in the houses on either side. Someone was waiting up ahead, just a shape on the grassy sidewalk, a man washing his car or getting cool evening air. Or a woman getting away from the kids.

At that moment she nearly saved her life, because she realized that she was hungry after all, and almost turned around to go back to her friends. But that was not possible. So she put her head down and walked up to the next corner, vaguely planning a route that would take most of the half hour she had of freedom. When she went past the shape on the sidewalk, she half-noticed that it was not a man but a fat bush.

The next street was shabbier, with two vacant lots between the mean houses like vast blots of darkness. Trees towered and loomed overhead, black and without definition. She heard slow steps behind her. But this was Arden and she did not begin to be fearful until something hard and blunt touched her back. She jumped and whirled around and when she saw the face looking at her she knew that the worst moments of her life were beginning.

4

At that moment I would have been skeptical about the odds on my returning to take up the bartender's invitation for Sunday, but twenty-six hours later I was in Freebo's, not this time at the bar but in a booth and not alone but in company.

I realized that I was drunk only when I found that I was pounding the VW along in second gear; chanting to myself, I messily, grindingly slotted the shift up a gear, ending the howl of anguish from the engine, and zoomed home, no doubt weaving through lanes as rakishly as Alison Greening had done on one night years before—the night I had first felt her mouth issuing warmth over mine, and felt all my senses rubbed by her various odors of perfume, soap, powder, contraband cigarettes and fresh water. About the time I reached the red thermometer in the Italian vista I recognized that the Strand girl's death had been the reason for the hostile stares I'd received from the Arden towns-people. After I spun into the driveway I left the car slewed at a telltale angle before the garage and lurched out, half-sprawling over the front fender. The maddening envelope and blank sheet of paper, along with several torn balled-up pages of Maccabee's book, bunched in my pocket. I heard footsteps inside the house, a door closing. I went unsteadily across the lawn to the door of the screen porch and entered. It seemed I could feel the chill of the boards even through my shoes. The cold house seemed full of noises. Tuta Sunderson appeared to be in two or three rooms at once. "Come on out," I said. "I won't hurt you."

Silence.

"It's okay," I said. "You can even go home, Mrs. Sunderson." I looked around, called her name in the direction of the old downstairs bedroom. Duane's furniture was immaculately cleaned and dusted, but no one else was in the room. I shrugged and went into the bathroom.

When I emerged, the noises in the old house had magically ceased. I heard only the singing of the plumbing in the walls. She had nervously decamped; I swore to myself, wondering what I would have to do to get her back.

Then I heard a cough unmistakably originating from my workroom. That I had yet to complete a sentence in that room made her offense against its privacy triply serious. I gave myself a shove toward the stairs.

But when I burst into the cold little room I stopped short. Through the window I could see the stout form of Tuta Sunderson huff-puffing down the road, her handbag bobbing on its strap; and seated in the desk chair, absolutely at ease, was Alison Updahl.

"What—" I began. "I don't like—"

"I think you scared her off. She was already pretty upset, but you finished her off. But don't worry, she'll come back."

Portion of Statement by Tuta Sunderson:

July 18

When I saw him get out of that car, I knew he was drunk, just pig drunk, and when he started that yelling I thought I'd better skedaddle. Now we know he was just back from that time he argued with the pastor on the street, down in Arden. I think the pastor was right in everything he said, next day, and he could have said it even stronger. Red was home from the police station by then—all shook by what he'd seen, of course—and he said, Ma, don't you go back to that crazy man, I've got a few ideas of my own about him, but I said his five dollars is as good as anyone else's, isn't it? I put that other two dollars under a lamp. Oh, I was going to come back, you can bet on that, he didn't scare me any. I wanted to keep my eye on him.

We stayed there silently for a moment—oddly, she made me feel as though I was intruding on her. I could see her assessing my condition. To forestall any comment, I said, "I don't like people in this room. It has to be kept private, mine. Other people louse up the atmosphere."

"She *said* she wasn't supposed to come in here. That's why I did. It was the only quiet place to wait for you." She stretched out her blue-jeaned legs. "I didn't take anything."

"It's a question of vibrations." At least I did not say "vibes." Alcohol cheapens the vocabulary.

"I don't feel any vibrations. What do you do in here, anyhow?"

"I'm writing a book."

"On what?"

"It doesn't matter. I'm stuck anyhow."

"A book about other books, I bet. Why don't you write a book about something real? Why don't you write a book about something fantastic and important that other people can't even see? About what's really going down?"

"Did you want to see me about anything in particular?"

"Zack wants to meet you."

"Swell."

"I told him about you and he was really interested. I said you were different. He wants to know about your ideas. Zack cares a lot about ideas."

"I'm not going anywhere today."

"Not today. Tomorrow around noon. In Arden. Do you know Freebo's bar?"

"I suppose I could find it on a bright day. Did you hear about another of your pals getting killed?"

"It's on all the news. Don't you pay attention to the news?" She blinked, and I saw the fright beneath her pretended indifference.

"Didn't you know her?"

"Sure I did. In Arden you know everybody. Red Sunderson found her body. That's why old Tuta was so touchy this morning. He saw her in a field off Highway 93."

"Jesus." I remembered how I had treated her, and then I could feel my face begin to burn.

So the next day I found myself entering the scene of my second disgrace in the company of Alison Updahl. Underage though she was, she sailed through the door as if, given any resistance, she'd knock it down with an ax. By now I of course knew to what extent this was purely a performance, and I admired its perfection. She had more in common with her namesake than I had thought. The bar was nearly empty. Two old men in coveralls sat before nearly full glasses of pale beer at the bar and a man in a black jacket sat at the last booth. The same fleshy gray-haired bartender who had been there yesterday leaned against the wall beside the cash register, surrounded by the flashing sparkling lights and perpetual waterfalls of beer advertisements. His eyes glided over Alison, but he looked at me and nodded.

I followed her to the booth, watching Zack as we went. His eyes flicked back and forth between us and his mouth was a taut line. He appeared to be charged with enthusiasm. He also looked very young. I recognized the type from my youth in Florida—the misfits who had gathered around gas stations, paying great attention to their hair, cherishing their own failure even then. Dangerous kids, at times. I didn't know the type was still in style.

"This is him," said my cousin's daughter, meaning me.

"Freebo," Zack said, and nodded to the bartender.

As I sat in the booth facing him I saw that he was older than I had at first taken him for; he was not a teenager but in his twenties, with those wrinkles embedded in his forehead and at the corners of his eyes. He still had that look of displaced, unlocated enthusiasm. It gave a sly cast to his whole character. He made me very uneasy.

"The usual, Mr. Teagarden?" asked the bartender, now standing at the side of the booth. Presumably he knew what Zack wanted. He avoided looking at Alison.

"Just a beer," I said.

"He didn't look at me again," said the Woodsman after the bartender had turned away. "That really slays me. He's afraid of Zack. Otherwise he'd throw me out on my butt."

I wanted to say: don't try so hard.

Zack giggled in the best James Dean fashion.

The bartender came back with three beers. Alison's and mine were in glasses, Zack's in a tall silver mug.

"Freebo's thinking of selling this place," the boy said, grinning at me. "You ought to think about buying it. You could snap it up. Be a good business."

I remembered this too: the ridiculous testing. He smelled of carbon paper. Carbon paper and machine oil. "For someone else. I'm about as businesslike as a kangaroo."

The Woodsman grinned: I was proving whatever it was she'd said about me.

"Far out. Listen. I think we could talk."

"Why?"

"Because we're unusual. Don't you think unusual people have something in common? Don't you think they share things?"

"Like Jane Austen and Bob Dylan? Come off it. How do you get your seventeen-year-old girlfriend served in here?"

"Because of who I am." He grinned, as though that were both Jane Austen and Bob Dylan. "Freebo and I are friends. He knows what's in his interest." I was getting a full dose of his sly enthusiasm. "But almost everybody knows what's in his interest. The Big One. Right? It's in our interest to talk, to be seen together, to explore our ideas, right? I know some things about you, Miles. People still talk about you up here. I was knocked out when she said you were back, man. Tell me something. Do people keep laying their trips on you?"

"I don't know what that means. Unless it's what you're doing now."

"*Hoo,*" Zack uttered softly. "You're cozy, man. Make 'em work, huh? I can see that, I can dig it. Make 'em work, yeah. You're deep. You're really deep. I got a lot of questions for you, man. What's your favorite book of the Bible?"

"The Bible?" I said, laughing, spurting beer. "That was unexpected. I don't know. Job? Isaiah?"

"No. I mean, yeah, I can dig it, but that isn't it. Revelations is it. Do you see? That's where it's all laid out."

"Where what is all laid out?"

"The plan." He showed me a big scarred palm, lines of grease permanently printed in it, as though the plan were visible there. "That's where it all is. The riders on the horses—the rider with the bow, and the rider with the sword, and the rider with the scales, and the pale rider. And the stars fell and the sky disappeared, and it all came down. Horses with lions' heads and snakes' tails."

I glanced at Alison. She was listening as if to a nursery story—she had heard it a hundred times before. I could have groaned; I thought she deserved so much better.

"That's where it says that corpses will lie in the streets, fires, earthquakes, war in heaven. War on earth too, you see? All those great beasts in Revelations, remember? The beast 666, that was Aleister Crowley, you know. Ron Hubbard is probably another one, and then all those angels who harvest the earth. Until there's blood for sixteen thousand furlongs. What do you think of Hitler?"

"You tell me."

"Well, Hitler had the wrong thing going, you see, he had all this heavy German stuff around him, all that shit about the Jews and the master race—well, there is a master race, but it's nothing crude like being a whole nation. But he was one of the beasts of Revelations, right? Think about it. Hitler knew that he was sent to prepare us, he was like John the Baptist, see, and he gave us certain keys to understanding, just like Crowley did. I think you understand all this, Miles. There's like a brotherhood of those who catch on to all this. Hitler was a screw-up, right, but he had insight. He knew that everything has to go smash before it get better, there has to be total chaos before there can be total freedom, there has to be murder before there can be true life. He knew the reality of blood. Passion has to go beyond the personal—right? See, to free matter, to set matter free, we have to get beyond the mechanical to, uh, myth maybe, ritual, blood ritual, to the physical mind."

"The physical mind," I said. "Like the dark seat of passion and the column of blood." I quoted these catch-phrases despairingly. The end of Zack's tirade had depressingly reminded me of ideas in Lawrence's writing.

"Wow," said Alison. "Oh, wow." I had impressed her. This time I nearly did groan.

"I knew it, man," continued Zack. He was just gleaming at me. "We gotta have more talks. We could talk for centuries. I can't believe that you're a teacher, man."

"I can't believe it either."

This sent him into such happiness that he slapped Alison on the knee. "I knew it. You know, people used to say all this stuff about you, I didn't know if I could really believe it all, about the stuff you used to do—I got another question. You have nightmares, don't you?"

I thought of being suspended in that blue drifting horror. "I do."

"I knew it. You know about nightmares? They show you the revelations? Nightmares cut through the shit to show you what's really going on."

"They show you what's really going on in the nightmares," I said. I didn't want him to analyze my dream-states. I had ordered another two beers while he ranted, and now I asked Freebo for a double Jack Daniel's to soothe my nerves. Zack was looking as though oil had come pouring out of his scalp, as though he expected to be either stroked or kicked. His face was wild and skinny, framed by thick sideburns and that complicated ruff of hair. When the whiskey came I drank half of it in one gulp and waited for the effect.

Zack went on. Didn't I think the situation had to be loosened up? Didn't I think violence was mystic action? Was selfhood? Didn't I think the Midwest was where reality was thinnest, waiting for truth to erupt? Didn't two killings prove that? Couldn't they *make* reality happen?

Eventually I began to laugh. "Something about this reminds me of Alison's father's Dream House," I said.

"My father's house?"

"His Dream House. The place behind Andy's."

"That place? Is that *his?*"

"He built it. You must have known that."

She was gaping at me. Zack was looking irritated at this interruption in his sermon. "He never said anything about it. Why did he build a place like that?"

"It's an old story," I said, already sorry that I had mentioned the place. "I thought it would have a reputation for being haunted."

"No, nobody thinks it's haunted," she said, still looking at me with determined curiosity. "Lots of us kids go there. Nobody bothers you there."

I remembered the mess of blankets and cigarette butts on the ruined floor.

Zack said, "Listen, I've got plans—"

"What was it *for?* Why did he build it?"

"I don't know."

"Why did you call it his dream house?"

"It's nothing. Forget about it." I could see her begin to look impatiently around the bar, as if to find someone who would tell her all about it.

"You've got to know about my plans—"

"Well, I'll find out from someone else."

"I've been doing some things—"

"Just forget about it," I said. "Forget I ever mentioned it. I'm going home now. I have an idea."

The bartender was beside us again. "This is an important guy, you know," he said, putting his hand on my shoulder. "He wrote a book. He's some kind of artist."

"Also," I said, "I think I'm going to give you some novels. You'll like them. They're right up your street."

"I considered we might see you in church today." Duane was still wearing his suit, the old double-breasted pin-stripe he had been wearing to church for ten years or more. But the new informality had touched him too: beneath the jacket he wore a tieless open-collared shirt, blue with patterns of lighter blue. Alison must have given it to him. "Do you want some of this? It's Tuta's day off over at your place, isn't it?" He lifted one big hand toward the mess that Alison had left bubbling on the stove—it looked like pork and beans, with too much tomato sauce. Like the general disorder of the kitchen, this too would have riled his mother, who had always prepared gigantic lunches of roasted meat and potatoes boiled so long they crumbled like chalk. When I shook my head no, he said, "You should go to church, Miles. No matter what you believe in, going could help you out in the community."

"Duane, it would be the most blatant hypocrisy," I said. "Does your daughter usually go?"

"Sometimes. Not always. I reckon she has little enough time to herself, taking care of me and doing for me the way she does around here, so I don't grudge her some extra sleep on Sunday. Or a couple of hours with a girlfriend."

"Like now?"

"Like now. Or so she says. If you can ever trust a female. Why?"

"I was just wondering."

"Well, she has to get along to see her friends sometimes. Whoever the hell they are. Anyhow, Miles, this is one day you should have gone."

Then I heard the emphasis I should have heard the first time. And wasn't it unusual that Duane was still wearing his suit an hour after the service? And that he was sitting in his kitchen instead of doing an hour or so of work before lunch?

"I'll bite. Why today, especially?"

"What do you think of Pastor Bertilsson?"

"I'll spare you. Why?"

Duane was crossing and uncrossing his legs, looking very uncomfortable. On his feet were heavy black brogues, immaculately polished. "You never exactly liked him, did you? I know. He maybe did go a little out of line when you and Joan got married. I don't think he was right to bring up all that old stuff, even though he did it for your own good. When I got married, he didn't talk about any of my old mistakes."

I hoped that his daughter would forget all about my reference to the Dream House—it had been a serious betrayal. While I was trying to think how I could tell him that I had let his secret slip out to his daughter without actually telling her anything about it, Duane got over his own nervousness and finally got to the point.

"Anyhow, like I was saying, he said a few words about you today. In his sermon."

"About *me*?" I yelped. My guilt disappeared like flash powder.

"Wait, Miles, he didn't actually name you. But we all knew who he was talking about. After all, you made yourself known around here, years ago. So I guess most everybody knew who he was talking about."

"You mean I'm actually having sermons preached about me? I guesss I really am a success."

"Well, it would have been better if you'd been there. See, in a community this size—well, a small community like this sort of draws together if any trouble happens. What happened to those two girls was a terrible thing, Miles. I think a man that can do something like that ought to be slaughtered like a pig. The thing is, we know none of us could have done it. Maybe some over in Arden, but none of us here." He shifted in his chair. "While I'm talking on this I ought to say something else. Look. It might be better if you didn't go around trying to see Paul Kant. That's all I want to say about that."

"What are you saying, Duane?"

"Just what I said. Paul might have been okay when he was a kid, but even then you didn't know him all that well. You were only here in the summers."

"To hell with that," I said. "Suppose you tell me what was the point of this sermon of Bertilsson's."

"Well, I guess he was just saying how some people—"

"Meaning me."

"—some people put themselves outside normal standards. He said that's dangerous, when everybody's got to pull together, times of trouble, like now."

"He's guiltier of that than I am. Now I wish you'd tell me what crime Paul Kant is supposed to have committed."

To my surprise, Duane flushed. He turned his eyes toward the pot bubbling on the stove. "Well, it's not a crime, exactly, not that you could say a crime, exactly. He's just not like the rest of us."

"He puts himself outside normal standards. Good. That makes two of us. I'll make a point of seeing him."

We stared at one another for a moment or two, Duane fidgeting, looking out of his depth. He appeared to be afflicted with moral uncertainty. In a dubious cause he had acted dubiously. He obviously wished that he had never brought up the questions of Bertilsson and Paul Kant. I remembered the idea I'd had in Freebo's Bar—an idea brought up by my tactless mention of the Dream House. "Shall we change the subject?"

"Hell, yes." Duane looked relieved. "Do you feel like having one of those beers?"

"Not now. Duane, what did you do with the rest of the stuff from Gramma's house? The old pictures, and all the furniture?"

"Well, let me think. I put the furniture down in the root cellar. It didn't seem right to sell it or throw it away. Some of that stuff might be valuable someday, too. Most of those old pictures I took down I put in a trunk in the old bedroom." That was the bedroom on the ground floor, where my grandparents had slept during my grandfather's life.

"All right, Duane," I said. "Don't be surprised by anything you hear."

Portion of Statement by Duane Updahl:

July 17

So that was what he said just before the really strange business began. Don't be surprised, something like that. Don't be surprised by anything. Then he went off toward the old house like a rocket was in his pants. He was all sort of excited—he was drunk some too, Sunday morning or no Sunday morning. I could smell the booze on his breath. Later I found out from my kid that he'd been over to Freebo's, down on Main. You know? He was just sittin' there with Zack, suckin' up drinks like it was Saturday night. Kind of funny, considering what he tried to do to Zack later. Maybe he was sort of trying him out, you know? Testing him? That's what I think, anyhow. I think maybe he was keeping his mind on Paul Kant too, to see if he could use him like he tried to use Zack. What a choice, huh? But I don't know. I don't understand that whole Paul Kant business. I guess none of us will ever know what happened there.

I found the trunk immediately. In fact, I had known where it was the moment Duane had said that it was in the old bedroom; it was an ancient Norwegian sea chest, not truly a trunk, a small brass-bound wooden case brought to America by Einar Updahl's father. It had carried everything he owned in a space just about large enough to hold four electric typewriters. It was a beautiful old thing—the wood was hand-carved, filigreed with scrolls and leaves.

But the beautiful old thing was also padlocked, and I was too impatient to go back and ask Duane where he'd misplaced the key. I slammed out of the house onto the porch and went down its length to the far door. In surprising heat, I tugged open the old sliding doors of the garage and went inside. It smelled like a grave. Damp earth smells, a general odor of mold and beetles. Old tools hung on the walls, just as I had remembered. Rusted saws from the log-clearing days, three ten-gallon gas cans, hatchets and hammers, all on nails driven into the walls. I took a crowbar off its nail and went back into the house.

The lip of the crowbar fit neatly into the gap between the lid and the body of the chest; I pressed hard on the bar, and felt wood yielding. The second time I pressed on the bar I heard a splintering sound; I put all my weight on the bar, and the wood above the lock popped away from the lid. I fell to my knees, the wound on my palm throbbing where I had unknowingly, unfeelingly been gripping it against the crowbar. With my right hand I banged open the lid of the chest. The inside was a disorder of framed and unframed photographs. After a second of pawing through them ineffectually and seeing several versions of Duane's square face and my vanished cowlick and many pictures of orthodontia at work on the toothy Updahl smile, I impatiently turned the entire chest over and sent the sheets and frames across the hooked bedroom rug.

It stared up at me from four feet away, self-isolated from the other photographs; someone had removed it from its frame, and it was curling slightly at either end. But there it was, and there *we* were, seen by Uncle Gilbert as we must have been seen by all, our spirits flowing toward each other, more one than two drops of blood in one bloodstream, no longer children but trapped in the beautiful amber chrysalis of the teens, our hands clasped and our faces smiling out in the summer of 1955.

If I had not already been kneeling, it would have brought me to my knees— the force of that face next to mine squeezed all the breath from me. It was like being punched in the stomach with the handle of a rake. For if we were both beautiful, stuck there in ignorance and love in June of 1955, she was incomparably more so. She burned my intelligent young thief's face right off the paper, she canceled me, she was on another plane altogether, where spirit is incandescent in flesh, she was at the height of being, body and soul together. This live trumpet-blast of spirit, this illumination, put me altogether in shadow. I seemed almost to be levitating, carried by the currents of magic and complication of spirit in that face which was her face. Levitating on my knees, my knees already rubbed sore by the hooked rug!

That face which was her face. By telepathy, we had been in communication all our lives—all my life I had been in touch with her.

Then I knew that all my life since our last meeting had been the project of finding her again. Her mother had retreated in shock back to San Francisco; after I had stolen a car and wrecked it in a spectacular crash not forty feet from the spot where the painted thermometer overlooked an Italian distance, my parents had clapped me in a prisonlike boarding school in Miami. She was in another state; she was in another condition. We were apart but (I knew) not finally apart.

After an incalculable number of minutes I rolled over onto my back. Moisture dripped into the hair at my temples. The back of my head was embedded in crushed photographs and long splinters of Norwegian wood. I knew I *would* see her, that she would return. That was why I was there, in my grandmother's house—the book had been an evasion. Wood dug into the back of my head. I had never intended to finish the dissertation. Spirit would not permit it. From now until she came, I would prepare for her coming. Even the blank letter was part of the preparation, part of the necessary trial of spirit.

I was in the final stages of the transformation (I thought) which had begun when I had torn open my hand on the VW's engine cover and felt the freedom which was her freedom invading and sluicing through me. Reality was not a single thing, it broke through the apparently real like a fist. It was this knowledge which had always trembled in her face. Reality is merely an arrangement of molecules held together by tension, a veneer. In her face was there not the face she'd had at six? Also the face of herself at fifty? As I lay sprawled on the hooked rug in a confusion of paper and splintered wood, the white ceiling above me seemed to dissolve into white sky. I thought fleetingly of Zack, and smiled. Harmless. Harmless clueless nut. When I lost normal consciousness, I dreamed not of being suspended adrift in a far blue horror, but of Alison swimming toward me.

This image rang through my suspended mind. Everything was a part of this surge of feeling, my ripped hand, the unimportant discomfort in my neck, even Zack's prattle about reality being thinnest in the Midwest, even my theft and destruction of Maccabee's terrible book. The proof would occur on the twenty-first of July. There were no impossibilities. I slept. (I passed out.)

And woke full of purpose. When I had said to Duane, don't be surprised by anything you hear, I'd had a plan which I now saw to be absolutely necessary. I had to begin the preparations. I had to be ready for the day. I had about three weeks. It was more than enough time.

I began by tearing a photograph out of the nearest frame that looked the right size and sliding the picture of Alison and myself inside it. Idly, I tore the other photograph in half, and doubled the pieces and tore it again. Dropping the torn bits of glossy paper and letting them flutter to the littered floor, I took the photograph into the living room and hung it where the first photograph of Alison had been.

Then I looked around at the room. Most of it was going to have to go. I was going to make an Alison-environment: I was going to recreate, as nearly as possible and with a few added embellishments, the room of twenty years before. Duane's office furniture could go down into the root cellar where my grandmother's old furniture now sat. I wasn't sure that I could single-handedly manage some of the heavier pieces down the rough steps of the root cellar, but there was no other choice. It was what I was going to do.

The doors to the root cellar were set into the ground at a slightly elevated angle just at the end of the porch. You swung them up and let them drop open to the sides—it was the most oldfashioned and rural of arrangements, and I suspected that Duane's dark cellar, though modernized by the introduction of a staircase leading down from the body of the house, was originally of similar construction. With some effort I pulled one of the doors up and open, nearly straining my back; time had cemented the two doors together.

The earthen stairs looked treacherous, half-crumbled away and very steep. Some of the damage was old, but Duane had shredded some of the steps when he had taken the old furniture down. I put one foot on the first of the stairs and tested my weight. The earth was reassuringly resilient and firm. After trying a few more steps I became careless and put my foot down without looking, and the earth gave way beneath it, sending me sliding three or four feet down across a terrace of crumbling dirt. When I was steady again I put my feet solidly on a thick step and braced my shoulder under the door and pushed with my body and legs. The door strained and flew open on complaining hinges. Now light entered nearly the whole of the root cellar. That wonderful old furniture lay in heaps and piles like stew bones. Like the garage, the cellar smelled like a grave. I began to pull my grandmother's furniture out of the dark hole of the root cellar and up into the sunlight.

I worked at this task of reclamation until my shoulders and legs ached and my clothes were covered with dirt. There was more furniture in the cellar than I had thought, all of it essential. I needed every footstool and end table, every lamp and bookcase. Too exhausted to continue, I went inside and made sandwiches from Saturday's groceries. When I had pushed down the food, I went back out with a pail of soapy warm water and washed off what was on the lawn; that completed, I went back down the crumbled steps and began to wrestle out more things. I could remember where every stick of it had been placed, I could see the room as it had been twenty years before and would be again. She had touched every bit of this furniture.

By the time the light had begun to fail, I had it all out on the lawn and washed. The fabrics were worn, but the wood was clean and shining. Even on the lawn beside the white house in the fading light, it all looked magically appropriate—that is to say no more than that it had the rightness of all things made and used with care. That beautiful worn old stuff could make you weep. The past was enshrined in it. Just sitting out there on the lawn in the dusk, it evoked the entire history of my family in America. Like them, it was solid, it was right.

Unlike Duane's office furniture, which merely looked naked and stunned and stupid when dragged outside. There was less of it than there had seemed. It had a negative relation to spirit.

I made the mistake of taking the lighter pieces, the dreadful pictures and lamps and chairs, down into the root cellar first. Under one of the lamps I found two neatly folded dollar bills. Under different circumstances, I might have admired the gesture, but it was proof of how badly I had acted. I finished with the light things in a disproportionately bad temper. That left me with the job of handling the heavy couches and the two heavier chairs when I was almost too tired to move them further, and in the dark. I had only the light from the porch and pale early moonlight, and the battered earthen steps, in many places now worn to a continuous pitted incline, were visible only at their top. The first chair went down easily; I carried it in my trembling arms and felt my way slowly along the ruined steps. But when I tried it with the second chair, I lost my footing on an incline of dirt and fell all the way to the bottom.

To complete that Buster Keatonish stunt I should have landed on the dirt floor seated comfortably in the embrace of the chair; but I landed sprawled half-over, half-under it, with pain radiating out from all of my left leg, ankle to thigh. It did not feel broken, but one of the chair's legs was, dangling from ripped fabric like a dead tooth. Cursing, I ripped it off and threw it into a corner. I disposed of the chair in much the same way.

After that, I had no patience with the couches. I was not going to baby them down the slope. I shoved the first up to the lip of the cellar, nudged it over until it was set, and let go of the arm. It crashed down to the bottom. I grunted with satisfaction and was turning to the second when I became aware of a flashlight bobbing toward me.

"God damn you, Miles," Duane said. The flashlight was held on my face. In a moment he had moved into the area of light from the porch.

"You don't need a flashlight to see it's me."

"No, even on a dark night I'd know it was you." He flicked off the flashlight and stepped closer to me. His face was savage. "God damn you. I wish you'd never come back here. What the hell were you thinking of anyhow? You fucking bastard."

"Look," I said, "I know it looks funny, but—" I realized that as far as anger was concerned I was an amateur. Duane's face seemed to be inflating.

"Is that what you think? You think it *looks* funny? Now *you* look. If you had to go and talk about that goddamn house, why did you have to talk about it with my daughter?"

I was too stunned to reply.

He glared at me for another long moment, and then whirled to the side and banged his hand against one of the porch supports.

That was when I should have started to worry—when I was given special dispensation.

"Don't you have an answer? You shit, Miles. Everybody's forgotten about that house by now. Alison was never going to find out. In a little while, the goddamn thing was going to fall over anyhow. She'd never know. Then you come along and tell her it was my 'dream house,' huh? Then she can get one of the drunken bums in Arden to tell her all about it, can't she? I suppose you wanted to get her to laugh at me, just the way you and your cousin used to do."

"It was a mistake, Duane. I'm sorry. I thought she knew already."

"Bullshit, Miles, bull *shit*. My dream house, isn't that what you called it? You wanted to make her laugh at me. You wanted to humiliate me. I should pound you into the ground."

"Maybe you should," I said. "But if you're not going to, then listen to me. It was an accident. I thought it was something everybody knew."

"Yeah, that makes me feel real good. I should break you up."

"If you want a fight, give it a try. But I'm apologizing to you."

"You can't apologize for that, Miles. I want you to stay away from my daughter, hear that? Stay away from her, Miles."

He might not ever have noticed the furniture around us if he hadn't thumped his hand into the couch. Pure furious astonishment replaced the rage in his face.

"Now what the hell are you doing?" he screamed.

"I'm putting back the old furniture," I said, my heart sinking and the foolishness of my entire project momentarily clear. "When I go you can change it all back again. I have to do it, Duane."

"You're putting back—nothing's good enough for you, is it, Miles? You have to spoil everything you touch. You know, I think you're crazy, Miles. And I'm not the only one around here who thinks so. I think you're dangerous. You oughta be locked up. Pastor Bertilsson was right about you." He flicked the flashlight on again and shone it into my eyes. "We're quits, Miles. I'm not gonna throw you off the place, I'm not gonna pound the crap out of you, but I'm sure as hell gonna keep my eye on you. You can't get away with squat from now on without my knowing it."

The light came off my face and played on the few items of furniture still dotted around the lawn. "God damn you, you're out of your skull. Somebody ought to put you away." For a moment I thought that he probably was right. He turned away without bothering to look at me. After he had stomped five or six feet away, I got the flashlight treatment again, but this time he was unable to hold it steadily on my face. "And remember, Miles," he called. "You stay away from my kid. Just keep off of her."

It was too much like Auntie Rinn.

I wrestled the other couch over to the abyss and savagely pushed it down. It crashed satisfactorily into the one already at the bottom. I thought I heard wood breaking. I kicked the doors over and shut. It took me another half hour to get the old furniture inside the old house. I just let it sit where I dropped it. Then I opened a bottle and took it upstairs.

5

All my life I have been engaged in Sisyphean and hopeless tasks, and given the ache and flutter in my muscles, it may not be odd that I dreamed of pushing my grandmother uphill in a wheelchair through an obscure territory. We were surrounded by brilliant light. My grandmother was surprisingly heavy. I felt great dread. The smell of woodsmoke burned my nostrils. I had committed a murder, a robbery, something, and forces were closing in. They were vague as yet, but they knew about me and they would find me.

—Talk to Rinn, my grandmother said.

She repeated—Talk to Rinn.

And again—Talk to Rinn.

I ceased pushing the wheelchair. My muscles could no longer bear the strain; we seemed to have been going uphill for hours. I placed my hand on her head and bent over. Gramma, I said—I'm tired. I need help. I'm afraid. The woodsmoke smell swarmed up, occupying the spaces within my skull.

When she turned her face to me it was black and rotten.

I heard three bare, cynical handclaps.

My screams woke me up—think of that, a man alone in a white bedroom, screaming on his bed! A man alone, pursued only by himself. My body seemed heavy and incapable of motion. My mouth burned and my head felt stuffed with oily rags. Result of abuse of magic substance. I gently swung my legs out of bed and sat up, bowing my back and holding my forehead in my palms. I touched the place where my hairline used to be, now smooth and oily skin instead of soft hair. My foot encountered the upright bottle. I risked a glance. It was more than half empty. Evidence of mortality lay all about me. I stood on long sensationless legs. Except for the boots, I still wore Sunday's clothes, now smudged and crusted with dirt from the root cellar. I could taste my screams.

The stairs were navigable as long as I planted my hands on the close walls.

The furniture at first startled me. It was the wrong furniture in the wrong places. Then I remembered the scene of the previous night. Duane and the

flashlight stitching into my face. That too seemed to have the quality of drunkenness. Effects can leak backward and forward in time, staining otherwise
innocent events. I sat heavily on the old couch. I feared that I could fall straight
through it into another dimension. On Sunday I had told myself that I knew
the precise, proper location of all my grandmother's things. Now I saw that
was an illusion. I would have to experiment until the room clicked shut like a
tumbler in a lock, itself again at last.

The bathroom. Hot water. Drinking water. I pushed off the couch and
avoided the haphazard furniture and came into the kitchen.

Alison Updahl was leaning against the counter, chewing something. She wore
a T-shirt (yellow) and jeans (brown). Her feet were bare, and I could feel the
chill of the floor as if it were penetrating my own feet.

"I'm sorry," I said, "but it's too early for company."

She finally finished chewing, and swallowed. "I have to see you," she said.
Her eyes were large.

I turned away, aware of the presence of a complication I was in no condition
to handle. On the table was an untouchable plate of congealed scrambled eggs
and shriveled bacon.

"Mrs. Sunderson made that for you, I guess. She took one look in the other
room and said she would clean in there after you decided how you wanted the
furniture. And she said you busted that old sea chest. She said that was a
valuable antique. Her family has one like it and a man from Minneapolis said
it was worth two hundred dollars."

"Please, Alison." I ventured another look at her. Beneath the tight yellow
shirt her large breasts hung heavily, comfortably. They looked like Claes Ol-
denburg torpedoes. Her feet, surprisingly, were small, white, slightly puffy,
beautiful. "I'm too wrecked to go public."

"I came for two reasons. The first is, I know I did a stupid thing by talking
to Daddy about that house. He really blew up. Zack warned me, but I went
right ahead and asked him anyhow. That was stupid, all right. What's the
matter with you, anyhow? Are you hung-over? And why are you putting all
that old furniture and stuff back upstairs?" She was speaking very quickly.

"I'm working on a project."

That stumped her. I sat down at the table and shoved the cold food away
before I could smell it.

"You don't have to worry about Daddy. He's real mad, but he doesn't know
I'm here. He's out in the new fields. That's way down the road. He doesn't
know about lots of things I do."

I finally saw that she was being very chatty—too chatty.

The telephone began to shrill. "Shit," I said, and weakly stood. When I
plucked the earpiece off the box, I waited for the caller to say something. Silence.
"Who is it?" I got no response. "Hello, hello." I heard a noise like wings, like
the whuffle of a fan, like beating air. The room was cold. I slammed the earpiece
down on the metal hook.

"They didn't say anything? That's weird. Zack says that telephones can lock you into these waves of energy from outer space, and he said that if everybody took their phones off the hook at exactly the same second all over the world you could get pure outer space energy coming in waves through the receiver. Another idea he had was that if everybody in the world called the same number at exactly the same split second, there'd be some kind of energy explosion. He says that electronics and things like telephones are all making us ready for the apocalypse and the revelations." There was a doll-like brightness in all of this.

"I need a glass of water," I said. "And a bath. That's a hint." I went to the sink and stood beside her while I watched cool water rush into a glass. I drank it in two or three large inhalations, feeling the water seem to sparkle along veins throughout my chest. A second glass failed to reproduce these sensations.

"Did you ever get any of those calls in the middle of the night?"

"No. I wouldn't answer it if I did."

"I'm surprised. It looks like a whole lot of people around here don't like you very much. They talk about you. Didn't something bad happen to you once a long time ago? Something did, didn't it—something all the old people know about?"

"I don't know what you're talking about. My life has been limitless bliss from infancy. Now I'm going to take a bath."

"Daddy knows about it, doesn't he? I heard him say something, well he didn't really *say* anything, he was talking about it without saying it straight out, on the telephone a couple nights ago. I think he was talking to Zack's father."

"It's hard to think of Zack having parents," I said. "He's more the head-of-Zeus type. Now scram. Please."

She wasn't going to budge. The water had awakened a sharp floating pain high behind my forehead. I could sense the tension in her, stronger now than my hangover. Alison crossed her arms over her stomach, consciously squeezing her breasts together. I caught her blood smell. "I said I had two reasons. I want you to make love to me."

"Jesus," I said.

"He won't be back for at least two hours. It doesn't take very long anyhow," she added, giving me more insight than I wished to have into Zack's sexual life.

"What would good old Zack think about it?"

"It's his idea. He said it was so I could learn discipline."

"Alison," I said, "I'm going into the bathroom now. We can talk about this later."

"We could both fit into the bathtub."

Her voice was light, her face miserable. I was terribly conscious of her thighs in the tight brown jeans, of the large soft breasts, the plump pretty feet on the cold floor. If Zack had been there, I would have shot him.

Mildly, I said, "I don't think Zack is very fair to you." She abruptly turned and wheeled out, slamming the door.

After my bath I remembered what my conversation with Duane on Sunday had resolved me to do, and I went immediately to the telephone book jacketed with the two small boys suspended over cold water. Paul Kant lived on Madison Street in Arden, but when he picked up the telephone his voice was so faraway and small that he might have been in Tibet.

"Paul, this is Miles Teagarden. I've been around for a week or so, and I tried to see you a few days ago."

"The women told me," he said. "I heard you were in town."

"Well, I heard *you* were in town," I said. "I thought you would have been off long ago."

"Things didn't happen that way, Miles."

"Do you ever see Polar Bears anymore?"

He gave an odd, bitter laugh. "As little as possible. Look, Miles, it might be better . . . it might be better if you didn't try to see me. It's for your own good, Miles. Mine too, probably."

"What the hell? Are you in trouble?"

"I don't know how to answer that." His voice was strained and very small.

"Do you need help? I can't figure out what's going on, Paul."

"That's two of us. Don't make things worse, Miles. I'm saying that for your own good."

"Christ, I don't understand what all the mystery is about. Didn't we used to be friends?" Even through the telephone I could detect an emotion I had begun to recognize as fear. I said, "If you need any help, Paul, I'll try to help. All you have to do is ask. You should have been out of that burg years ago. It's not the right place for you. Paul, I'll be coming into Arden later today. Could I drop in to see you at the store?"

"I'm not working at Zumgo's anymore."

"That's good." I don't know why, but I thought of the Woodsman.

"I was fired." His voice was flat and hopeless.

"Then we're both out of a job. And I'd think it's an honor to be fired from a mausoleum like Zumgo's. I'm not going to force myself on you, Paul, I've gotten involved in something that will probably take up nearly all of my time, but I think I should see you. We were friends way back then."

"I can't stop you from doing what you're determined to do," he said. "But if you're going to come, it'd be better to come at night."

"Why do you—"

I heard a click, a second of the silence Zack had told my cousin's daughter was laden with waves of energy from outer space, and then the noncommittal buzz of the dial tone.

While I was pushing the old wooden furniture around, trying to reconstruct the sitting room as it had been twenty years before, I heard from the second of my two old Arden friends. I set down the chair I had been moving across the room and answered the telephone.

A man asked, "Is this Miles Teagarden?"

"That's me."

"One moment, please."

In a few seconds another telephone lifted. "Hello, Miles. This is Chief Hovre."

"Polar Bears!"

He laughed. "Not many folks remember that anymore. Mostly people call me Galen." I had never heard his real name before. I preferred Polar Bears.

"Doesn't anyone dare call you Polar Bears anymore?"

"Oh, your cousin Du-ane might. I hear that you've been making a few waves around here since you came in."

"Nothing serious."

"No, nothing at all serious. Freebo says if you went in every day he wouldn't have to be thinking of selling his bar. Are you workin' on another book now, Miles?"

So Freebo had passed on my impromptu story about Maccabee's book. "That's right," I said. "I came up here for the peace and quiet."

"And walked smack into all our troubles. Miles, I was wondering if I could arrange to see you sometime soon."

"How soon?"

"Like today?"

"What's it about?"

"Just for a friendly talk, you could say. Were you going to make it in here today?"

I had the disturbing feeling that he had telepathically overheard my conversation with Paul Kant. "I thought you'd be pretty busy these days, Polar Bears."

"Always time to spare for an old buddy, Miles. How about it? Could you drop in for a talk sometime this afternoon? We're still around the back of the courthouse."

"I guess I can make it."

"Looking forward to it, Miles."

"But I wonder what would happen if I said I couldn't."

"Why do you think something would happen, Miles?"

But *why?* It sounded almost as though Polar Bears (Galen, if I must) had been monitoring my movements since I had come to the valley. Had one of Paul's enemies seen me pocket Maccabee's fraudulent book? If so, they would surely have stopped me before I left the store.

Still thinking of this, a little upset by the seriousness of Polar Bears' tone, I went upstairs and into the workroom and sat before the panel desk. It all felt unbelievably remote, as though another man had removed those diamond-faceted doorknobs and set the flat door upon the trestles. My pitiful notes, my pitiful drafts. I flipped open a folder and read a sentence. "Recurrent in Lawrence's work is a moment of sexual choice which is the choosing of death (or of half-life) over fully engaged, personalizing life." Had I actually written this sentence? Uttered stuff like this before students? I bent down and scraped a random lot of books off the floor. I tied them into a bundle with twine and went out of the house and up the path.

"I'll never read these," Alison Updahl told me. "You don't have to give me anything."

"I know. You don't have to give me anything either." She looked at me unhappily. "But at least this was my own idea."

"Would you mind—would you mind if I gave them to Zack? He's the big intellectual, not me."

"Do anything you want with them," I said. "You're just saving me the trouble of throwing them away." I started to turn away.

"Miles," she said.

"It's not that I wasn't tempted," I said. "I find you extremely tempting. But I'm too old for you, and I'm still your father's guest. And I do think that you ought to get away from Zack. He's screwy. He'll never do anything but injure you."

She said, "You don't understand." She looked terribly unhappy, standing just outside the door on the concrete steps and holding the little heap of books.

"No, I guess I don't," I said.

"There isn't anyone else like him around here. Just like there isn't anyone like you around here either."

I wiped my hand over my face. I was sweating like a band drummer on a hot night. "I won't be here long, Alison. Don't make me into something I'm not."

"Miles," she said, and stopped, embarrassed. Her habit of assertion saw her through. "Is something wrong?"

"It's too complicated to explain." She did not reply, and when I looked into her blunt face I saw the expression of another person whose problems were too complex to be fit easily into verbal patterns. I wanted to take her hand, and nearly did. But I could not lay claim to the spurious authority of age which that would imply.

"Ah . . ." she said as I turned to go again.

"Yes?"

"It was partly my own idea. But you probably won't believe me."

"Alison, be careful," I said, meaning it as much as I have ever meant anything in my life.

I went back to the old house through the sunlight. My hangover had receded to a not unpleasant sensation of light emptiness. By the time I reached the VW parked before the frame garage I realized that the sun was warming my face and shoulders. Twenty yards to my right, the mare grazed in the torn uprooted field, pretending for the sake of a full belly that it was a cow like its neighbors. The walnut trees ahead of me were thick and burly, emblems of long health. I wished the same for Alison Updahl and myself. I could feel her back there on the concrete porch, watching me go. I wished that I could do something, something strong and direct, to help her. A hawk swung far above the hills across the valley. Down the drive and across the road stood the birdhouse mailbox on its metal stalk. Tuta S. had probably left before the arrival of the mailman in his dusty Ford.

At the box I pulled out a thick pad of folders and envelopes. One after the other I sailed into the ditch letters addressed to Occupant. The last of the letters came in the same envelope as the one addressed to me, and it was written over in the same flowing handwriting. For a moment I thought I read my name on it. Like the previous letter, it had been posted in Arden.

When I finally saw what the envelope said I glanced across the cornfields to the beginning of the woods. No figure stood there gazing with waiting aloof Olympian calm. My hands were trembling. I looked again at the envelope—I was not mistaken. It was addressed to Alison Greening. Care of (my name), RFD 2, Norway Valley, Arden. The sun seemed to penetrate behind my pupils and give me a searing touch. Clumsily, still trembling, I inserted a finger beneath the flap and tore it open. I knew what I would find. The single sheet unfolded itself in my hands. Of course. It was blank. Neither a heart pierced by an arrow nor a black spot nor anything but creamy paper.

Down the road, her handbag pumping at her side, Tuta Sunderson toiled toward me. I waited, gasping with emotion, as long as I could and then ran toward her.

"Something come for you?"

"No, yes," I said. "I don't know. Mrs. Sunderson, you can't clean the living room yet. I'm not through in there. You might as well go home. I have to go somewhere." Remembering the phone call of the morning, I added, "If the phone rings, don't answer it." I pelted up the road toward my car.

Smashing the gears, making the VW howl in torment, I shot across the lawn, twisting the wheel at the last moment to avoid the walnut trees. I came rocketing out onto the valley road in the direction of Highway 93. Fat Tuta Sunderson still stood where I had left her; mouth open, she dully watched me zoom past.

But this was not how I wanted to meet Polar Bears, I could not be dragged manacled before him by a slack-faced Arden constable, and I slowed to forty descending the hill past the R-D-N Motel. By the time I reached the flat near the high school, I was proceeding at an almost-legal thirty. People were visible on the sidewalks, a cat cleaned itself on a windowsill, other cars trolled before mine: Arden did not have the deserted, eerie look it had had on my earlier visit, but was a normal small town in a normal condition of sleepy bustle. I pulled into an empty spot before Zumgo's and stopped as gently as a dove. I felt like a man poised on an eggshell. The folded envelope distended my pocket. I knew only one sure way to conquer that awful weightless expectant eggshell feeling. Hearing no wingbeats but the sound of voices, I crossed the pavement to enter Zumgo's.

Happily, the store had a good crowd of women shoppers. Mostly overweight, dressed in obscene halters and skirts excessively short, they would be the audience for my autotherapy. From them rose a mass smell of compost and barren backyards, of dime taps of Leinenkugel beer and soggy pretzels. I began to drift, in an attitude of abstracted busy specific search, through the aisles and around the tables. The women, including the harridan of my previous visit, scarcely noticed me. I was some husband on some errand. I thought and felt myself into this role.

I am no kleptomaniac. I have a letter from an analyst setting that down in black and white, pica type. I took a ten-dollar bill from my wallet and folded it between the second and third fingers of my right hand.

* * *

Now it is time for two comments. The first is obvious. I thought that I knew the handwriting on that envelope. I thought that Alison Greening had sent it to me. This was crazy. But it was no crazier than that she would return on the twenty-first of July to keep her vow. Perhaps she was signaling to me, telling me to hold out until that day. The second comment has to do with stealing. I do not think of myself as a thief—except perhaps at a gritty subconscious level that pumps guilt up into my dreams. I hate stealing. Except for Maccabee's book, I had not stolen anything for at least fifteen years. Thinking of the thefts of my boyhood, I once asked an analyst if he thought I was a kleptomaniac. He said, of course not. Put it in writing, I said. He told me it was my fifty minutes and typed it out on a piece of notepaper. Yet at moments of great unease, I know that I can put my mind right—if at all, if at cost of a wider displacement—by only one means. It is like eating—like stuffing food down your throat long after your hunger has died.

So what I intended doing was a repetition of my mime of thievery: I was going to surreptitiously pocket goods and then drop the ten dollars at the cash register on the way out. Temptation struck first in household novelties, where I saw a corkscrew on a table. Next to it lay a rank of clasp knives. I hovered over the table, ignoring a dozen opportunities for palming the corkscrew and one of the knives. The whole business suddenly seemed labored and stupid.

Revulsion for the charade made me turn away. I was too old for these tricks, I could not allow myself to be so foolishly self-indulgent. But still I suffered. I went upstairs where the books were kept.

Slowly I revolved the rack: you will not steal again, I said to myself, you will not even pretend to steal. Romantic novels with jacket pictures of girls running from castles predominated. I could see no more copies of *The Enchanted Dream*. Finding even one had been fantastic luck. With feigned idleness I scanned the spines side-view. Still nothing.

And then I saw a natural second choice. There, crammed in one of the bottom divisions, was a novel written by Lamont Withers, who had been the gabbiest, most annoying member of my Joyce seminar at Columbia and now taught at Bennington—*A Vision of Fish*, an experimental novel disguised by its jacket drawing of two embracing androgynes as a romance. I extracted the book and examined the back of the cover. "A sensitive tour de force . . . *Cleveland Plain Dealer*. Stunning, witty advance . . . *Library Journal*. Withers is the coming man . . . *Saturday Review*." My facial muscles contracted; it was even worse than Maccabee. Temptation reared up, and I nearly tucked the book between arm and elbow. But I would not give in to this gluttony; I could not be ruled by the responses of twenty years past. I gripped the book in my hand. I went down the stairs. At the cash register, an orderly man, I paid for the book and accepted my change.

Breathing hard, flushed of face, at peace, I sat in my car. Not stealing was so much a better feeling than stealing, or mime-stealing. Not stealing, as I had in fact known for years, was the only way to shop. I felt like an alcoholic who has just turned down a drink. It was still too early to see Polar Bears, so I touched the folded letter in my pocket and decided to go—where else?—to Freebo's, to celebrate. In the midst of death and breakdown, a successful mission.

As I walked across the street, a sharp atom neatly bisected my back between the shoulder blades. I heard a stone clatter on the surface of the road. Stupidly, I watched it roll and come to rest before I looked at the sidewalk. People were there, still simulating that sleepy small-town bustle, walking from Zumgo's to the Coast to Coast Store, looking in the bread-filled windows of Myer's bakery. They seemed to be avoiding looking at me, avoiding even looking in my direction. A second later I saw the men who had probably thrown the stone. Five or six burly middle-aged men, two or three in dungarees and the others in shabby business suits, stood in front of the Angler's Bar. These men were watching me, a general smile flickering between them. I could not stare them down—it was like the Plainview diner. I recognized none of them. When I turned away, a second stone flew past my head. Another struck my right leg.

Friends of Duane's, I thought, and then realized I was wrong. If they were merely that, they would be laughing. This businesslike silence was more ominous than stone-throwing. I looked over my shoulder: they still stood, bunched together and hands in pockets, before the dark bar window. They were watching me. I fled into Freebo's.

"Who are those men?" I asked him. He came hurriedly down the bar, wiping his hands on a rag.

"You look a little shook up, Mr. Teagarden," he said.

"Tell me who those men are. I want their names."

I saw the drinkers at the bar, two thin old men, pick up their glasses and move quietly off.

"What men, Mr. Teagarden?"

"The ones across the street, standing in front of a bar."

"You mean the Angler's. Gee, I don't see anybody there, Mr. Teagarden, I'm sorry."

I went up to the long narrow window overlooking the street and stood beside him. The men had vanished. A woman with her hair in curlers pushed a baby carriage in the direction of the bakery.

"They were just there," I insisted. "Five, maybe six, a couple of farmers and a few others. They threw rocks at me."

"I dunno, Mr. Teagarden, it could have been some kind of accident."

I glared at him.

"Let me get you a drink on the house," he said. He turned away and put a shot glass beneath one of the upended bottles. "There. Put that inside you." Meekly, I drank it in one gulp. "You see, we're still all upset around here, Mr. Teagarden. It was probably because they didn't know who you were."

"It was probably because they did know who I am," I said. "Friendly town, isn't it? Don't answer, just get me another drink. I have to see Polar Bears,

Galen I mean, in a little while but I'm going to stay in here until everybody goes home."

He blinked. "Whatever you say."

I drank six whiskeys, taking my time over them. Several hours passed. Then I had a cup of coffee, and after that another drink. The other men in the bar regarded me surreptitiously, shifting their eyes toward the mirror when I raised my glass or leaned on the bar. After an unendurable time of this, I took Withers' book out of my jacket pocket and began to read it on the bar. I switched from whiskey to beer and remembered that I'd had nothing to eat.

"Do you have sandwiches in here?"

"I'll get one for you, Mr. Teagarden. And another cup of coffee?"

"And a cup of coffee *and* another beer."

Withers' book was unreadable. It was unbearably trivial. I began to tear out pages. If you find a pattern, you should stick to it. Now the other men in the bar no longer bothered to conceal their stares. I recognized in myself the buzzing frontal lobes of intoxication. "Do you have a wastebasket, Freebo?" I asked.

He held up a green plastic bucket. "Is that another one you wrote?"

"No, I never wrote anything worth publishing," I said. I pitched the ripped pages into the green bucket. The men were staring at me as they would at a circus ape.

"You're shook up, Mr. Teagarden," Freebo said. "See, it won't help any. You've had a few too many, Mr. Teagarden, and you're kinda upset. I think you ought to go out in the fresh air for a little bit. You're all paid up in here, see, and I can't serve you any more. You oughta go home and have a rest." He was walking me toward the front of the bar, talking in a low, calming voice.

"I want to buy a record player," I said. "Can I do that now or is it too late?"

"I think the stores just closed, Mr. Teagarden."

"I'll do it tomorrow. Now I have to see Polar Bears Galen Hovre."

"That's a good idea." The door closed behind me. I was standing alone on a deserted Main Street; the sky and the light were darkening, though it would not be dusk for at least two hours. I realized that I had spent most of the day in the bar. Signs on the bakery and department store doors read CLOSED. I glanced at the Angler's Bar, which seemed from the outside to be as empty as Freebo's. A single car went past in the direction of the courthouse. Once again, I could hear the beating of pigeons' wings, circling way up above.

At that moment the town seemed haunted. The Midwest is the place for ghosts, I realized, the truest place for them; they could throng up these wide empty Main Streets and populate the fields. I could almost feel them around me.

With these thoughts in my mind, I started when I heard footsteps behind me. I looked over my shoulder and saw only an empty street lined with cars like the deserted hulls of insects. When I turned my neck, I again heard the footsteps, a crowd of them. I began to walk quickly, and heard them follow. The street lay wide and deserted before me, lined with empty cars and blank deserted shops. I heard the electric buzz of a neon sign in the window of a kitchen supplier's. Reality's veneer seemed on the verge of dissolution, even the pavement and the brick storefronts were stretched taut over a drumming void. I began to run, and heard them running behind me. I turned my head again, and was almost relieved to see a crowd of thick-waisted men making down the street toward me.

The courthouse was four blocks away, in a straight line up Main Street, but I didn't have a chance of getting there before they caught me. In the brief glimpse I had, some of them seemed to be carrying sticks. I pumped around the next corner and doubled back into an alley. When I reached the rear of Freebo's I hunched down beside a group of large silver garbage cans; I did not have time to reach the end of the alley. The group of men had clearly divided; two of them appeared at the alley's entrance and began to half-trot toward me. I crouched as low as I could get behind the big silver cans. Their footsteps approached, and I heard them breathing hard. They were even less accustomed to running than I was.

One of them distinctly exclaimed, "Shit."

I waited until I heard them returning; they passed my hole, and then clattered toward the alley's entrance. When I peeked out, I saw them turning right to follow the rest of the group. My back to the buildings, legs ready to spring, I edged down the alley's length. I looked cautiously out at Madison Street. Two blocks down, they were rocking an old car parked before a peeling, shabby house. One of them swung at the car with a long stick, ax handle or baseball bat. Glass popped and exploded.

I couldn't make sense of it. Were they just rowdy drunks looking for the nearest target? Hoping that the noise they were making while destroying the car would keep them from hearing me, I ran across Madison Street into the alley on the other side. Shouts and yells told me that they had seen me. I nearly fell down in terror. I pelted through the alley and came out on Monroe Street, turned right with the thick boiling noise gathering behind me, and wheeled around the corner back onto Main. At the last possible second, I yanked at the door handle of a car and rolled inside. Then I scrambled over the seat and lay, heart pounding, in the well before the backseat. A candy wrapper fluttered before my nose; dust seemed to pour dryly up from the floor, acrid and foul. I closed my nostrils with my fingers, and after a time the impulse to sneeze left me. I could hear them coming quickly up the street, banging with fists or clubs on cars in frustration.

The edge of a greasy shirt passed the window I could see. A hand pressed against it, flattened and white like a dead starfish. Then I saw only darkening sky. I thought: what if I die here? If my machinery fails and dumps my corpse into this odorous car? Who would find me? It was an image of utter hopelessness. After a while I was strong enough to sneak a look over the top of the seat. They were not far down the block, evidently confounded by my disappearance. There were only four of them, fewer than I had thought; they did not look like the men who had stoned me. They were younger. They ran ahead a few steps. Then they began to walk up Main, looking from side to side, rapping their bats on the sidewalk. They were the only people on the street. When a car passed, they bent to examine the driver's face. I waited until they had gone several blocks past the courthouse and then I crawled over the seat and came crouching out onto the sidewalk.

The four men were across the street now, far up ahead, nearly to the bridge over the Blundell River. The courthouse lay about halfway between us. I began to walk toward it. The men had reached the bridge, and I saw them leaning on it, talking, lighting cigarettes. Bent over, moving as quickly as possible without running, I gained another fifty feet. Then one of the men threw down his cigarette and pointed at me.

I lifted my elbows and knees and discovered for the first time in my life what running was. It is rhythm, all rhythm, long easy beats made by coordinating every muscle. They were confused that I ran toward them, but when I reached the courthouse and turned easily on one leg and pounded, stepping high, to the back, they flew shouting after me. I fisted my hands and made arcs in the air with them, my chest bowed out and my legs sailing across the asphalt parking lot. I reached the police cars just as they came into the lot. I heard them slow down, scuffling, calling out to me.

The words were unaudible. A roaring sound kicked to life in the corner of the parking lot, and I saw a black-jacketed man tear off on a motorcycle. It looked as though it could have been Zack; I wasn't sure. The sudden noise made my followers panic. By the time I reached the yellow door with thick glass inset above the word POLICE, they had scattered. My throat felt like burning paper.

The uniformed man rolling a sheet of paper into a typewriter turned his chubby face toward me. I closed the door and leaned back against it, breathing hard. Still holding the paper in his hands, he half-rose, and I saw the stumpy pistol strapped to his hip. "My name is Teagarden," I said, "and I have an appointment with the chief."

"Oh yeah," he said, and lowered the paper with deliberate slowness on top of the typewriter. My chest was heaving.

"I just won a race. Try not to shoot."

"Just hold it right there." He came around to the front of the desk, not taking his eyes from me nor removing his hand from within panic distance of the revolver. His left hand found the telephone; when he had the receiver to his ear, he glanced at the row of buttons at the base of the phone and punched one and then dialed a single number. "Teagarden's here." He set the phone down. "You can go right in. He's been waiting for you. Take that door right there, and then it's the door marked 'Chief.' "

I nodded, and moved toward the door "right there." Polar Bears' office was at the end of the hall; it was about ten by twelve, mostly filled with green filing cabinets and a worn old desk. Most of the rest of it was filled by Polar Bears.

"Sit down, for God's sake, Miles," he said, waving at the chair before his desk. "You look like you had a hard old day." Looking at him, I could see the difference in our ages more clearly than I ever had before—he had been nearly Duane's age, though his cheerful rowdiness had made him younger in my eyes. In this solidly massive man with a serious square face I could see few traces of the boy who had spitballed Bertilsson's sheep. Even the reason for his name had vanished: his furry cap of astonishingly white hair had darkened and receded to a brownish dusting from his ears to his rubbery-looking scalp.

"You look like you've had a hard old life, but it's nice to see you again," I said.

"Yeah, we had some good times together, didn't we? Some real good times."

"I had an especially good time on the way over here. A gang of your citizens chased me with baseball bats. I barely made it."

He tilted his head back and pushed his lips out. "Would that be the reason you're sort of late for our reunion?"

"Our reunion is the reason I'm here at all, and not broken up in the alley behind Freebo's. They only stopped chasing me because I made it into your parking lot."

"You were at Freebo's. I'd say you spent quite a time in there."

"Does that mean you don't believe me?"

"Some of the bucks around town are getting all riled. I can believe you, Miles. I don't suppose you saw these boys close enough to identify them."

"I was trying hard not to get that close."

"Simmer down, Miles. They're not going to get you. You're going to be safe in here, having a little talk. Just simmer down. Those boys will leave you alone."

"Some others of your local boys threw rocks at me this noon when my back was turned."

"Is that so? You get hurt any?"

"It's so, and no, I didn't. Do you want me to forget about that too? Just because they didn't dent my skull?"

"I don't want you to go getting yourself worked up over a bunch of hotheads. I'd say that some of the good people decided that you'd be better off leaving town."

"Why?"

"Because they don't know you, Miles. It's simple as that. You're the only man in about a century and a half had a sermon preached about him. You weren't thinking of being run off, were you?"

"No. I have to stay here. I'm involved in something."

"Um-hum. Real good. Any idea how long that might take you?"

"Until the twenty-first. After that I don't know."

"Well, that's not far away. I want to ask you to consider staying up there at Duane's until we get some things straightened out around here. Is that all right?"

"What the hell is this all about, Polar Bears? Don't leave town until the police give me permission?"

"I wouldn't put it like that. I'm asking you for a favor."

"Am I being questioned?"

"Hell no, Miles. We're having a talk. I want your help on something."

I leaned back in the stiff chair. I couldn't feel the alcohol anymore. Galen Hovre was regarding me with a half-smile which held little warmth. My senses were confirming a theory of mine, that when a man's nature changes his essential smell changes with it. Polar Bears once had carried a dense, pleasant odor of closely packed earth, strongest when he was racing a jalopy at seventy down the curves of Highway 93 or stuffing a mailbox with rocks; now, like Duane, he smelled of gunpowder.

"Can I count on your help?"

I looked at this large square-faced man who had been my friend, and didn't trust a thing he said. "Sure."

"You've heard about these girls who were killed. Gwen Olson and Jenny Strand. Your neighbor Red Sunderson found that Strand girl, and she wasn't a pretty sight. My deputy, Dave Lokken out there, lost his cookies when he saw her."

"He's still upset," I said.

"Any normal man would be," Hovre said amiably. "Truth is, we're all upset around here. This crazy son of a bitch is still walking around. He could be anybody, and that's the one that gets them by the nuts, Miles. We pretty well know everybody, and folks don't know what to think."

"Don't you have any ideas about who it might be?"

"Oh, we're sort of keeping an eye on someone, but even he's not very likely, according to the way I see it. Now I'd like to keep this local. I've been chief here for four years, and I want to get reelected so I can keep my family in hamburgers. Now you're new around here. You might see things we don't notice. You had a good education, you're observant. I wonder if you've seen or heard anything that might help me out?"

"Wait a second," I said. "Do those people who chased me think I did those things? Those killings?"

"You'd have to ask them."

"Christ," I said. "I've scarcely even thought about them. I've been busy with my own problems. I didn't come here for this."

"Seems to me it might help you out too if you could think of anything."

"I shouldn't need that. I shouldn't have to help myself that way."

"Seems to me should doesn't have much to do with it."

He had a point. "Okay, I can see that. I don't think I've noticed anything. Just a lot of people acting queer, afraid. Some of them hostile. I met one strange kid, but . . ." The "but" was that I did not want to say anything that would bring suspicion on Zack or Alison. Zack was just a nutty theorist. Polar Bears lifted his eyebrows in a gesture of uninvolved patient anticipation. "But he was just a kid. I don't even want to name him. I don't know what I could say that would help."

"Not yet, maybe. But you might remember something. Just keep it in mind, will you, old buddy?"

I nodded.

"Yeah. We could have this all on a plate by the twenty-first, so don't do any unnecessary worrying. Now I got a few other little points to bring up with you." He put on a pair of thick black glasses, making himself look like a scholarly bald bull of melancholy temperament, and took a sheet of paper off a messy pile. "I guess you got into a little trouble over in Plainview a while ago. I got a report on it just yesterday. A fellow named Frank Drum took the number of your car."

"Jesus," I said, thinking of the slinking little clerk who had been dispatched out of the diner.

"This was after an incident in Grace's Restaurant over there. Do you remember it?"

"Of course I remember. They were like your gang of happy hooligans who tried to beat in my head with bats."

"Who chased you." He looked sharply up from the paper.

"It's the same thing. What happened was ridiculous. I saw these guys listening to a radio and they looked like some trouble had happened and I asked what it was. They didn't like my face. They didn't like my coming from New York. So they threw me out after they took my license number. That was all. It was around one of the day somebody found the first girl."

"Just for the record, do you know where you spent the previous night?"

"Somewhere. In a motel somewhere. I don't know."

"You don't have a receipt or a check stub?"

"It was in a crummy little dive off the freeway. I paid with cash. What the hell do you want to know for?"

"I don't want to know. There's a cop named Larabee over there who wanted me to ask, that's all."

"Well, tell Larabee to shove it up his ass. I was in a crummy motel in Ohio."

"Just fine, Miles, that's fine. Real good. No need to get lathered up all over again. How did you hurt that hand of yours?"

I looked in surprise down at my bandaged hand. The tape was filthy and beginning to unravel. Loose wispy trails of dirty gauze leaked from beneath the tape. I had nearly forgotten about Duane's bandage. "I had an accident with my car. On my car. I cut myself."

"Dave Lokken can fix you up with a new bandage before you leave. He's real proud of his first-aid skills. When did that accident happen?"

"That same day. After I left the diner."

"According to another fellow in that restaurant, a fellow named Al Service— he's the official weedcutter in that part of the country—you made a funny remark before you left. According to Service, you said you hoped another girl would be killed."

"I didn't mean that. I was angry. I didn't even know anyone had been killed then. I just said something like, 'Whatever it was, you deserve to have it happen again.' Then I ran like hell."

He took off the glasses. He rested one jowl in his meaty hand. "I guess that makes sense, Miles. They got you riled. It happens to everybody. Why, you even got old Margaret Kastad worked up, I hear."

"Old who?"

"Andy's wife. She gave me a call after you left the store. Said you were writing pornography and I should run you off."

"I won't waste time talking about that," I said. "She holds a few ancient mistakes against me. I'm a different person now."

"All of us are, I guess. Guess it doesn't mean we can't help each other out. You could do something for me right now, and write out what happened in that restaurant and date it and sign it so's I can have a copy sent to Larabee. It's for your own good." He fished around on his desk and pushed a sheet of paper and a pen across the surface. "Just in general terms, Miles. It doesn't have to be long."

"If I have to." I took the paper and wrote down what had happened. I returned the paper to him.

"You'll give me a call whenever you remember or notice anything?"

I put my hand in my pocket and felt folded paper. "Wait. Just wait a second. Here's something you can help me with. Who do you think sent this to me? There was a blank sheet of paper inside it." I took out the envelope and smoothed it on his desk. My hands were shaking. "It's the second one. The first was addressed to me."

The glasses went back on, and he bent over the desk to take the envelope. When he saw the name, he glanced up at me. It was the first genuine response I'd had from him. "You got another one of these?"

"Addressed to me. With a blank sheet of paper in it."

"Would you let me keep this?"

"No. I want it. What you can do is tell me who sent it." I had the sense of taking a great risk, of making a huge error. It was strong enough to weaken my knees.

"I hate to say this, but it looks like your writing, Miles."

"What?"

He held up my statement alongside the envelope and then turned them so I could see them together. There was a certain superficial similarity. "It's not my writing, Polar Bears."

"Not many people around here remember this particular name anymore."

"All it takes is one," I said. "Just give me the envelope back."

"Whatever you say. Only experts can really tell about these handwriting things anyhow. Dave!" He was bellowing at the door. "Get in here with your first-aid kit! Pronto!"

"I heard you callin' him Polar Bears. Not many does that anymore."

Lokken and I were walking down Main Street in the late humid darkness. The few streetlights had come on; I could again hear the buzz of neon signs. Lights burned in the windows of the Angler's, spilling a rectangle of yellow onto the sidewalk. My hand was encased in gleaming white.

"We're old friends."

"You'd have to be. That name Polar Bears just drives him up the wall. Where's your car at, anyhow? I think you'd be safe now."

"I'm not taking the chance. He said for you to walk me to my car, and that's what I want you to do."

"Shit, there's nothing to be ascairt of. There ain't nobody out."

"That's what I thought last time. If you don't call him Polar Bears, what do you call him?"

"Me?" Lokken guffawed. "I call him Sir."

"What does Larabee call him?"

"Who?"

"Larabee. The chief over in Plainview."

"Excuse me, but you musta lost some of your marbles, Mr. Teagarden. There ain't nobody named Larabee over there in Plainview and even if there was he wouldn't be chief because Plainview ain't even *got* a chief of police. They got a sheriff named Larson, and he's my second cousin. Chief Hovre calls in there once or twice a week. It's his jurisdiction, like all these little towns roundabout, Centerville, Liberty, Blundell. He's chief of it all. Where's your car at, now?"

I was standing motionless in the middle of the wide dark street, looking at the VW and trying to assimilate what Lokken had said. The condition of my car made it difficult.

Lokken said, "My God, that's not yours, is it?"

I nodded, my throat too dry to form words.

The windows were smashed, the top and hood bent and battered. One of the headlights protruded like an eyeball on a thin stalk. I ran to look at the front tires, and then went around in back. They were untouched, but the rear window had been smashed in.

"That's property damage. You want to come back and tell the chief about it? You should fill out a report. I gotta make a report too."

"No. You tell Hovre about it. This time he'll believe me." I could feel anger building up in me again, and I gripped Lokken's arm and squeezed it hard, making him yelp. "Tell him I said I wanted Larabee to handle it."

"But I just told you my second cousin—"

I was already in the car torturing the ignition.

The dangling headlight clattered onto the street before I had gone a block, and as I gunned the car up the first of the hills, just past the high school, I heard a hubcap roll off into the weeds beside the road. Through the starred windshield, I could see only a quarter of the road, and even that was fogged and blurred by the condition of the glass. My single headlight veered between illuminating the yellow line and the weeds, and my emotional condition swung wildly about a giant sense of betrayal. Larabee, was it? Was it Larabee who wanted to know how I'd cut my hand? Was it Larabee who wanted to get reelected?

I suspected that it was Larabee who would not push very hard to find the men who had tried to attack me, and who had wrecked my car in their frustration.

Fighting the shuddering car around a tight, ascending curve, I realized that the radio was playing: I had accidentally brushed the button some miles back, and now it was unreeling yards of drivel. ". . . and for Kathy and Jo and Brownie, from the Hardy Boys, I guess you girls know what that means, a good old good one, 'Good Vibrations.' " Teenage voices began to squeal. I slammed into a lower gear, trying to watch the turning of the road through the web of the windshield as the announcer inserted a voice-over. "The Hardy Boys, far out." Headlights raced toward me, then slipped past, flaring like the car's horn.

The next car flipped its lights up and down twice, and I realized that my single headlight was on bright; I hit the dimming button with my foot.

"Too much, really too much. Those were the good old days talkin' at ya. Now for Frank from Sally, a real tender one, I guess she loves you, Frank, so give her a call, huh? Something from Johnny Mathis."

On the rises I could see nothing but black empty air beyond the roadbed; I kept the accelerator to the floor, releasing it only when I had to change gears or when the bolts in the car's body began to shimmy. I flew past the Community Chest thermometer, seeing it only for a second in the headlight. All the beautiful green distance was one-dimensional dark.

"Hey, Frank, you better watch that little fox, she's gonna get you, baby. She's just stone in love with you, so be cool. Little change of pace now—for the junior gym class and Miss Tite, a blast of soulful Tina Turner, from Rosie B—'River Deep, Mountain High.' "

My tires complained as I suddenly braked, seeing a high wooded wall of stone before me instead of the black road; I cramped the wheel, and the back end fished out and then righted itself in that way which suggests that an automobile is constructed of a substance far more elastic than metal. The oil light flashed and went dead again. Still going dangerously fast, my mind filled with nothing but the mechanics of driving, I came over the last hill and began the straight slope down to the highway in a deep well of unheard music.

Without bothering to brake I spun out onto the deserted highway. The music pulsed in my ears like blood. Over the low white bridge, past where Red Sunderson must have found the second girl's body; then a sharp left onto the valley road. I was breathing as hard as if I'd been running.

"Whoo-ee! Tell that to anyone, but don't tell it to your gym teacher! All the weirdos are out tonight, kiddies, so lock your doors. Here's something for all the lost ones, I kid you not, that's what the card says, for all the lost ones, from A and Z. Van Morrison and 'Listen to the Lion.' "

At last I became conscious of the radio's noise. I slowed, passing the narrow drive to Rinn's house. Dark mounted high on either side—I seemed to be entering a tunnel of darkness. From A and Z? Alison and Zack? "Listen to the Lion"—that was the name of the song. An untrained high baritone glided through words I could not distinguish. The song seemed to have no particular melody. I switched the radio off. I wanted only to be home. The VW sped past the shell of the old school, and a few moments later, the high pompous facade of the church. I heard the motor grinding arhythmically, and pushed the button to bring the headlight back up to bright.

Before the Sunderson farm the road makes a tight bend around a red outcropping of sandstone, and I leaned forward over the wheel, putting all my attention onto the two square inches of clear glass. The beam of yellow light flew over the corn. Then I saw something that made me slew the car over to the side of the road and brake. I hurriedly got out and stood on the ridge beside the seat so that I could look over the top of the car to the end of the fields.

It had not been a mistake: the slight figure was there again, between the field and the black rise of the wood.

I heard a screen door bang shut behind me and looked up over my shoulder, startled. Lights in the Sunderson home showed a tall husky man in outline on the high sloping lawn. I looked back across the fields, and it was still there. The choice was simple because it was not a choice at all.

I jumped down onto the road and ran around the front of the car.

"Hey!" a man shouted.

In the next second I was over the ditch and already running down the side of the cornfield, going toward the woods. Whoever was up there was watching me, I thought, letting me approach.

"Stop! Miles! Wait up!"

I ignored him. The woods were a quarter of a mile away. I could almost hear music. The voice behind me ceased to shout. As I ran toward it, the figure went backward into the woods and disappeared.

"I see you!" the man shouted.

I didn't bother to turn around: the vanishing of the figure into the woods made me run even harder, even more clumsily, forgetting the technique I had learned in the police parking lot. The ground was hard and dry, covered with a light stubble, and I pounded along, keeping in view the place where the figure had last been. Beside me, the corn was higher than my head, a solid dark mass beyond the first rows.

The boundary of the first row of fields, from the highway to the farm just beyond Duane's, is formed by a small creek, and it was this that gave me my first difficulty. The plowed and farmed land ended about eight feet on either side of the creek; when I reached the end of the corn planting, I looked to my left and saw an area of beaten-down tall grass and flattened weeds where apparently Duane customarily drove the tractor through to the upper fields. When I ran there and began to approach the creek, I saw that the ground had been churned by the tractor so that the whole area was a muddy swamp. There the creek was four or five feet wider than anywhere else, spilling out into the depression the tractor had made. I walked back along the bank; birds and frogs announced themselves, joining the cricket noises that had surrounded me since I had left the road. My boots were encased in soft mud.

I pushed tall fibrous weeds apart with my arms and saw a narrowing of the creek. Two hairy grassy bulges of earth made an interrupted bridge over the water; the bulges, about a yard and a half apart, were supported by the root systems of two of the cottonwood trees which grew all along the creek's length. I circled one of the trees and edged out on the root-hump and jumped across, banging my forehead and nose into the trunk of the tree on the opposite side. Crows took off in noisy alarm. Still clutching the tree with both arms, I looked back over the cornfield and saw the VW parked on the valley road before the Sunderson house up on its hill. Light came beaming out from both house and car—I had forgotten to turn off the engine. Worse, I had left the key in the ignition. Mrs. Sunderson and Red were standing at one of the windows, cupping their hands to their eyes and staring out.

I jumped down from the humped tangle of roots and, after struggling through another area of thick weeds, began to jog up through the next field. I could see the place where I thought the figure had slipped into the woods, and pushed myself up over a rise where alfalfa gave way to corn again. In a few minutes I was at the beginning of the trees.

They seemed sparser, less a thick homogeneous mass than they had appeared from the road. Moonlight made it possible for me to see where I was going once I had begun to run through the widely spaced trees. My feet encountered the edges of large rocks and the yielding softness of mould and beds of pine needles. As I ran deeper into the trees the impression of sparseness quickly diminished: the ghostly pines and birches slipped behind me, and I was moving between oaks and elms, veterans with rivered barks which blocked out nearly all the light. I came to a jog and then stopped, hearing an excited rustle of movement off to my left.

I turned my head in time to see a deer bounding for cover, lifting its haunches like a woman leaving a diving board.

Alison. I plunged blindly off to the right, hindered by my heavy boots. She had appeared to me, she had signaled. Somewhere, she was waiting for me. Somewhere deep in the darkness.

A long time later and after I entered a circle of trees, I admitted that I was lost. Not finally lost, because the slope of the forest's floor told me which way the fields and the road were, but lost enough not to know if I had been circling. More disturbingly, after I had fallen and rolled against a lichen-covered boulder, I had become unsure of lateral direction. The woods were too dark for me to see farmhouse lights in the distance—in fact, distance did not seem to exist at all, except as an infinity of big close dark trees. I had edged my way into one clearing, perhaps half a mile back; but it may have been *up*, not *back*, and was at least some distance up, for I had come down the slope before going right again. All in all I thought I had been looking for nearly an hour, and the trees about me seemed familiar, as if I had been at this same spot before. It was only the little clearing, blackened at its center with the cold ashes of a fire, which proved I had gone anywhere at all, and not turned and turned in the same place before the same trees until I was lost and dizzy.

Because, really, it did look familiar—the giant bulge of a trunk before me had been before me earlier, I had looked up at an identical thick curve of branch, I had knelt on an identical shattered log. I shouted my cousin's name.

At that moment I had an essentially *literary* experience, brewed up out of Jack London and Hawthorne and Cooper and Disney cartoons and Shakespeare and the brothers Grimm, of panic which quickly passed into fear. The panic was at being lost, but the fear which rushed in after it was simply of the woods themselves, of giant alien nature. I mean that the trees seemed inhabited by threatening life. Malevolence surrounded me. Not just nature's famous Darwinian indifference, but active actual hostility. It was the most primitive apprehension of evil I had ever known. I was a fragile human life on the verge of being crushed by immense forces, by forces of huge and impersonal evil. Alison was a part of this; she had drawn me in. I knew that if I did not move, I would be snatched by awful twigged hands, I would be shredded against moss. I would die as the two girls had died. Lichen would pack my mouth. How foolish we had been to assume that mere human beings had killed the girls!

From this frozen encounter with spirit it was terror that finally released me, and I ran blindly, plungingly, in any direction I could find—in far greater fear than I had run from the hooligans in Arden. Low branches caught my stomach and brought me crashing down, rocks skittered under my slippery feet, twigs clutched at my trousers. Low leaves rustled at my eyes. I was just running, glad for running, and my heart whooped and my lungs caught at breath.

I fell many times. The last time, I peered up through creepers and nettles and saw that the malevolence had gone; the god had departed; human light was darting into the vegetation, the light which represents our conquering of unreason, and I brought my body complaining up into a squatting position to see from where the light was coming. I could feel Alison's letter in my pocket. My personality began to reassemble. Artificial light is a poem to reasonableness, the lightbulb casts out demons, it speaks in rhymed couplets, and my body began to shake with relief, as if I had stumbled into the formal gardens of Versailles.

Even my normal cast of mind returned to me, and I regretted my momentary betrayal of belief. It was betrayal of Alison and betrayal of spirit. I had been spooked, and spooked by literature at that.

As this specific Teagardenish guilt whispered through me, I finally saw where I was and knew the house from which light fell. Yet my body still trembled with relief when I made it stand and walk through the domesticated oaks.

She appeared on the porch. The sleeves of a man's tweed jacket hung below the tips of her fingers. She was still wearing the high rubber boots. "Who is that out there? Miles? Is that you?"

"Well, yes," I said. "I got lost."

"Are you alone?"

"You're always asking me that."

"But I heard two of you."

I just stared at her.

"Come on in, Miles, and I'll pour you some coffee."

When I came up on the porch she scrutinized me with her good eye. "Why, Miles, you're in a terrible condition! You're all over dirt. And you've torn your clothes." She looked down. "And you'll have to take off those boots before you can come into my kitchen."

Gently I removed the mud-laden boots. I was aware of numerous small aches and sores on my face and hands, and I had somewhere banged my leg in the same place I had when I had accompanied the chair down the stairs of the root cellar.

"Why, you're limping, Miles! What were you doing out there at night?"

I lowered myself into a chair and she placed a cup before me. "Auntie Rinn, are you sure you heard someone else in the woods? Someone besides me?"

"It was probably one of the chickens. They do get out and make an awful ruckus." She was sitting poised on a chair across the old wooden table from me, her long white hair falling to the shoulders of the gray tweed jacket. Steam from the cups rose wispily between us. "Let me take care of your face."

"Please don't bother," I said, but she had already bounced up and was at the sink, dampening a cloth. Then she took a covered pot from a shelf and returned. The cloth was cool and soothing against my cheekbones.

"I don't like saying this to you, Miles, but I think you should leave the valley. You were troubled when you first came here, and you are more troubled now. If you will insist on staying, I want you to leave Jessie's house and come to stay here."

"I can't."

She dipped her fingers in the pot and dabbed a thick green mixture on my cuts. It made my entire face throb. A woodsy fragrance snagged in my nostrils. "This is just an herbal mixture for your cuts, Miles. What were you doing out there?"

"Looking for someone."

"Looking for something in the woods at night?"

"Ah, yes, someone broke most of the glass on my car and I thought I saw them running up this way."

"Why were you trembling?"

"I'm not used to running." Her fingers were still rubbing the green mixture into my face.

"I can protect you, Miles."

"I don't need protection."

"Then why were you so frightened?"

"It was just the woods. The darkness."

"Sometimes it is right to fear the dark." She looked at me fiercely. "But it is never right to lie to me, Miles. You were not looking for a vandal. Were you?"

I was conscious of the trees bending over the house, of the darkness outside her circle of light.

She said, "You must pack your things and leave. Come here or go back to New York. Go to your father in Florida."

"I can't." That thick smell hung over my face.

"You will be destroyed. You must at least come here to stay with me."

"Auntie Rinn," I said. My entire body had begun to shake again. "Some people think I have been killing those girls—that was the reason they attacked my car. What could you do against them?"

"They will never come here. They will never come up my path." I remembered how she had terrified me when I was a child, with that look on her face, sentences like that in her mouth. "They are only town people. They have nothing to do with the valley."

The little kitchen seemed intolerably hot, and I saw that the woodstove was burning, alive like a fireplace with snapping flames.

I said, "I want to tell you the truth. I felt something monstrous out there. Something purely hostile, and that's why I was frightened. I guess it was evil I felt. But it all came out of books. Some toughs chased me through Arden, and then Polar Bears shook me up, as he would say. I know the literature about all this. I know all about Puritans in the wilderness, and it caught up with me. I've been repressed and I'm not myself."

"What are you waiting for, Miles?" she asked, and I knew that I could prevaricate no longer.

"I'm waiting for Alison," I said. "Alison Greening. I thought it was her I saw from the road, and I ran up into the woods to find her. I've seen her three times."

"Miles—" she began, her face wild and angry.

"I'm not working on my dissertation anymore, I don't care about that, I've been feeling more and more that all of that is death to the spirit, and I've been getting signs that Alison will come soon."

"Miles—"

"Here's one of them," I said and took the crumpled envelope out of my pocket. "Hovre thinks I sent it to myself, but she sent it, didn't she? That's why the writing is like mine."

She was going to speak again, and I held up my hand. "You see, you never liked her, nobody ever liked her, but we were always alike. We were almost the same person. I've never loved any other woman."

"She was your snare. She was a trap waiting for you to enter it."

"Then she still is, but I don't believe it."

"Miles—"

"Auntie Rinn, in 1955 we made a vow that we would meet here in the valley, and we set a date. It's in only a few weeks from now. She is going to come, and I am going to meet her."

"Miles," she said, "your cousin is dead. She died twenty years ago, and you killed her."

"I don't believe that," I said.

III

I LIGHT OUT FOR THE TERRITORIES

1

"Miles," she said, "your cousin died in 1955 while the two of you were swimming in the old Pohlson quarry. She was drowned."

"No. She drowned," I said. "Active verb. I didn't kill her. I couldn't have killed her. She meant more to me than my own life. I would rather have died myself. It was the end of my life anyhow."

"You may have killed her by accident—you may not have known what you were doing. I am only an old farm woman, but I know you. I love you. You have always been troubled. Your cousin was also a troubled person, but her troubles were not innocent, as yours were. She chose the rocky path, she desired confusion and evil, and you never committed that sin."

"I don't know what you're talking about. She was, I don't know, more complicated than I was, but that was part of her beauty. For me, anyhow. No one else understood her. And I did not kill her, accidentally or any other way."

"Only you two were there."

"That's not certain."

"Did you see anyone else that night?"

"I don't know. I might have. I thought I did, several times. I got knocked out in the water."

"By Alison's struggles. She nearly took you with her."

"I wish she had. I haven't had a life since."

"Not a whole life. Not a satisfied life. Because of her."

"*Stop it*," I shouted. The heat of the kitchen was building up around me, seeming to increase with every word. The stuff on my face was beginning to burn. My shout had frightened her; she seemed paler and smaller, inside all those wrinkles and the man's baggy jacket. She slowly sipped at her coffee, and I felt a great sad inevitable remorse. "I'm sorry. I'm sorry I shouted. If you love me it must be the way you'd love some wounded bird. I'm in a terrible state, Auntie Rinn."

"I know," she said calmly. "That's why I have to protect you. That's why you have to leave the valley. It's too late now for anything else."

"Because Alison is coming back, you mean. Because she is."

"If she is, then there is nothing to do. It is too late for anything. She has hooks in you too deep for me to remove them."

"Thank God for that. She means freedom to me. She means life."

"No. She means death. She means what you felt out there tonight."

"That was nerves."

"That was *Alison*. She wants to claim you."

"She claimed me years ago."

"Miles, you are submitting to forces you don't understand. I don't understand them either, but I respect them. And I fear them. Have you thought about what happens after she returns?"

"What happens doesn't matter. She will be in this world again. She knows I didn't kill her."

"Perhaps that doesn't matter. Or perhaps it matters less than you think it does. Tell me about that night, Miles."

I let my head drop forward, so that my chin nearly touched my chest. "What good would that do?"

"Then I will tell you. This is what Arden people remember about you, Miles. They remember that you were suspected of murder. You already had a bad reputation—you were known as a thief, a disturbed, disordered boy with no control over his feelings. Your cousin was—I don't know what the word is. A sexual tease. She was corrupt. She shocked the valley people. She was calculating and she had power—I recognized when she was only a child that she was a destructive person. She hated life. She hated everything but herself."

"Never," I said.

"And the two of you went to the quarry to swim, no doubt after Alison had deceived your mothers. She was ensnaring you even more deeply. Miles, there can exist between two people a kind of deep connection, a kind of voice between them, a calling, and if the dominant person is corrupted, the connection is unhealthy and corrupt."

"Skip the rigamarole," I said. "Get on with what you want to say." I wanted to leave her overheated kitchen; I wanted to immure myself in the old Updahl farmhouse.

"I will." Her face was hard as winter. "Someone driving past on the Arden road heard screams coming from the quarry and called the police. When old Walter Hovre got there he found you unconscious on the rock ledge. Your face was bleeding. Alison was dead. He could just see her body, caught on a rock projection down in the water. Both of you were naked. She had been . . . she had been abused." Her complexion began to redden. "The inference was there to be made. It was obvious."

"What do you think happened?"

"I think she seduced you and died accidentally. That she died by your hand, but that it was not murder." Now her blushing was pronounced: it was a ghastly effect, as if she had rubbed rouge into her cheeks. "I have never known physical love, Miles, but I imagine that it is a turbulent business." She raised her chin and looked straight at me. "That is what everybody thought. You were not to be charged—in fact, many women in Arden thought that your cousin had gotten just what she deserved. The coroner, who was Walter Hovre in those days, said that it was accidental death. He was a kindly man, and he'd had his troubles with his own son. He did not want to ruin your life. It helped that you were an Updahl. People hereabouts have always looked up to your family."

"Just tell me this," I said. "When everybody was silently condemning me while hypocritically setting me free, didn't anyone wonder who had made that phone call?"

"The man didn't give his name. He said he was frightened."

"Do you really think screams from the quarry can be heard on the road?"

"Evidently they can. And in these times, Miles, people remember your old story."

"Goddammit," I said. "Don't you think I know that? Even Duane's daughter has begun to hear rumors about it. Her crazy boyfriend, too. But I'm bound by my past. That's the reason I'm here. I'm innocent of the other thing. My innocence is bound to come out."

"I hope with all my heart that it does," she said. I could hear the wind rattling the branches and leaves outside, and I felt like a character from another century—a character from a fairy tale, hiding in a gingerbread house. "But that is not enough to save you now."

"I know what my salvation is."

"Salvation is work."

"That's a good Norwegian theory."

"Well, work, then. Write! Help in the fields!"

I smiled at the thought of Duane and myself mowing hay side by side. "I thought you were advising me to leave the state. Actually Polar Bears won't let me leave. And I wouldn't, anyhow."

She looked at me with what I recognized as despair. I said, "I won't let go of the past. You don't understand, Auntie Rinn." At the end of this sentence, I shocked myself by yawning.

"Poor tired boy."

"I am tired," I admitted.

"Sleep here tonight, Miles. I'll pray for you."

"No," I said automatically, "no thanks," and then thought of the long walk back to the car. By now the batteries had probably run down, and I would have to walk all the way back to the farmhouse.

"You can leave as early as you like. You won't bother a dried-up old thing like me."

"Maybe for a couple of hours," I said, and yawned again. This time I managed to get my hand to my mouth at least halfway through the spasm. "You're far too good to me."

I watched her bustle into the next room; in a moment she returned with an armful of sheets and the fluffy bundle of a homemade quilt. "Come on, youngster," she ordered, and I followed her into the parlor.

Together we put the sheets on the low narrow seat of her couch. The parlor was only marginally cooler than the kitchen, but I helped her smooth the quilt over the top sheet. "I'd say, you take the bed, Miles, but no man has ever slept in my bed, and it's too late to change my habits now. But I hope you won't think I'm inhospitable."

"Not inhospitable," I said. "Just pig-headed."

"I wasn't fooling about praying. Did you say you've seen her?"

"Three times. I'm sure I did. She's going to come back, Auntie Rinn."

"I'll tell you one thing certain. I'll never live to see it."

"Why?"

"Because she won't let me."

For a solitary old woman close to ninety, Rinn was an expert in the last word. She turned away from me, switched off the lights in the kitchen, and closed the door to her bedroom after her. I could hear fabrics rustling as she undressed. The immaculate tiny parlor seemed full of the smell of woodsmoke, but it must have come from the ancient stove in the kitchen. Rinn began to mumble to herself.

I slipped off my jeans and shirt, sat down to remove my socks, still hearing her dry old voice rhythmically ticking away like a machine about to die, and stretched out between the papery sheets. My hands found one nubbly patch after another, and I realized that they had been mended many times. Within seconds, to the accompaniment of the dry music of her voice, I passed into the first unbroken and peaceful sleep I'd had since leaving New York.

Several hours later, I woke to two separate noises. One was what seemed an incredible rushing clatter of leaves above me, as though the woods had crawled up to the house and begun to attack it. The second was even more unsettling. It was Rinn's voice, and at first I thought her praying had become a marathon event. After I caught its slow, insistent pulse I recognized that she was saying something in her sleep. A single word, repeated. The whooping clatter of the trees above the house drowned out the word, and I lay in the dark with my eyes open, listening. The smell of woodsmoke hung unmoving in the air. When I heard what Rinn was saying, I folded the sheet back and groped for my socks. She was pronouncing, over and over again in her sleep, my grandmother's name. "*Jessie. Jessie.*"

That was too much for me. I could not bear to hear, mixed up with the windy racket of the woods, the evidence of how greatly I had disturbed the one person in the valley who wanted to help me. Hurriedly I put on my clothes and went into the kitchen. The undersides of leaves, veined and white, pressed against the back window like hands. Indeed, like the pulpy hand of one of my would-be assailants in Arden. I turned on a small lamp. Rinn's voice went dryly on, scraping out its invocation to her sister. The fire in the woodstove had died to a red glowing shadowy empire of tall ashes. I splashed water on my face and felt the crust of Rinn's herbal mixture. It would not wash off: my fingers simply bumped over it, as over the patches on the sheets. I inserted a fingernail beneath the edge of one of the crusty spots, and peeled it off like a leech. A thin brown scale fell into the sink. I peeled off the rest of the dabs of the mixture until they covered the bottom of the sink. A man's shaving mirror hung on a nail by the door, and I bent my knees to look into it. My heavy bland face looked back at me, pink in splashes on forehead and cheek, but otherwise unmarked.

Inside a rolltop desk crammed with the records of her egg business I found the stub of a pencil and paper and wrote: *Someday you'll see I'm right. I'll be back soon to buy some eggs. Thanks for everything. Love, Miles.*

I went out into the full rustling night. My mud-laden boots felt the knotted roots of trees thrusting up through the earth. I passed the high cartoon-windowed building, full of sleeping hens. Soon after that, I was out from under the dense ceiling of branches, and the narrow road unrolled before me, through tall fields lighter than the indigo sky. When it traversed the creek I once again heard frogs announcing their territory. I walked quickly, resisting the impulse to glance over my shoulder. If I felt that someone or something was watching me, it was only the single bright star in the sky, Venus, sending me light already thousands of years old.

Only when the breeze had dissipated it over the long fields of corn and alfalfa did I notice that the odor of woodsmoke had stayed with me until I had gone halfway to the road, and left Rinn's land.

Venus, light my way with light long dead.

Grandmother, Rinn, bless me both.

Alison, see me and come into my sight.

But what came into my sight as I trudged down the valley road was only the Volkswagen, looking like its own corpse, like something seen in a pile of rusting hulls from a train window. It was a misshapen form in the dim starlight, as pathetic and sinister as Duane's Dream House, and as I walked toward it I saw the shattered rear window and the scooping dents on the engine cover and hood. Eventually it hit me that the lights were out; the battery had died.

I groaned, and opened the door and collapsed onto the seat. I passed my hands over the pink new patches of skin on my face, which were beginning to tingle. "Damn," I said, thinking of the difficulty of getting a tow truck to come the ten miles from Arden. In frustration, I lightly struck my hand against the horn mechanism. Then I saw that the key was gone from the ignition.

"What's that for?" asked a man approaching me from the high slope of the Sunderson drive. As he crossed the road I saw that he had a thick hard belly and a flat face with no cheer in it. He had a pudgy blob for a nose, signaling his family connection to Tuta Sunderson. Like the hair of most men called "Red," his was a dusty tobaccoish orange. He came across the road and laid an enormous hand on top of the open door. "Why do you wanta go honkin' that horn for?"

"Out of joy. From sheer blinding happiness. My battery's dead, so the car won't move, and the damned key's gone, probably lying somewhere in that ditch. And you might have noticed that a few gentlemen in Arden decided to work over the car this evening. So that's why I was honking the horn." I glared up into his doughy face and thought I saw a glint of amusement.

"Didn't you hear my callin' you before? When you jumped out of this-here jalopy and tore on up toward the woods?"

"Sure," I said. "I didn't have time to waste."

"Well, I been waitin' on the porch to see you come back. I sacked out up there a little bit—didn't think you'd be so long. But just in case, I took your keys out of your jalopy. And I turned off your lights to save your battery."

"Thanks. I mean it. But please give me the keys. Then we can both get to bed."

"Wait up. What were you doin' up there anyhow? Or were you just runnin' away from me? You were sure goin' like a jackrabbit. What are you tryin' to get away with, Miles?"

"Well, Red, I can't really say. I don't think I'm trying to get away with anything."

"Uh-huh." The amusement became more acid. "According to my ma, you been doin' some pretty peculiar things up to Updahl's. Says that little girl of Duane's been hangin' around more than she should. Specially considering the problem we got here lately. You kinda got a *thing* about hurting girls, don't you, Miles?"

"No. I never did, either. Quit wasting my time and give me my keys."

"What's so good you got up in those woods?"

"Okay, Red," I answered. "I'll tell you the truth. I was visiting Rinn. You can ask her yourself. That's where I was."

"I guess you and that old witch got somethin' going."

"You can guess all you want. Just let me go home."

"This ain't your home, Miles. But I guess you can go back to Duane's. Here's your keys for this piece of shit you're driving." He held them out by extending one big blunt finger protruded through the keyring so that ring and keys looked dwarfed, like toys. It was a gesture obscurely obscene.

Portion of Statement by Leroy ("Red") Sunderson:

July 16

It was just eatin' at me that Ma had to be working in the same house as that Miles Teagarden—I'll tell you, if I'd been in Duane's shoes, I wouldn't of let my daughter hang around a man with a reputation like that. And some say he learned, good. I'd have run him off first thing, with a load of birdshot. So I thought, let's see what we got here, and started comin' down the drive to talk to him as soon as I saw his car begin to slow down outside below our house. Well Miles he jumps out of his car and looks away like he was seein' things, and he just begins to run like crazy. When I yelled he just kept on running.

Now there's two ways of looking at that. Either he was in one hell of a hurry to get at something in these woods, or he was runnin' away from me. I say both. I'll tell you, he was scared as hell of me when he came back. And that means he sure as hell was plannin' out what was gonna happen up in those woods—see?

I just said to myself, Red, you wait on him. He'll be back. I went down and switched off the lights in that beat-up junker of his. Then I waited for him. Ma and me both looked out for him for a little, and then she went up to bed, and I laid out on the porch. I had his keys, so I knew he wasn't going anywhere without me.

Well, a long time later, he comes back. Steppin' light. Loose as a goose. Walkin' like a city nigger. When I got up close to him he was workin' away at his car, swearin' and bangin' on the horn. Then I saw his face. He looked all burned or something—he had big red spots all over. The way Oscar Johnstad did when he got alcohol poisoning a few years back. Maybe somebody coulda been scratching on him.

I said, well Miles, what the hell you been up to?

I been makin' myself happy, he says.

I says, up in the woods?

Yeah, he says, I go up there to make myself happy. I been seein' Rinn.

How do we know what those two was up to? Funny things go on with these old Norwegians in the valleys around here—I'm a Norwegian myself, and I won't say a word against 'em, but some of those old people get up to crazy things. And that Rinn was crazy as a coot all her life. Sure she was. She was just about the only friend Miles had around here. You remember about old Ole, down at the Four Forks? Well, he was related to half the people in this valley, me included, and when he started going crazy he tied that half-wit daughter of his to a beam up in his attic and he started usin' his other daughter as his wife. On Sundays he stood there at the back of the church lookin' like an angry chunk of God that happened to land near Arden. That was twenty-thirty years ago, but funny things still go on. I never did trust Rinn. She could put the spooks in you. Some folks say Oscar Johnstad started drinking heavy because she put the evil eye on a heifer of his and he was afraid he was next.

The other thing you got think about is Paul Kant. Pretty soon after this, no more than a couple of days, is when he saw Paul. And then he tried to kill himself, didn't he?

I think he wanted to get out of it, fast—maybe Rinn told him to do it, crazy as she was. Maybe little Paul did too. Well, if he didn't he sure was sorry later. I mean, whatever Paul Kant did to make himself happy, he didn't go up into the valley woods at night to do it.

I feel all involved in this, you know. I found that poor Strand girl and talked to you fellows a couple of hours that day. I almost puked too, when I saw her—I knew nothing normal had been at that girl. She was damn near ripped in two. Well, you were there. You saw it.

So after we finally found out about the next one I got a call from one of the boys who drinks down at the Angler's, about that car idea, and I said, sure go ahead, I'll give you all the help you want. You set it up, and I'll help over at this end.

By the time I got the car into the driveway, my face had begun to burn and itch; my eyes watered, and I left the car just past the walnut trees and walked diagonally across the lawn, pressing the palm of my unbandaged hand to my face. It felt as cool and healing as water. My face was blazing. The night air too seemed ovenlike and composed of a million sharp needling points. I was moving slowly, so that the rush of hot gelatinous air would not scrape at my face.

As I approached the house, all the lights came on at once.

It looked like a pleasure boat on dark water, but it made me feel cold. I lowered my hand from my face and went slowly toward the screen door. The mare in the field to my left began to whinny and rear.

I half-expected a jolt from the metal doorknob. I almost wished that I were back on that bed of mold, beneath those giant dark trees.

I crossed the porch, hearing no noise from the interior of the house. Through the mesh of the screen, I looked sideways to see the mare's body plunging up and down, scattering the dumbfounded cows. Then I swung open the door to the sitting room and looked in—empty. Empty and cold. The old furniture lay randomly about, suggesting an as yet unlocated perfect order. All the lights, controlled by a single switch beside the doorframe, were burning. I touched the switch, aware that the mare had ceased her whinnying. The lights went off, then on, apparently working normally.

In the kitchen the overhead bulb in its shade illuminated the evidence of Tuta Sunderson's work: the plate of cold food had been removed from the table, the dishes washed and put away. When I touched the light switch, it too worked in the usual fashion.

The only explanation was that the wiring had gone massively wrong. At the moment that this possibility came to me I became aware that something— something important—was out of place in the living room. And that my face was still reacting painfully to contact with air. I returned to the kitchen and turned on the taps over the sink and splashed water over my forehead and cheeks. The feverish sandpapered feeling began to lessen. The only soap within reach was dish-washing liquid, and I squeezed a green handful into my right palm and brought it to my face. It felt like balm. The stinging disappeared. Delicately I rinsed away the soap: my skin felt tight, stretched like canvas over a frame.

This transformation, temporary as it was, apparently also made me more acute, for when I was in the living room again, I saw what had caused my earlier sense of dislocation. The picture of Alison and myself, the crucial picture, no longer hung on the nail over the doorway to the stairs. Someone had removed it. I looked around at the walls. Nothing else had been changed. It was an unthinkable violation, a rape of my private space. I rushed into the old bedroom.

Tuta S. had evidently been at work. The mess I had left on the floor had been bundled back into the broken sea chest and the splinters of wood from the chest's lid were laid out beside it like gigantic toothpicks. I knelt to open the chest and threw up the lid to see Duane's unhappy mulish countenance scowling at me. I lowered the lid gently. Pandora's box.

Unless it had been stolen, there was only one place where the photograph could be, and it was there I found it—in fact, even while I was ascending the narrow staircase I knew where I would find it. Propped between wall and desk, beside the earlier photograph of Alison.

And I knew—if the unknowable can be at all said to be known—who had put it there.

Following what seemed to be a general rule about nights spent in the old Updahl farmhouse, my sleep was interrupted by a succession of disturbing dreams, but all I could remember of them when I awoke—too late, I noted, to witness the parting of the lovers on the road and Alison's athletic, comic entrance through her window—was that they had made me start into wakefulness several times during the night. If you cannot remember them, nightmares lose all of their power. I was as hungry as I could remember ever being, another sign of renewed health.

I was as certain as if she'd left a note that Alison Greening had moved that photograph, and the information that she had influenced another hand to do it for her did not alter my conviction.

"You don't mind my moving that picture, do you?" said Mrs. Sunderson when I came down for breakfast. "I thought since you had that other one up there, you might want them both. I didn't mess with anything in that writing room of yours, I just put the picture on your desk."

Startled, I looked at her. She was working her fat arms over a frying pan. Grease spat, flames jumped. Her face was set in an expression of sullen obduracy.

"Why did you do it?"

"Because of the other one. Like I said." She was lying. She had been Alison's agent; it was also clear that she had disliked having the photograph within her view.

"What did you think of my cousin? Do you remember her?"

"Not to speak of." She went firmly back to the eggs.

"You don't want to talk about her."

"No. What's past is past."

"In one sense," I said, and laughed. "Only in one sense, my dear Mrs. Sunderson."

The "my dear" made her look toward me with magnified goggling eyes. More brooding, puzzled silence over the sizzling eggs on the gas burner.

"Why did you tear up that picture of Duane's girl? I saw it when I straightened up your mess in the front bedroom."

"I don't know what you're talking about," I said. "Oh I do remember. I didn't really know what it was. It was a random gesture. A reflex."

"So some would say," she pronounced as she brought me the eggs. "Maybe some would say the same about that car of yours."

I could still taste those eggs two hours later when I stood on the asphalt of the Arden filling station beside a squat young man with *Hank* blazoned over his heart and listened to him groan about the condition of the VW.

"This is some mess," he said. "I sure hope you got insurance. First off, we ain't even got a man these days who can beat out those dents for you. And all these is foreign parts. This glass here, and that headlight and missing hubcap. They might be a long time in coming. It's gonna cost plenty."

"You don't have to get them from Germany," I pointed out. "There must be a VW agency around here somewhere."

"Maybe," the boy reluctantly agreed. "I heard about one somewheres, but I can't remember where it is right now. And we're all backed up on work. We're doubling up."

I looked around at the deserted gas station.

"You can't see it all," Hank said defensively.

"I can't see any of it." I was thinking that it must have been at this station that the Polish lover of Duane's fiancée had worked. "Maybe this will help you squeeze it into your schedule." I took a ten-dollar bill from my pocket and folded it into his hand.

"You live here, mister?"

"What do you think?" He just coolly regarded me. "I'm a visitor. I had an accident. Look. Forget about the dents, they're not too important, just get the glass and headlights repaired. And take a look at the engine to see if it needs any work. It's been acting up."

"Okay. I need a name for the slip."

"Greening," I said. "Miles Greening."

"That Jewish?"

The boy reluctantly parted with one of the garage's loaners, a 1957 Nash that steered like a lumber wagon; further into Arden, I took the precaution of parking it in a side street in an area where the houses appeared to be at least moderately prosperous.

An hour and a half later, I was listening to Paul Kant say to me, "You put yourself and me in trouble just by coming here, Miles. I tried to warn you. You really should have listened. I appreciate your friendliness, but there are only two people that the good folks around here think could have done these crimes, and here we are together. Cozy. If you're not scared, you should be. Because I'm terrified. If anything else happens, anything else to a child I mean, I think I'm a dead man. They took baseball bats to my car last night, just to let me know they're watching."

"Mine too," I said. "And I saw them working on yours, but I didn't know whose it was."

"So here we are, waiting for the other shoe to drop. Why don't you just get out while you have the chance?"

"I can't, for several reasons. One of them is that Polar Bears asked me to stay put until everything is over."

"Because of the Alison Greening business?"

I nodded.

He let out an enormous, scooping sigh, too large for his small body. "Of course. Of course. I didn't even have to ask. I wish my sins were as far in the past as yours." I looked up, puzzled, and saw him trying to light a cigarette with a trembling hand. "Hasn't anybody warned you about being associated with me, Miles? I'm quite a notorious character."

"Hence the ritual."

"It's been a long time since anyone in Arden used a work like hence, but yes, hence the ritual."

I had come to Paul's by way of Main Street, where I first stopped in at a shop to buy a portable record player. The clerk looked at the name on my check and disappeared with it into an office at the rear of the shop. I was aware of my presence causing a little flurry of attention among the other customers— they were pretending not to look at me, but they moved with that exaggerated carelessness of people trying to catch every nuance. After a while the clerk returned with a nervous man in a brown suit and a rayon tie. He informed me that he could not accept my check.

"Why not?"

"Ah, well, Mr. Teagarden, this check is drawn on a New York bank."

"Obviously," I said. "They use money in New York too."

"But we only accept local checks."

"How about credit cards? You don't refuse credit cards, do you?"

"Ah, no, not usually," he said.

I yanked a lengthy strip of cards from my wallet. "Which one do you want? MasterCharge? American Express? Diner's Club? Mobil? Sears? Come on, you make the choice. Firestone?"

"Mr. Teagarden, this isn't necessary. In this case—"

"In this case, what? These things are as good as money, aren't they? Here's another one. BankAmericard. Take your pick."

The other customers by now had dropped the pretense of not listening, and a few were threatening to come forward to take a closer look. He decided to accept MasterCharge, which I could have predicted, and I waited while he took one of the portable stereos from stock and went through the usual business with the card. He was sweating by the time he had finished.

I spent some time looking through the record racks at Zumgo's and the Coast to Coast Store, but could not find what I needed for the Alison-environment. At a little stationery shop a block from Freebo's I found a few of the books I remembered Alison had liked: *She*, *The White Guard*, Kerouac, St. Exupéry. These I purchased with cash, having conquered for good that other childish business.

I cut through side streets to get back to the Nash, locked my purchases inside it, and then went back to Freebo's.

"Can I make a phone call?" I asked him. He looked relieved, and pointed to a pay phone in the rear corner. I knew by his demeanor what his next words would be before he spoke them.

"Mr. Teagarden, you been a good customer here since you came in town, but some people came to see me late last night, and I wonder if . . ."

"If I might lay off? Take my business elsewhere?"

He was too embarrassed to nod.

"What did they say they'd do? Break your windows? Burn your place down?"

"No, nothing like that, Mr. Teagarden."

"But you'd be happier if I quit coming in."

"Maybe just for a week, just for a couple of days. It's nothing personal, Mr. Teagarden. But, well, some of 'em decided—well, it might be better to wait it out for a while."

"I don't want to make trouble for you," I said.

He turned away, unable to face me any further. "The phone's in the corner."

I looked up Paul Kant's number. His whispery voice greeted me hesitantly. "Stop hiding," I said. "This is Miles. I'm in Arden, and I'm coming over to talk about what's happening to us."

"Don't," he pleaded.

"You don't have to protect me. I just wanted to prepare you. If you want people to draw conclusions from the sight of me banging on your front door, then let me bang away. But I want to find out what's going on."

"You'll come even if I say not to."

"That's right."

"In that case, don't park near my house. And don't come to the front door. Pull into the alley between Commercial Street and Madison, and then walk up through the alley so you can come around to the back. I'll let you in the back door."

And now, in the dark shabby living room, he was telling me that he was a notorious character. He looked the way you'd expect one of Freud's case studies to look—frightened, his body a little shrunken and bent, his face prematurely aged. His white shirt had been worn too many days; his face was small and monkeylike. When we had been boys, Paul Kant had radiated intelligence and confidence, and I thought that he was the person my age in Arden whom I most respected. On summers when Alison was not at the farm, I had divided my time between raising hell with Polar Bears and talking with Paul. He had been a great reader. His mother was an invalid, and Paul had the grown-up, responsible, rather bookish demeanor of children who must care for their parents. Or parent, in his case—his father was dead. Another of my assumptions had been that Paul would get a good scholarship and shake the traces of Arden from him forever. But here he was, trapped in a shabby musty house and a body that looked ten years older than it was. If he radiated anything, it was bitterness and a fearful incompetence.

"Take a look out the window," he said. "Try to do it without being seen."

"You're being watched?"

"Just look." He stubbed out his cigarette and immediately lit another.

I peeked around the edge of a curtain.

Halfway down the block a big man who looked like he could have been one of the party which had shied stones at me was sitting on the fender of a red pickup, directing his eyes at Paul's house.

"Is he there all the time?"

"It's not always him. They do it in shifts. There are five, maybe six of them."

"Do you know their names?"

"Of course I know their names. I live here."

"Can't you do anything about it?"

"What do you suggest? Telephoning our benevolent chief? They're his friends. They know him better than I do."

"What do they do when you go out?"

"I don't go out very often." His face worked, and ironic lines tugged deeply into his skin. "I suppose they follow me. They don't care if I see them. They want me to see them."

"Did you report that they wrecked your car?"

"Why should I? Hovre knows all about it."

"Well, *why*, for Christ's sake?" I burst out. "Why all this fire in your direction?" He shrugged, and smiled nervously.

But of course I thought I knew. It was what had occurred to me when Duane had first suggested that Paul Kant was better left alone: a man with Duane's history of sexual suppression would be quick to react to any hint of sexual abnormality. And a town like Arden would maintain a strict nineteenth-century point of view about inversion.

"Let's just say I'm a little different, Miles."

"Christ," I blustered, "nobody's different anymore. If you're saying that you're gay, it's only in a backwater like Arden that you'd have problems because of it. You shouldn't allow yourself to be terrorized. You should have been out of here years ago."

I think for the first time I understood what a wan smile was. "I'm not a very brave man, Miles," he said. "I could never live anywhere but Arden. I had to drop out of life to take care of my mother, and after she died she left me this house." It smelled of dust and decay and damp—Paul had no smell at all. He was like something not there, or there in only one dimension. He said, "I've never really been . . . what you're implying. I thought I was, I guess, and I guess other people thought I was. But the opportunities here are rather limited." Again I got that pale, self-mocking half-smile that was only a lifting of the edges of the mouth. He was like something in a cage.

"So you just sat here and put up with Zumgo's and what your neighbors whispered about you?"

"You're not me, Miles. You don't understand."

I looked around at the dim room filled with old lady's furniture. Lumpy uncomfortable chairs with antimacassars. Cheap china figurines: shepherdesses and dogs, Mr. Pickwick and Mrs. Gamp. But there weren't any books.

"No," I said.

"You don't even really want me to confide in you, do you? We haven't seen each other since we grew up." He stubbed out the cigarette and scratched his fingers in his tight black curly hair.

"Not unless you're guilty," I said, beginning to be affected by the air of despairing hopelessness which surrounded him.

I suppose the sound he uttered was a laugh.

"What are you going to do? Just wait until they break in and do whatever it is they have in mind?"

"What I'm going to do is wait it out," he said. "It's what I'm best at, after all. When they finally catch whoever it is, maybe I'll get my job back. What are you going to do?"

"I don't know," I admitted. "I thought we might be able to help each other. If I were you I'd scram out of the back door in the middle of the night and go to Chicago or someplace until it's all over."

"My car won't move. And even if it did, I'd be picked up in a day or two." He sent me that ghastly smile again. "You know, Miles, I almost envy that man. The killer. I'm almost jealous of him. Because he wasn't too afraid to do what he had to do. Of course he is a beast, a fiend I suppose, but he just went ahead and did what he had to do. Didn't he?" The small monkey's face was pointing at me, still wearing that dead smile. Mixed in with the smells of dust and old lady's possessions was the odor of long-dead flowers.

"Like Hitler. You sound like you should talk to Zack."

His expression altered. "You know him?"

"I've met him."

"I'd keep away from him."

"What for?"

"He can hurt you. He could hurt you, Miles."

"He's my biggest fan," I said. "He wants to be just like me."

Paul shrugged; the topic no longer interested him.

I said, "I think I'm wasting my time."

"Of course you are."

"If you ever need help, Paul, you can come out to the Updahl farm. I'll do whatever I can."

"Neither one of us can help the other." He looked at me blankly, wishing I would leave. After a moment he spoke again. "Miles, how old was your cousin when she died?"

"Fourteen."

"Poor Miles."

"Poor Miles, bullshit," I said, and left him sitting there with the cigarette smoke curling around him.

Outside the warm air smelled unbelievably fresh, and I recognized that my chest was tight, clamped by an emotion too complex to identify. I inhaled deeply, going down Paul's wooden steps to his tiny yard. It seemed to me that I could almost hear the paint peeling off that hopeless house. I looked both ways, knowing that if anyone spotted me I was in trouble, and saw something I hadn't noticed when I had come in. In a corner of the yard beside Paul's low fence was a doghouse, empty and as in need of paint as the house. A chain staked to the front of the doghouse trailed off into the weeds and bushes beside the fence. The chain seemed taut. The hairs on the back of my neck rose, and

I was aware of the texture of the shirt next to my skin. I did not want to look, but I had to. I took two steps across the dying lawn. It was lying in the weeds with the chain around what was left of its neck. Maggots swarmed over it like a dirty blanket.

The tightness in my chest increased by a factor of ten, and I got out fast. The dreadful thing stayed in my vision even when my back was turned to it. I went through the gate and began to walk quickly down the alley. It had been a wasted gesture, the visit. I wanted only to get away.

When I was no more than thirty feet from the end, a police car swung in front of me, blocking off the alley. A big man sat at the wheel, twisting his body to look at me. I was in full light, fully visible. I automatically felt guilty and afraid, and swiveled sideways to look down to the alley's other end, which was clear. I looked back at the man in the police car. He was motioning for me to approach him. I walked toward the car, telling myself that I had not done anything.

When I got closer, I saw that the man was Polar Bears, in uniform. He swung open the passenger door and circled a forefinger in the air, and I walked around the front of the car and got in beside him. "You've had brighter ideas," he said. "Suppose someone saw you? I'm trying to keep you from getting your head busted in."

"How did you know I was here?"

"Let's say it was a guess." He looked at me in a kindly, almost paternal fashion which was as genuine as a glass eye. "I got a call about an hour ago from a boy works at the filling station. Boy named Hank Speltz. He was a little upset. It seems when you brought in that VW, you gave him a phony name."

"How did he know it was phony?"

"Oh, Miles," Polar Bears sighed. He started up the car and rolled away from the curb. At the corner he swung into Main Street and we purred gently along past Zumgo's and the bars and the bakery and the Cream City brick facade of the Dairyland Laboratories. "You're a famous man, you know. You're like a movie star. You have to expect to be recognized." When we reached the court-house and the city hall, he did not pull into the police parking lot as I had expected, but kept going on over the bridge. On that side of Arden, the shops drop away fast, after you pass the bowling alley and the restaurants and a few houses, and you are back in open corn country.

"I don't think it's a crime to have a car repaired under an assumed name," I said. "Where are we going, anyhow?"

"Just for a ride around the county, Miles. No, it's no crime, that's right. But since damn near everybody knows who you are, it's not very effective either. It just makes boys like Hank, who aren't too well supplied upstairs, sort of suspicious. And Miles, why in *hell* did you use that name?" On "hell" he banged one of his fists into the steering wheel. "Huh? Answer me that. Out of all the names you could have picked, why the devil did you pick Greening? That's what you don't want to remind people of, boy. I'm trying to keep all that in the background. We don't want that to come out."

"I think it came out the first second I showed up in Arden."

Polar Bears shook his head, disgusted. "Okay. Let's forget it. I told that Hank kid to forget about it. He's probably too young to know about it anyhow."

"So why are you upset?"

"Forget about my problems, Miles. Let's see if we can get any work done. You learn anything talking with Paul Kant?"

"He didn't do anything. He certainly didn't kill anybody. He's a sad frightened man. He isn't capable of anything like those killings. He's too scared to do anything but shop for his groceries."

"Is that what he told you?"

"He's too frightened even to bury his dog. I saw it just when I was leaving. He couldn't kill anybody."

Polar Bears tilted his hat back and hunched down further on the seat. He was too big to fit comfortably behind a steering wheel. By now we were well out in the country, and I could see the broad loops of the Blundell River between trees. "Is this where the fishermen found the body of the Olson girl?"

He tilted his head and looked at me. "No. That was a couple miles back. We passed the spot about five-six minutes ago."

"On purpose?"

"On purpose for what?"

I shrugged: we both knew.

"I think our friend Paul might not have told you all the truth," Polar Bears said. "If he was going out grocery shopping, wouldn't he manage to buy some dogfood?"

"What are you saying?"

"Did he offer you anything when you were visiting? Lunch? A sandwich? Coffee?"

"No. Why?" Then I saw why. "You mean he doesn't leave his house? You mean his dog starved to death?"

"Well, it might of starved, or somebody might of helped put it out of its misery. I don't know. But I do know Paul Kant hasn't been out of his house in about a week. Unless he sneaks out at night."

"What does he eat?"

"Damn little. I guess he must have some canned stuff in his kitchen. That's why you didn't get any lunch out of him. He's screwed down pretty tight."

"Well, how the hell can you—"

He held up one hand. "I can't make a man go out and buy groceries. And as long as he doesn't actually starve, it might be better this way. Keeps him away from trouble. You maybe saw one of our local vigilantes watching his house."

"Can't you chase them away?"

"Why should I? This way I know what the hotheads are doing. I think there are some things you ought to know about Paul, Miles. I doubt that he'd tell you everything himself."

"Everything he needed to."

Polar Bears swung the car into a crossroads and began to go back in the general direction of Arden. We had gone nearly as far as the little town of Blundell, and we had not seen another person yet. The police radio crackled, but Hovre ignored it. He drove still at the same unhurried pace, following the line of the river through the valleys. "I wonder about that. You see, Paul's had a few problems. Not the sort of thing a man is proud of. He's been in a little trouble. You know how he lived in that rundown old place with his mother for years—even dropped out of school to nurse her and work so he could pay her doctor bills. Well, when the old lady died, Paul hung around town for a little bit, sort of lost, I guess, but then he packed up and went to Minneapolis for a week. About a month later, he did the same thing. He sort of settled down into a pattern. The last time he went, I got a call from a police sergeant over there. It seems that they had Paul under arrest. It seems they'd even been looking for him." He glanced over at me, savoring the denouement. He couldn't keep from smiling. "Seems they had a character used to hang around Boy Scout meetings—in summer, you know, when they meet in school playgrounds. Never said anything, just watched through the fence. When some of the kids walked home, he'd sort of amble on behind 'em, not saying anything, just trolling after these kids. After a fair number of times, say half a dozen, one of the parents calls the police. And the guy ducks out of the way—police couldn't find him. Not then. Not until he tried something in a park with lots of mommies and kiddies and cops around. He damn near exposed himself. When they came up on him, it was old Paul, with his hand on his fly. He was their boy. He'd been going over to Minnesota to release his urges, you could say, and then coming back here until he had to do it again. He confessed, of course, but he hadn't actually done anything. But he was scared. He committed himself voluntarily to our state hospital and stayed put there seven months. Then he came back. He didn't have anywhere else to go. Now I suppose he forgot to tell you about that little episode in his life."

I just nodded. Eventually I thought of something to say. "I'll have to take your word that what you told me is correct." Hovre snorted with amusement. "But even so, what Paul did—what he *didn't* do, rather—is a million miles from rape. The same person wouldn't commit both kinds of crime. Not if I understand people at all."

"Maybe so. But nobody around Arden is going to rule it out, you understand? And there are things about these killings that people generally don't know. What we have here isn't a straightforward rapist. Even a rapist who kills. We got something a little fancier. We got a really sick man. Could be impotent. Could even be a woman. Or a man and a woman. I go for the single-man idea, but the others are possible."

"What are you telling me?"

We were back on the fringes of Arden now, and Polar Bears was homing in toward the Nash as if he knew where it was.

"I got a theory about this boy of ours, Miles. I think he wants to come to me, he wants to talk about what he's been doing. He's got all that pressure, all that guilt building up inside of him. He's bursting a gut to tell me about it. Wouldn't you say?"

I didn't know, and told him so.

"Just consider it. Sick as he is, he's a mighty lonely man. He probably doesn't even enjoy what he's doing to these girls. But he knows he's going to do it again." Polar Bears looked at me; he was smiling and confidential and helpful. "There's a big head of steam in our boy. He's got to blow it off, but he knows it's wrong—sick. I'm the one he has to talk to, and he knows it. I wouldn't be surprised if he's someone I see now and then, someone who's around here and there, ready to share a few words. I might have seen him two or three times this week alone." He pulled up to a stop sign; across the road and down the block sat the Nash. I wouldn't have known how to find it. "Well, speaking of luck, Miles, isn't that Nash the loaner Hank gave you?"

"Yes. What are you going to do about the men who wrecked my car?"

"I'm looking into it, Miles. Looking into it." He rolled across the street and pulled up beside the old Nash.

"Are you going to explain what you said about the killer? About his not being a straightforward rapist?"

"Sure. Why don't you come over to my house for a bite to eat some night this week? I'll tell you all about it." He reached across me and opened the door. "My cooking won't kill you, I guess. I'll be in touch, Miles. Keep your eyes open. Remember, you can always call me."

His flat ingratiating voice stayed in my ears all the way home. It was almost hypnotic, like having your will taken from you. When I got out of the car at the farmhouse I was still hearing it, and I could not shake it even while I was pushing furniture around. I felt slightly engulfed by Polar Bears, and I knew the furniture would not come right, lock into the correct position, until I was free of him. I went upstairs and sat at my desk and looked into the two photographs. Eventually everything else went away, and I was left with Alison. Dimly, far away, the phone was ringing.

And the third time it happened like this:

A girl walked out of her home in the late afternoon and stood in the humid motionless air for a moment, wondering if it were not too hot to go bowling with her friends. Perspiration seemed to leap from her scalp. She remembered that she had left her sunglasses in her room, but she could not waste the energy to go back in and get them. She could feel her body sagging in the heat: and the pollen count was up nearly to 200. She would be sneezing by the time she got to the Bowl-A-Rama.

Maybe it would be better to simply stay in her bedroom and read. She was small for her age, and her pretty face had a piquant, passive cast which looked utterly at home in front of a book. She wanted to be a teacher, an English teacher. The girl looked back across the brown lawn to her house, and sunlight bounced off the plateglass window. There was not a shadow in sight. She sneezed. Her white blouse already adhered to her skin.

She turned away from the glare of the sun off the picture window and went toward town. She was following the direction she had seen Chief Hovre's car travel, two or three hours earlier. Girls in Arden did not like going anywhere alone since the death of Jenny Strand: friends waited at the bowling alley. But surely in the daytime one was safe. Galen Hovre, she thought, was not intelligent enough to catch the killer of Gwen Olson and Jenny Strand: unless the big man she had seen sitting beside the sheriff was the murderer.

She idled along looking at the ground, her thin arms swinging. She admitted to herself that she disliked bowling, and did it only because everyone else did.

She never saw what grabbed her—there was only an awareness of a shape coming swiftly out of an alley, and then she was slammed against a wall and the fear was too bright in her mind for her to speak or cry out. The force with which she had been lifted and moved seemed scarcely human: what had touched her, what was bearing down on her, scarcely seemed the flesh of a fellow creature. Surrounding her was the pungent smell of earth, as if she were already in her grave.

2

My arms and legs could not move. Yet in another dimension, they were moving, not lying still on the floor of my workroom but taking me toward the woods. I witnessed both processes impartially, both the internal (walking into the woods) and the external (lying on the workroom floor), thinking that the only previous time such an experience had been given to me was when I had burst open the sea chest and looked at the photograph she had directed to be put on my desk. The air was sweet, perfumy, both in and out. The lights had all gone out and the fields were dark. At some point in the immeasurable, unreckonable amount of time since I had stood up to see why the mare was terrified, night had come. I was walking across the dark field toward the cottonwood trees; I parted thick weeds, I walked out onto a grassy root-hump and jumped easily across the creek. My body was light, a dream-body. There was no need to run. I could hear the telephone, owls, crickets. The night air was soft, so sweet it seemed liable to catch in the trees, like fog.

I passed easily beyond the next area of fields and entered the woods. Birches gleamed like girls. Who had turned the lights out? My right index finger registered the sensation of polished boards, but it was touching a ghostly maple. Leaving it behind, I walked on a mulch of leaves. The gradient began to change. A deer plunged deeper into the woods somewhere to my right, and I turned in that direction. Uphill. Through trees closer and closer, high life-breathing oaks with bark like rivers. I touched the flank of a dead maple, down across my path like the corpse of a soldier, and lifted myself with my arms so that I sat on it and then swung my legs over and let myself fall onto the springy floor again. My knees absorbed the shock. There was still the light problem, but I knew where I was going.

It was a clearing. A clearing perhaps sixteen feet across, ringed with giant oaks, the ashes of a fire at its center. She was there, waiting for me.

Magically, I knew how to get there: all I had to do was drift and I would be taken, my feet would guide me.

When the trees approached too near, I shoved them aside with my hand. Twigs caught in my jacket and hair, pulling at me as a thorny weed had captured my foot outside the Dream House. Leaves stirred in the thick perfumy air. Where my feet had been were sucking black holes. On the perpendicular sides of trees hung glistening mushrooms, white and red. I waded through ferns as high as my waist, holding my arms as if they cradled a rifle.

There was a darkening of the spirit. Going closer to where I had to go, I saw the edges of starlight on the bark-rills and began to be afraid. When I passed through a gap, it seemed to close behind me. The breathing life of the forest expressed an immensity of force. Even the air grew tight. I climbed over a lightning-blasted trunk. Living stuff coiled around my boots, golden roots proliferated over them. I stepped on a mushroom the size of a sheep's head and felt it become jelly beneath my weight.

The rough hand of a tree brushed my face. I felt my skin tear along my jaw, and crack like a porcelain cup. Branches closed over my head. The only light leading me was from leaves and ferns themselves, the light plants produce like oxygen. Another tree clicked into place behind me, blocking the way back. I went to my knees. By scraping along the soft damp forest floor, I got beneath the lowest branch of the sentinel tree. My fingers touched grass and stones; I pulled myself into the clearing.

When I stood, my shirt was green with moss. The bandage was gone from my left hand. I could feel snapped twigs and dried, crumbling leaves in my hair. I tried to brush them away, off, but my hands could not move, my arms could not lift.

The trees jostled and whispered behind me. The blackness was edged and pierced by a thousand sharp silvery lights on leaf-edge and the curve of tendrils. The clearing was a dark circle with a darker circle at its center. I could move, and went forward. I touched the ashes. They were warm. I smelled woodsmoke, and it was heavy and sweet. The dense forest behind and before me seemed to grow taut. I froze beside the warm ashes, bent forward over my knees and in total silence.

What will happen after she comes back? Rinn had asked me, and I felt a terror deeper than that of the first time in the woods. A high rustling whistling noise was coming toward me from where the leaf-light was strongest, a whispery sound of movement. My skin felt icy. The sound dragged toward me.

Then I saw her.

She was across the clearing, framed between two black birches. She was unchanged. If anything had touched my thin layer of cold skin, I would have cracked open, I would have shattered into a heap of white cold fragments. She began to move forward, her motion slow, unstoppable.

I called her name.

As she drew nearer the noise increased—that high whispery whistling scratched in my ears. Her mouth was open. I saw that her teeth were water-polished stones. Her face was an intricate pattern of leaves; her hands were rilled wood, tipped with thorns. She was made of bark and leaves.

I threw my hands back and felt smooth wood. Air lay in my lungs like water. I realized I was screaming only when I heard it.

*   *   *

"His eyes are open," a voice said. I was looking at the open window above my desk, the curtains blowing and small papers lifting in the warm breeze. It was day. The air was its normal weight, unperfumed. "His eyes are wide open."

Another voice said, "Are you awake, Miles? Can you hear?"

I tried to speak, and a rush of sour fluid poured from my mouth.

The woman said, "He'll live. Thanks to you."

I sat up suddenly. I was in bed. It was still daytime. The telephone was ringing downstairs. "Don't worry about it," someone said. I turned to look; beside the door, her pale eyes reflectively on mine, the Tin Woodsman was closing a book. It was one I had given Zack. "That phone's been going all night and morning, I guess. It's Chief Hovre. He wants to talk to you about something. Was it an accident?" On the last sentence her tone changed, and her head tilted up. In her eyes I saw the fear of a complex betrayal.

"What happened?"

"You're lucky you weren't smoking. Pieces of you would probably be on top of Korte's barn by now."

"What happened?"

"Did you leave the gas on? On purpose?"

"What? What gas?"

"The gas in the kitchen, dummy. It was on most of the night. Mrs. Sunderson says you're alive because you're up here. I had to break a window in the kitchen."

"How was it turned on?"

"That's the big question, all right. Mrs. Sunderson says you were trying to kill yourself. She says she should have known."

I rubbed my face. It was unscratched. The bandage was still on my left hand. "Pilot light," I said.

"Blown out. Or gone out. Both of them. Boy. You should have smelled that kitchen. So *sweet*."

"I think I smelled it up here," I said. "I was sitting at my desk, and the next thing I knew I was lying on the floor. It was almost as though I left my body."

"Well, if you didn't do it, it must have happened by itself." She seemed relieved. "There's something wrong with this house. Just when you got home two nights ago, all the lights went on, all over the house."

"You saw that too?"

"Sure, I was in my bedroom. And last night, they all went off at once. My dad says the wiring never was any good in this old house."

"Aren't you supposed to be keeping away from me?"

"I said I'd leave as soon as you were all right. See, I was the one who found you. Old man Hovre phoned our house. He said you weren't answering your phone. He said he had important news for you. My dad was asleep, so I came over myself. It was all locked up, except for the porch. So I pushed up the window in the front bedroom downstairs, and that's when I smelled the gas. I went around to the kitchen and broke a window. To let air in. Then I held my breath and climbed in and ran into the living room and pushed up the window. A little later I came up here. You were on the floor in the other room. I pushed open the window in there too. I thought I was going to be sick."

"What time was this?"

"About six. This morning. Maybe earlier."

"You were still up at six o'clock?"

She tilted her head again. "I just got home. From a date. Anyhow, I just waited to see if you were alive, and then Mrs. Sunderson showed up. She went straight to the phone and called the police. She thought you did it on purpose. Tried to kill yourself. She'll be back tomorrow, she says. If you want her today, you're supposed to call her up. In the meantime, I told old man Hovre you'd call him when you felt better."

"Thanks," I said. "Thanks for saving my life, I guess I mean."

She shrugged, then smiled. "If anyone did, it was old man Hovre. He was the one who called me. And if I hadn't found you, Tuta Sunderson would have. Eventually. You weren't ready to die."

I raised my eyebrows.

"You were moving all over the place. And making noises. You knew who I was."

"What do you mean?"

"You were saying my name. At least that's what it sounded like."

"Do you really think I tried to kill myself?"

"No. I really don't." She sounded surprised. She stood up and tucked the book beneath her elbow. "I think you're too smart to do anything like that. Oh. I almost forgot. Zack says thanks for the books. He wants to see you again soon."

I nodded.

"Are you sure you're okay now?"

"I'm sure, Alison."

At the door she paused and turned toward me. She opened her mouth, closed it, and then decided to speak after all. "I'm really happy you're okay now."

The telephone began to trill again. "Don't worry about answering the phone," I said. "Sooner or later I'll get it. Polar Bears wants to invite me to dinner. And Alison—I'm very happy you were around."

"Wait until we're comfortable before you start asking the serious questions," said Galen Hovre two nights later, cracking ice cubes from a tray into a bowl. My intuition had been at least partially correct. I was seated in a large overstuffed chair in Polar Bears' living room, in that part of Arden where I had parked the Nash. Hovre's was a family house without a family. Newspapers several weeks old were piled on one of the chairs, and the red fabric of the couch had become greasy with age; the coffee table supported a rank of empty beer cans. Polar Bears' pistol hung in its holster from the wing of an old chair. The green carpet showed several darker patches where he had apparently made halfhearted stabs at washing out stains. On end tables on either side of the couch, two big lamps with stands shaped like wildfowl cast murky yellowish light. The walls were dark brown—Hovre's wife, whoever she had been, had fought for unconventionality. On them hung two pictures not, I was willing to bet, of her choosing: a framed photograph of Polar Bears in plaid shirt and fisherman's hat, holding up a string of trout, and a reproduction of Van Gogh's sunflowers. "I generally have a little drink after dinner. Do you want bourbon, bourbon or bourbon?"

"Fine," I said.

"Helps tamp down the grease," he said, though in fact he had surprised me by being an adequate cook. Pot roast, reasonably well made, may not be notably elegant, but it was not what I had expected from a two-hundred-and-seventy-five-pound man in a wrinkled police uniform. Burned venison steaks were more like it, I had thought: virile, but badly executed.

One reason for the invitation had been immediately clear: Polar Bears was a lonely man, and he kept up a tide of chatter all during the meal. Not a word about my supposed suicide attempt, nor about the girls' deaths—he had talked about fishing. Tackle and equipment, bait, sea-water vs. freshwater fishing, fishing then vs. fishing now, boats and "People on Lake Michigan claim those coho salmon taste pretty good, but give me a river trout any day," and " 'Course there's nothing like dry fly fishing for sport, but sometimes I like to take my old spinning rod and just sit by the shallows and wait for that wily old granddad down there." It was the talk of a man deprived by circumstances or profession of normal social conversation and who misses it badly, and I had chewed my way through several slices of juicy beef and a mound of vegetables in thick sauce while he let the tap flow and the pressure decrease.

I heard him tip a stack of plates into the sink and run water over them; a moment later he came back into the living room carrying a bottle of Wild Turkey under his arm, a porcelain bowl of ice cubes in one hand, and two glasses in the other.

"Something just occurred to me," I said as he grunted, bending down over the table, and set down glasses, ice, and then the bottle with a deliberate thump.

"What's that?"

"That we're all men alone—single men. The four of us that used to know each other. Duane, Paul Kant, you and me. You were married once, weren't you?" The furnishings and the brown walls made it obvious, even the ducks mounting up one of the side walls; Polar Bears' house existed, it occurred to me, in symmetry with Paul's, except that Polar Bears' bore the traces of a younger woman's taste, a wife, not a mother.

"I was," he said, and poured bourbon over ice and leaned back on the couch and put his feet on the coffee table. "Like you. She ran off a long time ago. Left me with a kid. Our son."

"I didn't know you had a son, Polar Bears."

"Oh yeah. Raised him myself. He lives here in Arden."

"How old is he?"

"Round about twenty. His mother left when he was just a little runt. She was no good. My boy never had much education, but he's smart and he works around town on a kind of handyman basis. Got his own place too. I'd like him to join the police, but he's got his own ideas. Good kid, though. He believes in the law, not like some of them now."

"Why didn't you or Duane remarry?" I helped myself to a good dose of bourbon.

"You could say I learned my lesson. Police work is hard on a wife. You never really stop working, if you see what I mean. And then, I never found another woman I could trust. As for good old Du-ane, I don't think he ever really did like women. He's got his girl to cook and keep house, and I reckon that's about all he wants."

I recognized that Polar Bears was making me feel very relaxed, giving me the spurious sense that this was nothing more than a casual evening between two old friends, and I looked at him from my chair. Light silvered the thick flesh on the top of his head. His eyes were half closed.

"I think you're right. I think he hates women. Maybe he's your killer."

Polar Bears gave a genuine laugh. "Ah, Miles, Miles. Well, he didn't always hate women. There was one that got to him, once upon a time."

"That Polish girl."

"Not quite. Why do you think his daughter's got that name of hers?"

I gaped at him, and found that his slitted eyes were watching me anything but sleepily.

"Truth," he said. "I think he even lost his cherry to that little Alison Greening. You weren't around every summer she was, you know. He was stuck on her, and I mean stuck. 'Course she mighta gone to bed with him, or done it standing up beside a haystack more likely, but she was too young for that to be public, and she treated him like shit most of the time anyhow. She just tore him up. I always thought that's why he went and engaged himself to the Polish girl."

The shock was still ringing in my chest. "You said he lost his virginity to Alison?"

"Yep. He told me himself."

"But she could have been no older than thirteen."

"That's right. He said she knew a lot more about it than he did."

I remembered the art teacher. "I don't believe it. He was lying. She used to laugh at him."

"That's true too. He was real burned up by the way she preferred you to him whenever you were around. Jealous. Crazy jealous." He bent forward over his belly and poured more bourbon into his glass, not bothering to add ice cubes. "So you can see why you shouldn't go tossing that name around. Du-ane might think you was deliberately rubbing salt in his wounds. Not to mention that you oughta think about protecting yourself. I hate to act like a spiritual adviser, Miles, but I think you might even try goin' to that church in the valley. People might let up on you if they see you acting more like them. Sit and absorb a little of Bertilsson's wisdom. Funny how all these Norskies took to that little Swedish rat. I can't see him for horse piss, but the farmers all love him. He gave me some story about your stealing out of Zumgo's. A book, he said."

"Ridiculous."

"So I told him. What's your side of this suicide business, anyhow, Miles? I don't suppose there's any truth in it."

"None. Either it was an accident, or someone was trying to kill me. Or warn me off." I was still mentally struggling to sit up.

"Warn you off what? You ain't *on* anything. I'm glad it didn't have anything to do with our talk yesterday."

"Polar Bears," I said, "did your father ever find out who called him, that night my cousin drowned?"

He shook his head, unhappy with me. "Get all that out of your head, Miles. Get it out of your system. We're talking about now, not twenty years ago."

"Well, did he?"

"Goddammit, Miles." He poured what was left of his drink down his throat and bent forward, grunting, to make another. "Didn't I tell you to leave that alone? No. He never did. That good enough for you? So you say this gas business was an accident. Right?"

I nodded, wondering what this conversation was really about. I had to talk to Duane.

"Well now, you see that's what I thought. I wish we could have kept Tuta Sunderson out of it, because she's bound to go around telling people what she thinks, and her version is a little hard on you. And right now, we've gotta take attention off of you. Aren't you gonna have any more of this good booze?"

My glass was empty.

"Come on. Keep me company. I gotta have a few drinks at night in order to get to sleep. If Lokken arrests you for drunken driving, I'll tear up your ticket." His big seamed face split into a smile.

I poured two inches into my glass and added a handful of ice cubes. The bourbon appeared to have as much effect on Polar Bears as Coca-Cola.

"You see," he said, "I'm tryin' my darnedest to keep you out of trouble. I like talking to you, Miles. We go back a long way. And I can't allow one of our good citizens of Arden to come in and sit here and see his police chief get sloshed, can I? We've got a good little understanding going. You forgive me for the Larabee business, and I'll listen to anything you have to tell me. I forgive you for boosting a book out of Zumgo's. You probably had a lot of things on your mind."

"Like getting anonymous blank letters."

"Like that. Uh-huh. Real good. And like your wife dying. And right now, we got another problem here. One that means you gotta keep a low profile, old buddy."

"Another problem."

He sipped at his drink, and slid his eyes toward mine over the rim like a card player. "It's what I was tryin' to talk to you about two nights ago, old buddy. A new wrinkle. Are you startin' to shake, Miles? What for?"

"Just go on," I said. I felt as cold as in the old Updahl kitchen. "This is what you've been leading up to all night."

"That's not entirely fair, Miles. I'm just a cop trying to see all around a case. Trouble is, it keeps on growing."

"There's another one," I said. "Another girl."

"Maybe. Now you're mighty clever to get that out of me, because we're trying to keep it quiet for the time being. It isn't like the other ones. We don't have a body." He made a fist and coughed into it, stringing out the suspense. "We don't even know there *is* a body. A girl named Candace Michalski, good looker, seventeen years old, just disappeared the other evening. Two-three hours after I dropped you off at the Nash a couple blocks from here. She told her parents she was going bowling down at the Bowl-A-Rama—we passed it going out of town, remember—and she never came back. Never even made it to the Bowl-A-Rama."

"Maybe she ran away." My hands were shaking, and I sat on them.

"Out of character. She was an honors student. Member of the Future Teachers of America. Had a scholarship to River Falls next year. That's part of the state university system now, you know. I took some extension courses in police science there some years back. A good girl, Miles, not the kind that lights out."

"It's funny," I said. "It's funny how the past keeps up with us. We were just talking about Alison Greening, who is still, ah . . . on my mind a lot, and you and Duane and I all knew her, and people are all remembering about her death—"

"You and Duane were a lot closer to her than I was." He laughed. "But you gotta take your mind off her, Miles."

My body gave a tremor. "And an Arden girl with a Polish name leaves town or disappears, like that girl of Duane's . . ."

"And you make a museum out of your grandmaw's house," he said almost brutally. "Yeah, but I don't exactly see where that gets us. Now here's my thinking. I talked to the Michalskis, who are all shook up, naturally, and upset, and I said that they should keep quiet. They won't tell anyone about Candy. They'll say she went visiting her aunt in Sparta—or anything like that. I want to keep the lid on it for as long as possible. Maybe the girl will write them a postcard from a nudist colony in California. Huh? Maybe we'll find her body. If she's dead, maybe we can smoke out her killer before anybody gets the chance to get all hysterical. I'd like a nice clean arrest, and I guess the killer would prefer that too. With the sane part of his mind, anyhow." He levered himself off the couch and put his hands in the small of his back and stretched. He looked like a tired old bear that had just missed a fish. "Why did you want to go and steal from Zumgo's, anyhow? That was shit-stupid. Anyone would think you were asking to be put away."

I shook my head. "Bertilsson is wrong. I didn't steal anything."

"I'll confess to you, I wish that boy would come up to me and say, I did it, now get it over with. He *wants* to. He *wants* me to get him. He'd love to be sitting right where you are, Miles. He's all screwed up inside. He's about ready to snap. He can't get me out of his mind. Maybe he killed that Michalski girl. Maybe he's got her hid away someplace. Maybe he doesn't know what to do now that he's got her. He's in a bad spot. I feel sorry for the bastard, Miles, honest I do. If we do get a suicide, I'll say, that was him. I missed him, dammit. But he missed me too. What time is it?"

I looked at my watch. Polar Bears moved over to his front window and stood leaning against the glass, looking out into night. "Two."

"I never get to sleep until four or five. I'm screwed up nearly as bad as him." The gunpowder odor seemed particularly strong, along with the smell of unwashed skin. I wondered if Polar Bears ever changed his uniform. "How's that project you mentioned? Comin' along okay?"

"Sure. I guess so."

"What is it, anyhow?"

"Historical research."

"Real good. I still need your help, though. I hope you'll stay with us until this is all cleared up."

He was watching my reflection in the window glass. I glanced at his revolver hanging in its holster from the side wing of a chair.

I said, "What did you mean the other day when you said something about the killer's not just being an ordinary rapist? That he might be impotent?"

"Well, you take rape, Miles," Polar Bears said, moving heavily across the room to lean on the back of the couch. "I can understand rape. It's always been with us. I'll tell you what I couldn't say to a woman. These cases didn't have anything to do with rape. These things were done by somebody with a bad head problem. Rape isn't perverted, the way I look at it—it's almost a normal thing. A girl gets a fellow all heated up so he can't control himself, and then she hollers rape. The way these girls dress is almost incitement to rape. Hell, the way some girls *look* is an incitement to rape. A fellow might misunderstand what some bottom-swinging little critter is all about, what she wants. He gets all steamed up and can't help himself. Fault? Both parties! That's not exactly a popular point of view these days, but it's sure enough the truth. I've been a cop long enough to see a hundred cases of it. Power, they say. Of course it's about power. All life is about power. But these cases now weren't done by any normal man. See, Miles, these girls didn't have any form of intercourse at all— the examiner at the state hospital in Blundell, Dr. Hampton, didn't find any traces of semen. They were violated by other means."

"Other means?" I asked, not really sure I wanted to hear any more.

"A bottle. A Coke bottle. We found one smashed up beside both Gwen Olson and Jenny Strand. On Strand, something else was used too. A broom handle, something like that. We're still looking for it in the field off 93. Then there was some knife work. And they were both beaten up pretty badly before the real fun started."

"Christ," I said.

"So it might even be a woman, but that's pretty farfetched. It's hard to see a woman being strong enough, for one thing, and it doesn't really sound like a woman, does it? Well." He smiled at me from his position behind the couch, leaning forward on his arms. "Now you know as much as we do."

"You don't really think Paul Kant did these things, do you? That's impossible."

"What's impossible, Miles? Maybe I did it. Maybe you did, or Du-ane. Paul's all right as long as he stays inside and keeps out of trouble." He pushed himself off the couch and went into the kitchen. I heard an explosive bubbling sound and realized that he was gargling. When he came back into the living room his blue uniform shirt was unbuttoned, revealing a sleeveless undershirt straining over his immense belly. "You want some sleep, Miles. Take care you don't run off the road on your way home. It was a nice evening. We know each other better. Now scat."

Through the huge magnifying lenses, Tuta Sunderson's eyes looked like goggling fish. Sulky, she forced her hands into the pockets of her gray cardigan. For the three days following my late-night conversation with Polar Bears, she had sullenly arrived every morning, noisily tramped around the kitchen, wordlessly cooked my breakfast, and then busied herself cleaning the kitchen and the bathroom while I experimented with the placement of the furniture. The old bamboo-and-fabric couch went against the far wall, to the left of the small shelves. The glass-fronted case (I remembered it holding Bibles and novels by Lloyd C. Douglas) faced into the room from the short wall by the porch door; the only thing resembling an easy chair sat on the other side of that door; but the other chairs and small tables seemed too numerous, impossible to place— a spindly-legged table with a magazine rack? A cane-backed chair? I was not sure I could even remember them in the room, much less where they had been situated. Perhaps a half dozen other small articles of furniture presented the same problem. Tuta Sunderson could not help.

"It wasn't always the same way. There is no right way."

"Just think. Try to remember."

"I think that little table there went sort of alongside that couch." She was humoring me, half-reluctantly.

"Here?" I moved it under the shelves.

"No. Out more."

I pulled it forward.

"If I was Du-ane, I'd have your head examined. He spent pretty near his whole rebate on that nice furniture. When he told my boy about it, Red went down and got some real nice bargains for me, too."

"Duane can move this stuff back downstairs when I leave. That table doesn't look right."

"Looks good enough to me."

"Because you don't understand."

"I reckon there's lots I don't understand. You'll never get your writing done if you do this all day long."

"Why don't you change my sheets or something? If you can't help me, at least you could get out of my way."

Her face seemed to fill with water, like a sack.

"I reckon you left all your good manners in New York, Miles." With that, she visibly gave up on me for the moment, and turned toward the window. "How long before that little car of yours gonna be ready from the filling station?"

"I'll try them in a few days."

"Then will you be leaving the valley?" She cocked her head, watching something on the road.

"No. Polar Bears wants me to stay. He must be bored with his usual company."

"You and Galen pretty close?"

"We're like brothers."

"He never invited anyone to his house before. Galen keeps himself to himself. He's a smart man. Guess you had a ride in his police car. Folks in Arden told Red."

I moved a chair to a spot beside the oil heater, then moved it nearer the bedroom door. "You seem to have cars on the brain today."

"Maybe because I just saw someone stop and put something in your mailbox. Not the mailman. It was a different car. Why don't you go out there where it's warm and see what you got?"

"Now you tell me," I said, and went toward the porch. I stepped outside into the sunlight. For the past two days, Tuta Sunderson had taken to wearing a sweater while she worked, in part to irritate me with the anomaly of a cardigan in hot summer weather, in part because the farmhouse was genuinely cold and damp: it was as if a breeze came slicing down from the woods to pitch camp in the house. Behind me I could hear her saying, just loudly enough for me to hear, "Some more of your fan mail."

Which, in the event, was what it turned out to be: fan mail. It was a single sheet of cheap lined paper torn from a school exercise book, and printed on it was BASTERD YOURE IN OUR SIGHTS. Yes, a familiar image from the movies; I could almost feel the cross-hairs centering on my chest. I looked down the road, saw the nothing I expected to see, and then leaned forward with my arms on the mailbox, making my breathing regular. Twice in the past two days I had received silent telephone calls, bringing me down from my new project to a noise of muffled breathing on which I could smell onions, cheese, beer. Tuta Sunderson said people all talk, and I could guess that there were rumors of the Polish girl's disappearance. Tuta's attitude itself, more abrasive since my "suicide attempt," showed that she had attended to these whispers: she had just thrown back to me my remark about Red's manners.

As I walked back toward the farmhouse I could see her mooning at me through the window. I slammed the porch door, and she scuttled over to the cupboards and pretended to dust the shelves.

"I don't suppose you recognized the car?"

Her flabby upper arms wobbled; her rump bobbed in sympathetic motion. "It wasn't from the valley. I know all the cars hereabouts." She peeked at me over her fat shoulder, dying to know what I had found in the mailbox.

"What color was it?"

"It was all dust. I couldn't see."

"You know, Mrs. Sunderson," I said, putting it very slowly so she would not miss a word, "if it was your son or any of his friends that came in here that night and turned on the gas, they were attempting murder. The law takes a hard line on that sort of thing."

Furious, baffled, she turned around. "My boy's no sneak!"

"Is that what you'd call it?"

She whirled around again and began to dust the dishes so vigorously that they rattled. After a moment she permitted herself to speak, though not to face me. "People say something else happened. They say Galen Hovre is going to get him soon. They say he sits down there in his office knowing a lot more than he tells." Then another wall-eyed peak at me. "And they say Paul Kant is starving himself in his mother's house. So if it happens again people will know he was inside and didn't do it."

"What a field day they're having," I said. "What fun they're all having. I envy them."

She shook her head maddeningly, and I would gladly have gone on in that vein, but the telephone rang. She glanced at it and then at me, telling me she would not answer it.

I put the sheet of paper down on the table and picked up the receiver. "Hello." Silence, breathing, the smells of onions and beer. I do not know if these were truly the odors of my caller, or if they were only those I expected from someone who made anonymous telephone calls. Tuta Sunderson pounced on the sheet of paper.

"You miserable boor," I said into the mouthpiece. "You have pigshit where you should have an imagination."

My caller hung up; I laughed at that and at the expression on Tuta Sunderson's face. She put down the misspelled note. She was shocked. I laughed again, tasting something black and sour at the back of my throat.

When I heard the porch door slam I waited until I saw her toiling up the road, the lumpy cardigan over one arm and the handbag jigging on its strap. After a long while she moved out of the frame of vision the window gave me, struggling in the sunlight like a white beetle. I put down my pencil and closed the journal. Standing on the cool porch, I looked up toward the woods—all was still, as if life stopped when the sun was so high. Sound told me that it did not: out of sight down the road, Duane's tractor put-putted from the far field, birds said things to one another. I went down the rutted drive, crossed the road, and jumped the ditch.

On the other side of the creek, I could hear crickets and grasshoppers, and small things whirring in the grass. I went up the bifurcated hill; crows took off from the alfalfa, screeching, their bodies like flak, like ashes in the air. Sweat dripped into my eyebrows, and I felt my shirt clammily adhering to my sides. I thumped down into the dip, and then began to rise again, walking toward the trees.

This was where she had twice led me. Birds twittered, darting through branches far above. Light came down in that streaming way it does only in forests and cathedrals. I watched a gray squirrel race out onto a slender branch, bend it under his weight, and then transfer to a lower, stouter branch like a man stepping out of an elevator. When the ground began to alter, so did the trees; I walked on spongy gray mulch between oaks and elms; I skirted pines and conifers and felt thin brown needles skid underfoot. As when I lay on the polished floor, I waded through high leafy beds of ferns. Berries crushed against my trousers. A lightning-blasted old ruin of an oak lay splintered and jagged in my path, and I jumped on top of it, feeling the softness of rotting wood. Filaments of green snagged and caught in the eyelets of my boots.

Going as I had gone in vision that night, I passed the thick unmoving trees until I saw where they seemed to gather like a crowd at an accident: I slid through a gap, and was in the clearing. The sunlight, after the filter of the network of the leaves, seemed violently yellow and intense, lionlike, full of inhuman energy. Tall grass tipped under its own weight. Insect noises hovered in vibrato over the clearing. A chirring unmoving noise.

At the center, in the charred place, the ashes showed a still red core, like the ashes in Rinn's old woodstove. It had Alison's warmth. Galen Hovre was wrong about Duane and my cousin. Or Duane, all those years ago, had lied.

Oddly, perhaps predictably, when I had dreamed about walking up into the woods the journey had a direct, palpable actuality, and when I actually went up there it felt like dreaming. I thought, almost fearing it, that I would sense some deeper closeness to Alison Greening if I approached the clearing where I had met her dreadful apparition in my vision; that space was hers, and I thought of it as the source of the chill which penetrated the old farmhouse. If there is another world, a world of Spirit, who is to say that its touch may not shake us to our boots, that its heat may not come to us as the cold of quarry water? But discounting that nightmare vision of Alison as a creature stitched together from leaves and bark, indirection brought me closer to her, evoked her more satisfactorily, than a crude search through the woods and clearing. I had begun a memoir, a task she had motivated (I could remember her telling me, one high summer day when we climbed the hill behind the valley and, carrying shovels, searched for Indian mounds, that she was going to be a painter, and I a writer), and it seemed to cement us even further, since—at the most obvious level—it meant that I thought about her even more than I might otherwise. She was the groundbass of what I wrote. It was as though I were reeling her in, sentence by sentence. And then, one morning after suffering through a breakfast presided over by a Tuta Sunderson, who had accepted seven one-dollar bills from me and then wordlessly handed back two as if they represented an immoral suggestion, I had driven the Nash loaner over the Mississippi bridge on Highway 35—a wonderful American sight, those islands showing their wooded backs like green water buffaloes in the brown river—to Winona, Minnesota, looking for the records necessary to the Alison-environment. If I'd had to, I would have gone all the way to Minneapolis. Albums on the Pacific label from the 'fifties are rare items. An initial glance through the racks in a Winona record store unearthed none, but then I saw the sign saying Second Hand Department Downstairs, and went down to flip through, in a basement illuminated by a single bulb, crate after crate of albums with worn sleeves and crumbled spines. Surrounded by cast-off Perry Comos and Roy Acuffs and Roger Williamses, two records shone like gold, and I grunted with such loud approval that the owner appeared at the top of the stairs to ask if I were all right. One was an old Dave Brubeck record I remembered Alison telling me she had loved (*Jazz at Oberlin*) and the other—well, the other was a true find. It was the Gerry Mulligan quartet album on Pacific which Alison had urged me to buy, the one with a cover painting by Keith Finch. Finding that record was like finding a message from her scrawled on a page of my manuscript. It was the record, above all others, which evoked her, the one she had most cherished. The owner of the record store charged me five dollars for the two records, but I would have paid twenty times that. As much as my writing, they brought Alison nearer.

"What *is* that stuff you play all the time?" asked the Tin Woodsman. She was standing on the porch on Saturday night, peering in through the screen door. "Is that jazz?" I put my pencil into my manuscript and closed it. I was sitting on the old couch downstairs, and the kerosene lamps shed a muted orange glow which softened her features, blurred already by the mesh of the screen. She wore a denim shirt and trousers, and looked more feminine, in that soft light, than I had ever seen her. "Look," she said, "it's okay. I mean, Dad's in Arden for some kind of meeting. Red Sunderson called him just before dinner. All the men are talking about something. They'll probably be at it for hours. I heard you playing that record the other day. Is that the kind of music you like? Can I come in?"

She entered the room and sat facing me from a wooden rocker. On her bare feet were tan clogs. "What is it, anyhow?"

"Do you like it?" I really was curious.

She lifted her shoulders. "Doesn't it all sound sort of the same?"

"No."

"What's that instrument playing now?"

"A guitar."

"A guitar? That's a guitar? Come on. It's a . . . um, a whatsit. Some kind of horn. A sax. Right?"

"Yes. It's a baritone saxophone."

"So why did you say it was a guitar?" Then she smiled, seeing the joke.

I shrugged, smiling back.

"Shit, Miles, it's cold in here."

"That's because it's damp."

"Yeah? Hey Miles, did you steal out of Zumgo's? Pastor Bertilsson's telling everyone you did."

"Then I must have."

"I don't get it." She looked around the room, shaking her head, her jaws working on a piece of gum. "Hey, you know this room looks really neat this way. It's just like it used to be. When I was a little kid and Great-Gramma was still alive."

"I know."

"It's neat," she said, still examining the room. "Didn't there used to be more pictures? Like of you and Dad?" When I nodded, she asked, "So where are they?"

"I didn't need them."

The gum snapped. "Boy, Miles, I don't know about you. You're really superstrange. Sometimes you remind me of Zack, and sometimes you just talk crazy. How did you know where everything went in here?"

"I had to work at it."

"It's sort of like a museum, isn't it? I mean, I almost expect to see Great-Gramma!"

"She probably wouldn't like the music."

She giggled. "Hey, did you really steal from Zumgo's?"

"Does Zack steal?"

"Sure." She made her sea-water eyes very wide. "All the time. He says you have to liberate things. And he says if you can take things without being caught, then you have a right to them."

"Where does he steal from?"

"Places where he works. You know. Stuff from people's houses, if he's working for them. Stuff from the gas station, if he's working there. You mean, you're a college professor and all and you steal things?"

"If you say so."

"I can see why Zack likes you. That would really turn him on. Some big Establishment guy ripping off stores. He thinks he might be able to trust you."

"I really think you're too good for Zack," I said.

"You're wrong, Miles. You don't know Zack. You don't know what he's into." She leaned forward, putting each hand on the opposite shoulder. The gesture was surprisingly womanly.

"What's the meeting in Arden about? The one Red and your father went to."

"Who cares? Listen, Miles, are you going to church tomorrow?"

"Of course not. I have my reputation to think of."

"Then try not to get stinko again tonight, huh? We gotta plan. We're gonna take you somewhere."

Portion of Statement by Tuta Sunderson:

July 18

Well, what my boy thought was that there was some kind of cover-up. That was the word he used to me, Galen Hovre, like it or not. Cover-up. 'Course it wasn't, we know that now, but look at what we had then—nothing! After those two murders, there's poor Paul Kant holed up in his mother's house, there's Miles batching it in his grandmother's house and riding around in police cars and who knows what all, turning that house into something Duane didn't want it to be, and people just thought something had to be done. And we all thought you were hiding something from us. And you were!

Anyhow, one of Red's friends had the car idea, and Red told him, let's wait until we know for sure what's going on, and let's have a general meeting to talk about it. All the men. They'd get together, see? To sort of piece out the rumors.

So they met in the back of the Angler's. Red says they had thirty-forty men at the meeting. They all looked up to Red, on account of his finding Jenny Strand.

Now, who's heard what? says Red. Let's get it all out. Let's get it where we can see it and not just gossip about it. Now, a few of the men had heard that the police were sitting on something. Let me see. Did one of the deputies tell his girlfriend? Something like that. I'm not saying it was that, mind. So one of the men says, who knows about anybody hiding away—not acting normal and neighborly.

And someone says, Roman Michalski hasn't been to work this week.

Sick? they ask.

No, nobody heard of him being sick. He's just holed up. Him and his wife.

Now, if we're talking about people being holed up, I could have told them about Miles. You bet. He just set there after he got all the furniture just the way he wanted it, the way his Gramma had it. He was real white, sitting there in that damp old house, drinking himself to sleep every night, and playing those goofy records all day. He looked like he was in a trance or something all the time. A big man like that, and he looked like he'd jump out of his skin if you said boo. And his language! Oh, he knew he wasn't going to get away with anything.

When I found out he'd had a girl in his bed I told Red right away.

Anyhow, like you know, Monday night some of the men paid a call on Roman Michalski.

After showering on Sunday morning I went upstairs and hugged my bathrobe about me while I examined my clothes. Mrs. Sunderson had wordlessly washed my muddy jeans and shirt and folded them on top of the bureau. The jeans had a quarter-sized hole at one cuff; looking at it awakened uneasy memories of my scramble through the woods; I was grateful that I had gone back to the clearing and found no more than a dying picnic fire. I fingered the hole in the jeans then withdrew my hand. I remembered a portion of Polar Bears' advice to me, and wandered indecisively to the closet where I'd put the one suit I had brought with me. It was seven-thirty; I had just time enough to dress and make the service. It had to be done correctly—I had to be dressed correctly, I could display no nervousness, my attitude must shout innocence. Just thinking about it while looking at the suit in the closet made me nervous. You're like Paul Kant if you don't go, stated a clear voice in my mind.

I took the suit from the hanger and began to dress. For a reason probably closely related to vanity, in New York I had packed, along with clothing appropriate to the farm, my most expensive things—eighty-dollar shoes, a lightweight pinstripe from Brooks, several of the custom-made shirts Joan, being nicely ironic, had once had made for me for Christmas. I certainly had not foreseen wearing them to Gethsemane Lutheran church.

After I had knotted a thick, glossy tie and put on the jacket I looked at myself in the bedroom mirror. I resembled a Wall Street lawyer far more than a failed academic or murder suspect. I looked innocent, big and bland and prosperous and washed in milk. A baby for the work of the Lord, a man who would absentmindedly mutter a prayer while sinking a difficult putt.

On the way out of the house I slipped the copy of *She* into my jacket pocket: a sliver of Alison for company.

I pulled the Nash into the last space in the gravel parking lot before the church and got out into the hot sun and began to walk over the crunching white stones to the church steps. As they did every Sunday, the men were standing on the wide high steps and on the concrete walk, smoking. I could remember them standing there, smoking and talking, when I was a child; but those men had been the fathers and uncles of these, and they had dressed in sober, poorly cut suits of serge and gabardine. Like the previous generation, these men had the badges of their profession, the heavy hands with stiff enormous thumbs and the white foreheads above sunburnt faces, but Duane's was the only suit among them. The rest wore sport shirts and casual slacks. Walking toward them, I felt absurdly overdressed and urban.

One of them noticed me, and his cigarette had frozen in mid-arc to his mouth. He muttered to the man beside him, and I could read the three syllables of Teagarden on his lips.

When I reached the concrete walk to the church steps, I here and there recognized a face, and greeted the first of these. "Good morning, Mr. Korte," I said to a squat bulldog-like man with a crewcut and heavy black glasses. Bud Korte owned a farm a mile or two down the valley from the Updahl land. He and my father had often gone fishing together.

"Miles," he said, and then his eyes shot wildly away toward the cigarette he was pinching between two fingers the size of small bananas. "Howdy." He was as embarrassed as a bishop just greeted familiarly by a hooker. "Heard you was back." The eyes shot away again, and landed with painful relief on Dave Eberud, another farmer I recognized, now looking in his horizontally striped shirt and plaid trousers as if his mother had dressed him in too much haste. Eberud's snapping turtle face, twisted slightly in our direction, snapped forward. "Gotta have a word with Dave," said Bud Korte, and left me examining the shine on my shoes.

Duane, in his double-breasted suit, its jacket unbuttoned to reveal wide red braces, stood halfway up the church steps; his posture, one foot aggressively planted on a higher step, his shoulders brought forward, plainly said that he did not want to acknowledge me, but I moved toward him through men who drew together as I passed.

When I began to go up the steps I could hear his voice. ". . . the last auction. How can I wait it out? If beef goes down below twenty-seven a pound, I'm through. I can't raise all my own feed, even now with that new land, and that old M I got is fallin' apart." Looming heavily beside him was Red Sunderson, who stared at me, not even bothering to pretend to listen to Duane's complaints. In the sunlight, Sunderson looked younger and tougher than he had at night. His face was a flat angry plane of chipped angles.

He said, "We're mighty fancy today, Miles."

Duane irritably glanced at me, and then shifted his cocked leg. The sunburnt part of his face was unnaturally red. "I considered we might see you here sometime." But it's too late now, his tone said.

"I said, we're mighty fancy today."

"It's all I brought with me besides jeans," I said.

"Ma says you finished playing with that old furniture."

Duane made a disgusted, angry sound with his lips. Behind me, a man drew in a hissing breath like a secret laugh.

"What's an old M?" I asked.

Duane's face became a deeper shade of red. "A goddamned tractor. A god-damned tractor with a busted gearbox, if you wanta know. Since you're through wrecking my furniture, maybe you'd like to junk up my tractors too, huh?"

"Been in the woods lately, Teagarden?" asked Red Sunderson. "Been gettin' any up in the woods?"

"What's that about the woods?" asked my cousin. Red was still staring at me from his flat chipped face incongruously mounted with his mother's blobby nose.

Some tribal signal was drawing the men at the bottom toward the steps; at first I thought they were coming for me, but when the first shouldered past without looking at me, I knew that the services were about to begin, and it was time to rejoin the women. Red turned away as if he could no longer bear to look at me, and I was left with red-faced furious Duane. I said, "I have to talk to you about something. About Alison Greening." "Hell," he uttered, and then, "Don't you sit with me, Miles," and stomped up the stairs with his friends.

I could hear them whispering as I followed them into the church. By either gossip or telepathy, they all knew who would be the last man to enter the building, and the women were all craning their necks to look at me. On several of their plain country faces, I caught expressions of horror. Duane went his shovel-handed way down to the right aisle. I went to the left, already sweating through the tailored shirt.

Halfway up toward the front I slid into a pew and sat down. I could feel their faces pointing at me, white and red, and tilted my head back and examined the familiar interior. White arched wooden ceiling, white chaste walls, four stained-glass windows on either side with Norwegian names at the bottoms: in memory of Gunnar and Joron Gunderson, in memory of Einar and Florence Weverstad, in memory of Emma Jahr. Up in Bertilsson's sanctuary behind the altar, a huge sentimental painting of Jesus anointing St. John. A white bird like one of the town hall pigeons hovered above the pale symmetrical face.

When Bertilsson popped like a figure on a German clock through his entrance at the front of the church, he unerringly looked at me first. The telepathy had reached him too. After that, much standing up and sitting down, much re-sponsive reading, much singing. A wizened woman in a purple dress gave abrupt, unmusical accompaniment on a small organ. Bertilsson kept watching me with oily eyes: he seemed to brim with a generalized emotion. His ears were very red. The four or five other people in my pew had moved farther and farther away from me, taking advantage of all the standing and sitting to shift a few inches each time.

My shirt felt like paper about to shred; a fly buzzed angrily, obsessively, somewhere up near the ceiling; whenever I leaned back, I stuck to the wood of the pew. Above the blond wood of the pew before me protruded a boy's vacant face, regarding me with dull eyes and open mouth. A drop of saliva hung on the full part of his lower lip.

After "O God Our Help in Ages Past" Bertilsson motioned for us to sit, using the gesture with which an actor silences applause, and moved to the pulpit. Once there, he deliberately removed a handkerchief from his sleeve, dabbed his shiny forehead, and replaced it. More time-wasting while extracting his sheaf of notes from within his loose garments. All this time, he was looking directly at me.

"The text for the day," he said, his voice light and confidential, "is James II, verses one to five. 'My brethren, have not the faith of our Lord Jesus Christ, the Lord of glory, with respect to persons. For if there come into your assembly a man with a gold ring, in goodly apparel, and there come in also a poor man in vile raiment . . .' "

I tuned him out and let my head fall forward, wishing that I had not taken Polar Bears' advice. What good could come of this? Then I was needled by a sharp awareness that Polar Bears had told me something far more important— a fact that connected to another fact. It was like a thorn in my side, nagging at me. I tried to go over the conversations I'd had with Hovre, but Bertilsson's sermon kept breaking in.

He had managed to wrestle the Good Samaritan into James II, I noticed, quite a feat even for someone as glib as Bertilsson. It seems the Samaritan was not a superficial respecter of persons. "But this works in reverse, my friends." I looked up at his odious, glistening moonface and silently groaned. He was still fixing me with his eyes. "Yes, my friends, we must not condemn the Samaritan to seeing but one side of the coin." I closed my eyes.

Bertilsson rolled on inexorably, and it was only his pauses while he rummaged for the ripest vocabulary that told me he was improvising. I looked up and saw him folding his notes, unconsciously making them into neat square packages with sharp edges. The boy before me permitted his chin to drop even further.

Then I realized what Bertilsson was going to do, and he did it while I witnessed the malice leaking from the glistening eyes and the rolling voice. "Is not there one among us in fine raiment, one who cannot hide his anguish beneath fine clothing? Is not there one among us needful of the Samaritan's touch? A man in pain? Brethren, we have with us a man sorely troubled, who imagines life not God's gift, as we know it to be. A sparrow's life, a child's life, all are precious to him. I speak of a man whose whole soul is a cry of pain, a cry to God for release. A sick man, my brethren, a man sorely ill. My friends, a man in need of our Christian love . . ."

It was unbearable. The fly still angrily thrummed against the ceiling, wanting out. I stood up, stepped out of the pew, and turned my back on Bertilsson. I could hear the glee in his voice, far below the message of love. I wanted to be up in the woods, holding my hands above the warmth of an ember. A woman began to chatter like a bird. I felt shock radiate between the white walls. Bertilsson rolled on, calling for my blood. I walked down the side aisle, going as quickly as I could. At the front of the church I swung open the big door and stepped outside. I could sense them all twisting their necks, looking at me. A vision of fish.

Back across the gravel to the ugly little car, and home in sweltering sunlight. I yanked off my jacket and threw it into the backseat. I wanted to be naked, I wanted to feel mulch and pine needles beneath the soles of my feet. Halfway to the farmhouse on the valley road, I began to shout.

3

As I went across the lawn toward the house I could hear the stereo going. Someone was playing the song "I'm Beginning to See the Light" on the Gerry Mulligan record. My anger at Bertilsson's inspiration left me all at once: I felt tired, hot, directionless. The smell of bacon cooking drifted toward me with the sound of Chet Baker's trumpet. I came up onto the screen porch and felt suddenly cooler.

Alison Updahl, chewing on something and dressed in her uniform, appeared in the doorway of the kitchen. Her T-shirt was pale blue. "Where were you, Miles?" I just went past her. When I reached the old bamboo couch I collapsed into it, making its joints creak and sing. "Would you mind if I turned off the music? I don't think I can listen to it now."

"You don't mind my—" She pointed to the turntable and lifted her shoulders.

"Not enough to actually object," I said. I leaned over and lifted the tone arm with trembling fingers.

"Hey, you were in church," she said grinning a little. She had noticed my necktie and striped trousers. "I like you in those clothes. You look sort of classy and old-fashioned. But isn't it early for church to be out?"

"Yes."

"What did you go there for anyway? I don't think they want you there." I nodded.

"They think you tried to kill yourself."

"That's not all they think."

"Don't let them bug you. You and old man Hovre are in real good, aren't you? Didn't he invite you to his house?"

The bush telegraph. "How do you know that? Did I tell you?"

"Everybody knows that, Miles." I sagged back into the couch. "Hey, it doesn't mean anything. Not really. They just talk." She was trying to lift my mood. "It doesn't mean anything."

"Okay," I said. "Thanks for the positive thinking. Did you come over just to play the records?"

"You were going to meet me, remember?" She pulled her shoulders back, smiling at me, and put her hands in the small of her back. If the clothing she wore had seams, they were straining. Her blood smell hovered between us, neither increasing nor decreasing. "Come on. We're going on an adventure. Zack wants to talk to you."

"Women would make great generals," I said and followed her back outside.

Minutes later I was driving past the church. The sound of singing carried all the way to the road. She looked at the cars in the parking spaces, stared at the church, and then turned to look at me with genuine astonishment. "You left early? You walked out?"

"What does it look like?"

"In front of everybody? Did they see?"

"Every single one of them." I loosened the knot of my tie.

She laughed out loud. "Miles, you're a real cowboy." Then she laughed some more. It was a pleasant, human sound.

"Your pastor seems to think I'm a sex murderer. He was shouting for the noose."

Her high approving good humor suddenly died. "Not you not you," she said, almost crooning. She twisted her legs up beneath her. Then she was silent for a long time.

"Where are we going?"

"One of our places." Her voice was flat. "You shouldn't have gone. It just makes them think you're trying to trick them somehow."

It was better advice than Polar Bears', but it was too late. She let herself slump over so that her head rested on my shoulder.

I had undergone too many swift alterations and swings of feeling, and this gesture nearly made me weep. Her head stayed on my shoulder as we drove toward Arden through the rising, sun-browned hills. I was looking forward to seeing her march into Freebo's as though beneath her sandaled feet were not wooden boards but a red carpet. This time, I considered, we would both need a mysterious protection of "who Zack was" to get into Freebo's.

Yet it was not Freebo's to which she was taking me. A mile outside of Arden we approached a juncture I had not yet permitted myself to notice, and she straightened up and said "Slow down."

I glanced at her. Her head was turning, showing her blunt profile beneath the choppy blond fringe of hair. "Left here."

I slowed the Nash to a crawl. "Why here?"

"Because no one ever comes here. What's wrong with it?"

Everything was wrong with it. It was the worst place in the world.

"I'm not going up there," I said.

"Why? It's just the old Pohlson quarry. There's nothing wrong with it." She looked at me, her face concentrated. "Oh. I think I know why. Because it's where my aunt Alison died. The one I was named after."

I was sweating.

"Those are her pictures in your upstairs room, right? Do you think I look like her?"

"No," I breathed. "Not really."

"She was bad, wasn't she?" I could sense her heating up again, pumping out that odor. I stopped the car. Alison said, "She was like you. She was too freaky for the people around here."

"I suppose." My mind was working.

"You in a trance or something?" She biffed my shoulder. "Get out of it. Turn up. Turn up the path."

"I want to try something. An experiment." I told her what I wanted her to do.

"You promise you'll come up afterwards? You won't just drive away? It's not a trick?"

"I promise to come up afterward," I said. "I'll give you five minutes." I leaned across and opened her door. She crossed the deserted road and began to march stiffly up the track to the quarry.

For two or three minutes I waited in the heat of the car, looking unseeing down the highway. A wasp flew in, all business, and bumped his head against the windshield several times before losing his temper and zooming by accident out the window on the other side. A long way down the highway a broiler farm occupied the fields to the left, and specks of white which were chickens moved jerkily over the green in the sunlight. I looked up toward a flat blue sky. I heard nothing but the mindless twitter of a bird.

When I got out of the car and stood on the sticky tar of the highway I thought I could hear a faint voice calling; if it was a voice, it seemed indistinguishable from the landscape, coming from nowhere in particular; it could have been a breeze. I got back in the car and drove up the track to the quarry.

The day I had returned to the Updahl farm I had expected a surge of feeling, but experienced only flatness and disappointment; the act of stepping out into the terrific heat of the flat grassy area near the quarry hit me with an only half-anticipated force. I anchored myself in the present by placing the palm of my right hand on the baking metal of the top of the Nash. It all looked very much the same. The grass was browner, because of the summer's dry heat, and the outcroppings of speckled rock appeared more jagged and prominent. I saw the same flat gray space where the workmen's sheds had stood. The screen of bushes above the quarry itself had grown spindly, the small leaves like brushstrokes, dry and brown, papery. Drawn up nearer to them than my car was a dusty black van. I pulled my hand off the hot metal of the car and walked on the path through the bushes to the rocky steps down to the lip of the quarry.

They were both there. Alison sat with her feet in the water, looking up at me with expectant curiosity. Zack, a bisected white exclamation point in his black bathing suit, was grinning, snapping his fingers. "It's the man," he said. "It's my main man."

"Did you shout?"

Zack giggled. "Wowee." *Snap-snap* of his fingers.

"Did I shout? I screamed my head off!"

"How long?"

"A couple of minutes. Couldn't you hear?"

"I don't think so," I said. "You screamed as loud as you could?"

"I'm practically hoarse," she answered. "If I yelled any longer, I would have ripped something."

Zack bent his legs and sat down on the black pile of his clothing. "It's the truth, man. She really hollered. What's it about, anyhow? What's your stunt?"

"No stunt," I said. "Just finding out about an old lie."

"You're too hung up on the past, Miles." His grin grew more intense. "Jesus, man, look at those clothes. What kind of clothes are those for a swim?"

"I didn't know I was going swimming."

"What else do you do at a quarry?"

I sat down with my legs before me on the smooth hot lip of rock. I looked up at the bushes overhead. They would have been hidden up there, waiting to jump down. That was where they had been. I wanted to be anywhere but where I was. I could smell the water and it was Alison's smell.

"I haven't been here for twenty years," I said. "I don't know what you do here."

"It's a great place to groove on ideas," Zack said, stretched out whitely in the sun. His ribs showed under the skin like sticks and his arms and legs were skinny and covered with thin black hair. His body looked obscene, spidery. Beneath the black strip of bathing suit lay a prominent sexual bulge. "I thought it was time we saw each other again." He spoke like a general summoning his adjutant. "I had to thank you for the books."

"That's okay," I said. I removed my tie and dropped it and the jacket I had been carrying by my side. Then I pulled my shirt out of my trousers and unbuttoned it halfway down to let air enter.

"Miles went to church," Alison said from the quarry's edge. "Old Bertilsson preached about him again."

"*Hah hah hah!*" Zack exploded with laughter. "That old fart. He oughta be making shitty little doilies, hey? He's a feeb. I hate that sucker, man. So he thinks you're the Masked Marauder, huh?"

Alison asked, "Did you bring towels?"

"Hey? Sure I brought towels. Can't go swimming without towels. Brought three of them." Zack rolled over on his belly and examined me. "Is that right? Am I right about him, my main man?"

"More or less." It was too hot for my heavy shoes, and I unlaced them and pulled them off.

The Woodsman said, "Well, if you brought towels, I'm sure going to swim. My throat hurts from all that yelling." She looked over her shoulder at Zack, who indulgently flipped his hand in a do-what-you-want gesture.

"I'm gonna go skinny," she said, and glanced at me. She still had not got over her desire to shock.

"You can't scare him, he's the Masked Marauder," said Zack.

She stood up, displeased, leaving dark high-arched footprints on the stone, and pulled the blue shirt over her head. Her breasts lolled large and pink against her chest. She pushed her jeans down unceremoniously, revealing all of her stocky well-shaped little body.

"If you're the Masked Marauder, haven't you been busy lately?" asked Zack.

I watched Alison go padding to the edge of the quarry and stand, judging the water for a moment. She wanted to get away from us.

"That's not actually funny," I said.

She raised her arms and then used her leg muscles to spring out into the water in a clean dive. When her head broke water, she began to breaststroke across the quarry.

"Well, what about that guy, anyhow?"

"What guy?" For a moment my mind blurred and I thought he meant Alison Updahl.

"The killer." He was lying on his side, gleeful. He seemed to be supercharged with sly, flinty enthusiasm, as if secrets were bubbling inside him. His eyes, very large now, appeared to be chiefly pupil. "He kinda turns me on. He's done something else, you know, something most people don't know about yet."

"Oh?" If that were widely known, Polar Bears' strategy was a failure.

"Don't you see the beauty of that? Man, that D. H. Lawrence would have. The guy who wrote those books. I been reading those books. There's a lot in them."

"I don't think Lawrence ever sympathized with sex killers."

"Are you sure? Are you really sure? What if a killer was on the side of life? Hey? See, I looked at that *Women in Love* book—I didn't read all of it, I just read the parts you underlined. I wanted to get inside you, man."

"Oh, yes." It was an appalling notion.

"Doesn't he talk about beetles? That some people are beetles. Who should be killed? You gotta live according to your ideas, don't you? Take the idea of pain. Pain is a tool. Pain is a tool for release."

"Why don't you stop talking and come in and swim?" Alison called from the center of the quarry. Sweat poured down my face.

Zack's intense black eyes focused unblinkingly on me. "Take your shirt off," he said.

"I guess I will," I said, and unbuttoned it the rest of the way and dropped it on top of my jacket.

"Don't you think the people who are just stupid beetles should be killed? That's why I dig this guy. He just goes out and does it."

We had left Lawrence a long way behind, but I wanted only to let him rant, so that he would be done earlier. "Has there been another one? Another murder?"

"I don't know, man, but answer me this. Why would he fuckin' stop?"

I nodded. Suddenly all I wanted was to be in the water, to feel the quarry's cold water about me again.

"Maybe my favorite part of the book was about blood-brotherhood," Zack said. "I dig that nude wrestling part between two men. You underlined almost all of that."

"I suppose I might have," I said, but he had switched gears again.

"He's free, you see, whoever this guy is, he's free as hell. Nobody's gonna stop him. He's thrown out all of the old shit holding him back. And if he thought anybody was gonna stand in his way, bang, he'd get rid of him."

This conversation was reminding me uneasily of my afternoon with Paul Kant; it was even worse. Where Paul Kant had been low-voiced and depressed, this skinny boy was simply shivering with conviction.

"Like Hitler did to Roehm. Roehm was in his way, and he just smashed him with his foot. The Night of the Long Knives. Bang. Another beetle dead. You see the beauty in that?"

"No," I said. "There isn't any." I had to get away from him, and when Alison shouted to us again, I said, "It's too hot for this. I think I'll swim a little."

"You gonna skinny-dip?" His mad eyes were taunting me.

"Why not?" I said, irritated, and shucked the rest of my clothing. Infuriatingly, Zack stood when I did, and slithered out of his skimpy black bathing suit. We dove into the water together. I felt more than saw the Woodsman watching us from the center of the pool.

The water hit me like an electric jolt. The memories of the last time I had been in the quarry hit me too, with an even greater force, and I could see her as I had seen her then, her hands and feet flashing. Then I recognized that I was seeing not *my* Alison, but my cousin's daughter, an altogether more adult female form. Underwater, I frog-kicked away, wanting to experience the rush of emotion away from the other two. It was like a clamp around my chest, and for a moment, fleeing the legs dangling in the water, I thought I would be killed by my own emotion. My heart fluttered, and I kicked away for another second and then surfaced, breathing noisily.

Zack's grinning face was four feet away, looking absurdly young beneath his streaming black hair. His eyes seemed to have no white at all. He said something inaudible, choked by his own pleasure.

Then he repeated it. "This is where it happened, isn't it, Miles?" He was exuding crazy glee.

"What?" I said, my stomach frozen.

"You and Alison's aunt. Hey?" His mouth was lifted in a loose insane smile.

I turned away and began to swim as strongly as I could toward the lip of the quarry. His voice was calling, but not to me.

Water was thrashing behind me. Now he was calling to me. "You don't talk, do you? You don't talk, do you?" His voice was loud and brutal.

Eight feet from safety I felt a hand catch my ankle. When I kicked out with my free leg, another hand grasped my calf, and then I was yanked backward and down. While two hands held my legs, other hands pushed my shoulders, and I felt a heavy body riding my back, beginning to squeeze my chest. The one on top leaned forward to wrap arms around my neck, and cushiony breasts pressed against me. I bucked underwater, but she clamped me with greater force, expelling the rest of the air from my lungs. Games, I thought, and breaststroked, thinking that my breath would outlast hers. Zack still clung to my ankles. I kicked idly, resolved not to give them the satisfaction of a struggle. Then I realized that she was close enough to the surface to raise her head and breathe, and a spurt of fear made me fight.

I shook violently, but she forced me deeper into the tunnel of water. The hands on my legs let go, and I knew that Zack too was going up to breathe. My chest fought for air. In moments, Zack appeared before me under the water and raised his arms to my shoulders. I swung at him, but the blow was ridiculously slowed by the water. He dug his fingers into my shoulders and held me helpless, prone in the water. Astride me, the Woodsman squeezed and squeezed.

If I had been alone with the Woodsman, I could have thrown or pulled her off, but while Zack held me and pinned my arms, I could do nothing but struggle, making my air problem worse. As I grew weaker, Zack moved in nearer and put his hands on the small of my back, pulling me down even further. I realized with shock and horror that he was erect when a fleshy club bumped my hip.

In the next instant I breathed in a gulp of burning water, and I knew that they were going to kill me.

Then their hands and arms fell away, the weight of Alison rolled off my back, and I was helped to the surface.

I held to the rock edge of the quarry, coughing painfully. Water came up like vomit. Getting out of the quarry was impossible; I clung with my weak arms and my head lolled against my shoulder. After a moment I could lever myself up far enough so that my forearms were flat on the hot stone, and I bent my head to rest on them. Through half-opened eyes, not really recognizing what I saw, I noticed Zack sliding out of the water and up onto rock as easily as an eel. Then he bent down and braced himself to take the arm of the naked girl. That bastard nearly killed me and it turned him on, I thought, and an emotion half fear and half anger gave me the energy to struggle up onto the edge of stone. I lay in the sun, shivering, my skin burning where it touched the hot smooth rock.

He sat down beside me. I saw only a spidery flank with thin black hairs streaming across white skin. "Hey, Miles. Hey, man. You okay?"

I rolled away, onto my back. The hot stone seared me. I closed my eyes, still coughing. When I opened my eyes, they were blocking the sun, standing above me. They were black against the flat blue sky. Alison knelt to cradle my head. "Let me alone," I said. I wriggled away. "Did you plan that?"

"It was just fun, Miles," he said. "We were playing."

"Poor old Miles, he 'most drowned," crooned Alison, and came toward me again and pushed herself against me. I was engulfed in cool wet skin. Involuntarily, I looked at Zack. "I'm sorry, man," he said, unselfconsciously manipulating his testicles. I turned my eyes away and found myself staring at Alison's soft heavy breasts and firm belly. "Give me a towel," I ordered. Zack stepped away toward the pile of clothing.

Alison brought her face closer to mine. "This is where it happened, isn't it?

You can tell Zack. You could tell him anything. That's why he wanted to meet you here. He heard about it at Freebo's. That's why he knows you understand him. He wants you to be brothers. Didn't you hear what he was saying before?"

I fought to stand up, and after a moment she released me. Zack was coming toward me, a pink towel in one hand. The other hand held an open switchblade. I stepped backwards.

When Zack saw what must have been in my face, he tossed me the towel and said, "Hey, man. I want to help you take off the bandage. It's not doing you any good anymore."

After knotting the towel around my waist, I looked at my left hand. It was caught in a soggy limp mass of gauze, a webby useless thing already half off my palm. Zack took my hand in his and before I had time to push him away, neatly sliced the mess of gauze away from my palm. Then he ripped away the tape in one quick motion.

Above the base of my thumb was a reddish triangle of new skin, defined by a thin red line on all three sides. I gingerly touched the spot with incurling fingers. It was delicate, but it had healed. Zack threw the drowned package of tape and gauze up into the bushes. I looked at him and his eyes were crazy and gleeful. His face was very young, framed by long smooth Indian's hair.

"You're my best friend," he said. He held out his left palm, and the image of him as a thin dead-white Indian lurched into stronger focus in my mind. He stood there, skinny, his ribs thrusting beneath his skin, dripping, dangling, armored in loony radiance. His dog's eyes filled with shining light. "I'll prove it to you, Miles. We can be brothers." He raised the switchblade like a scalpel and deliberately sliced his left palm. Then he dropped the blade and continued to hold his palm out toward me, inviting me to press mine against it. Alison screamed when she looked up at the sound of the knife clattering and saw blood dripping onto the flat rock.

"Miles!" she screeched. "Go to the truck! Get the bandages! Go!"

Zack's face did not alter by a millimeter: he was still encased in the armor of crazy light. "You did it," I said, still grasping the dimensions of what I had seen. "It's you."

"Miles," Alison sobbed, "run, run, please run."

Zack stood shining at me with dog's eyes and loose smile. To escape the light of the smile I ran around him, around the Tin Woodsman who was rushing toward Zack, and sprinted in bare feet and flapping towel up to the black van.

When I yanked down on the handle of the rear doors and pushed them open, something that had been wedged against one of them fell out into the dust. I looked down and saw a familiar shape just ceasing to roll. It was one of the old wide-hipped eight-ounce Coke bottles.

"What did you do that for?" she asked, still naked, the water dried by the sun from all but her darkened hair, as the paperback of *She* began to sink into the water of the quarry. I was conscious of Zack behind us, standing near his dropped knife on the hot stone, and I was aware of having too many reasons to be able to roll them up into a single answer. I was sending a chip of Alison into the place where she had died; I was furious with them both and with myself for not knowing how to reckon with what I suspected, the sight of the Coke bottle having brought back clearly what Polar Bears Hovre had told me; I was simply overcome with anger and disgust and throwing away something I valued was the simplest way to express that I had looked into the face of damnation. When I had crawled into the back of the van, I had seen, glittering amidst the rubble of spare parts, one of the thousand-faceted doorknobs I had removed from my desk.

"Get away from him," Zack said. "Ally, get your ass over here."

"Why?"

"Alison," I said softly, "Zack is in trouble. I think you should keep away from him."

"You don't understand him. Nobody does."

"Just take my advice," I said, "please," very aware in spite of everything of the Maillol-like body of the naked girl I was bending toward.

That night and the next I dreamed of being back in the drifting blue horror, suspended, dead, guilty beyond the possibility of help or forgiveness. It was the quarry, the deep pitiless water of the quarry, and it was where I had let her die, the greatest sin of my life, the one before which I had been most helpless, and the greatest crime I knew. The crime for which she could not forgive me. Even in sleep I believe I wept and ground my teeth. They had been up there, and I had not been able to send them away, those murderers of both her life and mine. It was a bottomless guilt. I would be freed of it only by her return. I had twice immersed myself in the cold water of the quarry, twice I had breathed it in, and both times I had emerged alive: that too was a crime, when she had not.

Sunday night I came miserably awake near two o'clock, smelled the air like a forest animal, and got downstairs in time to turn off the gas cocks on the stove. The recurrence seemed to prove that the cause was a simple mechanical failure, if one that could have had fatal results. What had awakened me, and therefore saved me, was the ringing of the telephone. I had once told Alison that if I got one of "those" calls at night, I would not answer it. But after twisting the handles on the stove and shoving open a window to admit the cool meadow air, I was in the perfect mood for handling Onion Breath. "Stinking skulking creeping weasel," I pronounced into the phone, "crawling cowardly weak crippled ugly snake." Incapable of syntax but with a good stock of adjectives, I went on until he (she) hung up. I could not then return to bed and that dominating nightmare. The kitchen was very cold; I waved newspapers to dispel the gas, and closed the window. After wrapping a blanket from the downstairs bedroom around my shoulders, I returned to the kitchen, lit a kerosene lamp and a cigarette, and combined some further elements of the Alison-environment, gin, vermouth, twist of lemon peel, ice. Her drink, with which I had been dosing myself nightly. Wrapped in the blanket, I sipped the martini and sat in one of the kitchen chairs near the telephone. I *wanted* another call.

Half an hour later, when the person might have judged me to have returned to sleep (I thought), the telephone rang again. I let it trill three, then four times, then twice more, hearing the noise of the bell spread through the cold farmhouse. Finally I raised my arm and detached the receiver and rose to speak into the horn. But instead of breathing I heard what I had heard once before, a whuffling, beating noise, inhuman, like wings thrashing in the air, and the receiver was as cold as the sweating glass of my martini and I was unable to utter a word, my tongue would not move. I dropped the icy receiver and wrapped the blanket tightly around myself and went upstairs to lie on the bed. The next night, as I have said, following the day which was the first turning point, I entered the same drifting guilt-ridden dream, but I had no anonymous calls, from either living or dead.

On the day—Monday—which marked my slide into knowledge and was the interregnum between these two awful nights, I came down from my work for lunch and asked a stony-faced Tuta Sunderson how to turn off the gas before it reached the stove. She became even more disapproving, and gruntingly bent over the range and pointed an obese finger down at the pipe descending from the wall. "It's on this pipe. What for?"

"So I can turn it off at night."

"Ain't fooling me," she muttered, or I thought she did, while she turned away to jam her hands into the pockets of her cardigan. More audibly, she said, "Made a big stir in church yesterday."

"I wasn't there to notice. I trust things went well without me." I bit into a hamburger and discovered that I had no appetite. My relationship with Tuta Sunderson had degenerated into a parody of my marriage.

"You afraid of what the pastor was saying?"

"As I recall he made a very sweet comment about my suit," I said.

As she began to lump herself toward the door, I said, "Wait. What do you know about a boy named Zack? He lives somewhere in Arden, I think. Tall and skinny, with an Elvis Presley hairdo. Alison's boyfriend. He calls her 'Ally.' "

"I don't know that boy. If you're going to waste good food, get out of the kitchen so I can do my work."

"Good God," I said, and left the table to stand on the porch. That cold breath of spirit which could only be felt on these twenty square yards was strongly present, and I knew with a certainty for once filled not with joy but resignation that Alison would appear on the date she had set twenty years before. Her release would be mine, I told myself. Only later did I recognize that when Tuta Sunderson said that she did not know that boy, she meant not that the boy was a stranger to her, but that she knew him well and detested him.

Yet if my release were to be total there were things I needed to know, and a series of bangs and clatters from the long aluminum rectangle of the pole barn suggested an opportunity for learning them. I left Tuta Sunderson's complaining voice behind me and stepped off the porch and began to walk through the sunshine toward the path.

The noises increased as I drew nearer, and eventually the sound of Duane grunting with effort joined them. I threaded through the litter of rusting parts and junked equipment at the pole barn's front end and walked onto the packed powdery brown dust which is the barn's only floor. Under the high tented metal roof, Duane was working in semidark, slamming a wrench on the base of a tractor's gearshift. His peaked cap had been thrown off earlier, and lay in the dust near his boots.

"Duane," I said.

He could not hear. The deafness may have been as much internal as caused by the terrific banging clatter he was making, for his face was set into that frustrated angry mask common to men who are singlemindedly, impatiently, making a botch of a job.

I said it again, and his head twisted toward me. As I stepped toward him, he turned his face away silently and went back to banging on the base of the gearshift.

"Duane, I have to talk to you."

"Get out of here. Just get the hell out." He still would not look at me. The hammering with the wrench became more frenzied.

I continued to come toward him. His arm was a blur, and the noise echoed against the metal walls. "God damn," he breathed after I had taken a half-dozen steps, "I got the son of a bitch off."

"What's wrong?" I asked.

"The goddamned gearbox, if you really wanna know," he said, scowling at me. His tan shirt was stained irregularly with perspiration and a black smear of grease bisected his forehead at the white line where his cap stuck. "It's jammed in first, and on these old M's you gotta go in from the top here and slide a couple of plates around to get the slots lined up, see, but what the hell am I talking about this with you for anyhow? You wouldn't know a gearbox if you saw it outside of Shakespeare."

"Probably not."

"Anyhow, on this one here, I have to take off the whole shift mechanism because everything's rusted shut, but in order to do that, you have to get the nuts off first, see?"

"I think so."

"And then I'll probably find out the battery's dead anyhow, and my jumper cables got burned to shit the last time I used them on the pickup and the plastic melted all over the terminals, so it probably won't work anyhow."

"But at least you got the nuts off."

"Yeah. So why don't you go break up some more furniture or something and leave me work?" He jumped up on the side of the tractor and began to twiddle the burring on the wrench down to the size of the nut.

"I have to talk with you about some things."

"We don't have anything to talk about. After that act of yours in church, nobody around here has anything to talk with you about." He glared down at me. "At least not for the present."

I stood and watched as he removed the troublesome nut, dropped it on a greasy sheet of newspaper by the tractor's rear wheels, and, grunting on the seat, lifted the shift levers and an attached plate up out of the body of the machine. Then he bent down and knelt before the seat. "Shit."

"What's wrong?"

"It's all grease in there, and I can't see the slots, that's what's wrong." His pudgy face revolved toward me again. "And after I fix this damn thing, the same thing will happen next week, and I'll have to do it all over again." He began to scrape oily sludge out with the point of a long screwdriver. "Shouldn't even be grease like that in here." He impatiently took a rag from the hip pocket of his coveralls and began to work it around in the hole he had opened up.

"I want to ask you about—" I was going to say, about Zack, but he interrupted me.

"Not what you said at the church. There's nothing to say about that."

"Alison Greening?"

His face hardened.

"You never slept with her, did you?" Looking at him kneeling like a squat filthy toad on the tractor, it seemed an impossibility. He began to scrub harder, his face frozen. "Did you?"

"Yeah. Okay." He plucked the rag out and threw it aside. "So what if I did? I didn't hurt anybody. Except myself, I guess. That little whore treated it like it was a new comic book or something. And she only did it once. Whenever I wanted to do it afterwards, she laughed at me." He looked at me, hard. "You were the golden boy, anyhow. What do you care? She made me feel like shit. She liked making me feel like shit."

"Then why did you name your daughter after her?"

He began to tug at something within the body of the tractor. He was trembling.

Of course. I had known it yesterday, when I had looked up at the dying bushes and seen a white shirt flitting in memory between them. "You followed us out to the quarry, didn't you? I know that that story about the driver hearing screams was a lie. I proved that you can't hear screams from up there down on the road."

His face, even the white parts, was turning red.

"So someone else was there, someone surprised us. It was you. Then you ran away and called the police when you knew she was dead."

"No. No." He slammed his fist into the tractor's seat, making a million small metal parts jangle. "God damn you, you had to come back here, didn't you? You and your stories."

"Twenty years ago, somebody told a story all right. And has been telling it ever since."

"Wait." He glared at me, his face still massively red. "Who told you about me and Alison, anyhow?" I did not speak, and saw comprehension battle fury in his face.

"You know who told me. The only person you told. Polar Bears."

"What else did Hovre say?"

"That you hated her. But I knew that. I just didn't understand the reason." Then he said too much. "Hovre talked about her?"

"Not really," I said. "He just let it slip that . . ." I looked at Duane's face, full of sly questions and frightened questions, and I understood. Understood at least part of it. I heard the cough from one side of the quarry's top, the whistle from the other.

"You try to go and prove anything," Duane said. "You can't prove a thing."

"Polar Bears was with you," I said, almost not believing it. "Both of you came to the quarry. And you both jumped us. You both wanted her. I can remember Polar Bears coming around day after day, staring at her . . ."

"I gotta fix my tractor. You get the hell out."

"And everybody up here thinks it was me. Even my wife thought it was me."

Duane stolidly replaced the gear levers and plate and started to tighten the nuts. He looked shaken, and he would not meet my eyes. "You better talk to Hovre," he said. "I ain't sayin' no more."

I felt, in the big dim dusty interior of the pole barn, as I had when the Woodsman and Zack had held me underwater, and I made it to an oil drum before my legs gave out. Duane was not bright enough to be a good liar, and his stolid stupid refusal to talk was as good as a confession. "Jesus," I breathed, and heard my voice tremble.

Duane had opened up the engine of the tractor; his back was to me. His ears flamed. As in the Plainview diner, I could sense violence gathering between us. At the same time, I was aware of the force with which sensory impressions were packing into my mind, and I clung to them for sanity: the big dim space open at either end, the thick powder of brown dust on the floor, fluffy and grainy at once, the litter of machinery lying around, discs and harrows and things I could not identify, most of it in need of paint, with rusty edges; in a corner, the high tractor; a sparrow darting through as I sat on the oil drum; my throat constricted and my hands shaking and my chest inflamed; the searing metal walls and high empty space above us, as though for a jury of observers; the man in front of me, hitting something deep inside the smaller tractor he was bent before, sweat darkening his shirt, dirt and grease all over his coveralls and the smell of gunpowder overtaking all other odors. The knowledge that I was looking at Alison's murderer.

"It's crazy," I said. "I didn't even come here to talk to you about this. Not really."

He dropped the wrench and leaned forward on the tractor's engine block, supporting himself with his arms.

"And it doesn't matter anymore," I said. "Soon it won't matter anymore at all."

He would not move.

"God, this is strange," I said. "I really came here to talk to you about Zack. When you brought up the other thing I thought I'd ask you about what Polar Bears said . . ." He pushed himself back from the tractor and for the space of a taut second I thought he would come for me. But he went to the side of the barn and returned with a hammer. And began to pound savagely, as if he did not care what he was battering or saw something besides the tractor beneath the hammer.

From down the path at my grandmother's house I faintly heard the screen door slam. Tuta Sunderson was going home.

Duane heard it too, and the sound seemed to release him. "All right, you son of a bitch, ask me about Zack. Hey? Ask me about him." He gave the tractor a thwacking, ringing blow with the hammer.

He turned to face me at last, his feet stirring up dust like smoke. His face was inflamed and explosive. "What do you want to know about that no-good bastard? He's as crazy as you are."

I heard the calls and whistles of that terrible night, saw the white shirt flitting behind the screen of bushes, heard the coughing of a boy hidden behind those bushes. As they watched with the hunger of twenty-year-old manhood the naked girl flashing like a star in the black water. The quick, quiet removal of clothes, the leap upon her and the boy. Then knocking him out before he even saw what had happened and hauling up his body onto the rock shelf before turning to the girl.

"Do you want to know what's funny about people like you, Miles?" Duane half-screamed. "You always think that what you want to talk about is important. You think that what you want to say is like some kind of goddamned present— huh?—to people like me. You think people like me are just goons, don't you, Miles?" He spat thickly into the dust and gave the tractor another ringing blow. "I hate you goddamned professors, Miles. You fucking writers. You people with your fifty-cent words and your 'What I wanted to say was really this, not this.'" He turned furiously away and reached inside the tractor to draw out a clamped pipe. This he rapped twice with the hammer, and I understood that something had broken off inside the clamp. He stamped, puffing up dust, his frustration growing. "I have half a dozen punches around here, and do you think I can find one of them?" Duane stamped over to the darkest section of the barn and rooted in a pile of loose equipment. "So you want to know about Zack, hey? What do you want to know about him? About the time he barricaded himself in his house and they had to go in with axes to get him out? That's when he was nine. About the time he beat up an old woman in Arden because she looked at him funny? That's when he was thirteen. About all the stealing he did, all along? Then there's the fires he used to go for, yeah, he went for 'em so much he sometimes didn't wait for other people to start 'em, and then there's—" He dipped forward suddenly, like a heron after a frog, and said, "God damn, I found one. Then there's Hitler, I thought we won that war and it was all over, but no, I guess if you're real smart, smarter than a dumb shitkicker

like me anyhow, you know Hitler was the good guy and he really won because
he provided this and that, I don't know. Understanding. Then there's the social
worker he had once, said because he didn't have a mother he grew up mean as
a snake—" Now he was approaching the tractor again, taking up the clamped
pipe—

—coughing, up behind the bushes, impatiently unbuttoning the white shirt
and unlacing his boots, hearing the signal of a whistle that now, in two minutes,
five minutes, they would jump on the girl and stop her contempt in the simplest
way they knew, hearing her voice saying *Do birds cough?*—

I heard him make a noise in his throat. The pounding stopped. The hammer
thudded to the ground, the pipe sprang back. Duane hopped away from the
tractor, gripping the wrist of his splayed left hand with his right, and moved
with surprising speed past me and out into the sun. I went after him; his body
seemed compressed, under a suddenly increased gravity. He was standing
spread-legged beside the rusted hooks and curls of metal, examining his hand,
turning it over. He had sliced the skin at the base of his thumb. "Not so bad,"
he said, and pressed the wound against his coveralls.

I did not know then why I chose that moment to say "Last night the gas
went on again," but now I see that his accident reminded me of mine.

"Everything's fouled up in that house," he said, holding his hand tightly
against the filthy coveralls. "I oughta tear it down."

"Someone told me it might be a warning."

He said, "You're liable to get all the warnings you can use," and stepped off
toward his house, having given me another as useless as the rest.

I went back to my grandmother's house and called the Arden police station.
What I wanted was not to accuse Polar Bears or to seek a futile revenge by
cursing at him, but simply to hear his voice again, with what I now knew or
thought I knew in my mind while I listened to it. I felt as bottomless as the
quarry was said to be, as directionless as still water, and I do not believe that
I felt any anger at all. I could remember Polar Bears striking his steering wheel,
enraged, saying, "Don't you know better than to use that Greening name?
That's what you don't want to remind people of, boy. I'm trying to keep all
that in the background." That was Larabee at work, keeping things out of
sight—he would say, using his Larabee-side as he had while defending it, for
my own good. But Hovre was not in his office, and Dave Lokken greeted me
with a cold reluctance which barely permitted him to say that he would tell
the chief that I had called.

Upstairs, my workroom looked very little as it had on the day I had set it
up. The books once piled on the floor were either given away or stacked in a
far corner to gather dust. The typewriter was in its case on the floor, and I had
thrown away all the typist's paraphernalia. I was writing my memoir in pencil,
being too clumsy a typist to be able to work at the speed required. All of the
thick folders of notes and drafts, along with my laboriously compiled packs of
file cards, I had burned a week and a half before. I read somewhere that birds

shit before they fly, and I was engaged in a parallel process, stripping myself down for takeoff, making myself lighter.

I often worked until I fell asleep at my desk. That was what I did Monday night, and I must have come awake about the time the men from Arden and the valley thrust their way into Roman Michalski's house and ruined Galen Hovre's plans by giving flesh to the rumors they had all heard. My eyes burned, and my stomach felt as though I had been swallowing cigars, a sensation precisely reproduced in my mouth. The room was icy, my fingers were cold and stiff. I stood up and turned to the window. I realized that Polar Bears had not called back. In half-light the mare tossed her head in the field. When I looked across the far fields I saw her again, standing in that vulpine way, not bothering with the shield of the trees, and staring directly at the house. I could not take my eyes from her, and stood in the blast of cold, feeling her energy come streaming toward me, and then I blinked and she was gone.

4

After the noise of Zack's receding motorcycle pulled me from the second night in a row of that dreadful dream, I lay in the gray light of early morning, experiencing what seemed an utter desolation. For the second time the thought of Alison Greening brought with it no current of joy and anticipation. The wrong things had happened; I was in the wrong room, the wrong place; I was the wrong man. It must be the way a young soldier feels when after he has enlisted out of a glorious mishmash of ideals, adventurousness and boredom, he finds himself cold, hungry, shouted at and on the verge of battle. I simply could not think of what to do. I had been going to tell Polar Bears what I knew about Zack—but did I really know it? (Yes. I did. Anyway, I thought I did.) But my relation to Polar Bears had irrevocably changed. I could remember all too clearly his telling me that rape was normal. Had he been telling himself for twenty years?

I saw that both Duane and Polar Bears must have hated my coming back to Arden. I was the last person they wanted to see again. Especially since I had begun speaking about Alison Greening almost from the moment I arrived in the valley.

And then I thought of the slight vulpine figure I had seen last night, leveling her face toward the farmhouse like a loaded gun, and thought too of the vision I'd had when the gas had almost killed me. And of the lights in my grandmother's house flashing on, all at once, making her place look like a boat floating out of its harbor. I was unforgiven.

I wondered how well I knew—had known—my cousin Alison. Again I saw that face of sewn leaves coming toward me, and I hurriedly left the bed, threw on my robe, and went downstairs.

I thought: now you are almost afraid of it.

And thought: no. You have always been afraid of it.

My bare feet were very cold.

When the telephone rang, I hesitated a moment before lifting the receiver from its hook. Polar Bears, up early from another sleepless night. *Do birds cough?*, that ardent high electric voice in my ears. But I smelled blubber, and knew that I did not yet have to solve the problem of what to say to Galen Hovre. She said, "Mr. Teagarden? Miles?"

"Present."

"I can't come to work today. I won't be there this morning. I'm sick."

"Well," I began, and realized that she had already hung up. Stupidly, I stared at the receiver, as if it could explain Tuta Sunderson's behavior.

The explanation came about an hour later, after I had dressed and was seated upstairs, trying to smother thought by the familiar tactic of concentration on work. I had succeeded in this often enough during my marriage. Intellectual labor is a common technique for the avoidance of thinking. Yet I had more problems fighting for mental space than Joan's infidelity with various Dribbles had given me, and I had written less than half a page of my record before I put my head down on the desk, my face damp with sweat and the desolation back in full strength. I groaned. The admission that I might—did—feel unease, disquiet, fear, all of those, at the enactment of the vow between my cousin and myself had opened up a vast psychic hole. I remembered Rinn's harsh words— I felt as though I were thrust back into the world of the "blue horror" dream, as though mere wakefulness could not separate me from it. I was still a guilt expert; that was a vocation which outlasted the academic.

Alison Greening *was* my life; her death had thrown me forever out of significance, out of happiness; but suppose Rinn was right, and that significance and happiness had been flawed and illusory from the beginning. Suppose that by returning to the valley I had brought death with me? Or if not death, its taint? The terror I had felt in the woods flicked at me again, and I pushed myself away from the desk and left the study. All the way down the stairs I felt pursued by that slight figure, that atom of the woods.

Downstairs, I was jerked back into the present. I knew why Tuta Sunderson had refused to come to work. They were there, out on the road, waiting like vultures.

Because that is what they resembled, vultures, sitting in their cars just past the walnut trees. I could not see their faces. They had switched off their motors. I imagined them assembling at the prearranged time, each pulling up on the road before the house, coming from all over Arden, all up and down the valley. Somehow, they had heard about Candace Michalski's disappearance. My throat dried. From where I was standing at the kitchen window I could see perhaps twenty of them, each alone in his car, all men.

At first, like a child, I thought of calling Rinn—of invoking that safety.

I swallowed, and went into the living room and opened the door to the porch. Now I could see them all. Their cars filled the road. Some of them must have gone down to Duane's driveway to turn around, because they were bunched in a thick pack, all facing the same way, three abreast in places where I could see only the tops of the farthest cars glinting light. From them rose wavy lines of heat. Menace came from them like a physical force. I stepped backwards into the dark of the room, and saw them still, framed in the doorway. The men in the cars visible to me sat twisted sideways on their seats, looking toward the porch.

One more impatient than the rest honked his horn.

And then I knew they would not leave their cars, for no one answered the single horn blast with his own: they were just going to sit out there.

I walked out onto the porch where I would be visible. Another car honked, one of those nearest the house. It was a signal: *he's out:* and I could see some of the hunched figures in the cars swing their heads sideways to stare at me.

I went back into the kitchen and dialed Polar Bears' office. A voice I recognized as Lokken's answered me.

"Hell no, he ain't in here. All hell's broke loose since last night. He's out with two of the others, lookin' for that girl."

"The news got out."

"It was that damn Red Sunderson did it, he and a lot of the boys called on the family last night, and now they got all stirred up, runnin' around and demandin' things and holy man, we been workin'—hey, who is this, anyways?"

"Get in touch with him fast and tell him to call Miles Teagarden. I've got some trouble here." And I know who did it, I said silently. "And I might have some information for him."

"What kind of information would that be, Teagarden?" I had ceased to be Mr. Teagarden.

"Ask him if a doorknob could have been used on those two girls," I said, and heard my heart thudding.

"Why, you lose a doorknob, Teagarden?" came Lokken's insufferable yokel's voice. "Whyn't you call up your friend Larabee and ask him to find it for you? You outta your skull or something. The chief ain't gonna do you no favors, Teagarden, don't you know that?"

"Just get him over here," I said.

Some of the men could see me telephoning, and I held the receiver for a few moments after Lokken hung up and stood directly in front of the window with the black cone of plastic to my ear. Two of the cars in front of the column came to life, and drove off after their drivers had tapped their horns. Two others crept up to take their places. I juggled the hook and then dialed Rinn's number. I could see the man nearest to me watching my arm move. He too tapped his horn and drove off in the direction of the highway. The front end of a blue pickup appeared in his space. Rinn's telephone trilled and trilled. I didn't know what I expected from her anyway. I hung up.

I heard cars gunning their engines and tires crunching the road. My throat felt looser. I took a cigarette from the pack in my shirt pocket and lit it with a kitchen match. Cars were still moving off and turning around out on the road, and as I exhaled I saw the blue truck move past the frame of the window, then two cars at once, tan and dark blue, then a gray car with spectacular dents in its side. For two or three minutes I waited and smoked, hearing them wrangle their way out, backing up onto the lawn, noisily bouncing on the drive to the garage, turning around.

When I thought they were all gone I saw the nose of a dark Ford pull into the frame of the window and stop.

I went out onto the porch. Three of them had stayed behind. When I pushed open the screen door, not really knowing what I intended to do, two of them left their cars. The third, whose pickup was nearest the drive, backed his truck around the last of the walnut trees and came about five yards up the drive. When he hopped out of the cab I saw that it was Hank Speltz, the boy from the garage. In front of the house, the lawn had been ripped into muddy tracks.

"Go on up that way, Hank, and we'll jump the ditch," called one of the two men out on the road. The boy began coming warily up the drive, his hands spread.

One of the men jumped the ditch and began coming through the line of walnut trees, the second following a little behind. They looked like the men I had seen outside the Angler's Bar, the men who had stoned me—big middle-aged roughs, with bellies hanging over their belts and plaid and tan shirts open past their breastbones. A circle of red just below the neck, and then the dead white skin usually covered by undershirts.

"Hovre is coming here," I called. "You'd better get out with the others."

A man I did not recognize called back, "Hovre ain't gonna be here in time to stop us doin' what we're gonna do."

"Where you got the Michalski girl?" shouted the man hanging back.

"I don't have her anywhere." I began to sidle toward the garage and the path to Duane's house. Hank Speltz, his face hanging openmouthed like a wrestler's, was coming up. I tossed the remaining two inches of cigarette onto the torn lawn, and went nearer the garage.

The man in the plaid shirt who had spoken first said, "Come at him slow," and Hank Speltz halved his pace, shuffling like a bear from side to side. "Get the hell on up here, Roy," he said. "Where you got her?"

"He's got her hid somewhere inside. I tol' you."

"I've never seen her." I kept moving to the side.

"He's going to that garage."

"Let him go. We'll get him there." He had a red hook-nosed face with deep lines, a bully's face—the face of the schoolyard terror who had never grown up. The two of them were coming at me slowly across the lawn. "Keep an eye on him in case he runs toward that Nash," shouted the man in the cap.

"Whose idea was this?" I called.

"Ours, smartass."

Then I was close enough to the garage and I hit the clip off the lock and opened the door. I looked at the curl of smoke coming from my cigarette and knew what I was going to try to do. "Go in there and we got you cornered," the leader crowed. Knowing that any sudden movement would make them rush me, I backed into the open garage and went into its gloom. The three ten-gallon gas cans were where I remembered them from the day I had broken open the sea chest. I picked one of them up: full. With my back to them, I bent down and screwed off the cap. When I emerged carrying the heavy can, one of them guffawed. "Gonna put gas in your car, Teagarden?"

Only the man in the plaid shirt saw what I was going to do. "*Shit*," he yelled, and began to run at me.

With as much force as I had, I threw the gas can toward the curl of smoke. I supposed that the odds were no worse than they were if I'd bet on a horse. Fluid began to spray out in wheels and loops.

For a moment we were all standing still, watching the gasoline come spraying out of the sailing can, but when the *crump* of the explosion came I was already running up the path toward Duane's house. I heard them shouting behind me. A bit of flying metal whizzed past my head. One of them was screaming.

I had just about time enough to get to the near side of Duane's house; when I glanced over my shoulder, I saw them coming through the fire, two of them. The man in the cap was rolling on the ground. Pieces of scattered fire dotted the lawn all the way to the row of walnut trees. Now they were stopping to kneel by the man in the cap.

If I had been right that Duane's basement was originally a root cellar like my grandparents', I would be able to get into it from the outside.

"Duane ain't gonna help you, you son of a bitch!" came a distorted, yelling voice.

I came running past the dogwood and sweet pea and onto Duane's lawn. "Cuz he's gone!"

I don't know what I was picturing: hiding down there, finding a burrow, defending it with an ax. As I raced across the short lawn I saw that I had been right. The white-painted boards of the entrance cover—the old access to the cellar—extended from the base of the house, just visible around the corner on the side facing the road. I came skidding around the corner and the door I yanked on swung easily upwards.

I fell down the earthen steps and rolled beneath the hanging axes. Then I remembered. The far wall, where my desk had been, in cases like mummies. I scrambled up from my knees and ran, crouching, over to the shotguns.

I took one up case and all and dipped my hand into the box of shells and ran back to the earthen steps. Like moving up from water into light, going back toward the slanting rectangle of blue air and sunlight.

I had the twelve-gauge out of the case as the men and Hank Speltz came running around the corner of dogwood and sweet pea. I broke the gun and slotted two shells into the barrels. "Stop right there," I said, and raised the gun and pointed it at the chest of the man in the plaid shirt. Then I rose up from my belly on the earthen steps and came out of the cellar. My breathing was so harsh that I could scarcely form words. They dropped their arms and stood momentarily still, shock and anger in their faces.

"Now get the hell out of here," I said.

They were beginning to circle. They were as wary as beasts.

"I've never seen that girl," I said. "I've never seen any of them. I only knew about the Michalski girl because Polar Bears told me she was missing." Put the gun against my shoulder, pointed it at the opening in the plaid shirt. Expected the recoil. "Get together and stay together. Stop moving around like that."

They obeyed. I could see the man in the cap limping up behind them, his hands in the air. His tan workshirt was flecked with black, blood leaking through some of the holes. His hands were blackened too. He stood by the dogwood with his hands up. "Walk backwards," I said. "All the way to your cars."

Hank Speltz took a step backwards into the dogwood, looked around wildly, and then began to edge around to the path. The others moved with him, following me with their eyes.

"If you're so innocent, how come you stuck around up here?" asked the man in the plaid shirt.

I gestured with the shotgun.

"Screwing that old crazy woman up in the woods," said Hank Speltz. "That's how come. And what about Gwen Olson and Jenny Strand?"

"You're asking the wrong man," I said. "Now I want you to start moving backwards toward the cars."

When they did not move I shifted the barrels to the right, flicked the safety, and pulled one of the triggers. The recoil nearly jerked the shotgun from my hands. The sound was louder than the explosion of the gas can. All of them moved smartly away from the dogwood. I saw that I had shredded the leaves and ruined the blossoms, leaving broken twigs and the smell of powder hanging. "You damn near killed Roy back there," said the one in the plaid shirt.

"What was he going to do to me? Move." I raised the barrels, and they began to step backwards down the path.

Over their shoulders I could see the mess of the long front lawn. A ragged, irregular black circle ten yards from the drive showed where the ten-gallon can had exploded. Smaller burned patches, a greasy yellow in color, were dotted all over the lawn, churned and rutted by their tires. A large hole had been blown in the mesh of the porch screen. The animals had disappeared down into the far end of the side field.

"We ain't through yet," said the man whose name I did not know.

"Hank, get in your pickup and drive out," I said. "I'll be coming in to pick up my car soon, and I don't expect any trouble."

"No," he said, and sprinted toward the truck in the driveway.

All three of us watched him roar away scattering dirt as he turned onto the valley road.

"Now you, Roy." The man in the cap looked at me glumly, lowered his hands, and walked heavily over the lawn to pass between the walnut trees. He stopped to stamp out the small flames licking up at the base of one of the trees.

"Now it's your turn," I said to the remaining man.

"Whyn't you just kill us?" he asked belligerently. "You like killin'. We all know about you. You got sumpun wrong in your head."

I said, "If you don't get out of here right now, you won't believe what's happening to you. You'll probably live for a minute or two, but you'll be glad to die when they're over." I cradled the gun in my arms and leveled it at his belt. And then I did an astounding thing—a thing that astounded me. I laughed. Self-disgust hit me with such force that I feared for a moment that I would vomit.

Portion of Statement by Hank Speltz:

July 15

I was standin' there watchin' Miles and I says to myself, boy, if you ever get outta this I promise I'll go to church every Sunday, I'll pray every night, I'll never say another dirty word, I'll be good forever, because you never seen anything like the way that Miles looked, crazy enough to chew glass, eat gunpowder, that's how he looked. His eyes they was just slits. His hair was flyin' all directions. When he let go with one of those barrels, I thought, uh-oh, the next one's for me. Because he knew me from the filling station. I didn't even wanna be there in the first place, I just went because Red Sunderson said, he said we'll all park in front of his place and scare hell out of old Miles. And we'll break him down for sure. He's got that girl put away somewhere. So I said, count me in. Then when the other ones all pulled out, I saw Roy and Don were stayin', so I thought I'd stick around for the fun.

He was a trapped rat. Like something mean backed up into a corner. Man. He blew shit out of everything with that gas can—he didn't care what happened. He coulda killed himself too!

So when he let me go I just took off, yessir, right off, and I figured, let someone else find that girl. But I did a little something extra to that beat-to-shit VW of his after I got to town. I fixed it real good. I fixed it so's he couldn't go but thirty-forty miles an hour, and wouldn't run very long at any one time too. One thing I am's a good mechanic.

But I knew that crazy sonofabitch done it. And if you ask me, he was askin' to get caught. Else why would he put that name Greening on the repair slip? Answer me that.

A screaming voice: "Miles, you bastard! You bastard!": Duane.

"Calm down." Another voice, deeper, lower.

"Get the shit out here! Now!"

"Just simmer down, Duane. He'll come."

"God damn you! God damn you! You crazy?"

I cautiously open the door and see that Duane in fury appears to be reduced in size, a small square jigging knot of red-faced anger. "I told you, goddammit! I said, stay the hell away from my girl! And second, what the hell is all this?" He whirls around, his rage giving him agility, and the gesture of his arms encompasses, as well as the greasy yellowish and black burns on the ripped lawn and the marks of the explosion—the gaping hole in the screen, twisted pieces of the gas can—the figure of Polar Bears in uniform behind him, and

Alison Updahl hurrying up the path toward her home. She glances over her shoulder, nearly there already, sending me a look, half fear, half warning.

"Just sitting in their cars, goddammit—just sitting out there—no goddamn trouble—and what the hell did you do? Make a goddamn bomb? Look at my lawn!" He stomps heavily, too furious to speak any longer.

"I tried to call you," I say to Polar Bears.

"You're lucky I don't kill you now!" Duane screams.

"I'm lucky they didn't kill me then."

Polar Bears firmly positions one hand on Duane's shoulder. "Hold your horses," he says. "Dave Lokken told me you called up. I didn't expect there'd be any trouble, Miles. I figured you could take a bunch of our country boys starin' at you from the road."

"Sittin' there—just sittin' there," Duane says, quietly now that Polar Bears is gripping his shoulder.

"I didn't think you'd declare war on 'em."

"I didn't think you'd go crawlin' around after my girl either," Duane hisses, and I see Polar Bears' fingers tighten. "I warned you. I told you, stay off. You're gonna get it—for sure."

"They didn't just sit there. Most of them left when they saw me dialing the telephone, but three of them decided to come for me."

"See who they were this time, Miles?"

"That boy from the garage, Hank Speltz, a man named Roy, and one I didn't know. One of those who threw stones at me in Arden."

"Stones . . . stones," hisses Duane, his contempt so great that it is almost despair.

"How d'ya manage all this?" He lifts his chin toward the lawn where tire tracks and brown muddy ruts loop crazily.

"They did most of it themselves. They drove all over it. I guess they were in a hurry to get out before you showed up. The rest I did. I flipped an open gas can from the garage on top of a burning cigarette. I didn't even think it would work. You knew they were going to be here, didn't you?"

"You got me again. Sure I knew. I figured they'd just help keep you—"

"Out of trouble. Like Paul Kant."

"Yeah." His smile almost expresses pride in me.

"You and Duane were together? With Alison?"

"Keep her name out of your mouth, damn you," Duane says.

"Just having a beer in the Bowl-A-Rama."

"Just having a beer. Not working on your story."

"Even a cop doesn't work all the time, Miles," he says, and I think: no. You do work all the time, and that's why you are dangerous. He takes his paw off Duane's arm and shrugs his shoulders. "I wanted to explain to Du-ane here that you and me are sort of helpin' each other out on these killings. That's a big plus for you, Miles. You shouldn't want to take that plus away from yourself. Now I hear you been talking to Du-ane about some crazy idea you got. You been talking about just the exact thing I told you not to talk about, Miles. Now that kinda makes me question your judgment. I just wanta be sure you've seen the error in your thinking. Old Duane here didn't tell you you was right, did he? When you hit him with this crazy idea?" He looks at me, his face open and companionable. "Did you, Duane?"

"I said he should talk to you."

"Well, you see, you got him all suspicious and worked up."

"I knew it out at the quarry, really. I had the girl shout. You couldn't hear her on the road."

Duane stamps in a furious muttering half-circle. "Undressed. You were undressed."

"Hold on, Duane, you'll make it worse. Old Miles will just go on drawing the wrong conclusions if you get sidetracked. Now, Miles, Duane says he never said you was right in your ideas. Now let's ask him. Were you out there that night?"

Duane shakes his head, looking angrily at the ground.

"Of course you weren't. It's all in the records my father made. You went out on 93 and turned the other way, toward Liberty. Right?"

Duane nods.

"You were mad at that little Greening girl, and you just wanted to get the hell away from her. Right? Sure," as Duane nods again. "See, Miles, if you just tell a girl to yell without her knowing anything about why, she's not liable to really give her best, like a girl would if she's bein' attacked. You see the error there? Now, I don't want you to go on talking about this, because you'll just dig yourself into a deep hole, Miles."

There is no point in prolonging this charade. "That little Greening girl," the figure of lean intensity I have seen leveling her muzzle toward the house? That little Greening girl, the fire in the woods and the blast of freezing wind? I can smell cold water about me.

I think that which I do not wish to think; and remember Rinn's words. My guilt drowns me.

Duane, for different reasons, also does not wish to continue. "To hell with this," he says. Then he straightens up and his pudgy red-and-white face flames at me. "But I warned you about seeing my daughter again."

"She asked me to come with her."

"Did she? Did she? That's what you say. I suppose you say you didn't take off your clothes in front of her."

"It was just for swimming. She took hers off first. The boy undressed too."

In front of Duane, I cannot tell Polar Bears my fears about Zack. I have already said too much, for Duane looks ready to flail out again.

I am trembling. I feel cold wind.

"Yeah, okay," Duane says. "Sure. Whatever you say." He turns his upper body toward me. "If you fool around with her, Miles, I won't wait for anyone else to get you. I'll get you myself." Yet there is no real conviction in this threat, he does not care enough; treachery is what he expects from women.

Polar Bears and I watch him tramping up the path. Then he turns to me.

"Say, you look kind of peaked, Miles. Must be all that skinny-dipping you do."

"Which one of you raped her?"

"Hold on."

"Or did you take turns?"

"I'm beginning to question your judgment again, Miles."

"I'm beginning to question everything."

"You heard me mention that hole you could be digging for yourself?" Polar Bears steps toward me, big and solid and full of serious concern, and I see dark blue blotches of perspiration on his uniform shirt, dark blue smudges beneath his eyes. "Jesus, boy, you gotta be crazy, throwing bombs at the citizens here, gettin' yourself in trouble . . ." He is moving with cautious, wary slowness and I think *this is it: he's going to break, he's going to fight me.* But he stops and rubs a hand over his face. "Pretty soon this is all gonna be over, Miles. Pretty soon." He steps back, and the sour combination of sweat and gunpowder engulfing me like smoke recedes with him. "Miles. Jesus Christ. What was that you were telling Dave Lokken about something like a doorknob?"

I cannot answer.

That night and every night afterward I turned off the gas where Tuta Sunderson had shown me. In the mornings, when she heaved herself into the kitchen and began to cough and stamp her feet and shuffle around and clear her throat and produce the entire array of noises expressive of sullen discontent with which I had become familiar, among them was always the sharp grunt of suspicious disapproval—and contempt?—that accompanied her discovery that I had done so. I would have fired her but for my certainty that, like Bartleby, she would have come anyhow. The day after the visitation by Hank Speltz and the others, I heard the coughing, feet-stamping, etc., and went downstairs to ask her if she had known what was going to happen. Foolish me. "Did I know what? What was going to happen? So what happened?" She had made no comment on the condition of the lawn or the hole in the porch screen. I told her that I imagined her son had been involved. "Red? Red doesn't get messed up in anything. Now how many eggs do you want to throw away today?"

For days I did nothing but work; and I worked undisturbed, for it seemed that no one would talk to me. Apart from her morning demonstrations of how much noise she could produce, Tuta Sunderson was silent; Duane kept away, even turning his head so he would not have to look at me on the infrequent times he passed the old farmhouse. His daughter, presumably beaten or warned off in a less physical manner, also avoided me. Sometimes, from my bedroom window I could see her crisscrossing the path to go to the equipment barn or the granary, her body looking rushed and inexpressive, but she never appeared downstairs in the kitchen or on the porch, chewing something from my larder. At night, I was often awakened from dozing at my desk, the martini glass beside me and the pencil still in my hand, by the sound of Zack's motorcycle cutting off when it came parallel to me. I wrote. I dozed. I drank. I accumulated guilt. I hoped that soon the Michalskis would get a postcard from their vanished daughter. I hoped that Polar Bears was right, and that it would soon be over. I often wanted to leave.

At night, I experienced fear.

Rinn had given up answering her telephone, and I kept telling myself that I would visit her tomorrow. But that too I feared. The anonymous calls ceased, both from Onion Breath and from the—whatever the other thing was. Perhaps there was a fault in the old telephone.

I received no more blank letters, and only one more bit of fan mail. It was printed on lined paper with torn perforations along one side, and it read WE'LL GET YOU KILLER. I put it in an envelope and mailed it with a note to Polar Bears.

It seemed to me that I had died.

Many times, I thought: you were wrong, back at the quarry. That he had Coke bottles in his truck is no proof; the doorknob taken from wherever I had put it is no proof. And then I thought of him slicing open his hand.

I said: it is not your problem. And then thought of his dedicating a record "to the lost ones."

And thought of Alison Greening coming toward me, a creature of sewn leaves and bark. But the thoughts which followed this could not be true.

It was impossible to talk with Polar Bears. He did not respond to my note or to the printed threat.

When the telephone finally rang on a Monday afternoon, I thought it would be Hovre, but when I was greeted by another voice pronouncing my name, I thought of a bent hungry man with tight curling black hair and aging face. "Miles," he said. "You told me to call you if I ever wanted help." His voice was dry and papery.

"Yes."

"I have to get out of here. I'm out of food. I lied to you that day—I said I went out, but I hadn't in a long time."

"I know."

"Who told you?" Fear made his voice trill.

"It doesn't matter."

"No. No, it probably doesn't. But I can't stay in town anymore. I think they're going to do something. Now even more of them are watching my house, and sometimes I see them talking, planning. I think they're planning to break in. I'm afraid they'll kill me. And I haven't had anything to eat for two days. If—if I can get away can I come there?"

"Of course. You can stay here. I can get a gun."

"They all have guns, guns are no use . . . I just have to get away from them." During the pauses I could hear him gasping.

"Your car doesn't work. How can you get here?"

"I'll walk. I'll hide in the ditches or the fields if I see anyone. Tonight."

"It's ten miles!"

"It's the only way I can do it." Then, with that ghastly wanness, that dead humor in his voice, "I don't think anyone will give me a ride."

About nine-thirty, when the light began to fail, I started to expect him, though I knew that he could not possibly arrive for many hours. I walked around the old house, peering from the upstairs windows for the sight of him working his way across the fields. At ten, when it was fully dark, I turned on only one light—in my study—so that he would not be seen crossing the lawn. Then I sat on the porch swing and waited.

It took him four hours. At two o'clock I heard something rustle in the ditch behind the walnut trees, and my head jerked up and I saw him moving across the ripped lawn. "I'm on the porch," I whispered, and opened the door for him.

Even in the darkness. I could see that he was exhausted. "Stay away from the windows," I said, and led him into the kitchen. I turned on the light. He was slumped at the table, panting, his clothing covered with smears of dirt and bits of adhering straw. "Did anyone see you?" He shook his head. "Let me get you some food." "Please," he whispered.

While I fried bacon and eggs, he stayed in that beaten position, his eyes fluttering, his back bent and his knees splayed out. I gave him a glass of water. "My feet hurt so much," he said. "And my side. I fell into a rock."

"Did anyone see you leave?"

"I wouldn't be here if they did."

I let him recover while the eggs fried.

"Do you have any cigarettes? I ran out six days ago."

I tossed him my pack. "Jesus, Miles . . ." he said, and could go no further. "Jesus . . ."

"Save it," I said. "Your food's about ready. Eat some bread in the meantime." He had been too tired to notice the loaf set squarely in the middle of the table. "Jesus . . ." he repeated, and began to tear at the loaf. When I put the food down before him, he ate greedily, silently, like an escaped convict.

When he had finished I turned off the light and we went into the living room and felt our way to chairs. I could see the tip of his cigarette burning in the dark room, tilting back and forth as he moved in the rocker. "Do you have anything to drink? Excuse me, Miles. You're saving my life." I think he began to cry, and I was glad the lights were off. I went back to the kitchen and returned with a bottle and two glasses.

"That's good," he said when he had taken his. "What is it?"

"Gin."

"I never had it before. My mother wouldn't let alcohol in the house, and I never wanted to go to the bars. We never had anything stronger than beer. And that was only once or twice. She died of lung cancer. She was a chain smoker. Like me."

"I'm sorry."

"It was a long time ago."

"What are you going to do now, Paul?"

"I don't know. Go somewhere. Hide. Try to get to a city somewhere. Come back when it's over." Cigarette glowing with his inhalations, dipping forward and back as he rocked. "There was another one, another girl. She disappeared."

"I know."

"That's why they were going to come for me. She's been missing more than a week. I heard about it on the radio."

"Michael Moose."

"That's it." He gave a crackly humorless laugh. "You probably don't know Michael Moose. He's about three hundred and fifty pounds and he chews peppermints. He's grotesque. He's got flat slicked-down hair and pig's eyes and a little mustache like Oliver Hardy's. He's right out of *Babbitt*. He imitates Walter Cronkite's voice, and he'd never get a job anywhere but Arden, and kids laugh at him on the street, but he's better than I am. To Arden. They think he's funny-looking, and they make jokes about him, but they respect him too. Maybe that's too strong. What it is, they take him as one of them. And do you know why that is?"

"Why?"

His voice was flat and bitter. "Because when he was growing up they knew he went out on dates, they know the girls, and because he got married. Because they know, or say, that he's got a woman over in Blundell who's a telephone operator. Red hair." The cigarette waved in the air, and I could dimly see Paul Kant raising the glass of gin to his lips. "That's it. He's one of them. You know what my crime is?" I held my breath. "I never had a date. I never had a girl. I never told a dirty joke. I never even had a dead girl, like you, Miles. So they thought I was—what they thought. Different. Not like them. Like something bad they knew about."

We sat there in silence for a long time, each of us only a vague form to the other. "It didn't start that way, you know. It didn't matter that I was less, shall we say robust, when we were all little kids. In grade school. Grade school was paradise—when I think about it, it was paradise. It got bad only in high school. I wasn't *cute*. I wasn't like Polar Bears. No athlete. I didn't chase the girls. So they started to talk about me. I noticed that people didn't want me around their kids about the time I had to leave school." He bent, and felt for something on the floor. "Would you mind if I had another drink?"

"It's right on the floor beside your chair."

"So now when this admirable character goes around ripping up little girls, they assume it's me. Oh yes, Paul Kant. He's never been quite right, has he? A momma's boy. Not quite normal, in a society that makes being normal the most virtuous quality of them all. And then there was another thing—some trouble I had. Stupid scum. They put me in a police station. They hit me. For doing nothing. Did they tell you about that?"

"No," I lied. "Not a word."

"I had to go to a hospital. Seven months. Little pills every day. For doing nothing. Stares when I got out. Only job I could get at Zumgo's. With those leering women. Jesus. Do you know how I got here tonight? Had to sneak out of my own house. Wind through the streets like a dog. Know about my dog, Miles? They killed him. One of them. He came up at night and strangled my dog. I could hear him crying. The dog." I could imagine the little monkey face contorting. The smell of gin and cigarettes drifted through the dark room. "Jesus." I thought he might have been crying again.

Then: "So what do you say, Miles Teagarden? Or do you just sit and listen? What do you say?"

I said, "I don't know."

"You were rich. You could come here in the summers and then go back to one of your private schools and then go to some expensive university and smoke pipes and join a fraternity and get married and get a Ph.D. and live in apartments in New York and go to Europe and wreck cars and buy Brooks Brothers suits and, I don't know, do whatever you do. Teach English in a college. I'm going to have some more of your gin." He bent, and I heard the bottle clinking against the glass. "Oh. I spilled some."

"It doesn't matter," I said.

"It wouldn't to you, would it? I'm getting drunk. Is it you, Miles? Is it you? Come on."

"Is what me?" But I knew.

"Are you the admirable character? Did you take time off from your *Atlantic Monthly* life to come out here and rip up a few little girls?"

"No."

"Well, it's not me either. So who is it?"

I looked down at the floor. Before I had decided to tell him about Zack, he was speaking again.

"No, it's not me."

"I know that," I said. "I think—"

"It's not me, no way is it me. They just want it to be me. Or you. But I don't know about you. Still, you're being nice to me, aren't you, Miles? Being so nice. Probably never had someone strangle your dog. Or do people like you have dogs? Borzois, wolfhounds. Or a cute little cheetah on a leash."

"Paul, I'm trying to help you," I said. "You have a ludicrous misconception of my life."

"Oops, sorry, oops, mustn't be offensive. Just a poor country boy, I know. Poor dumb pitiable country schmuck. I'll tell you why no way it's me. This is it, boy. I'd never go after a girl. That's why. You hear what I'm saying?"

I did, and hoped he would not torture himself by going further.

"You heard that?"

"I heard."

"You understand?"

"Yes."

"Yes. Because I'd do it to boys, not girls. Isn't that funny? That's why it isn't me. That's what I've always wanted, but I never did that either. Never even touched one. I wouldn't hurt any of them, though. Never hurt them."

He sat there, slumped in the rocking chair, the cigarette glowing in his mouth. "Miles?"

"Yes."

"Leave me alone."

"Is it important to you to be alone now?"

"Get the hell out of here, Miles." He was crying again.

Instead of leaving the room, I got up and walked past his chair and looked through the window facing the porch and the road. I could see nothing but the darker square mass of my own face reflected in the glass and the torn meshes of the screen beyond it. Beyond that, everything was black. His mouth made noises on his glass. "Okay," I said, "I'll leave you alone, Paul. I'll be back though."

I went upstairs in the dark and sat at my desk. It was three-fifteen. There was the morning to worry about. If the men from Arden broke into Paul's house and found that he had gone, the news, I was certain, would reach Polar Bears almost immediately. And if they were going to break into his house, it could only mean that they had been persuaded somehow that he and not I was responsible for the girls' deaths. But then they might think of looking for Paul at my house—and I could see nothing but disaster for both of us if a gang of Arden hooligans stormed into the house and found the two of us. A shotgun from Duane's basement would not rescue me again. I heard the sound of a car starting up outside, and I jumped. It faded.

Fifteen minutes passed. Time enough, I thought, for Paul to have recovered. I stood up, and recognized how weary I was.

I came down the stairs into the dark room. I saw the tip of a cigarette glowing at the edge of the ashtray. The odors of gin and smoke seemed very thick in the air of the cold small room. "Paul?" I said, going toward the rocking chair. "Paul, let me get you a blanket. I have a plan for tomorrow."

And then I stopped. I could see the top of the rocker against the window, and it was unbroken by the silhouette of his head. The rocker was empty. He was no longer in the room.

Immediately I knew what had happened, but I switched on one of the lights anyway, and confirmed it. The glass and three-fourths empty bottle sat on the floor beside his chair, the cigarette had burned nearly to the rim of the ashtray. I went into the kitchen, and then opened the door to the bathroom. He had left the house shortly after I had gone upstairs. I swore out loud, half in anger at myself for leaving him, half in despair.

I went through the porch and out onto the lawn. He could not have gone far. And I remembered the sound of the car that I thought I'd heard upstairs, and began to run across the lawn.

When I got to the road, I turned right by reflex and pounded down toward the Sunderson farm, in the direction of Arden, for perhaps forty seconds. But he could have gone the other way, deeper into the valley—I didn't even know what lay in that direction; and I recognized that he could also have gone into the fields, as he had done on the way from Arden earlier that night. I thought of him hiding behind a building or crouching in a field, riven by fear and self-loathing, and told myself that he had nowhere, really nowhere to go. He would come back before daylight.

I turned around on the dark road and began to trudge home. When I reached the drive to my grandmother's house I hesitated, and then walked a bit further up the road in that direction. It was hopeless. I could see nothing. I could find him only if he allowed me to. I turned back and went up the drive and sat on the porch swing to wait. An hour, I told myself: it won't be as much as an hour. I would sit and wait. As tired as I was, it was unthinkable that I could fall asleep.

But an hour later I was jerked awake by a sound I could not at first identify. A high agitated wailing, the sound of mechanical fury, mechanical panic, it came from somewhere off to my right, but was loud and near enough to distort my sense of place: for a moment I thought I was in New York, awake before dawn in New York. It was a New York sound, and as I gradually located my surroundings I located the sound too. It was the siren of a fire engine.

I found that I was standing up on the porch in the gray light of very early dawn, listening to a fire engine. Fog lay across the fields, and carpeted the valley road. As I listened, trying to position the sound of the fire bell, it abruptly cut off. I wheeled around and banged open the door to the living room. Bottle and glass on the floor, dead cigarette on the rim of the ashtray. Paul Kant was still gone.

Numbly, knowing that I had to hurry, I stepped down the porch's single step. Fog lay in the ruts on the lawn and concealed its burned patches. I went stumbling toward the drive, completely forgetting the car I must have walked right past, and went out onto the road. Then I began to run. Just visible down the road, in the direction of the highway, red suffused the dark gray air.

By the time I reached the Sunderson house I had to stop running, and I walked as quickly as I could without increasing the pain in my chest until I reached the shell of the schoolhouse; then I jogged as far as the church. The red sandstone bluff hid the redness of the sky. *Andy's*, I thought, and forced myself to run again. I heard men moving, machinery working. When I came around the sharp corner of the bluff I began to run harder. The fire engine was drawn up into the parking lot beside Andy's and a police car had pulled in slightly ahead of it, to the side of the gas pumps. I heard fire, that terrible raging noise of devouring. But it was not Andy's that was burning. I could see the flames jumping behind the high white front of the general store.

I thought, remembering: it might have been a motorcycle I heard, not a car. I had been too groggy to tell the difference.

I rushed past the front of Andy's and around the side.

At first I saw only the blazing facade of the Dream House, rushing into extinction as Duane must so often have wished it to do. It looked transparent, skeletal. The frames of the doors and windows hung darkly, like bones suspended in the red-orange flames. Three firemen in rubber boots and iron hats played a useless hose on the blaze. Steam rose with the smoke. Then I saw Polar Bears calmly watching me from beside the fire truck; he was out of uniform, dressed in a shapeless sports jacket and brown trousers, and I could tell by looking at him that he had not been to bed. His insomnia had kept him up, working at his bottle of Wild Turkey until the call from the fire department had come. It was still dark enough for the flames to redden the ground and the sky and the back of Andy's store, and as I walked nearer, I felt the heat. Dave Lokken, in uniform, stood talking to Andy and his wife, both wearing bathrobes and shocked unmoving faces, directly at the back of the store. The fire stained their faces peach. All three noticed me at the same time and stared at me as if I were a ghoul.

Polar Bears motioned me to him. I kept watching the fire; the first boards collapsed inward, sending up a huge shower of sparks.

"Fire bells wake you up?" he asked.

I nodded.

"You got here in a hell of a hurry. Sleeping in your clothes?"

"I wasn't in bed."

"Me neither," he said, and gave me one of his sad paternal smiles. "Care to hear the story? I'll have to tell you anyhow. You'll be interested."

I was looking dumbly at a mess of gray army blankets thrown in a heap halfway between the burning Dream House and the back of Andy's, and I nodded.

"Of course these boys aren't really going to do anything with that hose," he said, "but they might keep the flames from jumping to Andy Kastad's store. That'll be the best they could do. The call came too late for them to save that little abortion of Du-ane's, but I reckon nobody'll be too sorry to see that go, least of all Du-ane. It should of been pulled down long before this. What happened was, Andy and his wife woke up in time to save themselves—claim they heard a noise and *then* they heard the fire. Both jumped out of bed. They look through the window. Get the scare of their lives."

I glanced back at Andy and his wife, and thought it was probably true.

"So old Margaret calls the volunteers while Andy runs out the back to do something—he doesn't know what. Piss on it, maybe. And he sees something. Can you guess what?"

"No." Polar Bears was using his favorite trick of building up suspense.

"No. No indeed. Say, by the way, Miles, I don't suppose you happened to see your friend Paul Kant tonight?" His head was cocked, his eyebrows raised, his manner entirely unembarrassed by the digression. Another favorite trick.

"No."

"Uh-huh. Real good. Anyhow, like I was saying, Andy comes boiling out of his back door, all set to pour beer or something all over the fire, and he sees this object in the doorway of the house. Now he's like you. He can't guess what it is either. But he thinks he'd better have a closer look. So he runs up, takes a grab and pulls it away. Half of it's on fire. And when he sees it good and plain, he runs back inside and calls me up too, only Dave and I are already rarin' out here."

"What's the point of all this folksy crap, Polar Bears?" The heat of the fire seemed to be intensifying, grilling the side of my face.

"I thought you mighta guessed." He put a big hand on my bicep and began to lead me toward the store. "The point is that you got nothing more to worry about, Miles. Everything's over. I picked the wrong horse, but you're out in the free and clear as of this moment. It's like I told you. I missed him, but he missed me too."

I stopped and looked up into his massive face and saw, operating far beneath the confidential tone and manner, bafflement and anger. He jerked me forward, commanding me to join his charade. I stumbled, and he gripped my arm more tightly. "We're at the sixteenth of July, old buddy, so if you got nothing holding you here after the twenty-first, I guess you'll be leaving us. That's less than a week. Long enough to keep your mouth shut, I guess."

"Polar Bears," I said, "I don't know what you're talking about, but I think I know who you're looking for."

"Who I was looking for," he said.

We were nearly at the heap of blankets, and I was aware of Lokken shooing Andy and Margaret Kastad away. They bustled off somewhere behind me, seemingly glad to leave.

"That was a man he found in there," Polar Bears said, and bent over like a man about to pick a coin off the sidewalk.

"A man?"

Wordlessly Polar Bears folded back the edge of the blanket.

I was looking at his face. Part of his hair was burned away and his cheek was bloody. His eyes were still open. I felt my knees try to vanish, and I remained standing up only by great effort. Polar Bears touched me across the line of my shoulder blades and I again felt his suppressed anger. It came out of him like the touch of a branding iron. I heard him say, "That's your ticket out of here, Miles," and glanced at his fire-reddened features and then back at Paul's body.

"What's that on the side of his head?" I asked, and heard my voice tremble. "It looks like he was clubbed."

"Falling board."

"They didn't start to fall until I got here."

"Then he fell down."

I turned away.

"One more thing, Miles," said Polar Bears beside me. He bent over again, flipped back the edge of blanket, straightened up, and used his foot to kick over another section of gray wool. "Look. Something else Andy pulled out." He took my arm and revolved me like a toy. It took me a moment to recognize what lay exposed beside the kicked-back gray blanket, because the metal had been blackened by the fire. It was the second ten-gallon gas can from the garage beside the farmhouse.

"How he started the fire," said Polar Bears. "Plain as day."

"What is? That gas can's from my home."

"Sure it is. He snuck out, stole that can of gas, came back here, spilled it around and set it alight. He might as well have confessed. He couldn't take it anymore."

"No, no, no," I said, "Polar Bears, he *was* at my place earlier. He was trying to escape before that gang of thugs beat him up or killed him. He wasn't guilty, he didn't have anything to confess."

"Give it up, Miles," Hovre said. "You already told me you hadn't seen him. It's too late to lie about it."

"I'm not lying now."

"You were before, but you're not now." His voice was toneless and disbelieving.

"He left my house a little after three. Somebody must have been following him all the time. Somebody killed him. That's what he was afraid of. That's why he ran. I even heard the car." My voice was rising.

Polar Bears scuffled a few paces away. I saw that he was struggling to keep himself under control. "Now, Miles," he said, turning around to face me again, "it seems to me, just to get back to reality here, that the coroner might go one of two ways on this one. You listening? He might judge this as suicide or accidental death in the commission of a crime, depending on how much he wanted to protect the reputation of Paul Kant. Either way he's got to weigh in the evidence of that gas can."

"Those are the only two verdicts you think he might consider?"

"Yep."

"Not if I can help it."

"You won't be able to do anything here, Miles. You better finish off that research of yours and get out."

"Who's the coroner here?"

Polar Bears gave me a flat angry triumphant glare. "I am."

I could only stare at him.

"In a county of this size, it didn't make much sense to have two men both drawing public salaries."

I turned wordlessly to look at the fire. It was much lower now and the doorframe and all of the roof had collapsed into the roaring heart of the building. My skin felt half-roasted, face and hands. My trousers were hot where they brushed my legs. I sensed the Kastads shying away from both me and the fire.

"He was at my house," I said. I could not bear it any longer. I started to walk toward him. "He was at my house, and you raped my cousin. You and Duane. You killed her. Probably accidentally. But this makes two deaths you want to shovel dirt over. This time it won't happen."

His fury was more frightening than Duane's because it was quieter. "Dave," he said, looking over my shoulder.

"You can't pin it all on an innocent man because he's conveniently dead," I said. "I know who it is."

"Dave." Lokken came up behind me. I could hear him walking over the gravel.

"It's that boy Zack," I said. "There's one other possibility, but it's too crazy . . . so it has to be Zack." I heard Lokken whisper something in surprise behind me. "He had those Coke bottles in his truck, and a doorknob . . ."

"Do you know who Zachary is, Miles?" interrupted Polar Bears, his voice flat as a tombstone.

"He likes fires too, doesn't he?" I said. "Duane said he liked them so much sometimes he didn't wait for someone else to start them."

Dave Lokken grabbed my arms. "Hold him, Dave," said Polar Bears. "Hold him good." He came up close to me, and Lokken pinned my arms back, holding me so tightly I could not move. "You know who Zachary is?"

"Now I do," I tried to say.

"He's my boy," said Polar Bears. "My son. Now I'm going to teach you when to shut up."

In the second before he hit me I saw his face irradiated with rage and I had time to wonder if Duane would have told me the final detail if he had not cut his hand. Then I couldn't think about anything but the pain. Afterwards he told Lokken to let me fall, and I toppled over onto the gravel. I could not breathe. I heard him say, "Lokken, get your fat ass out of here fast," and I opened my eyes and saw his shoes. One of his toecaps lifted and came down on my face. I could hear Lokken running off. Polar Bears' odor poured over me. The foot lifted from my face. His voice came straight into my ear. "You would have been a lot better off if you hadn't never come here, Miles. And I think you better act like you know it." I could hear him breathing hard. Wild Turkey mingled with the smell of gunpowder. "Miles, God damn you, if you say one more word about those goddamned *Coke* bottles or goddamned *doorknobs* I'll break you in half." His breathing became ragged and harsh, and his belly strained out against his belt with the force of it. "And your cousin died twenty years ago, Miles. You say one more word about her and you're through. Now remember this and remember it good. Whoever it was that was there when your cousin died saved your life by dragging you up onto the shelf. Maybe they wouldn't repeat the favor. Maybe they'd just drop you back in the water." Then he grunted, standing up, and was gone. I closed my eyes. I could hear tires spraying gravel.

When I opened my eyes again I touched my face. I felt slick blood. Then I sat up. I was alone. Duane's Dream House was only a burning jumble of boards emitting a plume of dark smoke. Paul's body was gone, and so was the heap of blankets. I was absolutely alone, lying on the white gravel beside a dying fire.

5

The final stage began.

When I reached home, I washed the blood from my face and went upstairs to bed and stayed there thirty-six hours. I was without friends—Paul was dead, Duane hated me, and Polar Bears had revealed himself as an enemy too complex to see clearly. I felt his touch burning me like a branding iron, and that touch was worse than his blows. My only protection was Rinn, a woman more than ninety years old. Yet if Polar Bears and Arden in general had absolved me of suspicion, why did I need protection? From Zack? I had done my worst there. I rolled under the damp sheets, groaning. I felt great dread.

I know that I waited, hearing nothing but the sound of my own voice saying to Polar Bears over the body of Paul Kant that there was another possibility, but it was too crazy, and knowing that it was there that my real dread originated . . . and lay rigid with tension. But nothing happened. There is no other possibility, I told myself. Gradually I calmed, eventually I went back to sleep.

I woke, aware of the smell of cold water inundating the room. "Alison," I said.

A hand touched my shoulder. This happened. I rolled over and reached out and touched—I touched the body of a girl. A slight cold body, much colder than my hands. I was in that condition of only partial wakefulness when reality is at its most tenuous. I was conscious only of having been forgiven, and of her presence. My hands went, on their own impulse, to her face and felt what I could not see, the taut cheekbones bracketing that wild contradictory magical face, then her smooth hair. I felt her smile loosing itself under my palm, and there was no doubt that it was the smile of Alison Greening. A great general feeling of blessedness suffused my entire body. I touched her slim legs, embraced her lithe waist, cradled my head in the dip of flesh at the base of her neck. I have never felt such joy.

Actually, I have felt precisely that joy, and for the same reason: during the years of our marriage, I would at times come groggily half-awake and brush against Joan and think *Alison*, and embrace her, feeling in her longer taller body as we made love the lineaments of the dead girl I needed. At such moments, I experienced the same numb ecstasy, the same blessing; but on this night, the sensations were even more particularized, and as I embraced her shoulders and entered her, the small hands on my back and the slender body beneath mine were undoubtedly Alison's. Everything else vanished, all the wretchedness of the past week. If we had been on a battlefield I would not have noticed the gunfire and exploding shells.

As her body warmed, the strangeness began. It was not that her body changed—it was not as crude as that—but that it seemed at times during the night double-exposed, shifting imperceptibly in shape so that in one half of a second it was that body I had seen flashing in the water and in the other half it was fuller, so that a leg drawn up against my flank seemed to increase in weight, to press with greater urgency. The breasts against my chest were small, then heavy, then small; the waist, slim, then sturdy; but it is more accurate to say that both were present at once and when I was aware of this double exposure I dully imagined it as a flickering between the two halves of a second.

Once, for only a moment that was submerged deep into an onrushing succession of longer moments—a moment like the smaller fraction concealed within a fraction—my hands seemed to touch something besids flesh.

Hours later I opened my eyes and saw young skin beneath me, a curve of flesh which resolved itself into a shoulder. Hands were kneading my back, a round knee lifted between my legs. The bed was a bath of odors. Sexual perfume, that raw, pungent odor, talcum powder, young skin, newly washed hair. And the smell of blood. I jerked my head up and saw that the girl beneath me, even now sliding her hand to excite me once again, was Alison Updahl.

I scrambled off. "You."

"Mnnn." She crept forward into me. Her eyes were flat and pale as ever, but her face was soft.

"How long have you been here?"

She laughed. "I wanted to surprise you. But last night you didn't even act surprised. Just starved. You really make a girl feel welcome."

"How long have you been here?"

"Since about one last night. Your face is all cut up where Mr. Hovre hit you. You know that dumb deputy he has, Dave Lokken? He's been telling everybody. About two days ago. About how Mr. Hovre hit you. How it was Paul Kant all along. So I thought I'd help you celebrate. Even though you tried to make him think it was Zack. But that was just stupid."

"I want you to leave."

"Oh, it's okay. I mean, he won't know anything about it. It's Thursday morning, and on Thursday mornings he always goes over to the Co-op. He doesn't even know I'm out of the house."

I looked at her carefully. She seemed to be entirely comfortable, unaware of any oddity.

"You were here all night?"

"Huh? Sure I was."

"You didn't feel anything strange?"

"Only you." She giggled, and put an arm around my neck. "You're pretty strange. You shouldn't have said that about Zack to Mr. Hovre. Zack really likes you. He even read some of those books you gave him, like he told you. He usually only reads books about crime, you know, murder and stuff. Did you say it because of out at the quarry? What we did? We were just fooling around. You were cute then. Even after, when you were mad, you were looking at me—you know. 'Course I didn't have any clothes on. Like now."

She grimaced, apparently having scratched herself on something in the bed, and brushed off her hip with her hand; the gesture uncovered all of her compact upper body, and I felt an involuntary flame of sexual interest—the Woodsman was right. I had been starved. I still felt as though I had not made love in months. I reached over and cupped one of her breasts. The smell of blood began to pour outward again. My only excuse is that we were in bed together, and that she was being deliberately seductive. It was an experience entirely different from that of the night before. Her body was altogether foreign to me, our rhythms did not match, and I kept being thrown out of stride by sudden charges and spasms from her. Eventually I rolled over and let her direct things, as she evidently wished to do. It was an awkward performance, I suppose unhelped by my doubts about my own sanity. I had been so certain that my partner had been my cousin; when I tried to recall the "double exposure" sensation, it seemed very vague. But one thing was certain—Alison Updahl was a sexual stranger to me, less melodic with her body.

When it was over, she sat up in the bed. "Well. Your heart wasn't in that one."

"Alison," I said, having to ask it, "did Zack do those things—the killings? Because Paul Kant didn't, in spite of what Polar Bears thinks."

Her tenderness had vanished before I had finished speaking. She swiveled her legs over the side of the bed, making it impossible for me to see her face. I thought that her shoulders were trembling. "Zack only talks about stuff, he never does it." She lifted her head. "Hey, what do you have in this bed anyhow, I was scratching myself on it all morning." She stood up, turned to face me, and threw back the sheet. On the bottom sheet lay a scattering of thin brown twigs—about enough to cover the palm of a hand. "Time you changed your sheets," she said, in control of herself again. "They're starting to sprout."

I looked with a dry throat at the small things beside me on the rumpled sheet. She turned away.

"Alison," I said, "answer something for me."

"I don't want to talk about those things."

"No. Listen. Did you and Zack request a song on the radio about two weeks ago? From A and Z, for all the lost ones?"

"Yes. But I said I can't talk about that—please, Miles."

Of course Alison had no notion of what those fingerlike twigs meant to me, and when I got hurriedly out of bed she at first ignored me as she dressed.

"Not exactly chatty, are you? Except for stupid questions," she said, yanking a T-shirt over her head. "Not exactly big on small talk, hey, Miles?" She squirmed into her jeans. "You just like to ruin things. Well, you don't have to worry. I won't invade your privacy anymore." Then, when I did not protest, she looked at me more closely. "Hey, Miles, what is going on? You looked just as spooked as you did that first day you came back."

"I'm not surprised," I said. "I have the same reason. For your own good, you'd better leave."

"For my own good? Jesus, are you ever a case."

"No doubt," I said, and she stamped her feet into clogs and clattered down the stairs without saying good-bye.

Other explanations—there had to be other explanations. I had picked up the twigs on my clothing as I had walked into the woods, or simply while walking around the farm. Or they had adhered to my clothing when Polar Bears had permitted Dave Lokken to let me fall. I stood up and brushed them from the sheets. Eventually I straightened the bed, dressed, went into my office and took a pencil and some sheets of paper downstairs to try to work at the kitchen table. Tuta Sunderson showed up not long after, and I asked her to change the sheets.

"Heard you was over at Andy's the other morning," she announced, hands on hips. "Lot went on there, I guess."

"Um," I said.

"You'll be grateful for some of it, I guess."

"Nothing like a good beating."

"Red says that Paul Kant should have been run off a long time ago."

"That sounds like good old Red."

"I think he killed himself. That boy Paul was always a weak one."

"Yes, that's one of your favorite theories, isn't it?"

Portion of Statement by Tuta Sunderson:

July 18

The way I saw it, I wasn't going to rush into thinking something just because everyone else did. There wasn't any proof, was there? I think Paul Kant just snapped—he was too weak to take the pressure, and he broke. He never even confessed, did he? No. And you still hadn't found that other girl yet. I keep an open mind.

Anyhow, I was goin' to keep on watching Miles. In case he decided to run or something. So I went over on Wednesday morning just like always, and I'll tell you what I was thinking about—that torn-up picture of Duane's girl I found. That just sat in my mind, bothering me. I mean, what goes through a man's mind when he tears up a picture of a girl? You think about that.

So, like I said, I saw the girl leave his house that morning just when I was walking up the road. I says to myself, you've been where you shouldn't be, little girl, and I stayed out there on the road a little bit so he wouldn't know I saw, and when he sent me up to change his sheets I knew just what they'd been up to. You can lie all you want to, and some do, but you can't fool the person who washes your sheets.

I made up my mind I'd talk to Red. I knew sure as shooting that he'd get real mad, but I wanted him to decide if we should tell Duane. He's the man now.

Half a dozen times that day I nearly left, got into the car and took off for someplace—it did not matter where. But I still did not have my car and I still thought there might be other explanations than the one which had leaked into my consciousness on the night when I had looked through the window of my room and seen that slight figure blasting cold jealous energy at me from the edge of the woods. That was when the conscious fear had started.

And it remained, refusing to be salved by theories. It followed me downstairs and upstairs, it was with me while I bolted my food, and when I sat and wrote, it stood behind me, sending its chill straight through my clothing.

She is your snare, Aunt Rinn had said. All of my life had demonstrated the truth of that statement.

Which put me where I had started, with the overwhelming memory of the terror I had felt, that night in the woods. I tried to reconstruct those moments. Later, I had explained it to myself as a fantasy cooked up out of literature, but *at the time*—that was important, at the time I had sensed nothing literary but instead the pure and overwhelmingly terror of evil. Evil is what we call the force we can discover when we send our minds as far as they can go: when the mind crumbles before something bigger, harder than itself, unknowable and hostile. Had I not courted that evil, by willing my cousin back into life? She did not promise comfort, I knew, thinking again of the figure at the edge of the fields; she did not promise anything I could comprehend.

I still could not admit to myself what I had begun to imagine. That night, the night which changed everything, began calmly enough, in the manner of most of my evenings. I had halfheartedly munched an assortment of things in the kitchen—nuts, a couple of limp carrots, some cheese—and then wandered outside onto the lawn. The night was warm and full of the scents of hay and mown grass, and I could hear crickets chirruping and invisible birds lifting off the walnut trees. I rubbed my face and went down to the road. I could not see the woods, but I knew they were there. From the center of the warm night, an icicle of cold reached out to touch my face. Now that the inhabitants of Arden and the valley had decided that I was innocent of the girls' deaths, I felt more watched, more under observation, than ever before.

I thought of the twigs in my bed, and went back up the drive.

I pulled my chair up to the desk. Mechanically, I began to resume writing. After some minutes I became aware of an intensification of the atmosphere: the air in the room seemed charged, crowded with unseen activity. The overhead light appeared to waver, darkening my shadow on the page before me. I blinked and sat up straight. I could smell cold water all about me.

A palm of cold wind struck the pencil from my hand, an elbow of wind cut into my body.

The light darkened as my shadow had, and I was immediately aware of Alison's presence fighting to enter me. My face and hands were icy. I tipped backwards in my chair, windmilling my arms. She was coming in through nose and eyes and mouth; I screamed with terror. A stack of paper shot up into the air and fragmented. I felt my mind become elastic, skidding, stretching out of my control. She was within my mind, within my body: beneath my animal terror, I felt her hatred and jealousy. My feet kicked out at the desk, and the door racketed away from the trestles. The typewriter thudded to the ground. My head struck the wooden floor. When my right arm found a stack of books, they geysered up into the air. I felt her hatred on all my senses: the darkness, the burning cold of my mouth and fingertips, the flooding smell of water, a rushing noise, the taste of fire in my mouth. It was punishment for the last sad copulation, that spiritless animal joining. She was boiling within me, and my arms thrashed and my back arched and slammed against the wood. I sent papers flying toward the window, toward the lightbulb. My body was sent rolling across the floor. Saliva, mucus, tears slid across my face. For an instant I was above my body, seeing it thrashing and writhing across the littered floor, watching my slimed face contort and my arms hurling books and papers, and then I was back in the boiling, thrashing mess, suffering like an animal in a fit. Her fingers seemed slipped into mine, her light, violent bones overlay mine. My ears were pressed forward, fluid filled my nose, my chest burst.

When my eyes opened it was over. I heard myself panting, not screaming. I had not sensed her leaving, but she had left. I was looking at a quiet edge of the moon through the window above the toppled desk.

Then my stomach violently unlocked itself, and I barely made it downstairs in time. A bitter brown colloidal juice shot upwards into my mouth. At that moment I was seated on the toilet, feeling watery liquid expel itself from the other end of my body with an equal force, and I turned my head toward the sink, my eyes closed and a sickly perspiration blossoming on my face.

When I came limply out of the bathroom into the kitchen I had to support myself by leaning against the sink as I drank glass after glass of cold water. Cold water. The smell pervaded the house.

She wanted me dead. She wanted me with her. On that night which seemed a century ago, Rinn had warned me. *She means death.*

And the other things—the girls' deaths? I looked that dread in the face, fully, for the first time. I sat in the room I had labored to prepare for her and numbly tried to accept what I had refused to think about before: the other possibility I had mentioned to Polar Bears. I had awakened Alison's spirit, that terrible force I had felt in the woods, and I knew now that spirit was rancid with jealousy of life. On the twenty-first she would appear—and would have anyhow, I now saw, even if I had not worked at reconstructing the old interior of the farmhouse—but as the date drew nearer, she was growing in strength. She could take life. That, she had been able to do from the day I had begun to draw near the valley.

I sat in the cold room, paralyzed straight down to the core. Alison. I thought: the twenty-first begins at midnight on the twentieth. One day away from the day just beginning to appear in stripes of dark purple over the woods blackening the hills.

As the morning drew closer I moved out onto the porch. The bands of purple increased in width; the wide fields, striped yellow and green, grew in visibility and detail. Fog lay upon them in trails of misty gray, wisps of cotton snagged in the corn.

Footsteps awoke me. My hands and feet were cold. The sky had become a flat uniform pale blue, and the mist was gone from everywhere but the very edges of the woods. It was going to be one of those days when the moon is visible all morning, hanging in blue sky like a white dead stone. Tuta Sunderson was coming heavily up the drive, trudging as though her shoes were encased in concrete. Her bag jigged at her side. When she saw me, her mouth clapped shut and her face hardened. I waited for her to open the screen door and come onto the porch.

"You don't have to come here anymore," I said. "The job is over."

"What do you mean?" I could see suspicion darken her goggling eyes.

"Your employment is terminated. I don't need you anymore. The job is *finis*. *Kaput*. Ended. Over. Finished. Done."

"You been sitting here all night?" She crossed her arms over her chest, an operation requiring an impressive amount of effort. "Drinking gin?"

"Please go home, Mrs. Sunderson."

"You afraid of my seeing something? Well, I've already seen it."

"You haven't seen anything."

"You look kinda sick. What did you do, swallow a bottle of aspirin or something?"

"I don't know how suicide ever got along without you."

"By rights I should get the whole week's wages."

"Indeed you should. In fact you should get two weeks' wages. Forgive me. Please take fourteen dollars." I reached in my pocket, drew out bills, counted out two fives and four ones and handed them to her.

"One week's, I told you. That's five dollars. You're paying for today, Friday and Saturday besides the three days I worked." She took one of the fives and dropped the rest of the money beside me on the porch swing.

"Splendid. Please go and leave me alone. I realize that I've been awful to you. I couldn't help it. I'm sorry."

"I know what you're doing," she said. "You're as filthy as any beast of the field."

"That was eloquent." I closed my eyes. After a while the noise of her breathing changed, and I could hear her turning around. I was getting better. Now I could smell anger. Thank you, Alison. The screen door banged shut. I kept my eyes closed as I heard her walking down the drive.

Who slept together?

One crushed an anthill.

One broke a chair.

One was afraid.

One swam in blood.

One had cold hands.

One had the last word.

When I opened my eyes she was gone. A dusty brown Ford, the mailman's car, came up the road and passed the impaled metal receptacle without braking. No more fan mail, no more letters from my cousin. Yes. It made sense. Her body—her skeleton, after twenty years—was in a graveyard in Los Angeles, beneath a headstone I had never seen. So she had to put herself together out of the available materials. Or be just a wind, the cold breath of spirit. Leaves, gravel, thorns. Thorns for tearing.

I stood up and went down from the porch. I said in my mind: thorns for tearing. I felt as though I were walking in my sleep. The door on the driver's side of the Nash had slipped out of alignment, and it dipped when I opened it, creaking loudly in a voice like rust.

For a moment I could not remember where I was going, and simply put-putted up the road, going slowly and serenely as Duane on the big tractor. Then I remembered. The last, the only help. I depressed the accelerator, made the car rattle, picked up speed as I went past the Sunderson house. Mrs. Sunderson was at one of the windows, watching me go by. Then the shell of the school, the church, the tight curve at the sandstone bluff. I passed Andy's, and saw him pumping gas. His face was like clotted milk. Behind him was a large black area of dead land. His clotted-milk face swung around, tracking me as I passed.

When I came to the narrow path going up between the fields to the trees I swung hard on the wheel again and began to bounce along, going in the direction of the sun. A few ears of corn in the row nearest the road had been struck down, broken off at the stalk, and they lay flattened and sprawling at the field's edge. Here and there, whole rows had been trampled down; stick-leg cornstalks tilted crazily. Soon I reached the first of the trees, and then the fields vanished behind me and I was threading between big oaks. The narrow early sunlight filtered by the boughs and leaves came down in ribbons. I parked on the slope beside the tall red henhouse. When I got out of the car I could hear the gabbling of the birds. A few terrified hens ran away into the woods, lurching from side to side.

I looked in the henhouse first. I pulled open the doors and stepped inside, hit once again by the stench. It seemed even stronger than on the day when I had clumsily helped her cull the eggs. Two or three birds flapped their wings, high up on their nests. Beaked heads swiveled, button eyes stared fixedly. Slowly, I backed out, the fixed eyes glaring at me from the sides of their old men's heads. I closed the door as gently as she had taught me.

Two chickens were roosting on the hood of the Nash. I went up the path toward her house. Here the sunlight was blocked from entering directly, and there was only a golden hovering rustle overhead, where the leaves formed another sky. The little house seemed dark and empty.

One had cold hands.

One had the last word.

On a counter in the kitchen stood a plate stacked with something wrapped in a red-and-white gingham cloth. I touched the cloth. It was dry. I folded it back, and saw mould sprinkled green on the surface of the top piece of lefsa.

She was in the bedroom, lying in the middle of the double bed. A yellowed sheet, a patchwork quilt, covered her. My nostrils caught an odor like a deep bass chord. I knew she was dead before I touched her and felt the stiffness of her fingers. The white hair was spread thickly on the embroidered pillowcase. Two, three days dead, I thought. She might have died while Paul Kant's body was being dragged from the flames of the Dream House, or while I was fitting my body within a ghost's. I put down her stiff hand and went back into the dark kitchen to telephone the Arden police.

"Uh, God damn," said Dave Lokken after I had spoken two sentences of explanation. "You're there now? With her?"

"Yes."

"You say you found her?"

"Yes."

"Any, uh, marks on her? Any signs of, uh, assault? Any indication of cause of death?"

"She was about ninety-four years old," I said. "I suppose that'll do for cause of death."

"Well, God damn. God damn. You say you just found her now? What the hell were you doing up there anyways?"

For the last protection. "She was my grandmother's sister," I said.

"Uh, family reasons," he said, and I knew he was writing it down. "So you're up there in those woods now? That's where her farm is, right?"

"That's where I am."

"Well, God damn." I couldn't figure out why he was so agitated by my information. "Look. Teagarden, you don't budge. Just stay there until I can get out there with an ambulance. Don't touch anything."

"I want to talk to Polar Bears," I said.

"Well, you can't. You get that? The chief ain't here now. But don't worry, Teagarden, you'll be talkin' to the chief soon enough." He hung up without saying good-bye.

Lokken had been like a being from another, more furious world, and I went back into Rinn's bedroom and sat beside her on the bed. I realized that I was still moving with the numbness which had settled on me during my almost sleepless night in the living room I had prepared for Alison Greening, and I nearly stretched out on the bed beside Rinn's body. Her face seemed smoother in death, less Chinese and wrinkled. I was conscious of the bones pushing through the skin of her face. I touched her cheek and then tried to pull the sheet and quilt up over her head. They were pinned beneath her arms; and I remembered Lokken's telling me not to touch anything.

It was over an hour before I heard vehicles coming up the drive from the valley road, and went onto her porch to see a police car drawing up alongside the Nash, followed by an ambulance.

Chubby Dave Lokken bounced out of the police car and waved angrily at the two men in the ambulance. They got out and crossed their arms and leaned against the side of the ambulance. One of them was smoking, and the leafage of smoke from his cigarette wound up to the dense covering of trees. "You, Teagarden," Lokken shouted, and I turned my head to look at him. For the first time I saw the rumpled-looking man wearing a suit who stood beside the deputy. He had a Marine crewcut and wore thick glasses. "Teagarden, get the hell out here!" Lokken shouted. The man beside him sighed and rubbed his face, and I saw the black bag in his hands.

I came down from the porch. Lokken was nearly hopping with rage and impatience. I could see his breasts bulging in his uniform shirt. "All right. What's your story, Teagarden?"

"What I told you."

"Is she in the house?" asked the doctor. He looked very tired, and as though Dave Lokken had begun to wear on him.

I nodded, and the doctor began to move up the path.

"Hold on. I got a few questions first. You say you found her. Is that right?"

"That's what I said and that's right."

"You got a witness?"

One of the ambulance men snickered, and Lokken's face began to flush. "Well?"

"No. No witnesses."

"You say you just came here this morning?"

I nodded.

"What time?"

"Just before I called you."

"I suppose she was dead when you got here?"

"Yes."

"Where were you coming from?" He put great weight on the question.

"The Updahl farm."

"Anybody see you there? Wait up, doc. I wanta finish here before we go in. Well?"

"Tuta Sunderson saw me. I fired her this morning."

Lokken seemed puzzled and angered by this detail, but he decided to ignore it. "You touch the old woman in any way?"

I nodded. The doctor looked at me for the first time.

"You did, huh? You touched her? How?"

"I held her hand."

His color darkened, and the ambulance man snickered again.

"What made you decide to come up here this morning, anyhow?"

"I wanted to see her."

"Just wanted to see her." His flabby incompetent face shouted that he would love to swing at me.

"I've had a rough morning," said the doctor. "Dave, let's get this over with so I can get back and write my reports."

"Uh-huh," said Lokken, violently nodding his head. "Teagarden, this here honeymoon of yours might come to a sudden end."

The doctor looked at me with an almost professional curiosity, and then he and Lokken went marching up to the house.

I watched them go, and then looked at the ambulance men. They were both concentrating on the ground. One glanced at me and then snatched his cigarette from his mouth and scowled at it as if he were thinking of changing brands. After a moment I went back inside the house.

"Natural causes," the doctor was saying. "Looks like no problems with this one. She just ran out of life."

Lokken nodded, writing on a pad, and then looked up and noticed me. "Hey! Get out of here, Teagarden. You ain't even supposed to be in here!"

I went out onto the porch. A minute later, Lokken bustled past me to wave in the ambulance men, who disappeared behind for a second and then reappeared carrying a stretcher. I followed them into the house, but did not go as far as the bedroom. They needed no more than seconds to place Rinn on the stretcher. The sheets and quilt had been replaced by a white blanket, pulled up over her face.

As we stood watching them carrying her down to the ambulance, Lokken was a symphony of small movements: he tapped a foot, buffed a shoe on his trouser leg, patted his fat thigh with his fingertips, adjusted his holster. I understood that all this expressed his reluctance to stand so near me. When the doctor came out saying, "Let's shake it, I got four hours' work on the other one," Lokken turned to me and said, "Okay, Teagarden. But we got people who will say they saw you going up into those woods. Don't you go anywhere but back home. Got me? Hey, Professor? You got me?"

All of which was explained by a visit I received later that day. I had been picking up the papers in my office, just gathering them up by the armful and dropping them into bushel baskets. The typewriter was useless now; the carriage had been bent so that the roller would not advance, and I threw the machine into the root cellar.

When I heard a car driving up toward the house I looked out the window: the car had already drawn up too close to the house to be visible. I waited for a knock but none came. I went downstairs and saw a police car drawn right up before the porch. Polar Bears was sitting on the near front fender, wiping his forehead with a big speckled handkerchief.

He saw me come out onto the porch, put his hand down, and shifted his body slightly so that he was facing me. "Step outside, Miles," he said.

I stood right in front of the screen door with my hands in my pockets.

"Sorry about old Rinn," he said. "I suppose I should apologize about Dave Lokken, too. Dr. Hampton, the county M.E., says my deputy was a little rough with you."

"Not by your standards. He was just stupid and pompous."

"Well, he's no mental giant," Polar Bears said. There was a quiet watchful quality—a restraint—to his manner which I had not seen before. We stayed where we were and regarded each other for a bit before he spoke again. I didn't give a damn for him or anything he said. "Thought you'd like to know. The M.E. says she died forty-eight, maybe sixty hours ago. The way he puts it together, she probably knew it was happening and just got into bed and died. Heart attack. Nice and simple."

"Does Duane know?"

"Yep. He got her transferred to the funeral parlor this afternoon. She'll be buried day after tomorrow." His big head was tilting, looking at me with squinting eyes. Beside him, his hat pointed toward me so that I could see light reflected from the star-shield pinned to the crown.

"Well, thanks," I said, and moved to go back inside.

"One more thing."

I stopped. "Yes?"

"I oughta explain to you why Dave Lokken was acting sorta extra uptight."

"I'm not interested," I said.

"Oh, you're interested, Miles. See, we found that Michalski girl this morning." He sent me one of his low heavy smiles. "Funny sort of coincidence there. She was dead, naturally. But I don't expect that's a surprise."

"No. Nor to you." I felt the dread again, and leaned against the screen door.

"Nope. I expected it. The thing is, Miles, she was right up there in those woods—not three hundred yards from Rinn's little cabin. We started workin' our way in from 93"—pointing with one arm —"and we just *pored* through them woods, see, lookin' at every little twig, and this morning we found her buried under loose dirt in a sort of clearing up there."

I swallowed.

"You know that clearing, Miles?"

"I might."

"Uh-huh. Real good. That's why old Dave was sorta salty with you—you were up there with one body, and we found another one so close you could spit that far. It's just a little natural clearing, got some campfire remains in the middle of it. Been used pretty regular, by the look of it."

I nodded. I kept my hands in my pockets.

"Could be you used to go up there. Now that don't make any difference but for one fact. Oh, and Miles, she was worse than the other two. Her feet were burned. Come to think of it, her hair was burned too. And, let me see. Oh yeah. She was sorta kept there. This friend of ours, he tied her to a tree or something and—I'm only guessing—went up at night to work on her. For more than a week."

I thought of the slight figure drawing me up toward the clearing, and of how I had taken the warm ashes as a sign of her healing presence.

"You wouldn't happen to have any idea about who'd do a thing like that, would you?"

I was going to say *yes*, but instead said, "You think it was Paul Kant?"

Polar Bears nodded like a proud schoolmaster. "Real good. Real good. See, that brings up the little fact that I mentioned before. What do we need to know?"

"How long she's been dead."

"Miles, you shoulda been a cop. See, we don't think she died of—our friend's little experiments. She was strangled. Big fucking bruises on her throat. Now our friend Dr. Hampton isn't sure yet when that might have happened. But suppose it happened after Paul Kant killed himself?"

I said, "It's not me, Polar Bears."

He just sat there blinking, feigning polite attention. When I said no more, he folded his hands into his lap. "Now, we both know who it isn't, don't we, Miles? I had a talk with your prime suspect yesterday. He told me that those Coke bottles came from Du-ane's cellar, where you could get at 'em pretty easy, and he says you threw out that doorknob yourself. They were Du-ane's. Says he doesn't know how they got in his truck. And I know he hasn't been up in the woods at night, because he confessed to me what he's been doing with his nights." He smiled again. "He and Du-ane's girl used to go down to that shack behind Andy's. Do pokey-pokey all night. Paul Kant sort of ruined their fun."

"Nobody living is the one you want," I said.

He squinted up his entire face, then let out a disgusted grunt and put his hat back on his head. "Miles, if you go crazy on me you're gonna ruin all the fun." On went his sunglasses. He pushed himself off the fender. He looked like something you'd run from on a dark night. "Why don't you take a little trip with me?"

"A trip?"

"A little jaunt. I want to show you something. Get into my car."

I just looked at him, trying to figure it out.

"Get your ass in the car, Miles."

I did as I was told.

He spun the squad car out onto the highway without speaking to me, his face a tight mask of distaste. All of those unhappy odors began to build up. We went toward Arden at a good twenty miles over the speed limit.

"You're taking me to her parents," I said.

He did not reply.

"You finally decided to arrest me."

"Shut up," he said.

But we did not stop at the police station. Polar Bears zoomed straight through Arden, and we picked up more speed as we left town. Restaurants, the bowling alley, fields. The farms and the corn took over again. Now we were in the same country he had driven me through before, the afternoon I had talked to Paul Kant: wide fields green and yellow, and the Blundell River shining through a screen of trees. Eventually Polar Bears took off his hat and sailed it onto the backseat. He ran a palm over his forehead. "Too damn hot," he said.

"I still don't get it. If you were going to work me over you could have done it miles back."

"I don't want to hear your voice," he said. Then he glanced over at me. "Do you know what's in Blundell?"

I shook my head.

"Well, you're gonna find out."

Exhausted-looking cows swung their heads to watch us pass.

"The state hospital?"

"Yeah, that's there." He would say no more.

Hovre hit the accelerator even harder, and we sped past the sign at the Blundell town limits. It was a town much like Arden, one main street lined with stores, wooden houses with porches on a small grid of streets. Lightbulbs on a string and a row of banners hung before a used-car lot, the banners too limp to flap. A few men in straw hats and working clothes squatted on the curb.

Polar Bears took the first road out of town, and then guided the patrol car into what looked like a park. The road turned narrow. It was edged with a long green lawn. "State hospital grounds," he said noncommittally. "But you and me ain't going there."

I could see the big gray buildings of the hospital complex appearing through the trees to my left. They had a Martian remoteness. Sun umbrellas dotted the lawn, but no one sat beneath them.

"I'm gonna do you a real favor," he said. "Most tourists never get to see this feature of our country."

The road divided, and Polar Bears turned into the left fork, which soon ended in a gray parking lot before a low gray building like an ice cube. Shrubs around the sides of the cube struggled in the hard clay. I realized where I was a half second before I saw the metal plate staked into the ground in the midst of the shrubs.

"Welcome to the Furniveau County Morgue," Polar Bears said, and got out of the car. He went across the tacky asphalt of the lot without looking back at me.

I reached the door just as it closed behind him. I pushed it open and stepped into a cold white interior. Machinery hummed behind the walls.

"This here's my assistant," Polar Bears was saying. I realized after a moment that he meant me. He had his sunglasses off, and he rested his hands on his hips. In the antiseptic cold interior of the morgue, he smelled like a buffalo. A short dark-complected man in a spotted white coat sat at a battered desk in an alcove and incuriously looked at him. The desk was bare except for a portable radio and an ashtray. "I want him to have a look at the new one."

The man glanced at me. It didn't make any difference to him. Nothing made any difference to him.

"Which new one?"

"Michalski."

"Uh-huh. She's back from the autopsy. Didn't know you had any new deputies."

"He's a volunteer," said Polar Bears.

"Well, what the hell," the man said, and pushed himself away from the desk.

WILD ANIMALS / 358

He went through green metal doors at the end of the hall. "After you," said Polar Bears, waving me through.

It was useless to protest. I followed the attendant down a cold row of metal lockers. Hovre followed, so close that he nearly walked on my heels.

"You braced for this?" he asked me.

"I don't see the point," I said.

"You pretty soon will."

The dark-complected man stopped before one of the lockers, took a ring of keys from his pocket, and unlocked the door.

"Belly up," said Polar Bears.

The little man pulled the long tray out of the locker. A dead naked girl was lying on the slab. I had thought they covered them with sheets. "God," I said, seeing her wounds and the scars from the autopsy.

Polar Bears was waiting, very still. I looked at the girl's face. Then I began to perspire in the icy room

Polar Bears' voice came: "She remind you of anybody?"

I tried to swallow. It was more than enough proof, if I needed any more proof. "Did the first two look more or less the same?"

"Pretty close," said Polar Bears. "That Strand girl was as close as a sister might be."

I remembered the violence of the hatred I had felt when she had seemed to storm inside me. She had come back all right, and she had killed three girls who had an accidental resemblance to her. I would be next.

"Interesting, isn't it?" said Hovre. "Close 'er up, Archy."

The dark little man, who had been standing with his arms braced against the front of the locker as if asleep on his feet, pushed the tray back into the locker.

"Now let's go back to the car," said Polar Bears.

I followed him out into the blast of heat and sunlight. He drove me back to the Updahl farm without saying a word.

After he turned up the drive he cut the patrol car onto the lawn before the porch and got out as I did. He came toward me, a big intimidating physical presence. "Suppose we just agree to stay put until I get the final word from the M.E."

"Why don't you put me in jail?"

"Why, Miles, you're my assistant on this case," he said, and got back into his car. "In the meantime, get some sleep. You look like hell." As he twirled the car into the drive, I saw the grim, entirely satisfied smile on his lips.

I woke up late in the night. Alison Greening was seated on the chair at the foot of the bed. I could just distinguish her face and the shape of her body in the moonlight. I feared—I do not know what I feared, but I feared for my life. She did nothing. I sat up in the bed: I felt terribly naked and unprotected. She seemed utterly normal; she looked like an ordinary young woman. She was looking straight at me, her expression placid and unemotional, abstracted. For a moment I thought that she looked too ordinary to have caused all the upheavals in me and in Arden. Her face was waxen. Then my fear came booming back into me, and I opened my mouth to say something. Before I could form words, she was gone.

I got out of bed, touched the chair, and went across the top of the house to my office. Papers still lay on the floor, papers spilled out of bushel baskets. She was not there.

In the morning I gulped down a half-pint of milk, thought with distaste of food, and knew that I had to get away. Rinn had been right all that time ago. I had to leave the valley. The sight of her calmly, emotionlessly sitting on the chair at the foot of the bed, her blank face washed in moonlight, was more frightening than the frantic assault on my room. I could see that face, drained by the pale light, and it held no feeling I recognized; the complications of emotion had been erased. There was no more life in it than there was in a mask. I set down the bottle, checked my pockets for money and keys, and went outside into the sunlight. Dew lay shining on the grass.

Highway 93 to Liberty, I thought, then down to where I could pick up the freeway to La Crosse, and then I'd cross the river and head for a small town where I would leave the Nash and telegraph the New York Chemical for money and buy a secondhand car and go to Colorado or Wyoming, where I knew nobody. I backed out into the valley road and picked up speed, heading for the highway.

When I checked the rearview mirror as I passed the church, I saw another car keeping pace with me. I accelerated, and it kept the distance between us steady. It was like the prelude to that awful night when I had lost her, the night when we had made the vow. As the other car picked up speed and came closer, I saw black and white and knew that it was a police car. If it's Polar Bears, I thought, I'll attack him with my bare hands. I pushed the accelerator to the floor, and yanked at the wheel as I went around the curve by the sandstone bluff. The Nash began to vibrate. The patrol car pulled up easily and began to nose in before me, forcing me to the side of the road. I spun into Andy's and went around the gas pumps. The patrol car anticipated me and moved ahead to block my exit. looked around, considering backing up and swinging around into the side parking lot, but his car would have caught the old Nash in thirty seconds. I turned off the ignition.

I got out of the car and stood up. The man behind the wheel of the patrol car opened his door and rose up into the sunshine. It was Dave Lokken. Walking toward me, he kept his right hand on his holster.

"Nice little race." He was imitating Polar Bears, even in his slow walk. "Where do you think you were going?"

I slumped against the hot metal of the Nash. "Shopping."

"You wasn't thinking about leaving, I hope. Because that's why I been sittin' out near your place for two days, to make sure you don't even think about it."

"You were watching me?"

"For your own good," he said, grinning. "The chief says you need a lot of help. I'm gonna help you stick around where we can keep an eye on you. The medical examiner is supposed to call the chief real soon now."

"I'm not the one you're looking for," I said. "I'm telling you the truth."

"I guess you're gonna tell me it was Chief Hovre's boy Zack. I heard you say that a couple of nights back. You might just as well of put a gun to your head. His boy is all the family the chief's got. Now get back and get home."

I remembered the pale mask looking at me from the foot of the bed; and then I looked up toward the windows of Andy's store. Andy and his wife were standing up there looking down at us, one face showing horror, the other contempt.

"Come on and help me get my car back," I said and turned my back on him.

After a couple of steps I stopped walking. "What would you say if I told you your chief raped and killed a girl?" I asked. "Twenty years ago."

"I'd say you was lookin' to get your head blown off. Just like you been doin' since you got here."

"What would you say if I told you that the girl he raped—" I turned back around, looked at his angry yokel's face and gave up. He smelled like burning rubber. "I'm going into Arden," I said. "Tag along."

I saw him driving along behind me all the way to Arden, at times speaking into his radio microphone, and when I haggled with the boy Hank Speltz, he stayed in the car and parked across the street from the garage. The boy at first told me that the "repairs" to the VW would cost me five hundred dollars, and I refused to pay it. He shoved his hands into the pockets of his coveralls and looked at me with sullen hatred. I asked him what he had done. "Had to rebuild most of the motor. Patch what I couldn't rebuild. Lots of stuff. New belts."

"I imagine you're being funny," I said. "I don't think you could rebuild a cigarette."

"Pay up or no car. You want me to get the police?"

"I'll give you fifty dollars and that's it. You haven't even shown me a worksheet."

"Five hundred. We don't use worksheets. People around here trust us."

It was my day for being reckless. I went across the street and opened Lokken's door and made him follow me back to the garage. Hank Speltz looked as though he regretted his remark about getting the police.

"Well," Speltz said after I had forced Lokken to listen to an account of our interchange, "I was chargin' you in advance for the body work."

Lokken looked at him disgustedly.

"I'll give you thirty bucks," I said.

Speltz howled, "You said fifty!"

"I changed my mind."

"Make out a bill for thirty," said Lokken. The boy went inside to the garage's office.

"It's funny," I told Lokken, "you can't do any wrong in this country if you've got a cop beside you."

Lokken waddled away without replying, and Speltz reappeared, grumbling that the new windows had cost more than thirty dollars.

"Now fill it up," I said. "It's on my credit card."

"We don't take out-of-state credit cards."

"Deputy!" I yelled, and Lokken glowered at us from behind the wheel of his car.

"Shee-ut," the boy said. When I pulled the battered car up to the pumps, he filled the tank and returned with the credit-card apparatus.

Out on the street, Lokken pulled his car up beside mine and leaned toward me. "I had some news on my radio a while back. I probably won't be watching you anymore." Then he reversed, turned around, and sped away down Main Street, going in the direction of the police headquarters.

I discovered what Hank Speltz had meant about rebuilding the engine when I pressed the accelerator going up the hill past the R-D-N Motel. The car died, and I had to coast over to the curb and wait several minutes before it would start again. This was repeated when I went up the hill toward the Community Chest thermometer and the Italian distance, and again when I was coming down the last hill toward the highway. It cut out a fourth time when I pulled into the drive, and I let the car coast to a stop on the lawn.

Another police car was drawn up in my usual place before the garage. I saw the chief's star on the door.

I began to walk toward the figure sitting on the porch swing. "Everything work out okay at the filling station?" asked Polar Bears.

"What are you doing here?"

"Good question. Suppose you come inside and talk about it." Part of the facade had been put aside: his voice was level and weary.

When I came up inside the porch I saw that Polar Bears was sitting beside a pile of my clothing. "That's a brilliant idea," I said. "Take away a man's clothes and he can't go anywhere. The riverbank school of detection."

"I'll get to the clothes in a minute. Sit down." It was an order. I went to a chair at the end of the porch and sat facing him.

"The medical examiner phoned in his report a couple hours ago. He thinks the Michalski girl died on Thursday. Might have been as long as twenty-four hours after Paul Kant meatballed himself."

"A day before you found her."

"That's right." Now he was having difficulty concealing his anger. "We were a day late. We might not have found her at all if someone hadn't decided to tell us that you liked to go up into those woods. Maybe Paul Kant would still be alive too if we'd been there earlier."

"You mean maybe one of your vigilantes wouldn't have killed him."

"Okay." He stood up and walked toward me, his feet making the boards squeak. "Okay, Miles. You've been having lots of fun. You've been making a lot of wild accusations. But the fun's almost over. Why don't you wrap it all up and give me a confession?" He smiled. "It's my job, Miles. I'm being real nice and careful with you. I don't want any sharp Jew lawyer from New York coming out here and saying I walked all over your rights."

"I want you to put me in jail," I said.

"I know you do. I told you that a long time ago. There's only one little thing you gotta do before your conscience gets a nice rest."

"I think—" I said, and my throat went as tight as Galen Hovre's face. "I know it sounds crazy, but I think Alison Greening killed those girls."

His neck was swelling. "She wrote, I mean she sent, those blank letters. The one I showed you and the other one. I've seen her, Polar Bears. She's back. The night she died we made a vow that we'd meet in 1975, and I came back here because of that, and . . . and she's here. I've seen her. She wants to take me with her. She hates life. Rinn knew. She'd . . ."

I realized with shock that Polar Bears was enraged. In the next second, he moved with more rapidity than I would have thought possible in a man of his size, and kicked the chair out from under me. I went over sideways and rolled into the screen. He kicked out, and his shoe connected with my hip.

"You goddamned idiot," he said. The smell of gunpowder poured over me. He kicked me in the pit of the stomach, and I jackknifed over. Splinters from the boards dug into my cheek. As on the night of Paul's death, Polar Bears bent over me. "You think you're gonna get out of this by playing crazy? I'll tell you about your tramp cousin, Miles. Sure I was there, that night. We were both there. Duane and me. But Duane didn't rape her. I did. Du-ane was too busy knockin' you out." I was struggling to breathe. "I hit her on the head just after Duane clubbed you with a rock. Then I had her. It was just what she wanted—she was only fighting because you were there." He picked up my head by the hair and slammed it down on the boards. "I didn't even know she was out until it was all over. That little bitch was teasing me all summer, the little cunt. Maybe I even meant to kill her. I don't even know anymore. But I know that every time you said that little bitch's name I could have killed you, Miles. You shouldn't have gone messing around with what's past, Miles." He banged my head on the boards once again. "Shouldn't have gone messing." He took his hand off my head and inhaled noisily. "It's no good your tryin' to tell this to anybody, because nobody'll believe you. You know that, don't you?" I could hear his breathing. "Don't you?" His hand came back and slammed my head down again. Then he said, "We're moving inside. I don't want anybody to see this." He picked me up and dragged me inside and dropped me onto the floor. I felt a sharp, bursting pain in my nose and ears. I was still having trouble breathing.

"Arrest me," I said, and heard my voice bubble. "She'll kill me." The weave of a hooked rug cushioned my cheek.

"You want things too easy, Miles." I heard his feet moving on the floor, and tensed for another kick. Then I heard him going into the kitchen. Water splashed. I opened my eyes. He came back drinking from a glass of water.

He sat on the old couch. "I want to know something. How did it feel when you saw Paul Kant on the night he died? How did it feel, looking at that miserable little queer and knowing he was in hell because of what you did?"

"I didn't do it," I said. My voice was still bubbling.

Hovre emitted an enormous sigh. "You're making me do all this the hard way. What about the blood on your clothes?"

"What blood?" I found that I could lever myself up to a sitting position.

"The blood on your clothes. I went through your closet. You got some pants with blood on 'em, a pair of shoes with what could be bloodstains on the uppers." He put the glass down on the floor. "Now I gotta take those to the lab over in Blundell and see if they come out the blood type of any of the girls. Candace Michalski and Gwen Olson were AB, Jenny Strand was type O."

"Blood on my clothes? Oh. Yes. It happened when I cut my hand. The first day I came here. It dripped onto my shoes when I was driving here. Probably on my trousers too."

Hovre shook his head.

"And I'm AB," I said.

"How would you happen to know that, Miles?"

"My wife was a do-gooder. Every year we gave a pint each to the blood center in Long Island City."

"Long Island City." He shook his head again. "And you're AB?" He pushed himself up from the couch, walked past me to get to the porch.

"Miles," he called to me, "if you're so simon-pure innocent, why are you in such a hurry to be put in jail?"

"I already told you that," I said.

"Kee-rist." He returned holding my clothes and shoes. I felt the pain in my head jump in anticipation as he came toward me. "Now I'm gonna tell you the facts of life," he said. "Word is gonna get around. I'm not going to do anything to stop it. I'm not even going to have Dave Lokken sitting on his fat ass down the road. If anyone comes out here to find you, that's all right with me. A little jungle justice wouldn't bother me a bit. I'd almost rather have you dead than in jail, old pal. And I don't think you're stupid enough to think you can get away from me. Are you? You couldn't get far in that beat-up car anyhow. Hey?" His foot came toward me, and stopped an inch short of my ribs. "Hey?"

I nodded.

"I'll be hearing from you, Miles. I'll be hearing from you. We're both gonna get what we want."

After I soaked for an hour in a hot bath, letting the pain seep away into the steam, I sat upstairs and wrote for several hours—until I saw that it had begun to get dark. I heard Duane shouting at his daughter. His voice rose and fell, monotonously, angrily, insisting on some inaudible point. Both Duane's voice and the oncoming of dark made it impossible to work any longer. To spend another night in the farmhouse was almost impossible: I could still see her, sitting in the chair at the foot of my bed, looking blankly, even dully, at me, as if what I were seeing were only a waxen model of her face and body, a shell a millimeter thick behind which lay spinning stars and gases. I put down the pencil, grabbed a jacket from my plundered closet and went downstairs and outside.

The night was beginning. The dark shapes of clouds drifted beneath an immense sky. Above them hung a moon nearly washed of color. A single arrow of cool breeze seemed to come straight toward the house from high in the black woods. I shuddered, and climbed into the battered Volkswagen.

At first I thought of simply driving around the country roads until I was too tired to go further and then sleep the rest of the night in the car; then I thought I might go to Freebo's and speed oblivion by purchasing it. Oblivion could scarcely cost more than ten dollars, and it was the best buy in Arden. I rattled onto 93, and turned the car toward town. But what sort of reception could I expect in Freebo's? By this time, everybody would know about the medical examiner's report. I would be a ghastly pariah. Or an inhuman thing to be hunted down. At that point the car went dead. I cursed Hank Speltz. I did not even begin to have the mechanical competence to fix whatever the boy had done. I pictured driving back to New York at a steady rate of thirty-five miles an hour. I'd need another mechanic, which meant that I would have to commit most of the money remaining in my account. Then I thought of the waxen face concealing stars and gases, and knew that I would be lucky ever to get back to New York.

That night I made an appeal to compassion, a second appeal to violence.

Finally I got the car started again.

As I sped down one of the Arden back streets I saw a familiar shape passing a lighted picture window, and I cut over to the curb and jumped out of the car before the motor was dead. I ran on the black asphalt in the middle of the road and crossed his lawn. I pressed Bertilsson's bell.

When he opened his door I saw surprise alter his features. His face was as much a mask as hers. He ignored his wife's calls of "Who is it? Who is it?" behind him.

"Well," he said, grinning at me. "Come for my blessing? Or did you have something to confess?"

"I want you to take me in. I want you to protect me."

His wife's face appeared over his shoulder, at some hidden opening in their house, a corner or a door. She began to march forward.

"We've heard the distressing details of the Michalski girl's death," he said. "You have a nice sense of humor, Miles, coming here."

I said, "Please take me in. I need your help."

"I rather think my help is reserved for those who know how to use it."

"I'm in danger. In danger of my life."

His wife's face glared at me now from over his shoulder. "What does he want? Tell him to go away."

"I rather think he's going to ask to be put up for the night."

"Don't you have a duty?" I asked.

"I have a duty to all Christians," he said. "You are not a Christian. You are an abomination."

"Tell him to go away."

"I'm begging you."

Mrs. Bertilsson's head jerked upward, her face cold and hard. "You were too sick to take our advice when we saw you in town, and we're under no obligation to help you now. Are you asking us to let you stay here?"

"Just for a night."

"Do you think I could sleep with you in my house? Close the door, Elmer."

"Wait—"

"An abomination." He slammed the door. A second later I saw the drapes meeting in the middle of the window.

Helpless. Helpless to help, helpless to be helped. This is the story of a man who couldn't get arrested.

I drove to Main and stopped the car in the middle of an empty street. I honked the horn once, then twice. For a moment I rested my forehead on the rim of the steering wheel. Then I opened the door. I could hear the buzz of a neon sign, the momentary beating of wings far overhead. I stood beside the car. Nothing around me moved, nothing demonstrated life. All of the shops were dark; on either side of the street, cars pointed their noses at the curb like sleeping cattle. I shouted. Not even an echo answered. Even the two bars seemed deserted, although illuminated beer signs sparkled in their windows. I walked down the middle of the street toward Freebo's. I felt drifting blue gather around me.

A stone the size of a potato was caught in the grid of a drain by the curbside. It might have been one they had thrown at me. I tugged it out and hefted it in my hand. Then I hurled it at Freebo's long rectangular window. I remembered throwing glasses at the wall of my apartment, back in the passionate days of my marriage. There was an appalling noise, and glass shivered down onto the sidewalk.

And then everything was as it had been. I was still on the empty street; the shops were still light; no one was shouting, no one was running toward me. The only noise was the buzzing of the sign. I owed Freebo about fifty dollars, but I would never be able to pay him. I could smell dust and grass, the odors blown in on the wind from the fields. I imagined men inside the bar, backed away from the windows, holding their breath until I left. Inside with the scarred tables and the jukebox and the flashing beer signs, all waiting for me to leave. The last of the last chances.

On the morning of the twenty-first I woke up in the backseat of the car. I had been permitted to survive the night. Shouts, angry yells from Duane's house up the path. His problems with his daughter seemed terrifically remote, someone else's problem in someone else's world. I leaned over the car seat and pulled the door release, pushed the seat forward, and got out. My back ached; I had a sharp, persistent pain behind my eyes. When I looked at my watch I saw that it was thirteen hours to dark: I would not run from it. I could not. The day, my last, was hot and cloudless. Sixty feet away, the chestnut mare leaned its head over the fence of the side field and regarded me with silky eyes. The air was very still. A big horsefly, greenly iridescent, began to bustle across the top of the car, concentrating on the bird droppings. Everything about me seemed a part of Alison's coming, clues, sections of a puzzle which would lock into place before midnight.

I thought: if I get back into this car and try to drive off, she will stop me. Leaves and branches would block the windshield, vines would trap the accelerator. My visual sense of this was too powerful—for an instant I saw the homely interior of the VW choked with a struggling profusion of foliage, and I gagged on the spermy odor of sap—and I snatched my hand away from the top of the car.

I did not see how I could endure the tension of the intervening hours. Where would I be when she came?

With the desperate foolhardiness of a soldier who knows that the battle will come whether or not he is prepared for it, I decided what I would do at nightfall. Really, there was only one place for me to be when it happened. I had waited twenty years for it, and I knew where I would go to await the final moment, where I had to go, had to be when the noise of rushing wind came and the woods opened to release her for my own violent release. There were no more last chances.

Time passed. I moved dazedly around the house, at times wondering vaguely why Tuta Sunderson had not appeared, and then remembering that I had fired her. I sat on the old furniture, and fell bodily into the past. My grandmother slid a pan into the oven, Oral Roberts declaimed from the radio, Duane slapped his hands together from a chair in a dark corner. He was twenty, and his hair swept upward from his forehead in a pompadour. Alison Greening, fourteen years old, magically vibrant, appeared in the doorway (man's button-down shirt, fawn trousers, sexual promise making the air snap about her), and glided through on sneakered feet. My mother, hers, talked on the porch. Their voices were bored and peaceful. I saw Duane look at my cousin with a look of hatred.

Then I found myself in the bedroom with no memory of having climbed the stairs. I was staring at the bed. I remembered the feeling of breasts against my chest, first small, then cushiony, how I had fit myself into a ghost's body. She was still moving downstairs; I heard her light footsteps crossing the living room, heard her slam the porch door.

You got into trouble again last year. My face had blazed. *Summer's lease is fading, dear one.* I went across into my office and saw papers spilling out of bushel baskets. *Do birds cough?* I saw only one conclusion. I was in check. Still, in memory, she glided downstairs. I felt as though absorbent cotton encased me, as though I were moving through treacle, thick dust . . .

I went back to the bedroom and sat in the chair which faced the bed. I had lost everything. My face felt mask-like, as if I could peel it off like Rinn's balm. Even as I began to weep, I recognized that my features had become as blank and empty as her own, the night I had seen her gazing carelessly at me from this chair. She has entered me again, she is downstairs drinking Kool-Aid in the bubble of time that is 1955, she is waiting.

*   *   *

Some hours later, I am sitting at my desk and looking out the window when I hear Alison Updahl scream. A moment later, my senses awakening from their fog, I see her tearing down the path to the barn. In the back her shirt is ripped, as though someone had tried to swing her around by it, and it flaps as she pelts away. When she reaches the barn she does not stop, but races around the side and goes over a barbed-wire fence to get into the back field and run in its declivities and grassy rises up toward the blanketing of woods on that side of the valley. These are the woods where Alison Greening and I, each carrying a shovel, had climbed to look for Indian mounds. When the Woodsman reaches a little rise and begins to run down into a hollow packed with massed yellow blossoms, she tears off the flapping T-shirt and throws it behind her. I know in that second that she is crying.

Then a secondary, nearer motion: I see Duane, dressed in his working clothes, coming indecisively down the path. He carries a shotgun under one arm, but he seems in an uneasy relationship to it. He marches forward ten feet, the shotgun pointing the way, and then he pauses, looks at it, and turns his back on me. A few paces up the path, then another turn and the resumption of the march in my direction. Then he looks at the shotgun again. He takes another three steps forward. Then he sighs—I see his shoulders lift and depress—and tosses the gun into the weeds by the garage. I see his mouth form the word *bitch*. He glances at the old farmhouse for a moment as if he is wishing that he might see it too in flames. Then he looks up at the window and sees me. I immediately smell gunpowder and burning flesh. He says something, jerking his body, but the words do not carry through the glass, and I thrust open the window.

"Get out here," he says. "God damn you, get out here."

I go downstairs and out onto the porch. He is pacing over the ruin of the front lawn, his hands deep in the coverall pockets, his head bent. When he sees me, he gives a powerful sideways kick to a ridge of dirt left by a skidding tire. He glares at me, then bends his head again, and swivels his foot in the ridge of dirt. "I knew it," he says. His voice is hoarse and choking. "Damn women. Damn you."

His face seems to be flying apart. His condition is unlike the fury I had seen earlier, and more like the suppressed dull rage I had witnessed in the equipment barn, when he flailed the tractor with a hammer. "You're filth. Filth. You made her filthy. You and Zack."

I come out of the porch into waning sunlight. Duane seems nearly to be steaming. To touch him would be to burn your hands. Even in my foggy state, concentrated on what will happen four or five hours later, I am impressed by the high charge of Duane's emotional confusion. His hatred is nearly visible, but as if suffocated, like a fire under a blanket.

"I saw you drop the gun," I say.

"You saw me drop the gun," he mimics. "You saw me drop the gun. Big fucking deal. You think I couldn't kill you with my bare hands?" With ten percent more pressure behind it, his face would explode and go sailing away in a hundred pieces. "Hey? You think you're gonna get away that easy?"

Get away with what, I could ask, but I am riveted by his despair.

"Well, you ain't," he says. He cannot control his voice, and it spirals up into falsetto. "I know what happens to you sex creeps in jail. They'll make hash out of you down there. You'll wish you were dead. Or maybe you'll be in a nut house. Huh? Either way, you're gonna rot. *Rot.* Every day you'll be a little sorrier you're still alive. And that's good. Because you don't deserve to die."

The quantity of his hatred awes me.

"Oh, it's gonna happen, Miles. It's gonna *happen.* You had to come back here, didn't you? Wave your goddamned face, your goddamned education, in front of me? You bastard. I had to beat it out of her, but she told me. She admitted it." Duane brings himself forward toward me, and I see the colors alternating on his face. "Guys like you think you can get away with anything, don't you? You think the girls will never talk about it."

"There was no 'it,' " I say, finally understanding.

"Tuta saw her. Tuta saw her come out. She told Red, and my friend Red told me. So I know, Miles, I know. You made her filthy. I can't even stand to look at you."

"I didn't rape your daughter, Duane," I say, scarcely believing that this scene is happening.

"You say. So tell me what happened, shithead. You're good with words, you gotta command of the language, tell me what happened."

"She came to me. I didn't ask her to. I didn't even want her to. She climbed into my bed. She was used by someone else."

Of course Duane misunderstands me. "Someone else—"

"She was used by Alison Greening."

"God damn, God damn, God damn," and he jerks his hands out of his pockets and strikes himself on either side of his head. "When they got you locked up to rot, I'm gonna burn this place to the ground, I'm gonna bulldoze it over, all you city people can go to hell, I'm—" He is calmer. He takes his fists from his temples, and his eyes blaze at me. They are, I notice for the first time, the same color as his daughter's, but as filled with abstract light as Zack's.

"Why did you decide not to shoot me?"

"Because that's too easy on you. You didn't come back here, stir it all up, just to get shot. The worst things in the world are gonna happen to you." His eyes blaze again. "You don't have to think I don't know about that little fucker Zack. I know about how she sneaks out. You don't know anything I don't, even if you buy 'em drinks and that. I got ears. I hear her crawling back into her room in the mornings—she's just dirt, like all the others. Starting with the one I named her after. They're all dirt. Animals. A dozen of 'em wouldn't make one good man. I don't know why I ever got married. After that Polish bitch I knew all about women. *Dirty,* like you. I knew I couldn't keep her and you apart. Women are all the same. But you're going to pay."

"Do you hate me so much because of Alison Greening?" I ask. "Pay for what?"

"For being you." He says this flatly, as if it is self-explanatory. "It's all over for you, Miles. Hovre is gonna put you away. I just talked to him. Twenty-four hours at the most. If you try to run, they'll get you."

"You talked to Hovre? He's going to arrest me?" I feel the beginnings of relief.

"You bet your ass."

"Good," I say, startling Duane. "That's what I want."

"Jesus man," Duane utters softly.

"Alison Greening is coming back tonight. She's not what she used to be—she's something horrible. Rinn tried to warn me." I look into Duane's incredulous face. "And she's the one who has been killing those girls. I thought it was Zack, but now I know it was Alison Greening."

"Stop-saying-that-name," Duane says.

I turn around and begin to sprint toward the house. Duane shouts behind me, and I yell back to him, "I'm going inside to call Hovre."

He follows me inside and glares at me suspiciously as I dial the number of the police station. "Ain't gonna do you no good," he mutters, stumping around the kitchen. "Only thing you can do now is wait for it. Or get in that heap of yours and try to run. According to Hank you can't do more than forty in her, though. You wouldn't get to Blundell before Hovre caught you." He is talking as much to himself as to me; his bowed back faces me.

I am listening to the ringing of the telephone, expecting Dave Lokken to answer; but Polar Bears' voice comes to me instead. "Chief Hovre."

"This is Miles."

Duane: "Who you talkin' to? Is that Hovre?"

"This is Miles, Polar Bears. Why aren't you on your way out here?"

There is a baffling pause. Then he says: "Why, Miles, I just been hearing about you. Seems you couldn't stop. I reckon your cousin Du-ane is there with you."

"Yes. He is."

"Fuckin'-A I am," says Duane.

"Good. Say, we got results on that blood. It's AB, all right. It'll take another day to break it down further to see if it's male or female, the lab boys say."

"I don't have another day."

"Miles old friend, I'd be surprised if you had another five minutes. Isn't Duane carrying a twelve-gauge? I told him to bring one when he went down to see you. The law can overlook some things a man might do, if he's been pushed too far."

"I'm asking you to save my life, Polar Bears."

"Some might say that you'd be a whole lot safer dead, Miles."

"Does Lokken know what you're doing?"

I hear the wheeze of his coughing. "Dave had to go all the way to the other end of the county today. Funny thing."

"Tell him to get out here now," Duane says. "I can't stand having you in the house anymore."

"Duane says you should come now."

"Why don't you and Duane keep up your conversation? Sounds real fruitful to me." He hung up.

I turn around, still holding the receiver, and see Duane looking at me with dull eyes in a flushed face. "He's not coming, Duane. He thinks you're going to shoot me. He wants you to do it. He sent Lokken off on a wild-goose chase so nobody will know how he arranged things."

"You're talking guff."

"Did he tell you to bring a shotgun?"

"Sure. He thinks you killed those girls."

"He's more devious than that. He told me about Alison Greening. He told me what happened. He'd rather have me dead than in jail. If I'm dead, I'm still guilty of the killings, but I can't talk to anybody."

"You shut *up* about that," he says, his arms swinging at his sides. "Don't say one word about that."

"Because you hate thinking about it. You couldn't do it. You couldn't rape her."

"*Huh*," Duane snorts, his face red and strained. "I didn't come here to talk about this. I just wanted to hear you admit you put the dirtiest part of yourself into my girl. Do you think I liked beating it out of her?"

"Yes."

"*What?*"

"Yes. I think you did enjoy it."

Duane whirls and presses the palms of his hands against a kitchen cupboard, supporting his weight on his arms, as I had seen him do against the engine block of a tractor. When he turns around again he is doing his best to smile. "Now I know you're crazy. Boy, that just says it all. Maybe I oughta kill you, like you say Hovre wants."

"Maybe you should." I am transfixed by his ghastly attempt at relaxation. His face is colorless now; it looks as though you could pluck gobbets off it, like clay. His personality, which I had thought as stolid and bull-like as his body, appears to be breaking up, shaking apart into its facets.

"Why did you let me come here at all?" I ask. "Why didn't you write back to say that someone else was staying in the house? And why did you pretend to be friendly when I first came?"

He says nothing; he simply looks at me, dull and sullen anger expressed by every inch and angle of his body.

"I'm as innocent of the deaths of those girls as I was of the death of Alison Greening," I say to him.

"Maybe that was the first warning you had," Duane says. "I'm gonna be listening for the sound of that junker of yours, so you'd best sit tight until Hovre comes to get you." Then a smile which appears almost genuine. "I'm gonna enjoy that." His gray face breaks, alters, as a perception hits him. "By God, if I'd of had my shotgun here, I would have cut you in two."

"Then Alison Greening would come for you tonight."

"It don't make any difference how crazy you pretend to be," Duane says. "Not now it don't."

"No. Not now."

When Duane left the farmhouse he said, "You know, my wife was as dumb as the others. That cow actually wanted it. She couldn't even pretend she was better than that. She used to yammer about how dirty I got out in the fields, and I used to say the dirt on me is nothing compared to what's in your mind. I just hoped she would give me a son."

When dusk began to devour the landscape, I knew that I had approximately three hours to get where I had to go. I would have to walk. Duane would hear the car, and telephone Hovre. They did not belong where I was going. The alternative was to wait in the farmhouse and take every creak of the boards for the sign of her coming. No. If she were going to appear and spring the trap of our old vow, the Pohlson quarry, where it started, would be where it would end. I had to go back, alone, to where it had begun, to see it as it was on that night, without the Woodsman and Zack, to stand in darkness on those flat slabs of stone and breathe that air. I felt almost that if I stood on that spot again, I might go back to the beginning and reverse things: might find an echo of the living girl, and reclaim myself and her in that salvation. Duane and his furious repressions, Polar Bears and his schemes, were tiny in the light of this immense possibility. I forgot them both five minutes after Duane left the farmhouse. Starving Paul Kant had walked through the fields; so would I.

It took me a little more than a quarter of the time it had Paul. I simply walked along the soft verge of the highway, going in dying light where I had to go; once a rattling slat-sided truck passed me, and I veered off into a cornfield until its red taillights disappeared around a bend. I had a pervasive sense of invisibility. No clumsy hothead in a truck could stop me; no more than I could stop my cousin from asserting her claim. Fear sparkled beneath my skin; I walked quickly, scarcely aware of the gravel over which I moved; at the top of the long winding hill I touched the wood of the Community Chest sign and felt the dampness of woodrot. Lights burned in a farmhouse just visible in a black valley. For a second I had the sensation that I was about to leap from the hill's sheer side and fly—a dream of the inhuman, a dream of escape. Cold hands brushed my sides and urged me forward.

At the base of the drive leading up the smaller hill to the quarry I paused for breath. It was just past nine o'clock. In the darkening sky hung the white lifeless stone of the moon. I took a step up the drive: I was a magnet's negative pole, the lunar pole. My feet throbbed in their city shoes. A random branch of an oak stood out with supernatural, almost vocal clarity; a huge muscle rolled beneath its crust of bark. I sat on the edge of a pebbly granite shelf and slid off my shoes. Then I dropped them beside the rock and, finding what I had to find to move, moved. The air breathed me.

On tiptoe, with wincing feet, I went up the drive. Gravel gave way to dry grass. At the top of the drive I eased down onto my heels. The flat brown area was before me, the line of dying bushes at the far end. The sky was darkening fast. I realized that I was carrying my jacket in one hand, and I pulled it up over my shoulders. Air caught in my throat. Alison Greening seemed profoundly *in* the landscape, a part of all of it. She was printed deeply into every scrabble of rock, every tick of leaf. I went forward, the bravest act of my life, and felt invisibility stir about me.

By the time I reached the other side of the flat brown space, it had become dark. The translation from dusk to night was instantaneous, a subdivision of a second. My stockinged feet found a smooth rock slab. A blister burned at my heel. Its redness mounted up my leg, I could see that color rising and staining me, and I went forward again over brown grass to the line of bushes. My mind fluttered, and I snapped my head to the right, and saw a pair of finches shooting off into the bowl of the sky. Moonlight touched them for an instant, then lay upon and silvered the threads and bones of the sparse bushes. I took another step, and was on the first rock, looking down at the cup of black water which was the quarry. It was the center of an intense, packed silence.

And of a great brightness. The moon, as medallionlike as Alison's face, shimmered and glowed from the water's center. My leg was shaking. My mind was no more than a flat plate of images. It would have taken me a minute to remember my name, that leap from slippery *Miles* to froggy *Teagarden*. The stone beneath me ground at my feet; I went down onto the next step, and felt myself pulled toward the brightness. That flat pane of water with its glowing center drew me on, brought me down toward it. Another step. The entire silent pool edged with smooth rock was as if humming—no, was humming, wedged in the divide between the bottomless dark of the water and the flat shining head of the moon. The world tipped to slide me down, and I tipped with it.

Then I was there, on the bottom of the bottom of the world. Cool rock pushed upward on the soles of my feet. Heat burned at my temples and crisped small hairs in my nose. Water slid across my wrists. My fingers touched my sleeves, and they were dry. At the bottom of the bottom of the world, my face turned to the moon's cold effigy, I sat in a hard unreal brightness.

When my body began to tremble I planted my hands on the shelf of cool rock and closed my eyes. The signs of her coming were unimaginable: it seemed to me that she might step out from the center of that gleaming disc on the water. Rock flowed under my hands; with my eyes clamped shut I was moving, part of a moving element, the rock which fitted itself beneath my hands and body like a negative, mirrored image. This sensation was very strong. My fingerprints folded into minute grooves in the stone, hand-shapes met my hands, and when I snapped open my eyes again I thought I would see before them a sheer rise of rock.

I centered myself in my body, centered my body on the slab of rock. I felt the rock lift with my breathing, the veins in my hands connect to veins in the stone, and I ceased to move. I thought: I am a human mind in a human body. I saw white unreal brightness on my knees and stockinged feet. High walls circled me, the water lay still, the only thing in the world beneath me. I knew that I had very little time left. The jacket lay across my shoulder like leaves. I had all the rest of my life to think; to wait.

But waiting itself is thinking, anticipation is an idea in the body, and for a long time even my pulse was charged with the energy of my waiting. I thought of hurtling through time; I was no longer trembling. My fingers slid into grooves in the stone. In the bowl of the quarry, the night was terrifically still. Once I opened my eyes and looked at my watch where dots by the numerals and slivers along the hands glowed green: it was ten-forty-five.

I tried to remember when we had started to swim. It had to be sometime between eleven and twelve. Alison had probably died near to midnight. I looked up at the stars and then back down at the water where the moon floated. I could remember every word spoken on that night, every gesture. They had been crowded into my mind for the past twenty years. Twice, while lecturing to my sophomores, I had spun backwards to those busy minutes and seen them all again while my disembodied voice droned on, being witty at the expense of literature. It was true to say that I had been trapped here, in that section of time, ever since, and that what had frightened me in my classroom was no more than an image of my life.

It was all still happening, in a space behind my eyes that belonged to it, and I could look inward to see it and us. The way she looked, grinning at me as cool air settled on my shoulders. *Do you want to do what we do in California?* Her hands on her hips. I could see my own hands working at my buttons, my legs, the legs of a thirteen-year-old boy, hanging pale and slim to the rock slab. I looked up and she was a white arc just entering the water, a vision of a leaping fish.

That would be printed on two other minds as well as mine. They had seen us: our bodies cutting the water, our arms white, her hair a sleek mass against my face. From their angle we would be pale faces beneath water-darkened hair, two faces so close as to be flowing together.

I shook all over. I raised my arm and looked at my wrist: eleven o'clock. A patch of skin on the back of my neck began to jump.

I closed my eyes again and the energy of the stone again rushed up to meet my hands, heels, outstretched legs. My breathing seemed overloud, amplified by the complicated passages within my body. The whole area of the quarry was breathing with me, taking in and releasing air. I counted to one hundred, making each inhalation and exhalation last eight beats.

Very soon.

I saw myself as I had been a month earlier, when I had only half dared to admit that I had returned to the farm to keep an appointment with a ghost. And brought a string of deaths dragging like a tail behind me. Despite the pretense of the boxes of books and notes, I had not done even three good days' work on my dissertation: I had given it up on the feeblest of pretexts, that Zack's foolish ideas were too much like Lawrence's. Instead I had almost willfully turned the valley against me. And I *saw* myself: a large man with thinning hair, a man whose face immediately expresses whatever emotion has hold of him, a man rampaging through a small town. I had insulted more people in four weeks than I had in the past four years. I witnessed all of this as from the outside, saw myself bursting into stores and giving crazy messages from bar stools, miming shoplifting, my face registering disgust. Even Duane had done a better job of disguising his feelings. From the morning of my arrival, I had felt Alison Greening's approach, and that fact—the vision of her hovering at the edge of the fields—had sent me sliding as irrationally as a pinball.

I said her name, and a leaf rustled. The moonlight made my body look two-dimensional, a figure from a cartoon.

It had to be nearly the time. Eleven-thirty. Pressure suddenly happened in my bladder; I felt my face grow hot. I crossed my legs and waited for the pressure to ebb. I began to rock forward on my stiff arms. Nerves in the stone responded to my movement, and echoed it so that at first the stone rocked with me, and then took all the motion and rocked me itself. The need to urinate built into an ache. I was rocked more intensely, and it vanished. I lay back and let the stone fit a hollow for my skull. My hands, stretched by my sides, found their true places.

Very soon.

A cloud covered half the stars and slowly scudded past the dead circle of the moon. My body seemed already to have given up its life, and the stone to have taken it into itself. The cold quarry water was breathing through me, using me as its bellows; I thought I heard her walking toward me, but a breeze skimmed past, and still the complications of life, the complications of feeling streamed from my body into everything around. I thought: it cannot last, it is too much, death is necessary, necessary. Suddenly it seemed to me, at the bottom of my fear like a flash of gold, that I had returned to the valley knowing that I would die there.

I heard music and knew it came from the electric point of contact between my head and the rock above the water. Soon, soon, soon. My death came speeding toward me, and I felt my body lighten. The tremendous forces about me seemed to lift me an inch or two above the rock, the music sounded in my head, I felt my soul contract into a humming capsule just below my breastbone. So I remained for a long time, gathered to split apart at her touch.

I witnessed my heavy profane sarcastic deathbound naive person hurtling through Arden, hiding within the body of my grandmother's house, quailing on the floor of a forest, half-raping a coiling girl; I gasped because the sensation of levitating, all my cells linked by moonlight in a contract to ignore gravity, had endured so long.

All my being told me when midnight approached. I could not a second time will away the quick pain in my bladder, a leaf rattled in a twist of wind, and warm fluid rushed over my legs in a delicious letting go. I reached out for her, every second of her time ticked along my body. I caught only bright empty air.

And fell back to earth and unliving stone. In that giant embarrassment, the music ceased and I was conscious of my lungs pulling in air, the rock inert beneath me, the water black and cold, and I pushed myself backwards to rest my back against the wall of the quarry. The wet legs of my trousers hung on my legs. I'd had the time wrong. It must have happened later; but I caught the edge of desperation in the thought, and I leaned back and looked through the bleach of moonlight to the greatest loss in my life.

It was two minutes past twelve. She had not come. The twenty-first of July had slipped into the past and she was not coming. She would never come. She was dead. I was stranded alone in only the human world. My guilt, moving under some impetus of its own, shifted hugely within me and came to a new relationship with my body.

I could not move. I had invented it all. I had seen nothing at the edge of the fields—nothing but my hysteria. I pulled the jacket tightly around me, obeying a reflex left over from childhood.

The shock endured for hours. By the time my trousers had begun to dry, I realized that my legs and feet had gone to sleep, and I leaned forward and bent my knees with my hands. Intense pain arrowed out from my knees. I was grateful enough for it to try to stand. For a time I drowned my awareness in pain, moving awkwardly on someone else's legs. Then I sat on one of the stone steps and looked again into loss. I could not cry: too much of the loss was of myself. Whatever I was going to be, whenever I could think about becoming something I could call myself, I was going to be different. I had made up a self which relied on the possibility of Alison Greening for its shadings, and now I felt like a Siamese twin whose other half had been surgically severed, cast away. The guilt which I had carried for twenty years had drastically altered its dimensions, but I could not tell if it had grown larger or smaller.

I was going to have to live.

I spent the entire night by the quarry's side, though I knew from the moment I had seemed to fall back to earth—even before I had looked at my watch— that Alison Greening was gone from my life for eternity.

During the last hour I spent mourning Alison's second and final departure from my life, I was able to think about Arden and what had been happening there. Duane, Polar Bears, Paul Kant, myself. How after twenty years we had come together again in a tragic landscape. How we had all been marked by women. I saw the patterns tying us together, like Zack's "lines of force."

And I saw something else.

At last I understood that the murderer of the girls had been my cousin Duane. Who hated women more than any other man I had ever met, who had probably planned the murders of the girls who resembled Alison Greening from the day I had written him that I was coming to Arden. Duane's were the old Coke bottles, the axes, the doorknobs: Zack must have stolen the one I had seen from wherever Duane had hidden them.

Sitting by the quarry's side, still numb with the shock of loss, I saw it with a brisk, heartless clarity. Alison gone, it could only be Duane. And his daughter had feared this, I saw—she had run from any discussion of the girls' deaths. What I had taken for a desire to appear more callous (therefore, she imagined, more adult) than she was made even more sense, given the fear that her father was a killer. She had really rebuffed any conversation about the dead girls.

I stood up: I could walk. A kind of strength blessed me. An entire era of my life, like a geologic period, was coming to an end—it would end with what I was going to have to do. I did not have the whisper of an idea of what I would do after that.

I walked down the side of the hill and found my shoes. In one night they had gone dead and curling, and when I forced my feet into them, the inner soles felt like the hides of dead lizards. They seemed not to fit, to have been shaped by another man.

When I stepped onto the highway I saw a high rattling truck coming toward me from the direction of Arden. It was a blood relative of the truck from which I had fled the previous night; I stuck out my hand, thumb up, and the man beside the wheel pulled up beside me. From the truck floated the earthy smell of pigs.

"Mister?" said the old man behind the wheel.

"My car broke down," I said. "I wonder if you're going anywhere near Norway Valley?"

"Hop yourself right in, young feller," he said, and leaned across to open the door for me.

I climbed in beside him. He was a wiry man in his mid-seventies, with white hair that stuck up like a scrubbing brush. On the steering wheel his hands were the size of steaks. "Up early," he said, not quite making it a question.

"I've been traveling a long time."

He started the truck rolling again, and its whole rear section began jouncing and squeaking.

"Are you actually going into the valley?"

"Sure," he said. "I just been taking a load of porkers into town, and now I'm going home. My boy and me farm a piece of land about eight-ten miles down the valley. You ever been that way?"

"No," I said.

"It's nice. It's real nice down there. Don't know what a healthy young feller like you is doing bumming around the country when you could settle down on the best farmland in the whole state. Man wasn't born to live in cities, way I see it."

I nodded. His words unlocked in me the knowledge that I was not going to return to New York.

"I reckon you're a salesman," he said.

"Right now I'm between jobs," I said, and earned a bright look of curiosity.

"Shame. But you vote Democrat, we'll get this country back on its feet and young men like you will have jobs again." He squinted into the road and the rising sun, and the bouncing truck sent wave after wave of pig over us. "You remember that, now."

When he turned the truck into the valley road, he asked just where I wanted to go exactly. "You might think about coming all the way with me, and we could set you up with a good cup of coffee. What say?"

"Thanks, but no. I'd like you to drop me off at Andy's."

"You're the boss," he said, perfectly equable.

Then we were slowing down before Andy's gas pumps. The seven-o'clock sunlight fell on the dust and gravel. As I pulled down the door handle, he turned his brush-topped head slyly toward me and said, "I know you were fibbing me, young man."

I just looked at him in surprise, wondering what he could have read in my face.

"About your auto. You don't have any auto, do you? You've been thumbing your way right along."

I met his smile. "Thanks for the ride," I said, and stepped down from the cab and the thick odor of pigs into warm light. He rattled away, going deeper into the valley, and I turned to walk across the gravel and climb the steps.

The door was locked. I peere in through the glass and saw no lights. Andy had no CLOSED sign on the door, but I looked at the bottom panel of glass behind the screen and saw a dusty card which said Mon–Fri 7:30–6:30, Sat 7:30–9:00. I pounded on the screen door, rattling it. After forty seconds of steady pounding, I saw Andy waddling toward me through the crowded tables, peering at me to figure out who I was.

When he got close enough to identify me, he stopped. "We're closed." I motioned him forward. He shook his head. "Please," I shouted. "I just want to use your phone."

He hesitated, and then came slowly up toward the door. He looked worried and confused. "You got a phone down at Duane's place," he said, his voice muffled by the glass.

"I have to make a call before I get there," I pleaded.

"Who you going to call, Miles?"

"The police. Polar Bears Hovre."

"What're you gonna say to the chief?"

"Listen in and you'll know."

He came the necessary two steps and put his hand on the lock. His face jerked, and then he slid the bolt and opened the door. "Screen door's still locked, Miles. I suppose if you're gonna call the police it's okay . . . but how do I know that's what you're gonna do?"

"You can stand right behind me. You can dial it for me."

He revolved the pinwheel catch. "Quiet. Margaret's back in the kitchen. She won't like this." I followed him inside. He turned his face toward me; he looked worried. He was used to making the wrong decisions. "Phone's on the counter," he whispered.

As he went toward it his wife called from the back of the store. "Who was it?"

"Drummer," Andy called back.

"For goodness' sake, send him off. It's too early."

"Just a minute." He pointed to the telephone; then whispered, "No. I'll dial it."

When he had the number he gave me the receiver and crossed his arms over his chest.

The telephone rang twice, and then I heard Lokken's voice. "Police?"

I asked to speak to Polar Bears. *If you want your killer*, I was going to say, *just do what I tell you. He'll be on his farm, driving his tractor or banging on some machinery.*

"Teagarden?" came the deputy's high-pitched astonished whine. "Is that you? Where the hell did you get yourself to anyways? You're supposed to be here, this morning. What the hell?"

"What do you mean, I'm supposed to be there?"

"Well, see—the chief sent me out on this damnfool errand yesterday afternoon. I didn't get what I was supposed to get because it wasn't there in the first place, it never even *was* there, he just wanted me outta the way I guess. Anyhow by the time I got back it was near to midnight and he was hoppin' mad. Duane called him up and said you run off somewheres. So the chief says, hold your horses, I'll know where he is. I think he went and got Du-ane to help him bring you in. So where are you now? And where's the chief?"

"I'm at Andy's store," I said. I glanced over at him. His worried face was turned toward the rear of the shop; he was afraid his wife would appear and find me. "Lokken, listen to me. I know who should be arrested, and I think I know where the chief would have gone. Pick me up at Andy's."

"You bet your ass I'm pickin' you up," said Lokken.

"You'll get your killer," I said, and handed the receiver back to Andy.

"Should I hang it up?" he asked, perplexed.

"Hang it up."

He clicked it down and then stared at me, becoming more conscious every moment of my beard stubble and wrinkled clothes. "Thanks," I said, and turned away and threaded past the tables and went out, leaving him with his hand on the telephone. I went down the steps and out into the early light to wait for Lokken.

In eight minutes, which must have been a record, the deputy's squad car came speeding down the valley road. I waved, and Lokken braked to a halt, raising a great white plume of dust. He jumped out of the car as I walked across the road toward him. "All right, what is this?" he demanded. "This just plain don't make sense. Where's Chief Hovre?"

"I think he imagined that I'd go back up to that clearing where you found the Michalski girl. Maybe Duane went with him."

"Maybe he did, maybe he didn't," said Lokken. His hand was on the butt of his gun. "Maybe we'll go there, maybe we won't. Why in hell did you call the station?"

"I told you." His hand curled around the gun butt. "I know who killed those girls. Let's get in the car and talk about it on the way."

Very suspiciously, he stepped away from the side of the car and permitted me to walk around its nose. We got in at the same time. I leaned back against the hot plastic of the seat. "All right," Lokken said. "You better start talking. If it's real good I might listen."

"Duane Updahl did it," I said. His hand, holding the ignition key, froze on the way to the slot and he swiveled his head to gape at me.

"I wasn't even in town when Gwen Olson died," I said.

"That's why I'm listening to you," said Lokken. I returned his glance. "We just heard this morning from the Ohio state police. The chief had them checking into your story about staying in a motel ever since you told him about it. They finally found a guy named Rolfshus says he recognized your picture. He runs a little place off the freeway. Well, this here Rolfshus says you might be someone checked in there that night."

"You mean Polar Bears was looking for that motel since the night I told him about it?"

"He's tooken statements too," said Lokken. "Lots of folks up here don't like you." He started the car. "I don't know what the chief would say, but it sure as hell looks to me like you're okay on that Olson killing. So why the hell do you say it's Duane?"

I gave him my reasons as we spun down the road. His hatred of women, his hatred of me. The physical evidence. "I think he set up the whole thing to get me a life sentence in the booby hatch," I said. "And Polar Bears was hoping he'd shoot me, so that I couldn't say anything about how Alison Greening really died. He sent you off so you'd be far away when it happened."

"Christ, I don't know," said Lokken. "It's crazy. What's this about Alison Greening?"

So I told him that too. "And I think Duane has been half-crazy ever since," I ended. "When I wrote him that I was coming back, I think he just snapped."

"Holy man."

"I sort of snapped too. Otherwise I think I would have seen it earlier. I had a crazy theory, but last night it turned out to be wrong."

"Everything about this is crazy," Lokken said in despair. He pulled the car up on the shoulder of the road beside the rows of corn. Polar Bears' car sat, facing the way we had come, on the other side of the road. "Looks like you were right about the chief, anyhow. You think they're both up there?"

"I think Duane would go with Polar Bears," I said. "It'd be too risky for him not to."

"Let's have a look. Hell, let's have a look." We got out of the car and jumped the ditch.

He said nothing, the run up toward the woods took much of his breath, but after we had forded the creek Lokken spoke again. "If what you say is right, Duane might of tried something on the chief."

"I don't think he would," I said.

"Yeah, but he might of," he said, and drew his gun. "I don't exactly remember where the damn clearing was."

I said, "Follow me," and began to work up over the rise and toward the beginning of the woods. Lokken crashed along behind me.

When I reached the first of the trees I began to trot uphill, going in the direction of Rinn's old cabin. I had no idea of how the scene would be played. For once, I was grateful for Lokken's presence. It did not make sense that Polar Bears would have spent the entire night in the clearing. Gradually the big gnarled trees drew closer. I slowed to a walk. In places I had to part branches and tall weeds with my hands.

"Do you notice anything funny?" I said after a time.

"Huh?" Lokken's voice came from a good distance behind me.

"There isn't any noise. No birds, no squirrels. No animal noises."

"Huh," said Lokken.

It was true. Other times when I had come up into the woods, I had been aware of a constant natural chatter about me. Now it was as though all the birds and animals had died. In that dark place, surrounded by the looming trees, the silence was decidedly spooky.

"Gunshot scares 'em off," Lokken said. "Maybe there was some trouble." He sounded as apprehensive as I felt, and I knew that he still had the gun in his hand.

"We're pretty close to the clearing now," I said. "We'll know soon."

A few minutes later I saw the ring of trees around the clearing. "Right through there," I said, and looked around at Lokken. His face was red with effort.

"Yeah. I remember now." He cupped his hands around his mouth. "Chief? You there?" He got not even an echo; he shouted again. "Chief! Chief Hovre!" He looked at me hard, angry and frustrated, sweat running down his face. "Dammit, Teagarden, shake your butt."

Though I felt cold, I too had begun to sweat. I could not tell Lokken that I was afraid to go into the clearing. Just then the woods seemed very potent.

"Come on, we saw the car, we know he's here," said Lokken.

"Something's funny," I said. I almost thought I could smell cold water. But that was not possible.

"Come on. Let's go. Move it." I heard the revolver click against a tree as he shook it at me.

I went toward the circle of trees; light hovered in the clearing beyond them.

Then I went through the sentinel trees and stepped into the clearing. The sudden dazzle of light at first made it difficult to see. Smoke came from the banked fire at the clearing's center. I took another step toward it. I wiped my eyes. There was no humming, vibrant noise of insects.

Then I saw them. I stopped walking. I could not speak.

Lokken noisily broke into the clearing behind me. "Hey, what's goin' on? Hey, Teagarden, they in here? You—" His voice ended as if chopped off with an ax.

I knew why Lokken had vomited when he had seen the body of Jenny Strand.

Polar Bears was in front, Duane behind him fixed to a shorter tree. They were pinned to their trees, both naked, their bodies blackened and hanging like crushed fruit.

Lokken came up beside me, making a noise in his throat. I could not take my eyes from them. It was the most savage thing I had ever seen. I heard the handgun thump onto the earth. "What the—" Lokken began. "What—"

"I was wrong," I whispered. "Jesus Christ, I was wrong. She's back after all."

"What—" Lokken's face had turned a glistening, cloudy white.

"It wasn't Duane after all," I said. "It was Alison Greening. They came up here last night and she killed them."

"Jesus, look at their skin," moaned Lokken.

"She was saving me. She knew she could get me anytime."

"Their *skin* . . ."

"She punished them for raping and killing her," I said. "Oh my God."

Lokken half-sat, half-fell into the tall grass.

"Now she'll be after Duane's daughter," I said, suddenly realizing that another life was probably lost. "We have to get down to the farm right now." Lokken was retching into the grass.

"How could someone—someone lift them two like that—"

"My crazy theory was right," I said to him. "We have to get to the farm right now. Can you run?"

"Run?"

"Then follow me as soon as you can. Go down and drive your car to Duane's place."

". . . place," he said. Then his eyes cleared a little, and he picked up the gun and waved it at me. "You wait. You don't go anywhere, hear?"

I bent over and pushed the gun aside. "I brought you here, remember? And do you think I'm strong enough to lift those two and pin them to trees like that? Now hurry up and get straight. If it isn't too late, we have to keep this from happening again."

"How—"

"I don't know," I said, and turned away from him, and turned again with an idea. "Give me your keys. You can hotwire Polar Bears' car."

When I got back down to the road I hastily got into the squad car and twisted Lokken's key in the ignition. The motor started at once. I rolled away from Polar Bears' car and stepped the accelerator all the way down to the floor.

A tractor chugged down the road before Bertilsson's church; it straddled two lanes. I blew the horn, and the straw-hatted overweight man on the tractors seat wagged his hand without looking back. I looked for the siren button and found it. The farmer jerked around on the seat, saw the car, and steered the tractor to the side of the road. I blasted the horn and zipped by.

When I drove up to the old farmhouse I could see nothing unusual—the mare grazed among the cows, the lawn lay ripped and burned, Alison was not in sight. I swallowed, turning into the drive, afraid that I would find her as I had found her father and Polar Bears. I braked as I cut the car onto the lawn, and jumped out before it had stopped rolling.

I could smell her—I could smell cold water, as if rain had just ceased to fall. My legs nearly refused to move, and in my stomach lay an iciness that fear had deposited there.

I began to jog up the path to Duane's house. A door slammed. I realized that Alison Updahl had seen the squad car pull into the drive. She came running around the side of her house. When she saw me instead of Polar Bears or Dave Lokken, she stopped running and stood hesitantly on the path, looking worried, pleased and confused all at once. The air seemed to tighten, as it had on my first night in the woods: it seemed to grow thick and tight with malevolence. "Run!" I shouted to the girl. I waved my arms, semaphoring. "Get going!" The smell of the quarry washed over us, and this time she caught it, for she half-turned and lifted her head.

"Danger!" I yelled, and began to sprint toward her.

Wind knocked me down as casually as a breeze flips a playing card.

"Miles?" she said. "My father didn't—"

Before she could say *come home*, I saw another woman, a smaller woman, appear momentarily on the path behind her. My heart froze. The shadowy second girl stood with her hands on her hips, looking at both of us. She vanished in the next instant. Alison Updahl must have felt some particle of the other's force, and she twisted her upper body to look behind her. I saw the terror begin in her—it was as though life and will had suddenly drained from her. She had seen something, but I did not know what. I got up from the dust and stones of the path. "Take off," I shouted to her.

But it was too late. She was too terrified by whatever it was she had seen, and she could not move. "Alison!" I shouted, and it was not the living girl I addressed. "Leave her alone!"

There was a whirring, typhoonlike noise of rushing, rattling wind. I turned in its direction, and was aware of Alison Updahl, stunned like a bird before a snake, turning slowly too. In the long grass before the road, wind was making a pattern: carving circles in flattened grass. Leaves and twigs began to fly together. Out on the road, stones and chunks of tarry asphalt lifted and flew toward the circling pattern.

I called to Alison Updahl, "Come toward me." She jerked herself forward, stumbled. The air was filled with small flying bits of wood, with tumbling leaves.

Through the leafstorm I ran toward her. She had fallen on the path, and a shower of small branches and stones came cascading down upon her. I grasped her hand and pulled her upright.

"I saw something," she muttered.

"I saw it too. We have to run."

The whirling pattern exploded. Most of the twigs and leaves filling the air were blasted soundlessly away, and spun lifelessly down to earth all over the area between the two houses. Only a tall skeletal superstructure, a vague outline of brown and green, remained towering; then it too blew away. A few stones rattled around us. The noise of screeching air, as if we were in a hurricane, stayed with us. Again the grass was printing itself into wide circles.

Her mouth opened, but she could not speak.

I took her hand more firmly and started to run. As we came hurrying down the path, Dave Lokken pulled into the drive in Polar Bears' car. He still looked like a man climbing out of a three-day drunk. He looked at the girl and me, running as hard as we could in his direction. "Hey," he said. "We gotta get those bodies . . ."

The circling pattern on the grass moved in his direction. Then I saw the figure of the girl, still shadowy, that I had seen on the path appear beside his car. Immediately, both windshields shattered. Lokken screamed and covered his face with his arms. A force I could not imagine pulled him from the car seat and through the open window at his side. He rolled across the gravel of the drive. His nose was pouring blood.

I tried to take Alison Updahl toward the side field, seeing that it was useless to try to hide in the house. We had gone three paces, me tugging, she stumbling, when our hands were torn apart and a wind that stank of the grave and rotting meat buffeted me aside and knocked me against the tree where my grandfather used to hang his scythe. Something started to move across the grass toward Alison Updahl.

It was as though the rind of the world had broken away, just sheared away, houses, trees, dogs, people, jobs, sunlight, all of it, and only the most primitive and the darkest life was left, what remains when everything comprehensible and usual, the rind, has peeled off and what emerges is like what you see when you flip over a long flat rock in the woods. Lokken, lying down in thick vines behind me, his nose still gouting blood, saw what I saw and screamed a second time. I knew that he was covering his eyes.

Alison got to the porch and rushed inside. Whatever it was that followed her vanished like a smudge on a pane of glass.

A spout of material—grass, leaves, pebbles—lifted from the lawn and shattered against the side of the house.

There was one gas can left in the garage. I saw it in my mind and felt the way the grip would fit my hand, and without knowing what I would do with it or how it would help, I made myself run into the garage and lift it. It was full, as I knew it would be. By itself, the weight of the heavy liquid seemed to draw me outside again, as if it were pulling me down a slope.

I went toward the house. You have already done this once, I told myself, you did it last night: but I knew that beside the quarry I had been ready to die and now I was not. I glanced back at Lokken; he was half crouching in the weeds into which she had rolled him, making noises in his throat. Blood covered his uniform shirt. No sound came from the house. I had a sudden mental vision of poor Duane, poor Polar Bears, pinned like fruit to the trees, their skin black and white, and obligation to the past—a feeling like love—moved me forward.

The smell was like water from graves, and it blanketed the porch. The gas can weighed heavily in my hand. I went through into the living room. Everything looked different. It was all there, nothing had been moved, but the room I had prepared for Alison Greening was now darker, meaner, shabbier; water stains blotted the walls. The smell was thicker inside than on the porch. Alison Updahl was cowering on a chair, her legs drawn up before her chest as if she would kick anything that came too close. I do not think that she saw me. Her face was a tight white shield. What she had seen when she had twisted around on the path was what Lokken and I had witnessed moving toward the house. "I'm not going to let her get you," I said. "I'm going to get you out." It was just noise.

I heard the windows breaking all over the house. The girl before me twitched: her eyes were all whites. "Stand up," I said. She put down her legs and tried to lever herself out of the chair. I turned away, satisfied that she could move and began to splash gasoline around the room. *If we have to go this way*, I thought, *it will be better than*—I saw the bodies pinned to the trees. I doused the furniture and splashed the gasoline on the back wall.

She was there, I knew; I could sense her in the house. It was that awareness of a hostile force I had had on the first night in the woods. Alison Updahl was up on her feet, her arms out in front of her like a blind woman's. The floor of the room was filmed with dirt; I saw a triangle of moss sprouting in a corner of the ceiling.

Then I saw a shadow against the gasoline-spattered wall. Small, formless, but essentially manlike. I dropped the empty gas can and it rang on the floor. Outside, a branch thwacked against the white boards. "Miles," Alison Updahl said very softly.

"I'm here." Useless words of comfort.

Leaves pushed against the broken kitchen window and forced it in. I heard them boiling in the corrupt air.

The shadow against the wall grew darker. I caught the girl's outstretched arm and pulled her toward me. Her eyes were fluttering, but I could see their pupils. "That smell . . ." She was on the edge of hysteria, I could hear it slice in her voice. She moved her head and saw the darkening shadow on the wall. The earth on the floor was stirring, moving in dervish circles.

"I'm going to light a match," I said. "When I do, I want you to run out on the porch and jump through the screen. "It's full of holes, it's weak. Then just keep running."

In horror she was watching the shadow darken. Her mouth opened. "I dug up a cow dog once . . . after I buried it . . ."

The shadow was three-dimensional, standing out from the wall like a relief. The rotten air filled with the rustling of leaves. With part of my mind I thought that the room looked like it had been pulled up out of a flooding river. I tightened my arm around Alison Updahl's shoulder. She seemed scarcely to be breathing. "Now get out," I said. "Fast." I pushed her toward the porch. My fingers shook. I twisted five or six matches out of the book and managed to scratch them in a general way against the lighting surface. They went up into flame, and I tossed them toward the back of the room.

Heat and light exploded there. Beneath the whooshing sound of the gas igniting I heard the porch screen letting go as Alison tumbled through it.

Standing across the room from me was no shadow, no circling pattern on the grass, no tall outline of sticks, no dark thing from beneath the world's rind, but a living person. Maybe if I were closer to her I could have seen the seams and imperfections, the rough vein of a leaf or the discoloration in the white of an eye, but from where I stood she looked as she had in 1955, a perfect girl of bone and skin and blood. Even then, she stopped my breath, with the fire beating in on us, beating in. It was that face composed of a thousand magical complications. Not a man in fifty could have looked at it without aching—for the pain it would know, for the pain it would cause.

She was not smiling, but it was as if she were. Her gravity encompassed and suggested all feeling. Only gravity, the grave composure of such a face, can do this. Behind her figure small and slim the fire beat upwards on the wall. My skin baked in the heat.

With moveless fascination I saw that the tips of the fingers on one of her hands had caught fire. Without passion, with a clear quiet gravity which promised more than I could know or understand, she held me with her eyes and face.

Upstairs the house let go with a noise like a sigh. Fire sucked in a flaming orange stream up the narrow staircase. I stepped backwards, away from the flames. My eyebrows were crisping; I knew that my face was burned as if by the sun.

I understood, being looked at by her or what looked like her, that a contract was being made. I understood that she would rather have me dead, but that Duane's daughter, her namesake, was the reason I would live. Now her entire hand was blazing, lost at the center of a glowing circle of light. Yes, there was a contract: I did not wholly comprehend it, I never wholly would, but I was bound to it.

She let me back away as far as the door. The expression on the face so much like her face had not altered by as much as a millimeter. The heat was unbearable, killing; I turned and ran, as much from the sense of bondage as from the fire.

Like Duane's Dream House, the old farmhouse was igniting behind me, and when I turned around on the lawn to watch it go up, I saw that it too was a dream house. I felt as though part of me was still inside it. I was bound to it, bound for life, as I had been for twenty years. Seven hours earlier I had thought I had come to a new accommodation, and I now saw—still only half-comprehendingly—that all accommodations are the same accommodation. I felt simultaneously heavier and lighter, with my face burned and my life returned to me freighted with the responsibilities I had always had because I had taken them, because I was simply the person who had them. My cousin's daughter was standing before the walnut trees, watching me with disbelief. When I noticed the expression in her eyes, I began to shake more noticeably. I turned away from her regard and watched the house. Dave Lokken lay whimpering behind us.

I thought of her in there, sealing me to my bargain. The whole upper and rear portions of the house were distorted by flame. I had laughed at Duane without recognizing that I too owned a dream house; and he had paid for my illusions, on the night when they were strongest in me.

"There was a—a person in there," breathed Alison Updahl. "I thought you were going to die."

"And I thought you were," I said. "I didn't know I could really do anything to stop it."

"But you could."

"I was here. That was enough."

The house was roaring now, making a vast devouring sound. She moved right up next to me. "I saw something horrible," she said. "Miles—"

"We saw it too," I told her, cutting off her gasp as she remembered. "That's why he's like that." We both glanced at Lokken, who was kneeling now and looking at the house with red stunned-looking eyes. Blood and vomit covered his shirt.

"If you hadn't come just then . . ."

"You would have been killed. And so would I. That's what it was about."

"But now that—*person*—won't come back."

"I don't know," I said. "I don't think so. She'll never come back like that, anyhow."

The whole house was in the last stage before collapse, and I could feel the heat beating against my face. I had to immerse myself in cold water. Blisters were forming on the palms of my hands. Behind the flames the old building was so skeletal that it looked as though it could float.

"When I dug up our cow dog it smelled like that," Alison said. "Like inside."

Boards and rafters began to tumble inward. The entire porch leaned against the wall of flames, sighed like a tired child, and soundlessly sank down into flatness.

"If she doesn't come back like that, how will she come back?"

"As us," I said.

"Your father and I loved her," I said. "I suppose he hated her too, but he named you after her because he loved her first, before he hated her."

"And he killed her, didn't he?" she asked. "And blamed it on you."

"He was just there. It was really Zack's father. He was the one."

"I knew it wasn't you. I wanted you to tell me, out at the quarry. I thought it was my dad." I could see her throat fluttering, jumping like a frog's. "I'm glad it wasn't."

"Yes."

"I feel . . . numb. I can't feel anything yet."

"Yes."

"I feel like I could talk a lot or not say anything at all."

"I know," I said.

The sides of the house were still upright, bracketing two open rooms of surging and twisting fire. At the center of a strand of flame stood an immovable shadow, a brief column of dark. Dave Lokken staggered to his feet.

"Is my father . . . ?" She took one of my hands, and her touch was cool.

"We weren't in time," I said. "Lokken and I found your father and Polar Bears. Up in the woods. I wish we could have done something. Lokken will bring them down."

The shadow I was watching as she clung to me darkened in the midst of the fire. Her tears flamed in the damaged skin at the base of my neck.

I led her to my car. I could not stand there anymore. His eyes stupid with shock, Lokken watched us getting into the VW. We too were in shock, I knew. My hands and face hurt, but I still could not feel the pain, it was only an abstraction of pain. I backed out into the drive and stopped to look at the house for the last time. Good-bye, grandmother, good-bye, dream house, good-bye, dreams, good-bye, Alison. Hello. Good-bye. Good-bye, Alison. Who would be back—as a gesture seen on a crowded street, or as a snatch of music heard from an open window, as the curve of a neck and the pressure of a pair of hands, or as a child. Who would always be with us, now. Neighbors were coming slowly up the road, some of them walking, holding dish towels and tools in their hands, some of them getting out of their pickups with taut, worried faces. Red and Tuta Sunderson were moving slowly across the lawn, going toward Dave Lokken. The old farmhouse was nearly gone and the flames were low. I backed the car through the people and swung it out on the road so that it was facing deeper into the valley.

"Where are we going?" asked Alison.

"I don't know."

"My father is really dead?" She put a knuckle in her mouth, knowing the answer.

"Yes. So is Polar Bears."

"I thought he was the one—the one who killed those girls."

"I thought so too, for a little while," I said. "I'm sorry. Polar Bears thought so too for a little while. He was the one that finally put the idea in my head."

"I can't go back, Miles," she said.

"Fine."

"Will I have to go back?"

"You can think about it," I said.

I was just steering, just driving a car. For a while her crying was a wet noise beside me. The road seemed to wind generally westward. I saw only farms and a winding road ahead of me. After this valley there would be another, and then another after that. Here the trees grew more thickly, coming right down to the buildings.

She straightened her back on the seat beside me. There were no more crying noises. "Let's just drive," she said. "I don't want to see Zack. I can't see him. We can write back from wherever we get to."

"Fine," I said.

"Let's go someplace like Wyoming or Colorado."

"Whatever you want," I said. "We'll do whatever you want." The curve of a neck, the pressure of a pair of hands, the familiar gesture of an arm. The blisters on my hands began truly to hurt; the nerves in my face began to transmit the pain of being burnt; I was beginning to feel better.

At the next curve of the valley the car trembled and the motor died. I heard myself begin to laugh.

UNDER VENUS

I

THE PAST IN THE PRESENT

1

1969, December: a cold domineering wind, the sense of snow—invisible snow—hanging in the air. It is the true weather of an ending. At the finish of a decade of great hope and great foolishness, the Denmarks are flying home to America.

The skyline of Plechette City, like that of Chicago or Detroit, is abrupt and jagged, unplanned. At night when airplanes circle out over Lake Michigan, homing in to General Steenborg airport at the city's southern extremity, the passengers can look out of their windows and see the massed office buildings—these defined by light—and department stores built up about Grand Avenue, the principal shopping street downtown, and the dark huddled shapes of factories, breweries, other office buildings spreading out on either side. The War Memorial building, which functions as the city's art museum and is its most interesting structure, is too low to be distinguished at night from the taller buildings behind it, and the aspects of the city most distinct to the airplane's passengers are the huge revolving four-faced clock atop the Chambers Denmark factory, lately purchased by the Globe Corporation, and the blinking flame-shaped light mounted on the Gas Company building. The flame is blue in December, for the light is a weather indicator, and blue means *cold*.

The big clock is illuminated from within; the intricate Gothic numerals and hands stand out on the turning faces a pure dense black. It is in the city's guidebooks, and postcards with its picture may be purchased at the airport and art museum, for the Chambers Denmark clock is the largest revolving four-faced clock in the world: in the nineteenth century, a point of civic pride. The Gas Company flame is a more recent feature of the city's night landscape; the Gas building was constructed in the nineteen-sixties, and constructed according to the strictest principles of Mr. Mies van der Rohe. This is a few blocks to the north of Grand Avenue. The big illuminated clock shines out over the southern sections of Plechette City, the old Polish ghetto and manufacturing district, lately overtaken by Puerto Rican immigrants. The two great lights, yellow and blue in the week before Christmas, face one another across the expanse of the city.

From north to south, roughly parallel to the indented contour of the lake, runs the Plechette River, named like the city after Jean-Marie Plechette, the French Jesuit who was its founder on the site of an Indian settlement in 1684. Father Plechette Christianized the Indians, regulated the fur trading—southern Wisconsin was at this time largely forested, and bear, fox, deer and beaver were everywhere numerous—and gave French names to the local landmarks. Within the next two hundred and fifty years, all of these names had been changed, and the only trace of Father Plechette's industry, apart from the town and the river renamed for him, was the mural in city hall which depicted the Jesuit, idealized and sternly handsome, stepping rather garishly out of a canoe into a circle of fierce braves. By the time the mural was executed, the Plechette River had been already so polluted that the only fish to be caught from the abutments of the Grand Avenue bridge were carp, and the bears and deer and beaver had retreated to the far north of the state, and on into upper Michigan.

When Elliot Denmark's great-granduncle, Brooks Denmark, the founder with Charles Chambers of the Chambers Denmark Corporation and the first man in Plechette City to envision the four-faced clock, took a solitary trip down the Mississippi River as a young man, he passed town after town where the inhabitants chiefly spoke French. Even in the mid-nineteenth century, the great period of French colonialism in America had left some perceptible residue. Think of the names of the towns: Racine, Prairie du Chien, Prairie du Sac, Fond du Lac. Brooks Denmark worked in little river towns, learned their language, and wrote back to his mother, sister and brother, *Dearest Mother, Eleanora, and Logan: My studies in the admirable language of the French progress apace, though I am uncertain of my ability to completely master the tongue. It is my most earnest desire to visit the homeland, the source of this language, where I feel with certainty that my studies would take on an even greater enthusiasm. My employer's family, the Mirceaus, speak of France as though it were the next state, and of Paris as though it were the home of all their finer sentiments. Perhaps we may all see it together someday in the future . . . Your loving son and brother, Brooks.* But this was to be Brooks Denmark's only *Wanderjahr*; he returned to Plechette City in the autumn, borrowed money from uncles and friends, and started his factory with Charles Chambers. In two years, he had forgotten all his French. When he was sixty, one of those boyish-looking, elated Americans in absurd shoes and Norfolk jackets who visited Paris in 1890, a little of his river French returned to him. He was shocked that no one understood it. But by then he was one of the leading citizens of a town which had tripled in size since his boyhood, he had ordered the construction of the huge clock which dominated one entire half of that city, he had helped found a private school and a hunt club, was a director of a hospital and a bank, and he knew that the value of his long-delayed trip to Paris lay as much in the allusions he would be able to drop into conversations as in the experience of actually being there. Yet he was stimulated by Paris, and at times almost intoxicated by it: like his great-grandnephew Elliot, not to be born for forty-seven years, he was responsive to what was beautiful, and was capable of a wildness, almost an abandon, in his apprehension of it. When

Brooks Denmark first saw the banks of the Seine and the bridges and avenues fanning out from it, he thought immediately of transforming Plechette City. Paris was the only beautiful city he had ever seen. If he considered that he might make his hometown equal to his clock by making it more like Paris, he might be forgiven. Unlike many men of his class and time—new Midwestern manufacturing tycoons—Brooks Denmark would not have been dismayed to discover that one of his family would grow up to become an artist, a composer of music that most people would never hear and would not understand if they did, and a voluntary exile, with his wife, in Paris, and that this descendant would speak French like a Parisian born. (Perhaps, that is, a Parisian born in Marseilles: Elliot had often been told that his French was marked by a southern roll.) Brooks may have felt that he was getting some of his own back for the time a waiter spat on the floor when he suddenly remembered, as if by inspiration, six consecutive words of his river French. Brooks had no feelings about music, either one way or the other.

Music in Plechette City was largely an affair of brass bands, accordions and zithers. Especially in Brooks Denmark's time, it was imitative of German bands. It is not a coincidence that the first fortunes in Plechette City were made in the mid-nineteenth century. During this period, the city's first great time of growth, Germans seemed to come into town with every train from the East. Established families like the Denmarks admitted them with some condescension, but were, on the whole, grateful for the revenue and employment brought in by the breweries. By 1900, German was almost officially the second language in Plechette City, and unofficially, almost the first. It was regularly taught in the schools until the outbreak of the First World War; clerks in the new department stores along Grand Avenue were hired only if they were proficient in German. (Later, Polish was nearly as necessary.) By the year of Elliot Denmark's birth, the families most prominent in Plechette City were named Schallspiel, Van Blank, Denmark, Laubach, Nieder, Hockbein, Usenbrugge, Steenborg.

On the east side of the city, north along the long curve of the lake, these builders and entrepreneurs constructed their huge anomalous houses: some built on the model of the great family houses in Bonn and Munich, severe stone piles capped by turrets and cupolas, some, during the next three decades, oddly Spanish, almost Californian, imitations of Neutra. Others of these houses, shading into the new suburbs far north along Lake Point Drive, were multi-leveled brash constructions of imported stone, native woods, and a great deal of glass. Like Brooks Denmark, who could appear to them both charming and ruthless, both generous and a terrifying snob, the first suburbanites of Plechette City had a notion of the beautiful, and again like him, they cannot be blamed if it was aggressive and magazine-ish. It was the same impulse that led the fathers of the city to construct a park every two or three miles, so that, beginning at the strip of green between the Lake Expressway and the lake itself, you can walk all day in Plechette City and always rest your feet in the grass near a park bench.

*   *   *

On the last bank the plane made before circling down onto the landing strip, the Denmarks could see the lights of the western suburbs and old townships now annexed to the city, and beyond these illuminated windows, the dark mass of Nun's Wood, the fifteen acres of forest owned by a convent. These acres, thick with trees and enclosed by a high fence, were pricked at their center with light: the convent house, the "mansion" which had seemed so terrifying to Elliot when, eight years old, he had climbed the fence and stumbled, following the curving drive to the tall stone building, through the forest to the clearing, and seen the black figures gliding past the windows.

"I don't think I'm ready for this," he said to Vera, who was looking out of the windows to the now already vanished lights of her parents' suburb. "Maybe we should just stay on the plane and go back."

She smiled at him. "Our parents would be awfully disappointed if we did. And I'm sure you can bear it for three weeks." Then she said, brightening, "You'd also disappoint the thousands of admirers who think of your concert as the event of the season."

"Couldn't have been much of a season," he said. He folded a detective novel into his jacket pocket.

A minute later, lights and asphalt beyond the window, a quick dropping; then a hushed gravityless second: the wheels smoothly hit the ground.

"There's something moving on the runway," Vera said, grasping his arm. "Some animal. It's a dog, I think." She bent forward to see. "Can you see it? It's running around in circles up there."

"What kind of dog?"

"I can't tell, it's so far out there, way ahead of us. A raggedy little dog, like a terrier."

Her hand tightened on his arm. "Elliot, it's running right toward us!"

He put his head beside hers and peered out the window at the long gray expanse of floodlit track ahead and to the side. "I can't see anything," he said.

"Neither can I, now."

"Don't worry about it, dogs are smart. He'll just bark at the wheels."

One of the airplane's great tires thumped against something. "No," Vera said. "We killed him!" The plane rolled on for several more yards, then halted. The lights overhead blinked.

A stewardess stretched above him, teasing her jacket up over her blouse, and plucked his coat from the luggage rack, then Vera's. "Is this yours?" she asked him. He nodded. She reached up again, and struggled the long score case, three yards of brown leather concealing Elliot's "secret" present to Vera, a bulky *Italian Renaissance Painting*, down onto his lap.

Vera propped herself on the armrest, her face tired in the beam of light from the panel above. "Didn't we just hit something?" she asked. "A dog? There was a dog ahead of us on the runway."

"Of *course* not," the stewardess crooned, professional. "Animals are kept off the runway." She turned away, saying, "You may deplane through the front exit." Deplane: was that a real word?

* * *

Elliot Denmark, now thirty-two, had lived with his wife in Paris for four years. While Vera had been in graduate school, they had lived largely on grants from the Field Foundation, a documentary-film score he had written through a friend's recommendation (this work he had loved, and wished to do more of it), and occasional royalty checks from RCA, who had recorded his orchestral suite *Five Introductions*, Boulez conducting. After a euphoric two months while it seemed that the album was to be titled after his piece, it was released under the cowardly title *Mainstream Modern*, and Elliot thought that an ironic, painful, and apt category. Just when the second year of the grant had elapsed and when there was no offer to go to one of the lucrative summer arts festivals—in a year leaner than most, he a *Wunderkind* of twenty-seven, Elliot had spent a summer conducting an orchestra in Aspen, Colorado—Vera got her degree and began to teach at the American College in Paris.

Six years before, neither Vera nor Elliot had wanted to move back to Plechette City when he had finished with graduate work in the Columbia music department: but Elliot had been offered a good position at the college there when jobs in composition were difficult to find, the school had a good string quartet and a developing reputation for its music department; and in the end, they had lived in their old hometown only two years. When the foundation grant had come through, they were released from the school and the sometimes oppressive proximity of their parents. And Elliot was released, half reluctantly, half with relief, from Anita Kellerman, the widow of Frank Kellerman, who had been the chairman of the Plechette City University psychology department at the time of his death in an automobile accident. From their new flat in Paris, Elliot had written to Anita once, but she had not replied. Anita was a stern woman. From the first—within weeks of the beginning of their affair—Elliot had felt that he was an actor in some complicated game, a masque, where he had been set down without fully knowing the rules. Anita's husband had been twenty years older than she, an abstracted behaviorist in pink eyeglasses who had spent most of his time with his white rats and his rabbits in his laboratory. In the only picture Elliot had ever seen of the two of them together, Anita's fierce handsomeness, her blaze of heavy blond hair and black eyebrows (in a way which would not become fashionable for another twenty years, a shade too thick for standard beauty), her height, had made Frank Kellerman, a slight scholar's face and attenuated body in baggy Bermudas and a pullover, seem to recede off the photographic plate. Anita was scowling at the ground, walking a few feet before him, her whole attitude one of command.

Elliot had met Anita Kellerman at a party in the home of a cellist, Nathan Himmel. It was the first month of his return to Plechette City, not long before the beginning of classes, a time of faculty meetings and mimeographed letters from Jaeger, the dean of fine arts—he threw them all away. "You won't stay here long, will you, Denmark?" Himmel had said. "This is no place for a real composer. Stick around for a few years, get some work done, and then get out. If you stay here, no one will ever hear of you. You'll be stuck in academic politics, you'll make a few recordings on unknown labels, you'll go dry. You could bitch up your life here but good. You could turn into another old craphead like ——." He named a famous, though academic composer. Himmel's beefy face, its muscles slack, had come close to his own. "You should see the letters Blamires at Columbia wrote to Jaeger, recommending you. They'd knock your eyes out. I *know* about your talent—it's a pretty talent, but you haven't begun to develop it. I'm telling you. Don't let this place grab on to you." The cellist seemed to inflate with sincerity.

"Why do you stay?" Elliot had asked him.

"I'm no composer, I'm a performer. The Melos Quartet is doing very well. We can tour during vacations, all summer if we want. I like teaching. It's a comfortable life. I'm making so much money I could throw wads of it out the window. Hell, I'm a professor here! But you're not even thirty yet, you shouldn't even want a comfortable life."

"Maybe I don't," Elliot said. "I don't think I care about that."

"Well," Himmel had said, "haven't you always had one?"

Everyone in the city knew about the Denmark family. Good Himmel, with his butcher's face, his advice and his touchiness about inherited wealth—in Elliot's case, largely unfounded—he was still there, teaching sweating young cellists throughout the winter, concertizing in the summers, earning his professor's salary. The previous June, Elliot had spent two weeks in London, and he went to Wigmore Hall to see the Melos Quartet play a concert of Schubert and Beethoven quartets, a killing program. Himmel sat splayed over his instrument, his meaty face tugged by concentration, sawing delicately, eyes closed, head wagging. Elliot had not the heart to go backstage after the concert.

"Does it give you pleasure, writing music?" Anita asked him at the party. "Doesn't it make it difficult to listen to other people's music?" She looked like a Viking, a conqueror. A tall, solid body, deep in the thighs and pelvis: he had immediately wanted to put his hands on her, to see what she felt like.

"Pleasure?" he asked. "That's a funny question. It's all I've ever done. Sure, I guess it does. It saves me from having to do anything else."

"What kind of pleasure is it?" There was no trace of humor in these odd questions. He began to feel abraded. "Pleasure in the doing or the having done it, having finished something?"

"That doesn't last long," he said. Faced with this Viking of a woman—was this just arrogance? he wondered—he had to accept her seriousness. "That feeling slides off into depression, eventually. You don't know where the next one is going to come from. The best part of it is being in the middle of a long piece, waking up with it in the mornings, knowing it's going well. Seeing all those clean little marks on the paper. You push it around, hear it happening in your head."

"Don't use the second person when you mean the first," she said. "I'm no composer. I want to know what it feels like." When she smiled at him, her entire face changed. *My God*, he thought, *she's really beautiful*. It was like a bright blond sun coming out over a long tan field: her face seemed to kindle toward him. He felt as though he had been touched.

He bent to her face as if for a kiss. "To tell you the selfish truth, it feels like being made the king of Sweden."

"I hope you stay her awhile," she said. "We could use you."

Near the end of the party, Himmel played one of the Ciccolini recordings of the Scarlatti sonatas and Elliot made his way to the turntable, set into bookshelves. Himmel was standing by the machine, looking abstractedly at his party. "I know," he said, "it's not background music—but then, everybody hates background music. It's a lovely record anyhow, isn't it?"

Elliot nodded. Scarlatti reminded him of his piano lessons. Yet Himmel was right: it was a lovely record.

"By the way," the cellist continued, "I saw you talking to La Kellerman. That woman can be a bit of a trial, if you're not used to her style of conversation. Did you know that she is a widow?"

Elliot had not known.

"Her husband and she lived two houses up from here. He was a dry old stick of a guy. I think she got that way of talking from him. 'Why do you do this? Why do you do that?' I guess he was pretty good in his field, but I used to go out and mow the lawn whenever he came over. Kellerman was the only man named Frank I've ever known who actually called himself Frankie. After he died, she wouldn't fade away, like most widows. The day after the funeral, she called up all their friends and said that she was going to keep on living the way she'd always lived. I never saw her shed a tear. You know what I mean? She's a tough woman. And she's got a tough job now, raising that kid and supporting herself besides. She's an assistant for the psych. department. The kid's a trial too, I guess—one of those problem babies. He never stops wailing. Well, I don't want to gossip. I like Anita, and she's a friend of my wife's. But something about her scares me. There's no bullshit about her."

"That shouln't be scary," Elliot said.

"Well, it's not that. What I mean is, she looks at you like she's figuring out which part to bite off first."

"It might be a pleasure," Elliot said.

"Oh, she's good-looking," Himmel said. "She's the real Ice Queen. Look, just to change the subject," the cellist said, touching his sleeve, "are you one of *the* Denmarks? The family that owns the factory?"

It was a question Elliot had grown used to, though Himmel's phrasing was cruder than the usual mix of deference and curiosity. He grimaced into his glass. "Not really. Those Denmarks are my cousins. My father is in the industrial-real-estate business. And those Denmarks no longer own the factory. It was bought by the Globe Corporation, Ronnie Upp's company, five or six years ago. I've never even met Upp. No—I take that back. I met him once. We talked about our bicycles."

"Upp's the whiz kid around here," Himmel said. "I think La Kellerman knows him. I suppose if you've got enough money, nothing scares you. Me, I don't move in those circles."

Bumping his way forward in the airplane's corridor, he thought about these conversations, that first party. How American these encounters were! It only now occurred to him. No other people in the world behaved at parties like Americans. It was the American idea of the authentic, of authenticity: unless you were direct, you were lying. The thing had to be pressed to your face, its whiskers and pores right under your eyes, its breath blowing in your nostrils. If it were not real authenticity, then at least false: the style of so many Presidents and politicians, of pitchmen. Bluff, one knows is a bluff. A complicated game. This is what I'm not ready for yet, he thought. I've forgotten how to act in that nerves-open thrusting way.

Vera dodged past two girls in fake fur coats to come up to him. She had slept brokenly during the flight.

"Don't worry about anything, Elliot," she said, as if she had seen into his mind. And then with the charity that could always surprise him with its insight, she asked, "You're going to call Anita Kellerman, aren't you?"

"Should I?" he asked.

"Of course you should. I think she'd be very hurt if you didn't. You really have to call her."

Vera had not known about the letter he had sent to Anita Kellerman during their first year in Paris: a long frantic aching foolish letter. *Darling Anita*—he had settled on the adjective after searching for something wilder and more passionate. *Every time I turn a corner in this unexpected city, I think I see you: I have fantasies about you coming here secretly, just walking along the streets or waiting in cafés, waiting for me to find you.* Yet even when he missed Anita most fiercely, he never thought of leaving Vera—Anita's sternness and Vera's deep skeptical comfort forbade that. This tension, the sense that he was committing a halfhearted betrayal, gave his first and only letter to his mistress its essential falsity. That was his word, the way he characterized his effusion immediately after he had slipped it into the letter box. Perhaps he had always been wrong about Anita. He could not be certain that he understood the territory into which she had led him; he could be certain however that his timing had been wrong. She did not reply. Then, for three years he had been silent. Except for stabs of imagery, the emotion seemed finished. Then, after the university had invited him to give a concert and Vera had been so plainly and simply pleased by the notion of a Christmas visit to their parents, he had spent a week of nights vividly dreaming of Anita Kellerman, and days working in a sweat of memories.

Vera had that first night seen the threat in Anita. Driving back to their apartment, only eight blocks from Himmel's house in the university area about the campus buildings on Leecham and Fenwick avenues near the lake, Vera said to him, "Who was that Nordic blond you were talking to?"

"A widow," he said. "Named Anita Kellerman. Her husband was a psychologist, and he was killed in an automobile accident. She's a neighbor of Himmel's."

"She looks dangerous to me," Vera said.

"Dangerous to bachelors," he answered. He did not tell her that he had in his pocket a slip of paper with Anita Kellerman's address and telephone number on it. Then, he did not think he would call her.

* * *

Carrying their coats and parcels, the Denmarks went through the metal orifice of the jet, Elliot ducking slightly to avoid bumping his head, and walked down the gusty canvas corridor to the airport. Crackling announcements filled the air, battling with the Muzak. He shifted his bundles, switched the score case to his other hand, and turned to look for Vera.

She was standing at one of the big tinted plate-glass windows, cupping her hands above her eyes to look out at the jet and the runway. Businessmen who had taken the shuttle flight from Chicago rushed by, discreetly glancing at her.

"Oh, I see it," she cried. "We didn't hit it after all. It's out there. Come and look."

He moved up beside her and looked down at the glowing airplane. Up toward the front of the long thick tube of metal, below where he could see the pilots rubbing their heads and drawing on cigarettes in the tiny-seeming cockpit, a small ragged dog skittered back and forth between the twin front tires and the props for the walkway to the upper levels of the airport.

The Glaubers were waiting for them in the lobby. Tessa held her arms out and permitted Vera to enter their circle. Taller than her daughter, hair skillfully kept to its ruddy shade of blond, severe strained dramatic face. "Vera! Vera! You're hours late!" Vera extricated herself from her mother's arms.

"We were held over in Chicago, Mother."

"Hello, Elliot." Herman Glauber, a stout man in a sports jacket of a crackling plaid, held out his hand. Elliot took it with gratitude. He had always liked his father-in-law. A big honest Germanic face, made owlish by his huge glasses.

"I told Tessa you'd be late, but would she believe me? I spent half of my week out here, seems like, waiting for some mucky-muck to come in and tell us what's wrong with our city, and they're never on schedule." His bald head shone with sweat. "The controllers in this country are going crazy, trying to juggle all the flights we got now. It's an impossible job, a man-killer. How was your flight?"

"Not too bad. Just long. I'm tired, though, Herman. I didn't sleep at all. How are you and Tessa?"

Tessa embraced him lightly. Long strong arms. He kissed her cheek. "Elliot," she said, "we fumble on. After the last elections, we collapsed for a week and a half. The Birchers almost caught up with Herman this time."

Herman, cradling Vera, looked up. "I'm in no trouble yet, though," he rumbled. "There's no danger of me having to go look for a job. I've been an alderman here since I quit delivering papers, I sometimes think. People have pity on an old man."

Disconcertingly, Herman Glauber shot an odd, nervous glance at his son-in-law. "Time for all that later," he said. "Let's get ourselves on the road. Honey, I'm so glad to have you *back*." He released his daughter, holding her shoulders for a moment. Then he dropped his hands and took the duty-free carton from Elliot's arms. "We'd better go down and get your bags," he said, "before somebody swipes them."

They rode down to the airport's main floor on the escalator. Tessa stood beside Elliot, gripping his free arm, Herman riding down before them on the same step with his daughter. "It's great to have you two guys back with us. I feel like I could stay up all night talking with you."

Elliot mimed staggering against the rail. "Not quite all night, Herman, unless you like talking to a sleeping man."

"Oh, you kids gotta get your rest. But I've been trying to set up a few things for you. Some publicity. Maybe I can help sell tickets to your concert, peddle a few records for you, maybe. Get your face around for the public to see it."

The baggage counter was directly to the left of the escalator on the ground floor. The suitcases were driven up on long flat carts and thrown out onto the pitched steel plane of the ramp, where they slid down to the waiting passengers. Elliot left Vera with her parents on the outer fringe of the crowd around the baggage slide and wedged through to the counter. A slight English girl who had been on the flight from Paris stood beside him, talking to a baggage handler.

"Please please be careful with my suitcase," she was saying. "I've got some glassware in it, and I'm terribly afraid it might be broken."

The handler, a fierce ebony black so dark his features seemed blurred, grunted. He muttered something the girl clearly could not understand.

"Excuse me," she said. "What did you say?"

"Ah know mah *job!*" he shouted at her. The girl jumped. The first cart pulled up and two uniformed men unloaded the bags, thumping them on the ramp and letting them slip to the bottom. Elliot felt an increasing pressure at his back. A fist, a hip dug into him.

Pale leather cases slid down the ramp. The girl pointed to them. "Those are mine, in fact. Could you get them for me?"

The man's face set deeper into rage. "It's *mah job!*" he bellowed. The girl flushed a pure pink. Elliot could tell that she still did not understand what the man was saying. The black man leaned out over the counter and wrenched the two cases up from the steel plane and in the same motion slammed them onto a cart. The girl seemed close to tears; her face loosened. "Please . . ." she began, but the handler had begun to bawl "CLEAH THE WAY," to violently shove the cart through the crowd.

2

"Food," Herman said. "We go nuts about food in this country. American food is the best in the world." Going westward, Jackson Drive was lined with small shopping centers, restaurants, Thom McAn shoes, cocktail bars—the Swordsman, Green Gables, Dillers, the Monte Carlo—hardware shops, furniture stores, big chain groceries with acres of parking lot, until Sixtieth Street, where the real west side began. There, Jackson Court, a ten-acre shopping center, sprawled, a nest of reddish brick buildings encompassed by shiny black asphalt; after it, a welter of McDonald's hamburger stands, miniature golf courses, pancake houses, Colonel Sanders chicken houses.

"A lot of this will be new to you," Herman said. "The franchise fad came in here in a big way about two-three years ago." They passed a series of prefabricated glass-fronted shacks blazoning famous names—impermanent-looking buildings. Their parking lots were neatly shoveled, the snow heaped into banks.

"*All* of this is new," Vera said. "There were some other shops here when we left, but I can't remember what they were."

"Who can? That's progress. Something comes down, something else goes up. That's what America means. If a ghost is standing in your way, you knock him down and get the job done. This whole stretch here is zoned for small businesses. Now, it might not look beautiful to you, but I think it's a good thing. You see, you get lots of guys in here, they're just looking for a break. These little franchise joints either make them some money or make them go bust. If they know anything about business, if they've got some training, some business education, they can make a better life for themselves. They've got the right to try. Of course, it's a little crowded here right now, I'd agree to that. But there you are, that's the zoning."

They passed a succession of flimsy neon-lighted buildings. The flaring signs marched down the long length of road. Elliot felt as though he had never seen this road before, as though he had been gone a decade.

Tessa twisted about on the front seat to face them. "Darlings, it's so lovely to have you back with us for the holidays. We've got a big Christmas Day party planned with your parents, Elliot, and I'm sure you've got tons of invitations to other parties while you're here. And Uncle Kai is very eager to see you."

"We'll call him tomorrow," Vera said.

Elliot looked out of the rear window, to his left, toward the south of the city. He could just see, revolving, the big gold top of the four-faced clock on its tower. It was miles away, on the other side of the industrial valley. It sent out great streams of light.

"You'd better call him," Herman said. "I've never seen him so pleased. He's finishing his book on Goethe, and I think he wants to talk to you about it. Hell, poor old Kai. He's such a recluse. I'll bet he never goes out of that gloomy apartment of his more than twice a week. Lately, the only times he talks to me he tells me how much he wants to die."

"Herman!" interjected his wife.

"Well, it's the truth. There's no sense in hiding it from the kids, they'll see it for themselves. He keeps going on about Germany. Germany! If I'd been through what he went through in Germany, I'd spit every time I heard the word."

Kai Glauber, Herman's older brother, now in his seventies, had been teaching at the university in Bonn during the twenties; and then, in mysterious circumstances, had been arrested and put in a camp. He apparently had false papers, and he had refused to leave the country. What had Tessa said? "Kai wouldn't believe in the war—he thought that if he ducked his head in some country town, it would blow away—typical. Kai runs away from things. If you want proof, just look at the way he lives!" Kai had been in the camp—"a small unglamorous machine, operating wholesale," as he would later say to Elliot— all during the war. When American soldiers came through in 1944, they had at first refused to believe that he was from the same country as they. He had forgotten all his English. During the five years in the camp, he had shrunk to seventy-five pounds, lost everything he owned, become another person. If Herman Glauber looked like an amiable spectacled bull, his brother Kai, by the time Elliot first met him, resembled an old sharp-featured fox. An enormous vein curled along one side of his forehead, knotting past the hard prominent lumps of bone. Long sleek white hair skimmed straight back across his skull. Since his return to America, he had never had a job, but lived on his brother's charity while working on the book about Goethe he had begun before the war.

A knotty, painful old man, Elliot had always thought. Kai was beyond judgment, in a sense, for he had been to the bottom of the world and had come back speaking another language.

The Glaubers' house was in the township of Richmond Corners, which name now applied principally to the little shopping center on the site of the old town municipal buildings.

"I'll bet it's nice to see your old neighborhood, isn't it, Vera?" asked Tessa.

"Sure it is," her father said. "It's always good to see your home. Isn't that right, Vera?"

"Of course, Daddy," Vera said.

"And you've got all your old friends from the college, you'll have a great time here. Elliot, I can't get over your father inviting us all over to his place for Christmas. Even Kai."

"Will he come?"

"You'll have to work that out with him. When I told him he was invited, he just sort of nodded. But I'll tell you something, I think it did him good just to be invited. Your father can be a thoughtful man—I'll say that for him. He's got good manners."

"Herman," said Tessa.

"Tell us about Paris," Herman said. "What the hell is it like in old Paree?" Elliot saw his clumsy hands, clad in brown perforated driving gloves, clasp and unclasp on the wheel.

As Vera talked, they drove through the old township and on to the Glaubers' three-story wooden house. On the old fields behind, Elliot could faintly see, whitely limned with snow, the skeletal beams of half-constructed houses. One building, the only home finished, was a dark undefined black before the night sky, dazzled with stars. The car slushed onto the driveway to the garage Herman had added to his house; the wheels spun on the ice before catching. Drifts on either side of the driveway stood five feet high. In the pale winter moonlight, they gleamed a bluish white.

Elliot had once done a serial composition based on houses like this, *To Walker Evans*. It was one of the first pieces he had done after his marriage. Their spareness, their linear quality, a Protestant dryness: images in a book of Evans photographs Vera had given him.

It had been Tessa's idea to buy the house, he knew. Herman's "study" was filled with maps of the city, his filing cabinets, a *Playboy* wall calendar, his overflowing desk. The rest of the house was furnished with spindly antique furniture, colonial tables and rolltop desks Tessa had found in farmhouses or at auctions. On every table there were ancient nutcrackers, old beaten bowls for ashtrays. Pewter mugs. A bed warmer like an elongated spoon leaned against the fireplace. Each room on the ground floor had several hooked rugs.

In the first year of the Denmarks' marriage, Elliot a first-year instructor fresh from Columbia, Tessa had shown him around the house. "This old table was such a treasure I couldn't pass it up. Only thirty dollars, and you know what's happened to prices! Oh, look here, I got these from an old brewer who was just closing down his brewery. I wish I could have bought *him*." She was pointing at a jumble of rusted bottle caps in a brass bowl. "Selig's Family Beer, Est. 1801" was stamped on each flaking metal piece.

"We're putting you in Vera's old room," Herman said. "I hope you won't mind sharing it with some stuff Tessa moved up here from the living room. There's room enough to move around in, anyhow. I turned the heat way down, because I figured you wouldn't be used to central heating anymore." He opened a door and set the case on the floor, grunting.

Vera came in behind them. "Tell Mother not to fuss around in the kitchen,

Daddy. I told her that we ate a big meal on the plane, but she went on in there anyhow. All I want to do is sleep. It's nice and warm in here. What's all this stuff?" She lay down on one of the twin beds. "*Umm*, delicious. Like sleeping in a warehouse."

Elliot laid both cases beside the beds and sprang open the locks.

"Well, it's ten o'clock," Herman said. "What time is it for you guys?"

"Four or five," said Elliot.

"Four," said Vera.

"You better get some rest. Elliot, first you should call your parents. Use the phone up here. The way we arranged things, you stay here a week and a half, then spend the last half of your vacation at their house. We'd love to monopolize you the whole time, but it didn't seem fair."

"I'll go downstairs and have a drink with you while I call," Elliot said. "I'm so tired I don't think I could get to sleep without one."

"Join me," Herman said. He had been pacing around the bedroom, dodging mirrors and chests like a huge plaid bee. "I can show you the publicity I arranged for you, the newspaper article."

Downstairs, Elliot dialed his parents while Herman made him a drink in the kitchen. The telephone was an old-fashioned wall model with a crank and separate mouthpiece and receiver which dangled from a cord. He heard the phone ring once, twice in his parents' home, and then his father's reedy voice came over the receiver.

"Hello, hello. Denmark residence."

"Hello, Father. It's Elliot. We just got in five . . ."

He heard his father calling "It's Elliot" off into space, and then heard the click as his mother picked up another phone.

"Hello, darling," she said. "It's so wonderful to hear your voice. Please talk lots. Did you have a good trip?"

"Oh, it was fine. But tiring."

"Well, it's fine to hear your voice again, Elliot," said his father. "How are you and Vera getting on at the antique fair?"

"Fine," he said.

Herman put a drink in his free hand, and he heard him slap a newspaper down on the table beside him.

"There's a silly article about you in the *Herald*. I assume your father-in-law was instrumental in having it written. We can only hope he didn't actually write it. Have you seen it?"

"No, not yet," he said. "It's here, though."

"Don't bother him about that, Chase. Elliot, can you and Vera come here for drinks and dinner tomorrow night? We are so anxious to see you. How is Vera?"

"I think she's asleep."

"Do tell her we're anxious to see her again, won't you?"

"Have you talked with Herman Glauber yet?" asked his father.

"Not really."

"He's said nothing about Nun's Wood?"

"Nun's Wood?" Elliot could hear Herman exhaling noisily, hearing the phrase. "No, nothing. Why?"

"Chase, I don't think you should go into that now," said his mother. "He'll be hearing about it until he's sick of it."

"Then he won't be the only one who is sick of it, Margaret," his father said. "Elliot, keep an open mind, and we'll see you tomorrow night. About six."

"Okay," Elliot said. "We'll be over. It'll be good to see you again. Good-bye for now."

"Good-bye, darling," said his mother.

"Good night, kid," said his father.

Turning from the phone, he saw Herman Glauber's broad plaid back going into the kitchen. He swallowed a mouthful of his drink and lifted the newspaper from the table. It was folded back to page three of the second section, the arts page, where a headline read BAD-BOY COMPOSER RETURNS TO GIVE CONCERT. The date was a week in the past. He skimmed the article. "Elliot Denmark, at thirty-two one of the country's foremost young composers and a native son . . . iconoclastic modernist . . . His music is tough going, except for the *au courant* . . . a series of puzzles . . . shockability . . . A spell at Juilliard led to . . . many performances at festivals . . . *Mainstream Modern*. Mr. Denmark is the son of Mr. and Mrs. Chase Denmark of Plechette City and Chicago, and the great-grandnephew of Brooks Denmark. On January 3, Denmark will conduct a program of his own works in the Usenbrugge Concert Hall of Plechette City University."

He took the newspaper into the kitchen. Herman was holding an ice tray under the hot-water tap, splashing the water on his sleeves. Herman glanced at Elliot through steamed opaque lenses, then turned his face back to the ice tray. He jiggled it. Ice cubes clattered out into the sink and began to diminish in the stream of hot water. "Damn," said Herman. "Do you want more ice in that drink? Or don't they use ice where you come from?" He fished in the sink for the slippery cubes. "You read the *Herald* article?"

"Yes, it's fine," Elliot said. "It might bring some people to the concert."

"That's what *I* thought. That 'bad-boy' stuff, I wasn't responsible for that. It was a cute idea of the city editor's. And I couldn't tell you why they ran it a week ago—a lot of people think you've been here that long. I gave them a little hell for that over the phone."

Elliot yawned hugely. "I'm sorry," he said. "I think I ought to get some sleep. Don't be worried about that article, Herman. It was good of you to think of it."

"One more thing. With a little help, I got a slot for you on Ted Edwards' TV show in Chicago. The taping is sometime next week, and we can just run down there for the afternoon and come right back. Is that okay with you? I know Edwards might not be to your taste, but it's a little more publicity, a TV audience. And since it's only a local show, not syndicated, there's nothing to be nervous about. How about it? You could probably cancel, if you want to."

WILD ANIMALS / 406

"No, that's fine, Herman." Elliot yawned again, then sipped at his drink. "It was good of you to arrange it. It might be fun to do." Privately, he had some reservations. He could remember the Edwards show. Ted Edwards was an intense snakelike man, handsome in a gangsterish fashion, known for harrying his guests, disguising his rudeness with a smooth delivery. Celebrities he fawned over. Still, in his exhaustion, Elliot thought that he could deal with Ted Edwards.

"Did your father see the article?" Herman fidgeted with the objects on the kitchen table: he slid a battered brass salt cellar back across the scarred wooden surface. "What am I saying, of course he did. Kai called me on the afternoon it appeared. He told me I was an idiot. What could I say? That I didn't write it?"

Looking at Herman Glauber's earnest puggish face, Elliot thought of his own father, his dandyish clothing, his dandy's white mustache, his slightness, his dryness. What was there in him to threaten Herman Glauber? Just that he was a Denmark, this man who had not done a single practical thing in fifteen years. ˑ e name continued to impress. His father had once been grand master at a Cnicago debutante's ball. Was anybody convinced by this nonsense anymore? Even Chase Denmark had become "relevant," had involved himself in committees on social thought, ecology; he sent checks to convicted black rapists and murderers. All of this had happened over the past two or three years.

"Herman, you're being too sensitive about something," he said.

His father-in-law tilted back his glass and drained it. Taking it from his mouth with a snap of his hand, he bumped the base of the glass gently on the roughened surface of the table.

"He mentioned the Nun's Wood business to you, did he?"

Elliot nodded. "But he didn't go into it."

"It's a little problem we're having out here. There's a question of sale and development. Ronnie Upp is involved. Ronnie and I have worked out a scheme that will leave as much of the woods intact as possible. We could get it rezoned in a minute, except that some people came into our first open meeting and made such a ruckus that Max Festlinger, the head of the planning commission, put off the whole thing for a public hearing." Herman looked grimly down at his own hands for a moment. "Look, it's four in the morning for you. You'll hear about this tomorrow, I'll tell you all the details. The main thing is that your father and I are on opposite sides of the fence in this thing. Look, let's hang it up for tonight."

He stood up abruptly and gathered some letters off the counter. "You might just want to look at these. It's the mail you got delivered here." He pitched the envelopes onto the table in front of Elliot.

"Do you promise to talk about this tomorrow?" Elliot began to say. "I don't think I understand the position . . ." and then he saw an envelope in the stack which was addressed solely to Elliot Denmark, in a stark black hand he knew. He tore it open. There was a single sheet within. In the middle of the page was typed *Call me sometime when you come in. It would be so good to see you. A.*

"What's that?" Herman said, standing behind him. "A? Must be a woman. Am I right?"

"An old friend. Anita Kellerman. We knew her at the university."

"Oh, I know her," Herman said. "That is, I met her. She came out here one evening with Ronnie Upp. A tall blond doll, good looker?"

Elliot fought with his surprise a moment before replying. "That's right, I heard she was a friend of Upp's."

"Maybe she wants to talk to you about this business. Come on, it's time to hit the sack. We'll see you guys in the morning."

They went up the stairs together in the dark.

In the morning Elliot's nose bled a thick syrup. He felt dizzy, disoriented. The room was surprisingly noiseless. The window at the opposite end of the room looked out to a clear featureless white. Everything was different. Blood flowed sluggishly toward the back of his throat, tasting of unsweetened chocolate and brass. His mind shuffled through a list of places. Then he saw the spindly chair on which he had hung his shirt and the stained desk behind it, a carved American eagle at its top between two in-curling wooden waves, and he remembered. He looked at his watch: ten o'clock.

"I feel terrible," he heard Vera say. "I'm so *dry*."

While Vera showered and dressed, Tessa told him the entire story. They sat in the dining room, and he ate the eggs and toast she had made for him. The dining-room window opened onto the back garden, and while Tessa talked he let his eyes rest on the soft pale length of snow, swollen over hedges and massed at the edge of the driveway. Snow capped the head of the stone cherub at the end of the garden. His white stone arms were dusted, like the branches of trees, with inches of snow.

"You know how Herman has fought to bring development into this ward," she said to him. "And I do mean fought. People think aldermen do nothing but smoke cigars all day and make promises at elections, but I can tell you how hard that man works. He couldn't even stay at home this morning, as much as he wanted to. He had to go down to his office. The big hearing is right after New Year's, and he couldn't rest, knowing how much work he has to do. And the phone calls! Every time a dog bites somebody, every time somebody sees a rat, not that we've got rats out here, they jump to their telephone and screech at Herman."

"So," he said, breaking into her digression, "this Nun's Wood business has something to do with development? I gathered that it was that from the little he'd tell me last night."

"Why, of course," she said. Her ravaged face was white with a morning tiredness. "Do you want some more coffee?" She poured a thin black stream into his cup. "That's what I was telling you. The convent is closing down. The superior heard from Ronnie Upp soon after she made it known that they were going to sell, and I guess he made her a very reasonable offer for it. He must be Catholic, don't you think? They like to do business together. Anyhow, since

Herman is on the planning commission, Upp called him to see what could be done about rezoning the convent grounds."

"What did he want to put up?" Elliot asked. "A subdivision?"

"No, it's much better than that," she cried. "If he were going to do that, it wouldn't have to be rezoned. The way he explained it to Herman was that he was going to build an industrial park. The emphasis is on the *park*. The old convent house could be used for one of the office buildings, and he's planning to put up two others at widely spaced intervals on the property." Elliot could tell that she was repeating someone else's words, whether Ronnie Upp's or her husband's. "It would be done as tastefully as could be. They would leave sixty percent of the existing trees standing, and the buildings would be set into the natural contours of the land features. There'd be IBM, a big life-insurance company, Ronnie's offices, lots of other big names, companies people respect."

"What's the problem with the plan?"

"The problem? What's the *prob*lem? The problem started with the families who live across Wiltshire Drive from the convent grounds. All these people, these six or seven families, they think their property values are going to go down. They think they have a God-given right to protect their little property values, like nobody else counted. Buster, it makes you take a long look at so-called democracy. They sent around a petition and got lots of names of people who didn't understand the plan at all! You live in a special world, you know. You don't come in contact with unreasonable people. These people, they packed the public meeting and forced the commission to delay the final vote for a public hearing. Then the newspapers started in. There have been articles all winter long about Nun's Wood. Well, the superior says she wants to sell before February, and if the commission is blocked from rezoning, she'll just sell to the highest bidder and some developer will get it—some Catholic developer. Then there won't be any park at all! There'd be another row of houses, a lot of imitation mansard roofs and carriage lamps, like Tudor Acres back here in the old hayfield. Not that Tudor Acres is the worst of them. Ronnie's behind it, and some taste has gone into it, judging from the model home. But anything that would go up in Nun's Wood would be worse than the industrial park. That's the part they don't understand."

" 'They' including my father, presumably," he said.

She ignored his invitation to tell him what he already knew: Tessa's tact was often misplaced. "They want the city to buy the land and keep it the way it is. Or they want Ronnie Upp, who's been an angel through this whole mess, who's been all over the papers, to just plunk down his money and donate it to the city as a park. Now, nobody's saying he can't afford it. But is that a reasonable thing to expect?"

"I suppose it isn't," Elliot said. He was thinking: he is doing it to thwart Ronnie Upp. He still cannot forgive him for owning the Chambers Denmark factory. Elliot could imagine his father hiding his rancor behind the curtain of a humanitarian motive.

Ronnie Upp had been sent to boarding school in Connecticut when he was just a child. Then, a boy, he had returned one summer on his vacation, and the awful thing had happened. Harrison Upp, the father, lived near the Denmarks in the Lake Point area on the east side. In that year, 1951 or 1952, there had been a series of burglaries in Lake Point homes. They were all supposed to be the work of one burglar. Elliot's parents had put new locks on the doors and installed alarms on the windows, which were connected to a panel in the Lake Point police station. Harrison Upp, more swashbuckling than Chase Denmark, had a pistol. Sometimes he carried it in a shoulder holster. Elliot could recall his shock of delight and fascination when Harrison Upp had negligently let his jacket slide past the roughened black butt of the revolver; he had been standing in the door of the Denmark house, leaning on the jamb, his face florid in the June dog-heat. On a July night of that year, Ronnie Upp had heard a noise from the outside. It sounded like a man softly, quickly crossing their lawn. He had raced to his father's room, snatched the pistol from a drawer, and fired through the bedroom window. When the police came, they discovered that he had shot and killed his own father. Quite suddenly, it seemed as if everyone were saying, "Of course, Grace is an alcoholic, she's not responsible," and when Grace Upp died by her own hand in a nursing home at the end of summer, no one had seemed particularly surprised. Ronnie had gone away to Connecticut, then to England, and had not returned until he was a grown man. He owned property in downtown Plechette City, houses and land in many other cities; and he was almost legendary for his wealth. Upp was a member of the country club, but was never seen there; the same was true of the Town Club, the Plechette City Club, the Athletic Club and the Hunt Club. Anita, four years ago, had told Elliot that he was "sad." "I thought you must have known Ronnie," she said. "Of course, he is a rather sad person. He is innocent."

Elliot could at least admit that Upp had strange psychic baggage for a tycoon.

Tessa took his breakfast plates into the kitchen. Elliot continued to look out at the snow-drowned garden. At the far end, before a hummock that was a buried hedge, the stone cherub lifted his fat white arms. Anita Kellerman's note was in his jacket pocket, where he had put it, folded in quarters, the night before. He tried to make out the features on the cherub's face: they looked blank and open. Soft parted lips. He heard the gurgle of the dishwasher beginning its cycle. There seemed to be a faint promise in the cherub's face, an expectancy for which the blank features were the expression. It looked, its arms lifted and weighted with snow, as though it would shortly ascend into the cloud-heavy sky. He decided to call Anita.

Elliot leaned forward over the table and peered into the kitchen. Tessa's back, her fluffy ruddy hair and long slim trunk, was turned to him. She was fussing with something at the oven. He swiveled to the phone and stood up to dial. Then he realized that he no longer knew her telephone number. He replaced the receiver on the hook, picked the directory, clad in a blue denim binding which bore the name of an antique dealer, from the top of the phone box and flipped through to the K's. Kellerman, A. The Leecham Street address. It pleased him that she had not moved. He dialed.

The phone rang once before he heard her voice. In the instant of its trill, his heart seemed to swim beneath his ribs.

"*Ronnie*," she said. "I want—"

He hung up.

When he looked away from the phone, Vera was coming through the door from the kitchen, dressed in blue jeans and a blue turtleneck sweater.

"You look like Jack Kerouac's girlfriend," he said, his hand still on the wooden box of the telephone.

"Were you calling someone?"

"Here." He fished the note from his pocket. "This came in a letter addressed here. Herman gave it to me last night with the rest of the mail, mostly Christmas cards, judging from their shape. I didn't open them." She unfolded the note and bent her head over it. "It sounds unhappy to me, so I just tried to reach Anita, but her line was busy. Your father thought it might have something to do with the Nun's Wood business."

"With what?" Vera's face showed both puzzlement and suspicion.

"Oh, Christ, you haven't heard about it yet. Just wait till I call Anita and I'll explain it to you."

"Ve-ra," her mother called from the kitchen.

"Oh, another thing," he said. "We are supposed to go to my parents' house tonight at six for drinks and dinner."

"Of course," she said, and went through the door to the kitchen. The door closed, and through it drifted Tessa's voice. "What's the point of staying here if you're going to go running across town on those icy roads . . ."

He dialed the number again.

"Hello?" her clear voice said.

"Anita, this is Elliot."

"Welcome back, Elliot Denmark!" Her voice was entirely friendly. "Was that you who just called?"

"No," he lied. Then, remembering that Vera might be listening, he said, "I did try to call you just now, but the line was busy."

"I was waiting for a call from Ronnie Upp," she said. "That's not important. I suppose you're calling because of the note I wrote you."

"I would have called anyhow," he said. "I'd like to see you sometime soon, if you're not too busy."

"What does that mean?" He could hear her smile. "Never mind. Elliot, dear, I was confused and tired when I wrote that note to you. I read that awful thing in the *Herald*. How is Vera?"

"Vera is fine," he said.

"You're not angry with me? I had a rough spell, but I'm over it now. Please call me later, when I'm not so rushed, will you, darling?"

"How is Mark?"

"Getting on. Getting older. He's seven now. Duck, I have to run now. It was lovely of you to call. We'll get together later in the week. All right? Good-bye, sweet."

The phone clicked and the dial tone began to buzz.

He hung up. The voices of Vera and her mother, Tessa's pitched higher, came from the kitchen. One of them had swung the door, and he could see Vera's blue back, standing straight and alone near the oven: she was shorter than her mother, but her legs were long in those jeans. Her hair fell darkly down from her shoulders. Elliot looked out at the cherub, still on the verge of ascent, weighted by the powdery snow, its lips open as if to utter some statement about all this surrounding matter. He went toward the women in the kitchen.

3

When Elliot began his affair with Anita Kellerman, he knew that the sense of infallibility she gave him was illusory, but he could not dampen the surge of confidence she had aroused in him. He knew too that the motives for this flaring out of emotion were entirely primitive: Anita Kellerman was a big-bodied powerfully attractive woman—she seemed to blaze with purpose and design— and she loved him; he possessed her, at least as much of her as was not given to her son. If the world could be divided into survivors and victims, Anita seemed chiefly a survivor. What she touched in him was the level of feeling that had been all his life given to music. Anita's relationship to his work seemed profound. Since adolescence, he had instinctively valued those composers in whom the disorderly eruptive life of the emotions was made unrhetorical and implicit in form. The strength of the work he did in graduate school made him a small name, at least among other graduate students. Blamires, his supervisor, had been enthusiastic about these works, and Blamires knew everybody, Virgil Thompson, Cage, Sessions, Foss, Schuller, Tippett, everybody. As Himmel had implied, it was Blamires who had gotten him his job. After Elliot began his involvement with Anita Kellerman, he wrote a song cycle based on poems by Theodore Roethke, and allowed himself to be wilder, looser, more ragged.

Yet even the new music was highly conscious: it was as though he could transport the spirit of Anita's masque directly into it. Performed at the Donaueschingen Festival in 1968, *Words for the Wind* was his first real success. *Five Introductions* was written later that same summer.

Elliot had left the note in his pocket for weeks after Himmel's party. His classes had begun, he and Vera were buying things for their apartment, they ate dinner with one set of parents every weekend; Elliot felt as though, after the long grind of graduate school and nighttime writing, he had at last moved out into an actual life in the world. He enjoyed the business of teaching, and for some months it occupied him fully. He spent his evenings working out his lectures and planning exercises for his students, who were all seniors and juniors— music majors. He knew within the first month that most of them would never compose a bar of music once they left his course. They were too lazy. Many of his students would take jobs teaching music in Wisconsin high schools. Some, like Himmel's best pupils, would find jobs in orchestras; others would drift on into graduate schools. None of them reminded him of what he had been like at their age: compulsive about writing music, always ducking off to a practice room to toy with a piano.

He taught Monday, Tuesday and Friday afternoons, and Wednesday mornings. Wednesdays, he fell lazily into the habit of eating in the student-union cafeteria with Roy Baltz and Susan Stringer, both students. Baltz was a big farmboy, not long out of a crewcut, emphatic in his judgments. He loved Bruckner and Wagner, but seemed to despise the work of all other composers, including Elliot Denmark. He let it be known that he was working on an oratorio for rock band and orchestra. "Pardon me, Mr. Denmark, but all this stuff being done now is *so* minor." He looked to lank-haired Susan Stringer for confirmation. She nodded solemnly. "Where's the inventive music of today? It's not coming out of the academy. It's not old-fashioned so-called 'modern' works by guys who never thought beyond Webern." (Elliot knew that this was, for Baltz, a polite reference to his own work.)

After a month of listening to Baltz, he remembered Anita Kellerman on a clean aching mid-November day. He left the room after one of the Wednesday sessions and went upstairs to his office to use the telephone. When he arrived at her house, fifteen minutes later, she met him saying, "The arrival of Elliot Denmark." He had looked at her, puzzled. She seemed almost angry with him. He was uncertain of his intentions.

A record was playing inside her house, and he could hear it from where he was standing, outside the front door. Some slippery, piercing thing: jazz. He had a quick mental flash of Harrison Upp, his seersucker jacket pulled carelessly back over the cross-hatched butt of a gun.

She led him into the kitchen. It was a sunny yellow room into which the music drifted from the hall. Anita gave him a drink. "I'm glad you came," she said. "I was waiting for you."

Watching her move across the sunny kitchen, opening a can of soup, putting a pan on the stove, Elliot was moved by the clarity of her gestures. She did everything surely, finally: her face taut, cheekbones almost Slavic.

"You know," he said, "I'm not quite sure what I'm doing here with you."

"Does it make you nervous, being here?" She turned her head over her shoulder as she stirred the soup. Her face looked anxious.

"No," he said. He felt as though he were soothing her, though he knew this was not the case. "I'm not nervous. What did you mean, you were waiting for me?" He felt a small flutter in his stomach. He had the sense that something definite was expected of him, an action he was not sure he wished to complete: sitting there in the bright kitchen with the jazz music floating through the door, and watching this tall solid blond woman pour soup into bowls, he felt as if there were a role here, a definition he was supposed to embody. Her gestures were delicate, precise.

She set the steaming bowl before him. Was she one of those women who collected musicians or academics? She did not look the type, but you could never tell anything by looks. He felt both foolish and irritated.

"I just wanted to talk to you," she said, sitting across from him. "Yes, I'm lonely. People are different when a woman becomes a widow."

In a short tan skirt and white blouse she looked feline and healthy. He was conscious of long sleek legs. Her being widowed gave her another dimension, took her somehow beyond his reach. He could not be responsible for so much past.

During lunch, he felt himself opening up to her, talking about his teaching, his music, his ideas. She delighted him with her intelligence—that too seemed graceful. "Have you ever been entirely close to anything?" she asked him. "Close enough so you have a total understanding of it as another life, something you can understand without wanting to own it or possess it or change it?"

"I don't know," he said. "Maybe the closest I get to what you are talking about is with music."

"Other people's music," she said.

"That's right. I've spent all my life listening to it and trying to understand it, analyzing it, but I could never feel that I owned it or possessed it."

"You've never had this with a living being?"

"Have you?"

"Perhaps with Mark," she said. "I can remember seeing him in the hospital, seeing his red wrinkly skin and his tiny hands and feet. I felt as though I were looking right through, to see his veins and his heart. He's alive, I thought, he's another life connected to mine that will outgrow mine. That's the closest I've ever felt to anything. Frank was already dead when he was born." Her voice was level, uncomplicated; directed to some internal point. Yet he was sure that she meant him to take this speech as a kind of metaphor.

As he had to, he asked, "May I see him?"

She led him upstairs. The backs of her knees were smooth and girlish above the tender bulging of her calves. Watching her legs ascend the stairs, Elliot felt the beginning of a sexual tension, a current between them. He wanted to touch her. At the top of the stairs, she moved softly to a closed door and peeked in. Then she soundlessly entered and motioned to him. Her hand was slightly knotted about the joints and knuckles, the long strong fingers nearly the size of his own. "He's still asleep," she said. He moved beside her to the small bed. Mark lay on his back, thinner than most babies. He stirred, flung up an arm. Elliot, unthinking, put his arm around Anita's unfamiliar shoulder. She moved closer to his body.

She said nothing, but looked at him gravely, a long direct gaze that touched him squarely. They left the room together. In the tiny hall she put her hand in his.

Then she smiled at him, making his legs weak. "A lot of men find me forbidding. I'm too uncompromising. I always know what I want."

He put his arms around her. She felt solid in his arms, a denser presence than Vera. Anita's broad face hovered before his own, looking up at him. She seemed illuminated, as if by a private joke. Her eyes really were green, and lighted with humor.

She led him into her bedroom, the door next to the baby's. "Oh, my God," Elliot said. "I've got to teach a class in half an hour."

"Then don't take long," she said. "There'll be another time." He could not think of another woman in the world who could have said that at such a moment.

In moments of detachment and self-loathing, he saw his whole life from a great height: his big unathletic body, his heavy intellectual face, racing between two houses and the school, all this shrunk into dollhouse scale, his figure going in and out of beds, panting, groaning, embracing with two women, one taut and blond, one soft, dark. In front of his classes, he gesticulated, mouthing words in a fury, sometimes seeing saliva spray in the light, words about *purity*, *neatness*, *form*. *Bareness*. All the while cherishing his tangle of emotions, seeing his panting, ridiculous self as flawless.

Vera and Anita met for the second time at an end-of-term party at the home of Jaeger, the dean of the fine-arts school. Anita had come with Himmel, whose wife was in bed with flu. Jaeger was a tall thin greyhound of a man with the manners of a Japanese diplomat. "He gives good parties," Himmel had told Elliot, "but his only other talent is being good-looking."

"I've been hearing great things about your song cycle, *Wind Words*, is it?" Jaeger said. "*Winter Words?*"

"*Words for the Wind*," said Elliot. "Benjamin Britten wrote *Winter Words*."

"Yes, that's it," Jaeger said. "I hope you'll excuse my memory. Nathan has told me that it's a fine solid piece of work. I hope it's a great success at that wonderful festival. Where is that again?"

"Donaueschingen," Elliot said. "But it's not this year, it's next year."

"Yes. Quite a significant place, I gather. You'll be staying with us here at the school for a number of years, won't you, Elliot? We need a man like you to make our fine-arts school the place I know it can be. You and the Melos Quartet make us a powerful draw." He withdrew, smirking gently, to the side of a famous abstractionist who had been hired for the summer session. "Ah. Mr. Raciewicz," Elliot heard him purr, "it was so good of you to leave New York to join us here in the provinces." The painter was a small dumpy man, sweating through his denim shirt. He customarily worked on twenty-foot canvases, and Elliot heard him begin to complain about the size of his studio.

Elliot moved across the room to Himmel's side. The cellist waved his glass at him. "Ah, your first year in serfdom draws to its close. Did you know that you'll get Baltz next year, in your graduate class?"

"He told me," Elliot said. "He says he wants to change the whole program. He's going to petition the dean to do away with the requirements."

"Jaeger will just throw it back on us. With an infinitely courteous note. Fortunately, the good Baltz is practically friendless, as far as I can see. If he could get a majority of the first-year graduate students on his side, Jaeger might feel that he had to think about it. Then we'd be in trouble."

"I hate this administrative jiggery-pokery," Elliot said.

"Didn't I tell you?" Himmel's face began to look as cheerful as it could. "Don't get involved in this business, Denmark, or they'll end up making you an assistant dean. Then you can watch your life going down the drain."

"Don't you have any worries about it happening to you?"

"Me? I'm a helpless fiddler." Himmel seemed to radiate joy. "One of the court servants." He looked around. "Where's my date?" Himmel pretended to hold binoculars to his eyes. "Oh, date! Date!"

"I think she's in the other room," Elliot said. He had consciously avoided Anita throughout the party.

"Then let us adjourn," Himmel said. "The good Kellerman will have something illuminating to say about the Oversoul. Perhaps she is the Oversoul." He took Elliot's arm. "Come on. She doesn't really bite. I tried."

Anita was in the other room, sitting on Jaeger's floral couch with Vera. Still gripping Elliot's arm, Himmel led him before the two women. "Ladies, your court," he said. "Your friends from the animal world. I represent the Canadian goose and Denmark here is the sole surviving platypus. Only a kiss will restore us to human form. Make me human with a kiss." He bent down, offering his slab of forehead. Anita kissed his head lightly. "Alas," Himmel said. "I'm still a goose. Now the squire's turn."

He pulled Elliot's arm, urging him toward Anita. Elliot glanced at Vera, who was smiling at him. He bent. Anita's cool lips grazed his forehead.

"Transformed!" hooted Himmel. "*Un miracle!*" He collapsed on the couch beside Anita. "My dear, grant me a moment of bliss before you once more deliver me to my wife. A stray pet, a stray tickle among friends."

"I think Squire Denmark and I will grant you a stray cup of coffee," she said. "Will you help me?" she said, looking at Elliot.

"If you need help."

"I don't think it's Anita who needs the help," said Vera. She looked with amusement at Elliot. "Some coffee might be a good idea."

I shouldn't go in that kitchen with her, Elliot was thinking. We have to be more careful than that.

"Well, come on then," she said. He followed her toward the kitchen.

She closed the door behind them.

"Now I've got you," she said. "I told you I was greedy."

"This isn't very smart."

"I don't care. When I kissed your forehead I thought I'd faint. I wanted to put my hand inside your shirt." She smiled at him: the orange sun, that warmth. "Once I had my horoscope read, and the old lady who did it said that I was lascivious."

"She wasn't far wrong."

"No. She was dead right. I'm a lascivious bitch, and I'd love to make love to you on Jaeger's kitchen table."

She moved forward and put her hands on his shoulders. Elliot touched her lips with his: but she was still cool, playful. "You'd better lock the door," she said.

He took his arms from around her and went to the door. The lock was a simple lever below the doorknob. He clicked it to the left, then tugged at the door. It held. He went back to Anita, who stood smiling at him with a cat's face, and put one hand to her breast, the other lightly to the small of her back. Her mouth flickered beneath his.

"Now let's make the coffee," she said.

She took the pot off the stove and carried it to the sink. It was half full of old grounds and cold coffee, which she swilled down the drain. Elliot discovered some Maxwell House in a cupboard, the cups on a shelf close by.

"What did you and Vera talk about?"

"I wanted her to talk about you. My masochism, maybe. I wanted to see how she thinks about you." She heaped three, four, five spoonfuls of the coffee into the percolator, clamped the lid down, and put it on one of the burners. Twisted a dial. "But I couldn't get far. I kept wanting to find out about *her*, too. You've never told me anything about her."

"What did you find out?" He felt uneasy, slightly invaded.

"She loves you. She's a lovely girl. She knows you're a good composer, and she wants you to quit teaching. I think she's the kind of girl who always is first in her English classes, but with more warmth than that type usually has—do you know what I mean? I guess I liked her. I just like you more."

"Vera doesn't like most women," he said. "She thinks they're vapid. I suppose you are the kind of woman she'd like, if she didn't feel overwhelmed by you."

The doorknob rattled. The door thumped slightly, pushed from the outside.

"Come in," Anita called.

"Is it locked?"

Hearing Vera's voice, Elliot smoothed his hair and went toward the door.

"I think it is," Vera said. "Why . . ."

Elliot opened the door. Vera's hand was still on the knob, her face pale, vulnerable.

"I don't know how it got locked," he said. "I think the coffee is almost ready."

"Nathan wandered away, and I got bored, so I thought I'd come in to see if I could help."

He saw her scrutinizing his face. Elliot felt himself beginning to flush. From the main room, he could hear Raciewicz, the abstractionist, bellowing about the teaching of art. "*Nobody* teaches painters," he was shouting. "Painters damn well teach their own greedy selves. Only pansies and hacks think you get anywhere by teaching art. You fucking well give the little sons of bitches pencils, and that's teaching art."

Jaeger's thin bland face appeared in the doorway. He smiled fractionally, a movement of his lower lip. "Our famous acquisition appears to be a little out of sorts. Have you really made some fresh coffee? I've never had such helpful guests before."

"I think it should almost be ready," Vera said. She moved to the stove. "I'll get it for him. Then I think we have to go home." She looked at Elliot. "Unless you want to stay and go home with Himmel."

"No, of course not," he said.

When they left, a woman was refilling Raciewicz's cup. A large brown amoebalike stain was spreading on the carpet where the painter had dropped his first cup.

They drove home in silence. Vera stared straight ahead through the windshield. As they put the car in the garage beneath their apartment building, Vera said, "Well, I've met your ideal woman, haven't I?"

"It'll work out," he blurted.

They lay together on the bed, the moonlight brightening the window through the white curtains.

"I don't know what to do about it," she said. "You must be in love with her, or you would never have done it."

"I am. It was just something that happened. But I love you too."

"How long?"

"Just a couple of months." Six? Seven? Nearly nine. His chest thudded under the weight of those nine months.

"It must be very good for you. She's beautiful, isn't she? Does she love you?"

"I think she does, yes. But I think she loves her son more than she could ever love anyone else."

"Elliot, how am I supposed to act, what am I supposed to do? I knew something was happening, but I couldn't bear to think about it before. When I talked to her, I just knew. I *knew*. And then it was so transparent—that kitchen business. How am I supposed to handle this, Elliot? It can't keep on."

"It won't keep on. You're right, it can't now. But . . . I do love her. I suppose I should feel sorry about that, but I don't. It makes me feel stronger. It's just love. She's good for me."

"It would help if you didn't assault me with my inadequacies."

He said nothing. What do we do? he wondered.

"You used to meet her during the day?"

He nodded.

"Did you make love every time you saw her?"

There was a long silence. Elliot watched the moon, hung like a button in the sky beyond their window.

"It makes me feel so degraded. I don't have any dignity anymore. I'm so uncertain. I feel weak."

"What I have to ask is that you let things go their own way for a time. I don't want to lose you, you know that. And I haven't left you. That would be impossible for me."

"I'm your *wife*," she said. "Your *wife*. I hate her."

He put one arm about her shoulder. Her body felt rigid, as if he had struck her.

*   *   *

Since the telephone's invention, adulterous lovers have required it. The next day Anita called Vera and spoke to her briefly on the telephone. Elliot had already phoned Anita while Vera was out of the apartment. "Yes," Elliot could hear Vera say, "yes. Perhaps we should. I don't know what I have to say to you though . . . I thought that. In Plechette Park, down at the lakefront . . . Five minutes." She hung up.

"That was your girlfriend. She could tell that I saw what was happening. She's very intelligent."

"You're going to meet her?"

"She wanted to. Along the lake. What am I supposed to say to her? That I want my husband back?"

"I don't know what you're supposed to say." He opened his mouth to speak, then realized that he had spoken the truth; he could not imagine what Vera might say to Anita. "You're brave," he said.

"I'm not brave. I'm shaking."

"You don't have to go." Yet inwardly, secretly, he felt as though this meeting would testify to some deep symmetry in things, a comprehensibility.

He stood by his desk as she left. He saw himself ascending, a feather borne up by his emotions. The two women, Vera Glauber and Anita Kellerman, walked beneath him by the edge of a huge body of blue water. The women talked, talked, came to some unimaginable agreement. They held his world together. He was saved. Music poured from his head.

4

Elliot moved his hands across the lid of the piano, miming the actions of playing. He was doing one of the Scarlatti sonatas, the E Flat Major, doing it reflectively, hearing the music ripple across his mind. Vera moved indistinctly to his right, looking at his father's books. His fingers thumped on the polished dark wood. *Cantabile.* He had never been anything but a competent pianist. Maybe if he had practiced more, as Ladnier, his piano teacher, had insisted. He saw withered old Ladnier moving him aside on the bench, touching the keys. "So," he said. "Play it so." "So," Elliot said, the word a totem. He ruffled his fingers: I'd have got it that time, Ladnier. He abandoned the Scarlatti, coming up against a blank space in his memory; he could hear the ghost of the music arching, effortless, in his memory. A small, perfect room. Now this hands were doing something curious: a pun. He was making big swing leaps with his left hand, Teddy Wilson piano, embroidery with his right. His father's music. Elliot folded the lid back and continued this on the keys. He sensed more than saw Vera turning toward him in surprise. "Tea for Two." He began, as a joke, deleting bars.

"The boys in dance bands used to do that when I was a young blade," said his father, coming through the door with a tray of drinks. His shirt gleamed a soft mauve. "They got bored. Most of the band leaders couldn't tell the difference, and the Lord knows that nobody they were playing to could. You're still a little stiff in the bass, by the way. Still no competition for Teddy Wilson. Take a drink and let me have a go at it."

Elliot stood up and moved to one of the couches, taking a glass from the tray. Vera sat beside him. Elliot caught a vibration from her, an uneasiness; Tessa had retold the Nun's Wood story that afternoon. In my parents' house, he thought, she should not feel herself on enemy territory. Elliot felt a tiny flicker of anger, then realized that it came from his own discomfort.

Elliot's father sat at the piano bench. "Now," he said, "I think we could use a little 'Sheik of Araby.' " His left hand moved effortlessly up and down, gently striking the chords. "This is the most elegant kind of jazz piano there is." To

Elliot, it sounded as trivial as it always had. Thank God Anita had not played this stuff. She was at least a bit more modern. What was all that about on the phone? She had sounded distant, offhand. *Ronnie.* He took Vera's small hand in his. His father's dandyish face, sprouting white mustache above his colorless lips, winked at him over the top of the piano. "Do you see what I mean, Elliot? Utter elegance. Of course I can't do what Wilson does."

His mother came in from the hall door. "Dears, I hope you'll excuse my absence. I just had to change clothes, and then I thought I'd supervise Robert in the kitchen. Chase, don't be antisocial. Come and join us."

Elliot's father ended by playing a series of runs, and smartly closed the lid of the piano. "Well, I hate to pass the blame on to my only son, but when I came into this room, he was doing things to 'Tea for Two' that would have made Teddy Wilson turn green!"

"I'm sure Teddy will forgive him," said Margaret. "Now join us and talk to the children." She patted the cushions beside her.

"We're having some of your old admirers in after dinner," she said. "Some of our friends are dying to see you again. Pierce Laubach practically begged me to have him over, and Hilda Usenbrugge, who is an old dear, of course, wanted very much to see you, so your father and I invited them both for later this evening."

"Sure," Elliot said. "It'll be a pleasure."

Dr. Pierce Laubach was a thin baldheaded man, acid as fresh grapefruit juice, recently retired. He had been a gynecologist practicing among the circle of his friends. One of the old ladies whose illnesses had made him rich had almost certainly been Hilda Usenbrugge, the unmarried aunt to a large brewing family that had been in Plechette City for a century and a half. Elliot could remember her only as a scatty, rather shy old woman, her face the wreck of what must once have been a striking girlish prettiness. She had never shown any particular interest in him, and he could not imagine why she wanted to see him now. Nor Dr. Laubach either, though he was closer to the family. In shiny black dancing pumps and a wicked-looking tuxedo, Dr. Laubach had haunted his parents' parties while Elliot was growing up.

Elliot's father tucked up the knees of his trousers with a remembered movement of his wrists and sat where his wife had indicated. "You're all settled in over at the Glaubers'? We've rearranged your old room for you here, you know, so it will be ready for you when you make your great move." He smiled at them, his fine old eyes, the color of an August sky, wrinkling at their corners. "Vera," he said, "you've heard about the little disagreement between your father and myself. That's an unfortunate thing—it's unfortunate, I mean, that Herman should be on the wrong side of the fence—but don't waste time feeling nervous about it. We'll give him a bit of a thrashing, or at least I hope we shall, but you must know the respect I have for your father."

"Thank you," Vera said. "I think the best thing for Elliot and me is just to stay out of that question. I don't really understand it, anyhow."

"You don't understand it, my dear? It's quite simple. A gang of developers is going to despoil ten acres of the finest woodland in the entire county for the sake of a few irrelevant office buildings. Total disregard for the land, total disregard for the average citizen. And, I should add, for the sake of slipping a few extra dollars into Ronnie Upp's pocket."

"*Chase*," Margaret Denmark said. Her powdery pretty face inclined toward her husband. "There will be time for all that later."

She turned to Elliot and Vera. "For weeks Chase has been involved in this Nun's Wood affair. It's all I've heard, morning to night. Lord preserve us from our husbands' enthusiasms, don't you agree, Vera?"

Vera wryly agreed.

"Not that Elliot has ever been terribly interested in anything but his music. Chase and I never thought that our son would go in that direction, but we could see from the time he was the tiniest little boy that it was his whole life."

"Of course, Vera," his father said, "even people in the arts owe something to the world of ordinary human beings. Responsibility. I can't tell you how forcefully I feel this. Now if someone of Elliot's stature were to declare himself on this issue we have here, I think it would do good for the entire city. I've been toying with the concept of getting the really re*spon*sible people, the responsible well-to-do people, together with those they can help the most. The blacks, the Puerto Ricans from the valley, the Indians. In this instance, the Wiltshire Drive people who could use an area of parkland. Rona Bender and her cohorts. I think we could raise enough money, if the people of this section of Plechette City could be stirred, to settle the Nun's Wood question for good and all."

His father's voice had taken on a stridency Elliot had rarely heard in it. Things really have changed, he thought. For a moment he pictured his parents' living room populated by angry blacks and Puerto Ricans in black berets, Indians in feathers and warpaint, haranguing sleek Pierce Laubach and dotty old Hilda Usenbrugge while his father played "The Sheik of Araby" as background music.

After dinner the six of them sat in the upper living room, where his father had drawn the drapes and made a fire in the big brick fireplace "to welcome home the prodigals." The room seemed much too warm to Elliot.

Dr. Laubach was even more saurian than Elliot remembered him, though, four years previous, he would never have worn striped trousers (and, Elliot noticed, trousers discreetly flared). Hilda Usenbrugge remained unchanged. She was still the type of the maiden aunt, shy, feathery, still carrying the unsettling wreckage of her prettiness. Elliot remembered, now that the reason for their inclusion in the evening had become apparent, that she had always had a penchant for lost causes. She had, years ago, formed a group to protect the Plechette River; before that, when he had been in prep school, there had been something to do with bird sanctuaries in marshes.

"Oh!" Her spotted ringless hands described a vague shape in the air. "Elliot, I can't tell you what your father has done for us."

"Just so," Pierce Laubach purred. "Without Chase's help we may never have got off the ground. All of us on the committee are very grate-ful for his help."

"Why, it's true!" Hilda Usenbrugge appeared to be startled by her own enthusiasm. "There were the concerned Wiltshire Drive people and the Landmark Preservation Society. They came to us first thing, you know"—and he did know, for she had repeated this several times—"and we were all just casting about before Chase gave us his help. He was a real strongman for us."

"The news-papers," Dr. Laubach drawled. "The lovely news-papers. The lovely pub-licity. With Chase's help, we've given them a good clean fight. Vera, my dear, you see the necessity for this kind of thing in our society, don't you?"

"Yes," Vera answered. She looked acutely unhappy. "But I think Elliot and I should remain uninvolved."

"It's your privilege, of course," said Dr. Laubach. "And nobody would misunderstand your reasons for doing so. But we are merely asking for your husband's signature on the newspaper statement to be pub-lished the day before the hearing. It's a small matter, a *small* matter."

"But not so small as all that, " his father said.

"Just one name among many." His eyes glittered at Elliot.

"And two days before the concert! Just think! It's a real chance to express yourself, to help us in what we're doing . . ." Hilda Usenbrugge's voice trailed off confusedly. "We must stop this young Upp."

"Or just give him a crown and the keys to the city and let him rule us," his father said. Elliot could see a delicate flush begin to ascend his father's face. "We could just turn everything over to him now and forget our responsibilities as citizens. But I for one am not prepared to do that."

"I'm just a musician," Elliot said. "I don't even live here." Uncomfortably, he remembered Himmel. "I haven't made up my mind on this whole thing yet. I haven't been here long enough. And I can hardly do what you ask without causing personal problems I'd rather avoid."

"There are responsibilities," his father said. His mustache sprouted whitely out of his delicately reddened face: a little flag, a call to arms.

"Con-sequences," said Pierce Laubach. He wiped his hands together, making a dry scraping noise. "Every action entails its consequences. I think you might consider what we ask for a few days before giving us your answer. I will mail you a copy of our statement. In the interim, you might stroll about in Tudor Acres and gain some insight into the alternative to the position the three of us hold. That is another of Upp's little extravaganzas of taste. Vera, my dear, have your parents expressed any opinion of that assemblage of ex-crescences?"

"No, they have not," Vera said. Elliot held his silence.

"As a composer's wife, you must have an i-dea of taste. I advise you as well to see what our friend is capable of putting up."

"As a composer's wife, I have an idea of keeping us in groceries," Vera snapped. Elliot, taking her hand, could feel her trembling.

Dr. Laubach blinked expressionlessly as a lizard.

His father might be more refined, Elliot thought, but Herman Glauber was certainly more civilized, if civility implied a regard for another person's provinces of feeling. In his father's house, detachment had always been a Golden

Mean, despite his mother's attempts to elaborate out of household ritual a kind of warmth. Elliot had never outgrown his childhood feeling that in the Denmark house he was a guest who had to ensure his tenure by politeness. At dinners all during his growing up, he was wordlessly expected to contribute one-third of the conversation: any digression into chatter about school was gently corrected. "*Not* very interesting," was his father's comment. That was in the settled days, when Chase Denmark was a vice-president of the Chambers Denmark Company, before the financial troubles he could catch, like a lake breeze against his skin, in his father's noncommittal letters, before Ronnie Upp had returned from his exile in England to purchase the factory—and before Chase Denmark had found himself out of a job at the age of fifty-one. After the great change in his life, he had studied for a realtor's examination and taken a job with a tennis friend; as far as Elliot knew, he had not sold a site in his nearly ten years with the firm. He possessed an office with an aeriel view of Plechette City, he inspected properties in his English suits, he took customers to his clubs—Elliot thought that his father's advantage to the firm might lie chiefly in the accident of his knowing nearly everybody of importance in the cities on the western shore of Lake Michigan.

During his two years of teaching at Plechette City University, when he had feared his marriage might at any moment dissolve into ether, to a harsh gas, Elliot had considered that a man might go to a normal father for advice or understanding. But with Chase it was a clear impossibility; Elliot needed neither irony nor a lecture. This had been a rough passage. It had been months before Vera told him the details of her talk on the shores of the lake with Anita Kellerman. During this period, Elliot had felt himself being drawn thinner and thinner, to a thread: it would not have surprised him if he had awakened, one of those mornings from June to September, to find himself unraveled on the floor. Anita spent the summer in Sweden, after saying on the telephone, their last conversation before she left, "You know my position, Elliot. I don't make compromises, and I'm certainly not going to compromise myself. You know that I love you. I'll see you when I get back." There was a therapist in Sweden who was famous for his work with disturbed children, and Anita wanted Mark to spend the summer with him. Mark was nervous, taut as piano wire. Elliot had once watched him digging in the yard behind Anita's house, and the boy had screamed for minutes after catching sight of his face in the window. When Anita had calmed him and discovered the reason for his panic, she explained it to Elliot: "Seeing you, he didn't think it was his house anymore." A worse moment was the boy's entering his mother's bedroom and, screaming, flinging himself upon Elliot; the screams had pursued Elliot for days afterward.

During the time of greatest immediate strain, the first period of adjustment to Elliot's unfaithfulness, neither Elliot nor Vera had many excuses to take them out of the house. He was teaching only four hours a week in summer school, and she was not teaching at all. Sometimes Vera's students came to visit them at midday, and these were the only occasions when they were drawn upward out of their personal miseries into at least the show of normality. Elliot dreamed of Anita nightly during the first weeks of her absence. He felt tremendous dislocations. Groggy at three-thirty in the morning, his mind still turning slowly from an embrace, he would touch his wife and think *she's here: what luck this is* and draw Vera to him, feeling in her lighter body the lineaments of the woman he had dreamed. Such moments were very nearly their only lovemaking. In his dreams Anita was saying "You go into that room, to the blue chair, and I'll be right with you." In the mornings, Vera said, "You kept saying her name last night. You must have been dreaming about her."

"I don't remember," he said. "I might have. I can't be responsible for my dreams, can I?"

By her pouchy eyes and loose facial skin, he knew that she was sleeping little. "It all comes back on me, then. You want too much."

There was no one beyond themselves who might offer insight or comfort. Elliot's closest friend at the school was Himmel, who would have been of no help at all, himself half-infatuated with Anita Kellerman. Vera's friends, with the exception of one girl named Joanie Haupt, were all over the country, most of them back in New York, some in London, California, or Italy, and if single— like Joanie Haupt—themselves relied on Vera's capacity for sense to aid them in their love affairs; if married, they had begun their families and sent letters which were single sheets of paper folded about photographs of their babies. At his worst moments, Elliot wished that he had a confidant, even if the other person were to do nothing but listen sympathetically: at those times, he thought of what his father might have been.

After three months he knew the worst was over. Vera began to regain her lost weight, and she became more explicable, less a tense blue sky in which electricity was latent at every point. The week before Anita was to return from Sweden, Vera finally told him what the two of them had said in their talk on the lakefront.

"I was so nervous," Vera said, "that I had to put my hands in my pockets so she couldn't see them. But at the same time, I felt very purposeful. I knew what I had to tell her."

"Was she nervous?"

"I don't think she's ever nervous, do you? She was already there when I got down to the lake, and she was eating a hot dog from the little stand. She even offered to buy me one. When I said that I couldn't eat, she finished it off and wiped her fingers with the napkin, and the two of us started down the beach. We just said what we both had to say, I guess."

"What did she say?" His real question, unspoken, was *what did she say about me?*

"She said I had to share you. She wanted me to understand that she knew how I felt, but that she wasn't going to stop seeing you. She loved you, she said. She even said that she loved *me*. That almost made me sick. There was lots of stuff about what she felt like when her husband died. I could see why you would love her. She seemed so vital, and those big green eyes almost touched me, they were so intense. If I were a man, I would have fallen in love with her."

"I'm glad you had that talk," he said. "I'm even happier that you can talk about it now."

"It's not easy. But let me finish. When we had nearly got as far as the overhead bridge, after what seemed like miles of walking, I finally said that she couldn't see you anymore. Not in that way. Or I'd go crazy. I told her that I'd never leave you unless you did something absolutely brutal to me. And she agreed."

"She agreed?"

"So that part of it's over. I want you to promise. Otherwise I wouldn't be able to stand it next year. I wouldn't be able to stand you. Us."

He promised.

It was, he thought, a promise impossible to keep. But when Anita returned, he was only partially surprised to discover that she had resolved to honor her word to Vera: it was a reversal so complex that he could not see to its bottom. "I'm not even going to do the abandoned-woman stint—asking you to make a decision. Don't think this is easy for me. I've gotten awfully used to relying on you, you know." Thus they had spent the following year seeing one another only at odd times. Anita had coolly retreated, it seemed, into the life she had lived before his coming, as if she had sewn up a seam that had only shortly parted for him. But he was constantly reassured of her love for him, by her looks, gestures, and tones of voice. It was enough of what he needed—just enough. His love for her, blocked in this way from any conventional resolution, remained undiminished.

"What I envy most about your way of life, Elliot," Dr. Laubach was saying, "is your apparent ability to live wherever you choose. Your proximity to wonders that to us appear hopelessly distant. You make me feel terribly pro-vincial." His skin wrinkled about his eyes in a smile, and Elliot thought for a moment that Pierce Laubach would not forgive any man who made him feel provincial.

His mother must have sensed some of this, for she broke in saying, "But, Pierce, you've traveled so much more than any of the rest of us. Surely nobody could make you feel that way."

"These days, of course," he purred, "I am primarily an armchair traveler. I find that my insight into the places I've been has deepened immeasurably. Think of the Florentines! The Japanese! One has too much to read, I've found. But you *will* think about signing our statement, won't you, Elliot?"

Well, he thought, if it means no more than that, perhaps I will. He decided to go out the next day to walk around the unfinished Tudor Acres. The name was an unfortunate omen. Surrey by Lake Michigan. Signing the document would please his father, newly interested in such things; in any case his natural inclination might be to sign, especially since he knew the cause was almost surely lost from the beginning. The last planning-commission hearing would almost certainly result in a victory for Herman Glauber and Ronnie Upp. Signing would do no damage. But why involve himself at all? He had seen

Herman and Tessa's seriousness about the Nun's Wood question: they would inevitably see his signing the statement as a betrayal. Perhaps Herman could be made to see the meaninglessness of his signature. He was free to make up his mind on the question, he decided.

"You will think about it, Elliot?" repeated his father. Looking at the slim figure in his Savile Row suit, he thought: He is after all my father. And it is a small thing.

"Elliot is already thinking about it," said Dr. Laubach.

"I don't know how I could have forgotten this," Hilda Usenbrugge said in her rushing, breathless voice. "I think I'm getting too old. Age is a terrible burden. I've had it on my mind all day, Chase."

Elliot saw his father shift his attention with the slightest signs of difficulty from himself to the old lady. Nobody else, except his mother, could have noticed Chase's irritation. He twitched the flaps out of his jacket pockets—a gesture as habitual as the upward jerk to the knees of his trousers before sitting—and regarded her. Hilda Usenbrugge was not at all his father's type. "Excuse me, Hilda?"

The old woman colored. "I should think it is important, for a Denmark. And for anybody, really, who is interested in the Plechette City heritage. Why, that tower . . . I don't know why these things come all in bunches. He may have planned it. To confuse us, don't you think? The Preservation Society is so busy now with the wood, and then when I heard about it today, I thought we might need to delegate a subcommittee . . . Oh, I haven't explained it yet, have I?" Her color deepened.

"No," said his father. "What is the problem, Hilda?"

"Young Upp, of course. He's making plans to remodel the clock tower, to modernize it. He's going to tear the whole thing down and put up a new one."

"By God, we'll stop him!" said his father. Elliot for a moment saw the four older people in the room gaping at one another, their eyes wide. His mother closed her mouth.

"He can't do it," she said. "We all know that. It's a trick."

"It's blackmail," said his father. "Pure and simple."

"Or else he's perfectly serious, as he does own the building," said Pierce Laubach. "We might pause to consider that possibility."

"I don't believe that for a moment," his father said. "Hilda is right. Upp is trying to deflect us."

"We'll ignore it," his mother said.

"I think I'd better decide what to ignore," said Chase. "How did you find out about this, Hilda?"

The old woman looked increasingly cheerful. "It's terrible, isn't it? Money without conscience, money without principle. Always dangerous. One of our secretaries at the Preservation Society, Maggie Huebsch, told me about it. Her sister is a secretary at the Globe Corporation, Upp's company, the one that—"

"I know what the Globe Corporation is, dear," Chase interjected.

"Oh, of course. Excuse me. As I was saying, Maggie's sister is a secretary for one of the men there, and she told Maggie that she had seen plans for the new clock tower. And the architect's drawings, the renderings I believe they are called, of the new structure. Maggie's sister was most surprised that the new tower will not revolve. It was quite an attractive design, she thought."

And very likely it would be, Elliot thought. At least, it could with little difficulty be more attractive than the clock tower his great-granduncle Brooks had designed, that square-headed Victorian monument that turned and turned, sending out its conspicuous light. When he was a boy, people were still speaking of it as a "triumph of engineering."

"That clock is a triumph of engineering," Chase said. "Anything put in its place would be sheer modern gimcrackery next to it. I wouldn't put it past him to plan some sort of outright obscenity, like that damned imitation flame on top of the Gas building."

"It's a crime," said Margaret. Elliot thought that she was overstating out of an insufficiency of interest in the question of the tower. He began to understand how the changes in his father mut have confused her.

"Criminal," agreed Chase. "Of course, old Brooks's tower has begun to look a bit old-fashioned by now." He had recovered his habitual manner: perhaps Margaret was not at all confused. Chase gazed distantly at his son. "Elliot, you seem to bring us excitement." Then his gaze flicked to Vera. "Dear Vera, perhaps you should not discuss our conversation this evening with your father. On Christmas Day I may have the opportunity to . . . sound him out on the matter of the clock tower. We will inevitably have some private words together, if I know your father."

Vera made no reply. Elliot saw that his father thought he had made a joke, and that Vera was upset by the reference to Herman's directness. She merely nodded; and then his father looked, if only for a second, offended. It came to him that the public commission meeting would be nearly on the night of his concert. The room seemed unbearably hot.

The telephone began to ring when the guests were leaving. Helping Hilda Usenbrugge into her heavy camphor-smelling fur, Elliot heard the telephone racketing in the back hall. After a moment Robert appeared by the hall door. Elliot caught his glance and knew that the call was for him.

He rushed back into the hall as soon as Hilda Usenbrugge and Dr. Laubach had been seen into the doctor's Lincoln, and the car had backed massively down into the street and begun to inch toward Lake Point Drive. Dr. Laubach was a notoriously slow driver.

In the moment he picked up the receiver, he knew who it was. "Hello, Anita," he said.

"Elliot. Elliot, come over here. I have to see you. I called you at the Glaubers', and Herman told me that you were at your parents' house. That's not far away. Please come over as soon as you can."

"What's happened, Anita?"

"Just come."

"Should I bring Vera?"

"No. Oh, do what you want. No, don't bring her."

He hung up silently, for a second seeing her wholly.

"Vera," he said, while his parents, rubbing their arms, went into the lower living room, "that was Anita on the phone. She's upset about something, and she absolutely ordered me to drive over to her place to see her. I can't imagine what's happened, but she sounded very upset."

"Then you'd better go, hadn't you?" Vera took his arm. "I didn't mean it that way. You have to go. Should I come along?" She looked at him intently, then said, "No, I guess I shouldn't. Try to calm her down, Elliot. But please, don't be gone too long."

"I'll be back as soon as I can," he said, impatient to leave. He kissed her. "It might not take too long."

He hurriedly explained to his puzzled parents that he had to rush out to see a friend, then left the house, calling good-bye. He threw on his coat on the way to the Glaubers' car, which was parked against a snowdrift at the side of the street. After the heat of the living room, the cold night air felt fresh and alive on his face. The car jerked forward, skidded a few feet on the packed snow, then moved smoothly the few blocks up to the stop sign at Lake Point Drive.

He turned west on Windmere, then south again on Leecham. Anita's three-story frame house was the only home on the block that was undecorated with Christmas lights. Himmel's, just down the block, was outlined in red and green blinking bulbs.

Elliot stopped the car and climbed out into the white street. As he crossed to her porch and ascended, he heard from the unlighted house the swift dark downpouring of the jazz music.

5

"You don't look married," Anita said, "but then you never did." Her taut Nordic face, above the strong column of her neck and the narrow green jersey the color of her eyes, was wan, white; she looked very tired. Anita had lost weight over the past four years. As she led him from the hall into her living room, he saw that her body was slighter in outline, more fashionably thin, than it had been when he was her lover. She had cut her hair to a severe mannish bob, still shiningly blond, which emphasized the smooth planes of her face. The music, that constant background against which she moved, was unchanged; it grew louder as they approached the living room, the rapid fluent chatter of a saxophone. It was so familiar to him, this being led into the room he knew, this counterpoint of the lyric jazz. His chest fluttered with recognition. *My woman.* She made him a drink, and he could see her hands shaking.

She sat facing him. She was almost colorless. For a moment that was like a panic, a moment of utter loss, he wondered if he still loved her, the real bodily woman who had continued living in Plechette City and had not answered his letter. Then he saw with a shock that her face was slightly bruised beneath the cheekbone, a faint trace of a discoloration. "What happened to your face?" he asked.

"An accident. It's not important. Thank you for coming."

"I thought you were putting me off for good, this morning on the phone."

"I was," she said. "At least I was trying to. But I can't ever act on the basis of principle. I always end up acting on the basis of need." She smiled at him: a brief flash of her old assertiveness, her warrior's humor. "I used to say that I had gotten used to relying on you, and it seems I still do. I just wish there were a way to do away with the unfairness."

"I think *I'm* unfair to *you,*" he said. "We've already worked all this out, a long time ago. My relation to you depends on our not being married." How much of this is only a role, a part I have learned to play and from which I am too lazy to escape? Perhaps my relation to Anita depends on not seeing her, he thought. But knowing the mechanism, is the emotion made invalid? He thought of how many times, in his first years in Paris, he had held her in thought, made love to her in memory. The emotion persisted, no matter how wrong its causes.

"The only time you were unfair was in that letter," she said. "It made me furious."

"*Why?*" He felt baffled by her again.

"It was dishonest. And I kept hearing this undertone in it that said, 'We can't ever meet, we'll never meet again, and that's why I'm whipping up all this emotion.' Well, I didn't feel that way. So I said, well, I'll be damned if I'll answer that kind of letter."

"Well, I didn't know what to say, after the main thing had been said. 'I love you and I miss you terribly.' That leaves a lot of blank page." He was deeply pleased by her response to his letter—it seemed to pin him again to a reality. "Then the more I wrote, the more hopeless the situation appeared to be. I could see you just drifting away out of my life. *That's* my unfairness. I want the old thing to keep steady between us, but I also want you to have a good stable life, to get married again, and to know that my affection is always there. At the same time, I have to say, I'd be torn apart with jealousy if you did get married again." It came out of him in a rush: he had not expected to commit himself so thoroughly. This must be the truth, he thought, it just says itself. He smiled at her. "But that would be only temporary."

"I'm never getting married again," she said. "Don't waste your time worrying about that. I feel like a nun."

This statement, superficially a relief, compounded his sense of guilt. "I see."

They sat in silence, regarding each other.

The music stopped, and Anita got up to turn the record over. An alto saxophone, disarranging "Indiana."

"Tell me what's wrong," he said.

"Mark is getting worse," she said. "He's too nervous to play with other children. He's being tutored at home now, and he has sessions with a psychiatrist—it's a kind of class—every week. I'm afraid that I may have to put him in full-time professional care."

"In a home?" Elliot was profoundly shocked, knowing Anita's devotion to her son.

"It's a possibility. Mark needs more care than I can give him. He's getting a lot of professional care now, but it doesn't seem to be enough. Emotionally, he'll always be difficult."

"Are you positive about that?"

"I don't want to be," she said. "Let's not talk about Mark."

"I want to talk about what's bothering you. If I can't help you with whatever it is, then everything that was ever between us is meaningless."

"Everything is meaningless," Anita said. "But I know what you mean. I'm grateful for it." She touched the faint bruise on her cheek.

"Herman said that you had been out to his house with Ronnie Upp."

"I've been seeing Ronnie," she said. "He's an old friend of mine. You never met him, did you?" When he shook his head, discounting an encounter with

Upp when they were both children, she continued. "I'm having a party next week, on the twenty-third, and I'd like you and Vera to come. Ronnie will be here. Some other people. Nathan and Helen Himmel, if Helen can bring herself to come." She leaned her head against the back of her chair and closed her eyes. "I haven't been getting any sleep."

"Will you tell me what's wrong?"

"I don't know what's wrong," she said. "Maybe it's just middle-aged loneliness. I'm being impossible to you, dragging you over here from your parents' house. I wondered if you'd come." She opened her eyes. "Your father is being a fool about this Nun's Wood business. He and his friends are just delaying the inevitable. They can't beat Ronnie Upp. He has too much money and too much influence."

"I know," he said. "But I can see their point too. They asked me to sign a newspaper statement."

"That won't make any difference. You don't know about people like Ronnie. They do anything they want to."

Then from upstairs came a sudden series of screams—he jumped, spilling some of his drink. He heard footsteps, an automatic-sounding, thudding noise on the ceiling. Someone was running. The rapid clatter of footsteps sounded wrong, disturbing in the subdued house. Elliot felt a brief irrational moment of fear.

"Mark," Anita said. "He walks in his sleep." She stood just as the door opened and a small thin boy in pajamas windmilled into the room. His face was distorted with terror. "Out!" he shouted. "Get him out!" His body shook as he stood motionless for a second, and then he catapulted forward again and dove behind a chair. Elliot was certain the boy's unfocused eyes had not registered his presence. Anita bent over the boy and stroked him gently, quietly making him stand. She spoke to him softly. Mark's eyes blinked rapidly.

"He got downstairs before I could get to him," said another woman's voice. Elliot wheeled, still startled by the boy's high-pitched screams, and saw a woman in the doorframe. She was dressed in a shabby blue nightgown missing half the buttons. Her bare torso gleamed whitely in the interstices.

"Andy . . ." began Anita.

"That's all right," the woman said. "It doesn't matter." When she walked into the light, Elliot saw on her face a beautiful tracery of red scars. She glanced at him as she led the boy back out into the hall, her ridged face careless, free of shame.

After the girl left with Mark, Anita seemed to recover herself and become more the woman he had known. "Andy French was a student of Frank's," she said, "but she left school after her accident. She was in a terrible automobile crash, and she went back to live with her parents in New York for two years. I think she was very bitter then. She wouldn't have been more than twenty-one. She came back two years ago, and finished work on her master's. She's a therapist, and she plans to work with disturbed children. She's very good with Mark."

"Does she live here?" Elliot asked. He was haunted by his sight of the girl, her red-traced face and white gleaming trunk.

"I knew she didn't have any money, so I asked her to live here and help me take care of Mark. As I said, she's wonderful with him. And when I have to work late or do research at the library, she can see that nothing happens to him."

"Your Andy looked very competent."

"Oh, she's competent," Anita said. "We probably know one another too well. There was some trouble about a boy, a medical student in New York. Apparently he ran away from her after she came out of the hospital. She was uncertain about him, she says, about his reaction to her. To her scars. But it was a terrible shock when it came. It decided her to go without plastic surgery."

"Have you tried to change her mind? She looks strong enough to know her own mind, I'll admit. And . . . . it seems odd, but she's still beautiful, in spite of it."

"I know," said Anita. "I know she is." There was an extra unplaceable resonance in her voice.

"I love you," he said, touching her hand. He raised his other hand to her cheek. In the same impulse, they stood. Anita's arms clasped him tightly. Her head buried against his jacket. "I love you too, Elliot. These stupid words we have to use. You're good for me." He could feel her face moving with the words. "It's late. You'd better go back to your nice wife. I won't ask you what you think of America, or how you like being home."

"Nobody's asked me that yet," he said, feeling both grateful for her words and rebuffed by them. He kissed her. A flash of the familiar playfulness in her mouth.

"I almost forgot how nice and big you are," she said. "But now it's time for you to go." She walked him to the front door.

"How long have you been here, anyway?" she asked. "Isn't it about a week?"

"This is my first full day," he said.

"Oh. Oh! I thought . . ." Her breath drifted in the dark air.

"What?"

"You're crazy, Elliot."

"Probably." This had been crazy.

Big damp drifts of snow fell onto the street. The cold air bit at his face. "Merry Christmas, Elliot Denmark," she said. "Call me tomorrow." She closed the door. He was alone on the cold porch.

Elliot walked down the porch steps to Herman's car. He looked at his watch. "My God," he whispered. When he looked back at the house, he saw, in an upper window, the white face of the girl, Andy, gazing expressionlessly down at him. Even on the street, he could hear a skirling ghost of the music.

6

In the jumbled green light of dreams, he was dreaming that he was standing on a long lawn, a summer drink in his hand. Two people were in front of him, listening to his conversation. At first the people were Herman and Tessa Glauber, but as he talked, they imperceptibly metamorphosed into Dr. Pierce Laubach and Vera. Andy French, her face unscarred, was talking to his father some yards away: he knew they were discussing him, for their faces kept swiveling toward him. His father looked amused and detached, Andy angered. Her words, imperfectly audible, came to him as ". . . make it stronger, stronger." Dr. Laubach was caressing Vera's hand. Faint and distorted, as if it were played across a body of water, *Harold in Italy* shattered and threatened; he had always disliked it. "Vera, why are they playing this awful stuff?" he said. Vera's mouth moved soundlessly. Feeling an irresistible urging in his bowels, Elliot felt himself toppling backward, spilling his drink. Immediately as he fell, he began giving birth to a series of puppies. They streamed out of him, smeared with his shit. Andy walked to his prostrate body and began to rub each little dog with a towel. They were small and black, with floppy ears like spaniels. "Push," she said, "push." Everybody's face was turned, greenly, whitely, toward him.

He woke with blood pouring from his nose. He put his hand where, in the Paris bedroom, the box of tissues would be, and felt the smooth leathery edge of a jewelry case. He fumbled, and it fell to the floor. Elliot sat up sharply, holding his hand to his streaming nose. Vera's bed was made. He was alone in the room. He threw back the messed sheet—during the night he had tossed off the blanket—and stood by the bed. His legs wobbled, and for a moment his eyes swam; he thought he might faint. The box of tissues was pushed far back against the wall on the bedside table. He wadded a handful of limp paper to his face. The thickened blood tasted on his lips. Elliot glanced at his watch: it was ten-forty-five. He tilted his head and walked slowly to the bathroom, using the wad of tissues to dab at his face.

By the time he came downstairs, showered, shaved and dressed, the nosebleed had stopped. Vera and Tessa were talking quietly in the kitchen. When he opened the door from the dining room, the women turned, smiling, to him. Vera's eyes were underlined with gray. They had suffered a short conversation about Anita Kellerman when Elliot had returned to his parents' house.

"We've just been looking at the tracks on the lawn," said Tessa. "What kind of animal do you think made them?" She poured coffee into his upheld cup.

He looked out the back windows of the kitchen. On the thick flawless carpet of snow, a trail of indistinct tracks dotted a thin line to the back of the garden. He stood up and looked closer. He carried his cup to the window. "A dog?"

"It may be a dog. But it looks like a fox's tracks to me. Everybody says there is a family of foxes in Nun's Wood. One of the neighbors saw one last week, running across his back garden."

"I thought all the foxes had left this part of the state years ago."

"You'd be surprised," she said. "Of course, they'd be better off leaving. Apart from the fields, Nun's Wood is the only really safe place for them down here, and that won't last long, as we know. A deer was killed on the I-94 to Chicago last winter. When I was a little girl we lived on a farm and I could hear the wolves howling up on the ridges, and that was only a day's drive away from Plechette City. The deer used to come down to browse in the fields, and I guess the wolves followed them. Sometimes winter drives them south. Once I saw a wolf from our kitchen window. He came stalking out of the edge of the woods into our land, and he gave me a real thrill of terror. He was such a shock! I can't tell you. It was like seeing a red Indian with a tomahawk. He was a big gray gloomy creature, skinny, and he just trotted along the edge of the fields. I never told my father, because I was afraid he'd shoot him. And do you know what? Someone claimed they saw a wolf in Meadow Heights last week, not five miles from here. There was a picture of it in the paper—the woman's husband took it. You could only see this big foggy blur."

Elliot turned back to look at the tracks. They led to the stone cherub, now more thickly dusted with snow. He seemed to be wearing a conical white hat; beneath the knees, his legs vanished into the powder. The expression on the plump knowing face was still of expectancy, promise. But there was a difference in it. The little smile seemed faintly sinister, as if the cherub were plotting some anomalous wickedness. The tracks led twice around the babylike figure and then went into an obscure place beneath some boughs.

"I'll go out and take a look," Elliot said. "Maybe I'll be able to see him."

"Oh, he'll be long gone," Tessa said. "You'll catch your death, Elliot dear." Prompted by an irrational, wheedling logic, she added, "And both of you look so tired and worn out today, from staying up so late last night."

"If you want a real worry, there's always my concert."

"It's your health I'm worried about, not your concert," she said, but he was already putting on his topcoat and going out the back door. He closed it gently.

In front of him to the left, the garage door gaped open, revealing Herman's Pontiac parked at an angle within. Lawn mowers and rakes hung from hooks behind it. Vera must have driven her father into town and returned with the car. He remembered that they were to see Uncle Kai that afternoon; presumably Vera wished to do some Christmas shopping that morning. To his right the snow-filled back garden bulked whitely in his vision. The air was surprisingly warm, compared to last night's bitterness; it was a clean abrupt chilliness which he immediately heard as a sound, a pure piercing held note on a French horn. He had forgotten about such days, and the sense of animal good health with which they filled him. He inhaled deeply.

Elliot walked across the asphalt turnaround, plowed that morning while he was still asleep, and plunged into the garden. His shoes sank to their tops in the snow. Tessa, visible in the back window, was mouthing the word "Boots." He waved, signaling that there was no need to worry, and pushed through the snow to the tracks. Lobed, fingered, with tiny claw marks. He walked beside them all the way to the statue. The brisk unsentimental air felt to him like his natural element, a blessing. The tracks reeled about the statue and then seemed to drift in series, as though the animal had many times trotted back and forth.

As he bent down to look more closely, he found himself only inches from the stone face of the cherub. The blank wide face, the half-smile, seemed devoid of any meaning at all, stupid with happiness. He brushed the snow cap from the cherub's head. There was a quick rustling noise from beneath the snowy hedge. Elliot propped himself on one hand and bent lower. Still he could only see the flurried tracks disappearing.

Tessa will have a fit, he thought, and lay down flat in the snow. He had forgotten to button the topcoat, and he felt the white powder fasten coldly to his neck. His hands and ears were tingling with their exposure to the chill air. Then he saw the fox, first as an undefined brownish-reddish mass in a little hollow beneath the hedge, and then, as his eyes adjusted, clearly. It was lying down, its legs out to the side, regarding him intently. Elliot seemed to see each hair of its hide, each quill-like, puffed hair of its thick tail. Its eyes were focused on his face, and the fox breathed in short, quick pants, the long mouth open and seeming to smile. It was a perfect, quick, alien little creature. "Hello, fox," Elliot whispered. The fox leapt to its feet and darted beneath the hedge before he had finished speaking. On the light covering of snow where it had lain was a pattern of glistening drops. It was a moment before he recognized that they were blood.

"Blood?" Tessa said. "Was it injured?"

"I couldn't really tell. The fox didn't look injured, and I was just about four feet away from it. It stared at me for a second and I stared back, and then it bolted away. I've never been that close to a fox before." He still felt his elation, liquid held within him as in a spoon, and he feared to lose it. "I can't really explain why it should be, but the sight of it affected me very deeply. It looked so bright and alive. In another second I would have tried to pet it."

"Oh *no*," Tessa gasped. "You might be dead of rabies right this minute."

"But it didn't look sick. That's why the blood was such a surprise to me."

"It must have been hurt," said Vera.

Tessa required a second of thought to take this in, and then her response was final. "I don't think we need discuss it anymore," she said. "It was just a poor beast. Vera dear, weren't you going to the shopping center this morning? I think I'd better start the laundry. What are your plans, Elliot?"

His elation was wholly gone—trying to talk about it had been a mistake—and Tessa's attempt to neatly package him into an approved plan for the morning depressed his mood even further. She often made him feel rebellious: he had forgotten this. "I was thinking of taking a look at Tudor Acres," he said. "I'm curious to see what it looks like."

"Please, Elliot," Vera began, but seeing her mother's sudden attentiveness, she hesitated. "Don't forget about our appointment with Uncle Kai this afternoon. Try not to get lost."

"Why, that's absurd," Tessa said. "Elliot can't possibly get lost. It's right in back of the house!"

"Yes, of course," said Vera. She gave him a direct, warning look. "Elliot's a darling, but he really does have no sense of direction. He can get lost walking to the corner."

Tessa set down her coffee cup with a smile, clearly not believing Vera's comments, though they were not untruthful, and said, "I'm sure you'll like Tudor Acres. We hated to see Fleischer's old field go, but I do think the houses Ronnie is putting up there are fine. Oh! I made a joke! Well, you'll see what I mean. They're going to be lovely old-fashioned houses. They will attract the right sort of people. I did love the old field, but . . . things go, I guess." She looked brightly at the two of them. "I'd better start the laundry if I expect to get to the auction in time."

She went upstairs to inspect the beds, then after a moment they heard her coming back down the stairs, crossing the hall, and continuing to the basement. The washing machine began to chug beneath them.

"Elliot," Vera said, "you aren't going to sign that ridiculous statement, are you?"

"I haven't decided yet. And we don't know it's ridiculous, since neither of us has seen it."

"Don't you think it would be better for us to stay out of it altogether?"

"Maybe," he said. "But it really does seem like a small matter to me. In six months, Upp will be bulldozing the woods, your father will have won, and nobody will remember whether I signed the silly thing or not."

She was right. But they both knew that he wanted to sign the statement.

Elliot called good-bye to Tessa down the basement stairs and went out the front door of the big frame house and along the walk to Willow Road. He had dressed himself warmly for the walk, pulling on a turtleneck sweater after he had come in from the outside that morning. He had also changed his damp shoes for Wellingtons, and in place of his topcoat had taken one of Herman's stouter many-pocketed khaki jackets, lined with fur, which was inches too short in the sleeves and bound him tightly across the shoulders while flopping and sagging in the front like an upright sleeping bag.

When Elliot had nearly reached the side street leading into the Tudor Acres lots, a blue Falcon passed him and turned into the Glaubers' driveway. It was the car of a Richmond Corners friend of Tessa's, with whom she was going that afternoon to an auction. This was at an old farmhouse that had belonged to a man named Romer who had died intestate and heirless the previous month. Herman had mentioned to Elliot that the city would put in a bid for the land. Tessa had invited them along to the auction, and she had seemed slightly hurt by their evident unwillingness to go; Elliot felt that only Vera's mentioning the afternoon visit to Kai had assuaged her feelings. Elliot had never understood Tessa's attitude toward her husband's brother. It mixed a protective, maternal solicitude and a kind of impatience. It was Tessa who talked most of getting Kai out of his apartment and prodding him into finally finishing his book on Goethe. She had told Elliot and Vera that he could easily get a university position again, if the book were published, and she seemed to feel that Kai needed this reengagement with the outer world. This vision seemed to overlook most of the salient points about Kai, his bitterness, his solitariness and fragility. Kai had retreated into his dark flat, into his mind, and, one supposed, into his memories; the attempt to bring him out seemed to Elliot a violation. The book would presumably be finished soon, and then, according to what Herman had said, Kai wished only to die. He lived beyond ambition and sex and the possibility of comfort; he was abrupt with his brother and Tessa—Kai had refused, in words of one syllable, to come to dinner at the Glaubers' "for a meal with the children"—and so was perhaps beyond even love. This reduction of customary human ends and solaces chilled Elliot. He thought he could see why the old man had so long delayed the completion of his book. And yet even that, over the past four years, had taken on an unreality. Elliot had heard brief allusions to Kai's work ever since he had met Vera, and he now recognized, walking in the brisk light December day, that he had gradually ceased to believe in it. He wanted more than ever to see Kai.

Elliot passed the giant TUDOR ACRES sign and found himself at an intersection of three raw, planed-out roadbeds. Unfilled ditches for sewer pipes lay on either side of the new roads, and the stiff heaps of dirt beyond the ditches were heightened by their covering of snow. Tudor Acres was circumscribed by the two outer roads, Laura Drive and Annabel Drive, which formed a dual crescent about the four acres of the property. The middle road, Carriage Avenue, led into a crossed network of similar raw streets in smaller crescents. On all of these were visible the gaunt frameworks of half-constructed houses. Elliot turned up Laura Drive. He could see the raised area of the prospective green, now only a jumbled mound of dirt and concrete blocks under snow, through the timbers of the houses.

He was moving toward the only fully constructed house in the subdivision, the model home behind the Glauber house. A long barnlike roof of some imitation "English" tile, half-timbering on the white stucco, wooden ornamentation on the windows, and a carriage lamp on a black iron stand at the end of the driveway.

His own country gave him culture shock.

He walked up the flagstones to the front door of the model home. Experimentally, he tried the doorknob and heard a *click* as the heavy door swung in. He was standing at the entrance to a hallway. A mellow red light suffused the interior, and it was a moment before he saw that it entered the hall from the room to the left, where he had noticed stained glass inserted at the top of the picture window. He stepped quietly onto the carpet. The house was entirely mute. Elliot softly closed the door and moved down the hall in the mild red light to the front room to his right. He saw with a shock that the house was fully furnished. Of course: he should have expected that. In the living room were a spiky black chair, three other chairs, these padded, about a small white table, a bowl of freesias, a sofa with a nubbly tweed covering, Utrillo prints on the wall. On a low stand near the entrance lay a *New Yorker* with a Eustace Tilly cover. Broken patterns of light, cast by the sun on the leaded windows, swam on the far wall above the fireplace. The room was like a suite in a pretentious freeway motel, and it made him appreciate Tessa's idiosyncratic furnishings. He prowled the room until the strangeness dissipated.

But when Elliot walked out again to the hall and glanced into the kitchen and dining room, the dreamlike feeling he'd had on entering the house returned. In these rooms the light could be seen to be not merely red, but laid with green and blue and yellow, in spangles and splashes against the wall and floor. It was impossible to see anything out of the tiny leaded panes, except for swarmy blotches of mass and color. Elliot felt as though he were transported to another dimension, suddenly made very small, as though he were drifting about in a dollhouse. He began to perspire inside Herman's coat.

On the carpeted stairs his feet made no noise. The stairs went up into a kind of tube, the narrow brown walls seeming to shrink together ahead of him. At the top was another door, past it a corridor stuccoed like the outside and flecked with paint in a manner that Tessa described as "taffeta." The plaster was drawn up into little points like whipped egg whites. Brown doors with odd gold doorknobs. He opened one of the doors at random. Except for a chair and bed set near the open window, the room was bare and very cold. A breeze from the window stirred up some feathers.

In the instant that he closed the door, Elliot heard a savage beating of wings—a big dark shape took off from the head of the bed. Elliot's heart stopped. His death seemed to be flying toward him, a hawk or owl, coming too quickly to be seen. When Elliot backed against the door, too frightened to think of turning his back to open it, the bird flew past his head, missing him by what seemed to be only inches. The bird seemed to blaze in the dim cold room. It made an appalling unearthly racket. Elliot felt paralyzed by Herman's binding, sagging coat. Then he saw that, grasped by the heavy claws, a rat hung limply down. Carrying its food, the bird beat once more about the walls of the room, and then suddenly dipped and escaped through the window. Elliot ran across to slam it shut, and for a moment he saw the heavy brown bird mounting over the rooftops of Richmond Corners, making for Nun's Wood. When he turned back to the room, he saw that the floor was littered with bird and animal droppings, to some of which were gummed thick coarse feathers. His entire body seemed to be trembling.

"One lives or one doesn't," Kai was saying, "one works or one does not. What happens to the individual is an irrelevance. I am satisfied with my life, and I resist anybody's attempt to alter it. Another man would be shamed by the necessity of living on his brother's charity. I am not. I like to think that it gives us both pleasure."

The white-haired old man looked more feline than ever, his face almost transparently white, his shoulders and arms under the red wool shirt thinner than Elliot remembered them. The whole effect of the man was of neatness and quickness, of mentality. It was as though he had been born at the age of seventy, enjoying the spectacle of all those other people who had entered life with passions and illusions.

Passions: Elliot had once asked Herman if his brother had ever had a mistress or girlfriend. "I never saw one," Herman told him, "but he was a good deal older than me. Kai was always a loner, though. Why don't you ask him?" But the tiny apartment, the drapes closed against the sunlight, could never have admitted a woman. It was spotless, as orderly as a ship's cabin. Even the desk where Kai was sitting was uncluttered. Kai's dictionaries, his editions of Goethe, Heine, Kafka, Paul Celan and Theodore Storm, were lined on two shelves above the desk. Beside the old blocky typewriter was a square pile of yellow paper. A squat gray filing cabinet stood beside the desk, its drawers marked MSS and CORRESPONDENCE—GOETHE. On the bottom drawer the label read PERSONAL. Kai's little box of a record player was stowed in a corner, his records stacked beside it.

"That's not true," Vera said. "And I know that you're trying to change the subject. I really think you should get out more. Daddy said you never even come over to their house."

"If I tried to change the subject, Vera, it may have been because the topic of my welfare had gone as far as it could." He smiled at her. "Yet I am grateful for your interest."

"You always make me feel like a child," she said. "I'll stop. I was only concerned about your happiness. I don't know how you could be satisfied with staying indoors all the time."

"I can assure you that I am happier in my room than I would be in this terrible weather." He patted her hand. "Do you want some tea? I think it must be ready by now." Kai stood up and went across the room to the kitchen, a stove and refrigerator concealed behind a curtain. "Sugar? Do you take something in your tea?"

"Milk and sugar."

"Elliot?"

"Nothing."

"I apologize for having no coffee. I have few guests." He reappeared with a tray in his hands.

"I hope you will come for Christmas at my parents'," Elliot said.

"I have not gotten so misanthropic that I enjoy spending Christmas by myself. I would like to come, yes."

"Thank goodness. I hate to think of you just sitting in here."

"Then do not think about it, Vera. Most of my sitting is done at my desk. Now that I am reaching the end, it takes up more time than ever before."

"It," of course, was the book on Goethe. "Are you really almost finished?" Elliot looked again at the neat desk. There was no sign of a manuscript.

"Very nearly. Have you read much Goethe?"

"Not much," Elliot confessed. "For a German course, I read *Faust* in college."

"At least you read it in German. Goethe was a genius at manipulating his own language. He was certainly the greatest genius of his century, and his century had a disproportionate number of them. The range of his interests! He became increasingly involved, as you probably know, in scientific problems as he grew older. Mineralogy, botany, zoology. Always the exact, and the love of the work. He was interested in light, and worked with prisms, trying to disprove Newton's optics. Do you see what excites me in this? He outgrew poetry even as he became a greater and greater poet, and turned himself to the world. All of this side of Goethe's life moves me. Yet I know much of his poetry by heart.

> *Durch allen Schall und Klang*
> *Der Transoxanen*
> *Erkühnt sich unser Sang*
> *Auf deine Bahnen!*
> *Uns ist für gar nichts bang,*
> *In dir lebendig;*
> *Dein Leben daure lang,*
> *Dein Reich beständig!*

If you were going to set poetry to music, Elliot, you could have chosen better than Roethke."

He ran his thin hands over his face, rubbing the tall white forehead where the vein curled into his hairline. "But I'm talking too much. And this interest of mine, this hobby—because it could never be more than that—is something I've lived with so long that it seems like another person, something entirely outside me."

"Shouldn't it be just the other way around?"

Elliot still heard Kai's harsh voice reciting the lyric. He had understood very little of the German, but the voice, chanting the poem, had nearly brought him to tears. He realized that Kai had not answered Vera's question. "That's what I would have thought too," he said.

"I can't believe that," Kai said. "Does a pianist become the music? And after reading these books for half my life, I've become almost bored with them. I'm certainly bored with my own work on Goethe. Poetry is for young men. Nobody reads Goethe now, but for a few scholars. Perhaps it is different in Germany. If I could afford the fare, I'd go to Germany to die."

Where he very nearly did die, Elliot thought. Even Tessa had never been able to learn from Kai what had happened to him in the camp.

"Germany is a sentimental country," Kai said. "But perhaps not more sentimental than America. Here the disease takes a different form. Elliot's father is sentimental about his family, Tessa is sentimental about worthless artifacts from the past, the young are sentimental about themselves. Huxley would be a sage if he were alive now, he'd have a television program."

They finished the strong sweet tea.

"Now I am tired, and you must go. I see so few people that talking tires me. And I have been egotistical, talking about my work, that fool's invention. Thank you for coming, my dear ones. Elliot, someday when you are not busy being written up in the newspapers you must return so that we can discuss music." He stood. "Before I saw that piece in the *Herald* I had no idea you were such a difficult composer."

"I know you didn't!" cried Elliot.

7

"Anita was going out for the day," Andy said, "and that's all I know. She doesn't tell me everything she does. In fact, I sometimes think she hides things from me, conceals things. It's not easy for two women to live together. It would be impossible if we were living in one another's pocket. So I just don't know where she is."

"But she told me to call her the other day. I had the feeling that something was wrong that she couldn't tell me about after I got there the night before last. The note she wrote me, her urgency on the phone, those things for me add up to some pressure she's under. I was just hoping that you could tell me about what is happening in her life, what she's been doing these past four years."

"And I just explained why I couldn't. If you need a reason."

Elliot was driving aimlessly west on Jackson Drive with Andy French; it was, from the first, an awkward meeting. When he had telephoned that morning Andy had said that Anita was out, presumably for the day. When he had pressed her, she had invited him over to the Kellerman house, saying, "Well, if you really want to talk, I suppose you can come over. Mark is at his weekly appointment this afternoon, and I'm all alone with nothing to do." He had been hoping that Andy could help him to understand Anita's contradictory behavior. Vera had gone out for lunch with her high school friend Joanie Haupt, so he was free to use the Glaubers' car. He'd had no clear idea of what he wanted to talk about with Andy French: the notion that he wanted to pump her for information about her friend and employer was repugnant; yet he admitted to himself that he was uneasy about Anita's situation. He was driven to know the truth about her.

Elliot knew that he was succumbing once again to Anita's complex appeal for him, that he was again being drawn into her masque. But perhaps his strongest reason for accepting Andy's grudging invitation was his curiosity about the girl herself, apart from her relationship with Anita and whatever she might know about Ronnie Upp.

"I'm a little jealous of your relationship with Anita," he said. "I'm puzzled by her, and when we lived here—well, I was puzzled by her then, too. She's the kind of woman . . ." That was an Anita Kellerman way of beginning a sentence. "She's very strong. When I knew her before, before we left for Paris, she seemed to be able to ride out any difficulty she had. And I think I was closer to her than anyone else was. I don't know what she told you about our relationship."

Andy was smiling to herself, looking straight ahead out of the windshield. Why do girls wear those big sunglasses on overcast days? he thought, and then said to himself: she wants to hide her face. "Very little. But I've seen enough to think that you're being a fool about her—I think you are the kind of man who, without intending to, disrupts things. You have a wife, don't you? I think you are acting in a foolish way."

"I haven't acted at all," he said.

"You came over to our house in the middle of the night, didn't you?"

He turned again to look at her. The girl seemed very distant, despite her frankness; the pattern of red scars was almost a veil.

"Well, I *am* fond of her, and I think you are too. We both want the best for her. I don't feel as though I have any hold on Anita at all. All I'm interested in doing is helping her in whatever difficulties she's having. And to do that, I need your help."

"Well, I've been trying to give you my help."

"Will you just answer some questions I have?"

She nodded. "Any reasonable questions."

"I suppose the first thing is, what is going to happen with Mark? Will he have to be institutionalized?"

She answered him squarely, without hesitation. "There's at least some doubt about it. I've been seeing Mark daily for two years and working with him, but his condition has deteriorated so much recently that he simply cannot play with other children. It's pathetic and terrifying, and it is a strain for Anita, not to mention what it does to the other children. Mark attacked little Saul Himmel last year—he went for him with a hammer. One way to deal with it would be to put him into full-time professional care. Anita is just delaying her decision until I go, I think. Whenever that will be, in a year or two."

"Will he ever be normal?"

"He will need a controlled environment for several years. Anita knows this by now."

"My God."

"But that doesn't mean that he can't be happy. 'Normal' is not a very helpful concept. Mark will be able to have a satisfying life as long as he can live in such a way that ordinary pressures and threats are reduced. Living in an ordinary home might be of enormous help. He's an intelligent boy, you know. He won't need professional care forever. I'm sure that he will be able to go it alone in a number of years, if the care is thorough enough. Does that answer your question about Mark? After two years, I'm involved with the boy too, you know."

"What about Ronnie Upp? What is his role in Anita's life?"

She gazed out of the window for a long moment before replying. "It's nothing for you to worry about," she said. "He is a very old, very good friend of Anita's. They help one another in many ways. I think he dotes on her. She talks to him about his problems." She ran her hand along the padded edge of the dashboard. Elliot saw the fineness of her hand, her slim beauty. He turned to see her face again. "I guess she helps him. I guess he wants help. Ronnie is not the kind of man who ordinarily has much use for women."

He felt an enormous rush of gratitude. Andy seemed to be holding something back, some deeper resentment than she showed him, but his relief momentarily overrode his desire to go deeper.

"You've heard about the Nun's Wood business?"

"Ronnie's been talking about it for months."

"What's going to happen? Do you know?"

"He'll get his way. I don't think that Ronnie can be defeated very easily, once he has decided he wants something. He has too much money and influence, and he's too devious. At least in principle, I'm for the people who want to save the park. Ronnie is getting the land cheap, and he's going to charge an enormous rent for the buildings. If he bought it at the agreed price, he could save a fortune in taxes by leaving it untouched. At least, that's what I've been hearing. It's been quite an issue here, you know."

"I guess we are on the same side," he said. "My father and some of his friends want me to sign a newspaper statement about Nun's Wood."

"Is Chase Denmark your father?" She gave him a quick scrutinizing look through the enormous sunglasses. "I wouldn't have guessed it. He's been on the news programs now and then, along with that incredible old woman with the funny name. Hilda something."

"Hilda Usenbrugge. And yes, Chase Denmark is my father. I never expected him to turn out to be such a concerned citizen."

"He doesn't look like the placard-and-leaflet type, does he?" They smiled at one another. The self-conscious figure of Chase Denmark helped to remove the awkwardness and tension Elliot had felt during the long drive. Only now, in fact, did he realize how long the drive had been, taking them almost to the Meadowbrook turnoff on Jackson Drive, past the white unbroken fields on either side.

"We can be friends, can't we?" he asked.

"If you want. Being friendly is no strain. I *would* like to go to your concert. I heard the piece you wrote for that Boulez record, and I thought it was lovely— I still think it's lovely. Anita bought the record the day it came out. Were you upset by the piece in the *Herald*? Anita was furious when she read it."

He was touched by this, her unspoken and unadmitted connection to him during the years when she did not write, and touched also by Andy's kindness in telling him. "No, I wasn't particularly," he said. "I'd be much more upset if you didn't come to the concert. I'll send you tickets."

"I'd come anyhow. I really am interested in it. I don't know much about music, except that I like what everybody else likes. Stravinsky, Beethoven—

you know. Living with Anita, I've learned to like jazz. I took some music courses at Hunter, but I'm utterly ignorant about theory or anything like that. Even about modern composers."

"Thank God," he said. "Otherwise we might have to talk about it." He passed the Meadowbrook turnoff. "I seem to be abducting you. It wasn't my plan to get this far out of the city. Should I turn around?"

"No, go on a couple of miles further. Since we're out here, there's something I want to show you."

The only car on the road, they continued down the straight length of road. A mile to the right, a huddle of houses he recognized as Richmond Corners appeared, then winked past them.

Andy rapped on the windshield. "There is a little drive just ahead, into this field. Turn in there and park."

The field was fenced by white rails, and looking ahead, Elliot saw the gap in the fence where the drive must be. The gate, when they approached it, had been left open, and Elliot turned off the main road onto the field. For about ten yards, the little drive was paved with stones, but it then degenerated into two rutted tracks—in summer there would be a grassy mound between them—that trailed off into the middle of the field, toward a line of trees at the far end. These were firs, and stood out a dark mossy green across the field of snow. Between the end of the drive and the trees were innumerable ridges and dells, lightly covered with the snow, cropping out at intervals into rises matted with last year's long grass, brown and hummocky. The white fence bordered three sides, and went into the firs at the opposite end. Looking at the hilly expanse of land, Elliot thought it must be at least twenty acres. He got out of the car. Andy, on her side, did the same. They looked at one another across the top of the Pontiac. The girl's beautiful scarred foxy face, between the upturned collars of her coat, was radiant with good humor—where did that come from? he wondered.

"It's warmer than I thought it would be," she said. "And the snow is sparse out here. Would you mind taking a walk up the path? I want you to see the whole thing. Come on, city slicker," she said. "You won't get your feet wet."

They set off together, walking in one of the narrow tracks, she a few feet ahead of him. The path went up a small rise, then down into a bowl and back up again. "All this land," she said, "belonged to a farmer who used it to graze his cattle. It takes in the trees at the back, too, and they run for at least four or five acres more. The new owner has not touched it, because he says he wants to keep it just the way it is, to preserve it. As you can see, it's practically useless for farming anyhow. But in the summer, it is beautiful out here. All the little rises are covered with Queen Anne's lace and wild daisies. We've been out here for picnics lots of times."

"So the owner . . ." he began. It was inevitable.

"Is Ronnie Upp. He bought it just a year after he came back from England. I wasn't here then, but Anita told me that he drove out here three or four times a week, just to get away from the city and enjoy the feeling of having preserved something from the developers. Having done *that*, he felt he was free to join them, I guess. Free to make another fortune by doing the very thing he objected to in the other developers."

Elliot wandered up the path, thinking. "It doesn't make sense. You are saying that if he could do this kind of thing once, there is no reason why he could not do it twice. I don't think that is being quite fair to Upp." He looked back at her, a slim brown-haired girl in a long carcoat. The beautiful violent face was looking at him intently.

"He didn't buy this as an entirely philanthropic gesture," she said.

"And I'm also thinking that you don't like him very much."

"I don't like him at all," she said. "I hope you are going to sign that statement for the papers. He once struck Anita in the face, and gave her a bruise she's still got. I think he's trying to get her to fire me—he thinks I'm too pessimistic about Mark, but the real reason is probably that I saw him slap her. He can be so charming, as you will probably see at Anita's party, but . . ."

"Well, for his own good then," Elliot said, smiling. The news about Upp striking Anita had gone through him with surprising ease: as if he had known it from the first. "My wife's family will probably never forgive me."

"Don't they forgive your missteps rather easily?" She glanced up at him. "Excuse me. I'm being bitchy, and I don't really feel that way at all. Maybe I'm jealous of the way you feel about Anita. I've only had one serious relationship with a man, and that ended with this." She lightly touched her face.

It moved him so much, this gesture of her fine hand to the beautiful marked face, that he blurted, "Don't worry about that, ever. You're lovely. In fact I think you are beautiful. I thought so the first time I saw you." Looking down at her, remembering, he said, "Listen. You weren't embarrassed then, so please don't be now."

"Oh, I know. I'm not embarrassed. Though I usually don't walk about practically half nude in front of strange men. I guess one of us had to mention it. Like my face. You have to talk about it once, and then it is out in the clear, and you can forget about it."

"Then talk about it." He brushed the snow off a flat slablike boulder, wide enough for the two of them, and sat. She really is just a girl, he was thinking. Andy sat beside him. Before them, the bowl leveled off in a long bumped whitish line to the trees.

"You can't think I'm angling for your pity, or that I want it at all. I detest pity."

"I'd never waste my pity on you."

"I've never liked weakness of any kind." She took the sunglasses from her face and put them in one of her coat pockets. "That's one reason Anita and I get on. We learn how to be tough from one another. We both like things to be clear." She darted a quick stabbing look into his eyes. "I was in an auto accident, of course, and I suppose I'm lucky to be alive. I'm sure I am lucky to be alive. I'll skip the details. But when I came to after the operation, I knew what had happened—my face felt as though it were on fire and I thought I must have been burned—and I would have been happier right then if I *had* died. I felt the same way when I first looked into a mirror. The horrid thing was that I knew my whole life had changed, and I couldn't know in what way. For at least a week, I was sure I was going to spend the rest of my life in a room. I can remember thinking: I'll never be vain again. When my lover defected I really hit bottom. He was so horribly polite, and I could tell that he was revolted and shocked by my face. He had a point, it was much worse then. He was a coldblooded doctor type, Mike Zeigler by name, and his reaction shattered me. But I didn't have a breakdown. My mother thought I was going to, and I think she was a little bit put out that she wouldn't have all those delicious months of taking care of me and talking about me with her friends. When I saw what sort of future I was likely to get, I determined to take my new face out into the world and let what would happen, happen. And I'll be damned if I'll have plastic surgery. This face has cleaned up my life unbelievably, and I'm not going to pretty it up."

"I don't think you should," Elliot said. "You're marvelous. In Africa you'd be a queen. Why don't you let me take you back to the city and buy you a cup of coffee?"

As they walked back to the car, Elliot glanced over his shoulder and saw a man come out of the firs and stand, a slight lean figure in a brown jacket, his arms akimbo. The figure was perhaps two hundred yards away and dwarfed by the distance. He carried a shotgun under his arm. The man seemed to be looking at them. He said nothing, but remained stock-still before the line of trees, watching. It must have been Upp. Tiny, so far away, the figure yet expressed amusement—it was in the body's carriage, the set of the small head, the loose handling of the shotgun.

In the car Elliot paused a second before backing out onto the highway, and bent forward, looking for the slight figure in the brown jacket, but it had disappeared, probably gone below one of the ridges between the gate and the line of trees. In the distance, he could hear a dog barking. Then he heard the far-off blast of a shotgun.

Andy slipped her hand into his.

II

VENUS AND MARS

8

DECLARE YOURSELF: SAVE NUN'S WOOD

Plechette City has a proud heritage of parks and green areas: it has long been a city which values natural beauty and tranquillity, given to us on trust from the past, and which has sought to achieve a balance between conservation and industry. Our lovely parklands and woods are one of our most distinctive and unique features as a city. We are aware of the rape of woodlands and wildlife by careless development in other areas of the country. Other cities have been heartlessly damaged by industrial blight due to lack of planning and the indifference of their citizens. We believe that the people of Plechette City will not countenance this tragedy at home—we believe that Plechette City must and shall fight the erosion of its heritage. THE DECISIVE COMMISSION MEETING ON THE NUN'S WOOD ISSUE IS AT CITY HALL AT 8:00 P.M., JANUARY SECOND. Attend this meeting if you have an interest in the future of your city—and DECLARE YOURSELF.

It was an uneasy statement, Elliot thought, written by committee. "Rape" and "heartlessly damaged" must have been contributed by his father, the acolyte to activism; "countenance" was pure Pierce Laubach: Elliot could hear the old man ticking off the syllables in his precise, affected voice. His ear, too, told him that "proud heritage" and "erosion of its history" came from Hilda Usenbrugge—they were quavery, old woman's phrases. He was sure that Hilda had written the final version of the statement from drafts and suggestions submitted by the two men. Elliot wished, for a gleeful wicked moment, that he could see the statement his father had submitted to Hilda.

The note accompanying the statement read:

Dear Elliot:
The enclosed, as promised, is our poor effort to awaken our fellows. Doubtless we are unlikely Paul Reveres, but the statement is at least a clear espousal of our cause. If you should decide to sign it, mail it either to me

or to your father. The other names, besides your own, will be those of doctors, lawyers, university people, prominent men in the city who support our position. Many thanks for your thought on this issue. I am certain you will do the right thing.

Yours,

Dr. Pierce Laubach

Dr. Laubach's letter had come that morning, and after reading it, he had folded it into his pocket, promising himself that he would later show Vera the statement. He had by now decided to put his signature to the paper: Elliot had felt Upp's presence on the snowy field as a blast of freezing Olympian air. He could not help thinking that the man had intended to frighten him, to warn him off, mockingly. And Andy's opinion of Upp was a further incentive. The girl interested him greatly: she burned with a fine clear fire of intelligence. They had gone for coffee at Longman's Hotel on Grand Avenue, where he and Vera had often gone during their two years in Plechette City, and coffee had lengthened out into lunch. He had been unsure of himself, taking her there; unsure for her sake, not knowing how Andy would take being subjected to stares in the self-conscious atmosphere of the Edwardian Room. It was on the top floor of Longman's Hotel, a dark circular chamber lined with windows where patrons could look out over all of Plechette City, the dim blue length of lake spreading out past the Art Center to the east. The men who regularly used the Edwardian Room were not his sort, nor, he was sure, Andy's. They were businessmen from midtown, lawyers, secretaries: beginning at five, the round oaken bar in the middle of the room filled up, with men in blazers and double-breasted suits, neat short haircuts and bright neckties. But at two o'clock, there was only a scattering of these, dining at tables littered, in these precomputer days, with graphs and lists of cost analyses. Andy had walked through their glances, a queen in her brown carcoat and loose brown hair, as if she did not notice. Across the room through the south windows, Elliot could see the four revolving, perhaps doomed faces of the Chambers Denmark clock. Their conversation, spun out over the coffee and then lunch, had been primarily about her. She was working in the charged, emotional territory between brain damage and child psychology, territory disputed by generations of therapists, and was planning to get a job in a clinic in a year or two.

What was Frank Kellerman like?

Like? A rabbit. A very dear, very intelligent rabbit. He was a weak, charming sort of man, and he was a surprisingly good scientist. He would have been much happier as a zoologist than a psychologist. Frank loved the lab. Also, I should add, he was a good teacher.

Is Anita?

In a brutal way. She hates it, you know. But she works very hard and she's quite clever, so it doesn't show up too glaringly. Ronnie is good for her because he takes her out of academe now and then.

Tell me more about yourself.

What's to tell? I was born in Queens. I guess I had a sheltered life, unlike what you hear about New York kids. I never fell in love until Zeigler, and you know what happened to that. Oh, gloom and doom, get me on another topic. That's your clock over there, isn't it?

Ronnie Upp's clock. Tell me—do you mind my asking about this?—What happened the time he hit Anita?

I thought we were going to talk about something cheery. No, I don't mind—but I don't really know what happened. I was out that day, and came in at the end of it. Ronnie was in a rage over something, I don't know what. She said something that made him furious, and just when I walked in, he slapped her. I could hear it all the way to where I was, by the door. When he saw me, he ran around the room, picking up his things, and left. Anita wouldn't explain. She was very calm. Her face, across the table from him, was slightly flushed from eating, and the raised tracery of scars less visible. *I think Anita has needed me this past year.*

That morning and the next he woke comfortably. The crowded room, a repository for Tessa's "finds" since Vera had left home (the "finds" were either moving downstairs, rediscovered, or up into the limbo of the attic), and for that reason bizarre with little wooden objects, nutcrackers and pepper mills and frail chairs, the walls hung with plaques and old advertisements, was cool and airy on these mornings, perfect for sleeping. He woke with a clear head, his dreams mere fragments and fragrancies and broken memories of broad fields through which he had been walking with a woman. He was relaxed, as he had not been since his return. After three days back in America he felt his distance from it as strong as ever, and was grateful for it, but the strangeness of the country had drained: it felt again like the place in which he had been born.

"Everybody envies us," Vera said to him. "You should have heard Joanie Haupt going on yesterday."

"What for?" Vera had mentioned little about her lunch with her friend.

"Joanie kept talking about how she would like to live in Paris—I'm afraid she might come to visit us next summer. She spent three days there once, on a tour. She kept talking about the Musée Grévin. There's another reason, of course." Here Vera looked at him wryly, half-deprecatingly. "She is having an affair with Lawrence Wooster. From Walkins School, remember him? Apparently he is married, and he's treating her badly. She wants to get away from him."

Elliot could remember Lawrence Wooster: he had been a cheerful outgoing dishonest boy at Walkins, a prefect, captain of the football team. A banker now. They had never particularly been friends. Elliot could remember a time two years after graduation from Walkins when Wooster had come to Columbia for a weekend from Brown—they met at a mixer in the dining room beneath John Jay Hall. Wooster was carrying a bottle of bourbon, and maintained a breathless awfulness throughout the evening. He had rushed about the room, still athletic in his stride, biting girls' behinds. Leaving for the bathroom, he had said, "Gotta bleed the lizard."

"I told her we could put her up," Vera went on, "if we were in town. There was no way I *couldn't* say it, and I wouldn't mind, anyhow. She's more interesting than she used to be. Even though she is being very dumb about Lawrence Wooster, she seems more intelligent than she used to be."

"Good for Joanie," Elliot replied. He remembered Joanie Haupt as a loud-voiced bouncy girl, devoted to Gestalt therapists, a reader of genteel detective novels, a faddist of health foods and popular music. "I don't suppose it's Wooster's influence."

Vera sat down opposite him at the table. "What are you going to do about that statement? I've been expecting it to come any minute. You are going to sign it, I suppose."

He took it from his pocket with the note and held it out to her.

When she read it, her face puckered with distaste—that was for Dr. Laubach, he knew—and she said, "I'm happy he is so confident about what the right thing is. Paul Revere." Her eyes slid toward him, and they both cackled with laughter.

Two days passed, a peaceful time in which Elliot and Vera stayed in the Glauber home, spending hours reading or watching television. Nathan Himmel called him, inviting them for dinner, but Elliot invented another engagement, wanting only to be by himself, separate from others for a time. In the end, he told Himmel that he would talk to him at Anita's party, then only six days away. The television interview with Ted Edwards was to take place a few days before that, and this and the upcoming rehearsals gave him an added excuse.

"We have some good kids in the university symphony now," said Himmel, "and I heard them rehearse for your concert once before vacation, so they should do a decent job for you when the time comes. They're all eager to meet the great man himself. You only get three rehearsals with them, will that be all right?"

"Will it be enough?"

"Sure," Himmel said. "Most of them will ignore your conducting anyhow. But the tenor, a guy named Rod Ettenheim, is the best thing we've had for years, so you won't have to worry about the singing. He's a difficult sort of guy, but the bastard really has talent. Don't worry about any of it, in fact. The laymen will love it no matter how it sounds, and your old colleagues will be quietly malicious, just as they always were."

"Do you see much of Anita?"

"La Kellerman? Not so much these days. Mark scared the piss out of our Saul last spring, and Helen's turned a little cool toward her. I see her around school now and then, though. Have you seen her live-in psychologist? The au pair Cerberus?"

"The girl—Andy? I've talked to her," Elliot said. "An interesting girl."

The next day Elliot parked behind a Jaguar, a low green car like a large old cat, which was drawn up before the iron gates around Nun's Wood. Across

Wiltshire Drive he could see a face peering around the half-closed drapes in the picture window of a white two-story house, a building that looked oddly detached from its neighbors—but all of these houses looked like that to him, used to row houses and streets which seemed to have been made all at once and by the same hand.

A woman came out of the white house just as he was approaching the gates to see if they were unlocked. She picked her way toward him across the street.

"Do you work for Mr. Glauber?" the woman called. Her voice was assertive, grating. Elliot saw that she was wearing only red house slippers on her feet. The woman was about his age, a short dark-haired aggressive figure pulling a heavy coat over her shoulders.

"No, I don't," Elliot said, turning to her. "I'm his son-in-law, Elliot Denmark."

"I saw you were driving his car." The woman scanned his face as if searching for a weakness. "That's Herman Glauber's car there."

"Yes, it is."

"You come out to inspect the wood before the bulldozers get at it?"

"Something like that."

She shot a bleak little look at him, then glanced downward, her face hardening. She moved her feet in the red house slippers.

"Didn't even have time to put my boots on. I might give myself double pneumonia out here." She moved her hand in a jabbing motion toward the gates. "I want to talk to you about that, if you'll listen. We're going to make trouble for your father-in-law, mister, and for you too if you're on his side."

"I'll listen to whatever you have to say," he said. "I don't have any real opinion."

"Well, you'd better get one, in one hurry too, if you don't mind my saying so. Herman Glauber is supposed to be our alderman out here, and he's selling us down the river. It's a double cross, and you . . . you can just go back and tell him so." She hesitated on the last phrase and looked down again at her feet. These must have been very cold. Elliot saw that there were fluffy red balls on the toe of each slipper. "He's our representative, but it looks to us like he's feathering his own nest, him and that Ronnie Upp."

Elliot sighed impatiently. "I don't believe that, Mrs. . . . ."

"Mrs. Bender. Rona Bender."

"Mrs. Bender, and I don't think you believe it either. I'm sure Herman has made the decision he thinks is the best one to make."

"Selling off the only wooded area close to Wiltshire Drive? Everyone around here knew that convent was going to sell, and we all want a safe area for our children to play in."

He looked at the white-covered trees beyond the fence.

"In summer." Mrs. Bender glared at him. "And has your precious father-in-law thought about the value of our houses? I said it was a double cross, and I'll say it right to his face. At the public hearing." She stamped the ground with her feet, making a soft squashing noise.

"I don't think you're going to get anywhere by being angry, Mrs. Bender," Elliot said.

"Being angry is the only way to get anything done in this country. Do you think that people pay any attention to you if you speak in a soft voice? You have to make yourself known, mister, you have to buy yourself a drum and bang on it. Look at the blacks." She touched his chest with a steely index finger. "Yeah, look! Bunch of welfare bums and work-dodgers, they make enough noise and the rest of us support them. You'd be angry too if you lived here. I'll bet you don't even live in this ward."

"No, I don't," he said.

She blinked, then tugged the coat more firmly about her shoulder. "I don't care where you live." Then she looked at him slyly. "You say your name is Denmark?"

He nodded.

"Are you related to Chase Denmark?"

"He's my father."

"And you just came out to get a look at Nun's Wood?"

"That's what I wanted to do."

"Well, you needn't think we can't draw conclusions," she said triumphantly.

The lock on the gate hung uselessly from one of the iron rods: at his push, the gate opened. The path up to the convent house had not been driven on since the last snow. Only two pairs of footprints marred the surface, dotting an irregular pattern on the path. Elliot set off, following the wandering, irregular pattern of footprints.

9

"Well, that was Rona Bender, all right," Andy said. "She's one of those frustrated housewives who go batty from minding the babies all day long. She was on television last spring, when all this started, and the newsman couldn't shut her up. That awful voice! And she has an ass like a horse's. You should have seen her in blue jeans, trotting around with a picket sign in front of your old factory."

"Was that on television too?" Elliot asked. They were in Anita's living room later that afternoon, the pale winter light showing a film of dust and fingerprints on the windows. Anita's housekeeping had slipped in these past few years. Books were heaped on the little table beside the couch, and a pile of papers, scrawled in a messy childish handwriting that must have been Mark's, was untidily heaped on the floor. Record sleeves lay atop a row of books near the turntable. Elliot felt depressed by this disorder; he wished suddenly that he were elsewhere. He wanted to open the window and let in the cool winter air.

"Oh sure," said Andy. "All of the Wiltshire Drive people were out there carrying signs. Anita, thank God, had sense enough to stay away. She was furious that they would picket Ronnie—and she had a point, you should have seen some of the signs. Mostly women, of course. Rona Bender was definitely the leader. One of the newsmen from WBAC was covering it, and she ran up to him—galloped up to him—and practically commandeered the microphone. She wouldn't let go of it."

Elliot had driven over to the house after he had left Nun's Wood, wishing to speak with Anita. She was at the library, Andy had told him, and Mark was out. He knew that.

"I'm happy I don't live here anymore," Elliot said. "My comrades in arms would just about do me in. Thankfully, in a year or two nobody will remember the Nun's Wood business, except for the fanatics. My father will have begun to dominate the local chapter of SDS, and everything will be back to normal."

"It's probably a good thing you don't live here," she agreed. "You're lucky, you know, in being able to live wherever you want. Artists have the best kind of life."

Elliot stood up and wandered to the bookshelves. He looked at the record sleeves scattered across the books: his own was not among them.

"Aren't you happy here?" he said.

"Very happy, as long as Anita is happy with me. I've got everything I want." Andy's voice, now that he could not see the beautiful tribal face, sounded somehow defiant. He could imagine himself answering such a question in that way, as if he were slamming a door.

"But not quite everything," he said. He ran his hands along the spines of Anita's books. "You must want more than this, living in someone else's house, being a graduate student."

She made no answer for a time. Then: "When I need to have my satisfactions questioned, I'll bring you in for a consultation."

"Who does the housekeeping?" he asked. His fingertips were gray with dust where they had brushed the books.

"We split it," she said. "Week by week."

"Wouldn't you really prefer to have your own place?"

"No," she said. "To be blunt."

He had driven over to see Anita about what he had witnessed in Nun's Wood, and this enforced conversation with Andy unnerved him, set him obscurely on edge. The girl had met him with evident unselfconscious warmth, but their conversation, lagging, had inexplicably become irritable. He thought he might be keeping her from her work, but when he mentioned this she said, "Don't be silly. If I wanted to work, I'd just excuse myself and go upstairs." Yet they were uncomfortable. He thought he might be making a fool of himself. He wanted to tell her what he had seen.

When he had pushed open the gate and followed the tracks down the snowy path toward the convent house, he had no idea that he was, in fact, doing just that: his intention was to look at the woods and try to decide to what extent Ronnie Upp's projected office buildings would destroy it; at base, to satisfy his curiosity about the woods themselves. In childhood, this had been forbidden ground, mysterious territory. That afternoon he had still the sense of trespassing.

After Elliot had gone fifteen yards up the drive, the trees on either side thickly branched and heavy with snow, he had found himself turning on the drive's gentle S deep into the woods, and the sense of an outer world beyond the gates had vanished. He soon felt lost. The convent grounds were perfectly quiet. Big leafless trees, the old oaks of Plechette City, interspersed with gleaming birches, spread, darker than the ground, before him. Elliot walked slowly up the curves of the long drive and felt himself disconnected from the civic problems caused by the wood. Even Anita and her obscure problem fell away from him. He did not wish to be seen, to be talked to: he was grateful for his momentary aloneness. Elliot had, in those first five minutes within Nun's Wood, a sense of secrecy, of isolation—the quiet wood itself, in which no motion could be detected, seemed to answer it. His heart kicked in his chest.

Then at the base of a tree not far from the drive he saw a quick stirring, a motion like that of a leaf, and directed by his feeling of inconsequence and isolation, he walked toward it, leaving the drive. The snow had hardened, here where it was not driven into white-gray slush, and it crisped beneath his shoes. Ahead of him—he had by now lost his sense of direction, and could not tell if he were going back toward the road or off into the acres of untouched wood to the west—he saw, for only an instant, the upflung insolent brush of a fox. The animal darted into an area of pure white, and was gone. His feet going *pock pock* on the snow, Elliot reached the tree where he had first glimpsed it. At the oak's base, rough sectioned bark and roots tangling half in and half out of the layer of snow, he saw a dark hole. He knelt to peer in. A stale, bitter odor floated to him. The smell was oddly pleasing.

Standing again, Elliot looked back at the path, fixing it in his mind. This made him feel foolish, for he knew he was no more than minutes from the convent gates, but the woods had so disoriented him that he wished to take no chances of getting lost and walking either straight toward the mansion or condemning himself to a long tramp in the wood, his bearings lost. Keeping the drive directly behind him, he moved deeper into the bare trees, using a thick white birch trunk before him as a landmark.

Within minutes, he was truly lost. The birch had become one of a stand of birches, and once he was within their ring, he could not tell which had been his landmark. His footprints were nearly invisible, except for the crushed, beaten layer of snow where he had walked back and forth within the ring of white trunks, admiring them. He could, of course, always find his tracks, so he was not absolutely lost: though the snow was light and hard, it cracked beneath his feet. By "lost," he meant that his sense of direction had apparently been reversed, for his instincts told him that he had come into the ring from his left, but the faint impress of tracks straggled off further into the wood on his right.

After he had backtracked, following the dim markings of boots, he saw that he had been mistaken. The tracks led to a narrow paved footpath which he had never seen before. This meant, he recognized, that instead of going back toward the drive, he had continued moving west: his original notion of direction had been correct. But now where was he? North of the drive, certainly—but he had no clear idea of how far north. Three hundred yards, perhaps more, he thought. The path itself had been shoveled since the last snowfall, which must mean that it was frequently used. This in turn might mean that it led directly to the convent house, or that it bisected the drive. In either case, people from the convent might appear on it at any time. It came to him with a shock that the footprints he had been following were not his own.

A black figure appeared before him on the footpath, as if it had been waiting behind one of the oaks. It moved forward slowly, its head bent, aware of him but not looking at him. For a moment, Elliot felt an absurd desire to run into the wood, to hide—but the leafless trees offered no refuge, unless he were to crouch like a thief behind one of the trunks. His heart pounding, he stood on the little square of pavement, waiting for the nun to address him. He could always say that he had been unaware that the land belonged to a convent, that he was from out of town . . . He stared off into the wood. Bright yellow daubs of paint on some oaks before him riveted his eye.

The nun looked up at him, and smiling, swept past. No words had passed between them. Elliot turned to watch her gliding down the little path, he exhaling a white ribbon of steam, until she turned, still following the path, deeper into the woods. Even then he could see her black outline moving between the trees.

The trees crudely marked with yellow, huge gaunt oaks, were scattered closely up a small hillside. The gaudy paint, trilled down between the coarse rills of bark, seemed to him to make the oaks more desolate and wintry. Of course, he thought: they are to be cut. One of the two new office buildings would be built on this hillside; presumably, the other would be set on the other side of the drive. The little pathway would be widened to a road. The nun must have thought that he was one of Upp's men, out inspecting the new property.

Elliot imagined that the nun must have been coming from the convent house; the path probably went back in the direction of the drive to come out somewhere at a smaller gate on Wiltshire Drive. He pushed his hands deep into the pockets of his topcoat, clenching them for warmth. He began to walk slowly down the footpath. Up in the boughs of an oak he saw the black mass of a squirrel's nest. Sparrows, scrappy city birds, tore out of a hollow, cheeping excitedly, high overblown flute notes, Bach's trumpets at the top of their range.

He went some thirty feet, near to where the path turned, and stopped. At his feet, trailing off the path into the snow to his right, was a smeared line of blood. Aloud, Elliot said, "The fox." The words instantly translated into warm gouts of steam. Where the path turned stood a large stone statue of Christ pinned to the cross, his face tilted sideways in pain or unconsciousness. There was a stone bench set before it. Looking further down the footpath, where it curved to make a gradual arc back up toward its origin—so it wound backward to the house—Elliot saw, intermittently blocked and revealed by the bare trunks, a series of statuary and friezes.

The fox had run this way. But the bleeding was not the spotting he had seen in the Glaubers' garden; it was wound bleeding, great splashes pumped from the body. The patch he saw before him trailed onto the snow, then another lay further on, back in the way the statues went, in the area of wood between the loop of the footpath. He left the clean squares of pavement and stepped onto the crackling of snow. The red gouted splashes, regular as the beats of a drum, made another path, a blazed trail, straight for a brush heap. Elliot moved slowly toward it. The tangled pile came clear in his eyes, as if drawn there, wrongly, overclear. He came close enough to pull at it, and thrust aside a snowy branch, hard as a steel pipe and brittle-seeming in his hands. He thought it would shatter like glass when he tossed it aside, but the branch thudded firmly into the crusted snow. Using both hands, he pushed smaller branches aside, leaves dead-brown and molded. The blood was a thin mapping on the ground, threading into the pile. Then, at the bottom, just now ceasing to breathe, the animal lay, its mouth baring the two rows of teeth. It was not the same fox he had seen before, this one bigger, more muscular in the doggy hind legs and shoulders. A male. A thin childish-looking arrow's shaft jutted acutely from its side. Voices, a man's and then a boy's, came to him from the right, where the loop of the footpath wandered past the statues to the convent house. Elliot crouched beside the still body of the fox, and saw a slim dark-haired man in a brown suede jacket approaching, his face working in anger; beside him was a small slight boy Elliot recognized as Mark Kellerman. Dangling from the boy's hand was a bow. The man talking softly, angrily, the boy sobbing, they moved quickly past him, going in the direction he had come.

"Ronnie gave Mark the bow last year on his birthday," Andy said. "Anita didn't want him to have it, and it seemed irresponsible to me too, giving a weapon to a boy with Mark's emotional problems. Even if it was a toy, it was still a weapon. Those arrows are not rubber—you saw the proof of that. Anyhow, she hid it, but Mark kept finding it. She probably should have broken it or burned it, but I suppose she knew Ronnie would ask her about it."

"Why didn't she just explain to Upp that she didn't want Mark to have the bow?"

Andy faced him very calmly. "I suppose she didn't want to hurt his feelings. Ronnie has never wanted to acknowledge Mark's problems. He adores the boy."

"It was a shock for me to see them together," said Elliot. "I knew that the man was Upp, although I hadn't seen him before. Well, that's not quite the truth. That day you showed me Upp's farmland, I saw a man coming out of those woods at the far end of the field. He was too far away for me to see his face, but I could see his jacket, a brown thing that looked like suede. I knew it had to be Upp."

Elliot sat on the floor beside her chair. It was now late afternoon, and the room had darkened. He could see her face by tilting back his head and propping himself on his elbows. The scars seemed to have darkened with the failing light; no longer red, they showed as brown across her temple and cheek.

A moment later Andy stood and moved to the window, where she was seen doubly by him, her slim back, the patterned shirt above her trousers, and a blurred light figure reflected in the window. Elliot rose from the floor and sat where he had been earlier, in the padded chair near the bookshelves. The car outside had already stopped, and they could hear the footsteps rushing along the walk to the porch. The outside door opened, then the second door.

"How cozy you look," Anita said. "I'm so happy to see you here, Elliot. I didn't get a thing done at the library. I think the students must be stealing all the books from the stacks. Though why they pick such obscure titles to run off with is beyond me. Maybe the resale value is higher!" She removed her coat and slung it over a chair, dislodging a stack of papers. "Oh, damn. There go the term papers. Get me a drink, will you, Andy dear? I'm simply exhausted. Is Mark back yet? Make a drink for Elliot too."

Andy went quickly to the kitchen.

"I just saw Mark this afternoon," said Elliot. "The circumstances were rather unusual. That's why I'm here, really."

"Oh? That's a pity. I thought you came here to see me. Or Andy. Were you properly entertained while I was out?" Anita was going across the room, ruffling her bobbed hair, to the turntable. She pulled a record from the shelf, took it from its sleeve, and set it on the turntable. The jazz boomed from the speakers. This was a wall between them; the music irritated him, as did the hard chatty brightness of her manner.

"Could you turn that down just a bit, Anita?" he asked. He held out his hand, twisting it in the air as if turning a dial. Anita's expression, as she went back to the components, was surprised: a tinge of mockery? She lowered the volume slightly.

"As I was saying, Anita, I really came because of Mark. Andy has been telling me that he and Ronnie Upp are close—something to that effect, anyhow. That Ronnie is trying to help Mark."

"That's not quite accurate," she said. "Ronnie likes Mark, and consequently he does help him. I knew they were going to spend the afternoon together, if that's what your news is." From the kitchen came the sound of ice falling into glasses. "They often do. I think Mark ought to spend some time with a man, don't you agree? There are too many women around him."

"Elliot's going to be on television," Andy called out. "Has he told you yet?" She appeared in the doorway, a tray in her hands. "I should have asked before. Is Scotch all right for everybody?"

"Elliot is a great Scotch drinker," said Anita. In fact, Elliot disliked whiskey. But he took the glass. Upp liked Scotch, he supposed.

"What are you going to do on television?"

"Not much," he said, exasperated by this deflection of his purpose. "It's just the Ted Edwards show. Herman Glauber roped me into it. I don't very much want to do it."

"Oh, that's just cowardice," said Anita. "Ted Edwards is a cream puff. He and Ronnie are friends."

He did not want to postpone his revelation any longer—it seemed to him that the events of the afternoon stood almost as an epitome. Once spoken, they must cause permanent change. He saw again the body of the dead fox, pierced by an arrow. Elliot repeated his story.

"How dreadful," Anita said. "It must have been awful for you. I'm sure it was an accident. That he hit it, I mean. Markie's only seven, after all. Ronnie must have thought it would be impossible for him to actually hit anything with the arrow. It was an unhappy accident for all concerned, including the fox. I am pleased someone was there to tell him off, aren't you?"

"Sure. But . . . I thought you'd show more concern."

"I'm showing as much as I feel," she said. "I am sorry that he found the bow again, and I wish Ronnie didn't encourage him to use it. Maybe now he will see why I don't want him to have the awful thing." She sipped at her drink, then looked at Andy. "Why was our dear Elliot in the wood in the first place?"

Andy turned her face to him. "Elliot and I agree about Nun's Wood." She smiled, and he was reminded again of her youth.

"That's unfortunate. You went out there to see what would be done with the property?"

"I suppose so," he said. "Pierce Laubach and my father sent me a statement they want me to sign, and I thought I'd better see what all the fuss was about before I made up my mind."

"Fair-minded Elliot," said Anita. "I suppose that's the reason we all love you."

"But you think I'm foolish to worry about it at all."

"It's your privilege to be as foolish or naive as you wish. Or concerned, if you object to those two words. But I can assure you that Ronnie will get that property."

"I won't argue with that," he said. "But there is still a meeting. It is still an issue." The two women seemed to be closing about him. It was impossible to talk to Anita alone; with Andy present, they had to shuttle back and forth on secondary issues—nearly everything but his love for Anita now seemed secondary. He wished that Andy would leave the room. This conversation, the music, their drinks, even the early darkness that had entered the room from the street, blurring outlines and suppressing details, seemed to imply that all was as it had been years ago, when he had lingered here on so many winter afternoons. In those days, however, there had been no Andy French to sit beside Anita, crossing her trousered legs, regarding him calmly. He felt like an intruder.

"I don't think I will like Upp very much," he said.

Anita glaced at Andy, then smiled at him, opening her face, all her warmth going toward him. "Now you *are* being foolish. You've never met him. I think, though," she added, "that a lot of people don't like Ronnie. He doesn't give the impression of needing many friends." Again, and despite the smile—her old smile, full of tenderness for him—there seemed to be a complicity between the two women.

"Mark will be back any minute," said Andy.

"That's fine," Elliot said. "I'm just going."

The momentary stillness broke: Andy took their glasses back into the kitchen, and Anita stood, turning on a lamp. Light fell in a pool about her couch. "We are friends," she said, leading him to the door. She hugged him once, her arms tight about his waist, then left him alone on the cold porch.

10

Roy Baltz joined Vera and Himmel in the empty auditorium seats during the rehearsal while Elliot was leading the symphony through the third section of *Words for the Wind*. After four hours of rehearsal, Elliot knew that the orchestra was nearly as bad as he had feared. It was no help, he knew, that he was at best an inexperienced conductor. Yet he knew, more than anyone else, how the music should go: and he had a good ear. The problem, apart from some misplaying in the sections that could possibly be remedied, was that the individual sections themselves had trouble hearing what the rest of the orchestra was doing. The Usenbrugge concert hall, a giant theater in one of the new university buildings, bounced the sound from the walls, distorting what could be heard from the stage.

"Cellos," he said, "you are going to have to get your cues from the tenor in this part, if you don't look up at me. I'll indicate the beat you come in on, but remember to retard a moment before your entry." They looked up at him, a black with a bushy Afro, two thin girls with glasses, then looked back down at their music. "Mark it in the music, if you can't remember. And look at only my left hand in this passage. I'll give you a signal on the beat before you come in."

He waited a moment for the rest of the musicians to look up at him. "If we had enough time, we'd go through it all the way from the beginning now, just so you could hear how it should fall into place. But you know the schedule as well as I do. So let's not waste any time fluffing." Again, they began. The tenor, picking up beautifully, glided into the time change at the cello's entry. They did their best.

"Second cello," Elliot said. "Keep your eyes open." The girl squirmed under his gaze.

They went through the passage again. Elliot could hear Himmel, behind him, talking to Vera.

"I want a little more noise from the percussion section," he said. "Percussive noise, if you can manage it. Tympanist, don't be afraid to really hit it. From number twelve, and those eight bars. Try it along with the cellos."

In two attempts, they had it. Elliot could feel their uneasiness, their weakness, and then saw the black student flash a V sign toward Himmel after they had finally drawn together. "No games," he said. "Himmel isn't grading you."

A laugh.

The tenor, Ettenheim, was as good as Himmel had promised: a controlled, thick voice—it seemed to come from the back of the throat—but the boy was extraordinarily attentive to phrasing, the real gift. His voice constricted in the top of the range, but he kept it afloat, a dense bell of sound, moving like a bird through the rhythmic changes. With Ettenheim, at least, he could be confident: the boy could manage anything. Just for the pleasure of hearing him sing, Elliot conducted the piece through to its end, beginning with the third section, the tenor gliding up the glissandi, using the proper harshness in the short phrases. The strings began to lose their place, the cellos again rushing their entrance, and faltered, trying to follow his hand signals, but Ettenheim did the last difficult section perfectly, ringing out the somber closing lines and harshly biting off the last word, so that the listeners mentally leaned forward, thinking there should be more.

"Interesting," Elliot said when they had finished. "If you let the tenor down in the performance, you should all be shot. I think we can pull it together. See you once more before Christmas. And for God's sake take your music home with you, so you can practice."

A few handclaps from the orchestra as he stepped off his stand. Elliot felt full of energy, larger than his true size. He looked for Ettenheim. The boy was picking up his coat, a battered toggle-buttoned parka, from the floor.

"I thought we weren't going to go all the way through it," the boy said. He was short, with black eyes that went up and down Elliot's person, seeming to dismiss him.

"You didn't mind, did you?"

"Mind? I suppose not."

The boy looked bristly, assertive. Elliot sought for something to say that would overcome the distance between them. He wanted to be as generous as the boy deserved.

"I'm glad you are here, Ettenheim," he said. "You'll make this a good concert."

"I suppose I'll do that," the boy said. He was buttoning his coat, and did not look up.

Afterward, in the empty auditorium, the four of them stood awkwardly, putting on their heavy coats. The janitor leaned against the wall, far up at the back where the doors were, his hand resting near the light switches. Baltz talked volubly, enthusiastically; he had not heard the orchestra's confusion. Perhaps he had heard it, and thought it was intentional. Baltz liked things aleatory. Elliot hesitated to go, looking at Vera, wishing to be rid of Baltz.

"Thank you," he said to his old student. "But we've got a lot of work to do before we punish people's ears with the concert."

Baltz turned to Vera, smiling: he looked as though she had just cashed a dubious check for him.

"Look," Himmel said. "It's still early. What have we got to look forward to but another long winter night? Let's go for a drink."

Vera looked briefly at Elliot; she too was wondering, he knew, how to shed Baltz. They went out by the side door near the stage, to a concrete slab on a graveled yard. The parking lot was close by, and they began to drift toward it past the lighted library. The sky was already dark.

"We'll follow you," Elliot said to Himmel. "Lead on." Baltz hovered by the door of the Denmarks' car, still talking about the rehearsal. In the end, they simply started the car and drove off, leaving Baltz in the freezing parking lot.

11

He had been cold yesterday with Baltz, willing himself to be distant and only half-friendly, and was unsure of his reason for it. He knew now that the concert would never be the perfect, disruptive event he had hoped for—it might, indeed, only lie passively before the audience, a poor wounded set of intentions—but that was only part of it. Nor could he excuse himself by blaming his rudeness on Rod Ettenheim and on the verdict he had read in the tenor's manner. That had been only an unpleasant shock. Ettenheim must have thought that Elliot had been unsure of his capacities and had been testing him by the decision to let the piece roll through to its conclusion. You should have trusted me, the boy had meant; if you were a musician you would have seen that I could leap through any fiery hoops you can put before me. And it was true: he had seen it.

Baltz's very manner had put him off. That had been a profounder annoyance than Ettenheim's assertion of his own ego, his own worth. Baltz's ignorant approval of what he had heard had offended Elliot; it was an implied assent, remembered well in Baltz, of everything done, every human activity, however sloppy, as long as it was new. Walking about in the long arcades and hot little chambers of the art center with Kai, Vera lingering in another room behind them, Elliot was grateful for Kai's own distance, his consciousness of standards and ironies. Erect, almost glamorous in his old gray gabardine suit and duffel coat, Kai had been unmoved by the current show, strolling among the dwarfed, rubbery sculptures in the shapes of hands, breasts, fetal figures, smiling faintly at it all. He had liked only one section of the new exhibition, a random-looking assemblage of metal pipes and tubes, some heaped and scattered on the floor and others fixed to the wall. It looked as though the builders, in the midst of some complex project, had left for their lunch. "This I find myself liking," he said to Elliot. "I hope you think that odd."

"I think it's stupefying," said Elliot.

"But it makes no demands, no assertions," said Kai. "All these other things"—he gestured around at the hands and breasts—"all of them, they are so importunate."

"It astonishes me that you're interested in that kind of art," Elliot said. "In antiart."

"I'll confess that I have little faith in the lyric impulse, Elliot. So many of those flowers turn out in the end to be plastic. There was a guard in my camp"— he looked down at Vera, who had stiffened. He put his free hand over hers. "The guard could quote Goethe as well as I. I think he was the last person I've met who had a positive enthusiasm for Goethe. And could you guess? It has become a commonplace to mention such men."

"Someday," said Vera, with more heart than tact, "someday, Uncle Kai, would you talk with us about what happened there? I'm sure it would . . . I want to say, help you, but I don't mean that you need help."

"My dear Vera," said the old man, now walking with them into the main galleries. "Perhaps. But not to you. To Elliot." He smiled at Elliot, his face white and ravaged, handsome, the sleek hair pulled back above the vein knotted at his temple. "Yet, in the end, I don't think either of you should be interested."

But even as he said this, even as he so clearly meant it, Elliot thought he could hear in Kai's voice, for the first time, that he wanted to break through all the silence he had built about himself for twenty-five years.

Then they divided and went through the rooms separately. For a time Elliot lost sight of Kai and Vera, and stared unseeing at the paintings, brooding on Baltz and Kai. Then he turned a corner, passed a dozing blue-uniformed guard, and saw them again.

Vera and Kai were standing before a Zurbarán monk. She loved it, he remembered. Kai too seemed to like the painting; he stood as if for once not impatient to move on, staring into the tiny flame cupped in the monk's hands, the entire shrouded body plucked out for the painting's long moment from the surrounding dark.

12

"I'm glad you've managed to spend some time with Kai," said Herman Glauber. "I worry about the old bastard. He was always older than I was—when I was a kid, Kai already seemed like a grown-up to me. He was in another world entirely. And Kai hated the old man, my father. We don't use the word 'enemy' much anymore, but that's what they were, enemies." His glasses glittered toward them. He put his fists up to his chin and jabbed the left into the air before him, quick punches.

"It wasn't really that bad, was it, Daddy?" asked Vera. She rocked slowly back and forth in her chair, her eyes on the fire.

"Well, it never really came to blows, as far as I remember. But it was that bad, it really was. Kai wasn't usually a demonstrative guy, but I can remember him storming around the house, slamming doors and kicking things. He wasn't even in the U.S. when our father died—he cleared out quick, once he made the decision. He lived here in town for a couple of years, then *boom*. Away he went."

"Don't forget his teaching," Tessa said. She had a dry, attentive look, flipping the pages of a catalog.

"I did forget. When he was somewhere in his twenties, he taught at a little school up in the western part of the state, near the Mississippi. Not far from Tessa's parents' farm. He always did just what he wanted to do. I'll say that for him. And now, when I think of him in that miserable little room down on Ward Street, working all alone, never seeing anyone, I wonder what good it was, all that independence. Those fights. He reminds me of the old man, in his last days before he passed away."

"How did your father die?" asked Elliot.

"Cancer," answered Tessa. "He was a wonderful man, a man who could do things. He knew how to be charming with women. It seemed like such a waste of a man when he fell ill. He was a big healthy fellow when I met him, and strong as a bull. He worked with his hands all his life. Like my father."

"Well, he did," said Herman. "But Tessa only knew him when he was getting old. Not that he ever really did get old. My father was only in his late fifties when he died. And then he was a changed person, a big wreck of a man. I'll never forget how he looked, lying there in the hospital. His face got so terribly thin. He was in constant pain, awful pain, and nobody could do anything for him. The nurses were terrified of him. An awful thing happened one of the last times I saw him there—he was no more than a shriveled old bag of sticks, and he wanted to die. I came in the way I always did, but he looked at me in a funny way. He looked uncomfortable to have me there, and I knew that he'd always welcomed my visits. Then he said, 'You came back, did you?' and I knew he thought I was Kai. I was terror-stricken. 'Are you happy now?' he asked me. I was thirty-four, and I damn near wet my pants. My father didn't live long after that, and he didn't want to live, either. Oh, it was bitter."

"It was a long time ago," said Tessa. "Kai is another man now. He's crawled inside and locked the door."

Vera smiled a little flickering smile.

"We never had any trouble with Vera," said Tessa. "She was the world's best girl. We could always depend on Vera. Herman's father felt the same way about him."

"Hell, I was the peacemaker," Herman said. There was a comfortable irony in his voice, and in the set of his hands folded before his large bullish face. He clasped them together, then ran the joined hands over his scalp. "I had to be. All the time I was a kid, I was in constant terror that everything was going to fly apart. I didn't know what was going on. At night, up in our room, I could hear my parents arguing about Kai, my mother's voice pleading, and then my father's big bass growl. You couldn't really hear their words, but I knew what they were talking about. Kai just sat at his desk ignoring it. Then later, when we knew he was in trouble in Germany—nobody knew about the camps then, and we tried desperately to get word to him—I used to think about those days. I realized what he must have been going through, hearing those arguments— but he never moved a muscle! God, emotions are awful things."

"Emotions are beautiful things," said Tessa, "as long as they don't go amok." She looked to Vera and Elliot as if for approval. "It's like sex in movies. Who can get pleasure from looking at naked people? That's what I call something running amok."

"It wasn't emotion killed my dad," said Herman calmly. "It was lung cancer. My mother died of a heart attack two years after."

"They were both beautiful people," said Tessa.

"I suppose so," said Herman. "Let me show you something." He left his chair and went out of the room. They heard him going up the stairs and crossing the wooden floors to his bedroom; the creak of a drawer.

"Did Kai look healthy?" asked Tessa. She had put the catalog down on an old wooden school bench near the window, and leaned forward, facing Elliot, the ruddy hair coiled tensely behind her ears.

"He looked fine, Tessa."

Vera nodded, rocking in her chair. To Elliot, she looked sleepy, and impatient with her mother.

Herman came back into the room with a manila envelope in his hand. He pulled from it three photographs, brown sheets in spotted holders. "These are pictures of my parents, and one of their wedding." He thrust them toward Elliot. "Vera's seen them already. The big one with the mustache is my dad."

After Herman had gone upstairs to bed, taking the old photographs with him, Tessa sat in the kitchen talking with Vera and Elliot. She was preparing the morning coffee and warming some milk to take with her sleeping pill. "You don't know what it's been like around here, these past months. Herman has been slaving, working his fingers to the bone trying to get the Nun's Wood business through the planning commission. He can sleep like a log. But you know he's a worker." She nodded her pale dramatic face at him, narrowing her long eyes.

"That's why he was going on so about Kai," she said. "About Kai and his father. He thought it would take his mind off his work. Do you know how long it's been since that man has talked about his family? Well, I can tell you. It's been since we were married. In all that time I have not heard him mention his family once. Oh, he loved them. You can bet on that, if you know Herman. But you heard what he said tonight—he lived in constant terror that everything would go to pieces. That was your Uncle Kai's work. Herman thinks that Kai was bleeding when he listened to his parents fighting about him, but he's wrong and I know it. Herman was the only one who was bleeding. Kai was just trying to get to the end of the chapter in his book. You uncle has always been a selfish man, and Herman has always been too good-hearted to recognize it." She turned down the heat beneath the milk. "You can see how all this is affecting *me*. I'll never get any sleep tonight."

"I don't understand you," said Vera. "You've always taken the side of Uncle Kai. When he lived with us, you took such good care of him. You're always trying to get him into things again, to get him out of his flat. It was you who first suggested that Elliot and I call him up, the day we got back."

"Of course I did," said Tessa. "Don't you think that I respect that man? That I respect his experiences, his mind? If it hadn't been for that foolish trip to Germany and all those years wasted on his book, Kai Glauber could have done anything. He could have been a college professor, one of the old-fashioned scholars, I mean, not one of these radicals." (The radicalism of professors was a concern of these times.) "He could have been a doctor, a partner in a law firm, anything he wanted to be. If Kai had gone into politics, he would never have stopped at the local level, I can tell you. He'd be a senator. And look what he is instead. An old man in one room, living off our charity, surrounded by Puerto Ricans down on Ward Street. That smelly fourth ward. I learned a long time ago that your uncle had brains but no judgment. He never got back into the mainstream again after he got back from Germany, and that's another thing that is eating at your father's heart. Kai has been wrapping himself up in that book, it's like a cocoon for him."

Elliot felt that she was expressing, in veiled fashion, her resentment against him as well as her disappointment in Kai—Tessa was never far from thinking that Vera was supporting him in an arcane and profitless hobby.

"I think you're overlooking what happened to him during the war," Vera said. "You can't expect a man to go through that and come out unchanged."

"Are you telling me that Kai couldn't get a *job?*" Tessa's voice was fierce. "Hansel and Gretel. When I look at you two kids, I think of fairy tales."

Tessa poured the warm milk into a cup and drank half. She took a red tablet from the table and swallowed it with the remainder of the milk.

"We know all about Kai," Vera was saying. "I can't imagine him teaching, I can't imagine him as anything but what he is. And you've been lovely to him."

"You don't know everything about him," said Tessa. "For example, you don't know that I met him a long time before I knew your father. He was teaching in the town near our farm, Highland Junction. This is something I've never told your father, Vera, because I knew how it would hurt him. You know what I mean—your father is a terribly sensitive man. I would have sworn that Kai and I were going to be married."

"You mean that you were in *love* with him?" It was nearly a gasp. She stared in astonishment at her mother.

"I didn't have any idea what love meant, I was just an eighteen-year-old girl. I *thought* I was in love. I didn't meet your father until two years later, when I moved down to Plechette City. He was a friend of my cousin Jacey's, and I met him at their house. Jacey said his name was Herman Glauber, and I said, are you related to Kai Glauber? I said I'd seen his brother in Highland Junction, where he was a schoolteacher, but I didn't want to say any more. I knew what kind of man your father was just by looking at him. We saw each other for two years before we were engaged, and then it was too late to tell him. Sometimes it seemed important, and other times I knew it wouldn't make any difference at all. But Kai was in Europe when we were married, and he never said anything about it in his letters to Herman—though there were few of *those*, you can be sure. There were reasons for his silence about me, and I knew he wouldn't tell Herman that we had met. And then he came back after the war, and he was already an old man. I wasn't sure if he even remembered."

"Well, what happened?" Vera asked.

"Nothing happened," said Tessa. "Nothing at all happened. I used to meet Kai near the school in the evenings, and he'd talk to me for hours. He knew everything, he'd read everything, he knew about history—oh, it was thrilling to listen to him! I was just out of high school, and I was so eager to find out about the world, to learn things. I was like you then, with all your dreams. I must have seen him nearly every day. I told him everything about myself, all my hopes. When I think about it now, it seems sad. He was only ten years older than I, and what had he done? But he knew so much! We'd go up into the woods near town with sandwiches and we'd spend hours just talking. He was very handsome then, not like the boys I knew at school, the boys from the farms. They were clumsy people without an idea in their heads. Kai was another world from that. He was reading all the people that were famous then—Fitzgerald, Sinclair Lewis, Joseph Hergesheimer."

Tessa had again astonished her daughter. Elliot guessed that Vera had never before heard those names in her mother's mouth.

"But then everything changed. Kai began to avoid me. He had a friend who started coming up to see him, a man his age with a big yellow car, the kind of car we used to call a roadster then. On the weekends I used to see the car parked outside the boardinghouse where Kai lived. Sometimes Kai and his friend would go off for days together, Chicago, St. Louis, and in the summers to New York, on the train from Plechette City. His friend's name was Harrison Upp."

Tessa had first seen Harrison's Upp's car on a Friday afternoon, traditionally a time when she and Kai went for a walk. She had, in the past year, been growing closer and closer to Kai Glauber, and now it was the beginning of the summer of 1925, a close, breathless summer in western Wisconsin, and Tessa thought that she knew the pattern of her future. It seemed inevitable that she and Kai would marry: they had spoken vaguely of moving south, to one of the big cities there, Plechette City or Chicago, and getting teaching jobs. Kai was restless in Highland Junction. Tessa knew that he wanted to move to a higher-paying school district, one close to good libraries, and then begin graduate studies. Tessa was dreamily thinking of herself as a professor's wife, living in a colonial home in Princeton or Cambridge, herself a part of the world she knew only from novels and Kai's talk. In her imagination, it was a world of good china services and fast clever conversation, of effortless achievement; women with white dresses and intellectual husbands, long dinner parties that would seem to pass in a moment. She already saw herself, her hair cut short and somehow clinging close to her head like a brilliant helmet—Tessa was vain about her hair—walking across a college green to her new home. She had no doubts of Kai's ability to achieve all this for her: it would be a natural consequence of his conversation.

The yellow roadster seemed an omen, a portent of this life. She had never before seen an automobile like it. The heavens had moved, and brought her closer to the gorgeous careless future: touching the shiny metal of its door, she felt confirmed in her hopes. She knew that its owner must be a friend of Kai's, that he already had some connection with the universe they would later inhabit together. No one else in town could know the man who owned that car. Standing in the dusty street before Kai's boardinghouse, she thought that she had never loved him so much. ("Later," Tessa said, "I was horrified that what I thought was love had so much greed in it. But maybe it always does.") Playful, she honked the big horn at the driver's side of the car, squeezing the black rubber bulb.

Kai appeared in the doorway of the boardinghouse, followed after a second by a florid balding man who was dressed in the most beautiful clothes she had ever seen a man wear. Tessa was startled, and looked up at the house in her embarrassment. The other lodgers were standing at the windows, peering down at her. They were mostly clerks in the shops or traveling men, people who seemed to her to have purposeless, eventless lives, like her parents. The newcomer—Kai's friend—made them all appear shabby, grimy from their years of doling out parcels and change, or of endlessly circling about the western counties in rattly old cars and buggies. She could have stepped into that car and never seen them again.

She did get into the car, helped by Kai's friend, and they drove to another town, to a restaurant. By this time she had been introduced to Harrison Upp; he was the most sophisticated man she had ever met. All during dinner, he talked about the places he had seen, cities in Europe Tessa knew she would never see unless Kai took her to them. He was nervously quick, sarcastic, talkative, leaning slightly across the table toward Kai or gesturing with one hand in a way that made Tessa think of the young men in novels she had read. He knew Paris, Austria, Switzerland, Germany, and latent in his descriptions and anecdotes was the implication that Kai would know them too. It was all a prodding kind of flattery which must have been attractive to the young man Kai was then, about to begin his thirties in a small midwestern town for which he had no love. Tessa, watching these two, felt an odd mixture of emotions: envy, excitement, an unlocalized kind of fear. She knew that everyone else in the restaurant was watching them. Back at home that night, she sat in front of her mirror trying to see in it the face of the woman she was to become, who would be able to enter a restaurant that way and concentrate it about herself.

But, as she told them, there had been an omen "all right," and she had not read it correctly. Kai's attitude toward her began to change. He became more openly dissatisfied with the town, with his job. When she talked with him a few days after Harrison Upp's car had swept out toward the trunk road, raising a great feathery plume of white dust, Kai said many bitter things to her—he savagely lampooned the school's principal, Royce Watkins, and the bank president, Walter Bumpers. He frightened her with his wit. She knew that he was in a rage to leave the town. The next week he and Harrison Upp went to Chicago, and Kai came back with new books and two new neckties. Tessa knew that Upp had bought the ties for him.

One day after Kai had returned from Chicago, Tessa walked into town and up the road to the boardinghouse. She could see Kai at his window, watching her approach the house. When she was about to walk across the porch, he motioned her to stay where she was, and in a moment, joined her outside. They walked out of town toward the fields. Kai was uneasy and uncommunicative. He thwarted her questions with brief replies until she asked if he would stay teaching in the town another year. It had been their plan, she thought, to move separately to Plechette City the following autumn, though they had never spoken of it directly. Kai said no, he could not stay on in Highland Junction; nor would he move to Plechette City. Everything was slipping past him, he felt. He had

UNDER VENUS / 473

to go somewhere where he could work on another degree, somewhere in Europe. Harrison Upp knew about these things: he had taken courses at the Sorbonne; he had friends in German universities. The two of them sat in the broad grassy field, plucking stems of grass from the matted ground. Listening to him talk, Tessa felt herself condemned to a lifetime of this, the confined little town, the fields that rolled on west to the river, all of it deadeningly familiar.

For the rest of that summer she saw Kai infrequently. It was clear that he avoided her. Too proud to chase him when the other boarders told her that he had gone over to the school to "read," she hovered across the street, watching from the windows of the general store. The yellow car appeared on the weekends and Tessa could catch glimpses of the two men in Kai's window, or out in the fields around the town, slowly walking, Harrison Upp wearing a bright straw hat. Their trips began soon after, sometimes lasting weeks. In August one of the men at the boardinghouse caught up to her on the street and gave her a note from Kai. He had moved out, and left with Upp for Europe. For three days she had been watching an empty room. Tessa went back to her parents' farm and began to make plans to move to Plechette City. Her mother reminded her of Jacey, her sister's boy, who had married a Plechette City girl and lived there with his family. He could help her find a place to live. On the winter day she finally left, her parents watched her pack with inarticulate astonished amazement: even her mother, she knew, had not expected that she really had the will to leave. It had taken her six months.

Not until she had met Herman Glauber the year following and known him for several weeks did she learn that Kai had never returned from Europe: he was then living in Harrison Upp's apartment in Paris, and attending classes at the Sorbonne. He stayed there two years, then broke with Upp and went alone to Bonn. He had little money, but in his infrequent letters to his family said that he was very happy. He had friends, he found a teaching job, he had begun to do research for his book on Goethe.

Elliot and Vera lay in their beds in the dark cluttered upstairs room. From the bedroom across the hall they could hear the deep fluttery snoring of Herman Glauber, echoed by a gentler snoring from Tessa. "In the morning," Vera said, "she'll tell us that she didn't get any sleep at all. She is at least that predictable." After a moment: "What are you thinking about?"

"That story."

"So am I. It's funny to think that I don't even know my own mother. I never thought about how it was for her on the farm with her parents. She always used to make it sound so idyllic—you know Mother. She made it sound as if I should be jealous. But she must have hated it, Elliot. The other strange thing is that Uncle Kai could have been my father."

"Not if I understand the story," he said.

"Your parents knew Harrison Upp, didn't they?"

"Sure. He was a neighbor of theirs. Of ours."

"What was he like?"

"A red-faced kind of man, very bluff, a jovial type. He drank a lot, I re-member. Both he and his wife were supposed to be alcoholics. He liked the way my father played the piano. I don't know what else. He had a little rim of white hair. His family was very rich, and he was very rich, and he took his whole family to Africa once when I was a kid. We got postcards from them. They were on safari. He was a flamboyant man."

"Do you think Uncle Kai knew about the shooting?"

"It was in all the papers. I'm sure he must have seen it. I can't imagine what he thought about it."

"Oh, Elliot," she whispered, "I can't wait to get home. To have all of this over with." She turned to face him across the space between their beds. "Will you come in with me?" she said softly.

Elliot had been thinking, during this conversation, of the afternoon two days ago at Anita's house. He had, he realized, obscurely enjoyed the close world he had felt about him. He wondered what the two women had talked about when he was gone. He had tried to call Anita the morning of the rehearsal, the day after he had gone to her house to discuss Mark, and Andy had been parrying, protective.

How is she? Can I see you sometime tomorrow?

Dear Elliot. Aren't you awfully busy now? Don't worry about us. Anita and I were going to go shopping tomorrow—we are both last-minute types. In the background, he had heard his record playing.

Do you like that? The record?

I think it's beautiful. It reminds me of you. You should do things like that all day long.

He slipped from his bed and crossed to Vera's. In the darkness, her oval face looked tired, pale, pretty.

"Tell me about Anita," she said.

If Elliot had forgotten about Ronnie Upp's plans for the Chambers Denmark clock, his father had not. Tessa met them at the door as they returned to the Glauber house, saying that Elliot's father was on the telephone. "He called just this minute," Tessa said, "and I told him that you two were out for a walk, but then I looked out the front window and saw you coming up the driveway."

Vera, at a look from Elliot, took her mother into the living room.

"What the devil did you say to Rona Bender?" His father's voice was reedy, crackling. "She's one of our best women out there. I got a call from her the other day saying that she saw you snooping—that was the word she used— around Nun's Wood at the same time that Upp scoundrel was there. She as good as accused me of selling out the people on Wiltshire Drive and making a clandestine deal with Upp."

"That's because I was in Herman Glauber's car. You could have explained the situation to her."

"I did, believe me." Elliot could hear his father make a sigh that might have signified amusement. "I told her that you were a musician. And she told me that she didn't know how I could let a thing like that happen. I think she imagines you are one of those witless guitarists. Perhaps you should get a haircut."

"It's too cold for a haircut," Elliot answered, smiling.

"And Rona Bender can be a bit much at times. She was receptive to reason, however. I think she was rather ruffled by the tone you took with her. Rona is accustomed to rather less *hauteur*, I should imagine."

"Well, I don't think I said anything to disturb her. She just wanted to complain about her property values."

"A great complainer," said his father, his voice amused. "An inspired complainer. We're counting on Rona for some fireworks at the commission meeting. All that is by-the-by, really. I got a call from Pierce this morning, Elliot."

"Yes?" he asked, knowing what was coming.

"He had not received your signature on our statement. You are planning to declare yourself on our side, aren't you?"

"I am, yes." He waited for an indication of relief or approval, but none came. "But before I do, I've got to talk with Herman."

"Tread lightly, boy, tread lightly."

"We have to drive into Chicago for a TV taping the day after tomorrow, and I think I'll bring it up then. I'm sure you'll be able to calm Dr. Laubach in the meantime."

"Pierce is unimaginable any way other than placid," Chase said. "Unlike the good Rona, who is his opposite number, as it were. People on the west side of town seem to be more impulsive than ourselves." It was this sort of judgment, so typical of his father, that rankled within Elliot. "Don't even bother to contradict me," Chase continued. "I know one can't generalize. Especially in these days. And perhaps there are special categories for creatures like Ronnie Upp." Chase paused significantly, as if waiting to hear the next beat.

"I don't think I followed that," said Elliot.

"I'm talking about the clock. I hope you have not forgotten."

"I think I had," Elliot said. He had a moment's flash of boredom with everything to do with Plechette City. "Is there anything new about that? Any new information?"

"Confirmation, if not information. Perhaps you have also forgotten about our spy in the embassy, Hilda's good coworker."

"I remember now," said Elliot.

"I should hope that you do. At any rate, the Huebsch girl has told Hilda that an agreement has been made with a firm to demolish my great-grandfather's structure, work to begin this spring, after the weather changes. That gives us time to plan our attack, even file suit, if necessary. Oh, we will stop him, I assure you."

"I'm happy you are so confident."

"Confidence is a necessity. Especially for us." Chase still sounded amused. "I've been to a lawyer on this matter, and he could give me little assurance that we could save the clock tower. It must be officially designated a historic monument. When I pressed him, he of course agreed that it was a historic monument. Hence the need for a citizen's group. We must present our case before the Monuments Commission, and then stir up public sentiment. Most of the members of the Monuments Commission are themselves monuments. Hilda tells me that the commission has not held a meeting for the past fifteen years. One can assume that they would love to be consulted again."

"Shrewd of you, Father." Elliot smiled. "Are they all still alive?"

"In body," said Chase. "You won't forget to inform Herman Glauber tactfully of your decision on our little matter, will you?"

"No, I won't," said Elliot. "Oh, there's one more thing I wanted to ask. What was Harrison Upp like—can you remember?"

"I'd rather forget," said his father. "He was a bit of a scamp, however. Why are you interested in the father?"

"You might call it psychology," said Elliot.

13

In 1963, Jefferson Glee, then a first-term Plechette City alderman and a creamily brown-skinned gold-spectacled raccoonlike man who owned a string of laundromats in the valley to the south of Grand Avenue, introduced at a Common Council meeting a bill to alter the name of Grand Avenue to John F. Kennedy Avenue. In 1945 an earlier alderman from the same ward, Roman Zawocki, had proposed renaming it Roosevelt Avenue; and in 1937 Route America had been proposed by Wilton Zamon, who later became the mayor and held office until VE Day, when he died of a heart attack at his desk, having just been informed that his son Roy had been arrested during a raid on a Booker Place nightclub described in the *Herald*'s account (which included a photograph of General Mark Clark pinning a Silver Star on Roy Zamon) as a "hell." Both of these bills, like Mr. Glee's, were defeated.

Grand Avenue had been for a hundred years the principal shopping area of Plechette City, a conservative mile of its largest and best shops. Second Street, intersecting it near the river, had been its chiefest rival from the early twentieth century to the nineteen-fifties; the big department stores had branches on Second Street, and many small businessmen had chosen to rent or build shops there. In the sixties, Second Street was gradually—and in the view of these men, fatally—overtaken by the blacks who had been displaced from the valley by Puerto Ricans. What the new shopping centers had begun, the black population finished; and after the riots of 1968 in which millions of dollars of property was destroyed and seven men killed, Second Street was lined with failing pawnshops, storefront churches, taverns, and the boarded-up facades of the department stores. Grand Avenue was the last, threatened center of urban life in Plechette City, and the city council did not wish to toy with it. Elliot had been therefore surprised to see in the *Herald* that a week after the mayor's Model City plan had been rejected, plans were being drawn up to close Grand Avenue off to traffic and make it a shopping mall: in the newspaper drawing, an arcade lined with trees and benches. A shopping center with nowhere to park. At the bottom of the page had been a curious paragraph (WOLF IN GARDEN) about a man named Leroy Zim, who had seen a wolf loping across his backyard. Zoo officials were summoned, but had been unable to find the animal. Mr. Zim described it as "no dog I ever heard of, not after I looked at it twice."

Another article in the same issue (OUR DYING DOWNTOWN) reported that the volume of pre-Christmas business had declined by eight percent from the year before. Elliot, in the midst of a thrusting mob within the Gimbels Grand, could only be grateful. He loved these big old-fashioned stores when he was a boy—he had loved, in fact, all the prosperous crowded length of the avenue—and had come shopping that afternoon with Vera to recover his old sensation of absorption into a varied and rushing mass bent on work and pleasure.

The store still had some of its old aura for him: those glass counters of expensive scarves and belts, the dark wood of the elevators and the paneling of the men's department. The elaborate women, brokenly seen through the crowd, behind the cosmetic counters. Tall boots on wooden wall ledges in an alcove. Going up on the narrow escalator to the second floor (Notions, Perfumes, Toys, Books, Women's Clothing II—Young Modes), Elliot looked over the crowded, rambling expanse of the floor below. A steady swell of people pushed through the revolving doors below the GRAND AVENUE sign and the enormous gilded iron clock set into the wall above it: three-twenty.

Women's Clothing II—Young Modes, an arcade of booths and counters exhaling rock music, butted against the elevator like a more exotic continent. Vera led him into a row of long dresses with Spanish collars and great puffed sleeves through to a second enclosure. This was lined with satiny calf-length clothes, green and pastel blues and yellows, soft tan shades. Thick brown belts studded with bullets draped from hooks in the walls. The thin pained voice of the singers filled the air about them: ". . . and the eagle flies with the dove," rushed by drums. Elliot wondered for a moment if it might be Roy Baltz. He had not even asked Baltz if he had made a record.

"I think my mother would be happy if you got something and charged it to her," Elliot said. "That's what she wanted you to do. And if it looks expensive to you, no matter what it costs, think of Paris and get it. She'll be pleased." The offer of the charge card, Elliot thought, was Margaret's way of apologizing for Vera's embarrassment at the Denmark house.

"Don't worry about me," he said to Vera. "I'll just browse around. Take your time and find something you like."

Vera turned to the dresses, her face skeptical and concentrated. Elliot moved toward the little room's entrance and nearly bounced into a salesgirl.

"May I help you?" A harassed-looking girl, blue smudges painted below her large eyes.

"Just browsing—and so is my wife," he added, to protect Vera. He smiled at the girl's tired face. She looked no more than high-school age beneath the clown's paint. He earned a brilliant smile in return.

"Ask me if you need any help," she said, and went into the next enclosure: sweaters, Elliot saw, following. More belts with bullets. A new voice began on the tape, boyish and thick: "I'd like to be . . . Under the sea," a cowboy's unlikely lament. ". . . in the shade," comically mournful.

"Can't you shut that crap off? What is this anyhow?" The stumpy woman before the counter was staring aggressively at the girl he had just spoken to, looming her heavy face up at the girl from beneath a wild mass of black hair. "I asked you, what is this? I been waiting fifteen minutes, listening to that crap." She leaned on a fluffy pile of sweaters, her arms in the shapeless blue coat jutting out at the elbows.

"I'm sorry," said the girl. "It's just the tape they play here."

"*Sorry.*" The woman glared at the girl. "I been waiting fifteen minutes, and you're sorry. That's a big deal, huh? All I get out of you is fifteen minutes of stupid music and a big sorry. Is that what you call service here?"

"I'm sorry you were waiting," said the girl. "I'll help you if I can."

"All you can say is sorry, is that right?" The woman pushed herself back from the counter with a fat jerk of her short arms and picked the top sweater from the pile. It was a small turtleneck, cut skinny in the chest: in the woman's hands, it looked no more substantial than a handkerchief. "I want to try this on," she said. "If you're over being so *sorry*, maybe you could show me the changing room."

The girl's tired face, now set into bored hostile lines which seemed to leak the blue eye makeup over large flat areas of her face, focused toward the skinny sweater, then back to the heavy little woman in the blue coat. "I don't think it looks like your size," she said.

"I'm trying to see if it's my size," she retorted. "It's the biggest you got, up in this section."

". . . in the shade," went the cowboy voice, filling the silence while the salesgirl put her hand to her eyebrows and Elliot hung indecisively by the entrance.

"Isn't that why you got changing rooms?" the woman insisted. "You don't expect people to just buy this stuff right off, do you?"

"But it's too small for you," said the girl. "Everything in this department would be."

"I don't have to take that from you," hissed the woman. "Someone who made me wait."

"This is Young Modes. The right department for you is downstairs." The girl leaned forward across the counter to take the sweater, balled in the woman's hand. Elliot knew that the gesture was a mistake.

"You're just one of those kids, aren't you? One of those filthy schoolkids. What makes you think that you can order me downstairs? Order me, *period?* You and your kids. Snotnose college brats. I'll bet you go to college, don't you?"

"Yes, I do," the girl said. "At night."

"I know what you do at night," crowed the woman. The girl looked toward Elliot, appealing for help. "Night, is it?" It came out like a dirty word. The woman walked backward two steps, still clutching the sweater. "Night's all you're good for, painted up like a whore." She followed the girl's glance toward Elliot, lighting on him with inflamed eyes. "What are you gaping at, mister? You stay out of this. This isn't your fight. And you stop staring at me."

"There isn't any *fight*," the girl said. "Just give me back the sweater."

The woman gave Elliot a wild, triumphant glare and, tilting her head very slightly, carefully spat on the sweater she held bunched in her hand.

"Oh, no," groaned the salesgirl, standing frozen behind the counter.

"Stare at that, mister," the woman said. She dropped the sweater to the floor. "Now I'll try another one on. A real nice one." She thrashed sideways and clutched another sweater from the stack beside her. "This one."

Vera appeared in the doorway beside him, gaping at the woman. "Get the manager, or a clerk, or someone," Elliot said. "Something's wrong with her."

"It ain't wrong with me," the woman shouted at him. "With this store. This little tramp who goes to college." Vera broke from him and disappeared down the line of arcades.

"Listen," Elliot began.

"You listen," she said. "You got no right to tell me what to do, you hippie." Her voice raised to an assertive command, a fishwife's edict. "You can get out, you got no business here. You don't belong up here anyhow, up here in the lady's department. A creep, that's what you are, a creep, a creep, a creep. Go on, get the cops. I know what you are." She closed her mouth like a bulldog, the mad black hair waggling about her head. "*You*. Don't make me laugh." The music, now a boy's wail over a strummed guitar, filled in again when her voice subsided—*I see rain*, sang the boy.

"He thinks he's seen rain," the woman said, more quietly, and moved forward toward the counter. Before Elliot could reach her—and just as Vera appeared with a tall broad man in a blue suit, a salesman's pacifying smile on his face—the woman had reached the counter and kicked her foot through the glass. Blood welled out through her stocking, down the thick gray leg. The woman fell heavily, rolled, scraping her leg against the broken edges of the glass. Her blood smeared against the disarranged, twisting sweaters within the counter.

"Where is my son?" she said. "Creeps and bastards. I'm hurt."

The salesman rushed forward. "Lie still," he ordered. "Phyllis, get me some bandages and tape from the office, and call the police."

"And an ambulance," said Elliot.

"No, just the police, Phyllis." The man turned around from where he was squatting on the floor beside the woman. "And will all you people please leave? Everything's in control. Just an incident; just an accident," he amended. "Nothing to see. Please leave the room."

Elliot took Vera's hand—she was gripping a GIMBELS GRAND shopping bag—and led her out into the row of arcades. Looking up from her shocked face, he saw Andy French and Anita Kellerman, close in talk and seemingly not noticing the knot of people pushing him and Vera from the enclosure. They paused at a counter stacked with gloves, lifted a pair striped like racing shoes, smiled at one another, and continued down the row of counters into the next arcade. Out of the enclosure, the music was quieter, a barely audible thrumming interleaving with the woman's groans. He led Vera toward the escalator, neither of them speaking.

* * *

"Vera isn't used to seeing things like that," Herman said, steering the Pontiac onto the interstate freeway toward Chicago. "She's always been a tender sort of person, maybe too tender for the sort of world we're stuck with. I guess she inherits that from me. Tessa has always been the tough one in our family. I'll tell you, Elliot, marrying that woman was the best decision I ever made in my life. She's kept me going through all the rough spots. The first time I ever met her, one afternoon at her cousin's house, I could tell that she was the girl I was going to marry. The old man fought it right down the line, down to the bone—he thought I was too young, there was Europe to worry about, and he chewed me out for weeks. Until he met Tessa. She won him right over. The old man, my father, knew a bargain when he saw one. He always liked a woman who could speak her piece. Of course, Kai was the important one, in *his* mind. It would have been the happiest day of his life if he could have gone to Kai's wedding, feeling that there was peace between them."

Herman stopped talking, obviously deep in thought about Kai, and the car sped down the freeway, now dense with cars and trucks going south toward Chicago in the cold morning sunlight. There was a lacing of frost on the edges of the windshield, and snow piled whitely, enormously in the space between the two branches of the freeway and in the long prairielike fields to their sides.

The Pontiac drew up to a toll booth, and Herman tossed the coins into the basket. He rolled up his window again, blowing out steam for a moment.

Herman said, "You remember that guy who went to the Chicago World's Fair a long time ago, or wherever it was, and came back saying, 'I have seen the future and it works'?"

Elliot nodded.

"The only difference between him and us is that we know he was wrong. The past works, not the future. We thought that we were going to go on and on, more and more freeways, more and more cars, more and more money—you name it. Airplanes, solar power. Monorails. Then we wake up and the city is full of crazies, nut cases, lunatics. You can't get out of your house at night. Everybody's scared of something—muggers, rapists. All the papers get to look like *The Police Gazette*. I sometimes wish I'd been born fifty years earlier, so I could have been around in the 1880's. The Gilded Age. The country was about power, making money, expansion—all positives. Then, everybody had some kind of ideal. Things might have been less easier materially, but the country was hopeful—hopeful in a crude way, but people had values. For wars, what did you have? Teddy Roosevelt charging up San Juan Hill, instead of this Asian mess nobody understands. Other times, of course, I can tell myself, listen. This is the most exciting time in the most exciting country in the world. You got a front-row seat on history. Problem is, I don't know if I believe it. But I don't think I could ever leave this country. I don't mean to offend you—you know that?" He twisted his big head to look at Elliot.

"Of course I do," Elliot answered. "I just thought there were things to be learned by living somewhere else. What did you think when Kai went abroad? Did that bother you?"

Herman grunted with amusement. "Kai always did just what he wanted to do."

"Good for him," said Elliot.

"I can respect that. What the hell, everybody's got his own life to live." He tilted his bullish head to regard Elliot. "There's just one thing I want. That's for Vera to be as happy as any person can be these days. Does she ever talk about coming home?"

"Now and then," he said. "We both do, Herman. But we've got jobs and advantages in Paris that we'd have to look for a long time here. In fact, Vera is probably more at home in Paris than I am—she speaks perfect French and has a good job at the American College. And we love our house." That wooden extravagance in which the pipes froze and there were too many rooms, always the threat of dry rot and damp—it was theirs only by luck. A colleague of Vera's at the college, Emmet Vevres-Moore, lived in the apartment next door with his seven children and efficient Ohio wife; when Poltovnin, the old Russian, had died, Vevres-Moore had shown them around the old man's crazy palace. They wanted it immediately: the wandering old apartment was so unlike them. Old Poltovnin had filled it with elaborate tea services, silver samovars, great wooden desks stacked with émigré magazines. Editions of Akhmatova and Push-kin alongside bound copies of *Nature*. Dickens and Trollope too, on those stout dark shelves. Elliot had first read *Emma* because Poltovnin's house had held it, and had spent a week carrying the book to his studio, to rehearsals, to restaurants, reading it all over again on the day he finished it. Most of these things they had kept, along with a framed copy of the front page of *Combat*, a Resistance paper, with a grainy photograph of Nazi officers stiffly watching a group of Russians herd into a railroad car.

"I worked in one of those flops once," said Herman, pointing his finger toward a Howard Johnson's Motel and Restaurant that was just now slipping over their heads, built across the freeway on an overpass. Herman's hand followed its progress until his finger was pointed at the car's roof. "It wasn't a Howard Johnson's, of course, and it wasn't built spreading its ass over a freeway, but it was the same kind of thing. Longman's Motor Court, out on the old highway fifty-seven. It was owned by the same people, the same family, that put up Longman's Hotel down on Grand Avenue. Old Bing Longman and his kids—the kids, at least the son, still run Longman's. It was one of those motels that was built during the war. Ten-fifteen little block buildings, all white or pink stucco, set up around a parking lot with a central office where the manager stayed. You just had a cot, a stove, and a crapper. Bing Longman was out for the fast buck, and he didn't even put a heater in the manager's cabin. Elliot, managing that motel was a full-time job. You got your rent free, and now and then Longman would pop for a case of beer and a few steaks, just to keep me happy, but I stayed out there from 1939 to 1943. When no one showed up in the cabins in the middle of the week except for some hotpants kid from Racine,

I would hightail it into town to see Tessa, but that was just strictly on the quiet. Longman gave me a hundred bucks every Christmas on top of salary, and I thought I was riding the world like a bicycle going downhill. Later, Tessa made me quit and get a job at he Penney's store in town, selling T-shirts and jockstraps. I'll tell you what I was like then. I was jumping around like a kid. Just about your age. I only grew up after I'd been married to Tessa for a couple of years."

Elliot tried to picture a young Herman Glauber—Herman at thirty. He seemed like a man who had always been gentle, slightly ponderous, in one place with a single life.

"I grew up somehow, at least," said Herman, "some because of Tessa and some because of that motel. It was far enough out of town so a lot of the politicians from Plechette City would go out there for a shack-up on the weekends. The best mayor the city ever had, Wilt Zamon, used to come out with a little doll who worked in the Gimbels store on Second Street. And his son, Roy Zamon, would park his car in the woods behind the cabins so his father wouldn't see it." He smiled at Elliot. "I never saw any Denmarks there, if you're worried. But I did see a lot of the kids from the east side—Jimmy Steenborg's boy, the one who died in Guam, Chip Schallspiel, one of the Nieder boys, Ralph, who later got a Silver Star in Germany and came home with one leg and shot himself in his girlfriend's bedroom. All those kids in high school and at Walkins who were just killing time until they got into the war. And there I was, ten years older, running ice to their cabins and cleaning out their shit afterward. With the rich ones especially, you had to get out of bed at five to make sure they didn't get out without paying. Sometimes you'd have to burn the sheets. You never knew what you'd find when you went in to clean up. Twice I found dead cats—one hanging from a lightbulb, one stuck down the toilet. I had to get it out with a knife. I must have called taxis for a hundred girls—black eyes, nosebleeds, faces all bruised up, their clothes torn apart all over the room. They were picked up at dances, usually by servicemen who were so screwed up by boot camp that they had to beat up on something that couldn't hit back. The poor little dopes thought they were going to bed with heroes. In 1940, a guy took a shot at me with a Smith and Wesson .38, and in 1943, another hotwire tried it with a service .45 that put a hole in the plaster you could hide a dog in. Both times I was trying to bust up a fight—you knew something was funny if they turned up Glenn Miller on the radio so loud I could hear it in the cabin. When I hear 'American Patrol' now, I think I'm going to have to shove some bleeding little girl into the showers so she can remember her name and address. Old Bing didn't give a damn what happened as long as we got the money out of their pockets and kept the place out of the papers.

"There's nothing you can name," said Herman, "that I didn't see or have to clean up afterward. My war. I'd read the newspapers in that rotten little cabin and see the pictures of the generals—Patton with his boots and pistols, that dictator, that fraud MacArthur, counting how many days until he'd be President—Willie and Joe washing their socks in their helmets—and in the morning I'd have to wash some GI's shit off the wall where he wrote 'Fuck You' with it. 'Kilroy Was Here.' If I could have met Kilroy, I would've strangled him. Who the hell else but Kilroy would hang a cat in a motel room? Or beat up dumb little girls from the farms who felt sorry for you? They thought if they could open themselves up wide enough, they could win the war."

Herman squeezed the Pontiac out from behind a truck and pushed his foot heavily on the accelerator. They cut across two lanes, the innocent white fields reflecting the sun seeming to career toward them, and swung into the furthest lane. Ahead were the turnoffs for the outer suburbs, doll villages on the left horizon, set down on the fields like tumbled blocks.

"I'll tell you how I lost my job at the motel. I quit, but it wasn't just because Tessa wanted me to work in town. I quit because I was going to be fired. They had my ass on a griddle.

"I told you about Wilt Zamon," he said, "a man I admired. He was an honest mayor and a good man, a man a lot like my father. He was liked and respected in every part of the city, except maybe the east side. Wilt got all his training in the unions, and that was a rough way to grow up, during the thirties. You had all the unions fighting with themselves, and the manufacturers fighting them. Some very hard boys came out of that situation. Anyhow, Zamon was a mayor when he used to come to the motel. Roy Zamon, his son, was about twenty-five, twenty-six then—the handsomest man I ever saw. He had a big curly head of hair, and shoulders on him like an ox. Roy had a closetful of medals. In those days, early in the war, you saw his name in the paper every other week. And he used to write a column back to the *Herald* about what the war was like, what the GI's were doing. Willie-and-Joe stuff, but people loved it. In April 1942, he came home with his left foot blown off but he got fitted out with an artificial foot and he was all over the *Herald* again. Mostly the social columns, but he also was busy making speeches all over town, VFW, the Legion halls, the Polish-American League. If he'd run for office in town, he would have won hands down. I used to read about him like anyone else. I guess I envied him. He couldn't do anything wrong. I always thought he was a little stupid—his speeches were just the usual wave-the-flag stuff—but he had enough glamour to put on a Broadway show all by himself, and if you stuck wires into him he'd light up the theater too. Well, the first time he came out to the motel he checked in with a soldier—I figured they were going to have a big party, so I told him to keep the noise down. Mr. Zamon, I said. He gave me a look that would grill a hamburger and pointed to the register. 'Mr. Clark,' he said. 'Mr. Bill Clark.' And that was the name he signed under. 'You call me anything else and I'll knock your teeth out for you.' Then he pulled his car around to the back of the cabins where no one could see it and he and the soldier went inside. They stayed in there two days, just going out for some food and a couple of bottles. When he checked out he gave me ten dollars over the tab and asked me my name. When I told him, he grabbed me by the necktie and said, 'Glauber boy, keep your mouth shut, or you'll be sorry.' Real gangster stuff. Then that big war-hero smile that was in the papers.

"You have to understand Wilt Zamon to understand what happened next," Herman said. "He loved his kid so much he couldn't stop talking about him. Zamon used to put his son into his campaign pictures, he made speeches about 'our fighting men,' all that kind of thing. Any scandal would have ruined him. And it did, eventually. Roy probably came out to the motel nine or ten times, each time with a different soldier, when he wasn't smart enough to go fifty miles down old fifty-seven to the next joint—he thought he could get away with anything anyhow. Where he went when he didn't come out there, I don't know, but I know he used to cruise the bars on the weekends, and he couldn't have gone without any too often. I guess he didn't understand rumors, that you can't kill them once they're started. No matter how many girls he got himself photographed with, he couldn't stop people's tongues. There wasn't much talk, you understand, but by 1943 there was enough to get back to Wilt. Wilt called Bing Longman and asked him about it. Old Bing denied everything. I can hear him do it, he was so smooth. Then Bing got out to me and asked me about it. I said I'd never seen Roy Zamon, whether with a girl, with a man, or with a sheep—that I hadn't seen him at all. Well, that was my mistake. I lied to protect that bastard, and in the end it bounced back on me. Wilt hired a detective to follow his son, and they got pictures of him driving in there. Must have been quite a scene in the mayor's house *that* day. Wilt must have been too ashamed to tell Roy that he'd had him followed, because Roy came back with blood in his eye, threatening to kill me. He thought I'd blown the whistle to his father. I talked with him for an hour and got out of it with no more than the black eye he gave me when he busted through the door. I had a gun under the counter, but I didn't want to bring it out: he would have grabbed it away in a second, gimpy or not gimpy. The next thing I knew both Roy and his father called Longman, ordering him to fire me. Wilt said to give me a thousand dollars to keep my mouth shut; you can imagine what Roy said. So I quit instead. I wouldn't take the money. And about a year later Roy was caught by the cops in something a lot funnier than an illegal card game, although that was all the papers said, and Wilt Zamon dropped dead at his desk, still holding the telephone. Roy got off with a fine, and left town after his father's funeral—he had guts enough to go to that, I'll say that for him, but he just vanished somewhere. He just went into thin air. California, they said.

"And here's the real ending to the story," said Herman. "When I was thinking of running for alderman for the Richmond Corners area, Bing Longman got in touch with me and offered to pay my campaign fees. If it hadn't been for that, I probably couldn't have afforded to run, not without mortgaging my soul. It's a screwy world."

"It's a good story, anyhow," said Elliot.

The interstate freeway had melted into a series of expressways dividing Chicago, and Herman crossed two lanes in the heavy traffic, horns erupting around them, to get onto the wide belt expressway going south along the lakefront, backed by miles of hotels and offices. The city looked deeply rubbed in grime, a heavy gray layer on the facades; to their left, the lake was an upthrown gray rib, a frozen curve.

"It's a better story now than it was then." Herman looked toward Elliot, his meaty face good-natured. "All that business out at the motel taught me one thing—you can't interfere with what people are. You can't change them. There's too much insanity in the way people live, too much unreason in the world. If you have some kind of design, you have to chip away at it, settling for expedients. Increments. But with your own family, I guess you always want something more than that. Listen, Elliot: the last thing I want to do is interfere between you and Vera."

"Yes?" said Elliot, surprised. "What is it?"

"She's been looking tense to me, the past few days. Tense and unhappy. Vera shouldn't be that way. Is it being home that does it to her?"

"No, Herman, not at all," Elliot said. "Of course not. It's probably this Nun's Wood confusion—my father working against you. They've asked me to become involved, and that's what is making Vera tense."

"Who is they? Chase? His sidekicks, Hilda Usenbrugge and that Bender fireball from Wiltshire Drive?"

"I suppose so, yes. And Pierce Laubach. They sent me a statement they want me to sign. I've been meaning to talk with you about it since it came, but I've never had the time. I wasn't sure how to bring it up."

Herman wiped his hand over his face, grinning. "Hell, go ahead and sign it. You can probably guess what I think of Chase's position, but what the hell? He's your father. I don't care if you sign the statement. I'll fix it up with Tessa. Everybody does what he has to do."

He looked over at Elliot again. "The battle is really over, anyhow, as far as I can see. We just have to get through the public hearing. Some speeches, a little ruckus, and it will be all over. In the past few weeks, I've got nearly a majority of the council with me. They'll go for the rezoning just to get me of their backs. The clincher will be the black vote, Jeff Glee and his two acolytes. Nobody knows which way they might jump. If they give Nay votes, we're blocked from rezoning. If they go Aye or Abstain, we're in. So we got two chances out of three." He smiled to himself. "Elliot, get that business off your mind. You got Ted Edwards to worry about now. We're almost at the studio."

14

Driving back from Chicago on the freeway, Herman sat silent beside him. His remarks on the Ted Edwards show had surprised them both, and clearly wounded and perplexed Herman. Edwards had begun by asking, "Mr. Denmark, does serious music have any relevance to us today? Aren't most modern composers simply working in a vacuum?" Facing the red eye of the camera, Elliot had unexpectedly relaxed: the question was so predictable, so various in its possibilities, that he had immediately shed his nervousness, the sense that he, sitting before the artificial background of a sitting room—a plaster wall painted to look like brick, a painted fire in a painted fireplace—was contingent, an accidental presence which could only simulate opinions and arguments. He had felt this unreality when Edwards had come into the dressing room where a girl was smoothing makeup into his face. Edwards stood behind them, smiling into the mirror at Elliot. "I'm Ted Edwards. Welcome to the catacombs. Denmark, your bit is fifteen-twenty minutes. Just a friendly chat about music, Plechette City, anything interesting. You get me?" His face was a shock: tauter and older than it appeared on the screen, smoothly suntanned, a corrupt face, just on the verge of disintegration. *Ronnie Upp*, Elliot had thought. His eyes, nostrils and mouth were all the same dark shape, as if they had been slit in his mask with a razor. "I think I get you, yes," Elliot said, unwittingly repeating Edwards' words. "All right, then, let's make it a knockers-up show. If you tighten up, I'll get you out of it, okay?" At Elliot's nod, he vanished from the mirror, and the girl's fingers resumed coolly rubbing the makeup into his face. Elliot saw that she had a small blue star tattooed on the back of her left wrist. Her breasts grazed the back of his head.

"It's just a competition thing," the girl said. "Don't worry about it. It only lasts fifteen minutes anyway."

"Did it hurt when you got your tattoo?" he asked, fascinated by its appearance and disappearance in the mirror.

"I didn't feel a thing," she said. "I was flying the whole time. I was real relaxed."

Elliot looked up at the girl's face in the mirror: wide, permanently startled eyes, a broad businesslike chin. He remembered the girls Herman had told him about, bedded and beaten by soldiers in motel rooms.

"Could you get me a job in music?" she said.

Seated near Ted Edwards on the couch between the cameras and the pasteboard wall, Elliot could see Edwards' face adjust itself to the unseen presence of his viewers; the razor slits in his face opened and formed questions, the man's brown mask signaling for the camera to roll toward him. Then he had talked—endlessly, it seemed. Edwards' face had changed during Elliot's long answers. *I'm serious*, it had signaled, *observe me listening*. Talking, Elliot could still feel on his face the girl's smoothing fingers: he was relaxed.

But what had he said? It had come out in such a rush, all that talk.

The first half of the interview had been easy.

"I don't know how you guys do it," said Herman. "I guess I'm just stupid. The average guy, he can't make head or tail of what you were saying about music. It has no meaning to him, what you were saying. The average guy hears a tune, he tries to hum it, and that's it."

"You could understand it if it were your job," said Elliot.

"Well, maybe. Spirals?"

"Oh, Herman, I was just talking. Gassing." This was a hidden reference to what he had said about Nun's Wood, and Herman took it up.

"Well, plenty of gassing is what I'm going to have to do with Tessa."

This time they passed the Howard Johnson's Motel without comment. Elliot switched on the radio as they sped through the flatland, and for a time they listened in silence to country music, songs about heartbreak and divorce and drunkenness. The flat white country layered out on both sides of the freeway.

"You should try writing this kind of stuff someday," Herman advised. "Then I'll expect a Rolls-Royce for a birthday present."

Both were grateful that Elliot was moving the next day from the Glauber home.

"I'll have to sort of warm Tessa up for the showing," Herman said.

For the twentieth time, Elliot stared at the blue wall: it was of a flat shining blue that looked metallic, like a tinted skin of aluminum. "Your father and I wanted to brighten your old room up a bit," Margaret had said. "We didn't take anything out except for some of that old furniture you had in the Walkins School, but we had the room repainted, and then had these bookshelves installed. Chase loves that blue. Don't you?"

"It's very contemporary," he said.

"*Tant pis*," Vera muttered behind him.

"What was that, Vera dear?"

"Suits me," she answered.

Now Elliot lay back in his bed staring at the blank shining skin of the wall while Vera silently took her clothes from her suitcase and hung them in the closet. *His* bed was familiar, despite the new mattress he could feel beneath him, but the companion bed across the room was not. His stereo components, lovingly assembled while he was in high school, were now concealed behind a sliding panel, as were his old records. Elliot had been agreeably surprised that his old stereo system still worked. *Petroushka* was now uncoiling into the room: he had always loved the beginning, two trumpets playing in different triads.

The new blue wall, the new bed, the new wallpaper, the tubular and the ovoid lamps, the glass table: clearly, his room was now a guestroom. It struck him as a feeble pun that he should now be its guest. The bed's guest, the wall's guest. His parents had taken his books from the carved and battered old bookshelf and arranged them by size on long sleek shelves mounted to the wall. Thus spread and scattered and interspersed by vases, pots of ivy, a bust of Freud *(Freud?)* his childhood and prep-school books had lost their look of familiarity and seemed vulnerable, open to judgment. Old textbooks, science fiction, Sinclair Lewis and John Steinbeck, biographies of Mozart and Beethoven, *Generation of Vipers, Le Grand Meaulnes, Conversations with Stravinsky.* They had the look of books in a library, of the unopened volumes in an advertisement for shelves.

Yet the room was his. It reminded him, by the disposition of its volumes, by its dimensions, of his childhood. The boy he had been hovered within his consciousness; a thinner self inhabited his body. Old Ladnier bending his strict white face to say *Clumsy, but you are capable of better. At least that.* He began to think of school. In those years he had been intense, happy, moderately popular. He had at times been cruel or offhand to other boys, but such behavior was almost encouraged by the school—the caste system at Walkins was heartless. In senior school, the prefects were always the tallest, blondest, most Anglo-Saxon of the boys, the earnest athletes, dullards. Lawrence Wooster was one of these: the masters had loved him, especially those who were ardent football fans. Wooster had been able to throw long accurate passes. Later, he had played for a year at Brown. Elliot could remember Wooster gently opening the top of his desk during French class, peeking at the crib sheets he had hidden within. Elliot had spent over five years with most of his friends from Walkins, and with a handful, all twelve years of his schooling there—within three years, he was seeing only two. The two old classmates who remained still his friends were William Pittman, now a twice-divorced novelist living in Alicante with three cats and a sixteen-year-old German girl, and Minor Van Blank, a brilliant student who had earned a Ph.D. in economics at Harvard in three years and was now making a fortune in consultation fees. He was on the board of a New York bank, and could outplay Elliot at the piano. When Elliot was in New York, they played four-handed duets. Pittman hated music, and talked with Elliot mostly about his wives; Van Blank could talk about anything. Apart from women, they were his closest friends. He quickly banished the image of Anita: too complex a problem for the moment—and Vera, closing the closet doors, was tense and hostile.

Too complex. No, that would not do. Yet he could not think about Anita now. Vera was sitting by the little mahogany desk, another new acquisition whose guest he was, glumly looking toward the window. In a moment, he thought, she will ask what am I thinking. Elliot knew that the quarrel was not serious: Vera was angry primarily for her mother's sake, and that was not motive enough for a drastic bitterness. But the lower part of her face was set like a statue's.

He closed his eyes, and was swept over by the sensation of being back in his old room: another deflection. The unaltered volume around him seemed to shrink to the size of his body. His fingers grazed the wallpaper. He began to remember a story his father told about Mr. Von Heilitz, an old man who had been their neighbor during the forties. Then he remembered another thing about the man. Chase had once killed Von Heilitz's dogs, two wheezing and odorous spaniels, who had been sleeping in the Denmark driveway when his father had backed out of the garage in the morning. Mr. Von Heilitz had raced to the end of his hedge and fallen on his knees at the bottom of the driveway. His white jacket had soaked a little in the blood. Elliot, running from the house, saw with horrified fascination the crumpled animals, the blood draining down to Mr. Von Heilitz's white-trousered knees. Chase had detested the two dogs, as Von Heilitz knew. When he opened his eyes, he was looking at the blue wall.

"What are you thinking about?" Vera asked.

"About my father," he said. "During the war, he ran over two horrible old dogs that belonged to a neighbor of ours. He killed them. It was an accident, but the neighbor, an old man named Lamont Von Heilitz, wouldn't believe it, even though he knew the dogs had been asleep in our driveway. He thought it had something to do with his being German."

"That sounds like your family." A grim smile, and a scorching glance. Meaning: anyone connected with you could deliberately run over a dog.

"And before that I was thinking about Walkins—about school."

"A real little orgy of nostalgia, wasn't it?"

"I suppose it was." He was determined not to be provoked by Vera, who had the right to some bitterness. "There was a cat named Moorish, the school mascot, that used to pace around the halls and the school grounds like one of the masters. It was a huge black creature. The smaller kids were traditionally afraid of him. I just remembered now that one day in geometry class I saw Moorish going very slowly across the front lawn toward a sea gull—he kept to the edge of the bushes, and then sort of circled in toward him. At the last possible second, he leapt at the bird; flew at him, really, and pinned him down with one paw. The sea gull fought and tried to escape, but Moorish had him captured. In twenty seconds he had him ripped from top to bottom. The bird exploded feathers like a burst pillow. And in ten minutes the sea gull was absolutely gone—nothing left of him—just eaten up. All you could see was a perfect ring of white feathers on the lawn. I was the only person who saw it. For weeks afterward, I had dreams about it: a black thing devouring a white thing. Ugh."

She bent her head to the desk.

"I also just remembered a funny story about old Von Heilitz and my father.

Do you want to hear it?" Any conversation was good. Drain off the tension in chatter.

"Elliot, did you *have* to talk about that Nun's Wood business on the program? In front of my father?"

"He knew what my opinion was. I told you that. We talked about it on the way down."

"That wasn't enough," she said, and he knew what she meant. It was not enough for Tessa. Tessa had not been prepared. Herman had tried to cushion Elliot's apostasy, but Tessa had not let herself be assuaged. "You aren't with us?" she said, her face strained and her voice high and incredulous. "You're not on Herman's side in this? Why didn't you tell us?" Then, at last, he had pulled the crumpled statement from his pocket and smoothed it out on the table. "And you actually talked about it on television?" She is overdoing it, he thought, but a look at her shocked face had dispelled the idea that she was acting. "It wasn't for very long," Herman rumbled. "Just a couple of minutes at the end." "Five minutes," he said. *"Five minutes!"*—as though the number of minutes he had spoken of Nun's Wood would be reckoned at the last judgment. "Calm down, Tessa, we talked about it in the car." "Nobody talked to *me* about it," she cried . . . on it had gone, Herman pacing around the kitchen, Tessa standing sternly by the table where he was seated, Vera nervously watching. "He was going to tell you about it, Mother," she broke in, "but Elliot didn't know for a long time if he was going to sign. He was under a lot of pressure." "Pressure," retorted Tessa. "What you two know about pressure wouldn't boil an egg." The evening had spent itself somehow. At dinner, Vera and her father carrying a limping conversation, Tessa had said, "You never understood what Herman's job has been. How could you? You gave up the only job you ever had." He had blazed out at her. Then raged at himself, and at his childishness in allowing himself to be provoked. "Well, I suppose I can't wait to see what Elliot actually said," Tessa crooned, "if he feels so wrought up by it." She smiled a wounded smile.

"She was defending my father," Vera said. "I know she was upset, but that was only because she thought she had to protect my father's feelings."

Elliot could feel the tension draining away into the ordinariness of talk.

"But I do think it was inexcusable of you to bring up Nun's Wood on a television program."

"Sweetheart, I didn't bring it up. He did."

"You didn't have to talk about it."

"He tricked me," Elliot said. "I feel like a fool admitting it, but that's the truth. We were going on talking about music, and then right at the end of my time, he sprang it on me. I fell right into it."

Vera went across the room to her own bed and lay down. "That ghastly wall," she said. "I hope it doesn't shine in the dark. Did you really see a cat eat a sea gull?" She tilted her head to look at him. "Then why didn't you do something to stop it?"

"I was inside a building. It was the middle of a geometry class. I like cats more than I like sea gulls." He closed his eyes again and rubbed his fingertips against the wallpaper. The blue of the wall lay like a veil within his eyelids: against it, he saw the ring of white feathers.

Elliot went downstairs soon after, relieved that the worst was over, and that it had been so easy. He wanted nonetheless to get out of his parents' house. The rooms downstairs were too thick with his past, clamorous with old responsibilities. He wandered from the smaller living room (his wedding picture on an end table, he striding—with what assumption of knowledge!—down the church aisle, Vera leggy, elegant, shining with hope, beside him), where he toyed for a moment with the piano, across the hall to the dining room, then up into the large-windowed room that looked out over Lake Michigan. The fireplace was roaring and crackling: logs tumbled together, blazing. The room was terribly hot. Elliot went to the windows and looked out at the dim lake, three hundred yards down the wooded bank and across the expressway. It looked vast and somehow depthless, like an endless plane of indeterminate pale blue, cold to the touch.

Margaret's "office," where she devised the week's menus and figured the household accounts, a small skylit glassy chamber filled with ivy and green creeping plants, was an alcove fixed like an insect to the back of the house on the second floor. In summer sixteen years ago, water-skiing behind the Van Blanks' speedboat, he could look up to his house and see his mother bent at her desk, the steel-rib supports of the shell's exterior gleaming as though they were molten. In that dazzle, the plants had seemed a solidity, a protection against gravity.

Now the tangled profuse greenery against the glass reversed his sense of the exterior: the great dim lake, framed by leaves, was a Japanese painting.

"Are you all unpacked?" Margaret asked, putting down her pen. "Is Vera feeling better?"

"Yes to both questions," he said.

"And your room is not too much of a shock? It's a guestroom now, of course, but it's still most importantly your room."

"I like the change," he said, grinning.

"Comfortable?"

"I'm sure we will be."

"At least you are not shunted off on the west side of town anymore." She had a tucked-in, curiously gratified smile. "Your crotchety old parents will be able to see you."

"That will be nice. I do have to fit in my rehearsals and the concert, however." He liked the way she looked now: strikingly pretty for her age, with her tender powdery face full of confidence for him.

"You'll have no problems with your concert. You're not really worried about it, are you?" Behind her head, the leaves broke the lake into a million ice-blue shards. The sun glittered for a moment on the seams and edges.

"A little," he confessed.

"Vera will be coming down later?"

"Sure." He did not wish to begin discussing the television program, and did not amplify on Vera's condition, though it was clear that Margaret wanted him to. The sunlight along the chips of lake made him stretch restlessly in his chair.

"We all have some little insecurity," said his mother. "When you see your father tonight, be sure to compliment him on his suit. My car is downstairs, if you want to take it somewhere. I had it filled up and washed this morning."

He would not go to Anita's house. She was a white uncertain lucency in his consciousness, a troubling presence. What were his responsibilities? It was a difficult question. Anita had presented a closed face to him—or so it now seemed—when he had last talked to her. That afternoon, and the memory of Andy and Anita pausing at a counter in the frantic pre-Christmas Gimbels Grand, their heads together, a suggestion of great closeness. It was as though she were willing him to think about her. Elliot felt as though he were physically being pushed back into the sensations of four years before: as if, over a great distance, he were being manipulated by her. He knew that she expected him to come to her house, and that when he arrived she would confound him once again.

He turned the car onto the entrance to the lakefront expressway; now he was long past the turnoff to Windmere Court and Leecham Street. He felt a twinge of guilt like a dentist's gentle prodding of a drill into a diseased tooth. His responsibilities clung. A flock of sea gulls dipped like a cloud over his car and settled on the tennis courts in the little park alongside the expressway. When the lights changed, he gunned the engine and fitted smoothly into the line of cars.

Aimlessly he followed the traffic as it swept around the War Memorial. The architect's extruded planes and angles seemed to tilt precariously toward him, slabs and edges brilliantly honed. In the forecourt stood the black glossy monolith carved with lists of names. When the car before his turned sharply left to enter the parking lot, he impulsively followed. He took the car through the gates, parked it, and walked back along a cleanly shoveled path to the pool and the monolith. The weather report on the radio had said that the temperature was twelve degrees, but in his short walk to the terrace, Elliot felt that it could not be so cold. His heels rang on the pavement, his breath ascended in clouds. When he reached the pool, he saw that it had been drained, and that the monolith was upended in a ruck of pulped newspapers, sandwich bags, soda bottles. He scanned the names for one he recognized. Capt. Charles W. Steenborg, between Capt. David Stedman and Lt. Horace F. Steermayer. Dead, they were soldiers for eternity. No Denmarks were named on the giant slab. His ears had begun to ache with the cold. Which of these had beaten the girls Herman Glauber laundered and sent home?

Slapping his hands together, he wandered slowly back along the path toward the parking lot. I know what I'll do, he thought: I'll visit Kai. He felt an overwhelming curiosity, compounded with respect, for the old survivor.

15

From the War Memorial he drove south, following the tracks of the old tram line down First Street all the way, past the cream-colored brick of the huge Mother Beilburg bakery, a series of stolid red brick apartment buildings that housed secretaries who worked in south-side offices and aged immigrant couples, Lithuanians, Poles, and Latvians, then past body shops and gasoline stations, small brick machine shops, the Curtis Etheridge shoe factory, and by then he was descending Mitchell Avenue past gray buildings, and there was a bitter smell of chocolate in the air from the chocolate factory. Mitchell Avenue continued its descent into the valley. Elliot could see ahead of him the great turning faces of the Chambers Denmark clock, a golden ornament above the tops of buildings; then he was truly in the valley and the buildings closed in about him, concealing the clock. Here the factories were dense, and the smell of chocolate was overtaken by something grittier, a smell more urban and metallic. For Elliot, it was this odor, hot and bronzy, which meant *city:* when he was at Columbia he had breathed it in the IRT stops, and felt at once at home.

Crammed in the streets between the factories were the tenements—these of a red brick so deeply stained as to be a dense dark brown—and small bright eateries, passed-over shops and family groceries, drugstores and movie theaters, of the Puerto Ricans. Elliot's first impulse was to push down the locks of the car doors, as his father had always done when driving through the fourth ward, and he smiled at this reflex. A brown Santa Claus rang a bell outside Woolworth's. Elliot turned onto MacArthur Avenue at the Pérez-Ricardo Loan Company office, which had plastered on its facing wall an enormous poster for Jefferson Glee. The earnest raccoonlike eyes peered out of the smooth face; one plump hand had removed the alderman's gold spectacles and held them, in a lawyer's pose, a little lower than his chin. REELECT GLEE. Beneath, someone had spray-painted the words BURN WHITEY. The poster was torn at the bottom, revealing an ocher strip of side wall.

He turned left again at the next stoplight, and was now on Ward Street, where fifty years ago Polish newcomers, then the inhabitants of the valley, had built an incongruous street of white frame houses with fifteen-foot lawns and white picket fences. Kai's room was in the third of these houses: they had all been broken into tiny rooms and apartments, and Kai shared his house with the sons and daughters and various cousins and aunts of the Méndez family.

Elliot parked before the house and opened the gate. Even here, on this deceptive quiet street, the odor of factories was in the air, a thin bitter acridity. He rang Kai's bell. The door was immediately opened by a thin black-haired teenage girl in a dark leatherlike coat. She eyed him thoroughly, making no signs of recognition. He could not remember if he had seen the girl before. "Miss Méndez?" he said.

The girl nodded, moving her mouth about her chewing gum. "What you want?" she asked. "We paid the insurance last week."

"I'm not here about the insurance. I came to see Mr. Glauber. Is he in?"

"The old man's always in." She stepped back, allowing him to enter. "I'm just goin' out. You know where his room is?"

"Second floor, on the left," he said. "Okay?"

"Okay," she said. "Go on up." She gave him a rapid, smirking look and sidled through the door.

He went up the dark stairs and knocked on Kai's door. There was only silence from the room. He knocked again, saying, "Uncle Kai, it's Elliot." When the sounds he had made dropped like stones into the silent room, he slumped with dejection. Another series of knocks had the same result. One more try before I leave, he thought: he may be asleep. He reached his hand toward the doorknob and touched it. The door parted silently from its frame and swung inward. The room was dark. Elliot could make out only the rigid silvery outline of Kai's desk. "Uncle Kai," he whispered, knowing that the old man was not there. A faint odor of age and perspiration drifted to his nostrils.

He stepped within and groped for the light switch. When he had found it and seen his shadow leap instantly to the wall, he turned to look into the room: his heart was accelerating, and he realized that he had thought, at some inner depth, that he might find Kai dead. But Kai was not in the room; the cot, neatly and tautly made up, was empty. Elliot groaned. He had been looking forward more than he knew to a long talk with Kai; at the moment, Kai seemed to possess some answer that would resolve his dilemma. From the ironic mouth, stitched in the upper lip with pain, would come some clear unsentimental phrase. Elliot was tired: the morning's move to his parents' house, a chilly Tessa supervising, had been a drain on his emotions, on his control. He closed the door, went toward the desk, and sat heavily, his topcoat still about him, in the chair. Kai would soon return. A minute later he shed his coat and threw it over the cot. The drapes were closed, as he had always seen them, and the room's atmosphere, hot and unfresh, seemed to settle upon his shoulders, in his hair. He turned to rest his elbows on the desk. The high old typewriter and the square pile of yellow paper were the sole objects on its surface. It looked just as it had when he and Vera had been in this room the week before. Even the stack of yellow paper seemed the same size. There were no signs of occupation or labor, no pencils or erasers, no notepapers, no file cards. It came to him again: he did not believe in Kai's book. Kai probably arranged, noted, wrote a few words each day, knowing that he would never truly finish.

Elliot looked at the metal filing cabinet beside the desk. He could confirm his suspicions with one glance, if the cabinet were unlocked. He glanced up at the top-right-hand corner and saw the key inserted upright in the holder: the cabinet was unlocked. Should he look? It was unfair to the old man to bare his secret, his self-deceit; but it could make no difference to how he felt about Kai. In fact, looking into the file might clear his suspicions by revealing an actual manuscript. He was rationalizing. This embarrassed him. What he wanted to do was to look into the file. His curiosity was enormous. Why not look? He pulled the chair toward the cabinet, scraping its legs along the floor, and pulled out the drawer labeled MSS.

Leaning over and peering into it, he saw only a flat yellow folder, untitled. He pulled it out and looked at it, then bent back the outer cover of the folder. Within was a much older folder, marked with water spots, small brown stains, the impress of a boot heel. The pencil lines were so faint that at first he could not see them; then, detecting the thin light lines, he squinted and read them. *Notes on Faust*. His heart plummeted. He turned back the covering. Inside the two folders were thirty yellowing pages, each numbered at the top. These too were covered by the faint markings of the pencil, and when he looked closely enough at one of the pages, he saw that the writing was in German.

Elliot tilted back his head and exhaled. Kai had not done any work on his book for twenty-five years. It was all an invention. He dropped the folder back into the drawer and closed it. The bleakness—Kai's bitter winter landscape— seemed utter, completed. There was no comfort to be given or received. Elliot felt horribly depressed. He stood up, pushing back the chair, and moved to the windows. He pulled the drapes apart. A cold gray light streamed into the room. The tiny backyard of the Méndez home, gray snow flecked with black, ended at a white fence a few yards from a solid black wall—the back of a factory. Pipes and fire escapes, an elaborate geometry crested with white. At the back of the little yard stood a Bernadette grotto, leftover from the Poles. Sparrows hopped erratically on the dirty snow. He pulled the drapes together and went back to the chair.

There was one more chance. Perhaps Kai kept his typescript in one of the other drawers. He opened the CORRESPONDENCE—GOETHE drawer. This was surprisingly full. He pulled out the thick top folder: it was filled with typed letters in German, most of them with university letterheads. Herr Professor Schiff, Herr Professor Fuerst, Herr Professor Lieberbalt: Heidelberg, Bonn, Freiburg. The letters were dated from 1951 to 1955. In the next folder, the dates began in 1949 and ended in 1951. Below this was another fat folder. He squared the papers and inserted the top two folders back into the drawer. The dating was decidedly odd: it suggested that Kai had continued to make scholarly inquiries long after he had abandoned work on the book itself, and that he had abandoned even this spadework fifteen years ago.

Only one drawer was left. The PERSONAL label deterred Elliot for only a moment. Having gone so far, he thought, I might as well finish it. "Poor old Kai," he whispered. Yet how could he pity the old man? In the general muddle, he had come through with at least an intact surface. The number of consolations one could expect the world to grant seemed to shrink with each decade. For Kai, perhaps simply to go on living was labor enough.

He pulled open the lower file and looked into it. No manuscript was within. At the bottom of the drawer lay an oddly familiar brown leather box with tooled sides and cover. His memory fumbled, then caught: his grandmother Denmark, a straight uncompromising woman with perfect eyesight and black hair when in her seventies, had owned such a box to hold thread, needles, pins—none of these had he ever seen her use. Even the raised pattern of the lid felt familiar to his fingers. The leather box was surprisingly light in his hand, as if it were empty. He put it on his knees and lifted the lid.

The bottom of the box was covered with old photographs. There seemed to be about twenty or thirty of these, yellowed and in-curling. At first they appeared to be all the same picture. He picked up a handful and turned toward the desk. There, looking more carefully, he saw the differences. In most of them, a young man was posed against an emphatic background: Elliot recognized the Paris locations, the tower, the Trocadéro, the steep steps of the Sacré-Coeur. In other photographs, the young man was in the garden of what seemed to be an Italian villa, or at the Schoenbrunn, or outside the Pitti Palace or leaning elegantly against an open automobile. In some of the pictures the young man was Kai, young and dark-haired, broad and deep in the chest, his face split with health and contentment; in others the young man was Harrison Upp, an intense-looking muscular man in lounge suits and Sea Island sweaters. He was only barely recognizable as the boozy acquaintance of Lake Point Drive. One of the photographs showed a spider monkey perched on his shoulders, the country beyond a veiled distance which must have been Tuscany. In several of the photographs, the two young men appeared together, standing loosely beside a river or a *Schloss*, their arms about one another's shoulders: in these pictures, especially those located in the gardens of the villa, the two young men shirtless, there was an almost unbearable sense of overwhelming physical satisfaction. The young Kai looked out at him from his unlined face, happy and (he saw) even then doomed by the ten years yet to come. Elliot dropped the photographs back in the box, the box back in the file. He could no longer stay in the room while Kai might return.

The face of the young man Kai had been flamed in his mind as he slammed the door to the stuffy little room and double-jumped the stairs down to the front door and the street. None of the usually unavoidable and gregarious Méndez family appeared, a small favor for which he was grateful. The face was wide open, as open as a sun; it was not mere contentment which had set that expression there, of a blessing given and conferred; it was, blindingly, the face of love. Elliot's bowels were tremulous, scalding. Was that the face Vera had seen six years ago, when he had unlocked the door to Jaeger's kitchen, the face she had questioned night after night for assurance? It was a bitter proof that these moments passed, that loss endures, cruel and natural as winter. He could not go much longer without seeing Anita again. And how had Harrison Upp's face looked, what was its expression? Nerviness, tautness, gloom and with it, something like mastery. The face of an uneasy king. The kind of man who would wear a pistol near his heart. Wingbeats loudly divided the air, as of a flight of angels. A monstrous possibility beat in on him, a mad speculation that had the force of Truth. He *must* talk to Anita, and talk to her alone, without Andy French: her violent face seemed turned against him.

He turned the car up Second Street at the traffic lights. Soon the factories had vanished behind him, and the shops were boarded, their facades still scarred by fire. The Gimbels marquee hung useless over chained doors; up to the third floor most of the windows had been broken into sawteeth or stars. Each breath brought to him the heavy odor of chocolate.

"We all have to act on faith," his father was saying, his voice a shade more playful than usual, "though of course we must exercise a fair degree of scrupulosity in defining its objects. It is a secular world, despite the efforts of men like my good friend Father Squier. He, by the way, has taken to allusions to the Diamond Sutra and the Upanishads in his sermons, and I must say it makes for an improvement. I was getting a little weary of the I-Thou relationship and the existential moment. Won't you take some more wine, Vera dear? I can recommend it." He offered the bottle, Robert having vanished momentarily into the kitchen, and delicately poured two inches into Vera's glass. "Some examples. Elliot has faith in his music, in music in general. Just think of Bach, of Beethoven or Schubert, all of those elitist sensibilities scratching their way through day after grubby day, surviving only because of some persistent voice inside repeating *I, I, I.* Elliot's friend Pittman, scribbling away in his hovel at yet another unreadable would-be masterpiece: *I, I.*" Margaret made a wry face at Elliot from across the table. "Elliot has to have faith in orchestras and musicians. They at least are external to him."

"I like Pittman's novels," said Vera.

"Not quite the universal response, I gather, but more power to you. My problem may be that I was overexposed to Pittman the adolescent, a pimple-laden jangly bundle of neuroses, when he and Elliot were classmates at Walkins, and consequently I cannot be serious about those massive heroes he puts in his books."

"Pittman is," Elliot said, smiling.

"Please," said Margaret.

"Think of Bobby Seale bound and gagged in a courtroom. Perhaps these things don't happen in Paris, but it is these terrible events which comprise the real experience of our moment in history. We owe a responsibility to such events, to our own moments—novels cannot keep up with our responsibilities. From what I understand of Vera's uncle, Kai Glauber, I think that he would understand me." He smiled at his son. "And you are dying to point out, Elliot, that this too is merely another faith."

"Well, *I* don't understand you when you talk this way," said his mother. "I don't think responsibilities are so abstract. And I wish you wouldn't sound so pompous when you explain your ideas."

"He's talking about unselfish awareness," said Vera, breaking in. Her illumination seemed to falter.

"Beautifully put."

"And he's implying that . . . oh, I don't know. That artists are selfish, and that old verities and values are obsolete. Like living for God or for a family, or for a job—"

"I think you are extending what I said too far, my dear. We can still pick and choose among objects for faith. Some things still stand. Teddy Wilson's piano. Scarlatti. Decent manners. A respectable mode of dress."

"I'm mad about your suit, by the way." Vera had remembered: Elliot saw the gratitude flicker over his father's face as his hand went involuntarily in the direction of his lapels.

"What do you have faith in?" asked Vera.

"I have faith in the Monuments Commission. I've made an appointment for tomorrow morning"—this with a quiet look to Elliot—"with the chairman, Walter Lyte. Walter is an old friend of Hilda's. And I have faith in Jefferson Glee. I have an unlimited faith in the probity of I. F. Stone."

"Well, I'm mad about him, too." Vera grinned, amused by these combinations.

"I can't read that man," said his mother. "I know I should, but can't. How *are* your rehearsals going, Elliot?"

"Don't ask," he replied. His father began to speak again. Robert entered from the kitchen with a tray. Presumably, Robert would be given the day off when his father filled the house with Black Panthers.

His thoughts stuck. "Our first loyalty is to our values," his father was saying, Vera looking relieved that he was not directly discussing Nun's Wood, Margaret anxiously glancing at him. He smiled at her, explaining with a look that nothing was wrong. ". . . because everything else proceeds from values."

The rehearsal that day still hung heavily within him, as did its astonishing aftermath. His uneasiness about Kai, about Anita, had made him unnecessarily abrupt with the musicians, some of whom had drifted in late. Ettenheim was the last to appear. His hostility to Elliot seemed to have grown since the first rehearsal. When they were finally set up to play—Elliot's temper already frayed, and the first orders given, his command, slapping his hand on the podium, that "You all come in on time from now on, you hear? On time!"—Ettenheim lounged through his first section, singing without expression or color. "This isn't *Sprechstimme*, Ettenheim," he said. A cool glance in return: "I'm aware of that. It's a rehearsal." In the transition passages, Ettenheim paced around the stage, throwing off his old duffel coat, peering into the theater where only Himmel sat, the boy grimacing when the first clarinet faltered. The grimace implied that bad conducting, not acoustics, was at fault. One of the tympanists giggled. Then, a bar before his entry, he was back at his music stand, hands on hips, ready to sing. He now had the proper degree of strength in his voice, a perfectly timed vibrato, as slow as the tides, his back-of-the-throat voice thrillingly powerful.

In the cold air,
The spirit
Hardens.

It had been a performance laden with contempt, an extra edge in the voice. When they had gone twice through the song cycle, Elliot called for another, simpler piece, one that had gone well in the first rehearsal. Ettenheim sighed and jumped down from the stage to sit in the first row of seats. He did not go near Himmel, Elliot noticed happily.

He heard in their playing that the cellos had been rehearsing together privately. Himmel must have been coaching them. They were playing together, with the right bite in their attack, and were attending carefully to his signals. Thank you, Nathan. The battle with Ettenheim continued. What would the boy say if he saw the Edwards television program? He would dismiss Elliot as a fraud, as a pretender to modernity.

"You're not Bjoerling yet, Mr. Ettenheim," he had said to the boy, then wandering about the theater, "and I suggest that you sit down and pay attention to what is going on here. This is a rehearsal for everybody." A few smiles from the musicians. The black cellist raised his hand in a fist and gave Elliot a companionable grin: right on, baby. Ettenheim moodily returned to his seat in the first row and began flipping through his music. They started again from number fifteen. From then on, things had gone reasonably well, though he could still sense the tenor's spitefulness, and this rankled like a sore on his lip, a persistent irritation.

"Don't worry about it," Himmel said to him later in the Edwardian Room, "the kid's a personality fuckup. He thinks he's got the world by the balls. And maybe he does. Just apart from his voice, maybe you've got it knocked when you're twenty-two. I can't remember anymore. But next year he goes out into the jungle, and the animals will mess him around a little."

By the time they left Longman's it had grown dark, and wind sliced through the open toplighted spaces of the car park, cutting deeply into him. Elliot was on the fourth level; Himmel had told him that he'd had to wind up to the ninth before finding a space. He trotted across the freezing length of concrete between the elevator and Margaret's car, squeezed in beside a pillar, and unlocked the door, his hand shaking with cold. The seat covers sent a chill radiation upward through his coat, a motion parallel to his anger, his tension. Elliot had a sudden vision of Anita weeping, her face roughened with tears. He punched the heater button, then turned on the radio. "Frosty the Snowman" by Ella Fitzgerald, Nat Cole singing "The Christmas Song." Himmel's white Cortina slipped past him in the rearview mirror, its headlights on. He waited until the end of "The Christmas Song" and then swung out backward and went slowly down the curving ramp.

On Grand Avenue the stores were still open, and light spilled from the giant windows. Above the street, arches of lights shaped like trees oxidized the night to purple. "Santa Claus Is Coming to Town" gave way to a commercial and he switched off the radio. Himmel, caught in the traffic, was only a block ahead, and Elliot slowed, driving up to Second Street, so that the light would change. The Cortina went over the bridge above the Plechette River and vanished around a curve as he braked, the lights yellow, in a cacophony of horns.

He drove the rest of the way to Leecham Street in a concentrated calm, passing the dark angles and abutments of the War Memorial and then going steadily north past houses picked with red and green lights. Listen, Anita Kellerman. Listen to me. We have been through much together, you and I. I will not allow this to drift away. We are all experts in loss, we all know how to harden ourselves to it. Now it is time for you to tell me. Is Ronnie Mark's father? Yesterday I saw twenty photographs of . . . What? Love's face, and the face of mastery. I do not want us to have to make that terrible choice. Love is the dread of loss, and the shoring up against it of a million acts of charity. All this I will never say.

The lake a dark definitionless volume to his side, a blackness between the bright houses, Lake Point Drive became Windmere Terrace, then the sharp turn on Leecham. On Himmel's white lawn Santa's whip curled frozen over the plastic reindeer. Elliot slewed the car up against a drift across the street from Anita's house and, jamming the keys in his pocket, jumped out. A dim light showed in a ground-floor window. The air tore at his ears, his hands. He ran across the street.

A loud pause from within the house after his ring, and then he heard footsteps coming toward the door. Listen to me. We must talk, my love, my puzzle, my sister.

Andy French opened the door.

Music was faintly audible behind her. "Telepathy," she said, and he recognized *Five Introductions*. He looked past her into the house, but the entry and hall were dark. A mild light emanated from the living room.

"You don't look very happy, Elliot." She smiled questioningly at him. "Why don't you—"

"Is Anita home? She isn't."

"—come in?"

They looked at each other, Andy puzzled. She shivered. "I'll give you a drink. It's too cold to stand out here."

"Yes, give me a drink." He stepped inside, clapping his hands together for warmth. "She's not at home, is she? I wanted to talk about something with her." Hanging his coat in the closet, he looked into the living room: a bottle and glass on the coffee table, newspapers strewn on the floor, one light casting a pool about a chair. His nervous anger lifted uselessly under her gaze, changed key.

"Anita and Mark are out, that's right. They went to Ronnie's for dinner."

He grunted. She took him into the living room.

"So I was playing your beautiful record and reading a book and getting quietly drunk. It was a novel. *Traveling Loose*, by—"

"By William Pittman," he said. "I read it." He saw splayed open on a chair the garish paperback cover of Pittman's book, a young hood in a motorcycle jacket embracing a naked blond.

"I like the descriptions." She seemed embarrassed.

Elliot sat down on the other side of the coffee table. He felt hopelessly like Kai, adrift. "What time will they be back?"

"Anita? I don't really know . . ." Her voice light, puzzled. "Sometime before twelve. Mark enjoys Ronnie, and it's always a struggle to get him to leave. It wouldn't be before eleven."

He looked up at her, and saw for the first time that she was wearing a loose green long gown that gathered softly at the waist and then fell softly to the floor. In this garment Andy resembled a witch, or a Druid. She hovered in his scrutiny for a moment, her hands going from breasts to waist. "I'm sorry," she said. "You wanted to talk to her."

"It's all right." He felt sour, disappointed. The question was still hot within him and he longed to utter: *Is Ronnie Upp Mark's father?* "Really, it's all right. I like your outfit. You are beautiful in it."

"Ronnie gave it to me," she said. "Admire our tree for a second, and I'll be right back with a glass for you." She smiled at him and nodded to the front of the room.

He turned in the chair and looked into the darkest corner of the living room, where the bookshelves met the front wall. In this corner used to hang the photograph of a blooming, full-sailed Anita leading Frank Kellerman across the lawn. Now he saw the dark mass of the tree. Andy, returning at once with a second glass, set it on the table. She moved to the tree and stooped to push in a plug. A glow of red and green, the tree went alight. "We bought it yesterday. Mark loves it so much he gets dizzy watching it."

Andy came back toward him and sat on the floor beside his chair. "That's the way I feel, sort of, listening to *Five Introductions*. I really do think it's beautiful, Elliot."

Not knowing what to say, he said nothing. Then: "I like the ending." The ending came. The next piece began. "Would you mind playing something else?" he said.

Andy stood, using his knee for a support, and carefully took his record off the turntable, put it in its sleeve, and pulled out another from the shelf. A jazz piano record, soft, with giant open chords. Elliot sipped at his drink.

"So you are stuck with me," she said, returning to the floor beside him. Andy looked up sideways, tilting her head, and smiled again. Elliot felt guilty for having ever regarded the girl as an enemy. He could smell whiskey, a biting sweetness in the air. "You don't mind anymore, do you? I've been sitting here for hours, just drinkng. I'm so happy you're here, Elliot." Her face still tilted toward him, she said, "Don't be foolish about Anita, Elliot." She took one of his hands. He remembered how he had felt about her the day they had driven out to the field; he remembered how he had first seen her. She stroked his hand. "That's the extent of my advice," she said. Her hand moved slowly on his.

Shortly afterward they went upstairs to her room. He could later remember the shock of his mouth meeting the roughened skin of her scars, the calculation of her movements, her cries. It was only when she staggered, removing her sandals, that he realized how much she'd had to drink. That, at least, was his explanation. But in the midst of her abandonment, at the last moment, she said, "I don't take anything—don't do it in me," and he poured himself out on her belly. "We'll never do this again," she said softly into his ear. When he looked down at her face, she was coolly smiling, already detached.

He could see no further than the events of the past two days. He had been angry, anxious, approximately lustful, curious, sarcastic, tender, confident, confused: it did not cohere. He had not asked his question. He looked across the table at Vera, still listening to his father with an expression of complete attentiveness.

"I was thinking yesterday about Mr. Von Heilitz," he said. "Tell Vera about the time he invited you to the party. It's a lovely story."

Margaret burst into laughter. "Yes, do tell Vera about Lamont's party, Chase. I'm sure Vera will want to hear it."

"Please tell me," Vera said. "He was the man who had the dogs, wasn't he?"

"Let's not rake that up," said Elliot, seeing his father irritably stroke downward at his necktie. "That's another story." He looked across the table at Margaret, who seemed even more mirthful, recalling the debacle about the dogs.

"No, let's not," said Chase. "Lamont never forgave me for hitting those ridiculous old dogs of his. For a time, he even thought I had done it deliberately, which was very foolish of him. It spoiled what had been quite a satisfactory relationship. In many ways, I quite respected Lamont. *There* was a man who took his values seriously."

"As the story proves," said Elliot.

After checking to see that Vera was still attending, Chase said, "It does, rather." He signaled for Robert to divide the small remainder of the wine between Vera and Elliot, and paused while it was being poured. "The others have heard this story, Vera, so I am telling it just for you. As Elliot indicates, it is significant as well as amusing." He had recovered his humor. "Two things should be remembered about Lamont Von Heilitz's party. The first is that this was in 1944, during the war—a time when everything seemed endangered in this country. We at home had to keep things humming, use our factories for war production, we had to maintain morale. When the news from Europe finally took a positive swing, there were balls the like of which have not been seen since, in my estimation. We saw this as our part—it may have an odd ring in these times, but I still think we did a real service. If we were fighting for anything, it was to preserve the way of life that we did our best to continue during those years. Of course we and the people we knew did much war work as well—running the factory to satisfy the government contracts. My cousin Walter directed the War Production Board for this area. The country was working as a unit, as a team, for perhaps the last time it was possible for it to do so. There were the occasional rogues, such as Roy Zamon, who made a career of an artificial limb—you children wouldn't remember him. But there were heroes as well. Ralph Nieder, a young man of good family and an acquaintance of mine, who won his Silver Star in Germany. He killed himself here in Plechette City when he came back shattered from the war, and his death shattered many of us, I may assure you of that. I damn near *saw* him shoot himself. And there were others. That was twenty-five years ago, and it was a different America, an America that could still believe in heroes and heroism."

"Lamont's party, Chase," said Margaret.

"I am explaining the background to the party, my dear. These days, we would see it all differently. Our priorities have changed. Well, a man in Chicago named Montana Kingsmill threw a party in the winter of 1944 that was one of the wartime's grandest statements."

"It was lavish," said Margaret, enthusiastic. "We were both young, and we appreciated that kind of thing then. Oh, the flowers! And the music! There must have been five hundred people at the Kingsmill party."

"And we knew most of them. Old Jimmy Steenborg was striding around with his cane, a handsome devil of a man in his uniform. That was the last time I saw old Jimmy, but he looked firm and erect as ever—like his son, a real man for the ladies. Bryce, the coffee millionaire, Simpson and Watkins, who invested heavily in MGM and were both squiring actresses, Phil Morgan-Lime, Lotte Ramp, Count Zlydockwyczk, Edgar Burren, the portrait painter, Len Gamble, Hal Fisch . . . I could go on giving you the names for an hour. Shipman Kylody, who knew more about money management than any man in Chicago. Half a dozen famous theater people. Wanda Wylie—her picture *The Millionairess* had just had its premiere. All of these people had glamour, the real substantial glamour that comes from doing things grandly and publicly. Montana had got Benny Goodman's band to play, *and* Guy Pollack. There hasn't been a ball like it since, despite all your Truman Capotes.

"I said you had to keep two things in mind," said Chase. "The other is the character of Lamont Von Heilitz. When we moved into this house in 1940, Lamont was in his late fifties, and he hadn't done a day's work in his life. His father had been a stock millionaire who had invested in the auto industry right at the beginning, and unlike many of the twenties millionaires, he had been a cautious man. The Von Heilitzes had houses in France, Switzerland, and Florida—another killing there, in land. As a young man Lamont had been to school in Geneva, and then went to Princeton. He married young, a girl named Rose Ten Broek from upstate New York—one of those dowdy wealthy girls of the time who never spoke above a whisper. After their marriage, Lamont devoted himself to living well. In this case, that meant living with the greatest possible propriety.

"He and Rose were living in the light of an ideal—an ideal that commanded certain ceremonies of them. Lamont changed his clothes three times a day. They both dressed for dinner every night of their lives. Lamont was the most ceremonious man I've ever met, and probably one of the dullest, and Rose simply retired behind him like a voiceless shadow. I think they lost any sense they might have had of how other people lived. They never read the newspapers, never owned a radio, Rose read only novels by Jane Austen and Rose Macaulay. When Montana Kingsmill had his party, Lamont and Rose were of course invited, and equally as expected, they declined. But some description of the ball must have got back to Lamont, for he—as gently as could be—began to pump me for information about it. This went on for weeks. When I went out for a walk, Lamont would suddenly appear from behind a hedge, asking me who had been invited, how people had dressed, if there had been decorations, what the food had been. Who were the musicians? When he asked me if it were 'done' to invite single women to large parties, I knew that he was planning to emulate Kingsmill. Why, I still have no idea. He and Montana Kingsmill were as unlike as any two men could be. But that was precisely what Lamont had in mind to do, and he began his preparations that April, planning the party for August of 1944. One afternoon he invited me into his house to see his guest list. Rose was standing in the dining room beside this enormous stack of papers. She looked as proud and regal as a newly crowned queen. When she lifted the top page, I saw that it was all one long roll of paper, folded like an accordion— there must have been something like a thousand names on it. I saw right away that the first three people on the list were dead. They were old friends of my father's who had died before the war. He and Rose were so pleased with their work that I could not tell them, and I hadn't the heart to look at the rest of the list. I went home with my head and my heart in my hands, let me tell you.

"He and Rose kept at it all during that spring. It was a beautiful spring too, the news from the front was encouraging, and the weather turned mild very quickly, as if nature were redressing the balance for the terrible winter we'd had. All during that beautiful spring, Lamont was making ready for his party. He hired Guy Pollack's band, on my recommendation, I recall. Each week he'd done something new. Planned the menu, hired the same caterers Kingsmill had used, rented roulette wheels. He was happy as a boy.

"Then the disaster struck. In the late summer of that year, we had a particularly vicious measles epidemic. You could see the quarantine notices all over the city. The Von Heilitzes were as good as in quarantine normally, living as they did, but somehow, in the last week of July, Rose was infected. She'd never had measles as a child. Lamont hung on until the last minute, hiring a nurse full time and caring for his wife as well as he could, and then he came down with something as well. Fatigue, I expect. Nervous shock. I didn't see him for a week. By the time he realized that he'd have to cancel his party, it was too late—the band was committed for the rest of the fall, the caterers had sent him a notice that they were beginning to prepare his order, the flowers had all been paid for. He had paid several thousand dollars in deposits and rentals. Yet all the spirit had gone out of it for him. Rose hadn't moved from her bed in a month. He was exhausted. In the end, two weeks before the date of the party he hired someone to send out regrets to the people who had accepted his invitation. I hate to think how many telephone calls he must have had from sons and daughters and nephews, saying that Father or Uncle had died five years before.

"For days trucks and vans were coming up to his house—we could see them at work in the back gardens, setting up tents and a bandstand. A team of gardeners resodded parts of his lawn. Colored fountains. Spotlights sunk into the lawn. The liquor was unloaded in *cases*, dozens of them. To use a phrase Elliot was fond of as a boy, 'the whole schmear.'

"Then the day came. Debeek's men, the caterers, began arriving about noon, an army of them, with boxes and crates containing the food and the silver and the glassware. Anything that wasn't rationed. The band came in a bus. It was all very peculiar to see, and very funny and very sad at once.

"Our phone rang about six. When I answered, I heard a faint whispery sort of voice—it took me a moment to recognize that it was Lamont. 'I would like to invite you to our little party,' he said to me. 'You may come at your convenience. Dinner will be at nine-thirty, Chase, but it is not necessary that you dress.' I thanked him, and he hung up. So: at eight o'clock I walked across the lawn to his house. The band was playing, waiters were waiting, the house was lighted up like a fun fair, and no one was there but me. I sat at a little white table under a striped tent and was served drinks while I listened to the band. I was sure that, somewhere up in the house, Lamont was watching. I applauded each number Pollack played. They did an entire show while I sat there. 'Honeysuckle Rose,' 'Flyin' Home,' 'American Patrol,' 'One O'Clock Jump,' the drummer danced on a drum, a girl singer named Florence McCall sang 'Green Eyes,' Guy Pollack told jokes between numbers. Nobody looked at me. They were as embarrassed as I, and I felt that they too could sense Lamont watching them from up in the house. At nine-thirty, Raoul, Debeek's headwaiter, escorted me into the dining room. He put me at the central table, before my name on a place card. It was like being the captain of a deserted liner—all that white linen and sparkling glass. 'Will Mr. Von Heilitz be joining me?' I asked, and he said, 'Mr. Von Heilitz will be dining in his room tonight, sir'—as though he oversaw scenes like this every week.

"The wine steward, also one of Debeek's men, greeted me by name and asked my preference in the wines. They were all from Lamont's cellar, and I knew he had a good Puligny-Montrachet and an equally good Margaux, so I asked for them and had a half of each bottle—that was for Lamont's sake. The dinner was superb. When I had finished with my dessert and coffee, I had a small glass of port—Lamont never took brandy after dinner—and walked back across his garden to our house. I waved good-bye up at the house, but didn't see anyone there. One fellow in the band waved good-bye to me. It was the damnedest evening I'd ever had in my whole life."

"And the next week . . ." Margaret prompted.

"The next week Lamont popped out from behind his hedge again as I walked by, trailed along silently for half a block, and then asked me if I enjoyed his party. 'I'm so very happy,' he said. 'I caught glimpses of you from my windows, and I thought that you had quite enjoyed the music.'"

He smiled at Vera.

"I thought it was going to be a funny story," she said.

"Sometimes it is," he said. "But you really cannot deny that it has a great deal to do with values."

16

The next day the mail brought a Unicef Christmas card from Joanie Haupt and two letters, each addressed solely to Elliot Denmark.

Dear Vera:
Just a note to thank you for how kind you have been to me. I don't know who else would listen so sympathetically to my wretched problems. The situation seems better now. Lawrence is very contrite—*not* the way I like him best. He gave me a dog named Marcuse. Cute? Let's meet for lunch sometime next week. Love to you and Elliot, and Merry Christmas. Have a happy. Thanks again.

All love,
Peace,
Joanie

Elliot:
Just shamblin' along, footloose/careloose/jobloose. We went to Philadelphia for a week's gig the day after your rehearsal (two days after? I don't remember) and it turned out that the place we were supposed to play in was run by some mafioso who said he'd smash our instruments if we didn't do four sets a night—us sweating ourselves into greasy little puddles for about thirty bucks—so we quit after two days and went straight on through to New York. Well, livin' the blooz, like the song says. We have a new manager, an ace, who says that he can get us good gigs and a record contract if we hang around here & do a lot of rehearsing. In the meantime, it's cold asses hustling down East Twelfth Street between our "loft" and the local greaseria. Mucho coffee, señor! Sí. Big grins here. I try to keep from getting panhandled by guys who look just like me. A genuinely freakish experience.

Yet, yet, yet—I really do love this city, gritty and bitter and hostile as it is. It's like one long speed experience. (We've been living on hamburgers and Cokes, and that might have something to do with it.) I'm in the middle of reading *The Glass Bead Game*, Hesse's great mindbender, and it's like going from your music to Jimi Hendrix, reading that while hearing the police cars scream by at night. We're rehearsing in what our manager calls a "loft," but in reality is a watery basement in a warehouse. It goes well, old teacher mine. We'll begin working before long, we've got lots of new songs (and a genius new bassist from Memphis) and I'm feeling like I'm finally getting into place, into what I should be doing. We're having a demo heard by Sextant records. I got the money from my parents to buy an echoplex outfit for my guitar, and it really makes fantastic sounds. MAKE MUSIC—that's the only thing.

All this means that I'll miss your concert, for which I here maketh my apologies.

Has anybody seen the wolf lately? I got a big lift out of reading about that big ragged creature patrolling around the suburbs. This may be due to my Hesse binge. What do you think the bastard lives on? I bought a dog the other day, a furry little bundle who eats potato chips and lima beans.

Well, *Dragnet* is on the radio now, four guys just got shot between commercials on the tube, another guy is playing B. B. King on the stereo, I just finished *Traveling Loose* by William Pittman, a strung-out novel everybody here is reading, so the context is mixed, as always. After all, I'm not William Bendix and this isn't *Beat the Clock* . . . or is it? I saw Roy Rogers selling a disease on TV the other night, just a day after copping an old 45 of "Happy Trails." When I was an *enfant pas terrible* I used to daydream about Dale Evans' boobs. *La vie imite l'art, hein?* (What *is* that verb?)

> Until we meet again,
> Roy Baltz

Dear Elliot,

It was quite a pleasant surprise to get your signature on our statement in the mails this morning, and I write to express my gratitude and appreciation. To reciprocate, I am planning a little surprise for you, one I hope you will like, so do watch for our appearance in the newspaper.

> With best wishes,
> Dr. Pierce Laubach

"That sounds unpleasantly sinister," said Vera. "When a man like that uses the words 'a little surprise,' I begin to wish I had someone to taste my food for me."

"I don't think it means anything. Maybe he put my name first on the list. He could use my picture for all I care."

"Well, you've certainly burnt your bridges," Vera said. She was referring to his argument with Tessa, and she smiled at him: Elliot knew that there was no rancor left in Vera over the incident. The Glaubers too seemed to have resolved to forget it. Elliot had spoken with Tessa on the telephone yesterday morning before the rehearsal, and she had twice called him "darling." The peace was official.

"When you were a boy, did you daydream about Dale Evans' boobs?" Vera asked, still smiling.

"I was more in the Jane Russell–Faye Emerson era," he said. Andy French, an uneasiness threading up his spine, came clearly into his mind. It had the flavor of defeat. He completely saw for a long moment her face magnified beneath him, the violent lines like arteries and rough to his lips.

We'll never do this again.

What?

You heard me. This is it. Sex this casual makes me feel like I'm back in college.

I'm sorry that you didn't like it.

I like it enough. She had grinned at him, stretching her arms above her head. *I loved it, in fact. You're considerate. Thanks for not mentioning the fact that I still am in college.*

You must be the only girl in America who doesn't take the pill.

Did I say I didn't take it? Poor Elliot. When he was buttoning his shirt, she said, *Lots of us don't take it anymore, Elliot dear. Don't worry.*

"Would you mind if I visited Uncle Kai alone today?" he asked. "I'd like to go over there sometime after lunch."

"Tomorrow night we go to Anita's party?"

"If you want to."

"I'd love to. You've been hiding her from me, you know."

"I don't think so," he said. "It just worked out that way."

She was silent for a moment, toying with a giant transparent cigarette lighter on the table. "Be easy with Uncle Kai, Elliot," she said.

"Who's going to make him be easy on me?"

"And I think you should have a talk with your father, too," she said quietly.

He only barely heard her. All centers of his guilt seemed to be converging; since he had seen the photographs, Kai was horribly linked in his mind with Ronnie Upp. Images of fistfights, raw bleeding flesh, purple bruises, filled his inner vision. He could not enter Anita's house as long as Andy French was there. Pale light washed over them, reflected from the ice shattered and heaved up at the edge of the lake.

His father was playing "Ain't Misbehavin' " on the piano in the lower living room, and he must have heard their voices, for he called out, "Aren't you children chilly in there? Why don't you make a nice crackling fire?" *Da da da bumpbump, da da da bumpbump,* the piano continued. "By the by, our northern visitor, the *lupus*, was seen again this morning, according to the news commentators. It crossed Jackson Drive in full view of several automobiles, and then streaked away into the fields. It was going generally southeast. Perhaps we should outfit ourselves with weapons."

Driving along the lake expressway toward the valley, Elliot tried to draw things into order. First, the rehearsals showed that the concert would at least not be an utter failure: with one more long run-through on the day of the performance, they could at least make it plausible. It was not enough, but it would be sufficient. Second, the moment with Andy had perhaps been inevitable. He had let the girl grow too large in his imagination. Andy was only a girl—no more than twenty-two or -three. A graduate student. Like many girls her age, she was apparently capable of controlling her emotions. Third, Anita. For an instant, he saw her as some white defenseless thing, trapped, caged, at the mercy of more powerful forces, frightened . . . Well, she had been frightened. Upp had slapped her hard enough to raise a bruise. They must have had a falling-out before she summoned him from his parents' house. Somehow, he would use her party to talk about it with her. He also promised himself that he would have a long talk with Upp. And some words with Andy. Then he felt his panic begin to rise in him again.

Elliot swung the car up the curve around the War Memorial—the lake, catching the sun behind him, flashed once in his car mirror—and crossed to the inside lane. Looking sideways to see if traffic were coming, he caught sight of a slender, elegant man in a short brown coat who was walking briskly before the leafless trees along First Street; he was instantly convinced that the man was Ronnie Upp. A flock of pigeons took off from the War Memorial's plaza to his right and wheeled away like the souls of the dead into the dark air. When the traffic light flashed green, Elliot accelerated, recrossing the two lanes in a blare of horns, to get closer to the figure in the brown coat. Just as he drew near, the man stepped jauntily into a side street, and Elliot, braking, saw his slim back join a crowd of people walking toward the festooned entrance to a department store. Elliot lost sight of the man and began to look desperately for a place to park.

He cut savagely into an alley, tires whining, and drove down to the other end past the rust-colored backs of buildings. Just as he slammed the car to a halt, he saw the man, partially hidden by shoppers, cross the alley's entrance. He jumped out. He had no idea of what he would say to Upp. He began to walk quickly down the crowded street. His body seemed to be plummeting. The man came into view, crossing the street, only fifteen feet away. Just then the pigeons banked overhead, their wings loudly beating, and the man turned his head to watch their flight. He had a bony beardless face, round-nosed. It was not Upp. It was only a boy. Elliot's relief was so great that he slumped against a shop window. Trembling, he drew his hands over his face. He realized that he had intended to leap at the man, to flail him with his fists. Shocked, he continued to knead his face.

"I was rather expecting you, Elliot," said Kai, opening his door.

The apartment was just as it had been two days before; the odor Elliot remembered drifted over him again, a snuffy sleepy smell of age. The drapes were closed against the depthless sun. The blocky old typewriter still stood on the desk; Goethe and Celan and Storm marched above it. Elliot looked guiltily for an instant at the filing cabinet he had rifled on his last visit: had Kai noticed anything? Seeing the elegant old man again—his actions on that day seemed utterly unwarranted, an invasion. Nothing he had done seemed the right thing. Kai smiled at him and gestured to one of his chairs.

"You look as though you had better sit, Elliot," he said. "You are shaken." He held his gesture until Elliot removed his coat, laid it across the cot, and sat in the chair. "To give you one more proof of my percipience, I'll tell you that I bought some coffee on my last shopping spree. You would like some coffee?"

"Thank you, yes," Elliot said. "I'd love some." Kai nodded briskly and went toward the curtain. He parted it and disappeared inside. Elliot heard the pounding of water into a percolator. Then the sliding of a tin from a shelf; the gas made its small explosion. Kai reappeared through the curtain.

"Now," he said. "Our only artist is here at last, but he resembles a fugitive from justice. Do you want to tell me what happened? If it is something private, I will withdraw the question."

"I guess I can tell you," said Elliot. "It isn't any earth-shaking thing, really." Where to begin? He could not recount his history with Anita. For a moment he feared he might be sick. "It's all tied in with a man named Ronnie Upp," he said. "I thought I saw him on the way down here, and it was like seeing someone who is supposed to be dead—some old enemy. I wanted to kill him. There are some personal problems of mine tied in here." He shot a horrified look at Kai, who seemed unmoved by the reference to Upp and continued to regard him calmly. "Well, I can't go into that. It's probably unimportant anyway. It has to do with an old attachment of mine. As I say, probably unimportant. But I'm feeling hemmed in by the man. And that thing in the car just now—when I went to follow him—it makes me feel soiled. Filthy. I'm terribly confused about what I'm doing."

"I think you could use your coffee," Kai said, and went again behind the curtain, returning with two cups on a tray, which he set on the table beside Elliot's chair. Elliot sipped from his cup: the coffee was rich and strong, and he drank it gratefully.

"Of course you know about the Nun's Wood business," he said. "I'm involved, really in only a small way, with that, acting against Herman. I blew up at Tessa one night when she nearly accused me of treason, and that could be part of it, I suppose. The scene created some uneasiness between Vera and me. That's only natural, and it's over by now. This Upp is one of the principals in the Nun's Wood matter. Lately, everything seems to be part of some plot, almost, a plot in which I'm just wandering around, trying to build meanings out of dropped cigarette butts and old envelopes. At times I think I'm on top of things, and then something happens, and I'm back again where I started." Elliot realized that he had probably not made much sense. Talking about it made him feel worse. Kai was leaning backward in his tall desk chair, his white hands folded on his lap. The foxy old face was tilted forward, concentrated on him. "I can't . . . I mean, I'm grateful to you for listening to all this gibberish. I thought I had more self-control. I wanted to jump on that man and beat him to hamburger. That's really why I'm upset—it was like finding an enemy inside me, someone vain, savage, deluded . . ." Kai did not move. He was watching Elliot very calmly. He is waiting for me to confess about the files, Elliot thought. "A couple of days ago, I wanted to talk about everything with you, to stage some sort of confession scene, I guess. But I don't think I have to do that now."

"No," Kai said. "Confessions are a luxury." He gave his wintry smile. "They are very old-fashioned. The absolution we can get from others is liable to be of little value."

Then we are all self-bound, Elliot thought. Miles of stony distance seemed to separate him from Kai. "I suppose you're right," he said. "But I distrust that kind of statement."

"I do too." Kai smiled. "I distrust the whole apparatus of defensiveness. Forgive me if I overemphasized your use of the word 'confession.' I merely felt that you were not saying everything you wished to say to me. Nor do I mean to imply that we can look no further than ourselves. That you are here, and that I am happy to have you here, should tell you otherwise. I do feel that it is necessary now and then to walk out of the confessional into the street, to see if the sun shines, if the several square miles we inhabit have altered in any significant way."

"They've altered, all right," Elliot said.

"And that is what you cannot talk about."

"Yes."

"That is fine. I do not wish to probe into your private life. And I think you are too young to have any confessions I would find essential." His glance here was ripe with irony. "You and Vera can go on undisturbed, can you not?" Elliot nodded. "Then you are better off not speaking."

It seemed to Elliot that their footing had subtly changed. He sensed some purpose in Kai that he could not decipher, a strategy. He hoped with his whole being that Kai had not noticed that his files had been violated.

"Herman told me the last time we spoke," Kai said, "about the arguments with Tessa, and he mentioned that he thought there was some trouble between you and Vera. This does not annoy you? He is merely solicitous of Vera's welfare. He always has been."

Elliot's panic began to ebb. Kai wished to talk about Vera, so he could not have noticed anything wrong with the files. "No, it doesn't annoy me," he said. "Herman can't believe that Vera is happy living out of the country."

"He never could believe that," said Kai. "You need not concern yourself with that shortcoming of my brother's. And"—he smiled again—"you do not."

"I cannot."

"No, we are not responsible for other people's illusions." Kai crossed his legs, and his hand rose to the curling vein on his temple. "Is the Ronnie Upp you mentioned earlier the young man who shot his father during the fifties? They lived quite close to your parents' house, I recall."

He does know about the files, Elliot thought. He felt sickened, exposed. "Yes, that was the boy, son of Harrison Upp," he said. "Uncle Kai, I have to explain . . ."

"No, I have to explain something to you," Kai broke in. Astonishingly, he took Elliot's hand for a moment, and then let it fall back on his lap. "I want to show you something." He lifted out the leather box and held it on his knees. "When I was in the camp during those years of the war, I thought I had learned a few hard lessons—learned them absolutely. After I learned them, I chose not to forget. Other men, even women, went through what I endured, and sealed it all off, to the extent that it could be sealed off. But to return into the dream of normal life was defensiveness, I thought—no, *knew*. I trusted the work I was doing, because that was an almost impersonal act of consciousness. It also kept me away from anything that might have diminished my sense of what I'd learned. If what I learned was painful, then I had at least to keep my pain alive." He opened the lid of the box, held it up for a moment while he looked within, and then closed it gently.

"All that time, I was half-harboring an illusion, a myth, without being conscious of it. And I only became aware, shamefully aware of it, when I read in the newspapers about the death of Harrison Upp. Listen to me: I ran outside, holding the newspaper, weeping with joy and at the same time for my own dishonesty. Half of what I had thought about myself was shown up for a fraud." He passed the tooled box to Elliot. "It was a terrible moment. It put me back into the camp just as though I had never left it." He looked wryly at Elliot, who held the box, awkwardly, on his knees. "Only then could I finish my book. I began again on it, and spent years doing it, but I finished it over a year ago."

"Your book is done?" Elliot gasped. "Where is it?" He turned his head to the files, then back to Kai.

"I detest those metal files," Kai said gently. "Herman gave them to me years ago, when he was purchasing some new equipment for his office in city hall. I made the labels to please him, but I've never used the files for anything important. I've been keeping everything up here." He rose from his chair and went to the closets on the other side of the room. He opened the double doors. On the shelf above his clothes stood a rank of red manuscript boxes. "All of my work is in these boxes. The notes, the drafts, the typescript, everything. I sent a copy off to a university press when it was finally done, and several months later they wrote to say that although it was contrary to their policy to publish works by people not affiliated with universities, they were pleased to accept my book."

"But why didn't you tell anyone?" Elliot heard himself nearly shouting. "Why didn't you tell Tessa and Herman?"

"Because I am old enough to act as I choose," Kai said, looking as handsome as Elliot had ever seen him. "And I chose not to subject myself to the miseries I knew would follow. Would you like to see the letter from the publisher?"

From the shelf where it had been lying next to the manuscript boxes, Kai plucked an unfolded sheet of paper with a letterhead Elliot could read across the room.

"No, Uncle Kai," he said. "That isn't necessary." He swallowed, and watched Kai replace the paper on the shelf. "What will you do when the book is published?"

"I will give them a copy. And that will be my absolution." Kai closed the closet door and went back to his chair before the desk. "Elliot, instead of sitting there in such evident discomfort, why don't you just open that little box? I want to talk about some things with you, and the photographs in the box are where I have to begin."

17

When I found myself out on the lawn of Herman's house, Kai said, with the *Herald* wadded up in my hand and me sobbing as I had never before done in my life, I was thrown back almost physically into the camp at Blini. I could see the rows of barracks, three long buildings hedged by barbed wire, the railroad line coming into the camp which was visible from the *Appelplatz* outside the barracks, the two large buildings to the west of them where we worked in the laundry or the kitchens or the prisoners' store—all of this area was called the *Wohnlager*, and it was all surrounded by wire. Because I could see the railroad line and the *Lazzarett* I knew I had been ordered out into the *Appelplatz:* and when one found oneself alone there it meant one thing only. You were to be executed for some minor infraction—for disobedience, for theft, for something of that sort. At five every morning we were led out to line up there, and the guards took a special delight in exempting from the formation any man who was to be shot that day. He stood apart from the other prisoners and watched, while the rest of us marched away and thanked God we were not in his place. I could see even the dusty pebbles of the gravel beside my feet. It was the only hallucination I have ever suffered, but my lack of practice did not save me from having it complete.

Yet it did not make sense, my being there. Executions were rather rare among the workers in the barracks, and I felt a horrible confusion because I could not remember what I had done. I wished that I had requested a transfer to the *Totenlager*, the upper camp where the ovens and burial tips were located. The workers there never lasted longer than a month or two, and men who were scheduled for execution could win another few weeks of life by pleading to be put up in that section of the camp. I could not imagine why I had been so stupid as to let that last chance slip by me. All of this took place in seconds, I am sure. My hallucination faded as completely as it had come. I sat down on the grass until my terror left me—that odd calculating terror which was so familiar—and until I felt that I was once more in control. I was very badly shaken. A huge globule of perspiration came up under my shirt and soaked me.

I spent the next two days in bed, trying to feel my way through what happened, though I had known immediately, sitting on the grass soaked in my own juices, that Harrison Upp, the father of the young man you have mentioned, was at its heart. Harrison Upp, and my relationship with Harrison Upp, and how that relationship ended, though I think it did not really end until that moment. I had gone on being Harrison's prisoner until the day I learned of his death.

I have loved and hated only one man in my life, and in the end the hate drove out the love, killed it so that it was no more than a dry little seed. Yet any strong emotion is a connection to its object. It took Harrison's death to free me of him. Curiously, it is similar to the feeling of having finished the book on Goethe. No purpose is left to me, no fuel—it is the sensation of being beached, run aground; a uselessness. To be fanciful, I could say that it is like being one of my sister-in-law's antiques: an old barrel, a brass bed warmer—those pathetic objects that lately have made me hate entering her home. As I tell Herman, I wish to die, but I do not wish to be reminded of my death by images of it.

The photographs in the box were taken from 1925 to 1933, the years I spent largely with Harrison Upp. Upp traveled a good bit on his own, returning frequently to America, but even toward the end of that time when we had to struggle to remain cordial and fought bitterly nearly one day of every three, he and I must have spent half of every year together. I wrote to Herman that I had "seen through" Harrison sometime in 1930, and that I had left him in Paris and gone to Bonn. That was a very careful lie, a prudent lie—and, as it happened, a prescient lie. By 1932, when I had become well established in Bonn, the situation with Harrison was unbearable. He tyrannized over me, and he was a cruel and capricious man whose tyranny was very inventive. "Seeing through" him, unfortunately, did not stop me from being tied to him. After every separation we were impelled to meet again—as though there were some thread we had to follow through to its end. The photographs show us in the exuberant moments when peace seemed possible, but those had become painfully rare by the thirties. Upp would arrive without warning from a visit to New York and demand that I leave with him for Paris: I'd argue and fight, very truthfully pleading my scholarly work as an excuse, I'd finally give in in despair and then at the last minute he'd leave again without warning. At times I would come home from the university to find him in my room with some girl he had brought there—and he would insist on taking us both out to dinner, torturing us both throughout the evening, and it would end with the girl scornful, sarcastic, upset . . . twice he amused himself by sending me home alone with one of these girls. There were, of course, other young men as well. Harrison gave a party in his Paris apartment in 1930 that was my first collision with his puppetmaster aspect. More than half of the guests were street boys, and Harrison made it clear that they'd have to vie for him. I was sickened by the scene that followed. The next day I tried to talk about it with him, to see why he had done that to me, and he answered, "I thought you might be amused by my little game, my dear Kai." I remonstrated as violently as I dared, and he merely shrugged. For weeks after, he humiliated me in small ways, constantly demeaning me. Yet we always returned to one another, and there would be one of those explosions of goodwill that cemented us even more firmly together. At some point, I recognized that although I had come to Europe because of him, I was in effect taking care of him, supporting him psychically, buttressing him, and that tied me to him even more firmly.

During one of those summers, Harrison bought a pistol, a beautiful little black Italian weapon, which he wore in a holster from a shop on the rue Passy. He used to lay it very delicately on the table when he was unusually playful or especially unhappy or vicious, always parodying the gestures of a man *in extremis:* at times, it was the performance of a madman, and it terrified me. He would toy with the pistol, aiming it at my head, and then flick it away. "I am going to be married in America," he said to me, "and, little friend, if you object, I will *plink* and *plink* with my little pistol until nothing is left of you." Then he turned up the butt of the gun so I could see that the clip was not in it. I would have been delighted if he had made a happy marriage, and he knew it.

He had a little monkey then, and the animal would run chattering up the drapes when Harrison enacted one of his dramas with his pistol. You can see the monkey in one of the photographs taken at the villa of Bruno Larella, the costume designer—it was a hypertense little beast, and it shat all over the floor when it panicked. One day in Bonn he set the monkey on a table and began toying with his pistol. "Do you see Fritzie, Kai?" he said. "Naughty little Fritzie? I'm sick of him." He pointed the gun at the monkey, and the animal scampered off the table, chattering, to make a run at the window ledge. "Should I kill him?" he asked, and I said, thinking that the clip was out, "You know I hate the beastly little thing. Do what you want." He played with it, pointing the gun and then dropping it, while Fritzie dashed screaming over every surface in the apartment. I couldn't bear the noise the animal was making—its terror. Finally the monkey hid himself behind the drapes. Harrison shot it twice through the draperies. I had really thought the gun was unloaded, as it usually was, and I jumped with the shock. The noise of the firing had seemed so small, almost insignificant. I had thought it would make a terrible explosion. But Fritzie was bunched on the carpet, bleeding, his body suddenly shapeless, like a pulpy rag. Harrison told me to wrap it up in newspapers and put it in the dustbin. He was drunk on that day, of course. I had always detested the little creature, and it was all I could do to touch it, but I opened an old suitcase I hadn't used in years and prodded it in with my foot. Then I took a tramcar and dropped the suitcase in a canal.

I had to use the tram because Harrison had ruined his automobile some months earlier while driving us back to Bonn from Remagen, in the Rhine valley. He insisted on driving on the smaller country roads, and on driving recklessly fast, especially when drunk. He never let anyone else drive his car, a Marmon he had brought back with him from one of the trips to New York. There was a young man with us, a boy really, whom Upp had picked up in our hotel at Remagen. He was a naïf, but a rather charming, witless sort of person. He was twenty, named Karl Frisch, and his mother had just married a horrid little official from Mainz; the mother was only too happy to be rid of him when Harrison proposed bringing him back to Bonn with us. A rather slight boy, blond, with a face like a crushed rose. Frisch had been drinking steadily during the day, and sat in the tiny backseat of the Marmon, singing and bellowing at the other cars and at the farmers driving their hay wagons. I was furious at Harrison for bringing the boy with us, and I was in a rage at the boy for behaving so boorishly—he was anything but charming that afternoon. He insisted we stop at a hotel in another village further up the Rhine for more bottles of hock, and Harrison pretended to be delighted with the notion. He was flattering the boy relentlessly, and I could see that, even drunk, he was enjoying seeing the way Frisch was making a fool of himself. Later, this would all be used as a lever against the boy. I could see Harrison exulting. We stopped at a *Gasthaus* for wine, and then, in a sudden shower, continued. The boy continued to drink, he and Harrison passing the bottle between them. Then just as we were heading toward the roofs of another village, down a slope from where we were, the rain increased heavily, and Frisch began to shout for more wine. He was delighted with himself, delighted with the car, the shower, the village where we would be able to get more wine—as he lurched forward to grab the wheel away from Harrison, I saw his face, and it was terrifyingly happy, bestially happy, the brain guttered out with speed and pleasure and egotism. He fell sprawling over the steering wheel, tumbling into Harrison, and the Marmon went straight for the side of the road, as I remember, Upp in his confusion pushing the accelerator instead of the brake. I saw his mistake, and could do nothing: I was frozen. We overturned, the car flipped onto a rock ledge and crashed down into a ditch. Frisch was killed when he fell half out of the car and was crushed against the ledge. The Marmon dragged him along beneath it when it went down the rocky face. I was thrown clear when we overturned, and fell onto the ledge—when I opened my eyes I saw Frisch being soundlessly mangled by the car, dragged down the slope by its weight. Harrison simply fell out and clung to the ledge.

He explained to the police that the boy was a friend, that he had tried to grab the wheel as a drunken prank—he seemed absolutely sober as he talked to the police. I, the Herr Professor Glauber, would act as witness. He arranged everything. We were held over three days, one of the farmers we had passed testified to Frisch's drunkenness, and afterward we continued on to Bonn by train. Harrison left for Paris several days later and stayed there for a week or two. In the interim, of course, he'd shot the monkey. I think he was in a bad psychological condition—all nerves and guilt and recklessness. Before he left, he mentioned to me, as if it were only a casual passing remark, that he wished *he'd* been the one to die. I knew it was more than that, and that made him even more restless to leave. And he knew that the accident stayed with me, and would stay with me a long time—I think he knew that I had resolved to make a final break from him. He wanted to allow the usual healing that took place whenever we were separated. But I could not look at him without seeing the Frisch boy. It didn't help that my motives were anything but completely moral and that I was disgusted with myself for the tangle of my own emotions.

After his return we fought about my leaving. I had already found another flat nearer to the university, and I planned to move at the end of that month. It was July of 1933. Bonn was bakingly hot, everything was unsettled in Germany, one saw appalling things everywhere. The country was just about to take its final lurch into disease. Yet I was determined to keep on at my work, somewhere in the south, apart from Harrison. We were on a tramcar going into the city when he said that he had finally arranged false papers for me—a necessity if I were to remain unharassed in the country much longer. "I'll take the papers because I need them," I said, "but I can't live with you any longer. I'm going to hide myself in some farm town to work on my book. You can do what you want, as long as you don't do it near me." Just as I was finishing my piece, which I had been practicing for weeks, waiting for him to return from Paris, an old rouged dandy in a white linen suit, an obvious toupee gummed to his scalp, boarded the tram. His eyes lit on Harrison. His hands fluttered. He spoke with a Berlin accent, in an educated, precise, drawling voice. "My dear Harry, what a delight to see you again!" he crooned, moving across the crowded tram toward us. "Such old friends as we should never have lost touch. . . ." On and on in this fashion. I could tell that Harrison, who'd had several large brandies before leaving the apartment, was flushing with anger. The old man's face had been powdered, and you could see the line on his neck where the healthy-looking makeup ended and his dead-white skin crept down into his collar. "You are looking well, your distinguished friend looks well, and I too am looking well today," said the apparition. "I must take my time . . . arranging . . . in the mornings, but we will all grow old. Yet art may provide where nature fails; we may all look young, with proper care." The old man was half-crazy. It was the pathetic craziness of those who cannot distinguish their reality from their performance, who are swallowed by their fantasy. He invited us to dine with him. "Not at the old place, Harry, I couldn't keep it up anymore, but at my flat on . . ." He named a decrepit street in the area near the city buildings. Harrison told him to shut up, just in that way—his voice was as chilly as a steel blade. He was in a rage, and I could recognize the look he got, his face red and indrawn, when he was on the edge of fury. "Shouldn't speak to me like that," the old man stage-whispered, so loudly that everybody turned to stare at us, "after everything I've done for you. You are a silly little wretch, Harry, a silly terrible little fool." His face was trembling, and he picked up one of his hands to touch Harrison. In a moment Harrison was on his feet, wrenching the old man out of his seat. He dragged him down the aisle to the door, the old man bent in half like an old piece of paper, and pushed him off the tram. I saw the old man go down on the tracks, smearing his suit with black from the cinders. He looked as though he were crying, muttering to himself. I wish I had in that box a photograph of that rouged old creature, crushed bit of human candy that he was; kneeling in the dust he looked like only a filthy bundle of clothes sporting a clown's face. An S.A. man on the tram laughed and clapped Harrison on the back. "You should have let me do him," he said. "All right," Harrison said, coming back to the seat, "I'll send you your damned papers. We'll finish this charade." Then he put his face beside my ear, in such fury and compression of movement that I thought he was going to bite it off. He patted his suit under his shoulder where he carried his pistol and hissed, "I'd like to shoot you, you know. Just shoot you dead, right here. But if you're fool enough to stay in this country, I won't have to." I got off at the next stop. At the end of the month I moved into the new flat. By summer, I had arranged to rent a farmhouse in the country west of Rüdesheim. I used the name on the papers Harrison had given me.

Within a year I knew that I had made a mistake. The farmers were suspicious and snooping, my work had lost its direction, and it became clear to me that Germany was the wrong place to be. But then it was too late to leave. I was arrested in 1934, kept in jail in Berlin for three years, and then removed to Blini. The name on the papers Upp had given me was Traum. Artur Traum. Arthur Dream. I thought that Harrison, who knew many Nazi officers, had betrayed me to them; and I thought that he had decided to do it that afternoon on the tram.

If you can give me more time, I want to tell you the rest of it. I have been silent too long. Try to picture the way rats live on a garbage heap, fighting for spoiled food, lifting their snouts for clean air, all of them carrying disease, living in it, in a strict hierarchy—except that we rats were directed by the officers at Tiergartenstrasse 4 in Berlin, Bouhler, Brock, Blankenburg, Professor Heyde, names none of us knew then.

III

THE BEGINNING OF THE CONCERT

18

The evening paper carried on the first page of the local section a brief story headed FALSE SHOT, DOG DIES, concerning a Mr. Georgiou Stampos, of 5580 Pearl Drive, Willowbrook Meadow subdivision, who had shot and killed with a .22 long rifle a German shepherd dog when it approached the fence at the back of his property. "We know the wolf was headed this way by what we read in the papers," Mr. Stampos said, "so we figured we had a right to defend ourselves. For the time being, people should keep their dogs locked up, or more unfortunate tragedies like this are going to happen." A special detachment of men from the sheriff's office, along with a volunteer from the Plechette City zoo, were spending the weekend patrolling the area south of Willowbrook in an effort to capture the wolf. Suburban gun owners were advised to lock up their weapons and telephone the police if they caught sight of anything resembling the animal.

"This business about the wolf is incredible, truly incredible," Chase said. "Incredible and poignant. Don't you see the potential in it? Old Simmons Speigner, the zoo director, is going crazy trying to capture the thing before somebody shoots it. Meanwhile, madmen with guns riddle their picture windows with bullets and shoot all the family dogs in sight. In the interstices between flying bullets and newspaper columns, the animal careers around the city, popping up here and there like the Scarlet Pimpernel. A loose wolf hasn't been seen within two hundred and fifty miles of here for a hundred years, maybe longer. We don't know how to deal with it. It's like science fiction, a time-travel story. In a way, it reminds me of what I was telling you last night about Lamont Von Heilitz." His gaiety seemed forced to Elliot, but Margaret overrode it.

"Oh, Chase, now you are being fanciful," she said. She looked around the dining room of the City Club, where they were seated at the "Denmark" table—theirs because Brooks Denmark had graced it—with Dr. Laubach. A black pianist, whose wispy melodic traceries of show tunes were upheld by a bassist and snare drummer, played dance music at the edge of the room's tiny dance floor.

"Elliot," Margaret said, tapping the back of his hand with a finger, "I think I see an old friend of yours across the room. Isn't that Lawrence Wooster there, with that lovely blond girl?"

"I hope not," Elliot said. He looked. "My God, it is. Don't catch his attention, please." He had no desire to trade banalities with Lawrence Wooster, now, as his mother had written him, a junior trust officer at the Guaranty Bank. "Oh," he said, "Lawrence Wooster," remembering, and looked at Vera. She seemed dismayed at the prospect of meeting Joanie Haupt's lover.

"No, please, Mother, he's not a friend of ours."

"It sounds as though you're hiding a deep dark secret," said Margaret, her expression piqued and amused at once. "I certainly don't mind your going out all afternoon without saying a word about where you've been"—Vera, who knew that he had seen Kai, slowly stirred the ice in her vodka martini—"after all, you're a grown man now, but I can't *imagine* what could be amiss with dear little Lawrence Wooster. Not that he was ever really little, but he certainly seemed harmless enough. Why, I can remember on your commencement day from Walkins how all the boys in your class smiled when he went up on the stage to get his diploma. *Cum laude*, too, as you were, Elliot. You were all grinning like Chinese cats! Mrs. Wooster wasn't three rows away from us, and she looked terribly proud."

His father surprised him then: he reached out to his wife and gently patted her wrist. "Let's not bother with Lawrence, if the children don't wish to see him." Even more surprisingly, his mother took the rebuke gracefully. She merely nodded, saying, "Well, it's just that he was at Walkins with Elliot." Chase received the sentence gloomily.

He had been uncharacteristically quiet all during the day, Elliot recalled. Shortly after coming in from some errand, he had gone into the lower living room and played the piano—played it for hours. Elliot had left the house shortly before lunch, and when he returned, frustrated and upset by Kai's long recital, Chase had gone upstairs to work. This was not unusual in itself, but what work could he possibly have on the twenty-third of December? Vera had wanted to hear about his conversation with Kai, but he had been unable to recount that long story. "Yes, he told me some things," Elliot had said to his wife, "but I think it was in confidence." Of course he could not tell her that the book was very nearly published; that much was certainly in confidence. "He said a lot of things about Harrison Upp. He thinks Upp might have betrayed him to the Nazis and had him put in the camp. Kai had false papers with a Jewish name." Vera looked sickened. "What else?" "He said they lived like rats on a garbage heap." Vera said, "I don't think I can hear any more about it. But did talking about it seem to help him? I thought . . ." Seeing his helpless look, his shrug, she had nearly cried. "I don't know, I just don't know," he answered. "I guess he had to talk about it, yes."

Elliot thought that Kai would never have told him his story if he had not blurted out his disconnected version of the Ronnie Upp affair, and, perhaps, if he had not been so shaken, arriving at Kai's apartment—or if Kai had not noticed that his files had been disturbed. But, that granted, what followed? Elliot could not help feeling that Kai had been doing more than unburdening himself of a complicated and painful memory; the old man was too reticent for that. He had almost certainly caught some echo of Elliot's affair with Anita; if not the affair, then his distress about his former mistress, and the long story had been intended as a reflection of that confusion. He had offered his own history as parable. Some insight seemed to elude him here, his brain could go no further, and he had given up. Elliot remembered ruefully the clarity he had felt that morning, driving along the edge of the lake. It had been no more than a respite: it was certainly not the grand summing-up he had thought. The false sighting of Upp, Kai's history, these had drowned that momentary optimism in doubt. All afternoon, he had longed to call Anita.

So his father's unexpected retreat into Fats Waller and then into the upper part of the house had not been unwelcome. He could have bantered with Chase only feebly, and that would have evoked irony, superiority, a lurking sadness. Chase was pleased that he had signed Dr. Laubach's statement; it was undoubtedly the reason for the doctor's inclusion in tonight's outing, though dinners at the City Club normally were almost overbearingly "family" occasions. The doctor, at least, seemed to have nothing serious on his mind. He had chattered to Elliot about music, flirted with Vera, and was now gaily talking to Margaret about, of all things, the Walkins School, where he and Chase had been classmates.

"It was discipline," he said, "that made Walkins a great school. Chase's grandfather and Brooks knew that if they wanted a first-rate private school in Plechette City, they had to have high standards in every department of school life. That is why they began with an entirely English staff, and I am convinced that it was no mistake."

"No one any longer thinks it was," said Chase.

"Of course not, Chase."

Years ago, Walkins had been known as "the English school," even after no more than two or three English masters remained on the staff. But, Elliot thought, why in the world did Pierce Laubach feel it necessary to utter this belated loyalty pledge? The label had helped, in time, to attract pupils: Brooks's whim had, like nearly everything else in his life, earned its way. Listening to Dr. Laubach go on about the school, Elliot was puzzled by the man's entire manner, which seemed propitiatory and soothing.

"A great school, and a real contribution to the community," he was saying. "It helped change the face of the city in an entirely positive manner. When it turned out artists, they were *real* artists, like your son, not layabouts and beatniks."

"The school was never intended to nurture composers or any other kind of artists," Elliot said. "What it wanted to make was businessmen. They might name Pittman and me in their list of distinguished graduates, but that's only to leaven the loaf. Everyone else is a banker, like our friend Wooster across the room, or something equally respectable."

"Well, you can't expect them to honor failures," said Dr. Laubach.

"No, Elliot is right," said his father. "Our goals might have been too narrow from the start. The school turned out four generations of real-estate salesmen and lawyers and manufacturers of roofing and siding. Babbittry, in a way." He reflectively sipped at his drink.

The club's manager, Jacques Mortrent, approached deferentially. In atrocious English, he said that the young lady's lobster would require another fifteen minutes to cook, and asked if they would care to order another drink before it came.

"Oh, *let's*," Margaret said. "We should celebrate. Elliot is going to be on television tonight." Chase gloomily nodded.

"Canadian Cloob for Mrs. Denmark . . ." He took their orders and left them, snapping his fingers at a waiter.

"Excuse me a minute," said Elliot, rising. "I won't be a minute." He walked out of the dining room, skirting the other tables and the polished tiny dance floor.

He rushed down the curving staircase to the ground floor, passing a portrait of Brooks Denmark glaring from a brass frame, and crossed the dark red carpet to the members' lounge. An adolescent in a striped waistcoat inclined toward him, but Elliot shook his head, smiling, and the boy again stiffened into military posture, glancing, as he straightened, at his wristwatch. The members' phones were on a table at the back of the lounge. He pulled the fat floppy book from the table and turned to K. In a moment he had found the name, and he began dialing. The waiter discreetly wandered to the farthest side of the lounge. Elliot heard the telephone ring twice in Anita's house, and looking up, saw himself caught in a huge gilt mirror. He looked distracted, out of place, his hair fluffed at the back of his head to puff out behind his ears. *Useless*, he thought. He began to smooth his hair. He did not know what he would say to Anita. Merely talking seemed of value. But as the trilling continued, he looked into the mirror again and saw himself staring out like a bushy simian in the zoo, and felt helpless, foolish. The telephone continued to ring.

His real place was upstairs in the dining room, with Vera and his father, helping them in their difficult evening. Both were unhappy, Vera with her usual sensitivity, Chase uncharacteristically somber and unironic. He had so far not uttered a word about Nun's Wood. The conversation had revolved, like a great clumsy dancing bear, about the Denmark family. Dr. Laubach had been at pains to describe the essential Denmarkness of Walkins School. It was as though the Nun's Wood battle had already been lost. It was lost, of course, but those two men would not admit it. They saw themselves as leading a squadron of wheelchairs and ball gowns up over the ridge, about to conquer the sharpies and carpetbaggers; holding the line, like pathetic Lamont Von Heilitz, like Hilda Usenbrugge's Preservation Society. The recollection of the

scattered old woman brought it back to him: Chase had mentioned an appointment with Walter Lyte, the chairman of the Monuments Commission. He had
tried to save Brooks's clock. Elliot had forgotten all about it—forgotten it once
again, and it was terribly important to his father. He smacked himself on the
forehead with his palm. His father must be feeling wretched. The boy across
the room jumped as though Elliot had shot himself. He lifted his eyebrows,
took a step forward. "No," said Elliot, "no thanks, I'm all right. I just remembered something."

When he entered the dining room and threaded back through the tables,
Lawrence Wooster and his wife, the wife in Elliot's chair and Lawrence back-
straddling another chair pulled away from the next table, were cozily seated
with the Denmarks. Vera, he saw, was in agonies. Lawrence leapt up and
embraced him.

"Ellie!" Wooster pounded his back, then held him at arm's length. "You old
sonofagun, I haven't seen you in years! You look terrific!" He scrutinized Elliot's
face like a drill instructor: Elliot saw the amused glance at his hair. Lawrence
Wooster, for his part, looked considerably more substantial than he had in prep
school or at the Columbia mixer. Now Wooster's semicrewcut had grown out
another inch and his waistline ten, his shirt sparkled, his teeth gleamed. His
jowls owned a bankerish heaviness. "Sylvie and I were sitting across the room,
and I said to her, 'I bet that's Ellie Denmark over there with his wife.' And
you know I had to recognize your father and mother, even after all this time.
Gee, Sylvie was a little shy about meeting you, she adores your music." Elliot
perceived Sylvie's hard glossy vapidity as she gave him a voter's smile, and
understood Vera's agony. "And she knew we were friends, so I promised to
introduce you. We've been having a nice little powwow with Vera while you
were away."

". . . away bleeding the lizard," he expected Wooster to say, but, like his
haircut, his manner had changed. He wanted Wooster to leave as quickly as
he could suggest it, but said, with a passable facsimile of sincerity, "How nice
to see you again, Lawrence. It's a pleasure to meet your wife. Hello, Sylvie."

The girl lifted the corners of her mouth. "An honor to meet *you*." She was
pretty in a blond, Breck-shampoo barbecue-clique way, but her voice was
mesmerizing. "We are both looking forward to your concert. Lawrence had
told me that he was a friend of yours from school, and I was so anxious to meet
you." Another alto like Andy, with a grainy New York accent.

"Well, tell me," Wooster said, "Ellie, how do you like being back in the
Fatherland? You going to stay over there forever?"

"I don't really know. How long is forever?" He wanted these people to leave.
His mother was looking at him with disapproval. "We have a nice home, so
we'll probably stay a few years. Vera's got a teaching job, and I can get a lot
of work done there."

"You've got to come out and see our new place," said Wooster. "I'll throw
a log on, and we'll have a real talk."

"Well, I'm not sure," said Elliot. "I'm a little busy . . ." He shrugged.

"No kidding, I'm really serious. How does the old country look to you? We were over in France ourselves last year—stayed in Sarlat, in the Dordogne valley. You know the place? I had two weeks off, and we just lazed around in the sun. Skipped all that tourist stuff they've got around there. Then we hit the Riviera for a couple of days, and then went back up to Paris. Paris is a really feline city, am I right? Of course, I love Gothic, and Sylvie's crazy about it, so we were right on home ground there. What I say is, you can't beat the food and the churches, but I sure didn't get anyplace with the citizens. You have that trouble?"

"No, we don't," Elliot said. He smiled.

"It helps if you can speak French," said Vera. She was enjoying Elliot's general awfulness.

"Well, anyhow, come on, pal, answer my question," said Wooster. "How does the old country look to you?" He tapped Elliot lightly on the arm. "Are you going to be one of these expatriates?"

"Technically, I suppose I am an expatriate, yes. I live out of the country." Chase looked disturbed, while pretending not to listen. "But I'm not sure what you mean by the word. I don't think of myself that way. I'm just trying to get my work done."

"That's my Ellie, always working." Wooster beamed down at Vera and his wife. "Can you folks make it out to my house next week? Let's nail it down for, say, Wednesday."

Vera looked up questioningly at Elliot. "I'm not . . ."

"I think I'll have to call you back about that, Lawrence. We have a number of important engagements, and I can't remember the dates."

Sylvie stood up. She was taller than either Lawrence or himself. Her face, seen in relation to her body, looked surprisingly petite, insectlike, less hard. "That's a pity, Mr. Denmark." Clearly, she had registered the rebuke to her husband, though Lawrence had not. "I'm afraid I've been sitting in your chair. Lawrence and I were just on our way out, and I don't want to keep you standing."

"Just give me one more minute, will you, sweetie? I haven't seen Ellie in years."

Dr. Laubach, patently bored with Wooster, turned back to his conversation with Chase.

"Have you seen any of the old Walkins crowd? Who have you been seeing? I mean you and Vera, of course. Catch up on any old friends?" Wooster crossed his arms over his chest, his smile a shade less confident.

Sylvie—really a towering woman, Elliot saw—went to her husband's side. She was clearly uncomfortable. She knows what the bastard is angling for, he thought. "I'll go to the powder room, Lawrence, and wait for you downstairs. Lovely to meet you both, and you, Mr. and Mrs. Denmark. Dr. Laubach." His father and Pierce Laubach stood in the same instant. Sylvie strode from the room, holding her head up. Her posture suggested tension, strain: Elliot remembered the bright glossy face she had turned to him, and felt a tingling of shame that she had seen his contempt for her husband.

"Join me just a second, will you, Ellie?" Wooster nodded to the entrance of the dining room.

When they were standing together in the hall at the top of the curving staircase, Wooster said, his whole being aglow, "I guess you've been talking to Joanie Haupt. So you know the story."

Elliot was wild with impatience, thinking of his father. "No, I don't. It's not my business, Lawrence. Why don't you go downstairs and join your wife? She seems to be in trouble."

Wooster was impervious to even blunt suggestion. He seemed radiant with pleasure. "Sylvie's okay. It's the rag or something. They lose a lot of calcium right around then, did you know that? Calcium loss makes them irritable—it's all in Adelle Davis. Sylvie's a good wife, but a little high-strung, you know what I mean?" Before Elliot could protest that he did not, Wooster continued. "I just don't want you to get the wrong idea about me and Joanie. She's been upset for a couple of weeks, but I want you to know one thing—I take care of her." He beamed at Elliot, then looked down at his shoes. "I know we weren't ever the closest friends in the world, but I've been following your career, Elliot. I bought your record, and I got tickets for your concert. I just want to speak my side of the story, that's all. Joanie and I had a little fight the other day, and she told me she was going to talk to Vera. You could have knocked me over with a feather. I didn't even know she knew you people. I begged her not to— Christ, I even slapped her. So she called me a sadist. That's all there was to it. Otherwise, we've got a terrific relationship, a really *human* relationship. It makes me feel bigger than life, Ellie. No shit, it's the greatest thing I ever did in my life. And listen—she's terrific in the sack. The best sex I ever had in my whole life, really *human* sex." He leaned back and put his hands in his jacket pockets. "Isn't that what it's all about, Ellie? Maybe I can tell you something for a change. Taking care of someone like Joanie, that's what it's all about, that's the body's message. Now don't you know that's right?"

"I know you have to be careful to restrain illusions from messing up facts," Elliot said. "I have to go back inside, Lawrence."

"In a minute. I just told you the facts. Sylvie's a Catholic, I can't get a divorce. Besides that, she is a child emotionally. I kid you not, Sylvie's a great woman in her way, but I'm married to the last Victorian lady. Believe me, I know what I'm talking about. She still believes in stuff you only find in books. Well, we're all sensual creatures, aren't we? It's got to be expressed. An artist like you, I don't know why I'm telling you. What I'm talking about is experience, and you must have seen plenty of it. Did you ever read *The Prophet*?"

"You're an ass, Lawrence," Elliot said. "I'm sorry, but I have to get back to my table."

Wooster straightened his back. "I'm going to forget you said that, Ellie. That's your temperament speaking, not you. Maybe you could use a good Reichian analysis. I might just be a clod of a banker, not some fancy composer, but I think you could do with some real experience in your own country. You might be getting a little out of touch." He brightened again. "*Touch*. Now there, you see—"

"Thanks for the advice, Lawrence." Elliot extended his hand. "I think you'd better join your wife."

"Just one more thing. I think your father is doing a bang-up job on this Nun's Wood business. Ronnie Upp is an egotistical little pain in the ass, and a cold-hearted bastard to boot. I'll tell you what your father has, Ellie. A social conscience. I signed his petition myself, and I was happy to do it."

"That's nice. I'll tell him," said Elliot wearily.

Instead of saying good-bye, Wooster held up the two first fingers of his left hand, and then went down the staircase to the ladies' lounge. It took Elliot a moment to understand what the gesture meant.

"Just because Lawrence Wooster's manners are execrable is no excuse for yours to be the same," said Margaret, neatly parting a section of duck from the bone. "He is a child and his wife is as high-strung as a kitten. I wouldn't be surprised if you terrified them both."

"I think that Wooster probably terrifies his wife himself," answered Elliot, "and I couldn't even make a dent in him, much less scare him. He gave me the peace sign when he left."

Dr. Laubach giggled. "Bankers are becoming very mo-dish," he said to Chase.

"Wooster is a lout and a bore, no matter how modish he is," said Vera. She looked glaringly up at Elliot. "And I'm sure I know what he wanted to brag about to you." She'd had another hysterical telephone call from Joanie Haupt that afternoon.

"I'm sure I don't care what it is," said Margaret. "His wife is much too good for him."

Elliot merely nodded. "Did she know anything about music?" he asked Vera.

"She plays the guitar."

"Modish bankers must have modish wives," said Dr. Laubach. "Lawrence Wooster is one of the signatories of our statement, Chase. He was the only man in his trust department to sign, I believe."

"Well, maybe Walkins did something for him after all." Chase did not appear to be elated by this possibility.

"Folk songs?"

Vera smiled. "John Dowland."

There was silence while they ate.

"Elliot," Chase said after a while, "there is something I must tell you. I'll try to put a good face on it, but it is bad news."

"I know what it is. I realized downstairs that you'd been unhappy all day." Looking over at Vera, he saw that she had noticed it long before. It was, he could see, the reason for her suggestion that morning that he talk to his father.

"Astute of you," said Chase. "Forbear from interruption, and I'll describe the morning's events. Pierce has been kind enough to join us tonight, and I'll have to ask his forbearance as well, for he already knows what I am about to say."

Dr. Laubach seemed to glitter with amusement. "Genre painting," he mystifyingly said. "A Dutch tavern scene, with glandular cases loitering in corners. Or a Goya court scene, with Walter Lyte as crippled king, and Ronnie Upp as *éminence mauve*."

"Oh, I'm sorry," said Vera.

"Pierce can always keep me amused." His father ignored Vera's condolence. "This morning I went early to Walter Lyte's house to speak with him about having the Monuments Commission give their sanction to Brooks's clock tower. Pierce joined me, at my request. Pierce and I were shown into the foyer, were divested by a mollusk of our coats, and left to admire the parquetry. In a moment, another old lobster showed us into a drawing room. He lifted a sheet from a couch and two chairs and mutely bade us sit. At this point, engulfed in the gloom of Victorian breakfronts and maroon carpets, I felt like a figure in a Charles Addams cartoon. The image was miraculously apt. A whirring noise emanated from the hall. Piqued, I went to the doorway and looked up the staircase.

"Shock followed shock. Gliding like Bela Lugosi down the banister and supported in an evil network of straps, a gnome was delivered to us in a chair. The gnome in his basket reached the bottom, fumbled peevishly at a lock, and was dropped gently onto the floor—still in his basket, of course. The basket began once again to purr, and brought him forward. As he motored toward me, I saw a gigantic dry old head, eyes nearly closed and as rimmed with black as though they were rubbed with kohl, two withered, palsied hands, a trunk and body that seemed no more substantial than the thin antlers on the drawing-room walls. All of this midpart was encased in a substance curiously like a winding sheet—or so I thought, until I realized that it was simply a shirt which had twisted about him so thoroughly that I could not see the buttons. He raised a sparrowlike paw to my hand.

"I escorted him back into the drawing room, where he stationed himself before the couch. Pierce and I sat there, in the dark sea of tartans and sheets, under Walter Lyte's Egyptian gaze. With some difficulty we brought our matter to his attention. He squinted up his face so that it appeared to be one huge spot, liverish in hue, and offered the information that a charming Mr. Hop had been to see him months before, and had obtained his signature on a paper. The Monuments Commission had mightily moved, and could not move again."

"A sub-stantially true account," said Dr. Laubach. "Though somewhat embroidered, my old friend."

"Upp had already been to see him?" blurted Elliot. "He took care of it before."

Shockingly, Chase's face dissolved. "He took care of it," he said. "We're finished. There's nothing I can do. That senile old man signed Upp's papers months ago. Upp convinced him that the tower was structurally unsound. He said it's a miracle that it's stood as long as it has." He held his hand over his eyes.

"Come, Chase," Margaret said firmly. "Let's finish our meal, and we'll go home to watch Elliot *do his thing* on television."

"He's a filthy plotter," said Chase, still holding his hand over his eyes. "Forgive me."

"He's been like that all day," said Margaret. "You know the pride Chase has in the family. He's never forgiven Robert Denmark for selling the factory to Ronnie Upp, and the tower was the last straw." She glanced sharply at Elliot. "He wanted to talk to you in private about it this morning, but when you went out without saying a word, he went back to pounding the poor piano."

"I would have stayed, if I had known," said Elliot. "The last thing I wanted to do was desert him."

"I know that, Elliot, but he doesn't. All that talk about Lamont Von Heilitz—don't you see that he thinks he's like that poor silly old man? Chase thinks the whole world is slipping by him. It's the worst thing that can happen to a man, to see himself as outmoded. Or impotent. Or useless. All of this sending out checks to criminals is his way of convincing himself that he is still in touch. That there is still something he can do." She nodded toward the bust of Freud on the bookshelves. "It's why he bought that bust. He wanted to show that he's at least in the right century." It was the first time in years that Elliot had seen his mother so angry. "Do you think that Pierce Laubach would react in the way your father has? That any of his old friends would? Chase is a deeper man than any of them. He's also an optimistic man, as you are, but the past few years have been hard on him. When he came in this morning with Pierce, he was ashen, positively white in the face." She sat straight-backed in one of the new chairs and looked at him sternly.

"What can I do?"

"Talk to him. Let him talk to you."

They heard a car door closing down in the drive, and Elliot went to the window. Dr. Laubach's Lincoln was taking its stately way out toward Lake Point Drive; the taillights flashed once, and the long car drifted like a barge northward.

"Letting people talk to me seems like the only thing I've done since I came here," he said. "When I buy a pack of cigarettes I think I'm going to get a life story with my change."

"I told you why he wanted to talk about Lamont Von Heilitz, Elliot," said Margaret. "Your father thinks he was born thirty years too late."

She stood and joined him at the window. Dr. Laubach's Lincoln was still moving northward, going heavily against the whiteness. He felt her hand smoothing the hair at the back of his head. "He's your father, Elliot," she quietly said. From the upstairs living room, the television set dimly burst into theme music. "Let's go see how you look on television," she said. "He's proud of you for this, you know."

Chase and Vera were seated before the set, where an oval-eyed woman was caressing a soapbox. From the couch, his hands toying with the huge transparent cigarette lighter, Chase gave Elliot an uncomfortable, embarrassed glance from the August sky of his irises. He smoothed down his necktie with one hand. "It just started," he said. "Mr. Edwards has promised us a 'slam-bang show for Christmas' and told three sub-Johnny Carson jokes." He looked critically at the crease in his trousers.

Margaret sat beside Chase on the sofa and took his hand. Elliot leaned on the back of Vera's chair, not knowing if he would be able to watch himself turning into a spouting didactic fool. "Are your parents watching this mess?" he said. Vera turned her head to him, and nodded.

"It's all right," she said.

A zoom shot: Ted Edwards in a chair before a fireplace, leafing through a magazine, then Ted Edwards' face, sleek and gangsterish, filled the screen, as if in amazement. The audience laughed. "I was just getting to the juicy parts." He opened his mouth, winked, closed his mouth. "Well, they won't let me tell you about it," he said. "But it's nothing that doesn't happen in kitchens all over America." More laughter. "Our first guest is a luscious bit of southern honey who graciously gave us a little"—a long pause—"of her time before she starts filming her next picture. One of the greatest actresses of our time: *Lola Walker!*"

To enthusiastic applause, a woman strode onstage. Her hair was achingly red. Halfway to her chair, she did a parody bump-and-grind, kissed Edwards, and mock-demurely sat on the guest's chair. "Ted dear," she wheezed, "I wanted to sit on your lap but the management said it was reserved." Whistles, laughs. "I *told* them there was room enough for both of us."

"Does anybody want a drink?" Elliot asked. Chase shook his head, and Margaret and Vera both said no. "I think I'll make one for myself, then."

A long pan of the audience, which Elliot had scarcely noticed when he was on the stage, walled behind the cameras and the lights: rows of women with open mouths, some waving hands, a poster reading FREMONT HS WOLVERINES, a few stunning girls in the front seats.

"I'm going to make that drink," Elliot said, and pushed off from the back of Vera's chair. A local commercial came on the screen.

Elliot went to the door as Edwards' face reappeared in mid-syllable, saying, "And now, something a little different. Plechette City, currently in the midst of a civic Waterloo, a blockbuster rezoning issue to decide the fate of many acres of woodland, is also the birthplace of one of our finest modern composers. I've been talking to this man downstairs, and I think you'll find him as charming and entertaining as I have. Let's have a hand for a real force in modern music, Elliot *Den*mark."

He walked before the camera: always a surprise to see yourself this way. Elliot hung just inside the door, watching his image shake hands with Edwards, his gestures a little stiff, then take his chair, jerking up his trousers as his father did. The image-Elliot, big solid face like his grandfather's and hair curling over his ears, tilted his head toward Ted Edwards, crossed his legs. Compared to Edwards, he seemed somehow unprofessional, unfree. "I never heard all that stuff about the city," he said to his parents and Vera. "I was away off to the side, and when he said my name, somebody gave me a push."

"Shhh," said Chase, who was leaning forward, his hand still held by his wife.

"That's what I thought," said Vera. She smiled at him.

"It's why they wanted you on the program," said Chase, his mustache bristling. "Pure and simple."

On the screen, Edwards' razor-slit eyes were narrowing, as if in concentration. Then, Elliot had not noticed the amusement in the man's face, the lifted eyebrows and nods: he looked like a man giving serious attention to a child. Then Elliot's own voice, as the camera stayed on Edwards' face for a moment: ". . . the breathing of the music." Edwards opened his eyes and took a conspicuous breath. Then a medium shot of the two of them, Elliot talking, moving his hands; but the damage was nearly total. Edwards had managed to communicate seriousness to him while the camera recorded urbane amusement. "Composers need system to characterize space," his voice was saying, "and they need not fall back on the tradition of the centralized hierarchy of triads. All this is Germanic and nineteenth-century, the kind of music we know best." "*Do* we?" said Edwards gaily, and the audience laughed again. Elliot left the room.

He made a drink in the kitchen and sat beneath the rows of shining pots on hooks. He tried to make his mind empty. What else could he do, except what he had done? But the fiasco of the interview seemed of the same fabric as his humiliation and confusion before Kai, Ettenheim's insolence, his perpetual turmoil over Anita, the whole business of the petition. Andy French. From the hall, he could hear Vera speaking quietly to her parents on the telephone. That was another mess. He finished his drink and moved into the hall, passing Vera. She winked at him.

The television set had been switched off. From the end of the hall he saw a spreading green-tinted light which meant his mother was in her office. Elliot continued back to the living room. Chase was standing by the big windows, looking out at the black lake, hugely visible through his reflection, and turned to him as Elliot entered the room. His change in mood was immediately apparent. He was beaming, his eyes clear and brilliant. "They'll have to get the ice cutter out soon," he said. "The whole harbor is icing up. Vera is talking to her parents? Your father-in-law must be something less than pleased by all this." He waved a hand in the direction of the blank television screen. "Herman has no one to blame but himself."

"No, Herman was very good about it," Elliot said.

"Of course. I had forgotten that he drove you down there for the taping." He was standing very straight before the windows. "Son, I've been in the dumps all day long, but you've lifted me right out of them. I can't tell you how proud of you I am. That was a very brave thing you did just now."

"Just now I went into the kitchen and had a drink."

"Whenever."

"And it wasn't very brave. I was just tricked into it. Edwards was playing me along and then when I was ready to say anything at all, he brought up Nun's Wood."

"But the way you did it!" Chase moved his arm emphatically down and across his chest, fingers balled. It was a gesture of forceful approval. "You put it so judiciously and yet so firmly. And I didn't know that Upp owned some land out near Richmond Corners—that was a very telling point."

"I'm not sure about it," said Elliot. He sat heavily on a chair. His reflection looked at him: skin the color of egg whites against the lake's flat blackness. "I mean, I'm sure about the land, but I'm not sure that it means anything. Or that my talking about it will change anybody's mind."

Chase went softly around the room, patting at his suit-jacket pockets. "Don't you fool yourself, Elliot. You've done us a real service by what you just said. We've been making news in Chicago too, if you're not aware of it. What we are doing in this city is significant, and you gave the reason for it precisely in what you said to Edwards. Upp's plan would be an ecological disaster."

"I know I said that." Elliot saw the dying fox, its small teeth exposed, at the bottom of the brush pile in Nun's Wood.

"Of course you did!" Chase had by now circled the room, moving exultantly, and he sat on the couch across from Elliot. He picked up the transparent lighter and tossed it in one hand. "I want to tell you something. While the women are out of the room is a good time, because I don't want Margaret to hear it."

He leaned forward and gently set the lighter back on the coffee table. "I've been in utter despair for this entire day. It seemed to me that everything I believed in was dying, on its way out, all the traditions of my family. I kept thinking about one of the boys I mentioned to you earlier, Ralph Nieder, who was the brother of George Nieder, a good friend of mine at one time, before he went off to Pittsburgh to buy into a chain-store operation. Ralph killed himself when he came back from Europe, you know. He'd been a hero—there was a picture in the *Herald* of Eisenhower himself pinning a medal on Ralph. Well, I was at the Nieder home when the girl, Ralph's girlfriend, called. She was hysterical. George kept telling her to calm down and explain what happened. Finally, he went sort of white, and shouted into the phone. *What? What?* He raced out of the house, and I followed him. We drove out to Lone Pine Lane, just past the Hunt Club, where the girl lived with her parents. Then there were as many farms out that way as houses, and Ralph's girlfriend lived in one of the new houses set back from the lake. Better frontage than we have, and a lot more of it. It looked pretty peaceful as we drove up, but when we got inside, the girl was screaming. She had blood on her fingers where she had touched him, and she was smearing it on the walls, on her dress—she looked crazy. George and I ran upstairs to her bedroom, and found Ralph's body up there, naked on the girl's bed. *On* it, not in it. He had broken in when she was at school, gone upstairs, taken off his clothes, unstrapped the false leg the army gave him, and shot himself on her bed. It was the worst sight I'd ever seen in my life, and it's stayed with me for the past twenty-five years.

"Now, listen to me. Today I was thinking, Elliot, if that might not be the right way to finish things off after all. I could see Ralph's point. But I was wrong, Elliot, wrong as wrong could be. And that's what you've done for me. Despair is no answer. I feel full of plans again."

Chase's new enthusiasm, couched in such terms, was nearly too much for Elliot. "I don't believe you were thinking of killing yourself," he said.

"Who said I was?" Chase drew himself up again and pursed his mouth. "I said I saw his point. That's all I said. The sight of young Ralph lying there made quite an impression on me, kid. No, no, no"—he was shaking his head vigorously—"suicide is a coward's way out, a low unmanly way of canceling your problems. And poor Ralph Nieder had his leg blown to bits by a German mine, and he couldn't deal with the adjustments back to peacetime. Two powerful motives—besides those, he'd been a boy who never thought beyond the end of his nose. If that is the organ in question. But today, I was thinking about him with more sympathy than I'd had before."

"I see," said Elliot, not wanting the moral lesson he knew would follow.

"Why, certainly you see. You're a Denmark. The way to conquer your problems in this life is to face them out, squarely, to take the worst and not knuckle under to it. . . ." There was more, but it was all familiar to Elliot.

When they were lying together in Elliot's single bed, Vera said, "Don't feel bad about that program, Elliot. Your father needed something like that. I was so *sorry* for him when he started to cry. By the end of the program he was back to himself again."

"So I learned."

"And my parents weren't too bad about it. You know how Daddy is—he said one more oar in the water wouldn't stir it up much more. Mother was a little bitchy, but in kind of a nice way. She says that more people are calling up about the wolf now than about Nun's Wood. They all want the alderman to rush over to their houses with a shotgun."

She put her hand on his chest: a light cool density against his skin. Elliot, sensing some ultimatum, bent his neck so he could see her face. "He said, 'If your husband is such a genius, why can't he buy me a Rolls-Royce for Christmas?' "

"Jesus, I've had an incredible day," Elliot said. In seconds he was asleep, still holding Vera to him.

In the morning he moved sleepily to one side and found that she was still in his bed. She tentatively moved her hand to him, and his mind just clearing from a dream, he entered the soft immensity of their mutual pleasure as if it were the means of restoring his coherence. For minutes at a time, he thought they were back in their house on Villa Beauséjour.

19

"How do you feel about this?" asked Elliot. He was parking his mother's car six houses down from Anita's house, before the only vacant curb space he could find on the block. "It looks like a big messy party." He gestured at the other cars illuminated by the soft nighttime shine of the streetlamps.

"I'm not sure," said Vera. "You're not really talking about the size of the party, are you?" Her face, lightly touched with makeup, which made her seem abstract to him, a harder and more complicated version of Vera, gleamed toward him in the light from the dashboard. A moon, a continent. "You've seen her a couple of times since we've been back, and I haven't seen her at all. You didn't sleep with her, did you?"

It was what she had wanted to ask the previous morning, before he had left for Kai's apartment. The question now seemed to come from the personality suggested by the makeup: yet it was merely another proof of her courage. "No, I didn't," he said. "I didn't even want to."

"Then she's just another woman who lives in Plechette City. A person I used to know. I suppose you're closer to her than I am. That's all."

"It's just a friendship now. I get a kick out of seeing her. And that's all for me." Saying this, having said it, he felt a yearning toward the condition he had just defined, as if the emotions he had felt rumbling and barking within him on the first night he had seen her again—a thinner Anita bearing the traces of a bruise—had been willed, created. Kai's story about Harrison Upp stirred within him, then dissipated like fog before strong sun. He would ask Anita his question. He would talk with Ronnie Upp: Elliot managed to stifle the feelings that arose with the name.

Vera leaned across the seat and kissed his cheek. "It's too cold to sit in the car when we have a nice messy party to go to. Let's go inside where it's warm." She turned her head toward the window, where heaped snow mounted to the top of the lock's thin column. "I'll get out on your side."

He climbed out onto the street. White narrow stripes showed the progress of the plow's razor, traces of snow above a glasslike ice interrupted by the duller material of the asphalt, and he said, "Watch out, it's slippery." He held out his hand and helped her from the car. Vera wobbled, lurching toward him, and then steadied herself. They moved slowly on the street between the twin rows of cars. Fifteen yards before Anita's house, Elliot released Vera's arm and ran ahead three long strides that became a swooping glide along the ice. The winter air needled at his face. He staggered, one of his feet slipping sideways, then windmilled his arms. "Elliot!" called Vera. He knew he was going to fall: he fell in that instant. The whiteness broke and dissolved before him into points of light. His back hurt. Elliot opened his eyes and was looking straight up toward the black sky. A single enormous star hung above him.

From the porch, in the cold anticipatory moment before the bell answered, they could see through the windows into the living room: the bright edge of the tree, a shifting mass of people holding drinks. A steady buzz of voices overlay the music swelling from the speakers. For an instant, it seemed to Elliot a summation of all the parties he had ever been to, lively, jumbled, a bright erotic confusion.

Anita, flushed, opened the door. "Elliot and Vera, come on in, dears, I was just wondering where you were. I'm so happy you came!" Elliot followed Vera through the door into the foyer, Anita taking Vera's arm.

They put their coats in Anita's study, across the little hall from the dining room, where the big dark table was covered with chafing dishes and plates of hors d'oeuvres, salads, spreads. A group of men had collected around the impromptu bar at the end of the room. As they walked by, shedding their coats, Elliot saw Rubin and Heldenweit, two of the members of the Melos Quartet, juggling plates and their drinks back across the main hall to the living room, but he said nothing. There was time ahead for all that. In the glimpse he had, the living room seemed as crowded as it had looked from the porch: a moving wall of people. Himmel glanced toward him, raising his glass. His mouth opened.

"Andy and I may have overextended ourselves," said Anita as she closed the door to the study. "You can see what kind of a madhouse we've got here. We just went around inviting people for weeks ahead of time, and unfortunately, I think they've all shown up!" She exhaled, leaning back against the door. "But here we are, together again at last. I'm so happy you're here. Let's just relish the few seconds we've got before all your other admirers sweep you away." Anita blazed out at them, her green eyes moving from Elliot to Vera, then flicking back. "Promise me you'll stay for a long time," she said. "I want to be able to talk to you."

She's overdoing it, he thought, but Vera surprised him by saying, "We'll probably stay until doomsday, Anita. It looks like a lovely party."

"At the moment it looks like Dante's fourth circle to me, I'm afraid. I just don't know what to do with so many people!"

"Let them take care of themselves," said Vera. "How are *you* doing?" In Vera's voice, lower than usual, and in her stance, her head a fraction forward, Elliot could read her impatience. She did not want a reunion scene.

"Dear friends and sweet people," was all Anita said.

"Well . . ." said Vera.

"It's time to feed you to the lions." Then she moved closer to Elliot. "You were wonderful on Ted Edwards' program. I was so proud of you, Elliot. You make me so happy, you really do."

"How did Ronnie think I was?" Still looking at Anita, he saw Vera, barely disguising her impatience, begin to move toward the door.

"Oh, Ronnie knew all about it. He was there in the audience when you did the taping." She reached sideways, still glowing at him, and took Vera's hand, intercepting her progress. Vera looked skyward. "You'll see him tonight, and he'll tell you about it. Ronnie is very eager to see you, in fact. Now—to the lions."

She opened the door and they went into the dining room; immediately they were swept into the party, and Elliot lost sight of Vera.

"This isn't a party, it's a menagerie," said Himmel. He gave Elliot a glass and half-filled it from a bottle in his hand. "La Kellerman and *la jeunesse* invited every other person in sight. Old-fogydom, us Agee-alcohol set, cheek to jowl with the with-its." Himmel splashed liquor into his own glass and then set the bottle on the bar table. "The with-its, Miss French among them, are blowing their minds out in the television room."

"Why are there all these kids?"

"Half the university symphony was invited. It's by way of being your party, Denmark. You're lucky Ettenheim isn't here to do his Tito Gobbi act in the midst of the festivities." Himmel's beefy face slackly indicated glee. "Where's the beautiful Vera?"

"I lost her getting through the dining room." Elliot looked over heads. In a crush by the door, he saw Vera talking to the dean. "She's talking to Jaeger," he said.

"The nincompoop? Watch out, my boy. He's going to try to hire you back, if he can remember your name correctly. Look—" Himmel grasped his arm and spilled some whiskey on his trousers. "Let's us scout around and see if there's any available maidenly beauty. My wife is at home minding Saul. She never quite forgave Anita's not apologizing for the time Mark hit the kid with a hammer. Nor Andy, for that matter. Andy damn near makes her shit in her pants."

"She does look a little wild," Elliot agreed.

"Wild? She glares like a hungry tiger. The only time I tried to talk to Miss French, she damn near scorched my eyebrows. How do you get on with her? I saw your car parked out in front here for a couple of hours when Miss French was home alone."

"I couldn't say," he said, wanting to change the subject.

A tall thin familiar-looking girl in glasses was touching his sleeve. She greeted them both by name.

Himmel's demeanor changed. "How nice to see you, Roberta. Have you been introduced?" The girl shook her head, tucking her lower lip between her teeth. "This is Roberta Potocky, Elliot. One of your cellists. I think she wants to tell you how wonderful you are."

"You're unfair," the girl said to him. "I just wanted to say—" Here she looked at Elliot, who saw that the girl had a fragile, brittle kind of prettiness. She reminded him of Sylvie Wooster.

"Thank you," he said.

"Well, that's all I really had to say."

"I'm happy you said it." The girl still hovered by, clearly hoping for more. "You don't think I'm too much an ogre at rehearsals?"

"I love it when you're like that," she said, and blushed so hotly he thought she would faint. "And I saw you on television yesterday night, and I thought you were wonderful. He *was* wonderful," she said to Himmel, looking for support, "wasn't he?"

"He was a dream."

"I thought I was a buffoon."

"Oh no, you were perfect." The girl smiled up at him, bit her lip again, and fluttering her fingers, said, "I'm looking forward to the concert." Then she backed away into the crowd. Elliot watched the top of her head move toward the living room.

Himmel clapped his right hand about the elbow of his left arm, raising his left hand in a fist. "Perfect!" he bellowed. "Perfect."

Carrying their refilled glasses, they elbowed through to the living room. Near the tree, Anita waved at them before turning back to a furry young man in a denim suit. He could not possibly be Ronnie Upp. "Bob Cratchit, believe it or not," Himmel breathed in his ear. "That's his real name. He's in the psych department. He and Kellerman have long tender discussions about white rats."

"Have you seen Ronnie Upp?"

"Wouldn't know him if I saw him," said Himmel. "Not unless he drove that Jaguar into the room. I see it parked out in front of here now and then. Cratchit now, he drives a dune buggy."

"*Here?*"

"No, you pedant. On the beach. He gave a lecture about the psychoaesthetics of dune buggies and tattoos to the Student Union Forum one night—what is he doing in this room, though? He ought to be snuffing out his consciousness upstairs with the kiddies."

"One of the new academics."

"One of the newest."

On the other side of the room, Elliot saw Vera talking to the black cellist from the university symphony. As he watched, she laughed at something the boy said, and held out her palm toward his own. "No *way*," he heard the boy saying, "no *way*." He and Vera both laughed.

"I'm telling you," Himmel said, "you could do worse than Roberta Potocky. A trifle skinny, but she's got a great little tush." He swirled his glass. "I'm dry," he said, and pushed his way back to the bar.

*   *   *

—You're Denmark. You're sweet.

He had maneuvered his way to the front of the room, looking vaguely for Anita, and turned to see an ample girl, her red-blond hair longer than Anita's used to be, bubbling up at him.

—You don't know me yet.

—Sweet sweet sweet.

"I don't like that adjective." He smiled at her starry eyes.

"Where's your head, sweet Denmark? Do you want to turn on with the real people?"

"No," he said. "I hallucinate."

The girl held her cupped hands up to her eyes. "I see you," she said. "I really, really see you."

"What do I look like?" He sought for a ready excuse to separate himself from the bubbly girl.

"A biiig bear." She made her voice gruff. "A coyote. A sad man."

"———"

Hearing a female voice enact a wordless slide from a perfect D flat to a perfect G, he turned, his ear tingling. Then he met disappointment. It was Rosa Heldenweit, chubby wife of Ernst Heldenweit, violist for the Melos Quartet. He had met her no more than three times before, once over thin sherry at a music-department party in Thatcher Hall (now uprooted and replaced by the concrete-and-glass of Usenbrugge Hall), once at a stuffy gathering at Jaeger's house where she had talked about her son Raymond, accepted on early admission to Harvard and a gangly surly lump he had later encountered at a party, the third of these, at Himmel's house, where Rosa had snubbed him, then an hour later confronted him with the words: "Why don't you ever invite us over? Ernst and I have been wondering." Quoth charmer Raymond: "Forget it, Mom, he's a snob." A worse disappointment was her company, two men standing as if in straitjackets, each expressing by rigidity his disdain for the surroundings. Wattman and Donadio, musicologists and coauthors of *The Poverty of the Modern*, where he had been given a caustic footnote. (Donadio, in the infinitesimal flurry after publication, had written an article for *Gramophone* on "Surveying New Composers" in which Elliot's work was described as "engagingly arid.") Wattman and Donadio looked no happier to see him than he felt seeing them, but Rosa Heldenweit, still pursuing a world of perfect sociability, put a plump hand to his wrist. "Elliot, I thought it was you. Ernst told me he'd heard you were back, but I forgot all about it until I saw you standing there." She smiled, full of baffled goodwill.

"Yes, it's me," he said.

"Denmark," said Donadio. Wattman twitched his shoulders in a gesture intended as a greeting.

"Hello, gentlemen," he said. "Still pursuing the good?"

Wattman showed his teeth. "Always the comedian."

"Ernst would love it if you would come to our house for cocktails," said Rosa. Elliot could imagine the Heldenweit cocktail hour: South African sherry and damp things on crackers, while Heldenweit mumbled complaints about Himmel. He invented an excuse.

"Hold on a sec there, Denmark," said Donadio. "Do you still like that stuff under Stravinsky's name in the *New York Review of Books*?" He was alluding to a dusty series of arguments, conducted with a choked fury on Donadio's part, from his second year of teaching. "Wouldn't you say the old boy has been getting awfully thin lately?" He smiled aggressively. "You subtract all that overrated wit, and how much content have you got?"

"About enough to make three other composers. Or twelve musicologists." Elliot laughed. "What are you working on now?"

"Caustic, aren't we?" said Wattman. "That's a pretty poor defense, I hope you know that."

"We're doing a book on Elgar. *Elgar's Musical Failure*."

"Maybe just *Elgar's Failure*," mused Wattman.

"I didn't know that he'd had one," said Elliot.

"You're going to have to learn," snarled Wattman, "that you can't joke your way out of serious discussions. I'm convinced that going to Paris was the worst move you could have made. That hothouse-Boulanger atmosphere, that superficial glossy chasing after fame, that worldly-wise atmosphere, that *avant garde* posturing, whatever, that's all bad for your work."

"You're beginning to talk the way you write," said Elliot.

"Hold on a sec there, Denmark, we're trying to make a point," said Donadio.

"Give me a call when you've made it," said Elliot. "Good-bye, Rosa."

He went back through the crowd to the bar and refilled his glass, took two long swallows, and then refilled it again. The whiskey ignited in his throat and burned unpleasantly down his chest. Someone in the living room changed the record. Elliot heard Roberta Flack sinuously gliding through a key change.

Elliot sipped again at his drink and started to walk away from the bar. "Oh, Elliot," he heard Jaeger saying, "what a nice surprise to see you here." The dean separated himself from a group and came toward him. "We've all been following your career very happily. You've done some very impressive things during your sojourn abroad."

Elliot thanked him.

"You've freshened your drink? . . . Then perhaps you wouldn't mind stepping into a quieter area to have a talk with me." Jaeger led him out of the dining room into the hall, where they could talk undisturbed. Several feet away, a boy Elliot recognized as the tympanist from the symphony was leaning up against a girl, prisoning her against the wall and talking to her in a fast undertone. When Elliot and Jaeger approached, he looked up and, glaring at Elliot, led the girl up the staircase. "I must say, I haven't been at a party quite this . . . exuberant in a number of years," said the dean. "It rather reminds me of my student days."

"It reminds me of my grade-school days," said Elliot.

"Oh, things have changed in the university," Jaeger said, not quite appositely. "Some of the formality that might have bothered you years ago has been erad-icated." Jaeger was thinking of the stir that Baltz had created, Elliot saw. "We've tried to follow some of the newer lines of thought, you know, in an effort to adjust to changing realities. For example we now have only three required courses for music majors—or is it two? Something in that line. And the piano requirements for the M.A. exam have been severely moderated. I don't know if you keep up with this sort of thing"—Elliot shook his head—"but I think you will find that we here are very nearly in the vanguard of educational reform. When I go out and talk to various groups, raising funds, you know, and ex-plaining our program, I'm quite surprised to see how radical we've become." He laid two fingers on Elliot's sleeve. "It may be an improper time to broach such a suggestion, Elliot, but I'd like to sound you out on possibly returning to the university. You were quite an asset to us in those days, my boy, and we'd be terribly proud to have you with us again. I'm sure everybody in your department would agree."

Elliot smiled wryly into his drink. "Well, thank you," he said. "But I'm doing quite well on my own, and teaching does take up a lot of time."

"I think you'd find the salary a recompense for any time lost," said Jaeger. "And of course, as a distinguished composer, you wouldn't be expected to teach more than four hours a week."

"Four hours?" asked Elliot. It was less than the chairman taught.

"If it meets your approval."

"What would the salary be like?"

Jaeger coughed delicately into his hand. "It's as yet an unofficial offer, Elliot, so I can't say anything definite. And you know that we've had budgetary problems for the past two years—cutbacks in federal spending play havoc with our salary systems. But as you'd be coming in with a good deal of substantial work behind you, and would perhaps be able to bring in other distinguished musicians and composers for brief visits, I think I'm free to name an approximate figure of about . . ." He named a figure which made Elliot with difficulty restrain a shout of triumph.

"How much?" he asked, for the pleasure of hearing it again.

Jaeger repeated the figure. He began to frame an elaborate sentence containing the words "pride" and "responsibility," when the boy on the landing above them shouted at the girl with him. "Come *on!*" "*No,*" the girl shouted back, "*I'm not going to,*" and began sobbing. The boy turned to glare at Jaeger and Elliot staring up at him, and then wrenched the girl into what Elliot knew was Anita's bedroom.

"That's quite a figure," he said.

Soon after, fortified by another drink, he went upstairs to the television room. Bob Cratchit and a handful of students were watching *Niagara,* and Elliot smelled the heavy perfumed odor of marijuana. Marilyn Monroe's figure was surprisingly lush, more Gibson Girl than Elliot had remembered. "You fucking zombies can't even see that face," Bob Cratchit was saying. "You were all wetting the bed when they made this movie." In the students' laughter, Elliot saw the bubbly girl he had spoken to downstairs. She said, "It's Mr. Coyote." Andy French, seated in the darkness on the couch, saw him, and left the room to join him. She kissed him in the hallway. "Hello, Mr. Coyote," she said. "Cheryl is right. That's who you are."

Then they were back downstairs, going through the dining room to the bar. "Miss French," said Himmel, bowing. "Be easy with me, Miss French." He was drunk. Bob Cratchit had followed them, and he threw an arm around Himmel's waist. "Let me introduce you two music pushers," he said to Nathan. He was being aggressive, edgy, and he looked at Elliot as though he wanted to fight, his teeth shining from his beard. "Two humanists," he said.

"Nathan, I think you need some fresh air," Andy said, ignoring Cratchit.

"Then walk me around the block," said Himmel. "Up and down and around and around. I'll take you away from this discount Hemingway."

"Your imagery is out of date, friend," said Cratchit.

Someone was touching Elliot very gently on his arm.

"Well, what do you know about Ravel?" asked Himmel. "What do you know about any music, for that matter? I won't be drawn into altercations with these *chazzers*."

Cratchit insinuated his bulky upper body between Himmel and Andy. Elliot saw with surprise that he was shorter than either of them. His furry head waggled; he seemed to be speaking into Himmel's jawline as though it were a microphone. "The trouble with you humanistic types is that you can't follow an argument," he was saying. For all his bristling, it was a weak rejoinder, and Elliot thought that the furry little man would not actually start a fight. "I don't care about that," Himmel said in a lordly way. "You are a gnat." Cratchit began to froth. There was some dialogue Elliot couldn't hear—people had begun to crowd around. A man put his hand on Cratchit's shoulder. "Systems are my lifeblood, Tiny Tim," retorted Himmel. Cratchit balled his fists, bent lower, and sent a left hook to Himmel's chin, sending him sprawling backward. A girl screamed.

The pressure on Elliot's arm subtly increased. A soft Oxford-accented baritone voice said, "Couldn't we go someplace quiet to talk, Denmark?" and Elliot turned around to see a short, suntanned, smoothly boyish man with a neat cap of hair which concealed his ears, square amber glasses, and he knew that the man was Ronnie Upp.

"We have a lot to talk about," Upp said. "I think you know who I am."

"Yes, I know who you are," said Elliot. Of whom did the grown Ronnie Upp remind him? It was not Ted Edwards, though they shared a sleekness which suggested that both men lived much of their lives before mirrors. Then he recalled an evening at a high-vaulted drafty French theater, and remembered an actor he had seen in a provincial production of *Hamlet:* a miscast elaborate young man, ambitious and uncomfortable in the role of Fortinbras. A tense black-tighted young man, an unlikely victor. But perhaps this was a new model for conquerors. "You're the man behind the scenes," he said.

Upp glittered at him, as if delighted by this description of himself. "Your imagination is not always that theatrical," he said. "Perhaps it's the setting." He moved his eyes, mockingly, toward Himmel. A girl was dabbing at the cellist's mouth with a handkerchief. Elliot saw that Himmel's chin was splashed with blood—he must have bit his lip when Cratchit's blow landed. "If we want to have a reasonable discussion, I think we should go elsewhere."

"Hello, Ronnie," said Andy, her voice cool. She left Himmel's side and came slowly toward them.

"Andy, my dear." Upp looked at Andy like a man keeping a disagreeable secret. Elliot looked around the crowded dining room for Vera or Anita, but saw only Donadio and Rosa Heldenweit, piling their plates with food from the table. The mood of the party downstairs had shifted: though the music was still raucous, the people were quieter, drawn into groups. Himmel had left his chair and was weaving into the kitchen. No more than five or six people had seen the fight. "I want a word with Elliot Denmark, and then I'll join your lovely party." He lifted one hand and placed it atop the other. "Before it dissolves."

"That will be sweet, Ronnie," said Andy. "Anita will be pleased that you are here."

"Let's go into the study," said Upp. He cocked his head toward the other side of the room. "I think we might take our drinks with us."

As they walked into the hall from the dining room, Elliot saw Vera and Anita, close in conversation, moving across the entrance to the living room. They were outlined by the pattern of books behind them. Neither woman looked in his direction.

Upp lifted the coats from a padded leather chair and dropped them on the floor. Elliot took the only other chair in the room, high-backed and hard before Anita's desk. It resisted the contours of his body, and this discomfort increased his unease at finally being in the same room with Ronnie Upp. The shorter man looked at him steadily, his dark eyes shining with amusement behind the big tinted lenses. "You don't look terribly cozy," Upp said, and Elliot remembered more accurately who it was Ronnie recalled to him: not the tense young Fortinbras, but the photographs he had seen of Ronnie's father, with his glittery edgy glamour. His hostility, brushed up like a cat's fur by Bob Cratchit, began to fade. "It's been a long time since we've met, Ronnie," he said.

"So it has. And in the meantime, nearly everything has happened. Everything of importance to either of us." Upp's smile was brilliant, boyish. "But I hope you don't mean to waste time reminiscing."

"Where do you want to start?"

"I think we could begin with Anita, don't you?" The smile continued. "She is important to you, I gather."

"I don't think that's your affair, but I don't see why I shouldn't admit it. She is important to me. She's a friend. I feel involved in Anita's problems, and I want to give her any help I can."

"And your notion of help is to talk about how much you love her. Then she tells you she loves you, and you both feel better." Ronnie's smile tightened. "Or you try to alarm her with horror stories about killing animals in Nun's Wood. Anita and I have few secrets from one another. We met in Cambridge— our Cambridge, not theirs—when Frank Kellerman was doing a year's research. I owned the house they rented. And we became friends there. Three people from Plechette City—we were very close. After Frank's death I took up much of the payment for Mark's treatment. That may be a surprise to you."

It was.

"That's because you don't understand money," said Upp. "Your entire attitude toward the Nun's Wood business says that. Elliot . . . that foolish performance on Ted Edwards' program!" Upp looked at him gently, chidingly. "Do you really believe in that sentimental soap opera about ecology your father has been deluding himself into believing? I can't really imagine that you do. I'll confess that I was distressed to see you rambling on like dear old Hilda Usenbrugge. She's scarcely a reputable model, do you think?"

"I wasn't aware that I had taken Hilda Usenbrugge for a model," said Elliot.

"Yes, I think awareness *is* the problem." Upp smiled as if he had some secret knowledge.

Elliot could not define Upp's attitude. His tone, a schoolmasterly unctuousness, mixed confusingly with the slightly menacing glee of his manner. Two weeks ago Andy had told him that Upp thought of himself as superior to other people, and perhaps it was this condescension which was the key to his attitude. Yet condescension was usually a fool's refuge, and Upp did not appear to be a fool. Nor did he appear merely condescending. He seemed to be deliberately setting out to create unease.

"What distressed you? That I talked about your other property out there?"

Upp put his hands in his jacket pockets and sank deep into the padded chair, his face showing a mixture of surprise and incredulity. "That? No, that scarcely seemed significant. And it is not really significant, is it? Tell me, if your father were not fighting us on the Wood question, would you have bothered bringing it up? And with such vehemence?"

"I would have been happy to ignore the question altogether. But my motives don't change the action."

"I'm not going to let you take refuge in evasions, Elliot. But your honesty on the point is refreshing. So I will be similarly honest with you. It wasn't at all your talking about the other property or even your misguided references to me that I found upsetting. I thought it was a pity that you're wasting your energies on a foredoomed issue."

"Is that all?"

"It's also a pity that you waste them on hostility to me. I could do a great deal of good for you."

Upp was still slouching deep in the chair, his eyes shining at Elliot. Elliot sipped slowly from his drink. He felt Upp's tension like a wind; but that was not all he could feel. Upp's manner was that of a man concealing a trump card. That, and the tension he could feel in the man, began to make Elliot nervous again. It was like talking to a betrayed husband.

When Elliot did not speak, Upp went on. "Your father-in-law and I had a long talk about you the evening I dined there. I suggested to Herman—out of Mrs. Glauber's hearing, by the way—that I thought it might be possible to arrange a place for you on Ted's program. Ted Edwards is an old friend of mine, and I thought he could put you on his schedule. There are a number of other favors I could put in your way, if you were to go back to your main concern, which is making delightful music."

"Herman didn't . . ." Elliot stopped. He thought that Upp had shown his trump card. "The favor rather backfired. Herman seemed unruffled, however."

"He's a sweet man," said Upp. "Herman Glauber is unencumbered by ancient grudges."

"Well, so am I," said Elliot. "But I think this conversation is getting tedious. I don't think you need to buy up Nun's Wood, but you're not interested in what I think about that. You could be a hero and buy the place as a park. Probably I'm boring you. Why don't you say what you want to say to me?"

When Upp stood and walked toward him, Elliot expected to be threatened. Upp's handsome boy's face maintained its affability only with effort. He stood no more than a few feet away from Elliot, his hands still in his pockets. "I think I've said most of it. Let me ask you a question. How much money do you make in a year? Don't bother to answer. Combining your income with your wife's, fifteen thousand? Twenty? Most of that would be her salary. About enough to pay for the mortgage on your romantic home and buy score paper." The smile deepened, became more malicious. "You're an industrious ant, Elliot. You don't even live in the real world. You made a tiny substitution for it and convinced yourself you're comfortable there. Let me tell you something about money. I'm an expert on money—I respect its energy. Money is a metaphor, it has its own will. People like you make the mistake of thinking that money is a term for leisure or ease, when it is really another term for electricity, for war—for a hurricane of will. Where there is money, engines turn, darkness scatters, because there's a tiger on the loose, and you've goddamned got to keep it fed. Because it's the biggest tool in the game, Elliot, the one hand you can play that makes everyone else put down his cards. It's too bad you were raised as a rich boy, so you could never see it."

"Weren't you raised as a richer one?"

Upp leaned against Anita's desk, crossing his arms over his chest. "Let me tell you how I was raised. I'll condense it into an anecdote, so it won't bore you." He leaned backward on the desk, letting his heels rise inches off the carpet. Elliot noticed that he was wearing high brown suede boots. A dandy, he thought, like my father. Upp squinted toward the light. "At the time of the anecdote, I am eight, and we are in Lausanne. My father is having our house there redecorated, and men are in and out all day long. My mother is usually in bed, resting. Sometimes there are parties, where lots of young men play with me. Since it is summer I'm not at the *école*, and I can stay up late at night. One night my nurse, Martine, brings in a sheep dog during one of my father's parties. It's my dog. A surprise for me. The young men fuss over it, put ribbons in its lovely shaggy fur, make it drink champagne from bowls. My nice doggy. I went to bed—fell asleep on the couch, actually—very late, full of dreamies about my doggy."

He looked down at Elliot from his perch on the desk and folded his feet under himself crosswise. "Take a little sip of your drink, because here comes the heartbreaking finale. I woke up on the couch headachy and ill. The dog was whining and shuffling around the floor, where people had spilled food. The room was a mess, not just the usual mess from the decorators, but a sort of last-days-of-Pompeii mess. Broken glasses, spilled drinks, cigarettes. I saw the dog sniff around a wine bottle standing on the carpet, nose it over, and then lap up what spilled out. It was whimpering and yowling, crying, making a terrific racket. My father came fumbling out of a bedroom and down the stairs, still tying his bathrobe about himself, and I could tell by the way he was walking that he had a hangover. He was in an evil mood, and I tried to run away, but he grabbed me and pulled me out into the backyard. Then he went back in and pulled out the dog, which was still whimpering. 'Which would you rather have,' he said, 'this dog or a thousand francs?' I started to cry. 'I asked you a question,' he said. When I didn't answer, he went back inside, and then came back with his pistol. 'Choose,' he said. 'You shoot that wretched animal, and I'll give you a thousand francs. You can do whatever you want with the money.' He held it out to me. He ordered me to hold it while I made up my mind." Ronnie looked teasingly down at Elliot. "I was fascinated with the pistol, of course. All kids are. He'd never let me touch it before. Well, the dog looked sick. It was sort of baying around the garden. So I tried to shoot it without looking at it. I fired and missed. The dog ran toward the fence, but it couldn't run very well. I aimed and pulled the trigger and missed again, and then my father took the pistol and shot the dog in the head. He was a wonderful marks-man. Later he gave me fifty francs in cash and put the rest in my bank account. Bye-bye doggie. But when I was holding the pistol, my arm numb from the first shot, I remember thinking that if I shot my poor old hung-over bastard of a daddy, I'd have it all." He smiled at Elliot. Perched on the desk with his feet tucked under his legs, he spread his hands, palms up, so that the light gathered on their smooth pink skin.

Upp raised one hand, leaned over, and touched Elliot lightly on the forehead.

"If you are asking me what I think you are asking me, I think the answer is yes. I've always thought so." Anita sat across the kitchen table from him and looked at him levelly, her short mannish hair catching and glowing with the light. Nathan Himmel was slumped where they had put him, in a chair near the oven. "It was the act of a terrorized young boy, and he has been paying for that act all his life. And there's another thing. I don't know how much you know about Ronnie's father—"

"Too much," said Elliot.

"Then you know that he probably deserved what he got. He was undoubtedly an ill man, but illness is not an excuse for what that man did, for the cruelty, falseness, and deception of his entire life." The green eyes, now seeming almost depthless, looked at him squarely. "I think he was lucky to live as long as he did. And probably he wanted to die. He was killing himself with liquor, and his wife, in what must have been an intolerable situation, was doing the same. When it finally happened, I don't think that Ronnie himself knew that he was doing it purposely. I am sure he thought, with the largest part of his mind, that he was doing what his father would have done, shooting at a burglar."

Elliot sat quiet for a moment. "I don't know why I'm talking to you about Ronnie, since you are determined to defend him."

"I'm defending him only because I know him much better than you do," she replied. "Dear one, for years I've been putting Ronnie together. Don't be foolish about Ronnie Upp."

"I'm trying not to be." After a moment, he said, "As I'm trying not to be foolish about you. What kind of thing do we have? What sort of connection is it between us?"

"Maybe that is up to you," said Anita. "But remember that for a year while we lived in the same city, you retreated into your marriage. What sort of connection did we have then?"

"A frustrated one."

"Because it was all we could have. You chose to have it that way."

"But it doesn't stop there," he said. "Sometimes I think I'm simply obsessed with you. I carry you around in my head. I probably think of you once every ten minutes. There's an area in me that simply belongs to you." Kai, and Kai's story, stood as a rebuke to sentimentality. "It might be that all we've got is friendship. Yet even if that's so, it is an exceptionally resonant friendship."

"One reason I love you is that you always say the right thing," said Anita, once more baffling him. "Dear Elliot, I love you. I depend on you."

"Well, you confound me." He rubbed his face with his hands. "You puzzle me. It's not a bad state—maybe just a sort of emotional polyphony. It's not always at the same strength, but it's always latent. At least I think it is."

Ronnie Upp's voice, rapid and gratingly English, came from the living room, followed by a burst of laughter. When the two of them had returned to the party, Upp had been immediately surrounded by Jaeger, Wattman and Donadio. Vera had been talking to Andy French, and both had looked questioningly in his direction when he and Anita had left the room together. Bob Cratchit and several of the students had left, but many others were dancing, in the small crowded space of the living room, to an old Beatles record. "All I wish is that you'd be more open with me."

He returned her steady gaze until Anita made a pouting gesture with her mouth and looked down at the table. "I've always been open with you, Elliot."

"Then why did Ronnie begin his spooky little tale by asking me about you?"

She did not reply. Her face down-tilted, she showed him only the broad plane of her forehead beneath the sideswept short blond hair.

He asked his question. "Is Ronnie Mark's father?"

She lifted a radiant, assertive face. "I don't know. He could be. Ronnie thinks he is."

Himmel, who had begun to snore, stirred in his chair. He lifted his head. "*La belle Denmark,*" he said. "What time?"

Elliot looked at his watch. "One-thirty," he said. Himmel nodded exaggeratedly, then leaned back to rest his head against the sink. "Hemingway," he muttered.

"I could never have told you," Anita said. "But I'm glad you thought enough about it to ask. I knew Ronnie for a long time before we met. He had the virtue of not being an academic. And I wanted an affair, and I had one. Oh, Elliot . . ." She glowed at him. "I really am happy that you guessed. Ronnie is no threat to us."

"His power doesn't go that far, you mean." He put his hand to his forehead, which had begun to throb. His back still hurt from the fall on the street. "Does Andy know about all this?"

"I've never told her. Andy works for me." That was Anita's gift: to imply that all other relationships were secondary, insubstantial. "And you know how she feels about Ronnie. I think she's a little jealous of him."

"Well, I'm not sure that I'm not jealous of him."

"You dear fool," she said. "I told you I felt like a nun."

Her statement filled him with an extraordinary relief. Anita's having a child by the odd, tormented Ronnie Upp could not shake his feeling for her. Now that she had freely admitted the truth of Mark's parentage, it lost the charged significance it had held for him. If the matter was of supreme importance to anyone, it would be Frank Kellerman, and he had slipped into history when his car had stalled on a freeway. Elliot thought that he could understand Upp now: he must have felt insecure in his relationship with Anita, on unsteady ground. Hence his bribes, his peculiar manner. He feared that Elliot would once more begin an affair with Anita, and injure his relationship with Mark. Yet at this moment he felt a grateful distance between himself and Anita—she was irretrievably apart from him. In all of this, there was a large, lifting, and complex relief.

Yes, Elliot thought, my real life is in Paris with Vera. Kai had been implying just this sense of detachment—it was the meaning of his story. He felt suffused with warmth. As he looked across the table at Anita, he felt an irresistible sexual stirring. He remembered the taut planes and soft hollows of her body, and wished to touch them again.

Anita was still talking about Andy. "She has been monopolizing me lately. Andy and I see one another for most of every day, you know. We work in the same department, and then she takes care of Mark when she's not with me. I'm afraid that the Kellermans have been absorbing most of her emotional life. I really have been unfair to Andy. Mark and I are a refuge for her, a sweet safe little den. We are very close, of course, but Andy has become sort of overprotective lately. I think it will be good for all of us when she finally leaves."

"And what about Mark?"

"Mark will be taken care of, one way or another."

"That's how you got *this*," he said, holding one hand up to his cheek. Anita nodded, her face defiant, almost warlike beneath the shining helmet of her hair.

"I was going to give Nathan some coffee," she said. The percolator on the stove was making a staccato popping sound. She walked around the table to stand beside him. "Why don't you come over here tomorrow?"

"If you want me to." His body seemed forcefully impelled to hers.

"Does your back hurt, darling? You've been rubbing it all night."

"I fell down in the street." He took his hands away from the small of his back and let them dangle, unsure of what to do with them. "It doesn't really hurt."

She began to stroke his back, slipping her hand underneath his jacket, with short intense caresses. Her hand was very warm.

"Oh, Elliot, have you seen the news? On television?"

"No," he said, "I've just been talking to Anita." But Andy knew that. She seemed gloomy and distracted. She had spoken to him as he walked past the sofa, carrying a drink, and when he looked down at her, she seemed small and defenseless, the tribal face showing an almost pathetic eagerness to talk to him. Elliot sat beside her. The couch was warm, as if someone had just left the place he now occupied. "What was the news?"

He could see Ronnie near the tree, talking to Anita and Roberta Potocky. Several yards away from them, and watching Ronnie Upp with great fascination, Wattman and Donadio were devouring the last of the food. When Wattman glowered at him, Elliot felt unreasonably elated.

"They showed your tower," Andy said. "That clock tower. The announcer said that new plans for it were approved, and then he showed an architect's drawing. It's going to be taller than the old one, but not so . . . grandiose. Did your father know that it was that final?"

"He just found out. He was upset at first, but he cheered up when he saw me on television."

"Because of what you said about Ronnie?"

He nodded.

"He's going to dedicate the new tower to Brooks Denmark, did you know that? With a plaque."

There were two reasons for her bitterness, and he chose the less complicated. "You are very unhappy with Ronnie, aren't you?"

"I'm unhappy, if that's the word, about his treatment of Anita. I'd like to see her free of him."

"I think she is free of him, in any important way," he said. When she merely looked at him, he said, "Why didn't you say anything about this when we went for that ride?"

"I didn't know how much I could trust you. How much you could be trusted."

"And now?"

"Now I know you can't be." Laughing, she patted his hand like a child's. "It's good that you can't, in that way. I wish the same could be said for Ronnie. Sometimes I think people should be a little more faithless. They'd be less screwed up." She smiled, still a little cool.

"I don't think I've seen enough of you," he said. It seemed to him that Andy had just echoed his thoughts.

But she looked at him as though she detested him. "Then why don't you come over tomorrow sometime? One or the other of us is sure to be in." Andy continued to hold her eyes on his. "Ronnie was just telling me you'd be around," she said. "I suppose he told you about trying to shoot that dog. It's what he tells people at parties."

"Well, I talked with your two women," said Vera. They were near the bookshelves, apart from the rest of the party. "And I had a short talk with Jaeger. Did he make you his offer?"

"He did, and it was a lovely offer."

"Are you going to take it?" Vera looked at him questioningly, her eyes full of danger.

"I don't think so. It was flattering, but I don't think I could live in Plechette City anymore. It's too complicated."

"Even with all your admirers?"

"I don't want admirers," he said. "There's something poisonous in it."

"She's pathetic," said Vera. She did not have to specify the "she." "There's something wrong with her. I feel sorry for her, and that's quite a reversal. It's like she's crippled somehow—or that she always was, but that she was too full of energy for anyone to see it. Or maybe she had you and whoever else she had to hide it. It was like talking to Joanie Haupt."

He could not meet the bitterness in her voice. "What about Andy? My other admirer?"

A light, amused look passed between them. Elliot was intensely curious about his wife's reaction to Andy French.

"Andy will do," Vera said. "Andy is straight. I like her. I think she should get out from under Anita's thumb."

In a little while there were only three or four people left in the room, and the Denmarks were not among them.

20

Elliot sat, holding a cup of coffee and the morning's *Herald*, in the dining room of his parents' house. Disturbed by his dreams, slightly hung-over, he had risen and dressed long before anyone else was up, and then gone down to the kitchen to put the pot on the stove. Now, fifteen minutes later, it was still only six-thirty and black outside. He'd had only four hours of sleep. Even Robert would not be up for another hour.

He had been pleasantly surprised to find the newspaper in the mail slot, entirely unsurprised by the contents of the front page. The headlines speculated about Vietnam and Cambodia. The President was to make a speech next week—when Elliot would be back, he thought with relief, in Paris. On the front page was a photograph of a captured Vietcong hung by his heels, surrounded by grinning South Vietnamese boy soldiers. He read the caption, skimmed the articles, and looked at a story on the bottom of the page. Simmons Speigner, the zoo director, had not found the wolf, which was thought to be wounded. One of the sheriff's party had apparently hit it with a long-range shot over the weekend. Speigner was quoted as saying that it might have found a secluded spot and died in the fields around the southern subdivisions bordering the airport.

The dining room was cold and oppressively dark. Elliot felt penned within it. He folded the paper under his arm, and took the cup and saucer across the hall, going up the short flight of steps to the upper living room. In the big-windowed room over the lake, he set the newspaper and coffee cup on a low table and pulled open the drapes.

The big room seemed immediately colder. Looking east across the black lake, visible as a denser darkness than the sky, he saw only a faint hazy ribbon of light on the horizon. The single lamp he had switched on glowed orange in the window, and Elliot could see the tall fluffy-haired outline of his body wrapped in a robe. Down at the edge of the lake, a few giant jagged blocks of ice shone a pale gray. His dream made it all ominous.

Kai's disturbing story was behind it, he knew—it weighed on him still. He had been walking through a grassy field, like those around the small farmhouse in Beynac he and Vera had rented one summer. The sky was black, shot with broad lurid threads of pink. Andy French had been walking up a hill about fifty yards before him; Elliot followed her, knowing that she was leading him to something appalling—he was impelled to go toward it. He smelled some sweet terrible odor. After walking a little of the way, he tried to run, but each step was made with great effort. After struggling uphill for some minutes, he saw what looked like one of the little prehistoric stone huts which had dotted the fields in Périgord. Andy looked at him coldly as he approached her. The scars on her face stood out as though they were about to come to life. He saw that there were bodies on the ground around the hut. He moved toward it, and saw that it was not a hut, but a pile of something shaped like one of the little stone constructions. It was burning. Small flames curled out at its edges like a hundred tongues. The odor grew worse. He bent to his knees in front of the burning pile, holding a hand before his face to shield it from the heat. In the tangle of arms and legs which made up the pile, he saw a corner of material, and pulled at it. One of the bodies came away. He pulled it out onto the grass and scattered ashes off its face. In the lurid glowing darkness he could not distinguish its features. It was a woman. Then he saw that it was Anita. He had come suddenly awake, his heart pounding and his mouth cottony, with an almost painful erection.

He had been dreaming of Anita for several nights in sequence. None of these dreams had been obviously erotic. Often he saw her alone in a room, her hair as long as it had been years before, spreading out in wild tangles over the white shoulders of her nightdress as she went around the room trying the doors and windows. Her face, even when she began to weep, retained an extraordinary calm, as if she knew she were a figure in a dream. In another dream a pigeon flew wildly back and forth in a skylighted chamber, battering itself against the windows at the top. He could not bear to think of the bird killing or maiming itself and he tried to catch it, but the pigeon was far out of his reach, skittering from window to window. There had been an odd specific terror in that dream, but last night's was the most harrowing. He had tried to fall asleep again, but the sense of threat and fear was so immediate that he could not. The blue wall on the far side of the room had seemed to be moving imperceptibly toward him through the darkness.

Anita still weighed heavily on his mind. But things seemed at last stabilized between them. His dreams to the contrary—and what were they but testimony to his sheltering sense of her importance to him?—Anita Kellerman had her own life in which she solved her own problems. His homecoming had shaken her weak connection with Ronnie Upp. This was teasingly satisfying to his ego. Beneath the sleekness and smoothness, Upp was an uncertain juvenile who resented Elliot's relationship with Anita. It was possible that he had undertaken the Nun's Wood business and the destruction of the clock tower to wound the Denmark family. No, that could not be true: his father had become interested only after Upp had made an offer to purchase the land. Now, however, Upp was no doubt delighted by the prospect of blocking the Denmarks.

Yet that was more his father's problem than his. In the cold gray darkness of the morning, Elliot felt that his own problems might be moving toward a clarification, a resolution. Anita had always possessed a significance for him that was nearly mythical; he had seen her as though she were a giant figure in an epical drama of liberation, and now he could approach her more practically, with a realistic love which honored their situation. Anita herself found no unfairness in the stringent conditions imposed upon them. He would have to see her again; if time could be found, today. His love for Anita, with all the distancing necessary in it, entailed like all love a responsibility: otherwise everything was loss and disorder and wild chaos.

He folded the first section in half and took up the second section of the paper, the local news. Alderman Jefferson Glee had given a speech at a black Catholic church citing the Nun's Wood affair as a white ploy to divert attention from the issue of civil rights. Was that good news or bad? Vandals had set fire to a fourth-ward junior high school. It was only six blocks from the school where Vera had taught, and Elliot felt a tic of relief that she was no longer working there.

Then his knee jumped as he saw his own name in one of the heads on the inside of the first page. COMPOSER DENMARK SPEAKS ON NUN'S WOOD. The story recounted his appearance on the television program, and laid great emphasis on his remarks about Ronnie Upp. "Ecological disaster," "reckless building," "the arrogance of wealth": he had actually spoken this drivel. The writer implied that he had spoken violently, decisively, as if he had used the Edwards program as a platform. Chase Denmark would be delighted by the story. Rona Bender would show the piece to her husband. All of this threw Elliot back into the dejection his dream had aroused in him, the sense that important matters were beyond his control. It must be the lack of sleep, he thought, but the idea only brought Anita's party back to him. In retrospect, it was a depressing evening. He saw Ronnie Upp's smooth face before him, talking about shooting a dog. He drank his coffee and reread the article, then pitched the newspaper to another chair and stared for a minute at the grim expanse of the lake. The room had become intolerable.

Upstairs, Vera still lay asleep in her bed, the pillow a little smudged with makeup. Elliot looked at her closely and then took off his robe and began to dress. He fumbled in a drawer for his old blue jeans and found them by touch. Then a clean shirt from the laundry, which he tucked into his jeans while sliding his feet into loafers. As an afterthought he pulled on a sweater. He closed the door and went softly downstairs. On his way out he took from the closet near the front door an old sheepskin jacket he had worn at Columbia as an undergraduate; worn and dirty, it suited his mood, and it was the warmest thing he owned.

It's too cold to walk far, he immediately thought, and decided to go only as far as the traffic lights at the eastern end of Jackson Drive, where it intersected Lake Point Drive. The *Herald* article was not enough to justify freezing oneself, though he could only guess at Tessa's reaction to it, and the discomfort she might cause. The evening he would have to pass at the Glauber house became gigantic in his mind, and he began to go south along Lake Point Drive, from time to time slipping on patches of ice, brooding about it. His nose and ears stung with the cold, but Elliot, far into his thoughts, scarcely noticed. He put his hands up over the collar of the jacket and held it close to his ears. When he reached the traffic lights, he absently glanced eastward, where the band of light above the lake had fractionally broadened. The streetlamps, still burning, canceled any sense that it was yet day. He continued walking. He remembered going to work this way years ago, driving in the winter darkness along the drive toward his morning classes. Now he could not recall what days he'd taught. His teaching life seemed impossibly long ago, the person he had been then lost. Everything was different and everybody had changed. He was a foreigner here. As if to confirm that he was alien, a cruising police car, the only automobile on the road, slowed as it went past, and the two uniformed men in it turned their heads to stare at him. Should he wave at them? They were clearly suspicious of him. Nobody walked down Lake Point Drive at seven in the morning.

Elliot remembered that he had no identification with him; it came to him that he did not even have a house key. The police car was now traveling so slowly that it was keeping exactly abreast of him. He was walking past the huge houses of Lake Point Drive, the great gray Gothic buildings. He could probably name the owners of three out of four of these houses—would that convince the police? One of them was talking into a radio. Elliot was suddenly aware of his ears and nose, now almost numb. One of the houses he was passing was almost certainly the home of Walter Lyte. Elliot shoved his hands deep in the pockets of the jacket and put his head down and continued walking.

The policeman on Elliot's side of the car negligently turned his head, and the car gradually picked up speed and pulled away from him. Humping his shoulders, Elliot continued on in the direction the car had gone. Now he was half a mile past the lights at Jackson Drive; the next traffic lights would be at the turnoff for the lake expressway. Far ahead he saw them glimmering red through the darkness, a little hazed by the oncoming of the sun. He had gone much further than he had expected to, lost in his brooding about the article and the party. But that the police had not stopped him had left him somehow buoyant, and he walked another block in a dislocated peace and lightness, almost relishing the cold. He began to walk consciously toward Anita Kellerman's home. It was much too early to find anyone awake or dressed, and he had no idea of what he would do when he got there. As Baltz had said, the activity was enough—he relished this walking, dressed in old clothes, to a woman's house. It was as though he had been translated out of his daily life into another existence, free of consequences—he felt fifteen years younger. He had a brief vision of himself and Anita talking about the newspaper article, both of them laughing: he was now so close to Windmere Terrace that turning off the drive toward Anita's home was irresistible. In any case, he had to stay away from his parents' house for at least an hour, so that Robert could let him in without waking the whole house.

Ten minutes later, when he was turning into Leecham, he recognized that the vision of Anita laughing with him in her old vibrant way over the reporter's misreading of his performance on Edwards' show was an impossibility. Ronnie Upp had interposed himself between them; he could no longer predict what might make Anita laugh. For a moment he felt as threatened as he had by the police car, a dark heavy helplessness. If everything—the country, his city, his parents—had changed, then Anita had changed most of all. Yet the optimism of his mood carried him into the reflection that the change in Anita was after all not an essential change—people could not alter so drastically. What he was feeling was much like the old rich emotional confusion she had caused in him, the product of what he had thought of as her masque. Now once more within it, he thought he understood its mechanism. Certainly none of *that* had changed: Anita was still Anita, and he was bound to her.

Her house seemed, like its inhabitants, unawakened. Looking at the quiet brick and wood of its face, he felt a wave of tenderness washing through him. The dislocations of being up so early in the morning! Elliot felt whole and entire, standing across the street from Anita's house. He forgot the newspaper article entirely. The house was much like its neighbors, all of them two-story modest structures with big Midwestern porches. Even in winter the brick's muted reddish-brown, interleaved with creamy mortar, seemed warm. His depression now seemed insubstantial—a vapor from the dream. The house expressed peace, comfort, mystery: Elliot was swept back into thinking of how many times, in what wildness or exuberance of feeling, he had entered it. Ronnie Upp was not Harrison Upp any more than Elliot was his own father, any more than Mark was Ronnie. One had to take short views, be grateful for temporary satisfactions. Herman's words, and Kai's, seemed to move in his bloodstream. He thought of Anita lying asleep in her familiar bed, her knees tucked up and her skin shining.

The sky had perceptibly lightened to a pinkish gray, a true city color, and the air smelled alive and clean. Whether he had meant it or not, Kai had said this, Elliot thought: he had cried not from hate but from love. Badly or ignorantly chosen, love remained, the best of all small satisfactions and stays against chaos. He remembered Anita's slipping her warm hand down the length of his back. Kai's story had been about the giving of love, and the sufficiency of the gift: any strong emotion is a gift of spirit to its object. After the death of Harrison Upp, Kai had been bereft of the person who had evoked the strongest response from him; and so was overtaken by a dim gritty tide of loss. Elliot felt charged with a rich emotional surge of meaning, everything understood; he felt once more American. He began to speculate on Kai's similarities to his father, and then saw with regret how far Kai had been diminished in his imagination. The world spun, a gaudy controlled toy, between Anita and himself.

He was freezing, freezing and awash in feeling. He could not merely stand on the street and watch Anita's house. In one of the upstairs windows, a light suddenly appeared. Someone was up. The streetlamps switched off with a surprisingly loud click. The day had begun. He crossed the street and went up the stairs to Anita's house, moving as if he were sleepwalking.

Before he touched the door he knew it would open. When he put his hand to the knob, it swung noiselessly in. He stepped quickly through. None of his actions seemed to entail consequences. He stepped across the narrow porch and gently pulled down at the old-fashioned handle of the next door, and moved into the hallway. The house was suffused with pinkish-gray light. The pale colors of the walls, the dark colors of the woodwork, were as if new to him, softened by the spreading light. He went forward in the hall and saw the ruined mess on the dining-room table, the cloth blotched and stained, plates and serving dishes strewn this way and that. A large silver spoon was stuck to the tablecloth with a congealed yellow mass that had been fondue. Three or four plates had been carelessly stacked at the end of the table, particles of food littered about them.

No attempt at all had been made to clean the living room. When Elliot went across the hall and stepped through the arch, his foot toppled a glass and released a gold spreading stain on the carpet. The smell of whiskey lifted to his nostrils like a ghost. There was a humming. From across the room he saw that the turntable was still revolving, the needle clicking uselessly within the blank end grooves. Elliot walked over the strewn floor and switched off the machine. Like the streetlamps, it made an abnormally loud clicking noise which hovered for a second in the air. The carpet was a mess, a bedlam. Overturned ashtrays, glasses, record sleeves, a necktie. Some white plates dotted the floor, two of them still half-piled with food. The whole house seemed to smell of ashes. In the odd light it all looked strangely beautiful, every object picked and defined by the beams easing in through the windows. Elliot went across the room to the source of the light, his old sheepskin jacket weirdly altered by it in color, and put his hand to one of the panes. The palm was black, his fingers nearly transparent. Our lovely temporary bodies. Then he pushed up at the frame and forced open the window. Cold air streamed over him.

When he turned away from the window and went around a chair back toward the center of the room, his foot crunched down on a pile of slippery black fragments. A record, he thought, stepping aside and looking down. It had been broken into quarters, then snapped piece by piece until it was in a dozen sections. He saw a fragment of the label. Printed on it was a dog cocking a floppy ear to the bell of an old gramophone. Red paper: RCA Red Seal. He idly separated the fragments with his foot. One piece bore the entire word MODERN. "Oh no," he whispered, and bent down. On another piece he saw:

MAINST
I Fiv
II Mom
RCA Sym
Pierre B

Marcas Regi
STEREO DYNAGROO

It was his record. Some of the grooves had been pounded into gray powder, and all were thickly fingerprinted.

Elliot jumped back to his feet and moved quickly to the shelf of records. The sleeve was lying flat across the tops of the other two records, and it was empty. In disbelief he went back to the small black heap beside the chair and looked down at it. Someone had deliberately broken up his record. The pieces lay in a jagged heap just now touched by the light. He could still see the word MODERN. The room's atmosphere had changed. The pinkish light seemed wrong, somehow sinister, threatening, as did the disorder on the carpet. He had to see Anita. His body did not fit the room. Stepping over the fragments of the record, he drove his ankle into a hard edge of the chair; a plate slipped away beneath his foot. He heard it crack. He felt sluggish, too large for the house.

For a second he hesitated at the bottom of the dark stairwell. A black line of shadow diagonally bisected the stairs: below, whiteness tinged with unearthly pink; above, dark gray of a lintel's shadow. Why had Upp destroyed his record? He could see the dapper little man effortlessly snapping the record, then grinding it with his boots—what for? He might have hurt Anita again. Elliot went quickly up into the darkness of the stairs.

On the next floor nothing suggested that anyone was yet awake. The hall was still night-dark, and Elliot kicked a small table with his shoe before his eyes adjusted. His ankle flamed again. A pot wobbled back and forth on the table's surface, rattling, and Elliot gripped it with his hands. Then he walked slowly down the hall to Anita's door. The doorknob was temperatureless to his fingers: the heat of a stone. He could hear no noise from within. He gently turned the knob and swung the door in.

Four identical eyes looked into his, two neat boyish heads lifted from pillows. They looked like brother and sister, or like sister and sister: when the man threw back the sheet, their bodies seemed for a second of clarity duplicate creatures, each pink, nearly hairless, molded . . .

The illusion broke when Anita scuttled back under the sheet in a frantic knifing movement and Ronnie came naked toward him across the small sunlit floor. "Go downstairs," he said, his voice powerful. "Now. I'll be with you in a second." In the next room Mark began to scream.

It was catastrophe. He collided with Andy in the hall, nearly knocking her down. She uttered something that sounded like "Poor Elliot," and then pulled her nightgown about her and rushed through the third door, from where came the high-pitched screams, as eerie and urgent, mechanical, as those of a rabbit in a gin.

The terrible screaming stopped when he reached the bottom of the stairs, cut off as if a pillow had been placed over the boy's face. The echo of the screams seemed a part of the walls, the high hysterical tone carried in the wash of pinkish light. Elliot cast back and forth in the living room, stepping on cigarette butts, feeling seared. His eyes burned. Had he known that Upp was in Anita's bedroom? Had he then invited this wretched confrontation? No, no.

"What are you doing to me?" he said when Upp, gathered into a blue silk robe and carrying the amber eyeglasses, padded into the room. He was as neat as a cat. "Where the hell is your goddamned car?"

"I'm freezing," said Upp. He ran his hand through his hair and gave a few dexterous fingerings which made it fall perfectly into place. He looked around, his mouth down-drawn, at the chaos, and slid the glasses over his eyes. The bows disappeared into thick hair at his temples. "The window," he said, and went across the room to close it. Elliot hoped he would struggle with the frame, but it came down effortlessly, as if on oil. "My car is where I left it, I suppose. There was such a crowd here last night that I had to park it blocks away, and then I had a beastly walk to get here. You throw off the heaters in these old houses, you know, if you let cold air get to the thermostats."

He shoved his hands into the pockets of the robe and stood watching Elliot. Beneath the hem of the robe his legs smoothly protruded, straight and hairless. He had small pretty feet. "You look terrible. I take it you've walked over— you're still carrying the cold with you. Why don't you sit down for a minute, warm up, and let me run you home?"

After a minute when Elliot sat in silence, staring at him, Upp said, "I like you. Let me take you home after you've calmed down. Neither of us wants the obligatory scene, so I can't think why we should suffer through it."

"I think you're despicable," said Elliot.

"No you don't. You're just upset." Ronnie stood gazing at him, his eyes soft behind the big lenses. "Isn't this room appalling? The worst thing about parties is cleaning up afterward. In fact, I only came last night because Anita very much wanted me to. I thought I should have the opportunity to talk to you longer, but as luck would have it I was captured by those two dreary musicologists."

"Wattman and Donadio."

There was a rushed rustling noise on the stairs, and Elliot looked up wildly, hoping to see Anita.

"Wretched polecats," said Upp. "Do people like that actually teach? They might be brothers."

Elliot was still numbly watching the door.

The complex noise continued, and Ronnie too turned his head, an annoyed expression on his face. Andy entered, half-carrying Mark, who was rubbing his face on the sleeve of his pajamas. When the boy looked up, he at first gaped at Elliot, his eyes wide and mouth in an astonished O. He began to scream.

"Stop that," said Ronnie. "Let him go, Andy."

The boy sagged, then went taut, his face terrifically red. His screams caught in his throat.

"Come over here, Markie," said Upp. He held out his hands, and the boy raced toward him, scattering a litter of ashes and cigarette butts from an upended ashtray. The soles of his feet were gray when Upp lifted him. "Nothing's wrong, Markie Markie. This is Mr. Denmark. He's a friend of your mother's, and Mother and Andy like him very much."

Andy glared at Elliot, challenging him to speak. "Is that all?" she asked, her eyes on Elliot.

"Yes, dear," said Ronnie. "Go upstairs and help Anita get dressed. Elliot's given us all a bit of a *turn* this morning."

Andy wheeled out of the room. When Mark stopped his sobbing, Ronnie took him back upstairs. In a little while he came down dressed, his suit and shoes different from those he had worn at the party. He drove Elliot home.

Elliot was back walking up the driveway at eight-fifteen, just in time for Robert to see him through the little window in the kitchen and to let him in the back door. "Cold for a walk, Elliot," was all Robert said. Elliot went upstairs and showered.

That evening at the Glauber home, Elliot saw that Tessa took his chastened manner as an apology for his remarks in the *Herald* article. "I suppose I'm the only one who thinks of Ronnie," she said. "He struck me as a very sensitive man." Vera, knowing that her mother intended this as the last word on a Delicate Subject, took her aside.

These were their presents: perfume, an antique brass bowl, a striped shirt, a nightgown, a copy of *Lives of the Composers* ("I told the clerk, give me something for someone interested in music. You can exchange it if you already have it," Tessa said), a John Updike novel, a game called Diplomacy. Elliot feigned suspense, surprise, gratitude, all the appropriate responses.

This is what Kai was telling him, he thought, *this:* you are your fate. He could not escape himself. His insights all seemed fledged, insubstantial, drained by the weak and corrupt creature he was. When he thought of Anita, he saw only the white pigeon of his dreams, battering against the windows. There was no emotion in it. Trumping him, Ronnie Upp had finished that.

21

Roy Baltz's question as to what the Plechette City *lupus* found to eat was drastically answered during the late evening of December 24, when the wolf attacked and severely injured a child, an eight-year-old girl, who had been making her way across a field near the airport. She had been playing with a friend and was coming home to dinner when the animal, starved and unseen, had come circling out of a ragged, dying stand of elms. The Christmas-morning edition of the *Herald* contained a picture of the field, rumpled and spotted as a bedsheet after lovemaking, interviews with the girl's parents, a photograph of the girl, thin and spectacled in her class picture, and an Olympian roar from the zoo director. A small army of sheriff's men was spending Christmas thread-ing the southern subdivision and airport fields.

"It's finished," Chase said, "it's dead already, blown away. Before this hap-pened, I was fond of the beast. It must be a glorious animal. If it had come down from wherever it came from in the summer, this would never have happened. One of Speigner's men would have shot it with a tranquilizer, and by now it would either be in the zoo or back where it belongs. A pity. Either way, a pity."

" 'Pity' is hardly an adequate word," suggested Elliot. "The girl will probably die."

"What else? 'Tragedy'? We don't have tragedies anymore. Our beliefs aren't large enough. Look at Vera's uncle downstairs. If anyone among us is qualified to use the word, it is he, certainly as much as the parents of that poor girl, but how does he spend his time? Writing a book about a dead poet. The man could be a witness, but instead he's elected to be a failed scholar. Though Kai Glauber does appear to be a charming man. He and Pierce Laubach would like one another, don't you think?"

Elliot did not answer, and both men looked for a time through the glass where Chase had parted the leaves and vines in Margaret's dark office. A single large bright star vibrated in the sky.

It was perhaps twenty minutes before dinner; Chase had left the upper living room, where the Denmarks and the Glaubers had been sitting uneasily over drinks, and when he had not returned, Elliot had gone upstairs to look for him. Chase had been muted all day, except for brief flashes of gaiety when, before the arrival of the Glaubers, they had exchanged gifts. Vera was delighted with the book of Italian paintings and he with the volume of Berg's letters to his wife she had given him. Then, Chase had been impish, dealing out the presents with barbed little jokes. With the Glaubers' arrival he had changed. When Elliot found him in Margaret's office, he was sitting beside his wife's desk, chin held in hand, looking out at the sky's first star, the room darker than the night.

"Earlier, only a few generations ago, everybody knew the stars," Chase said. "Earlier still, they were figures. Myths. The only constellation I can now distinguish is the Big Dipper. My father once pointed out Orion to me, and it looked like a great white-handed giant, but now I wouldn't know Orion if I held a chart of it in my hands. We don't read the Greek plays not only because they are not close to our experience, but because they are scarcely comprehensible. Margaret and I saw a performance of the *Oresteia* in Athens years ago, and it might as well have been a ballet—lovely movements, nothing more. It was like a trip to a costume museum." He fell silent.

"Are you going to come back downstairs?"

"And stop sulking up here. I take your meaning, Elliot. But I don't want you to think I'm merely sulking. Perhaps I'm just catching my breath—charging my batteries. Tessa Glauber is a bit of a burden. She's been lowering her eyes at me all evening, when she was not sitting there frozen-faced, and I was finally so uncomfortable I thought I'd come up here for a bit. This is one part of the house where there is always a feeling of purpose and accomplishment. How is your mother doing downstairs?"

"Perfectly."

Margaret had immediately made Herman and Kai feel easy in her home, guiding them by instinct into conversations where each could freely talk; an easier task with Herman than Kai, but she had kept it flowing by tying it to Elliot and Vera, and Kai could always talk about Elliot's music. He had been gentler with Elliot's work than was his habit. Only Tessa had resisted Margaret's efforts. She had a self-possessed, icy edge to her, smiling only with her mouth. Yet even Tessa had loosened after seeing that Herman was not going to be insulted. Elliot saw also that part of her stiffness was a fear that Kai would embarrass her. He explained this to his father.

"Then the woman's a fool," said Chase. "Kai is even a more old-fashioned man than I." He pulled open a desk drawer after switching on a lamp. "I really came up to find these old photographs of you and some of the places we've been." He took an old album from the drawer. "Looking at dull pictures is a marvelous way of calming the nerves. Let's go downstairs, son."

Somehow, the evening passed. After dinner—Tessa uncertain of how to deal with the problem of Robert, and solving it with an elaborate steely politeness—Chase led them all back to the smaller living room. After preparing them all with drinks, he began to play the piano. For Elliot, the success of this ploy was astonishing. Tessa was as pleased as a child by his father's rattly bouncy jazz, and after he had played "Ain't Misbehavin' " and "Rosetta," she began to call for other songs. "A Fine Romance," "The Lady Is a Tramp." "Oh, Chase," she said, her whole being expressing pleasure, "this is such a treat. I can see where Elliot gets his musical talent. Do you remember 'This Year's Kisses'?"

"One of the finest," said Chase. "Just you wait to hear how we old masters play it."

Where Tessa led they all followed. Herman, his face gleaming with amiability, a brandy glass prisoned in his fist, sat down on the bench and began to sing. Later, after Chase had left the piano, he led him aside and the two men had a long quiet discussion on the couch. At Tessa's request, Margaret took the other woman back to the upper living room. "I love your views," said Tessa. "Have you ever thought of changing to colonial?" Elliot and Vera went to Kai. When the two men went up to join their wives, Elliot could hear his father's light dry voice beginning to tell the story about Lamont Von Heilitz's party.

"Your father has worked a miracle," the old man said. "He's won Tessa completely."

"Uncle Kai," said Vera, "I think you're the miracle. Imagine what she would have been like if you weren't here."

"That's only partially the truth. Tessa has been afraid all evening that I might use the wrong fork or commit some other dreadful social solecism. Yet"—he smiled at them—"her real fear is not that I might be awkward, but that she might. At some level, she's proud of me."

"Oh, I know," said Vera. "Dear Kai."

"Just the usual mixture of feelings," he said, still smiling. "Tessa is too powerful for her own good. She has too much force to function as smoothly as she'd like."

"Well, she's honest," said Vera.

"She and your husband."

"No, Elliot is like you," said Vera. "You both have secret lives. Mother would like to, but she's not subtle enough." The rebuke in her words was modified by her kindness, and Elliot saw that she was talking entirely to Kai, not to him.

"If I have any secrets, they are all out-of-date by now," Kai said. "But even that no longer seems significant to me." He seemed relaxed, a little tired, paler than usual. "What we keep secret," he said, "isn't really half as important as what we tell."

Vera took his hand.

Kai was right, Elliot knew. He had been half-consciously waiting for Anita Kellerman to telephone, but he thought that none of that would ever happen again.

The Glaubers left soon after. Margaret stood waving in the door, but Chase went outside with Elliot and Vera as the others went to Herman's car.

"Thank you again for coming," said Chase. "When all of this is over, this upset, I do hope that we can see more of each other."

Tessa nodded and said, "We owe you a dinner now."

"We'll be sure to collect." Chase had not even winced.

"Too bad it's such a long haul out to Richmond Corners," Herman rumbled. "And I don't suppose you think much of the sights along the way. We should try to meet for dinner at a restaurant somewhere in between."

"A marvelous idea, Herman. Let's try to do that. When all of this is over. And thank you again for your offer. We'll arrange a meeting about it after the kids leave."

"You got your meeting," said Herman. "I always said there should be no hard feelings from this business. I was annoyed as hell at the start, but . . ." His voice dropped, and he shrugged his shoulders. "I suppose you were too. We just have to see how things go at the hearing."

They were all shivering with the cold, and the night hung massively above them. Tessa went around to the passenger's side of the car and let herself in. The lights were off in Lamont Von Heilitz's old house and in the lower floors of the two houses visible across the street. Chinks of yellow shone through blinds in the bedroom windows. When Elliot turned back to look at his parents' house, he saw his mother standing inside the first-floor windows, still waving. Vera went up to hug her father, and Chase moved toward Kai, who had been standing a little apart.

"You're probably the only man among us who can answer my question," he said. Kai bent his head, smiling. "When I went upstairs to find the photograph album, I saw a large single star or planet right through the glass in the back of the house—my wife's office. It was the only star in the sky. Is that the North Star?"

"No, that was more likely to be Venus," said Kai. "The evening star. It is always more conspicuous than any other, and it is the first to appear."

"I thought you'd know," said Chase. His whole body expressed satisfaction. Both of them—and Elliot, his chest constricting, imitating—lifted their faces to look. The December wind blew about them.

"Come on, you people, get back inside," said Herman. "It's too cold to stand around out here stargazing." "Especially this close to the lake," came Tessa's muffled voice. Herman opened the car door, bent the seat back for Kai, and then got in himself. "Merry Christmas," he called to them. They were already on their way back up the drive to the house. "Merry Christmas."

"Merry Christmas."

"Merry Christmas."

"Merry Christmas."

When the doorbell rang the next morning, Elliot was working at the piano, trying to rough out the new piece he had begun several days before, a setting for the Theodore Roethke poem *The Waking*. It had to be kept to the simplest essentials, just piano and voice, with a six-verse structure which would modulate by intricate repetitions from the quiet dreamlike beginning to something more somber: an unfolding from the villanelle's rhymes to a swelling baritone-register conclusion. He had heard it from the first as for a baritone, with a patterned series of lifts and surprises in the music. When completed, the song could stand as a synthesis, an epilogue, to *Words for the Wind*, another voice entering to dominate. But the simplicity had to evolve from a tough density of tone which would advance the tenor's insistence in the earlier work. He had done three of the verses, then stuck at the fourth.

This morning it was going better. Normally he did not work at a piano, but spun it out in his head, testing the alternatives with his inner ear; the change was temporarily exhilarating. When the bell rang, he ignored it, thinking that Robert would answer. Then he realized that Robert had the day off. Vera was still upstairs. His parents had gone to visit Pierce Laubach and his sister: a "brunch," Dr. Laubach had said, the quotation marks audible in his voice indicating his disdain for his sister's vocabulary.

The bell rang again. He looked at his watch: ten to eleven. He was pleasantly surprised that had been working so long, nearly two and a half hours. He decided to save Vera the trouble of coming downstairs. Just as he was crossing the room Vera called from upstairs.

"Oh, Elliot, what a bother. Do you want me to answer it?"

"I'll get it," he said, and went to the door.

At first he did not recognize the good-looking hippie-ish girl outside. Then she said shyly, "Elliot," and he saw that it was Joanie Haupt. In five years she had grown up. Even red-faced, as now—from the cold? from crying? she was pouched beneath the eyes—Joanie was remarkably prettier than she had been. Perhaps it was merely that she no longer looked innocent. Her hair was much longer, and her face had a strained, sleepless quality that made her look in some way doomed. Momentarily, Elliot felt a shade more sympathy for Lawrence Wooster. He asked her to come in.

"I don't want to disturb you," she said, "but I had a terrible day yesterday. I had a really black Christmas. I thought I'd come to see Vera. I was in the car for half an hour, debating whether or not to ring the bell. I saw your parents leave. I didn't want to come. I'm sorry." She looked down at her feet. "I don't even know you very well."

"Don't be silly," he said. He took her coat. "Vera's upstairs somewhere. She'll probably be glad to have someone to talk to. I've been working down here all morning, and she's just been keeping out of my way."

"Oh, you're *working*," Joanie wailed. "I'm interrupting you. Baby, be still."

"Excuse me?"

"I had to bring him with me because he hates being alone in the house, and then it was so cold in the car." From one of the deep pockets of her coat she lifted a small liver-colored dog. The dog squirmed in her hands. "This is Marcuse," she said, holding the squirming little dog out so he could see it. She appeared to be a little less mournful. "Larry bought him for me. He's fully grown, and he only weighs four pounds. Isn't he *tiny?*"

Elliot agreed that Marcuse was tiny. He glanced back toward the room with the piano.

"Marcuse keeps me company. Maybe what I really needed all the time was a dog, not a man. Larry keeps *hounding* me, and I can't keep hanging up the telephone when I hear his voice." She looked at him again, the dog struggling in the crook of her elbow, and he saw that she was on the point of tears. "Should I go?"

"No of course not, come on in," he said, looking around for Vera.

He was holding Marcuse when Vera came into the hall. "Vera, I had to come," said Joanie. "I'm sorry."

"There's nothing to apologize for," said Vera. "Come on upstairs. We'll keep out of Elliot's way, and then the old ogre will be able to work." Elliot gave the wriggling dog back to Joanie, and Vera led her firmly upstairs. She cast Elliot an apologetic look before disappearing.

Elliot washed his hands and splashed water on his face and then returned to the piano. Marcuse began to bark, off in the direction of his bedroom: a yappy two-syllable popping. He played the song setting through from the beginning. An idea formed. The barking stopped, resumed, stopped again. He could very faintly hear Joanie Haupt's soft full bruised voice.

Twenty minutes later—two lines of music which were a dissonant variation on the second verse—he heard a car coming into the driveway. The door punkily closed: since it did not continue into the garage, it was not his parents' car. He stood up from the piano and went to the window. Anita Kellerman, her hair ruffling in the wind, was striding up the walk.

He went to the door and opened it just as she was about to ring the bell. Her eyes swam luminously toward him.

"I had to see you," she said. "When you didn't call, I decided to come over. Do you mind?"

"No, come in. I was working, but . . . come on in."

"I'm so happy you were working," she said. "You're so much better than the rest of us. What's that noise? It sounds like someone is breaking bottles."

"It's a dog. A friend of Vera's just came over and she brought her dog."

"You look spiky today." Anita's face was questioning, uncertain. She fidgeted in the hallway, and he drew her in and removed her coat.

"No, come in," he said. He felt tired. They went into the living room. Anita went toward the couch, and watched him moving around the room.

"I wish that hadn't happened, that morning," she said. "You won't understand it, and it's going to change everything. Oh, damn. I wanted to say something else, and just looking at you I can see that everything I wanted to say was wrong."

He sat on a chair. He looked at the piano. "You don't have to explain anything. I shouldn't have just come in that way, of course. I was in an odd mood—a disconnected sort of mood. The night before, I hadn't had much sleep; then I saw a piece about me in the *Herald*, an absurd story. I had to get out of the house, and I started walking, and I wound up at your house. So I came in."

"As easily as that."

"Yes."

Neither of them spoke for a second.

"You think I've been lying to you," she said.

She had never seemed more distant to him—sitting there before him, she seemed packed with history, with her past that was her life.

"I suppose you're right. For a while, I thought you might be sleeping with Andy."

She laughed gloriously, holding her fingers over her mouth. "Dear Elliot. What should I say? What Hollywood people say, I guess. We're just good friends."

He felt a great self-loathing: his remark, utterly factitious, had been intended to wound her. Then he recognized that, at various points in the past two weeks, he had indeed wondered about the relationship between Andy and Anita. He had never quite allowed this fear to become conscious.

"Andy says that people should be selectively unfaithful. She said something like that to me at your party. I guess she was trying to help me along to enlightenment."

"Oh, I can't bear you when you're being so heavy and ironic." Anita was very confident. "I wish you hadn't come barging into my bedroom, but since you did, I don't want it to damage what we have together." She looked at him questioningly. "Don't be so distant from me, Elliot. I can't bear it."

"All right. I won't be distant." He looked at her: her short hair shining, the forceful face turned squarely to him. "None of this makes any sense," he said. "I don't have any claims on you. But I guess I took you too literally when you said you felt like a nun."

"I meant you to take it literally. I do feel like a nun."

He caught a faint whiff of her meaning: a purpose cold and direct as a bullet.

"Elliot . . ." She looked as though she wanted to take his hand, and he slumped deeper into the chair. "Elliot darling, I've always rejoiced in your marriage. *Rejoiced* in it. And I've always loved Vera—I told her that once."

From upstairs, over Marcuse's *yap yap*, Joanie Haupt's voice was faintly audible.

"I don't know much about you and Upp," he said. "I don't want to know much about it. But I don't like your 'rejoicing' in my marriage. That makes me feel invaded. It's intrusive and presumptuous. You don't know Vera at all. You just made a little model of the perfect wife, someone discreet, sympathetic, not too bright to be threatening, and you pinned Vera's name on it. That's not Vera—that's not any real person at all."

"And you don't know Ronnie. Nor Mark." There was a flicker of appeal in her eyes, but the tone of their conversation had irrevocably darkened, and the appeal became depthless as he waited for her to continue. "Ronnie loves Mark, and he always has. You're a childless man. Mark is unreal to you. You couldn't begin to know how to deal with him. With all Ronnie's problems, he is terribly supportive for Mark. I'm beginning to think that we might be able to keep Mark at home, if Ronnie can spend more time with him. This year has been a wasteland for all three of us, but I think Mark might be coming out of his terrors. Ronnie may be right. I'll at least give him the chance to try. You wouldn't do as much."

"I think I would," he said. Yet perhaps Anita was right. He could not imagine himself as Mark's father; he might repeat the pattern he had set with Baltz.

Then her anger softened. "Ronnie was afraid of you, Elliot. He didn't know what might happen when you came back. He's still uncertain. That was the reason he struck me, a month ago. I'd just heard that you were coming home, and I couldn't help looking pleased. I think Ronnie has always been afraid you might come back."

The history of this sentence slowly beat in on Elliot. Upp had known Anita long before he had first returned to Plechette City.

"Nothing has changed," she said. Marcuse, upstairs, barked. "And after all, dear one, it's you who live in Paris. Not me."

He stood up smartly, moved around the couch to the piano and struck a series of chords. He tried one of the runs from the Scarlatti sonata in E flat major, but misfingered it badly. He played it again, willing it to be right. The second time, it was technically correct, but sounded wooden to him, lifeless.

"That was beautiful," said Anita.

He sat on the bench and looked over the top of the piano at her.

"Play for me what you're working on," she said. "I'd love to hear it. What is it?"

"A song setting. Another Roethke poem—the villanelle called *The Waking*. I'm not satisfied with it so far, though."

"I'd love to hear it," she said. "I always love your music. Will you play it for me?"

He nodded. He was in a savage mood. He played through the first four verses—the morning's idea came back to him as he struck the last two lines of the fourth verse—and then, without a break, thinking of the shattered record on her carpet, he played "Ain't Misbehavin' " out of tempo, in no key.

"Elliot, that's the loveliest thing you've done yet," she said. "It's just beautiful."

"I like the ending," he said.

When he took her to the door, she put her arms about his neck and said, "I know everything will be the same. Tell me you love me."

"I love you," he said. "What difference does it make?"

She misunderstood him gloriously.

Ten minutes later, seated back at the piano, he again heard wheels crunching against the snow at the side of the drive, followed by the closing of a car door. Andy, he thought; he did not desire Andy French's sympathy. Elliot walked around to the windows and, looking out, saw a red Porsche parked outside. Whose? Another intruder. The doorbell rang.

When he opened the door, furiously impatient, Lawrence Wooster, coatless and in a blue pinstripe suit, strode in, his pink face flushed and embarrassed. "Ellie baby!" His hand was damp. "I'm on my lunch hour, Ellie, and I tried to get in touch with Joanie. When I didn't get her at her place, I had a quick bite at the club and thought I'd take a swing around this way. I spotted her car outside your place here. Is she . . . ?" He paused. His breath suggested that the quick bite had included more than a little gin.

Elliot nodded. "She's upstairs with Vera. Do you want to go up?"

Wooster surprised him by blushing. "Gee, I don't know, Ellie. Maybe I ought to let her talk it out, do you think?" He was standing nervously in the hall, rising and falling on the balls of his feet. "It's awkward of me to show up here, I know, but I've been trying to get ahold of Joanie for a couple of days now, and she won't cooperate. Jesus, Ellie, I'm going out of my mind. Do you suppose I could just stay down here with you for a little while?" He tweaked the hair at the nape of his neck.

Wooster looked as though he might explode, and Elliot wished to cushion him. "Sure, come in and sit down," he said. "I'm trying to get some work done, so I won't be able to talk, but if you just want to wait a few minutes . . ."

"Yeah, I'll take a pew," Wooster said, badly imitating what must have been his habitual manner.

Elliot returned to the piano. Before he had played the ridiculous ending to Anita, he'd had a minute needling of what to do with the fifth verse, and he began to toy with it, bar by bar, trying to ignore his visitor.

Wooster left the chair and wandered about the room. He picked up Elliot's wedding picture, sighed, and put it back on the table. "Sorry," he whispered. "Can't seem to stay still." He went back to the couch. "Say, could I make myself a drink?"

"In a cabinet in the kitchen. To the left of the oven." Elliot kept his head down, and his hands on the keys. Wooster said, "Gee, thanks," and moved heavily across the room and into the hall. Elliot heard him discover Robert's swinging door which led back and forth between the kitchen and the dining room. A sound of cabinets being opened and closed. Marcuse barked, but Wooster seemed not to hear. Then the clatter of an ice tray rapped against the sink.

Wooster reappeared in the living room, pink-faced, a short glass with a bobbing olive in his hand; he looked too young for his suit. "What's it like, working at home?"

"That depends." Elliot looked speculatively at Wooster, who was now back at pacing the room. "Sometimes it's a little difficult."

"Jesus, I envy you. No office to go to, no regular hours, no boss. That's the way everybody should live. But you know? I think most people in the U.S. aren't ready for that kind of life. They're whipped into line by their jobs so . . ."—he groped for a word—". . . much . . . that they wouldn't know what to do without them. Take anybody you can name at the bank. Take the trust department. If those guys tried the *vie bohème* like you, they'd go to pieces." He sat on the edge of his chair. "Take me. I make one step out of the pattern, and they call me on the carpet."

Elliot looked up. "Joanie?"

"Hell, no." Wooster glanced at the ceiling, then brought his round blue eyes back to Elliot. "I mean that damned thing I signed for your father. Walt Clement, the head of the trust department, called me into his office yesterday and gave me a long powwow about steering clear of public issues—said my future could be at stake. I think someone in the department squealed to him. Ronnie Upp's a big investor with us, you know. Clement sees him three times a year. When I said I was trying to use my social conscience—I had your father in mind there, Elliot—he damn near took my ear off."

Wooster gulped at his drink. "Indirectly, sure. Indirectly, Joanie's probably been affecting my work. A load like this is a tough thing for a man to carry. Then I spent a couple of months in analysis, and my whole head was turned around. Elliot, I saw things. I saw things you never dreamt of in my philosophy. Joanie's been a great help to me—the sex alone has changed my life. All my values changed. I was never a deep thinker, but now I'm into things that make me take a whole new look around. Some examples." He spread his hands as if he were opening a portfolio. "I used to be a straight-down-the-line party Republican. Straight ticket, all the way. Back our boys in Vietnam. Had a flag decal on the station wagon—the old Stars and Stripes. Then after I met Joanie, I started to blow a little grass with her friends. I started to think it couldn't be *that* bad. Hell, she was doing it, and *I* was doing it. I got in touch with Dr. Loomis, my therapist. Gave the wagon to Sylvie and bought myself the Porsche. Grew my hair a little. Ellie"—his eyes grew charged with sincerity—"I read books. I subscribe to *Rolling Stone*. I began to see what it was all about. Sure, I stayed within the system, but I figured that was the way to change the system. Picture hundreds of guys like me, thousands of us, working in banks, lawyers' offices, brokerages . . . Elliot, you wouldn't believe the talks I've had. I used to think of Joanie as my teacher. I learned things about love I never learned in eight years of marriage with Sylvie. Oriental things—Indian things. Joanie went the same way I did, you know, but she started earlier, when she went to college at Madison." He gloomily stared into his drink.

Elliot closed the lid of the piano. "You think Upp tried to get you fired?"

Wooster came back from his reverie. "Something like that. He swings a lot of weight down at the bank. Clement told me that if my work didn't pick up, and if there was one more incident like this, I'd be in the market for another job. He said I'd better make my image fit in a little closer with the bank's. Then I come home, and Sylvie is playing her damned guitar or talking to some priest or giving me some shit out of the nineteenth century. I give her a good home, a car, a social life, every credit card under the sun, but she's not satisfied. She wants to stand in the way of my development. She tries to hold me down. She hates my friends. And now, things are going to hell with Joanie. I didn't think she'd ever want to get away from me, but it looks like I have to chase her all over town just to talk to her." He looked pleadingly at Elliot.

The dog's barking carried faintly down the stairs. "Jesus, that's Marcuse," Wooster said. "I gave her that dog for Christmas, and now I think she loves the dog more than she loves me. I even named it for her. I better go up." Wooster had suddenly come close to tears.

"No, sit still," Elliot said. "I'll go up instead." Wooster regarded him lovingly with his round eyes. Elliot left the piano and went into the hall. He could now hear more loudly the dog's insistent *yap yap yap* and Vera's voice calmly, lowly talking. He went up the stairs.

Joanie, her head propped against the wall, jumped when he entered the room. She was leaning weakly back in a chair; her face looked powdered, dead white. The clean lines of her mouth and jaw touched some internal point in Elliot. "You scared me," she said.

Vera stood up: he saw that she had had enough of Joanie.

"Has he left yet?" she asked.

"No, he wouldn't leave," said Joanie. "I can't get rid of him. He buzzes around me like a fly. When he can't get me at home, he calls me at work. He's absolutely, utterly like glue. I feel so *harassed*." She carefully smoothed her forehead with one hand. "You people are so good to me," she said. "Larry was so sweet when we started—I used to think of him as being so straight and dependable. He was so innocent. Everything he did, he acted like it was the first time anybody had ever done it. 'I'll take care of you,' he said to me, 'just let me take care of you.' But now I feel like I somehow created him. He never stops talking about how much I mean to him. He sort of went all mystical. He's not very bright. He confessed to me one day that he cheated his way all through high school. In college, he bought term papers from his fraternity— they had files. I was so excited by what I could do for him! But damn him, he won't stop talking about it."

Vera, standing near, put her hand on Joanie's shoulder. "What do you want to do about it now?"

"I just . . . just . . . just don't know." She faced Elliot, using her eyes. "If I go down now, he might hit me. There's a whole side of him that's in a terrible darkness, and you never know how the darkness will express itself. Marcuse, get down from there."

The dog was rooting in a stack of score sheets beside Elliot's bed. Hearing his name, he lifted his head and looked worriedly around at Joanie. "Get off," she said sharply. He sprang from the pile of papers to the bed and began to roll on it.

"I had to get away," she continued. "But getting away is killing me. Sometimes I feel like I'm in this terrible sort of physical slavery to him. I love him. When he's all strong and quiet and just touching me, he's the most wonderful man. But then he starts to talk about it! He jumps up and reads something out of a book. I don't *want* him to be like that. I don't *want* him to talk the way my friends talk. When I hear him on the phone, he's all gruff and serious to begin with, the way he should be, and then he ends up all whiny and pleading. Oh, I hate that."

The dog was still rolling on Elliot's bed, rotating the small stick of his tail; the bedcovers puckered and bunched about him. The score sheets lay in a rumpled heap.

"Lawrence Wooster isn't going to hit you," said Vera. "I think you should go down. We'll come with you." She moved toward the door and took Joanie's hand. Over her shoulder, she threw Elliot a look of wild impatience. "Come on, Joanie."

Together, they took her to the staircase. Halfway down, Joanie began to weep. "Marcuse," she sobbed, and raced back up to the bedroom. Cradling the wriggling dog in her arms, she reappeared and started again down the stairs.

Wooster met them at the bottom of the stairs. "Joanie . . ." he said, unable to continue.

"Don't be so *pathetic*," she snapped at him, and clasping the dog in her arms, sailed past, snatching her coat from the rack in the hall before running out. They could hear Marcuse squealing as if injured.

Wooster goggled at Elliot and Vera and then blushed furiously. "Excuse me," he whispered, already moving toward the door. He dashed outside, and they heard Joanie's car starting up and going off down the street. "Ellie, thanks for the drink and your company," he called to them from the doorstep, then slammed the door behind him. In a moment the Porsche roared, and Elliot heard its wheels whining for a second on the road.

"He's nineteen years old," he said to Vera, still astonished.

She said, "So is Joanie." She put her arms about his waist. "Elliot, let's get away from these people."

22

Elliot moved from landscape to landscape, turning the pages of the book he had given Vera, virgins succeeding nymphs on the big colored plates, Ucello's snaked line of soldiers overwhelming a smooth Botticelli girl, half-asleep in a thick wood. A long-haired man, his muscles lovingly delineated, slept near. It was Mars. Beside Elliot lay a bookmarked *Bech* and a proof copy of Pittman's latest novel, sent with a note from Alicante. *Inge's packing to leave, as sick of me as I knew she would be, as sick of me as I am of her. She uses tiny leather bags no larger than her ass. Go, go—it makes me feel like Papa Lowry, hung upside down in an amusement park, watching everything he owns fall out of his pockets to the roof of the car. Inge-less, I'm dedicating this to you. Take it and run.* The note was taped to the green backside of the flap, two pages away from his name. *For Elliot Denmark.*

Some of the paintings recalled the photographs he had seen in Kai's room. The pale green misted landscape of the Domenichino frescoes—lush Daphne extruding leaves from her fingers to evade rapacious Apollo—and the lyrical long plane, softly brown, of Pollaiuolo. He deliberately flipped the page, and the plate fluttered. Here was a perverse, delicious Piero di Cosimo, half the canvas filled with dogs—aimless patient creatures. Had Kai walked along that lake? His past was as formalized as the paintings, concentrated to a pattern Elliot had read. He looked in the index, then opened the book again at the Botticelli *Venus and Mars*, two languid figures in a wood. At the right, his head thrown back, Mars was about to be blown to life by a fat goat-satyr puffing into a shell, a horn: an instrument. Elliot looked closely at the first satyr, and knew he had been right. Its impish chubby face was that of the cherub in the Glaubers' garden.

And the Bellini portrait of the doge, an image which had haunted him for weeks, that stern amused old face was Kai's. Indeed, had he not known it from the first? Kai the survivor—the face rebuked him.

Anita said, "The entire subject is something we shouldn't talk about. It'll ruin what we have together, and I wish you'd be more reasonable about probing and prying into what's only an old story. I love you. I need to love you. If I also need to love Ronnie, and you'll remember that I told you that on the first night I saw you after you returned, you've always had Vera. I'm selfish about my needs, but all needs are selfish anyhow. When I came to your house the day after Christmas I thought we had settled all this. Elliot, I'm heartbroken to see you still upset. Count on me, Elliot. Depend on me. Trust me."

"I trust you to *be* you."

"So you really don't think that I've been honest."

"No, but I don't think that I have either."

"Oh, but you are," she said. "You're honest, and you're fair, and you're not a fool."

Elliot signaled to the waiter for another drink, and turned to look at the turning faces of the clock. By summer it would be a heap of shattered brick. Further south loomed the two golden domes of a Polish church, and, to their right, the bare winter beach, visible between buildings, of a south-side yacht club. "For a behaviorist, you're being awfully mystical," he said. Then he knew it was a mistake. She liked his talking that way.

"You might be right," she said, smiling. "What I mean is that if you hadn't come back here, I would have shown up on your doorstep in Paris one afternoon, just to keep you in my orbit. I can never lose you, Elliot."

There were chords enough, he saw, but they were the wrong ones.

"Ronnie was never really paranoid. He was just frightened. He remembered what happened when you came back here from Columbia years ago. We'd had a rift, a falling-out. I hadn't seen him for weeks when I first met you. And I kept him away all during our first year together. But then when it was over, and I met Ronnie in Sweden, I knew that everything would hold. That we were all tied together."

Where he had looked for a clear hard vein of purpose—in Anita—he had found the deepest nonsense. Seated across the polished table from her in the dark circular room, their glasses half-empty, he wanted most to throw a switch to cause some hard bright illumination over all of them, a light impossibly clear—other people were always as hidden as not, always objectifying one another into emblems and excuses. He wanted to abstract himself, to complete the wounded retreat of his emotions.

Yet he could not be so arbitrary. It was the impulse to go back into his work, into the house on Villa Beauséjour rich with old Poltovnin's possessions. Perhaps he was more like Tessa Glauber than he imagined.

"You've just gone away," said Anita. "Come back."

On New Year's Eve the Denmarks went to a party at Nathan Himmel's home, and Anita, who had spent much of the first half of the evening speaking quietly with Vera, found Elliot in Himmel's study, where he had been letting Roberta Potocky, the student cellist, assure him of his artistic magnitude. Under the barrage of her compliments, Elliot had grown increasingly uncomfortable. He saw that she was pleading with him—she wanted to impress him with her seriousness. She was just finishing her work at the university, and she was looking for a symphony position: he knew that she was clumsily preparing to ask for a recommendation. When Anita entered the room and gave one glance at Roberta the girl scampered through the door as though she had been seared. Elliot felt annoyed, relieved, pursued.

"How did you make her leave like that? It was very impressive."

Primed with assurance, Anita glided magnificently toward him, eyes and face alight. He thought she would embrace him, and he unconsciously stiffened, but she stopped a foot away. In her elegant simple clothing, a rich modulated ocher which brought out the depth of her eyes and the starkness of her face, Anita was the most breathtaking woman at the party; Elliot thought it possible that Roberta Potocky had been literally shamed from the room. She gave him a deep humorous glance. "I only have you for a few more days," she said. His old illusion: she looked like the woman by whom all others must be judged.

From the living room Elliot could hear a faint buzz of voices, and over them, Glenn Gould playing the fourth Bach partita. Strong steely music. "Why isn't Upp here?"

"He wanted us to have some time together. He knew I'd rebel if I couldn't see you alone some more before you left."

"And Andy?"

"She's at home with Mark." Anita gave her answer almost shruggingly: as though everything were finally understood between them. "Vera is still uncertain of me, but we basically like one another. I can't tell you how much I want Vera to like me. All of us are friends now." Her glance meant that "friends," between them, was code.

It was nearly nightmarish, her misreading of his mood. She was convinced that he would be in love with her for life.

She came toward him, and he, countering, drew her toward the door. When he glanced at her face, he saw that rejoining the party was precisely what she wished to do. It suited her masque: if he were surly, it would suit her masque; if he kissed her—the taking for granted of her implications—she would be distant. Ronnie Upp and Vera were now part of her internal ordering. It was easier to leave the study. The partita's brisk gigue, its last movement, accelerated, slowed, accelerated through the low voices.

"Now that you've finished the song, what are you going to work on?" They were just entering the living room. Vera, on the far side of a crowd of faces, was talking to Himmel, who held one meaty hand on her shoulder. Anita would always assume that he was "going to work" on a new piece.

"I've had something in mind," he said. "Something for an unaccompanied chorus, with big blocks of sound. Almost medieval in feeling."

"What is it?"

"More poems," he said. "I'm thinking of calling it *Four Hymns to Marriage*." She showed puzzlement only for a second. "It's perfect," she said. "You couldn't do anything else."

At midnight, when everyone blew out razzing raucous blasts on noisemakers,

Wattman and Donadio sulking beside the bar, Himmel set on the turntable a violent cheerful piece by Shostakovich, and in the blare of sound, faces bending to kiss all about him, Elliot looked for Vera but found himself being turned by a firm female hand on his shoulder and then beneath his lips those, a little sticky from champagne, of Rosa Heldenweit.

"Please come over to our house, Elliot," she breathed to him. She stumbled, and he was forced to catch and hold her with the length of his body. "Please do come. I'm so sorry."

Italian Renaissance Painting lay beside the chunky pop-art cigarette lighter on the coffee table, a folded newspaper and three glasses the only other objects on the table's smooth expanse. It was the late evening of New Year's Day; far out in the lake, Elliot could see the red lights of a harbor ice cutter inching southward. It had been at work all during the day, casting back and forth and moving toward open water.

"So you have seen the *Herald*," said Dr. Laubach, nodding toward the paper. "My little surprise for Elliot. Hilda thought of inserting it in the January first issue instead of the January second. A marvelous in-stance of feminine connection to yearly rhythms, the woman's sense of symbolism. I am forever observing this in my sister.

"A new year, a new beginning. We have this impulse when we make resolutions for the new year. We know we can't change our skins, but at least it *feels* as though we might. Perhaps the community as a whole might alter its priorities. Especially when advised by so luminous a character as yourself, Elliot." Dr. Laubach gave his thin saurian smile.

A week ago, the newspaper statement would have infuriated Elliot; today he was calmer. His picture looked somberly up toward the ceiling, the same photograph to be used on posters and programs for the concert. Its distracted, rather shifty appearance did not well suit the italicized comments beneath it, which had been taken from his interview with Ted Edwards.

"It's a good thought, Pierce, and good of you to have given Elliot such prominence in the ad, but I'm afraid we are on the losing side of this battle. On Christmas Day I talked to Herman Glauber, and he intimated to me that he has five certain votes on the commission. Jeff Glee is our only chance, and he's a slender reed." Chase tugged at his cuffs. "Of course, we've had a decent exercise in participatory democracy, and that may be of value in itself. At least Upp did not clear us off the board in one move, as he did in the clock-tower business."

"Hold on to the faith," said Dr. Laubach. "Hold on to the faith, baby." He grinned wickedly at Elliot. "Did I say it correctly?"

"Ask Lawrence Wooster," said Elliot.

Dr. Laubach looked from Chase to Elliot, then back to Chase. "I take it that you do not entirely approve of my redesigning of our statement."

"Oh heavens, Pierce," said his father. "I think it's lovely."

"It's fine by me," said Elliot. "I wish there were a photograph that made me look less like a butcher with his thumb on the scale."

"You look the image of your grandfather," said Dr. Laubach, "and a good deal like old Brooks with long hair. We put in the quotations at the last minute—another of Hilda's inspired notions. They improve the layout, don't you think?" He held up the paper and turned it toward Elliot.

"The layout is fine."

"Fine," echoed his father.

Dr. Laubach put the paper aside and took the huge book onto his lap. He opened it near the middle. Then he took his eyes from the Uccello which Elliot could see upside down, glare from the lamp obscuring half the plate so the warriors marched into a dissolving whiteness, and said, "We are all working together on a serious issue. Don't be defeated now."

"I'm proud of the *fight*," said Chase, "but I don't think I care anymore who wins it."

Far out beyond the crisp outline of his head the red light of the armored harbor boat swung inward for the last time.

"It seems from the evening news that the wounded girl will live," said Dr. Laubach. "She will have a few scars, but plastic surgery can fix anything these days, I gather. Ah!" He propped the book up with his hands. "Florence!" It was meant as a general accolade to the arts, and as the ice cutter's red light inched toward the frame of the window, Elliot ironically bent his head.

23

"You have only a few days left among us. Andy will miss you," said Ronnie Upp, grinning pleasantly at Elliot from behind the giant ornate mahogany relic that had once been Brooks Denmark's desk. Everything else about the office had been changed from the times when Chase had taken Elliot as a boy up to the suites on the top floor of the factory. Where an old richly colored Turkish carpet ("Make a wish and you'll be able to fly on it," his grandfather had said. "If it is the right wish.") dully glowed from desk to door, there was now a single dark patterned green sheet like a country-club lawn after a summer shower; the walls had been repainted from their old sober colorless color to a light snapping blue, interrupted at regular intervals by large abstractions—black whisked over white—signed with a famous name. Brooks's delicate mono-prints of Paris, preserved by the Chambers family and the various Denmark cousins who had used this office, were gone. Wood and aluminum in strong linear patterns: if the old office had implied labor, moral seriousness, an idio-syncratic Francophilia, it now suggested coolness, distance, vistas. Only the desk and the great windows to the east remained. Immediately beyond them the side of the clock tower gigantically revolved. Seen so closely once again, it reminded Elliot of a still from a Harold Lloyd film—a little man hanging from a huge clock hand. "We will all miss you, naturally. But particularly Andy, I think."

"Because she will lose an ally."

The two men looked at one another with self-conscious irony. Upp had welcomed Elliot into his office with no coolness—the magnanimity of a man who had won every hand. Elliot, sitting across from him in this cool transparent office, felt vestigially shabby, displaced. Upp was dressed in the manner of a wealthy young English viscount with a fondness for Tommy Nutter and Savile Row. Even his secretary—a beautifully elegant young man—had regarded Elliot with a limp superiority. Yet Upp had seemed unsurprised to see him, had even appeared to be expecting him, this morning after the disastrous public hearing.

"Let's not be nasty," said Upp. "I'd never hold that absurd newspaper thing against you. In fact, I'm sure that wasn't your doing at all. You're not that kind of man. I am certain that your father's cohorts thought of using those quotations from the Edwards taping. It was typical misplanning. That kind of thing does more harm than good in Plechette City. And you are not really a Savonarola type, are you?"

"It seems not," said Elliot. "That was never one of my problems." He looked at the edge of the clock.

"You've just proved my point, Elliot. One of the things I've learned from Anita is that there are two reactions to stress, fight or flight. That's the jargon of her trade, but it is accurate. You choose flight. That's fine! If things had worked out differently, I think we could have been friends. Perhaps we still can."

"I didn't come here to be your friend," said Elliot. "I just wanted to get another look at you."

"Curiosity?" Upp's smile was now nearly intolerably superior. "You once caused me a year of misery—I wouldn't be human if I weren't interested in the man who was capable of that. You must know that Anita picked you blindly. Willfully. You were an accident, Elliot. No more than that. You know, our friend Anita is incapable of living without a man. Before me, there was one of her husband's colleagues, before that a graduate student. I fear that Bob Cratchit may be the latest of these footnotes. Don't be shocked. After all, you know Anita's temperament. She must have told you about the astrologer who told her she was lascivious. Anita's proud of that."

"So you're contemptuous of her." Elliot felt sickened.

"No, I'm hardly that," Upp answered. "I know her too well. Anita fulfills a necessary function for me. When I need a hostess she is a good one—she is an impressive woman. I really cannot do without her. For years we've had a good firm relationship. It's tricky at times, but what relationship isn't? I tolerate her foibles, she tolerates mine. Elliot, you should be grateful you can see the true situation at last. I was almost grateful when you walked in on us that morning. I thought, now we can all begin to build from here. Don't look so downhearted. We both want you to think of us as friends. I'd like to look you up when she and I come to Europe next summer. I know a clinic in Geneva that can do wonders for Mark."

Upp stood and went around the desk. He touched Elliot lightly on the shoulder and then motioned toward the door. "You have your last rehearsal to fit in today, if I remember correctly. It's a pity we can't have lunch together, but some other time. And, Elliot"—going back around the desk, he slid the glasses back over his eyes—"remember this. We all got what we wanted." He smiled. "Perhaps you should call on your father before your rehearsal."

Elliot had one more question. "Why did you shatter my record?"

The other man surprised him by grinning. "Oh, did you see that? I'm terribly sorry. But I am not your culprit. Mark broke it, I fear. And I'm sure he picked it utterly at random. It was on top of the other records. The boy used a hammer.

Much better that he attack objects than people or animals, don't you think?" Upp waved him out of the office.

Elliot parked in the lot behind the Moore Building on upper Grand Avenue, pushed down all the locks, and walked swiftly, turning up his coat collar, toward the back entrance. His feet were damp from the gray slush. Against the building someone had set a beer bottle, and it had frozen during the night, so that now it was like the still frame of an explosion; brown shattered glass buried in thick brown ice. He kicked it over with his foot, and the misshapen thing snapped in two. He had gone to Upp's office in a tigerish mood, but had failed—the man had evaded him as neatly as a fish slipping around the edges of a net. In his muted eggshell of an office, he was impenetrable. Anita was his. The hearing, despite Rona Bender's feverish verbal assaults, had gone smoothly beneath its frantic surface. The wood too was Upp's. And now, thirty minutes before the last rehearsal, he was following Upp's advice and going to see his father.

Still, for all Anita's mysticism—it was how he thought of her faith in the permanency of love—he felt that she was stronger than Upp. Upp's smoothness, his blandness, his air of bullying superior graciousness, these fitted him less well than did his foppish clothing. For all his calculated air, Upp broadcast a sense of pain. Anita would not see this. Entering the elevator in the immense brown lobby of the Moore Building, Elliot remembered what he had said to Upp. "I didn't come here to be your friend," he repeated with satisfaction. A man with a swollen jaw—the lower floors of the Moore Building were a phalanx of dentists—visibly started, and Elliot realized that he had spoken aloud. He looked down to his ruined shoes, to the filthy winter floor of the elevator, then shifted his gaze to the panel above the door. *Next stops 4 6 7 12.* When the elevator stopped, *4* vanished and the other man moved very quickly out into the hall. Elliot watched while all the numbers before *12* went black.

Jefferson Glee had been his father's last hope on the commission. There were twelve aldermen seated on the platform above the audience in the hearing room, and Herman Glauber had told Chase that nearly half would vote for the proposed rezoning, no matter what comment came from the audience. With one exception, the others were uncommitted. Archie Holton, Chase's alderman, and perhaps two or three others would vote against. "You never know what Glee's going to do," Herman had told Chase. "He got elected by making speeches about the white devil, and he never stopped making them, even while he was doing deals right and left with white men. And whatever way he goes, the other two black aldermen will follow. The trouble is, Glee's slippery. He can't look like he's playing up to the whites or he'll lose face in his ward. But if he goes with me, maybe he'll think that I'll support him on programs for his ward. And maybe I would. Glee and I have never got along very well, to tell you the truth. If he goes your way and votes no, you could tie it, and we'd have to schedule another hearing."

Chase had been silent throughout the speeches. To his son, he looked gray and already defeated. When the new sound system in the hearing room sputtered and squealed, he held his hands over his ears. Dr. Laubach, in contrast, rushed around the chamber like a ferret before the start of the hearing, speaking to each uncommitted alderman, seating Rona Bender and her friends in a bloc at the front of the room before the platform. When Elliot came in with his parents, he saw Dr. Laubach leading Jefferson Glee toward a quiet corner. Glee's face was stony and aloof. He was older, more grizzled than his posters indicated, and his eyes were a lionish yellow around the irises. When Glee mounted the platform and sat behind his microphone, Dr. Laubach scurried around to Chase. "I think we may have him," he said. "Glee is too can-ny to say it now, but in the end I think he'll go with us. One thing the minorities hate is middle-class suburbanites, and he'd have no interest in putting companies out there to lower their tax base." Chase merely grunted.

Rona Bender, scanning the room, saw Elliot in the back of the chamber. She signaled to him with a commanding wave, and when he went up to the front of the room, she stood to meet him like a man. Rona's manner had altered from their first meeting. She seemed still hypertense, aggressive, but beamed at him with an overwhelming goodwill. When she began to speak, he saw that he had become a hero. "You really told 'em," she said. "Boy, did you ever tell 'em. And now we're going to squash them flat. I've got a whole list of arguments right here"—she lifted her purse—"in case I forget any. I really have to hand it to you. Boy, you really laid it on the line. When I first saw you I wasn't sure about you, but I take it all back. I agree with everything you said. You're your father's son, Mr. Denmark. I should have seen what you were doing that day out at our place. You were getting that Ronnie Upp's number. I should have seen it then. I don't see him here, do you?"

Elliot said that he did not think Upp was in the chamber.

"Because he's afraid to show his face. Oh, we've all got his number now, Mr. Denmark. He knows what's going to happen to him tonight." Rona's voice was rising, and her face was a little flushed. People in the near rows stared at the chunky little woman. He was reminded uncomfortably of the madwoman in the department store. "I'm a great admirer of straight talk, Mr. Denmark, and you talk straight, and all of us are going to talk straight tonight. You can tell that to your father." She had clamped onto his wrist. An angry-looking man in a turtleneck was coming toward them, his eyes fixed on Elliot; behind him, others followed. Elliot removed his wrist from her grasp. "I'd better get back to my seat," he said. He nodded at the rest of the people who were gathering around him, and then glanced up at the aldermen's table. Jefferson Glee was looking down impassively, his gold spectacles twinkling in his hand. To Elliot, the crowd of people in the chamber seemed brilliant and tense, volatile; whenever the loudspeakers hummed or sputtered, the noise level rose.

The council meeting began calmly, then disintegrated into disorder. Rona Bender began to heckle other speakers in the audience. The microphones and amplifiers wailed like electric guitars. The head of the planning commission, an old alderman named Max Festlinger, gradually ceased banging his gavel and let the arguments rage. He supported his chin on his fist and pointed into the crowd to select the speakers. At the epicenter, Rona Bender put on her glasses and fished in her purse. She stood and shouted down a man in the middle of the room who was rambling about taxes. Clippings fluttered in her hand. "I've got some advice for you, mister," she called. "And for you too, Mr. Festlinger." Elliot never heard what the advice was, because her next sentence was drowned in a storm of booing from the right of the chamber. Jefferson Glee and the other two black aldermen swiveled their heads from side to side, expressionlessly, like observers of a tennis match. None of them had spoken. Then Elliot heard, with a shrinking feeling of horror, his own name. Rona Bender began to read from her clippings.

In the end, three hours later, when Rona's voice had become unbearably shrill, a hoarse Max Festlinger silenced the audience and called for a vote. Herman Glauber calmly recorded an Aye. The four aldermen to his right did the same. Archie Holton showed the first Nay. Then one more, then another. Then the sixth Aye. When the next man showed a Nay, Rona and her section of the audience applauded, cheered. Chase, too, dryly clapped his hands.

"Mr. Glee," called Max Festlinger. Elliot heard his father stop breathing.

"Abstention," said Glee, very calmly and clearly.

Dr. Laubach, on the other side of Chase, patted his fingertips together. "The son of a bitch," he whispered.

The final vote was six to four in favor of the proposal to rezone the land. "Mr. Festlinger, you've murdered our children," screamed Rona Bender. Boos, shouts, applause.

Elliot and his father, along with a silent Pierce Laubach, left the council chambers soon after. Out in the corridors of the vast building, Elliot noticed that all of city hall smelled of floor wax and tobacco smoke. Walking through the lobby, trailing his father and Dr. Laubach, Elliot paused to look at the murals of Jimmy Steenborg icily regarding Père Plechette and his ring of muscular braves. Someone had recently retouched them, and they shone gaudily in the harsh light. Then they were outside, going down the rank of marble steps to the plaza, and hunching their shoulders against the black cold.

"Democracy is overrated," said Dr. Laubach before he left them to go slowly up the plaza in the bitter wind toward his car.

Elliot waved to his father's secretary and opened the door to his office. "Welcome, son," said Chase. He was seated gray-faced behind his desk. "It's good of you to come." He went to one of the leather chairs, motioning Elliot to another. When Elliot sat, he noticed on the far wall of the office, near the windows and facing the aerial view of the city covering one wall, the prints of Paris which had once belonged to Brooks Denmark. So that was where they had gone; it was odd he had never noticed them here before. But for the prints and the two opulent chairs, Chase's office was as bare and neat as Kai's room.

"Pierce is very bitter," said Chase, crossing his legs. "He was even more involved than I in the effort to stop the rezoning. Hilda and he were in it from the first. They were the real soldiers. I think I was just a sort of hanger-on. I gave them a few ideas. Looking back, I'm not sure I ever thought we'd really stop them. The world's changed too fast for me. Years ago, I suppose we would not have even considered trying to do anything about Nun's Wood. We would have let that side of town go on about its own business."

"I wish you weren't so damned discouraged," said Elliot. "Maybe it's better to be bitter."

"I'm too realistic for that," his father snapped. "We were amateurs fighting the professionals. Nothing could have won it for us. Upp knew from the beginning that if he got Herman Glauber on his side, he'd eventually get a majority vote from the planning commission. The hearing was just a sideshow. Herman told me as much on Christmas Day. A less worthy man would have gloated, but Herman didn't permit himself that satisfaction. He was admirably level with me. Fifty Rona Benders screaming at the tops of their lungs wouldn't have changed the final vote, except to alienate more of the commission. From the beginning Upp had all the cards. *Finis.*"

He looked glumly out of the window. "I keep wondering what my own father would have done. I think he would have invited Jeff Glee and his whole family to dinner, and sent a case of Scotch around afterward. Don't look disgusted with me, Elliot. I should have seen from the beginning that Glee was the key to our winning or losing. Pierce thought all along that he'd go with us. If we hadn't been so stupidly optimistic, we would have sent round petitions, forced a referendum."

"You could still do that."

"No, we've lost our moment," said Chase. "Pierce, Hilda, the Wiltshire Drive people, I, all of us are antiques now. Dusty things in a lumber room. We'd be split up for kindling if we kept it up any longer. Ronnie Upp is the new man now—he's stolen all the best Denmark methods."

Though he recognized the truth in what was said, Elliot laughed aloud, amused by his father's self-consciously despairing language; Chase shot a single bright glance at him. "Laugh at me, you decadent lounger," he said. "I used to wonder if you'd ever understand me."

"No, I don't think so," said Elliot, still smiling.

"The Denmarks have always been contradictory types," said his father. "Your grandfather would have bought up that acreage himself and sold it off for a fortune, and then agonized about it, wondering if he'd done the right thing. Old Brooks would have done the same, but made a speech about contributing to the progress of Plechette City. At least young Upp spares us that. You are smarter than the lot of us. You make your own world. I wish I could say the same."

Elliot went on looking out the window, where a parade of flat roofs heaped with snow led off to the bright blue glowing tear of the Gas Company's flame. The sky shone white.

"Have we given you and Vera a good Christmas?" came his father's voice.

"Of course," he said.

"I've been thinking about Harrison Upp lately. Your mother and I used to see him now and then, you know, in the days when you were just a boy. Your asking about him on the telephone the other day started me off, and since we've been locking horns with his son, I've found myself recalling him, little things he did."

Elliot was now facing his father, and something in his glance made Chase smile. "Silly, isn't it? The man's been dead how long? More than fifteen years. Nearly twenty years. It doesn't seem that long ago to me. The fifties are quite present to me—it was a good decade, better than it is represented these days. Certainly better than the sixties. Less surreal. I've read all the books, all the new books, and I know that we're not supposed to think this way. In some ways though, I think the books are wrong. In the fifties a certain surface calm prevailed, but currents were always present under the surface. It was probably the last of the America we used to know, but all the mutations and variants were cropping up. Didn't that fellow Ginsberg begin writing in the fifties? All that gloomy talk about the Bomb. At the time, none of us could read phenomena of that sort. What I've been thinking lately is that Harrison Upp was a sort of harbinger, in his own way. Then, we used to think of him as simply 'wild,' you know, and some people went further than that. He was not a universal favorite.

"I rather liked him," said Chase, "because like Lamont Von Heilitz, though a Lamont turned one hundred and eighty degrees about, he had his own sort of code. I think perhaps he was a moralist, and I think I should have paid more attention to him."

"What do you mean, a moralist?" said Elliot.

"Well, I now think that Harrison Upp possessed the kind of sophistication that never allows itself to be violated. He invariably knew what he thought and what he wanted—he was like a chess master. He seemed so immensely vital as a man. Do you remember his taking his family on safari in Africa? That was pure Harrison Upp—he nearly got himself killed, trying to get a lion. When I went past his house at night, out for a walk, I'd see cars all up and down the block, jazz music would be pounding out the windows, there'd be throngs of people who claimed to despise him, but who couldn't stay away. And he loved shooting, hunting—it was the way he loved drinking. Harrison had built up his father's fortune the way his son has built up his own. He sold all the property he owned on Second Street when land there was at the height of its value. I'm sure that he saw then what would happen there—Jeff Glee was a sort of protégé of Harrison's. Upp sold off his properties to men who were convinced that there'd be a larger market down there eventually; the expansion principle, I suppose. Upp knew better. In fact, he *always* knew better in business matters. He saw what industries would begin to make money, and he saw it a few steps ahead of anyone else. Many people hated him for that, when they couldn't afford to despise him.

"I don't want you to think he was a Gatsby," said Chase. "Harrison was too self-possessed and too violent. All those guns! But he did have, I gather, a past as disguised as Gatsby's. He'd traveled everywhere, met everyone. Vera's uncle has something of this air about him—of more experience than most of us have seen, as though most of what is significant about the man is hidden. Maybe what I felt was that the most important part of his life was in the past: that his future could never be as substantial. For all Upp's bearishness, I always felt that he was calculating his actions, keeping himself concealed in some essential way. He was like a survivor of the twenties, with his drinking and his safaris and his parties; but it was his attitude of mockery about it all that made it compelling. It was like he didn't give a damn about it, or about his fabulous success, and like he thought that was funny too."

"He does sound interesting," Elliot admitted.

"I rather think old Brooks Denmark and Harrison Upp would have liked each other. If I were your age now, I might like Ronnie Upp. Twenty years ago I was too narrow-minded."

"I thought you said you did like the father."

"I said, I think, that I rather liked him. It was a highly qualified affection," said Chase, smiling to himself. "Unlike most of the people we knew, unlike Margaret and myself, I don't think Upp liked the fifties at all. He was too conspicuous. It was no secret that he liked boys as well as girls—in those days, it was a thing you hid, it put you pretty much beyond the pale. Harrison flaunted his differences, but, again, I now think that he did it from a kind of ironic sense. That was what made him so glamorous. He never seemed exactly happy, even at his wildest. What does cruelty come from? Some kind of desperation? That may be merely a liberal's answer. Whatever it was, it could be unsettling. He mistreated his wife very badly; he humiliated her at parties. Margaret still cannot mention him without showing her loathing. But many women found him devastating. You'd be shocked if I listed all the respectable women from this area who chased after Harrison Upp. And who caught him."

"Is that what you meant when you said *nihil nisi bonum?* Queerness? Promiscuity?" A flight of heavy gray pigeons dropped diagonally past Chase's window; they settled on one of the ledges below, pecking and cooing. In their midst, plumper than the others, was a beautiful soft brown bird, its coloring so subtly varied that it appeared to have been laid on with a paintbrush.

"No, not really," said his father. "It was a feeling I had. Nothing I should talk about."

"Well, for God's sake don't clam up now," Elliot said. He was torn between leaving for his rehearsal, scheduled to begin in fifteen minutes, and hearing whatever last insight into the dead Harrison Upp his father could give him. The pigeons were wheeling away again and dropping down further toward the street. The beautiful little brown bird among them was lost to his sight, somewhere far down among the buildings.

"I suppose it doesn't make any difference what I think," said Chase. "And although I appreciated Upp's skill at managing people and events, I was always a little intimidated by him. I thought buying that pistol was an outright mistake, especially since he didn't keep it locked up with his other guns. He wasn't in any sense a careless man, and that troubled me, leaving the pistol lying around.

Carrying it in a holster. His reputation at that point was as low as it ever got—the men who'd bought into Second Street were beginning to feel the first slump in their business, and people were talking about Upp and a young man, a brainless kid from Chicago who had just tried to kill himself. The last time I went to one of his parties, he drunkenly told me that he'd given his son permission to use his pistol to defend the house anytime he was out. 'He's a weak little shit,' he told me when I tried to argue that it was irresponsible to give a child license to handle any weapon. 'It's one chance in a hundred,' he said. Upp looked terrible, his skin seemed to be on the point of falling off his face, he was drunk, and I didn't understand what he was talking about. And I was afraid to press him—he was still capable of violence. A couple of weeks earlier, he'd been beaten up in a fight in a very sordid bar on Booker Place. So you see my point. When he was killed, it crossed my mind that he'd almost planned for his son to shoot him. I think he'd been taunting his son for months. His motives? I don't know, couldn't begin to guess, apart from what I've just told you. I think it no longer mattered to him if he lived or not."

"My God," uttered Elliot. "If that's true, how can you say he was moral?"

"Maybe you don't understand your own country as well as you might," said Chase. "You'd better go off to your rehearsal."

"But you're saying that he was mad. Crazy."

"Yes, I suppose. Crazy." He smiled thinly, and stood. "But he always got what he asked for, and in the end, I imagine that he got the last thing he had been asking for. And his family got the fortune in insurance, not that they needed it, which a suicide would have taken from them. Hadn't you better rush? I'll see you at dinner. Robert is going to outdo himself in cooking some sort of tribute to your concert, so be sure to demonstrate your appreciation." Before he went back to his desk, he added, "It was just an idea I had at the time. I could easily be wrong. But that I could think it at all shows you something of what kind of man he was." He went back behind his desk, and Elliot left the office, rode down in the dark elevator, cut through the lobby, and walked out into the cold white air.

Of all the results plotted separately and jointly by Herman Glauber and Chase Denmark, one had unequivocally occurred: standing in a passageway far behind the stage in the Usenbrugge Auditorium, Elliot could hear, unmistakably, the sounds of a large crowd assembling. For nearly half an hour, people had been streaming into the auditorium where, during the past two weeks, he had seen only Vera and Nathan Himmel seated—two small white faces in a sea of rich red and gold. Now it was a beehive of voices, a perpetual buzzing and humming. His stomach momentarily fluttered. Was the music on the podium? Elliot's knees seemed fluid, watery. Of course it was there. He had spoken to the boy twice. Most of the musicians were raggedly gathered in the gray-block cavern behind the stage, some still carrying their coats. (The architect had apparently forgotten that culture did not hibernate during winter, and on the far wall of the cavern hung a single short rack of curved hooks. A huddle of coats lay beneath, crumpled, trod upon, arms folded or outflung.) The musicians too seemed nervous, but brilliantly nervous, as though they were hosting an important party. The last rehearsal had been the best to date, with no faltering in the sections, no hesitations or gingerliness; some of the pieces had sounded really right for the first time. When they had given the entire program a final run-through, he had been deeply pleased by their playing. Now if they could only conquer their jitters—and he, his—to duplicate that last performance.

In their suits and long dresses they looked different than they had during the course of the rehearsals. He had, unthinkingly, been expecting tuxedos or tailcoats—his own had been meticulously pressed by Robert that afternoon— to be worn by the males; now he was grateful they were not so formal. Some did not even wear suits, but came in the same sweaters and jeans they had worn to rehearsals. Ettenheim was seated on the concrete floor with his back against the hard wall, his eyes closed. The others bounced on the balls of their feet, laughed at some comment from the stringy-haired exuberant boy who played first trumpet, or talked loudly with their friends. Another group of musicians clustered around the edge of the aperture which allowed them to see the audience. Their arms rested loosely across their backs and shoulders—like Kai and Harrison Upp, both squinting shirtless in the sun and the camera on the terrace of a villa. While one part of his mind snagged on the memory of the photographs, another section recorded that he had never been made so aware that they were students.

"May I?" He was at the edge of the cluster around the aperture. Roberta Potocky was sarcastically describing her mother's dress, and the giggling ceased when he spoke. *Why*, he thought, *this is more an event for them than it is for me.* They broke apart as if he had shouted. "Oh, it's wonderful, Mr. Denmark," said Roberta Potocky, turning her nervous, glancing face toward his. "We're nearly filled! I've never played to so many people before. Just look at them all! I even saw my mother, and she never goes to concerts—she's in the tenth row, wearing her schoolteacher dress—a purple dress. The only thing she ever went to before was my Master's recital. Which she didn't even like!"

"Will she like this?"

"Oh, I don't know," giggled Roberta. "She'll probably like the singing."

"Well, I like the singing," said Elliot. The students glanced at one another, as if he had uttered a significant admission. "As of four hours ago, I like the playing too," he added. Pep talk, paternalism. He bent to the aperture and looked out at the audience. The vast middle portion of the orchestra section was nearly filled, and more people were still stepping down the side aisles.

The complimentary tickets must have been all from the same roll. His parents were seated in the third row, on the right side, next to Herman and Tessa Glauber. Herman looked flushed, hot, delighted; Tessa fumbled in her bag beside him, and took out a comb and ran it through her hair. Chase leaned across his wife and made some comment to Herman which caused his bullish face to split with good humor. Vera, beside her mother, smiled too, and reached over to touch her father's hand.

Then he saw a moving flash of yellow hair coming down the far aisle and knew before he saw the face that it was Anita Kellerman. He had not thought that she would come; that, he saw, was foolish. Slim, preoccupied, she was marching down the aisle unguided by an usher; Andy came behind, carrying the tickets. She was comparing the row numbers with those on the flimsy paper tickets, and kept turning her head from side to side as they came forward, her lips pursed, her forehead drawn up. Men stared at her face. Anita moved like a distracted queen straight for the correct row. Her certainty released a bubble within him: he could not maintain his hostility. They were, after all, friends. As he watched, Anita paused at a row a little back from the Denmarks and Glaubers; Andy, checking the tickets, nodded sharply. They went in toward the middle of the hall and took two vacant seats beside a placid heap of a woman in purple.

"I see your mother," he said to Roberta, who hovered beside him.

"You saw that awful dress? It's what she wears to *functions*. It makes her look so ghastly, like someone at a funeral. Let me look." She bent her head close to his. "Oh, dear Mother," she whispered. "Now she's got those two exotic creatures beside her, I suppose she'll be nervous and not hear a thing. Wait. Isn't the blond one Mrs. Kellerman?" Her face, half an inch away, registered dismay. "I'm sorry, I didn't . . ." She turned half-hysterically back to the opening. "I mean I think Mrs. Kellerman is beautiful. When I was an undergraduate, boys took her classes just to look at her for an hour. She's a good friend of yours and Mr. Himmel's, I know . . ."

"It's all right," he said to her profile. "You didn't say anything."

"My goodness! Look at that! That couple up in the boxes. If music is the food of love, they'd better leave right now." She giggled again, and trying to point, dropped her music on the floor. Elliot leaned over to put his head where hers had been, and looked up at the row of boxes. Most were empty. You could see only half the stage from there, and with the hall's acoustics, you'd be lucky to hear even that. He saw a tangle of hands, two heads together in a kiss. The man browsed along the woman's lips, her cheek. Since they were seated, only their heads were visible above the plush railing, giving them a Punch-and-Judy look. The man—it was Lawrence Wooster—broke apart from the woman and traced a finger down the side of her jaw. Joanie Haupt caught his finger and slipped it in her mouth. Elliot turned away from the aperture, full of chagrin and amusement. Roberta Potocky was still stooping above the concrete, assembling the loose pages of her music.

"I saw you on television," said Ettenheim. He had stationed himself two feet away, and looked as though he might break into a run. "You were okay. I thought what you said made a lot of sense."

"About Nun's Wood?" Elliot was incredulous.

"No, what you said about music. I'd like to hear some of your newer work sometime. I mean, I was really persuaded by what you were saying. I've been thinking along those lines for about a year, and when you were talking to Ted Edwards, you made a lot of things fall into place for me."

Roberta, now kneeling on the floor, looked up at Ettenheim with amazement.

The boy jammed his fists into the pockets of his jacket and glared at Elliot. "I mean, it's just the way I felt. I was just wondering what kind of thing could be done with a vocalist in the sort of music you were talking about. We don't talk about really new music very much here, and I kind of feel like I've been stumbling along in the dark. Is there anyone I could write to?"

"You could write to me," said Elliot. He fumbled in his pocket, but found no pen, no paper. Ettenheim handed him a shabby notebook with a ball-point clipped to the springs, and he put down on a blank page his name and address.

Then everything happened. Roberta finally finished assembling her pages and fluttered across the cavern to where the musicians were lining up to go onstage; Ettenheim shoved the notebook in his pocket with a perfunctory thanks and took his own place in the formation. At a signal, they swept onstage. Elliot watched them take their chairs, bathed in light and applause. When they had finished flipping the pages before them and the applause had nearly ceased, the ritual of tuning completed, he started to walk out of the wings toward the podium, head back, using long determined strides—the conductor's march; but before he had even properly begun, Nathan Himmel appeared from nowhere and embraced him. "You can't lose," Himmel whispered, and released him. Elliot grinned at his friend, turned his back toward the lighted stage, and walked out in his normal manner, as if he were going down the block to buy flowers. The moment he stepped out into the light, he was drowned in renewed applause. None of the faces he dimly saw looked familiar.

One last glimpse of Elliot Denmark: he is seated by the window in the backseat of his father's immense black automobile, so crowded by his mother, whose knees project upward in a clean elegant nylon line, her feet placed on the floor's central hump, by Tessa, who is all elbows-in and hurtled together, and by Uncle Kai, of whom only the outline of a gray sweater and a gray tweedy angle of legs are visible, that he is jammed up against the rear door, his side dug by the armrest. The front seat is less crowded. Chase and Herman Glauber sit, with enough room to turn and gesture, on either side of Vera.

"Are you sure you have your tickets?" Tessa leans forward abruptly, forcing Margaret to list to the left, and transfixes Elliot with her long eyes. While Elliot assures her that he has them in his pocket—the long holders rest there beside a letter from Baltz (a demo made, a girlfriend, another dog, two weeks in Max's Kansas City)—he sees his father tighten with impatience. It is the third time Tessa has asked about the tickets.

Herman rumbled with laughter. "You don't want to have to say: I wish the grand piano were here."

"Oh, I know that one," Margaret sang out. "They are at the Harvard-Yale game, and you can't get a seat for love or money because it's the crucial game of the season."

"A shortcut," says Chase, turning the car at the War Memorial building to follow First Street down into the valley.

"You don't use the expressway?"

"I'm sure this way is faster. The expressway takes you so far east that you lose all the time you gain while you're going south."

"Just check to see if you've got the tickets, Elliot. To put my mind at ease."

"He *has* them, Mother. Jesus Christ."

"I always use the expressway myself. You can really belt along until you get to the Pulaski Avenue turnoff."

"And the wife says, why do you wish the grand piano were here?"

"Oh, I did forget something," said Elliot.

"I knew it."

"No, he has them, Mother. I saw him put them in his pocket."

"It was the proof copy of Pittman's novel. I just remembered that I left it up on one of the beds."

"If your mother finds it first, she'll burn it."

"I hate to put you to the trouble, but could you mail it to us?"

"Is that the book Vera was telling us about? It sounds wretched."

"Then he says, because that's where I left the *tickets*."

They were sailing down the long hill to the valley past a billboard for Jefferson Glee; everyone in the automobile but Kai looked at it as they accelerated past.

"You don't have to break the record, Chase, we're in plenty of time."

"Better safe than sorry."

"It's been wonderful to have you here, dears."

"Maybe we can come back next summer."

"Your mother and I will probably come over if you don't. I haven't seen Paris since I was twenty."

"Oh, have you been to Europe? I envy you."

"Don't encourage them, Tessa, they'll never come back."

The gold top of the Chambers Denmark clock revolved above the buildings, showed its gleaming faces, then was lost among the rising gray and red brick of factories.

"You kids today have all the breaks."

"Now *you're* encouraging them."

"I wish you could stay longer."

"How is your book coming, Kai?"

"It's a secret."

Soon they were out of the city. The houses scattered apart as if a bomb had dispersed them, little frame buildings made to look like dwarf ranch houses. Fields hemmed them in with barbed wire.

"A lot could be done with this ward. Already, a few companies are making noises about relocating out here, to take advantage of the land price."

His father and Herman began to talk about the planning commission, the new proposals for extension of the expressway. Elliot looked out of the window to the sparkling fields. "Now they think it was a dog that attacked that girl," said Margaret. "Did any of you see that in the morning paper? One of the neighbors had a savage dog that he kept to guard his home. It's such a ghastly thing. The dog ran away on the morning the girl was injured. The man was afraid to tell anyone, but his wife made him go to the police." he and Tessa, crowded shoulder to shoulder, tried to remember what breed of dog it had been. Doberman? German shepherd? Off to his right, dashing across the field, Elliot saw a swift dark shape. It was loping, not running; in mid-stride, it rolled over on its back like a puppy and squirmed deliriously in the snow, nosing, writhing. When it got to its feet again, now dusted with white, it ran, keeping pace with the car for a few moments, then fell back. The animal looked like no dog he had ever seen. No one else in the car had noticed it. Herman pointed his finger upward at the windshield; a giant silvery jet was planing away eastward, seeming to move very slowly and trailing plumed white ribbons. After a second they were hit by its sound.

EPILOGUE

5 Verbena Blvd.
Boulder, Colorado
29 November 1970

Elliot Denmark
6 Villa Beauséjour
Paris XVI
France

Dear Elliot,

I don't really know why I'm writing to you, unless it's because I see both of us as Anita's victims. At times last December, I could almost see your brain working, see all the wheels and judgments and decisions whirling around, trying to grasp how she and I related, how you fit in. I wanted to protect you—to keep you from seeing what you were eventually made to see. Maybe it would have been kinder, on the day in the field, to have explained everything; but I couldn't, I could not be certain that it would not be a kindness for the sake of cruelty, and you were too open, too vulnerable for that. I wasted too much time in being jealous of Anita, jealous about you, about Ronnie, about Mark—she seemed to have engineered everything, to have made everything possible for herself—and in the end I simply became superfluous. She wouldn't understand this, with her gift for optimism. (Perhaps I should say, with her gift for power—but that may be residual malice. In the end, I was fired, although she tried to disguise that reality. I didn't know how you could fire someone from friendship.) I always felt very ordinary beside Anita, like something small and cosseted, and this is miles away from my normal conception of myself.

I'm finding this a very difficult letter to write. As you will have perceived, it's taken me months to get organized enough even to try. And maybe I'm still confused, metaphorically out in the cold, away from the circle of Anita's affection, friends, lovers—maybe, I mean, she was our victim and not we hers. But if that's true, neither of us will ever be certain. That gift of hers for optimism and illusion-making might be our blessing as well as hers. I suspect that we both still love her. (Oh, a little voice says, didn't you know? I had the classic little-girl/gym-instructress crush.)

Life here in Colorado (observe, she said, the rapid change of scene and subject) is pleasant, unhurried, purposeful; the university near to mountains and clean air. In the summer it smells of mountain flowers and streams. I have a half-time job in a good clinic, the people I work with are to a man Western and gregarious and friendly. A gang of them climbs mountains on weekends. Nobody ever wears a necktie. My boss is the exception, and he wears one of those string ties you see on country-and-western singers. *Autre temps, autre* neckwear. I expect none of this interests you, though I think you'd like the sheer peculiarity of the landscape. It's jumpy and lyrical, unexpected, like your new record. *Marriage Hymns*, indeed.

I'm going to mail this now before I change my mind, and then to the library to add another fifty or sixty notecards to my vast mound of them. Please don't feel that I expect an answer.

All in love,
Andy

P.S. I'm almost glad the sixties are over. It's like: *Now* I can start growing up. Which I guess you have to leave home, or whatever you replaced it with, to do.